The Surgeon's Apprentice

Also by John Biggins

A Sailor of Austria
The Emperor's Coloured Coat
The Two-Headed Eagle
Tomorrow the World

JOHN BIGGINS

The Surgeon's Apprentice

www.johnbigginsfiction.com

PUBLISHED BY JOHN BIGGINS 2010

Copyright © 2010 John Biggins

All rights reserved. No reproduction, copy or transmission of this publication may be made without written permission. No paragraph of this publication may be reproduced, copied or transmitted save with the written permission of the author or in accordance with the provisions of the Copyright Act 1956 (as amended). Any person who does any unauthorised act in relation to this publication may be liable to criminal prosecution and civil claims for damages. Requests for such permission should be addressed to info@johnbigginsfiction.com

John Biggins has asserted his right under the Copyright, Designs and Patents Act 1988 to be identified as the author of this work

ISBN: 978-0-9565423-2-8

Printed by Lightning Source

The cover artwork shows *La defensa de Cádiz contra los ingleses* ("*The Defence of Cadiz Against the English*") by Francisco Zurbarán, 1634, original in the Prado Museum, Madrid; and also the constellations Orion, Taurus and Gemini from Johann Ellert Bode's *Cosmographia*.

www.johnbigginsfiction.com

HISTORICAL NOTE

This note has been written to explain certain behaviour on the part of the characters in this novel which may be perplexing to 21st century readers brought up to think in terms of nationality and nation-states, neither of which existed in any very developed form in the Europe of the early 17th century.

The Netherlands and the Spanish Netherlands

At the end of the Middle Ages, under Burgundian rule, the seventeen provinces of the Low Countries – the "Nieder Landen" – enjoyed a degree of political cohesion in addition to the unity imposed by language (the various Low-German dialects which evolved into modern Dutch) and by geography (the marshy delta of the Rhine, Meuse and Scheldt rivers). But this all began to unravel after the last Duke of Burgundy died in 1477 without a male heir and his lands passed to the House of Habsburg, then in 1555 to the Spanish branch of that family. In the 1560s a series of revolts broke out in the northermost cities and provinces. In the beginning these were local rebellions against a centralising government in Madrid imposing new taxes and persecuting Protestants. But by the early 1580s they had turned into something like a war of national liberation, and the rebel provinces had grouped together into a *de facto* Dutch state, the Republic of the Seven United Provinces of the Netherlands, led by its wealthiest province Holland and governed via a national assembly called the States-General acting in concert with the Stadhouder, a sort of hereditary president drawn from the princely House of Orange.

For the first thirty years or so of the war the ultimate aim of the Dutch rebels was to drive the Spaniards out of all seventeen provinces and form a unified Netherlandic state. But by the early 1600s doubts about this project had surfaced on both sides of the battlefront. Decades of persecution and forced emigration had cleared Protestants out of the southern provinces of Flanders and Brabant, leaving them solidly Catholic and very doubtful whether they wished to be liberated by northern Calvinists even if their would-be liberators did speak approximately the same language. Likewise the northern Calvinists had by now begun to question whether they really wanted to win more territory from the Spaniards if the result would be a state where Catholics would be the majority and Antwerp would be a serious commercial rival to Amsterdam. In these years two distinct identities began to emerge: a northern "Dutch" one (town-based, commercial, republican and tolerantly Protestant) and a southern "Flemish" one (rural, conservative, aristocratic and devoutly Catholic). Likewise the language soon began to diverge under the two different political systems: in fact it was not until 1980 that a commission of scholars finally decreed that Dutch and Flemish are not separate languages but sister-dialects of Netherlandish.

By the time of the truce with Spain in 1609 the Dutch Republic was an independent state and recognised as such by most of Europe. This left the status of the southern provinces very uncertain; so when Philip II died in 1598 Madrid granted them semi-independence as the Spanish Netherlands under the Habsburg Archduke Albert and his wife the Archduchess Isabella (Philip II's daughter) with their court in Brussels. This arrangement lasted until 1713 when the Spanish Netherlands – or what was left after successive chunks of territory had been annexed by the French and the Dutch – passed to Austrian rule, then became Belgium in the early 19th century.

HISTORICAL NOTE

Armies

Throughout the Eighty Years' War between the Dutch Republic and Spain, from 1568 to 1648, most of the fighting was done by mercenaries, so that at no time did the "Dutch" Army of the States-General ever consist of more than 25 per cent Dutchmen or the "Spanish" Ejército Real of more than about 20 per cent Spaniards. For the rest the two armies were made up of an extraordinary mix of nationalities: German, Italian, Swiss, Scottish, Flemish, French, Irish and English. Soldiers served on contract, and if – as frequently happened – they were left unpaid for more than a couple of years they would not hesitate to change sides if ready cash were offered. Set-piece battles were few and usually happened by accident, so the war consisted mostly of sieges separated by long periods when nothing much happened because one side or both had run out of money. In fact between 1609 and 1621 the Low Countries were entirely at peace thanks to a twelve-year armistice concluded because both Spain and the Dutch Republic were too hard up to continue fighting.

When they were not fighting – which is to say, most of the time – the soldiery on both sides lived off the land, a polite term for robbery and extortion, and were billeted on the local towns and villages. Permanent armies wearing uniforms, regularly paid, living in barracks and eating government-supplied rations were a late-17th century innovation and quite unknown at this period.

Navies

Throughout this period of pretty well continuous sea warfare between the Dutch and Spain, then the Dutch and England, then the Dutch and France, there was never in fact any such entity as the Dutch Navy. The Seven United Provinces were defended at sea by no less than five separate fleets each controlled by its own admiralty, and with only a very weak central command structure.

HISTORICAL NOTE

When the Dutch Republic took shape in the mid-1580s the States-General, instead of setting up a national admiralty to oversee naval matters, decided that it would continue the existing makeshift naval organisations in the three coastal provinces of Holland, Zeeland and Friesland. These would provide the bulk of the money for naval defence, while the inland provinces of Utrecht, Overijssel, Gelderland and Groningen would vote funds each year as their contribution. In practice, however, this arrangement never worked well. The inland provinces seldom paid their allotted sums on time, complaining that they had expensive border fortresses to maintain, whilst even within the coastal provinces naval administration was extremely complicated, with numerous overlaps.

The common fleet was made up of ships built – or more usually chartered – and equipped by the five naval administrations using money voted by their provincial parliaments. The five admiralties were Zeeland, based in Middleburg; the Maze (Maas) based in Rotterdam; Holland based in Amsterdam; West Friesland (also called the the North Quarter) which alternated between the towns of Hoorn and Enkhuizen; and Friesland based in Dokkum, later Harlingen. But the provincial contributions to the common fleet were very unequal, with most of the ships, men and money being furnished by the wealthy cities of Amsterdam and Rotterdam. Zeeland and West Friesland provided fewer and fewer ships in the second half of the century, while poor, rural Friesland never had more than a half-dozen vessels in commission at any one time. Among the five admiralties there was constant bickering over precedence between Amsterdam (the wealthiest) and the Maze (the oldest), while extremely able commanders like De Ruyter and the Evertsen brothers found themselves blocked for promotion to the Republic's top naval job, Lieutenant-Admiral of Holland and West Friesland, because of the reluctance of Hollander captains to take orders from a Zeelander.

In the English Royal Navy until 1653 the order of seniority among the squadrons in a fleet was red, blue and white, not red,

HISTORICAL NOTE

white and blue. Royal Navy warships at this period were still almost always commanded by a nobleman land-officer and sailed by a ship's captain. Aboard Dutch ships however the near-invariable practice by the 1620s was for the most senior officer to be a sailor.

Spellings

Dutch/Flemish orthography in the early 17th century was quite as chaotic as English. The practice in this book is therefore to use modern spellings except when quoting book titles etc.

Place-names

Along the French-Flemish linguistic border usage as regards place-names was highly variable, with most towns and villages having a Flemish name and a French one: for example Lille (in Flemish "Rijssel"), Tournai ("Doornik"), Arras ("Atrecht") and Mons ("Bergen"). Where there is a generally accepted English spelling that is used – for example "Dunkirk" rather than "Dunkerque" or "Duinkerken" – and for the rest the probable usage of the period is followed, given that much of west Flanders was annexed by France in the second half of the 17th century and place-names were gallicised by decree. That being said, usage still varied quite a lot between the educated and the illiterate: even Dutch sources of the period sometimes refer to the town of s'Hertogenbosch as "Bois-le-Duc".

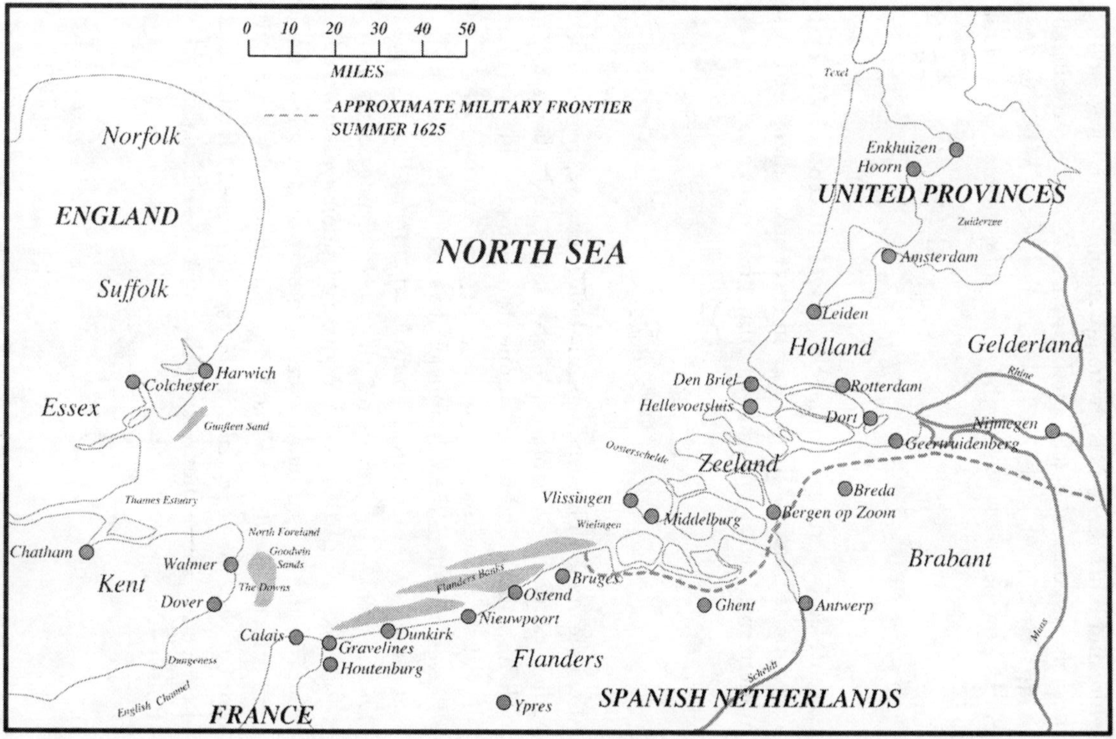
0 10 20 30 40 50
MILES
APPROXIMATE MILITARY FRONTIER
SUMMER 1625
Norfolk
ENGLAND
Suffolk
Essex
NORTH SEA
Harwich
Colchester
Gunfleet Sand
Thames Estuary
Chatham
Kent
Walmer
Dover
North Foreland
Goodwin Sands
The Downs
Dungeness
English Channel
FRANCE
Calais
Gravelines
Houtenburg
Dunkirk
Nieuwpoort
Ostend
Bruges
Flanders Banks
Flanders
Ypres
SPANISH NETHERLANDS
Ghent
Antwerp
Scheldt
Wielingen
Vlissingen
Middelburg
Oosterschelde
Zeeland
Bergen op Zoom
Breda
Brabant
Den Briel
Hellevoetsluis
Rotterdam
Dort
Geertruidenberg
Nijmegen
Rhine
Maas
Holland
Gelderland
Leiden
Amsterdam
Zuiderzee
UNITED PROVINCES
Hoorn
Enkhuizen
Texel

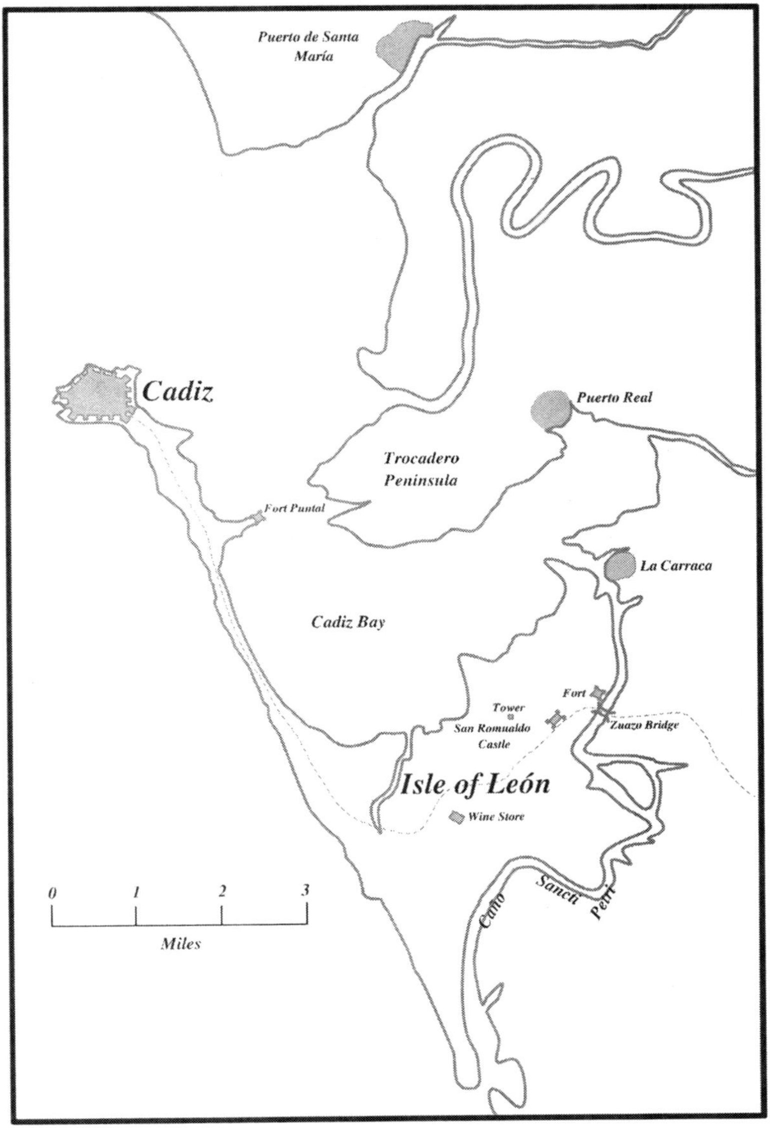
Puerto de Santa María
Cadiz
Puerto Real
Trocadero Peninsula
Fort Puntal
La Carraca
Cadiz Bay
Fort
Tower
San Romualdo Castle
Zuazo Bridge
Isle of León
Wine Store
Caño Sancti Petri
0 1 2 3
Miles

The Surgeon's Apprentice

CHAPTER ONE

The twenty-fifth day of December in the year of Our Lord sixteen hundred and ten: the Feast of Our Blessed Saviour's Nativity. In the chill hours before dawn the midwinter stars still twinkled cold and remote in the great indigo vault of sky above the sedgy water-meadows of west Flanders. Amid the early-morning darkness there was still no visible token of human presence other than the tiny pinpoint of light seven or eight miles distant in Dunkirk where a lantern burned on top of Saint Eloi's belfry to guide mariners out on the wintry North Sea.

The year before, the King of Spain and his former Dutch subjects had concluded a twelve-year armistice after fighting one another hammer and tongs for the previous four decades. So ships making their way among the sandbanks of the Flanders coast now faced only the hazards of routine piracy or being driven ashore by a westerly gale. The country hereabouts had likewise become part of a vague, provisional entity called the Spanish Netherlands – chiefly to distinguish them from the Netherlands that were no longer Spanish. And meanwhile the inscrutable stars shone in the heavens above, majestically aloof from the scuffling knaveries of pirates on water and monarchs on land. The giant Orion – by this hour of the morning sunk up to his waist in the sea – brandished his mighty club at the fishes. The bright dot of Venus shone low on the eastern horizon as the first glimmerings of daylight began to suffuse the sky. Out beyond the fringe of sand dunes the salty grey waves lapped sullenly on the shore after days of being driven against the beaches by a north-westerly gale. The wind had veered eastwards during the night, and occasional flurries of snowflakes now fluttered out of the darkness to gather among the ice-locked reed stems that bordered the drainage ditches and sluggish meandering streams of the Flanders marshes. A few miles southwards that dark, inchoate plain of swamps and rivermouths that extended down the coast all the way from Denmark came to a sudden stop against the chalk hills of Artois and the forest of Éperlecques, where wolves still made their lairs and wild boar rootled for beechmast among the black leaf-mould as they had done since the last Ice Age. Some centuries before the Romans arrived this land had emerged from the sea, only to be submerged again a few centuries after they left, so that in the days of the old Counts of Flanders ships could sail up the River Aa as far inland as Saint Omer. Within the collective memory of the country folk the Bredenarde had been a shallow estuary where fishermen cast their nets and wildfowlers set their traps for duck and widgeon. But then – as though the land were some giant snoring gently in his sleep, each breath lasting a millenium or more – the sea had retreated again, and this time had sealed its decision for posterity by trailing a line of sand dunes up the coast from Calais; each winter's storms extending the dunes a further mile or so until the whole of the Flanders marshes as far north as the Scheldt were cut off from the sea and rendered suitable for drainage by land-hungry peasants and the ingenious monks of the abbeys, toiling for centuries with spades and wheelbarrows to raise the dykes and dig the orderly grid of canals that would discipline wastrel swamps into docile hard-working ploughland and meadows. Yet for all their efforts the land hereabouts still seemed only a provisional and temporary thing; no more than water solidified for a while into earth, but always ready to turn back to its original element if the dykes were not maintained and the sluice-gates were allowed to rot: a congealed sea lapping against the foot of the chalk hills where pasture gave way to cornland and Flemish to French as the language of the country folk.

Before long there was sufficient light for vague shapes to emerge from the early-morning darkness. A long, black smudge was already visible among the water-meadows: too high and too solid to be yet another grove of alder trees. As the sky lightened it revealed a jagged outline of roofs: some of them in the middle high, crow-stepped gables of brick while others towards the edges were the low reed-thatched ridges of wooden houses, then mere cottages, then hovels which might equally well provide shelter for men or for beasts. Above the roofs towards the eastern side of the smudge there became visible against the lightening sky a dark, rectangular bulk which slowly assumed the form of a great squared-off church tower with a pinnacle at each corner and a truncated turret in the middle like an overgrown pepper pot. Soon there was light enough to discern a little walled town standing on the banks of a slow-meandering, reed-fringed river winding its way through the marshes as though it was still in two minds about whether or not it should join the sea. Judging by the three church towers that rose above it, the town might once have been a place of some note, but was evidently no longer of any great consideration.

Here along the border between France and Flanders the towns had always been fortified. Half a century of intermittent warfare between the Kings of France and the House of Habsburg meant that the more important municipalities along the frontier were now surrounded by elaborate lace collars of ramparts and bastions traced out according to the latest fashions decreed by the military engineers of northern Italy. But as for the town of Houtenburg (or "Audainbourcque" as French-speakers called it), despite being situated less than a mile from the French frontier the place had not been deemed of sufficient importance for the Archduke's government in Brussels to spend any money on improving its fortifications. Turreted medieval walls of brown brick still surrounded it just as they had done two hundred years earlier in the days of the town's prosperity; before the sea retreated, when English wool ships had lain moored four abreast along the quaysides of a River Lommel now so choked with mud and reeds as to be scarcely navigable by a market-gardener's punt laden with cabbages; when the streets rang all day to the clacking of weavers' looms and the river changed colour every evening, red, green, yellow or blue, as the cloth-dyers drained their vats at the end of the day. All that wealth and glory had long since departed. Plagues, wars, the sea's retreat and changing fashions had put paid to the town's trade in woollen cloth and eaten away at its very fabric. Being constructed mostly of timber with thatched roofs, Houtenburg's houses had burned nicely during each of its regular pillagings by warring armies; and even if they could be replaced quickly enough afterwards, each successive fire saw fewer of them being rebuilt, so that miserable squatters' shacks and empty spaces full of willow herb now occupied much of the town's back streets. The town council still met and municipal life still functioned after a fashion: buildings were patched up as they crumbled, and every few years yet another impressive-sounding but poorly-performing Italian or Dutch engineer was expensively hired to cut a canal through the marshes and the strangulating sand-dunes to reach the North Sea.

But with each year that passed there was less conviction in any of it and more of a sad, dispirited sense that there was no point any longer: that Houtenburg's great days were gone beyond recall and that its decline was now as irreversible as that of an old man with some wasting disease. One tower of the arched and turreted gateway on the Calais road had collapsed some years before, picked apart by ivy and winter frosts, and the rest was now shored up with timber scaffolding. As for the other gate, on the road leading across the marshes to Bergues, it was only kept in repair because it served as the town's gaol. But this hardly mattered any longer: the walls were nowadays only of symbolic value in distinguishing a small town from what might otherwise be a large village, and a battery of siege cannon would surely have pounded them to brick-dust in the course of a morning. The gates were still shut and barred at nightfall and opened again at dawn by the town sergeant self-importantly jingling his iron keys while the town drummer rattle-tat-tatted along behind him. But this was done nowadays only as a display of municipal pride, and to keep out the marauding beggars who had plagued the Flanders countryside ever since the Dutch truce and the disbanding of the armies. If a hostile force of soldiers came that way – or a theoretically friendly one, which amounted to much the same thing for anyone unlucky enough to be on its line of march – then Houtenburg was effectively as naked and at its mercy as the poorest hamlet out in the surrounding platteland.

Thin tatters of cloud straggled across the sky as the stars began to fade. The east wind swayed the frost-rimed, crow-picked corpses of two highway robbers hanged the previous August which still dangled raggedly from the gallows on the mound known as the Galgenheuvel, across the river from the Calais Gate where the old Roman road to Cassel had crossed the Lommel and where the Counts of Flanders had later built their wooden fort – the Houten Burcht – to deter the Vikings from rowing inland towards Saint Omer. As yet nothing stirred within the town walls, for today was a church holiday and in any case at this darkest season of the year the hours of daylight were too few for the spinning of linen thread, which was Houtenburg's staple industry nowadays, and there was likewise little work to be done in the fields which came almost to the foot of the town's walls. But before long a faint glow could be seen making its way up the spiral staircase in one corner of the great church tower, appearing at each window slit in turn as the panting sacristan Nollekens, candle-lantern in hand, climbed the four hundred and thirteen steps leading up to the wooden belfry. There was a pause as he took off his cloak and regained his breath, sweating from his exertion despite the early-morning chill. Then a harsh, discordant clanking like the beating of a soup ladle inside an iron cauldron began to echo through the sleeping streets below as he lugged at the rope of the church's only remaining bell: a cracked iron one which had been used for sounding the Angelus until the year 1592, when Queen Elizabeth's soldiers had ransacked the town and taken the church's magnificent peal of six bronze bells back to England to melt down for cannon. There had been talk ever since of replacing them; but given the present sorry state of the town's finances there could be no question of it. So for want of anything better the dismal iron bell continued to set the townsfolk's teeth on edge eight times a day, ringing out the hours of the church offices to regulate their lives in a town still without a municipal clock. Today though, it being a holy day of obligation and Mass having already been celebrated at midnight, Matins was being rung an hour later than usual.

Most of the townsfolk still lay snoring in their beds: many sleeping off the effects of kerstbier; the dark, potent brew with which Christ's birthday was traditionally celebrated in this part of Flanders. But some were already up and about. Just inside the Calais Gate, in a cowshed leaning against the wall of the town's principal inn, the *Cheval Noir*, a lantern guttered in the draught while sounds of distress came through the clapboard walls. It was the voice of a young woman; evidently in some pain. Her moans became cries, competing with the strident clangour of the church bell, until they reached a climactic shriek. There was silence from the cowshed for a few moments, then the indignant squalling of a baby justly outraged at being so rudely thrust from the dark, heart-thumping warmth of its mother's womb into the chill air of a winter's morning. The bell ceased its clanking at last, and as it did so the door of the miserable shed opened to reveal a man in his forties silhouetted against the flickering lamplight, bleary-eyed and with his blond beard and short-cropped hair uncombed, carrying a leather bag and with a cloak thrown around his shoulders against the cold since he was still in his shirtsleeves. He turned to speak with a stocky, middle-aged woman as she wiped her bloodied hands on a piece of rag.

"Very well, Vrouw Anna, I shall entrust her to your care since there seems to be no further need for my services. A fine lusty boy, the mother young and strong and the birth without complications; so I imagine that both of them will fare well or ill enough from now on without my aid."

"I'm sorry to have had to call you out at this hour, Mijnheer Willenbrouckx, and on Christmas morning too, but the matter was beyond my competence. An incision had to be made, and the town council would take away my licence if I'd done it myself."

"Think nothing of it: being called out at all hours is part of the surgeon's lot." He smiled. "But certainly it's a singular enough occurrence, to have a virgin giving birth in a stable on the twenty-fifth of December. It reminds me of a story I once heard somewhere..."

"Come now, mijnheer, not so very much out of the ordinary. Five years ago I had to attend a gentlewoman near Rieteghem who was in childbed though still *virgo intacta*. Her husband was a notorious fool, and I was called upon later to testify in the bishop's court when she petitioned for an annulment. I had to explain in great detail to those lascivious old priests how a woman could fall pregnant even though her maidenhead was still unbroken – though I still think they neither understood nor believed me."

"Indeed so: though this case was what we call *hymen septatus*, which is a different matter from simple *hymen intactus* resulting from a feeble husband. As you saw, it was an extra membrane between the vaginal walls. But there; all that it called for was a simple snip with my scissors and the child's head came out without any further trouble. Do you have any idea who the woman might be, though? As municipal surgeon I shall have to make arrangements for her and the child to be lodged, then admitted to the Hôtel-Dieu if they have no other means of support. For the moment though we'll place her in the inn: mere Christian charity forbids us from leaving her lying in the straw of a cow-byre on Christmas day when the snow falls outside. Did she give you any hint of who she might be and where she comes from?"

"Not in the slightest, Mijnheer Willenbrouckx: I was called to attend her only an hour ago. The ostler Pieterken came knocking on my door and said that a woman was groaning in labour in the cowshed and what was he to do? And by the time I reached her the poor soul had more pressing matters on her mind than giving me her name. I thought at first that she must be some beggar's drab come into the town rather than give birth in a wayside ditch: Lord knows there's been enough of those lately. But I saw that she wore a good dress, though torn and bespattered, and likewise heard that her speech was of the better sort and not of the fields and muddy hovels: perhaps a lady's maid seduced by her master and left with child then cast out when her belly could no longer be hidden. What brought her to Houtenburg, though, I've no idea. She must have come into the town as the gate was closed yesterday evening and tumbled into the first nook she could find to be out of the wind and snow."

The surgeon nodded sadly in agreement. "A common enough tale in these times, Vrouw Anna. The poor creature isn't the first; and I very much doubt whether she'll be the last." He clutched his cloak together at the collar. "Anyway, please to bring me the bill for your services so that I can submit it to the council after the holiday. And in the mean time speak with Vrouw Cellier to provide her a room with a bed and firing: also swaddling clothes for the infant against an invoice."

"Begging your pardon, mijnheer, but I think the council may well refuse to honour my bill, or Vrouw Cellier to give me credit since so many other bills have been refused of late. The échevins may well say that Houtenburg's poor-chest is for succouring the folk of Houtenburg and not for every vagabond in Flanders who comes knocking at our gate."

The surgeon sighed, and fumbled in his purse to extract two silver shillings. "More than likely; so as usual I shall have to attend their next sitting and plead the woman's case like Pericles before the council of Athens to prise a few miserable coppers from their grasp. They will gravely inform me that times are hard in Flanders by reason of the peace – as they were formerly hard by reason of the war – and that charity begins at home; if indeed it begins even there. So pay Vrouw Cellier in advance, and I shall seek reimbursement later on. By the time our worshipful échevins have reached a decision on the matter the boy will probably be in breeches and fathering brats of his own."

The midwife curtsied. "You're a munificent gentleman, Mijnheer Willenbrouckx, and the whole of Houtenburg says as much."

"I'm not a gentleman, just a barber-surgeon; which is a trade not a calling and therefore confers no gentility. And behind its doors the whole of Houtenburg will say that I am either a gullible fool to pay the bills of the rabblement from my own pocket, or that I dispense largesse to the undeserving poor because I hope to be elected mayor one day, though I've often said that I would sooner be ducked in the Lommel with a dead cat hung round my neck than fill that office. Anyway, see to it that the woman and her infant are looked after, and bring the bills and dockets to me at my house after Mass." He turned to leave. "Oh, and my best wishes to you and Meester Boudewijns on the occasion of Our Lord's nativity."

The surgeon departed, and the midwife returned to the young woman lying in the straw on some hempen sacks beneath an old horse blanket. She was exhausted, and her dark blond hair had come loose and hung in straggles over her shoulders. But she seemed happy enough as the blood-smeared morsel of life that had just fought its way out of her lay sucking blindly at her breast. Vrouw Boudewijns made sure that all the afterbirth had been expelled, then carefully collected it and the umbilical cord in a wooden pail; partly from fear that it might be taken by witches and used for casting spells; partly because there was a ready market for dried umbilical cords among the fishermen at Gravelines, who wore them around their necks as a talisman against drowning.

"Are you comfortable now, my dear?" she asked. "That's a fine lusty boy you have there and well worth all your pain and trouble. Just look at his red hair."

The young woman smiled weakly. "Thank you for your help to a poor stranger. I must pay you…"

"No need for that now: I'll speak with the landlady of the inn and have you moved to a bed as soon as you're strong enough to walk; also have the kitchenmaid warm you a bowl of water to wash the child with."

"But I can pay you; only that I have no money about me now: I had to leave Sottebecque yesterday evening in haste. But once I can send word to my friend there…"

"Stop this babbling about payment, child" (the woman was about twenty-two and Anna Boudewijns nearing fifty). "When children decide to be born they will be born, and take no heed of whether there's money enough to pay for it. It was ever so since Eve gave birth to Cain – and as you yourself now know, since this was plainly your first child." The midwife paused, not quite sure how to put the next question, which was none the less an important one since it would determine how the woman would be viewed by the poorhouse guardians: whether as a respectable person fallen upon misfortune or a cozening vagrant imposing upon the town's charity. "Do you have a husband?" she asked at last. "That you were still a virgin makes me suppose not."

The young woman looked shocked. "No, this is no bastard infant. I am – or was – a married woman, as you may see by this ring on my finger" (she indicated a ring of brass or some such paltry metal, already brownish and discoloured). "I'm a widow who lost her husband some seven months ago, in France, only three weeks after we were married. My husband and I lay together but once, and it was then that he begot my child. But he married me afterwards. And now I am his widow."

"Who then shall I say that you are? If you wish for this town's charity I shall have to give a name to the poorhouse guardians, and likewise arrange for your child to be baptised like a good Christian." The young woman's reply caused the midwife to catch her breath suddenly.

"My name before my marriage was Catherine Maertens. But now I am the Widow Ravaillac".

It was ten o'clock, and the High Mass for Christmas Day was coming to an end in the great draughty, echoing nave of the abbey church of Saint Wolverga; so splendid in the days of the town's wealth but now as meagre and shabby as the rest of that decayed municipality of perhaps two thousand souls. It had been intended as the greatest church in west Flanders, its tower five hundred feet high so that it could cock a snook at Saint Eloi's in Dunkirk and Saint Winoc's in Bergues, and indeed be visible on a clear day from as far away as Ypres or even Ghent, lifting its head high above the flat countryside to proclaim Houtenburg's wealth and prestige to the whole of Flanders and beyond. But even before the River Lommel began to choke with silt, about the year 1420, the tower had run into difficulties. Despite being built by the best stonemasons using the finest limestone brought by ship from Caen, it became clear as the tower rose that the marshy ground beneath it was simply too soft to bear its massive weight. By the time the masons had reached three hundred feet it was already leaning four or five degrees out of true. Attempts were made to correct the tilt by means of heavy weights and by digging beneath the foundations on the high side. But in the end the opinion of all the experts was that the tower might topple over if it went any higher. So a halt was called, leaving a leaning, squared-off edifice surmounted by a pinnacle at each corner and by a timber belfry clad with lead.

But further misfortunes had followed. A raid inland by the Dutch rebels in 1574 had led to the abbey's treasures being looted and the buildings set alight. Scarcely recovered from that calamity, the church and town had again been pillaged and burned by the English in 1592 during an Anglo-Dutch attempt to take Dunkirk from the landward side. A fire caused by a bolt of lightning the following year had consumed much of the roof, already stripped of its lead by the English to make musket balls. The town was plundered once more in 1596 by the troops of Henri IV of France pursuing their war against the Spaniards, then set on fire in 1601 by Spanish soldiers mutinous after being left unpaid for the past four years. The great church consisted now of a whistling-bare nave and two ruinous aisles boarded up against the weather, all the gilded reliquaries, the fine carved and painted altars and the brocade hangings having long since been stolen or burned or used as blankets to drape horses stabled in the sanctuary. All that remained of its former splendour was the ornate stone tomb of Saint Wolverga who had been beheaded by the still-pagan Flemings near Watten about 600 AD, and had then picked up her head and walked with it under her arm all the way to Houtenburg where – for reasons best known to herself, since she had just covered five or six miles in a headless state – she finally dropped dead and was buried, to the universal wonderment of the people: and their considerable profit in the centuries that followed, once she became the saint of first resort all over Flanders for the healing of boils, carbuncles and other pustular lesions of the skin. Her feast was still celebrated on the 15th of September each year with a three-day fair which brought visitors from all over the region to buy and sell their goods and partake of the town's local speciality: Wolvergapuisten or Furoncles de Sainte Wolvergue*: little round choux-pastry buns filled with saffron-tinted custard and a dab of cherry jam.

The vigil Mass at midnight had been the feast-day's main religious event. But the town's échevins were nowadays mostly the local landed gentry, and a journey along muddy country roads in the black of a midwinter night would have been unreasonable to expect of them. So the quality had came into Houtenburg for the Mass on Christmas morning, to see and to be seen and for their wives to appraise one another's toilettes, and then depart back to their manor houses having performed their annual civic duty. The Mass itself was a perfunctory affair and the townspeople were left afterwards to spend the day as they chose. This was a holy day of obligation, so guild regulations forbade work and most of the menfolk would sit in the taverns after Mass drinking their pewter quart-pots of kerstbier, which was famously provocative of violence towards wives and servants once the drinkers had stumbled their way home. The town's seigneur Achilles van Beausart de Roblés, the mayor Antoine Cabeljauw and the congregation of notables and their wives were gathered towards the front of the nave in their feast-day finery, the ladies seated – insofar as the hoops of their farthingales would permit – on stools by kind permission of the Abbé Gosaerts in recognition of their degree and

---

* Saint Wolverga's boils.

sex, while Houtenburg's meaner sort stood graded according to their rank and condition towards the back of the nave, finishing near the great doorway with the beggars, cripples and whores who laughed, gossiped, cracked hazelnuts, scratched themselves, farted and cast dice throughout the Mass even during the elevation of the blessed sacrament. The abbé gave his benediction, and the congregation filed out of the church into the square.

Snow was now falling in a half-hearted sort of way, the flakes collecting in the crevices of the brick paving as the wind scurried them along. On the church steps the quality bowed and curtsied and doffed their hats, or received bows and curtsies and had hats doffed to them according to their rank and their degree of their kinship and affinity, since the town's burghers and the gentry from round about were now bound to one another by two centuries' worth of cousinships and intermarriage, so that it was scarcely possible any longer to separate the landed squires with their coats of arms and their Spanish patents of nobility from the old burgher families whose great-grandfathers had made their money as master weavers and wool merchants. For their part the gentlefolk were happy to let the menu-peuple leave the church first rather than rub shoulders with them. It was December now and the frosts had set in: fleas were somnolent and people no longer stank as badly as they had in August. But there were still plenty of contagions to be caught, not to speak of other people's lice which the physicians were unanimous in declaring to be much more pernicious than one's own since, being generated from alien sweat, they might contain all manner of corrupted humours. Even so, it was still doghouse-cold inside the great draughty church, and the ladies in their décolletéd satin gowns and starched ruffs were by now visibly shivering, anxious to don their cloaks and return as soon as possible to their domestic firesides.

As the acknowledged heads of local society, Monsieur and Madame de Roblés left first, she to climb into the ponderous family coach with the coat of arms on the doors and he to hoist himself stiffly on to his horse, since though the gout plagued him nowadays he was still a former officer of King Philip, and for a military man to ride in a coach like a priest or a lady's maid would fatally undermine his dignity. The rest of the town's notables then followed them down the church steps in a cascade of holiday black. Michel de Willenbrouckx, his wife Laetitia and their only surviving child Regulus, a solemn little boy of five, exchanged their bows and seasonal greetings with the rest of Houtenburg's better sort. In this world of infinite gradations of rank a mere barber-surgeon, however competent, came well down the scale of social acceptability even if he did have a "de" to his family name (though he seldom used it) and his wife was also of gentle birth, a Collaert no less, a member of that great Dunkirk dynasty of ship owners and occasional pirates who had married into most of the landed families of west Flanders. This entitled him to the courtesy title of "mijnheer" instead of plain "meester", since she was a "mevrouw" by birth and her husband must therefore be of equal degree and consideration with her. He knew perfectly well though that the cordiality shown towards him was a result not so much of his social rank as of his calling. For whether kings or beggars, we are all children of Eve and equally heirs to the ills and accidents of the flesh, so that even the most fanatical sticklers for hierarchy and precedence will usually take care to stay on friendly terms with the man who might one day have to set their broken leg or pull out an aching tooth. So it was joyeux Noël Monsieur et Madame le Chirurgien, and an affable enough nod from the seigneur and his lady as they departed (though they still had a bill outstanding for one of her teeth extracted at Martinmas) and goede morgen Mijnheer en Mevrouw Willenbrouckx, and even some perfunctory doffing of hats from the lowest ranks of the quality as the couple made their way down the steps and across the square, Laetitia muffled in her new wine-red cloak with the fox-fur collar and Regulus in his best Sunday suit of black velvet with a fine beaver-felt hat on top of his blond curls.

At the foot of the church steps Vrouw Boudewijns and her husband the town's apothecary greeted the surgeon. While Laetitia consulted Meester Boudewijns about a powder for her migraines (her health having been poor for some years past) the midwife took the surgeon aside.

"Mijnheer Willenbrouckx, the young woman who was delivered of a child this morning..."

"What of her? Is she well?"

"Perfectly well, pleasing your honour, and now moved to a room in the inn as you instructed me. But there's more to this than first appeared. The state of the poor woman's head troubles me more than that of her body."

"What do you mean?"

"I asked for her name, to have Vrouw Cellier make out a docket for the poorhouse guardians. And she told me that her name is the Widow Ravaillac."

"The Widow *who*...?"

"The Widow Ravaillac. She says that her husband died in France some seven months ago, after they had been married only three weeks, leaving her with child."

Willenbrouckx considered for a while. "Well, I suppose that she *might* well enough be a widow though still a virgin: stranger things have been known. And as for the Ravaillac part, the name's uncommon enough to be sure, but still not the sole property of that villain who stabbed King Henri. When I studied surgery in Paris years ago I knew a canon lawyer called Charles Raffailac from Poitiers who died from having a stool broken over his head in a wine shop after he threatened to excommunicate the landlord for refusing him credit."

"By your leave, mijnheer, that's not all. After I left her I met with old Goosens from the toll-house on the Calais road. And he says that as darkness was falling yesterday a crowd of some thirty or forty of the rabblement from Sottebecque came along with sticks and stones chasing a young woman heavy with child, calling out that she was a witch and a whore and bore the Devil's whelp in her belly and much else such nonsense besides. He dropped the barrier pole across the road and demanded what their business was on the King of Spain's territory. So she ran ahead of them, and anyway it was growing dark and beginning to snow. So after some shouting and calling of names and throwing a few stones after her they quit their pursuit and went home. Likewise the town sergeant says that just as he was closing the Calais Gate yesterday evening a woman in great terror with a nine-month belly and her hair hanging down and her clothes all torn and spattered begged him to let her through so that she could find a hole to hide in. He thought that she must be a mad beggar-woman and let her through the postern, but lost sight of her after that."

"Hmmm, how very singular: not every poor vagrant woman who comes into this town to drop her child bears the name of a regicide, or arrives chased by a mob seeking her life. I fear that, as you say, her trouble may be an addled head and an incontinent tongue. To provoke people as dull and lethargic as the Sottebecquois into chasing her to the gates of Houtenburg on Christmas Eve when they should have been drinking themselves insensible certainly argues a certain talent for stirring up trouble."

"And the name Ravaillac? Should that set people against her so long afterwards and so far from Paris?"

"Vrouw Anna, it's still less than nine months since the French lost their king to that madman's dagger – and were left with a nine-year old boy as his heir, and four or five rival claimants for the throne. It was only by good luck and the infinite mercy of God that they avoided a new civil war over the succession. If I were a subject of young King Louis I'd certainly be mighty neuralgic about some foolish woman bandying around the name of Ravaillac. Anyway, see to it that she and her child are comfortable and lack for nothing – but counsel her that in future she keeps a wiser tongue in her head unless she wishes to be chased out of this town as well. For I think that the name she lays claim to is one that will win her few friends even here in Flanders."

As the family walked back to their house *De Salamander* on the Kortestraat the surgeon was thoughtful. The dramatic events in Paris the previous May had come to the ears of the folk of

Houtenburg a week or so later only as a distant rumbling, like that of a thunderstorm too far off to menace the local crops: someone else's misfortune for once rather than their own. For months past it had been rumoured that Henri IV of France had been massing an army to go to war with the Emperor Rudolf over some obscure duchies in the Rhineland; which would certainly have meant his going to war sooner or later with the Emperor Rudolf's Spanish cousins and invading Flanders once more. The townsfolk knew only too well that when armies were on the march, whether those armies were French or Spanish would make but little difference to a small frontier town like Houtenburg too poor to defend itself but still rich enough to have something worth stealing. So although no one was imprudent enough to say so (all God-fearing folk being agreed that regicide was the foulest crime imaginable short of murdering God Himself) the news of the French king's sudden death had been greeted with a certain quiet relief. The week before the assassination folk working in the fields – or so they said afterwards – had seen an army of ghostly warriors fighting in the evening sky above the distant hills of Artois, which certainly betokened trouble for someone. It was reported likewise that a prodigiously large fish had been brought ashore at Mardyck with mysterious markings upon its flanks which scholars said spelled out "Woe Unto Men" in Hebrew on one side (the signification of which was plain) and "Thrice Times Thirty" on the other in Greek (which might mean anything at all). In the last days of April a traveller passing through the town on his way from Brussels to Calais had announced to the drinkers in the pot-room of the *Cheval Noir* that the French king had been stabbed to death in Paris: which was singular to say the least of it, he being still very much alive at the time, and caused the wiseacres to say afterwards that clearly Spain and the Jesuits must have had some hand in the matter. Then in the third week of May came the authentic news of the assassination, and an apprehensive week or two afterwards, with two English gentlemen on their way home from Italy reporting that Amiens and Doullens had shut their gates for fear of civil war. Around the middle of June a band of twenty or thirty French gentlemen, diehards of the Catholic League, came galloping on to Spanish territory near Audruicq pursued by the Governor of Calais's horsemen after they had tried and failed to start an uprising in the town. But in the end it had all blown over and young Louis was duly proclaimed King with his mother as Regent until he came of age. As for Henri's war against the Emperor, nothing more was heard of it and the great army camped near Mézières was quietly disbanded, which led many to suspect that His Majesty's liege subjects might themselves have been less than happy with the idea and had perhaps looked the other way as the assassin followed the royal coach through the streets from the Louvre.

Willenbrouckx himself had treated one of the English travellers for a toe gone septic after a horse had trodden on it in an inn yard. They talked in a mixture of Latin and French while the Englishman puffed at his tobacco pipe; a habit by now very widespread among that strange island people but still sufficiently novel in Flanders for people to turn and point in the street. It appeared that Sir Giles Bassingbourne, Member of Parliament for Oakham in the county of Rutland, had been in Paris on the very day of the murder.

"Of course sir," he said, "you may be sure that the whole place was soon as alive with rumour as an Irishman's beard is with lice. People said that for certain the Jesuits were behind it all, and that those artful knaves had contrived for two wagons to block the street ahead of the King's coach. Others said that Queen Marie had hired the murderer, outraged by the King's endless adulteries. But others said that no, it was not the Queen repaying the King for his mistresses, but his former mistress Madame de Verneuil revenging herself on him for marrying Queen Marie when he had previously undertaken to marry herself. Others still said that the murderer's sister had been seduced by the King and left with child, then abandoned by him: but all discounted that tale since though old Henri was marvellously incontinent and wherever he went bastards sprang up afterwards in his footsteps like asphodels in Apollo's..." (Sir Giles paused for a moment so that the surgeon could admire the elegance of this classical allusion) "...no man ever knew him behave ungenerously towards his doxies or refuse to acknowledge the children he had begotten. So in the end, sir, everyone and no one was the culprit, and you might have fancied that perchance His Majesty was grown so tired of life that he hired the assassin himself. But for my own part..." he paused with a knowing air to pack down the tobacco in his pipe, then blew a puff of smoke "...I give but little credence to such idle conjectures, and think that the murderer was rather a plain madman: a great red-haired lummock of a fellow all dressed in green whom I think I once saw myself loitering beneath the arcades outside the Louvre. For all concur that, since no man saw him strike the blow, he could easily have slipped away afterwards and no one the wiser; but instead he stood there like a poor silly sheep – *stultus ovis simul* – with the dagger all bloody in his hand waiting to be seized."

He laid the pipe aside. "I ask you, sir, does such seem to you to be the behaviour of a hired assassin? My own father served with Sir John Norris in the Low-Country wars and was in Delft when the Prince of Orange was shot dead by the villain Gérard. Yet even though that rogue was as desperate a fanatic as ever lived, as he demonstrated by his steadfastness under torture and afterwards on the scaffold, even he had a pair of inflated bladders with him so that he might swim the palace moat, and a horse waiting saddled on the other side, and would infallibly have made his escape if Sir Roger Williams had not run after him and brought him to the ground. Yet this Ravaillac fellow of ours was no such man of violence: indeed by all accounts was uncommonly pious and had never so much as hurt a fly in his whole life before; a lawyer's clerk turned schoolmaster, if you please..."

Willenbrouckx paused in his work and looked up, smiling. "If that is true, then I hope that on the Day of Judgement it will be considered by the Almighty as a plea in mitigation."

Sir Giles looked at him uncomprehending. "What do you

mean, sir...?"

"I meant, that though many who have the charge of schoolboys must consider homicide twenty times a day, the wonder is that so few actually pass from the thought to the deed. The brats must have provoked the poor fellow beyond all measure, that instead of killing one of them he went and stabbed the king instead."

The Englishman looked bewildered: neither his French nor his Latin were quite equal to such conceits. He laughed nervously. "Yes...yes...Indeed so: a most judicious observation to be sure. But whatever the fellow's motives, there's no denying that his execution provided a rare spectacle for the people of Paris. You could scarcely move in the streets for the crowds that came to watch – though I suppose that precious few of them can have seen anything. Our landlady doubled the rent for our room, declaring she could find a thousand who would pay as much. They say that the roof of a house near the Hôtel de Ville collapsed from the number of people that had paid to perch upon it. And such lamentation and weeping of crocodile's tears as you never heard in all your days! 'Le pauvre bon roi Henri!' and 'Ce scélerat d'assassin!' from folk who when we had sat at supper with them two days before were calling for anyone who loved God and his holy church to put an end to the life of such a heretical adulterous tyrant, and were there no men left in France to wield the knife? The French – saving your honour sir, because I take you by your name to be Flemish – are a fickle and changeable people, inconstant as so many weathercocks, and nothing good is to be expected of them."

The Willenbrouckx family arrived home and were greeted by the housekeeper Anke Scarlakens, a sturdily built Flemish peasant woman in her mid-fifties who had managed the household with formidable competence these past fifteen years – and as well that she could too, now that Mevrouw's health was so fragile and she confined so often to her bed. After dinner Willenbrouckx went to his study to read, lighting a tallow candle as the early winter dusk descended. He read for a while, a chapter or two of the *Scriptores*

Historiæ Augustæ concerning the Emperor Commodus Antoninus, who seemed by all accounts to have been a most egregious oaf, then tired of it and took out his lute to pluck a few tunes since, as befitted a medical man, he was a tolerably good amateur musician.

The end of another year in the town of Houtenburg, he thought to himself, marked in suitable style by the arrival of yet another deranged beggar-woman to place a further charge upon the public purse. He was forty-three now, too old to advance much further in his profession. He had come to it as most surgeons did, by following his father's trade in a barber's shop in the town of Poperinghe, though the family were minor landed gentry come down in the world, which gave them the "de" in their name though he himself never used it except on official documents. But then at the end of his apprenticeship the desire to see the world beyond Flanders had gripped him, and he had signed articles as a surgeon's mate aboard one of King Philip's ships, the galleon *San Isidoro*, at Lisbon in the fateful spring of 1588. There had followed a three-month waking nightmare of fighting their way up the English Channel on the far left flank of the Invincible Armada, battered for days on end by the heavier guns of the nimbler English ships until the orlop deck was a charnel-house of the dead and dying, stinking of vomit and gangrene. Then the chaos off Calais, where they came to anchor at last to await Parma's invasion barges – only to cut their cables in panic as the English fireships drifted in among them. And afterwards the confused mêlée off Gravelines, and the terrible gale-battered journey up the North Sea and around the Shetlands, then back south again wallowing in the storm-driven Atlantic breakers off the west coast of Ireland – which the ship missed by a hair's breadth while the *Santissima Trinidad* was driven on to the rocks of Blasket Island before their horrified gaze with the loss of her entire crew. Then coming ashore again in Santander ninety-four days later, starving, filthy, wasted away with sickness and rotten provisions and treated like so many malefactors for their failure.

There had followed years as a military surgeon with Verdugo and Farnese and a half-dozen lesser commanders floundering among the waterlogged meadows and ditches of Holland; at Zutphen, Deventer, Gronigen and Breda; battles, skirmishes and sieges; each one exactly like the last with only the rain-sodden autumns and the ice-bound winters to separate campaign from campaign. The blaring of trumpets and horses' neighing above the thunder of artillery and the rattle of musketry; powder smoke rising into the summer sky among the wheeling swallows; shot-torn flesh and dying men's groans: tighten the tourniquet, detach a flap of skin to cover the stump, then cut round quickly with the curved knife to sever the muscles; saw through the bone and sear the ends of the blood vessels then leave the assistants to dress the stump and on to the next ; sorting those who might still live from the wretches whom only the chaplain could help while two hundred other such unfortunates lay outside the surgeon's tent beneath the sun's glare or the weeping Dutch drizzle, imploring his help. Good training, to be sure, in making rapid and accurate assessments; a quick and certain hand with knife, saw and bullet probe; many injuries that no civilian surgeon would ever be called upon to deal with; and also some quiet satisfaction that so many of his patients survived to be discharged and spend the rest of their lives begging outside the town gates of a dozen kingdoms. He was even modestly proud to have contributed somewhat to the art of battlefield surgery by devising a probe with a white porcelain tip, since the sound that it made tapping against a bullet was subtly different from that when it encountered a fragment of bone and likewise the lead of the bullet left an unmistakable streak of grey upon it.

But to build up a proper career as a surgeon, he now saw, it would have been better to have joined the guild in Ypres at twenty-five not thirty-five, to have married a nice girl from a surgical family and to have established his practice in a wealthy town rather than in this impoverished hole of a place. True, the office of municipal surgeon which his wife's relatives had secured for him in Houtenburg was by no means a contemptible one; for though the town itself was poor and down-at-heel, there was the countryside round about and the local gentry as customers, who preferred to be attended by a surgeon with refined manners and clean fingernails who spoke good French and Spanish as well as Flemish. Though no one at the time saw any connection between the two, the fastidious cleanliness which so many of his fellow surgeons laughed at meant that the death rate from infection among his patients was gratifyingly low, and he had even begun of late to build up a remunerative practice in cutting for bladder stone, with perhaps only one in ten of his patients dying of blood poisoning afterwards, whereas with other lithotomists it might be half or two-thirds. Likewise the post carried a small official salary and brought a certain prestige, even at the price of constant conflict with the town physician Doctor Gilbert Hooftius who, having himself had his natural ignorance enhanced by studying medicine at Louvain and the Sorbonne, despised all surgeons as unlettered empirics no better than so many cobblers or wheelwrights. But when all was said and done it was still a dismal backwater with few prospects for anything better. His once-blond hair now turning grey, he felt that life had passed him by, sitting in a dreary, damp little provincial town in an obscure province with an ailing wife – her suffering all the worse because he loved her so dearly – and four out of their five children now lying in their graves. It was sad. But life was a sad and painful business ending always in death, as a surgeon had more reason than most mortals to know. At last he snuffed out the candle and went to bed, on his own to avoid disturbing Laetitia's sleep. In a few days yet another year would end. And yet another one would begin: in all probability exactly the same as the one before it and the one after it, and be thankful only if things got no worse.

At eight o'clock the next morning, Saint Stephen's Day, the midwife knocked on the door of the surgeon's house.

"Mijnheer Willenbrouckx, if you please, I've come about the young woman."

"What's the matter, Vrouw Anna? Does she now claim to be the widow of some other great villain? Perhaps Gilles de Rais this time or the Emperor Caligula?"

"She claims no such thing, mijnheer, but babbles a great deal of other nonsense. I fear she has childbed fever."

"Well then, call Doctor Hooftius and not me. That learned fool should soon usher her into the next world with his hired knaves Galen and Aristotle to help him."

"By your leave, mijnheer, she asks in particular that you should attend her. She says she has an important charge to entrust to you, and no one else can be relied upon to do it."

The surgeon snorted. "What, must I put on my cloak and turn out of doors in the snow at the whim of every mazy-headed pauper that comes through the gates of this town?"

"She's very insistent, Mijnheer Willenbrouckx. And by the look of her I fear that she may not be with us much longer. Childbed fever has carried off many a woman hereabouts these past few months."

In this the midwife was perfectly correct: despite her intelligence and her expertise in the delivery of children she had no way of knowing that after attending each woman with puerperal fever she would as often as not transfer the infection to her next patient; in this case from a miller's wife at Kwaadhove who had died of the fever on the afternoon of Christmas Eve and whom she had helped to wash and lay out. It was a form of blood poisoning which progressed rapidly and was usually fatal.

In the end Willenbrouckx was overcome by his better feelings, and having had no other patients to attend to that day beyond a few festive beer casualties, went with her to the *Cheval Noir*, where he found the young woman bright-eyed and flushed with fever, though the baby lying beside her in a makeshift cradle was sleeping peacefully enough.

"You wished to speak with me." Willenbrouckx said, "And seeing that you are clearly a person of some consideration, I felt that I must attend you." He sat down on a stool on one side of the low bed and the midwife at the other side.

Catherine grasped his hand. "Promise me, mijnheer, as you love God, that you will have my baby baptised tomorrow as a good Catholic…"

"Of course I promise: we shall take him to the church to be christened as soon as a priest can be engaged."

"… and that you will name the child in memory of my poor late husband."

Willenbrouckx looked apprehensively across at the midwife, who seemed as nonplussed as himself. "And what name would you have us give the boy? I fear that…"

"François Ravaillac, the child's father, who is dead now and burned to ashes; who has no tomb for any to weep over, and none to bear his name, which all men execrate, nor anything else in the world except myself, a dying woman with his ring still on my finger, and this poor innocent babe of his."

"But such a name as that: how can we…?" She clutched his hand so fervently that the bones creaked.

"Promise me this! Promise this to a woman who may die this very night! For the sake of Our Saviour and the Blessed Virgin his mother, promise me this last thing!"

Vrouw Boudewijns tried to calm the young woman, who was plainly growing delerious, mopping her brow with a damp towel. But she only fell to sobbing so grievously that a Tartar would have taken pity on her. So in the end, before the surgeon administered her a calming draught and they left, they had both promised to name the boy as she desired. After they came out of the room they conferred for a while on the dark staircase.

"Mad. Quite mad." The surgeon said. "The Widow Ravaillac indeed: such moonshine stuff as never was."

"But she said it as well when I attended her after the delivery" the midwife replied, "even when the cord was scarcely cut. She was certainly not raving then; in fact most calm and composed for a woman who had just given birth. Why do you suppose she said it, if it were mere fancy?"

"Vrouw Anna, the two of us have worked together for many a long year attending to the sick in body of this town, and likewise to the sick in mind. So you know as well as I do that mad people will often seek to redeem the wretchedness of their condition by associating themselves in their fancy with great persons or notable villains. Not five years since we had a young woman arrive in the Hôtel-Dieu most insistent that she was the surreptitious child of the Archduchess Isabella stolen by gypsies and afterwards brought up in a cellar by the Jesuits. And despite old Hooftius attaching a whole jar of leeches to her brows to draw off the madness and purging her to the very gates of the underworld, she persisted a good six months in her nonsense and narrowly escaped being hanged for sedition. Likewise two years since when the brigand chief Bleektandt was broken on the wheel at Steenvoorde, with thirty cudgels hung afterwards around the rim to signify the number of his victims, there were a half-dozen women in this town who claimed to have been his mistress and to be with child by him. But now we've both gone and indulged this poor madwoman in her deranged fancies. I fear no good can come of it."

"What else were we to do?" the midwife asked. "The poor creature was fairly raving and implored us so that I thought my heart would break. But what now? If we do as she wishes then we might as well christen her child Judas Iscariot and have done with it."

"I wish I knew: I've often been given deathbed commissions, but never one as strange as this. Anyway, go along now if you please, and speak with Canon Blanchard to appoint a time for the child's baptism. As for a christening robe, use the old one that we keep for such charity cases. But for the moment, say nothing of the child's name. I must consider what to do."

So they parted, and Willenbrouckx returned home, went to his study and called for Anke. She brought him a pewter mug of beer warmed at the kitchen fire.

"Anke" he said, "I would ask a small favour of you."

"Ask, mijnheer, and as always I shall do my best to oblige you."

She said it without irony: though they were master and servant their relationship was a long and mutually respectful one, with Anke never hesitating to speak her mind on family matters.

"I know that you collect pamphlets and broadsheets, since every time a peddler comes to the kitchen door I see you scrabbling for a shilling in your purse."

Anke sniffed. "I may be only a humble housekeeper, mijnheer, but I still like to know what goes on in the great world." This was true: unusually for a serving-woman Anke was literate; and not just in Flemish but in French as well. And she did indeed like to keep up with events: especially wonders and prodigies, and also executions, which she never missed and would often walk long distances to attend if there were none in prospect in Houtenburg. She would often say that for children, one good hanging was a better lesson in morality than a hundred sermons.

"Your interest in public events is most commendable, Anke. So might I ask you to lend me your store of such literature for an hour or so? There's something that I need to be quite sure of."

"Certainly, mijnheer." She curtsied and bustled out, happy that such a learned gentleman as Mijnheer Willenbrouckx should be seeking her advice on matters requiring more informed judgement than the collection of bacon fat or the removal of moths from woollen bed-curtains. Her position as housekeeper to the municipal surgeon gave her considerable prestige among the wives in the Market Place, who would often seek her advice on their various ailments, so it was doubly gratifying now for the master to be seeking her advice as well. She returned a few minutes later from her room in the garret carrying a brass-hinged limewood box, which she placed on the table before returning to the kitchen. Willenbrouckx opened the box and found inside it two bundles of folded papers, one tied up with red ribbon and the other with green. He untied the green bundle and found that it consisted of pamphlets relating to prodigies: *True Relation of a Two-Headed Foal Born Lately Near Wormhout*; *A Mighty Whale Washed up on the Strand at Nieuwpoort*; *The Great Stone of Iron That Fell from the Sky at Hazebrouck on Trinity Sunday*; *A Bull-Calf with the Face of a Man Lately Born Near Tongeren*; *A Man-Child with the Face of a Bull Lately Born Near Waereghem*, and so on and so forth. He tied it up again and opened the other bundle, which consisted of broadsheets relating to notable crimes and their consequences: usually crude woodcuts of the deed and the subsequent retribution accompanied by the malefactors' last words from the scaffold – real or invented – and concluded by doggerel verses pointing out the moral of the story. The titles were predictable: *Authentic Narration of the Atrocious Poisoning of Her Husband by a Tallow Merchant's Wife of Bailleul and Her Subsequent Trial and Burning*; *Ten Murdering Brigands Broken on the Wheel at Rijssel, with the True History of their Foul Crimes*, and so forth.

The surgeon leafed through the twenty or so sheets of paper until he found what he was looking for. It was a quarto sheet folded in two and bearing eight successive panels, two per side, each depicting a scene and accompanied by a caption in French, Dutch and Latin. The quality of the copper engravings was fine and minutely detailed; the work (he noted) of "*Willem Swaanenberg, Leiden, anno 1610*". Willenbrouckx saw at first glance that Swaanenberg and his assistants (for the work was too much for one engraver to have done in so short a time) had more than a passing acquaintance with the public buildings of Paris: the Louvre palace and the Hôtel de Ville which he remembered well from his student days. The pamphlet was entitled *A True and Authentic Narration of the Most Horrible and Unnatural Murder of Henri IV, King of France and Navarre, in the Rue de la Ferronerie in the city of Paris on the 14th day of May 1610, and of the Subsequent Execution of the Monstrous Regicide François Ravaillac on the Place de la Grève on the 27th day of the Same Month*.

The first panel showed the Devil looking on approvingly from above the housetops as a man in a broad-brimmed hat and cloak standing on the wheel of a coach lunged in through the window to stab the King seated inside.

I. *Urged on by Satan his master, the foul and unnatural murderer Ravaillac plunges his dagger into the breast of the father of his people, that best and most benevolent of princes King Henri IV of France.*

II. *Blood pouring from his mouth, the king is carried by his attendants back to the Louvre but expires on the way. The monstrous villain Ravaillac is meanwhile seized with the fatal dagger still dripping in his hand. Despite being put to the severest torments he maintains that he acted alone.*

III. *Following his condemnation, with a torch in each hand the hellish parricide Ravaillac is carried in a tumbril from the Conciergerie Prison to the Place de la Grève before a vast crowd thronging the streets.*

IV. *Clutching the knife with which he committed his detestable crime, the unnatural monster Ravaillac's right hand is burned off in a brazier of pitch and sulphur. Flesh is then torn from his breast, arms and thighs with red-hot pincers, after which boiling oil, burning resin and molten lead are poured into the wounds. Despite these torments and the urging of his confessors he still refuses to name his accomplices.*

V. *Four horses are harnessed to pull the foul assassin Ravaillac asunder. After an hour, the beasts having proved unequal to the task, the onlookers help them to complete their work.*

VI. *Driven mad with grief and rage, the crowd hurl themselves upon the hellish miscreant Ravaillac's dismembered trunk and limbs and tear them to pieces. His remains are afterwards gathered up and burned and the ashes fired from a cannon.*

VII. *The monstrous regicide Ravaillac's father and mother are commanded to leave the realm within thirty days and never to return. Meanwhile the cottage where he was born in the village of Touvres and the house where he lived in the town of Angoulême are pulled down, and the places where they once stood are made into dunghills and places of everlasting infamy.*

Willenbrouckx paused here. In itself, the doleful catalogue of horrors described in the pamphlet moved him very little. Pain was an inescapable part of every man's life, and no one knew that better than a surgeon, who had every day to slice into living flesh, set broken bones and cauterise ulcers without the slightest regard for his patient's sufferings: who indeed would be failing in his professional duty if he paid any heed to their cries beyond instructing his assistants to hold them down more firmly. Though himself the kindest and most benevolent of souls, he had to inflict atrocious pain as part of his job for the simple reason that the consequences would otherwise be far worse. And though he avoided such melancholy ceremonies himself and felt a certain distaste for people who treated them as an entertainment, he took a very similar view of the execution of criminals: as the painful but necessary cutting out of diseased tissue from the body politic. He had himself studied surgery in France during the Wars of Religion which old Henri had brought to an end; had seen with his own eyes the refugee-crammed towns stalked by plague and famine and the deserted countryside with its burnt-out, ransacked villages amid fields covered by thistles. So he considered that on balance the maniac whose wanton deed might well have plunged the country back into such misery had got off lightly. No, he took no view on the rights or wrongs of the matter; he was looking for something else entirely. And in the very last panel he found it: a hall full of venerable bearded gentlemen in ruffs, counsellors' robes and tall hats; many of them with a hand raised as if to make a point or to indicate agreement.

VIII. *Sitting in solemn session, the Parlement of Paris decrees that from now until the end of time, under pain of death, no person in the King of France's domains shall ever again bear the accursed name of Ravaillac.*

Willenbrouckx laid down the pamphlet and reflected. So if it was now a hanging matter to be called Ravaillac in the King of France's territories – whose border was not a mile away from where he now sat – then it would be no less than a felony to give that name to a new-born child; effectively placing a noose around the infant's neck along with its chrisom robe. But he had made a promise to a dying woman, and the surgeon was (all were agreed) a man who took his promises very seriously indeed. So he took a piece of paper and a lead pencil and began to scribble various combinations of christian and surnames. At last an idea came to him: the distant memory of a poor little hamlet amid the heaths and peat bogs of Drenthe near the town of Hardenberg where he had been billeted for five rain-soaked months in the winter of 1591, after the Dutch rebels had taken Gronigen and Verdugo had sought to take it back from them, until brimming rivers and an empty pay-chest had obliged his army to go into winter quarters. He wrote out the name three or four times, holding the paper at arm's length to consider it critically since his eyesight was now starting to grow dim with advancing years. At last he was satisfied, and called Anke up from the kitchen to return the box of pamphlets and thank her for her assistance. To salve his conscience and exonerate himself at the Last Judgement of the charge of promise-breaking he could (he thought) always plead hardness of hearing, for having spent so many years practising surgery with cannon thundering next to his tent he could truthfully lay claim to a certain dullness in the ears, which was on balance an advantage rather than a handicap for a surgeon. In any case it mattered little, since the child's mother would soon be dead of fever, so only Vrouw Boudewijns would survive as a witness to his undertaking.

And so the next day, the 27th of December 1610, in the abbey church of Saint Wolverga in the town of Houtenburg in the county of Flanders, before the required two godparents Michel de Willenbrouckx, surgeon, and Anna Boudewijns, midwife, a male infant was duly and perfunctorily baptised *in nomine patris et filii et spiritus sancti* by the young Canon Blanchard, who had three more brats to christen that morning. The boy bawled loudly as the icy font-water was dribbled on to his forehead. And afterwards in the vestry his name, distorted from "Frans van Rawijk" by the vagaries of Flemish orthography, was inscribed in the great parish register as "Frans van Raveyck, firstborn child of the Widow Catherine van Raveyck, traveller; place of abode unknown; currently lodged at the *Cheval Noir* inn".

And thus inauspiciously began the history of one of the most original and inventive minds even of that century so replete with exceptional spirits and mighty talents. For we must all be born somewhere, and in the end it is not where or how we begin our life that matters but what we do with it afterwards.

* * * * * * * * * *

Though I might quibble with his remarks regarding the name "Rawijk", and cannot think how he came by that information, since my stepfather always told me my name was derived rather from the barony of Raveyck which is near Turnhout in the county of Brabant (though its castle is long since demolished), I must agree with our chronicler's wise observation that how a man lives his life is more important than how he begins it. For many notable fools were born in palaces, while many who later did great things in the world first saw the light of day in surroundings every whit as unpropitious as my own. Throughout my life the knowledge that I share the day of my nativity with Our Saviour Jesus Christ, and likewise the outward appurtenances of it, such as a stable in a poor lowly little town to be born in and a virgin for a mother, has always been a singular source of strength to me. For like myself, Our Lord was subject to calumny and vilification throughout his life on Earth and suffered much opposition from those who remained wilfully blind to the truths that he revealed to them. To be sure, unlike Jesus I have not been put to death (though I came quite close to it on a number of occasions) while it remains to be seen whether I shall be able to rise from the dead on the third day. But despite those discordancies Our Saviour and I were always borne up alike by the knowledge that even if the outward circumstances of our birth were lowly, our paternities were unusual to say the least of it.

The same stars preside alike over castles and cowsheds, and over the nativities of princes and beggars. As soon as I was of an age and wit to have some understanding of these matters I cast my own natal chart, having the advantage of a precise time for it since my mother remembered that I came into the world at around ten minutes past seven o'clock on the morning of the 25th of December, as the church bell finished ringing for Matins. And I discovered with no great surprise that the course of my later life could easily have been foretold from the constellation that presided over my birth. Sagittarius ascending with Jupiter its ruler in the seventh house portended a life of great successes, but of equally great checks, when the largeness of my designs would prove greater than the means for carrying them out: one where passion and the urge to master the elements would be accompanied by great mutability and sometimes – I freely confess it – a facility in too many matters for me ever to be truly the master of any of them, so that flux, movement and the great watery vastness of the ever-shifting sea would be the common themes of my life. The Sun being in the first house decreed that I should be fiery, proud and full of vigour in whatever I essayed, impatient of the timid little souls of clay that so often surrounded me. But the conjunction of warm, generous, abundant Venus and dry, melancholic old Saturn in the second house was an unfortunate one, since it meant that my facility for gaining wealth would be equalled only by my aptness to lose it all again, and that like the tides of the ocean gold and silver would flow away from me just as readily as they flowed towards me. Likewise the moist and fickle

Moon predominating in the fourth house indicated that my life would be one of movement and journeying, never tarrying long in one place, and always restless so that no sooner had I arrived somewhere and set down my bags than I would be up again and off somewhere else. The heavens rule our destinies, and could we but read them aright all things in past, present and future would be plain to us.

My name likewise, though given to me quite fortuitously in order to disguise my paternity, turned out to be so aptly and prophetically chosen that I was never in the slightest tempted to change it from mangled Flemish to its pristine French form even if it were not still, I assume, a hanging offence to bear that name in the King of France's domains. For the name Raveyck, though my stepfather chose it for its similarity of sound to "Ravaillac", is in itself most apposite since it is derived (scholars agree) from the conjoining of the two words "raaf" – which is to say, "raven" in the Netherlandish tongue – and "eyck" which signifies an oak tree. Throughout my life these two components in my name have shaped my earthly destiny as inexorably as the stars themselves. The raven, though by common consent the wisest and most subtle of birds (Athene's owl is a mere fool by comparison), is also reputed both in the legends of the ancients and in the fireside tales of our country boors to be a bird of ill omen; the bringer of bad tidings and the tatler of secrets. It was the raven who brought Apollo the news that Coronis had made a cuckold of him, and was therefore the cause of Aesclepius his son being entrusted to the centaur Chiron, who taught him the art of medicine, which I suppose should make that bird the emblem of all us doctors: not least because many a husband since Apollo has first learned of his wife's playing him false from a physician examining his water in a flask. In the epics of the old Goths two such birds, Hugin and Munin, sat upon the shoulders of Odin and spoke wise counsels into his divine ears. And the raven, like myself, is a perpetual roamer and though he does not migrate at set seasons or along regular paths in the sky like the storks or the swallows, never stays long in any one place but continually ventures afield in search of new domains. And the other part of my name, the oak tree? Why that signifies steadfastness and fortitude against the battering of the rowdy storms, so that our word "robust" comes from the Latin *robur*, signifying oak wood: a debt which I duly acknowledged when King Louis ennobled me by taking a raven sitting in an oak tree as my coat of arms, and likewise when I built a house in France, named it "Corbeauchêne". The choice of an appropriate Latin name however, once I began to correspond with my fellow virtuosi in that language, caused me no small amount of head-scratching. At first I considered "Franciscus Roboreus"; but that made me sound a dull wooden fellow, as though my feet were rooted in the soil and leaves sprouted from my ears. Then I tried "Franciscus Corvinus", which though it sounds scholarly enough with its suggestion of flapping black robes and musty libraries, entirely omits the oak-tree part. So in the end I settled for "Franciscus Ravecius". But you may know me throughout these histories as plain Frans Michielszoon van Raveyck while in the Low Countries (the "Michielszoon" I added later on to honour my stepfather, though patronymics were by that time somewhat fallen out of favour) or François de Ravècques when in France, or Doctor Francis Ravick in England. But in the end, as Monsieur de Montaigne so justly observes, what does a name signify other than that which men have agreed among themselves that it shall signify? I am who I am; I could be no one else even if I desired it; and I fancy that no single hair on my head would change its colour were I to have been christened either Woodlouse or Zeus King of the Gods.

CHAPTER TWO

By rights Catherine Maertens – or la Veuve Ravaillac if one gave credence to such addle-headed stuff – should never have lived to see the year 1611. Childbed fever was as untreatable as most other diseases were in those days, and usually killed its numerous victims within three or four days. But this robust young woman, fruit of a long line of sturdy Flemish peasant farmers, proved to be cut from solid cloth and stitched together with double seams. Her fever soared throughout the third day of Christmas, so that by late afternoon Vrouw Boudewijns was about to send for a priest to administer extreme unction while Vrouw Cellier made sour-faced arrangements for laying out the body of a guest so lacking in elementary courtesy as to die while lodging at her inn. But with devoted nursing from the midwife and Laetitia Willenbrouckx – who though in poor health herself, had gone to the young woman's bedside once she learned of her plight – the crisis passed about the time that the bell rang for Vespers, and by dawn on the fourth day Catherine had sunk into an exhausted but peaceful sleep. Although she would never know it, she had been saved from death by the happy chance that Doctor Hooftius was away in the countryside visiting relatives over Christmastide and refused to be brought back to Houtenburg to bleed and purge a mere vagrant woman – though for a while he did consider making the journey in order to try out the new drug antimony on a patient with no next of kin to complain to him afterwards. The fever left her weak and drained, but by Saint Sylvester's Day she was making a good recovery. Her infant son had meanwhile been placed with a wet-nurse in the Heilige Bloedstraat and was completely unperturbed by any of this, as one might expect with a child only three days old now safely received into the bosom of the Holy Catholic Church so that he might escape the fires of hell and receive Christian burial if – as was more than likely – he failed to survive his first year.

As Catherine convalesced in the first week of the new year she was rarely without anyone to sit by her bedside. Vagrant women giving birth in ditches and sheepcotes were two a farthing, now that the armies had been disbanded following the Dutch truce and the heaths and woodlands of Flanders swarmed with ex-soldiers and their dependants trying to subsist by begging and highway robbery. But this young woman clearly had neither part nor lot with that lousy thieving rabble, being instead a person of respectable birth and cultivated manners fallen upon some misfortune which had temporarily unhinged her mind. It was not that she was a great beauty or particularly delicate in person: "solidly handsome" would better describe her, with her honest, squarish countenance, her sturdy country girl's body, her grey-blue eyes and her darkish blond hair which she was very particular about keeping braided up even as she lay in bed. It was rather that she had about her a quiet refinement quite unlike either the affected airs of the meaner sort come up in the world or the foolish arrogant braying of so many gentlewomen-by-birth. Her hands were small and her fingers slender, and their movements precise and measured as those of a professional lacemaker. Likewise she was remarkably devout, asking as soon as she had emerged from her fever that the *viaticum* might be brought to her, and clutching at the little locket (which must surely contain some saint's relic) that hung on a chain about her neck when Vrouw Boudewijns tried to remove it in order to bathe her. And in conversation with her it was plain that she was either a person of the quality herself, or had long been in contact with such. Though evidently a Fleming – from the Tournesis to judge by her accent – she also spoke court French perfectly and with only the faintest whiff of Flanders cow-dung about it, to a degree where even Laetitia (who preferred French to Flemish and was very proud of her diction) began to feel somewhat self-conscious when talking with her.

And there was still the abiding mystery of what had brought

her to Houtenburg in the first place. Apart from the periodic fires, epidemics and pillagings little that was remarkable ever happened in such an insignificant town, so that a dog being skewered by an icicle falling from a house-eave or a pig escaping from the butcher's block to take refuge in the abbey church became major sensations and were talked about for weeks afterwards. Thanks to the Dutch truce and King Henri's recent mishap the planet Mars was in the descendant for the time being, and likewise there had been no public executions since last summer to give the town something to talk about. So the nocturnal arrival of a woman big with child being chased along the road from Sottebecque by an angry mob was bound to excite gossip; particularly on the following market day when some women from that town came into Houtenburg to sell their produce. Yes, they said: stories of witchcraft and wild rumours among the town's rabblement that "the villain Ravaillac's whore" had come among them to bring plague and misfortune. Nine months pregnant too, so that their utterly undistinguished little town might soon have the distinction of being the Antichrist's birthplace, which was hardly likely to increase the desirability of its sheep's-milk cheeses in the marketplaces of west Flanders. A violent thunderstorm on the night of the winter solstice had not helped matters either, since lightning had struck the church tower and set it ablaze. The final straw (they said) was a mare giving birth next morning to a foal with six legs, which though no one had actually seen it or counted the legs, must surely be a sign of God's extreme displeasure. So in the end the usual small-town mob of idlers and good-for-nothings had assembled to drive the woman out before her presence brought any further calamities upon them.

Before long such idle gossip was causing murmurs in Houtenburg as well, among the vulgar and ignorant sort who seem to spend their lives in search of some new foolish thing to believe. So in order to forestall a mob gathering in front of the *Cheval Noir* – since like garden weeds, evil rumours are best rooted out before they flourish and produce seed, and nothing drives out a nail more effectively than another nail – Vrouw Boudewijns and Laetitia Willenbrouckx used their connections and their prestige as persons of judgement to have it noised abroad that, contrary to idle gossip now circulating in the town, the young woman lying at the inn was in fact a good Flemish Catholic and a former lady's maid, later married to a master stonemason called Joris van Raveyck from Maastricht (which town they hoped was far enough away for people not to ask questions) who had been killed by a collapsing wall while working in Paris on the new frontage of the Hôtel de Ville, leaving his pregnant wife a widow after only a few months of marriage and obliging her to lodge with a cousin in Sottebecque. Her misfortunes had distracted her mind for a while, and the proverbially foolish people of that town* – who everyone in Houtenburg agreed had no more brains between them than a herring – had seized upon her name as a reason for chasing her across the border into Flanders. But she was now safely delivered of a fine healthy child, God be praised, and was making a good recovery among her own people with wholesome beer instead of noxious French wine to drink and good honest Flemish countryfolk around her once more instead of the mincing and affected Fransquillons. These counter-lies did their work most efficaciously, such is the natural credulity of the ignorant sort as apt to believe one arrant falsehood as another, and within a few days the malicious rumours had faded away to be replaced by a mild and generally benevolent curiosity, with people congratulating themselves that though it was only a poor obscure little town, Houtenburg had a generous heart and could always be counted upon to look after a daughter of Flanders fallen upon misfortune in a foreign land.

Even so, some delicate matters remained to be resolved as Catherine returned to health. In the first place someone would have to break the news to her that her first-born child was not

---

* Sottebecque (from Flemish "zoutebeek", salty brook) means something very close to "foolish gob" in old French.

named François Ravaillac as she had implored – a mad conceit if ever there were one – but Frans van Raveyck according to the law, three witnesses and an entry in the parish register: likewise that by dint of the same process she herself had become de Weduwe van Raveyck. And there was also the small matter of what was to be done with her and her child once the lying-in was over and she would have to be supported either by her own work or by public charity.

Of these two sensitive subjects, the first and thorniest turned out in fact to be the easiest to resolve. It was left to Laetitia to broach the subject of the child's baptism and to explain why, in view of the Parlement of Paris's late decree, bearing a formally attaindered name meant that it would be death for her – and her son as well, once he had reached man's estate – ever to put their noses across the French frontier; likewise that even in Spanish Flanders it would hardly be prudent to saddle an innocent newborn babe with the name of a man condemned and executed not eight months since for murdering his lawful sovereign. Laetitia expected tears and recriminations. But in the event the young woman took the news calmly and seemed to see the perfect reasonableness of not giving her child a name that might one day lead him to the gallows. In fact she seemed much less insistent on the Widow Ravaillac business than she had been a few days before, which led Laetitia to hope that the hysterical fancies that had filled the young woman's head during the last days of her pregnancy had now redescended to her womb and been expelled with the afterbirth. She herself, after all, had been a mother five times and well remembered the strange cravings and odd imperious notions that had gripped her when she was with child. Or perhaps (as Doctor Hooftius might explain it) the burning heat of her late fever had acted on her brain to dispel the hot, moist vapours that had clouded her reason as a result of the Sun, the Moon and Venus conjoining in the third week of December.

That evening Laetitia spoke with her husband over supper, once Regulus had gone to bed. "I confess, she's a strange young woman and a complete enigma to me. But still I think that I never met a better-hearted or more sincere creature in all my life. God alone knows what trials and afflictions brought her to her distracted state. But I think she may now be recovering her proper mind at last."

"What makes you think so? As one of the Lay Sisters of Charity you minister to mad people in the Hôtel-Dieu with a rope girdle round your waist and sandals on your feet in the depth of winter – though I've long maintained that your health is too fragile nowadays for such mortifications – so you know as well as I do that not all lunatics rave and thrash about in the straw: in fact the most frightening ones of all are those who are quietly insane."

Laetitia drank some more table beer – she was permanently thirsty of late – and wiped her lips with a napkin. "True enough, Michel. But did you ever see or hear of a maniac, challenged in their most cherished delusion, calmly consenting to accept a lesser delusion in its place?"

"What do you mean, madame?" Willenbrouckx always used this form of address to tease his wife, raising one eyebrow as he did so.

Laetitia put down the beer tankard. "I meant, monsieur, that she wished you to have her child baptised as François Ravaillac – which you will surely agree is as ripe an insanity as ever there was – yet calmly consented a week later to the boy being given a made-up Flemish name as though it were the most natural thing in the world, and if you had christened him The Man in the Moon or Till Uylenspiegel she would have been just as well content. It's as though a madman who believes himself to be Our Lord Jesus Christ should reflect upon his folly, and then agree that perhaps he is not Jesus after all but merely John the Baptist instead. My own experience of lunatics is that confronting them in their madness merely drives them further into it."

"Do you mean, then, that you believe this Ravaillac nonsense of hers?"

"I mean that, though I don't entirely believe her, neither do I entirely *disbelieve* her. Certainly something very strange and singular befell her."

"Indeed it must have done: it falls to the lot of very few of us to be pursued along the roads of Flanders on Christmas Eve by a mob seeking our life. But from your talking with her, do you have any notion of who she might really be?"

"No more than you: we've spoken but little about her family and circumstances, having had more pressing matters to occupy us, like bringing her back from the churchyard gate and caring for her child in the meantime. But she's certainly of the better sort: the daughter of a substantial farmer or perhaps a petty gentleman in the Tournesis. And quite plainly she also spent some years in Paris in a great household: I can tell that from her speech. I think that she was most likely a lady's maid or a seamstress, because she has already had Anna Boudewijns bring her linen and needles and thread and is busy sewing shirts for the child, with as neat and as deft a stitch as ever I saw in my life. From what little she's told me of herself I understand that she was educated at a convent in Tournai, and that she has some skill in lace-making, because she asked me to bring her a cushion and some bobbins so that she can make cuffs for the child's robe."

"So what are we to do with her? Does she have a family in Tournai that she can return to, or must this town support her and her infant? Before long I shall have to make a recommendation to the poorhouse guardians whether she and the child are suitable recipients of our meagre charity, or whether we have the pair of them whipped out of the gates to beg their bread elsewhere."

Latetitia sighed. "Yes, you will. But even if our most worshipful guardians were to agree, I think the Hôtel-Dieu is scarcely the place for her, heckling flax for two liards a day with nothing but scabby beggars, pox-raddled harlots and drooling idiots to keep her company. To send her and her child there would be to condemn both of them to death within the year."

There was little gainsaying Laetitia's poor opinion of the old abbey hospital, the Hôtel-Dieu. Though it had once been one of the most admirable institutions in the whole of Flanders as regards caring for the poor, the sick and the lame in body and mind, it now shared in the decayed fortunes of the town itself. In the days of Houtenburg's prosperity money from tolls and market dues had poured into the municipal coffers, while the endowments of rich cloth merchants intent on buying their way out of purgatory had built the abbey church of Saint Wolverga. In the Hôtel-Dieu the Benedictine brothers could minister to the unfortunate without having to keep too close an eye on the cashbox, washing the sores of lepers with rosewater and dressing them in fresh linen bandages rather than with sorry grey rags which had already bound up a hundred other sores. But the storks, bringers of good fortune, had long since spread their wings and departed from Houtenburg's turrets and house gables. The raid in 1574 by Willem van Lumey's Sea-Beggars* had left the abbey in flames and such monks who had been unable to escape nailed by their hands to its doors or hung disembowelled from the arches round the cloisters like so many Christmas geese, such was the reforming zeal of those Calvinistic pirates and their hatred of Popish error. The Benedictines had not returned to Houtenburg afterwards, preferring to remain a safe distance inland at Saint Omer, so the burnt-out abbey buildings were passed to the municipality to continue the work of the Hôtel-Dieu and the Latin School as best it might. Which is to say, not very well at all. The passing of the woollen trade had left Houtenburg with the spinning of linen thread as the only means to earn its living. Seen from across the fields in early July when the flax was in bloom, the little town seemed a miniature version of the celestial city, floating on clouds of ethereal blue. But in every other respect linen was a poor substitute for wool, causing the ditches round about to stink

---

* In the early years of the Dutch war of independence the Sea-Beggars (Watergeuzen) were part-freedom fighters, part-pirates who harried the Spaniards all along the North-Sea coast. Their most notable exploit was the capture of the town of Den Briel in 1572, which gave the Dutch rebels their first secure base on land.

abominably in autumn as the flax stems were left in the water to rot, demanding huge labour to beat and haggle the stems into fibre – and bringing in precious little revenue for people's trouble at the end of it all, since the thread went to Mechelen and Ghent to be woven into cloth, and the Archduke in Brussels would not grant the town a licence for linen-weaving without a contribution to his war-chest much larger than it could afford to pay. So the destitute were constantly beating on the door of the Hôtel-Dieu, especially when wars disrupted trade or the harvest failed (which seemed of late to be every other year) and bread was dear. The town still allotted enough money to save people from starving to death in the streets: though grown threadbare, municipal pride was still not entirely worn through at the elbows. But it had no funds to provide them with anything better than a straw mattress in the chilly damp cloisters, a coarse barley loaf per day and employment haggling flax stems into raw linen – which in itself caused ill feeling, since employing paupers at such a task merely depressed the wages of those who were doing exactly the same work outside the walls of the poorhouse. Hard times were normal in this fallen world. But Houtenburg's hard times seemed by now to have become the permanent state of affairs.

Even so, one man's disease or a whole town's may at the same time be another man's fortune. And as far as Michel Willenbrouckx was concerned the surgical practice was prospering well enough as Houtenburg entered upon the year of Our Lord 1611, its collective head still throbbing from twelve days' imbibing of kerstbier. Willenbrouckx was a proficient surgeon and known to be such, and now had enough patients to occupy all his time, so that the barbering side of the business had lately been leased out to a shop further down the street and surgical patients no longer had their woes increased by out-of-tune madrigals villainously accompanied on the lute by those waiting their turn in the barber's chair. Human misfortune and folly being pretty well constant at all times and in all places, the supply of patients was little diminished by the town's decayed fortunes. The surgeon had made the happy discovery, which had so far evaded even such economists as Doctor Copernicus or Sir Thomas Gresham, that medical care defies the laws of the market in that the greater the supply of it, the greater likewise is the demand.

The good thing about practising in such a small town (Willenbrouckx reflected with suitable gratitude) was that he had very little competition. For the physician Doctor Hooftius was widely distrusted in spite of his fur-trimmed gown, his imposing physical bulk, his little pointed beard and his impressive parchment degree of *medicinæ doctoris* from Louvain University with all its seals and signatures. Though Flanders country people were greatly in awe of the educated and would pay a good deal to be mumbled over in Latin and Greek, they were still peasant-shrewd enough to make the practical observation that untimely death was alarmingly frequent among the doctor's customers: or as folk put it, "Where Doctor Hooftius goes the sexton soon follows, and he were as well carry a spade with him in his physic bag." Though he meant well enough, Hooftius was a diehard Aristotelean, foolish as only a well-educated man can be, and would doggedly explain every symptom within the framework of the four humours and the movements of the stars, so that he was said once to have refused even to look at a flask of urine red as claret wine on the grounds that the patient's temperament was clearly phlegmatic not sanguine and that Pisces (which is a cold watery sign) was in the ascendant when the sample was taken, so any alleged redness could only be the result of eating stewed beetroots. He had recently won local notoriety by bleeding a new-born infant so savagely that the poor mite expired, then bleeding the mother to death to accompany her infant, then maintaining that since Mars was in opposition to Saturn his only fault was not to have bled them enough, and the distraught father had to be bundled out of the house to prevent the doctor from bleeding him as well for good measure. He would allow of no treatments other than blood-letting, emetics and purges, and had lately become a great exponent of antimony, which although mentioned by neither Aristotle nor Galen and advocated by the charlatan Paracelsus, made up for those shortcomings by being so violent an emetic that patients given a few grains of it in a glass of wine were soon vomiting up their kidneys in a most satisfactory manner. The result was that in recent years his medical practice had dwindled to that of an astrologer giving consultations on the most auspicious times to conceive – a great interest of his, about which he would question his female patients in minute detail – and the most favourable days for people to take their annual bath; but otherwise anyone with a doit's worth of common sense would go to Mijnheer Willenbrouckx or to Vrouw Boudewijns. The town midwife, being unencumbered by a university education, had laid up a store of useful observations over the years, such as the effect of an infusion of witch-hazel bark in reducing fevers and the use of a tisane of foxgloves in the treatment of heart palpitations. Which Hooftius, when he learned of it, dismissed as the merest empirical quackery since the ancient authors made no mention of witch-hazel, and likewise infusions of foxgloves ran clean contrary to the Doctrine of Signatures since that flower bore no conceivable likeness to the heart. He then did his best to have the midwife deprived of her licence for trespassing on the territory of physicians.

It also had to be admitted, even by the most hardened doomsayers in the tap-room of the *Cheval Noir*, that the town's fortunes, though scarcely flourishing, had at least got no worse over the past year or so. Trade had picked up a little following the Dutch truce, now that the agents for the Haarlem linen weavers could freely purchase Houtenburg thread, which was much cheaper than in Holland where the manufactories were booming and wages were high. Likewise the last two harvests had been adequate, so bread was cheaper and people had a little more money in their pockets; not just for surgery but for the things that led to it. In a land where a gallon or more of strong beer was part of every man's daily diet, where every gentleman wore a sword, where every farm labourer carried a knife and where every beggar could tear a cudgel from a thicket, the call for a surgeon to sew up knife wounds and repair cracked skulls was constant over and above the more usual accidents of this sublunary world such as collapsing walls, toppling ladders, falling chimney pots and harvesters' scythes swung without due care and attention. The days following fairs and church festivals would see the benches in the hallway crowded with rustics nursing broken heads and stab wounds, while the Corpus Christi procession in July and St. Wolverga's fair in September were particularly rich seasons for a surgeon.

And there was now also a growing demand for the dressing of gunshot wounds, which made Willenbrouckx grateful for his time as a military surgeon. Decades of intermittent warfare had introduced Flemish country people to gunpowder, and likewise left the meadows littered with discarded muskets which could be cut down by a village blacksmith to make a crude fowling-piece. Recklessness and bumpkin stupidity did the rest. Every autumn and winter careless loading and drink-fuddled imprecision of aim produced a rich harvest of shot wounds for the surgeon to treat, compensating in no small measure for the seasonal decline in farm injuries and festive knifings. The rustics were usually well enough satisfied after Willenbrouckx had picked the swan-shot out of their buttocks, suffering that operation with their customary grunting stoicism and afterwards dropping their silver shillings into the copper pot by the door with only half-hearted attempts at haggling down the price. The Flemish peasant's pig-headed obstinacy (he reflected) was a nice generator of revenue for the surgeons and lawyers who had to deal with its consequences. As the local saying put it, "I'll have what I like!' said the farmer, and roasted butter on a spit": an apposite enough motto for stubborn fools who would cheerfully fill a glass bottle with gunpowder, then drop it on to the kitchen fire to demonstrate that gunpowder will not explode unless flame touches it; and commonly for no better reason than that some other stubborn fool had maintained that it will.

Not the least of the reasons for Willenbrouckx's high reputation was that the wounds which he dressed hardly ever became seriously infected; dribbled a little pus perhaps (which was only to be expected and was a normal part of the healing process, so that its absence was a bad sign rather than a good one) but rarely became so inflamed and stinking that further flesh had to be cut out and eventually the whole limb might turn gangrenous and have to be amputated. By nature a fastidious person, his experience as an army surgeon had taught him the importance of cleanliness in his work. Likewise his time with the Spanish fleet had brought him into contact with a Neapolitan ship's surgeon who had introduced him to a fluid called spirits of wine, distilled from grape brandy in a succession of alembics. The Neapolitan – who claimed on dubious authority to have learned the practice from the Arabs in Baghdad – swore that dipping the instruments in the spirit and then setting them alight over a candle to burn for a few seconds with a quiet blue flame had the effect of drawing off the earthy moist humour that hung about the steel and reacted with the patient's blood to poison wounds; as might indeed be predicted from first principles since Mars, the ruling planet of iron, stands in direct opposition to Jupiter the ruler of the sanguine humour. Over the years Willenbrouckx had suffered much mockery from his colleagues on account of this eccentric practice; but despite its doubtful basis in theory he had persisted with it to the great profit of his surgical practice, remarking as he counted the day's takings that so far as he was concerned the iron of Mars and the tin of Jupiter might strive with one another as much as they pleased, provided only that the Sun's gold and the Moon's silver lived harmoniously together inside his purse.

The previous year a chance gunshot wound had proved the making of the practice, when a gentleman from Watten was brought to him lying in the straw of a farm cart with a steel rod transfixing his right eyeball and passing clean through his brain to emerge from the parietal bone on the left side. It was the ramrod of a pistol which he had been cleaning and which, unknown to him, had still contained a charge of powder when he squinted down the barrel to see what was obstructing it, then pulled the trigger. It was a hideous wound and his life was despaired of. But with great care and trouble Willenbrouckx had managed to extract the ramrod – which by some miracle had touched no major blood vessel – then remove the damaged eye and close the hole in the patient's cranium with the original fragment of skull, which the gentleman's daughter had had the presence of mind to retrieve from a flowerbed and had brought with her wrapped in a damp handkerchief. The patient made a full recovery, though the damage to his brain meant that he could no longer speak either French or Flemish, but only Spanish; which was unfortunate because he detested the Spaniards and everything connected with them and some years later (it was said) hanged himself in a barn because his very name had mutated in his mouth from Jeroen de Vischer to Jerónimo el Pescador. The fame of the operation spread throughout Flanders, and the surgeon's reputation was made. As he would often say to Laetitia when no one was about to overhear, "If we had need of one, the motto on the gable-stone of our house would be *'Pecunia ineptorum merces prudentorum'* * ".

Thus it was that in that cold January, as the sun moved into Aquarius and hung low over the ice-covered water meadows, the Willenbrouckx household had reason to feel as prosperous and secure as any family could in those days of wars, famines, pestilence and every form of sudden and arbitrary death. In that particular month the surgeon had more time than usual to attend to his municipal duties. Blood-letting was in abeyance, since most people chose the spring for that operation, as the sun climbed in the sky and the sanguine humour accumulated in their veins along with the sap rising in the trees. The short winter days and the slackness of work in the fields meant that farmyard injuries were few: at most a farmer with his guts hanging out from being gored by a bull, or the stump of a finger to dress where some fool had cut it off while chopping firewood. So the surgeon could sit in his study with a charcoal brazier (for his blood was thinning with age and chilblains plagued him every winter) dealing with his papers and

---

* "The money of fools is the reward of the wise"

casting up accounts for the next meeting of the poorhouse guardians. He was still out of pocket for the stay of the Widow van Raveyck and her infant at the *Cheval Noir*. It would have been grossest barbarity to have moved the poor woman so soon after her confinement and the fever which had nearly taken her life. But move she must before the end of the month; either to private lodgings if she could pay for them or to the Hôtel-Dieu if she could not. As to the mysterious friend or cousin of hers in Sottebecque, a messenger had been sent after New Year to the address she gave in that town and was informed that the woman who lived there, a certain Demoiselle Lemaire or Le Merle (no one seemed quite sure which) had left in great haste at Christmastide, at dead of night and without telling anyone where she had gone. Catherine's family near Tournai were either dead or untraceable. So it looked as though for want of funds it would have to be the Hôtel-Dieu.

Willenbrouckx shared his wife's dismay at this latter option. The guardians did their best with the limited funds available to them; but the truth of the matter was that the place was nowadays no more than a sink of thieves, rascals, whores, the incurably diseased, the syphilitic, the incontinent old and the babbling-insane: a refuse pail that gaped to receive all those unable to make their way in the world – and from which, once they had fallen into it, there was little likelihood of anyone ever climbing out again since even the honest poor, once they had entered the Hôtel-Dieu's crumbling portals, tended in a matter of weeks to become as debauched and worthless as the other inmates. It was certainly no place for a woman of refined sensibilities; while as for her child, once the infant was weaned it would be taken from her and set to work picking flax with the other verminous brats in the adjacent Weeshuis, seeing its mother only on Sundays for as long as it lived; which would in all likelihood not be very long since epidemics of measles and whooping cough ravaged the orphanage every couple of years. Clearly, something must be done. But what?

As Willenbrouckx pondered, gazing out at the snow-covered

roofs across the street, Laetitia came in bearing a cup of mulled wine for him, then sat down beside him in her fur-trimmed dressing gown. Since Three Kings' Feast her health had taken a turn for the worse, but she said that she felt a little better now and was able to get up. As so often happened, she seemed to know her husband's thoughts before he ever uttered them.

"The Widow van Raveyck again?"

The surgeon sighed. "Yes, my love: the Widow van Raveyck again. The last day of the month approaches, and I must either apply to the guardians to have her admitted as a pauper, or see her sent on her way to become a pauper in some other town."

Laetitia was silent for a while, then spoke. "I have an idea. Could we not take her into this household?"

The surgeon look puzzled. "Why should we? The woman is no kindred either of yours or mine except through common descent from Adam and Eve. And though the practice prospers well enough, there are still charges on it, with Regulus going to the Latin School before long. We'd be hard put to it to feed another mouth even if the obligations of family required us do so."

"I know that. I meant, could we not engage her as a servant? Anke says that Mayken is likely to give us her notice before Eastertide: off to Madrid this time to have her scrofula touched by King Philip."

Willenbrouckx groaned and held his head in his hands.

"Dear God, not again! Why Madrid ? Was the fortnight's holiday we gave her to go traipsing to Reims for King Louis's coronation not sufficient?"

"She says that King Louis's touching failed to cure her; probably because he's still only a child of ten despite his anointing, and the power to touch for les écrouelles has yet to pass to him when he comes of age. As for King James of England, though by all accounts he often touches for scrofula, quite apart from all the bother of getting herself to London she says that he's plainly disqualified by reason of being a Protestant heretic, which might well cure her bodily ills only at the price of winning her soul a place in hell. So Madrid it must be."

The servant girl Mayken's scrofula and possible cures for it had been a staple of conversation in the Willenbrouckx household ever since she had first developed the unsightly weeping lumps on her neck two years before. Willenbrouckx had tried all manner of salves and had even considered cutting out the infected lymphatic glands. But in the end it had come down to the donation by Saint Remigius to the old Kings of France – and by extension to all the other princes of Christendom – of the power to cure the condition by laying on of hands. Except that here in Spanish Flanders in 1611 there was (it seemed) no properly qualified monarch nearer than King Philip III in Madrid. So a two-month journey to Spain appeared to be the servant girl's only hope of a cure.

"So do you propose that we engage the Van Raveyck woman as a kitchenmaid?" Willenbrouckx enquired. "She seems to me to be a cut above that, and unlikely to take for long to drawing water from the well and scrubbing floors."

"Only for a short while, Michel. Anke is getting old now and talks of entering a béguinage in Bruges this year or next. She could teach her duties to the Widow van Raveyck, then retire and leave her as our housekeeper. The woman is intelligent and cleanly in her person, and young and strong besides, and gives me the impression that she would be most diligent about her duties. And of course, she's as deft a seamstress as ever threaded a needle. We have a great need for new linen and bed-hangings, now that my eyesight prevents me from sewing and Anke's hands are stiff with rheumatism. So I think that if we let her depart from this town we might afterwards go a great deal further to find a servant and fare a great deal worse."

Willenbrouckx smiled wearily. "And do you not fear to have a young woman here in the house with me? Many a wife would."

"Not I, Michel: I know that you could never deceive me: not because of what I am but because of what you are." She laughed, suddenly shedding the permanent weariness of the past few years to become as bright-eyed and vivacious as when they were courting. "And anyway, a silly impotent old fool like yourself would be no hazard to a housekeeper's chastity, though she possessed the charms of Aphrodite herself."

"You speak no more than the truth there, " he replied, "My member serves me now only to pass water, and that but fitfully. She would be as safe here as one of the Great Turk's wives among his eunuchs. Very well then: go speak with her tomorrow and make a proposal."

So on Ash Wednesday 1611 the Widow Catherine van Raveyck duly entered the household of Michel Willenbrouckx, barber-surgeon, in the capacity of serving-woman and seamstress at a wage of thirty Flemish pounds per annum, payable each Lady Day, plus her board and lodging. Since she could not have Frans with her in the house the boy was put out to a wet nurse in the nearby village of Veldeghem: a good solution, since his mother's wages were adequate to cover the charge and it was in any case better for a baby to grow up in the wholesome air of the countryside than amid all the stinks and contagions of a town. The wet nurse, Bette Cortsteert, was an honest woman with four children of her own, in good health and free from scrofula, rickets or other visible diseases, and her small farmstead – her husband was a sailor and away at sea most of the year – would be a good place for little Frans to spend his first years. His mother slept meanwhile on a straw mattress in her tiny room under the eaves, seeing her child every Wednesday afternoon and the whole of each Sunday after Mass. And in the meantime she scoured pans and scrubbed floors with a will and a strong Flemish farm-girl's arm, to Anke's complete satisfaction though she was the severest of judges in matters of household management.

As the March days lengthened and the ascending sun entered the sign of Aries, Catherine began her campaign to sew the new bedlinen and shirts and petticoats and curtains that the household had long needed, sitting tranquil in the spring sunlight by the great window that looked out on to the Kortestraat as the howls and roars of the surgeon's patients echoed down the brick-paved hallway (which was disturbing at first, she found, like living next to a slaughterhouse, but one soon grew accustomed to it). She was grateful to have found safe haven at last after a tormented, terrible year, and as she sat plying her needle in-out-turn-pull-in-out-turn-pull her troubled mind, soothed by the regular motion of stitching as a baby is by the rocking of its cradle, began to arrange the crazy jumble of things that had befallen her during those twelve months which now seemed more like twelve whole years. She wondered sometimes whether she might have been bewitched, or perhaps have dreamed it all in the delerium of her fever. Yet there were parts of it that were undeniably, terribly real: the pangs of giving birth in a freezing cowshed; and seven months earlier, seeing the child's father for the last time, being drawn through the streets in front of Nôtre Dame in a cart before a crowd howling for his blood, in his shirt with a burning torch in each hand and still pale and half fainting from being put to the extraordinary question in the Conciergerie not an hour before, while stones and filth flew about his ears and the Archers and the Swiss Guards struggled with their halberds to prevent the roaring mob from storming the tumbril and tearing him to pieces. She would slam the lid of that box shut and resolve to think of it no more: but still the memory would not go away. So, being literate and writing a neat hand which the sisters had taught her at the convent in Tournai, she began before long to procure sheets of paper from the housekeeper's accounts drawer and write things down, to record them before they faded from her mind altogether. And as they were written, a sheet every few months, her recollections were hidden away in a double-locked wooden box secreted beneath the floorboards in her room. By writing down fearful things (she discovered) we can sometimes render them less fearful to us.

★ ★ ★ ★ ★ ★ ★ ★ ★

I am grateful to the writer of this history for having supplied us with the foregoing information, because I myself – though, unlike him, I was actually there at the time – was but an infant in arms and unconscious of what was going on about me, or else my memory too inchoate and unformed for me to have any precise recollection of it afterwards. As he informs us, when my mother entered the Willenbrouckx household as a servant in the early months of the year 1611 I was placed out to foster with a household of boers in the village of Veldeghem a mile or so outside the gates of Houtenburg, amid the polderland on the road towards Cassel, and lived there happily enough for the next three years or so with my mother coming to visit me several times a week. Nourished by a Flemish foster-mother's milk, and later by good cheese and vegetables – and much fish too, since we were only an hour's walk from the sea – I grew up into a sturdy well-knit child with handsome red-gold hair which my mother said I had inherited from my poor father who was no more; though as I shall relate in due course, it was not until much later that I learned the reason for his no-moreness. I began to walk, and to babble prettily in Flemish (though my mother and I would usually converse in French when we were together), and played happily about the farm with my nurse's two sons and two daughters. I suffered the usual maladies of infancy such as measles and pertussis, and shrugged them all off without further detriment, having – praise be to God – inherited from both my parents a robust constitution which has supported me throughout a lifetime of adventures and tribulations. In short, I grew up to be a lusty small boy competent to swim in the canals and meres in summer with the other village children, and skate along them with mutton bones tied to our clogs when they froze over in winter; to climb the alder trees beside the reedy brooks and catch frogs and eels in the fenny meadows. I dare say if left thus in my half-savage rustic state I might have grown into a passable Flanders boer, clumping along the roads in my buttoned leather gaiters and doffing my hat as I passed each wayside crucifix, sitting over a pot of beer in a tavern on market days and cursing the price of oats indiscriminately whether it be high or low; scarcely less rough and unschooled than the two naked wild-men with clubs – "woodwoses" I think you call them in English – who support Houtenburg's coat of arms on the front of the Radhuis with their loins wrapped in green foliage. But neither my birth nor the fate inscribed in the stars that attended my nativity would ever permit me so cloddish a destiny.

By the time I approached the age of reason, at about four or five years, it was evident that I was not cut from the same homespun cloth as the country children around me, my nature already princely and dignified so that my companions were in no little awe of me. Not that I was a heavy child in any way: the rule of Saturn was limited in my natal chart, and the influence of dull heavy lead therefore small in proportion to that of Jupiter's tin and Venus's ruddy copper which smelt together in the furnace to make noble bronze, and of the Sun's bright gold. On the contrary; I was a quick and lively boy, aware of everything around me and possessed of a great curiosity to know and to grasp objects in my hands, even trying once to snatch glowing coals from the fire because they shone so prettily, which caused me to howl most piteously and have my infant fingers smeared with butter and wrapped in bandages a good week afterwards. I had about me even this early in my life a kingly dignity which pleased the goodwife Cortsteert and her village gossips as much as it perplexed them, though it was not until many years had passed that I would discover why.

My nurse told me years later that when I was a toddling child there was much talk among the villagers that whereas they discounted the talk of my being the regicide Ravaillac's child as so much stuff and nonsense, occasioned no doubt by the ignorant folk of Sottebecque hearing the words "de Weduwe van Raveyck" through their ears half blocked with louse droppings (it signifying the same thing in Flemish as "the widow *of* Raveyck"), they still thought that from my bearing and temperament I must be some French nobleman's child fathered upon the poor Juffrouw Catherijn, and she obliged to invent a dead husband for herself to hide her shame on returning to Flanders with a belly greater than the one she took with her. In our childish games I became the ruler, as ordained by Jupiter predominating at my birth; not through imposing myself upon my fellows as a tyrant (which I might have done if Mars and Scorpio had ruled the heavens at the hour of my birth) but rather through them freely recognising me as their monarch, which it is said that even silly elephants will do if they happen upon a king, dropping down on one knee and reverencing him with their trunks. Yet for all that, I lacked learning; and as a mere serving woman's child I looked set to remain so beyond such little instruction as a parish school might give me: that is to say, barely enough to sign my own name beneath a bill of sale on market day or reckon the price of a pound of cheese if it be three shillings the stone. My fancy was too lively and my apprehension too quick for them to be satisfied with such coarse rustic fare. And here the stars ordained that I should receive an education just as soon as I was ready to profit from it. But even so, it still makes my heart heavy to think upon the doleful chain of events by which that very same constellation – so benevolent for me but so malign for another – would unlock the gates of learning.

CHAPTER THREE

Year after year, life went on in the town of Houtenburg much as life had always done and in all probability always would do until the Day of Judgement brought all earthly things to a close: ploughing sowing and reaping; spring summer autumn and winter; Corpus Christi and Saint Wolverga's Fair; Shrovetide and Candlemas; the passing hours of the day marked by the cracked iron bell of the abbey church clanking out over the fields for Prime and Matins, Angelus and Vespers in a world with little competing noise other than the lowing of cattle in the meadows and the cawing of rooks in the alder groves, the clinking of a blacksmith's hammer on an anvil and the lumpy rumbling of iron-tyred cart wheels on the rutted country roads, the quotidian hum of spinning wheels turning flax into linen thread, the nasal skreeling of bagpipes at a wedding feast and the town drummer's rattle-tattle echoing through the streets when a proclamation was to be made. At the end of March, predictable almost to the day, the storks would arrive to build their untidy nests, always on the same chimneys and barn roofs, which brought the householders good luck and also protection against lightning. The great white birds would spend the summer gorging themselves on the frogs that pullulated in the damp Flanders meadows. Then in September, always on the same day, they would flap into the sky to return to wherever it was that they spent the rest of the year: by the Nile in Egypt, according to a few intrepid travellers who had seen them there. And another year would to draw to an end as the days shortened, the leaves fell and Orion the Hunter rose in the heavens.

To be sure, there were small, geologically slow changes to the daily round. In the year 1612 the heads of the Archduke Albert and the Archduchess Isabella appeared together on the fine new silver patagon coins struck to replace the old Flemish chaos of reals, guilders and livres in which every town minted its own money. And in the same year the municipality purchased a second-hand clock from Bailleul, which was rebuilding its town hall, and installed it in a hole cut in the façade of the Radhuis on the Market Place. It was a clumsy old-fashioned affair driven by great weights hanging on chains, but it had a carillon of five bells to chime the hours and was an affirmation of Houtenburg's municipal status even though most of the townspeople regarded it as a frivolous innovation and a waste of public funds, since everyone knew what time it was without a clock to tell them and what was wrong with the church bell and a good honest sundial such as their grandfathers had used? The town walls crumbled a little more each winter; flax was harvested in the autumn to be left rotting all winter long in the ditches, then haggled, combed and spun into thread. Fools died, and other fools were born to take their places. Beer was brewed, bread was baked and oxen were slaughtered; pots were made and pots were broken and thrown out to be replaced with other pots; shoes and pewter plates were bought, and wore out, and new shoes and plates had to be bought in their stead. Such was the sublunary world, such the sublunary world had always been, and only the archangel's peremptory trumpet blast at some unspecified date in the future would ever put an end to the daily round and the annual procession of the sun through the signs of the zodiac. Those who could read – a growing number in Flanders these days – bought their crudely printed almanacs from the peddler and pored over them at their kitchen tables, laboriously tracing out the letters with their calloused forefingers and muttering the words to themselves under their breath: the numinous predictions that "*in this year there shall be droughts in divers places, and floods in others. Great events shall happen, and many that were mighty shall be cast down while others that were hitherto of little consideration shall be raised up.*" Winters were cold – old people said far colder than in their youth – so that in most years by early January the ditches and canals had frozen over solidly enough for people to skate upon them with mutton bones strapped to their shoes if poor, or the new-fangled steel blades imported from Holland if more affluent. Hard winters bore heavily on the poor in their draughty hovels; but at least they kept the plague at bay by freezing the hot, moist humours that engendered it, and while lesser fevers abounded, that most terrible emperor of all earthly misfortunes had not visited the town for ten years or more. Winter or summer, most of Houtenburg's inhabitants lived and died as their parents and grandparents had also lived and died, seedtime and harvest world without end amen, and thought little into the future beyond their next pot of beer.

In the Willenbrouckx household domestic life continued much as before once Mayken had departed for Madrid to be touched by King Philip. She would be gone for at least six months, and had talked before she left of afterwards entering a convent in Spain, a nun's habit having always seemed very stylish to her and there was now an order of Flemish sisters in Toledo. Catherine took over the servant-girl's duties, and proved very proficient at them. And as well that she should too, since Laetitia's health was deteriorating and her domestic responsibilities had to be placed on the shoulders of the servants. Mijnheer, after all, could not be expected to concern himself with day-to-day management of the household; not when his waiting room was full every day with folk from miles about nursing cuts, broken bones, aching teeth, ulcers, boils and all the infinite variety of ills and injuries which the flesh is heir to. In any case, the surgeon was now often away from home for several days at a time, riding out into the countryside with his apprentice Pompeius de Vos as far afield as Hazebrouck and Licques to cut for bladder stone, which was far more common in the chalky country of Artois than on the Flanders marshes. It was an operation which took him far more to the manor houses and chateaux of the rich than to the hovels of the poor, since only the quality could afford the considerable fee for having their bladder cut open, and were anyway more prone to calculus than the meaner sort since their diet, mode of life and social status plainly disposed them to it. Bile, after all, was the bodily humour that most corresponded to the noble warlike estate, and bladder stone was no more than a concretion of bile, as might readily be ascertained at post-mortems by the frequent presence of stones in the biliary duct. As the surgeon would remark to his assistant (though not within earshot of his patients), "Well-water and oatmeal never yet engendered calculus nor the gout, Pompeius, so the fees that we charge to cut for the stone are but a tax on the rich that allows us to treat the poor for nothing." His practice prospered, and his professional standing grew with it, to a degree where it was widely predicted that despite the poor and obscure little town in which he lived, he might well be considered one day for election as Master of the Surgeon's Guild of Saints Cosmo and Damian in the town of Ypres.

He had little competition nowadays from Houtenburg's only other surgical practitioner, the public executioner. Although Bartolomeus Nooten had enough to do in these hard-up times performing the duties for which the town council and the seigneurial court paid him his stipend (and also a patch of land and a cottage outside the town walls, since no one would live next to him), he could not subsist from his main employment alone. Perhaps twenty times each year he would hang malefactors, or occasionally break them on the wheel or burn them if the court's judgement specified it, and in between whip lesser criminals through the streets at the tail of a cart, brand them or put them to the ordinary question in the cellar of the Bergues Gate as directed by the investigating magistrate. In themselves, however, the duties of public minister of retribution no longer paid well enough to support a family and two assistants. Nootens worked as a contractor to the town council rather than its employee, and although the municipality furnished the tools of his trade like the town gallows and the seldom-used beheading sword (beautifully made in Solingen a hundred years before when Houtenburg still had cash to spare, with the motto TIMOR LEGIS SALUS REIPUBLICAE* en-

---

* "Fear of the law is the health of the community"

graved down the blade), the consumables, like rope for hangings and faggots for burnings, had to be provided by the executioner himself out of his fee. And since that fee had not increased in a century, while the price of everything else had doubled or tripled, there was a constant temptation to scrimp. Often with most lamentable consequences, as at the burning of an Anabaptist woman in 1612 when the amount of wood purchased by the executioner was quite insufficient to do the job, leaving the wretch standing among the embers charred but still alive, and even the customary bag of gunpowder hung round her neck too little and too loosely packed to end her sufferings, so that in the end someone had to fetch a musket and shoot her. While the onlookers agreed that Anabaptists were the very spawn of Satan and would bring hailstorms and the plague to any community that tolerated them, the whole sorry episode brought discredit both upon Houtenburg as a town of penny-pinchers and upon Nooten himself as a hapless bungler. He had inherited the job from his father, but in truth he had never had much enthusiasm for it, having always wanted to be a saddler, and in addition was seriously astigmatic and short-sighted. Judging the weight of his victims was always a problem for him since they appeared to him much shorter and fatter than they were, with the result that Nooten usually turned the unfortunates off the ladder too low for the drop to break their necks, so that members of the crowd had to come forward and swing on their feet to complete the job.

Executioners had always supplemented their income by healing the poor and simple; partly from an ancient superstition that those who dealt out death also had the power of life; partly from an entirely empirical observation that if a broken leg needed setting or an aching tooth had to be pulled out, then someone with a strong wrist, a sure eye and a sovereign indifference to other people's suffering was the best man for the job. All who remembered him agreed that old Balthasar Nooten had been a master of his trade; able to decapitate a man so deftly (people said) that the victim knew nothing of it until he sneezed and his head fell off.

And he had been a notable healer as well, once reduced to tears when he was called upon to behead the very criminal whose fractured skull he had mended so neatly the previous year. But over the years his miserable son had steadily lost the family's surgical clientele, his poor eyesight invariably causing him to wrench out two or three healthy teeth before he located the offending one, and setting broken bones so incompetently that on several occasions Willenbrouckx had been obliged to rebreak them with a mallet and wedges so that he could set them properly. One customer had died of blood poisoning after Nooten extracted a splinter from his thumb, so in the end Willenbrouckx had petitioned the town council to forbid the executioner from practising surgery or bone-setting and restrict him instead to less dangerous procedures like laying on hands and selling his used nooses as a cure for sore throats. The petition was refused: ancient rights were ancient rights and anyway, as town physician Doctor Hooftius could be guaranteed to block any measure intended to safeguard the health of the public. But Willenbrouckx was still quietly glad that Nooten had now effectively put himself out of business, after having monstrously botched a beheading in front of a huge crowd come from all over Flanders for the occasion. A gentleman highway robber, a discharged army ensign, had demanded a death appropriate to his rank; very unwisely as it turned out since Nooten's first stroke missed his neck and cut into the base of his skull, while the second almost severed his arm at the shoulder, whereupon the unfortunate got up and stumbled bleeding about the scaffold until he fell off it, being at last wrestled to the ground by Nooten's assistants and his head hacked off with a butcher's knife like a sheep in a slaughter pen. His last audible words were "You bloody villain! Did I pay you five ducats to mangle me so?" The crowd's hoots and cat-calls turned to lumps of filth and then to stones, and it was only the intervention of the town's musketeers that saved Nooten from being thrown into the river or worse. Houtenburg was soon the laughing stock of all Flanders. At the next meeting of the town council Willenbrouckx suggested that if the fool kept his job, then to avoid any further such embarrassments he should at least be provided with a pair of spectacles at the town's expense. After the matter had been put to the vote Nooten retained his office and likewise remained without glasses, since the council felt that having a bespectacled public executioner might expose Houtenburg to even greater ridicule than before. But as for his practice as a healer, his mystical aura was quite gone and his patients now took their ailments to a proper surgeon. Like the divinity of kings, the magical aura of hangmen can never be restored once it has been lost.

Yet for all his growing prosperity and renown, by the autumn of the year 1613, as the declining sun passed through the equinox, domestic concerns were looming on Michel Willenbrouckx's horizon, huge and dark as the angry stormclouds driving in from the North Sea. Laetitia's health, long fragile, was now worsening visibly from one day to the next: permanent exhaustion, fainting, constant thirst yet constant passing of water so that two, then three chamber pots had to be placed beneath the great bed every night. And now failing vision and suppurating sores on her feet as well. Much against his better judgement, Willenbrouckx consulted Doctor Hooftius, who to no one's surprise – and without even examining the patient – recommended a regime of bloodletting and purgatives so ferocious that the public hangman himself would have baulked at applying it. The surgeon paid the doctor's fee without demur, thanked him and left his house, then sent a message to an old colleague from his student days in Paris, the physician Doctor Philippe Renaudot in the town of Abbeville in Picardy, who for friendship's sake rode two days' journey to Houtenburg along the muddy November roads. The doctor examined Laetitia, took some of her urine, then in the privacy of the surgeon's treatment room boiled a little of it over a candle in a pewter spoon until the watery constituent was all gone, leaving a sticky yellowish-brown residue which he then tasted. He shook his head sadly.

"As sweet as honey. Michel, my friend, your wife has *diabetes mellitus*, from which sentence there is no reprieve, nor any holy water or invocation to the saints that will cure her. Here, taste it for yourself."

Willenbrouckx dipped his tongue gingerly into the sour-smelling deposit; it was indeed little more than sugar syrup.

Renaudot sighed. "Before you ask me that which as her husband you must ask me, I see no hope for her. In thirty years' practice as a physician I have never known any patient to recover from a sweet consumption of this kind. Diet, blood-letting, fasting, purging, emetics, laxatives, astringents, poultices, cataplasms: none is of the slightest efficacy. Prepare yourself as best as you can for widowerhood. And instruct my lady your wife to make herself ready for the life to come, for this one is nearly over for her."

"How long will it be?"

The physician shrugged. "Who can say? Five months: perhaps six? The sweetness will spread through her body, starting at the extremities, and in the end turn her limbs to candied orange peel, causing the small blood vessels to atrophy and the flesh to die from lack of nourishment. All that you can do is comfort her and ease her end as best you can."

The doctor's prognosis turned out to be entirely accurate. Necrosis of Laetitia's feet set in during the weeks before Christmas, leading to blackening flesh and a hard, dry gangrene which Willenbrouckx had to cut away every day until the bones themselves were exposed. Laetitia drank until she seemed near bursting, but was still tormented with thirst, and her sight grew dimmer by the day as the retinas of her eyes broke down into bloody pulp. Anke and Catherine and a hired nurse did their best for her, but by the Feast of Saint Agatha in the year 1614, when the snow lay thick outside, the battle had clearly been lost: her legs were now gangrenous and stinking to the knees so that amputation seemed the only course. Yet what good would that agony do her, except allow her to suffer a few days longer? And what husband who loved his wife could saw her two legs off above the knees with his own hands? In the end there was nothing that Willenbrouckx could do but summon Hooftius once more and tell him that, after giving the matter his most earnest consideration, he now saw that he had been wrong and the physician right and that heroic blood-letting was the only means by which the corrupted bloody humours that had accumulated in his wife's legs might be drawn off. Hooftius smiled his fat little smile, and remarked that he was glad that the surgeon – whom he always addressed pointedly as "meester", not "mijnheer" – had now come round (albeit belatedly) to recognising the wisdom of the ancients and the time-hallowed therapies which their writings enjoined upon those who had Latin and Greek enough to read them in their entirety, and not just selected extracts put together for ignorant empirics who fancied themselves physicians. Swallowing the insult for the sake of a greater good, Willenbrouckx acknowledged his fault and instructed the doctor to do what was necessary – except that he asked as a special favour, since it would be too painful for him to wield the fleam himself, that the doctor's own assistant might open his wife's veins and he not be obliged to look on. Since it behoves victors to be magnanimous, Hooftius graciously consented to this and left the bedchamber while Willenbrouckx spoke with his wife for what he knew would be the last time. They held hands as they had done when they were courting twenty years before.

"Michel, my love: promise me something."

"What is your wish, madame?" She smiled weakly, as though even that action now fatigued her.

"My wish, monsieur, is that when I am dead and buried..." (the surgeon winced) "...you will marry Catherine."

"How could I marry anyone after losing you?" He was tempted to say "enough of such foolery: you will be up and about by Easter" but he knew that neither she nor he would believe it any longer. "I'm forty-seven now: an old man fit only to sit by the fire and maunder about the days of my youth. I would sooner remain a widower for the rest of my days."

"Don't be such a silly old gander! You need a wife to look after you all the more now, and Regulus a mother." With infinite effort she raised herself on to one elbow and looked at him with her by now almost blind eyes, seeing only his dim shape in the candlelight. "Anyway, why do you think that I suggested bringing the young woman into our household three years ago, but for your sake and his? I felt my strength draining away even then, and wonder only that it took me so long to reach my present state. When I am gone, marry her, and even have more children by her. The woman is not even thirty yet; healthy, strong and as honest as daylight." She laughed, a faltering ghost of her old merry peal of laughter. "...And anyway, what more suitable wife could an eminent surgeon have than the widow of the late Ravaillac, who once let blood from the King of France himself?"

Willenbrouckx was horrified. "Laetitia, you speak blasphemy: spit that out and have a care for your soul."

"The dying are allowed to say what they think, Michel: the condemned man's speech from the ladder is our most notable form of public rhetoric here in Houtenburg, and usually the most interesting to listen to. I dread to think what turgid stuff our rederijkers* will put together for my funeral and shall thank God only that I am lying dead in my coffin and not able to hear it. No, Michel, I beseech you now as you loved me when we were both young: marry her when your time of mourning ends, and perhaps you may grow to love her too, and make her as happy as you have made me all these years."

Doctor Hooftius coughed and shuffled outside the door, his assistant having now arrived bearing the fleam and the phlebotomy basin with the section cut out of the rim for the patient's arm to rest in. Willenbrouckx squeezed his wife's hand and kissed her, and left the bedchamber with tears in his eyes, pausing only to make sure that the nurse had placed blanket-wrapped hot bricks in the bed as instructed so that Laetitia would not shiver as the vital heat left her body along with the blood. Ten whole pallets

---

* Town rhetoricians, charged with the task of putting on municipal celebrations and entertainments.

of blood were duly removed from her arm and thighs, then another eight pallets that same evening, after which she fell asleep and never woke again. Hooftius was entirely satisfied with this outcome, which exactly confirmed his diagnosis of the patient's condition and also his prognosis that the blood-letting was likely to be fatal since the Moon was waning in the sign of Aquarius, the ruler of the lower limbs. He deplored only that the patient's conceited ignorant coxcomb of a husband had not allowed him to intervene a month earlier and administer antimony, which would surely have set right the disordered decoction of natural blood in the patient's liver. But at least (he said afterwards) the silly fellow was properly repentant, and had even gone so far as to kiss his hand in thanks when he left the house.

Laetitia was buried on the evening of the 10th of February 1614 in a lead coffin in the vaults of Saint Wolverga's Church, wearing the habit of the Lay Sisters of Charity, with a rope girdle around her waist and sandals on what remained of her feet. There was a funeral oration composed by the rederijkskamer; as turgid as the dead woman had predicted, and stuffed with clumping but still (Willenbrouckx thought) fitting and sincerely meant allusions to Laetitia the Roman goddess of joy and laughter. He and Regulus, now nine years of age and full of a solemn gravity that won the hearts of the onlookers, had led the funeral procession through the dark streets, followed by the town musicians with their muted cornets and sackbuts playing a sad, slow pavane by the Leiden composer Schuyt, and then a cortège of local dignitaries and members of the deceased's family, since although she had been the wife of a mere barber-surgeon she came from the house of the Collaerts who were related to the De Roblés and all the other leading families of west Flanders.

Weighed down by sadness more than he had ever expected, Willenbrouckx was grateful in the weeks that followed for a larger than usual stream of patients in order to distract his mind since (as he would say) "There's nothing quite like extracting a stubborn wisdom tooth for putting one's own petty griefs into perspective".

His time was also taken up with commissioning a memorial to his dead wife: a bust of finest marble, taken from her death mask by the Florentine sculptor Giambatista Carracio at his studio in Antwerp, and also a splendid Latin panegyric written for him by Præceptor Luytens the schoolmaster whose proficiency in the turning of elegant verses in pure Ciceronian Latin was so famous throughout the region that grieving relatives from as far away as Amiens would commission epitaphs from him.

On the last day of February 1615, his year of mourning over, Michel Willenbrouckx was duly married to the Widow Catherine van Raveyck, née Maertens. She had accepted his proposal of marriage with some reluctance at first, fearing that in such a small town a mere servant who had married her master would afterwards have all manner of unpleasantness to deal with: sneering remarks in the market, disdain from the better sort and insolence from the servants; for as the local aphorism so elegantly put it "A widower who marries his housekeeper were as well shit in his own hat then clap it on his head again". But Catherine had never been much like other servants, whilst Willenbrouckx was greatly respected in the town and everyone commiserated with him for the loss of the wife he had loved so dearly. Matters therefore resolved themselves with surprising ease, everyone moving along a little like passengers on the benches of a trekschuit* to accommodate a new traveller, with a little grumbling and resentment at first just for form's sake, but soon followed by matter-of-fact acceptance.

In any case, even before she married her former employer the Widow van Raveyck had become visible in her own right within Houtenburg's little society. She was a proficient lace maker, that having been her mother's trade in Tournai before she married and likewise her own special skill at her convent school. And she was only too happy to pass her knowledge on to poor young orphan girls in the town's Weeshuis who would otherwise have few pros-

---

* Horse-drawn canal barge for passengers, current in Flanders from about 1590.

pects once they left that dreary institution beyond whoredom or scrubbing the floors of farmhouse kitchens, or perhaps whoredom *and* scrubbing the floors of farmhouse kitchens if they happened upon a particularly bad employer. In fact she had lately created a small college of dentellières whose products were delicate and artfully wrought enough to catch the eye of merchants' commissaries from Ghent and even from the Dutch provinces. Orders followed, for the new Houtenburg lace was fine and subtle as the frost on apple boughs in winter, and likewise considerably cheaper than the Bruges or Valenciennes patterns. Before long a sizeable part of Houtenburg's linen thread was being worked up in the town instead of being woven into cloth elsewhere. The town council began to take an interest in lace manufacture as a means of dragging Houtenburg out of the mire of poverty in which it had floundered for most of the previous century. After all, lace was valuable but it weighed very little, so that a whole month's production might be carried on the back of a single packhorse. The old lace-making towns might of course go to the Archduke's court in Brussels and demand a ban on competition, which the Archduke would be only too ready to grant if they poured enough money into his treasury. But sufficient unto the day was the evil thereof, and for the time being lace-making grew and flourished.

In the house *De Salamander* domestic life resumed under the new mistress. At Candlemas 1615 Anke retired at last amid great sobbing and lamentation to her béguinage in Ghent, promising to say masses daily for the soul of poor Mevrouw Laetitia and the prosperity of the new ménage. Catherine came to the great bed, and to his surprise Willenbrouckx found his blood warming again, the desires of the flesh returned after many years of absence like the springtime sap rising in some orchard tree long since given up for dead. Catherine's embraces were loving, and within three months she was pregnant, giving birth to a boy who lived barely long enough to be baptised, then in 1617 to a healthy little girl whom she chose to call Henriette.

The Ravaillac business was never mentioned nor alluded to

now: that was years ago, and whatever fancies or sorcerer's spells had clouded her reason in those distant days, they had long since dispersed and had never returned. Willenbrouckx sometimes wondered to himself what torments of body and spirit could ever have led his wife into such folly, she being a person of such sound judgement and exemplary common sense. But he was tactful enough not to ask, so the matter was never mentioned between them even on those mornings – perhaps once or twice a year – after she had been moaning and crying strange things in her sleep and woke sweating to clutch her husband against her as though all the demons of hell were crowded into their chamber and lifting the bed-curtains to peer at the sleeping couple with their eyes of fire.

As for Frans, now four years old, he now returned from Veldeghem to live in the house in the quality of the master's new stepson. Such an elevation was far from unusual: sudden, early death and frequent remarriages meant that few households in Houtenburg (or in Flanders or the in whole of Christendom beyond) were without a step-something-or-other, and new families cobbled together from the remains of old ones were the rule rather than the exception; as normal as patched dresses handed down from mistresses to servants, or new houses built with the timbers of old ones, or old leathern bottles converted into shoe soles. Regulus meanwhile accepted his stepmother with the gravity that came so naturally to him, like some little monarch offering his hand to be kissed by a new chief minister kneeling before the throne. He had progressed some two years since from a dame-school to the Latin School beside Saint Wolverga's Church – though in truth he showed more aptitude for scribbling sketches than for pounding geometry and Latin declensions into his head. His new younger brother, presented to him ready-formed like one of Jason's warriors sprung from a dragon's tooth, plainly won his whole-hearted approval. Frans had been formally taken out of petticoats and breeched on his fifth birthday as was the custom, and had started attending school to learn reading and writing, solemn and dignified in his new estate as second son of the town surgeon. He accepted his new family and household with scarcely a qualm, while as for Willenbrouckx, unlike many stepfathers he treated his new son with as much affection and consideration as if he were the child of his own body, so that apart from one having a different surname there was no difference in their treatment between his two sons. For his part Regulus, an amiable boy though somewhat dreamy, was very protective towards his younger brother when he too started to attend the Latin School at the age of seven; a year sooner than was normal in recognition of his lively intelligence and quick apprehension.

As to the delicate matter of his true paternity, his mother unfolded that grievous truth to him delicately and gradually, explaining it to him little by little as she tucked him up in bed in the evenings and recited his prayers with him that he was not the son of her present husband, but of another who was now dead. And on the 27th of May each year she went with him to the abbey church to have a mass said for a private intention and light a candle in front of the image of Saint Francis.

★ ★ ★ ★ ★ ★ ★ ★ ★

That I would go early to the Latin School was no surprise to anyone: least of all to myself, since it had been plain from my very earliest days that I was a child of rare wit and ingeniosity; quick to apprehend everything I was taught and of insatiable curiosity regarding my surroundings. By the time I was five I could scribble passably well on a slate, and likewise read both Flemish and French, soon scorning the simple horn-books of the dame-school in favour of Anke's almanacs and sinnepoppen, which are collections of moral tales with little woodcut pictures hawked from house to house by peddlers in the Low Countries. I soon passed on to Latin learned from my mother's breviary (which had the two texts side by side, Latin and Flemish), then on to simple tales from Ovid and Aesop, so that before long the gods and heroes of

Greece and Rome were as much my companions as the Houtenburg urchins. Lysander and Perseus played with me in the Flanders meadows and bestrode the night sky above me when I would gaze into the heavens and see Andromeda and Pegasus frozen for ever in the immutable stars, as familiar to me as the tower of the abbey church or the distant lantern on top of Dunkirk belfry.

Likewise that which lay beneath my feet excited my infant curiosity as much as that which was above my head: frogs, toads, spiders, flies and slow-worms as I grew older and marked where they would hide themselves in the damp summer grass; soon learning to distinguish an adder from a culverin* by the black mark on the back of its head. Folk said fie upon me for meddling with such loathsome creatures, and some years later it would go very ill with my parents on account of this interest of mine. But I begged to disagree with them, and at the age of seven or thereabouts had my ears soundly boxed by Canon Blanchard in a cathetical class in the Latin School for suggesting to him that toads and flies were not generated from corrupt matter as all men believed, but came from eggs like hens or sparrows, which I myself had seen by patient observation: that fly maggots were but a stage intermediate between a fly's egg laid in rotting flesh and a new fly, and that if one prevented flies from settling on a dead carcass by covering it with muslin (as I had done lately with a dead rat) then no flies would emerge from it but the corpse merely bloat up and then collapse in on itself as it dried. Which practical experiment of mine, when I related it to him, merely caused the canon to remark that I was an impudent young fool to disagree with what the ancient authors had written and every man knew besides, and that I would surely end my days on the gallows, whereafter I might illustrate the spontaneous generation of blow-flies using my own carcass as an example.

Our human anatomy likewise intrigued me. Unlike many surgeons in those days, who were (and still often are) as ignorant as

---

* Grass snake.

hogs in the mire and no better than so many shoe menders as regards the theoretical part of their trade, my stepfather was a man of wide and profound learning and possessed a goodly library of anatomical works for me to consult: our fellow-countryman Vesalius's *De Humani Corporis Fabrica* with its wondrous copper-plate engravings and the *Oeuvres* of the surgeon Ambroise Paré, whose student my father had been in his youth and for whom he had an unbounded admiration. Without my ever thinking about it, I settled from my earliest years into a surgeon's way of thinking and never contemplated any other calling. Though I held the basin for him at blood-lettings as soon as I was seven or eight years old, my stepfather was insistent at first that I should continue at Latin School until I was old enough to go to university to study physic, "For though the physicians are for the most part egregious asses" (he would say) "with their Latin and their Greek and their Galen and Aristotle, and kill their patients more often than they cure them, yet physic and surgery are two sides of the same coin, which is the well-being of the patient. So a surgeon would do well to study medicine first and sift out the few grains of wheat that it contains amid so much worthless chaff, then apply himself to gain his surgeon's licence, which will in the end do his patients a great deal more good." In the end, however, my stepfather decided that I must be trained up by him to become a surgeon before I went to study physic, the reason for this being that my stepbrother Regulus had an invincible horror of blood and wounds and swooned at the merest glimpse of them, whereas I myself was never in the smallest degree squeamish at such spectacles. My stepfather tried to habituate Regulus to it by degrees, since he wished naturally that the son of his loins might become his apprentice and inherit the practice from him when he retired. But in the end we cannot go against nature, harnessing a lion to a plough or forcing an owl to hunt at noonday; so by the time my stepbrother was eleven or twelve years of age my stepfather had settled it in his mind that I and not Regulus would succeed him in his surgeon's practice, while Regulus would be apprenticed to a painter of pictures in Holland where he might be trained up to that profitable trade, since he had not only a neat hand and an exact eye but also a good schooling in the Greek and Roman histories and in Holy Scripture which, with his elegant deportment and good manners, might equip him to become a court painter in Flanders or even in France once he had completed his apprenticeship and travelled in Italy to see the great ruins of antiquity. A cousin of my stepfather's was an intimate of Meester Rubens in Antwerp and said that whilst that notable painter – who was even then much talked of – had no room for any more apprentices in his workshop, a journeyman painter might well find employment there to paint the humdrum draperies and antique colonnades, the naked figures (for his canvases each contained a half-acre of dimpled flesh whether they were a *Judgement of Paris* or a *Martyrdom of Saint Cecilia*) and so on and so forth, and thereby gain advancement and estimation in his profession. For "il Maestro" (the cousin reported) did only the faces nowadays, or an occasional woman's breast if it pleased him (he being mighty fond of women's breasts), and left all the rest of the work to his thirty or more operatives so that he could spend his days out hunting with the Archduke's courtiers and thus secure further commissions for his workshop.

So on Michelmas day in the year 1619, to my great sorrow, my stepbrother, who was just past his fourteenth birthday, departed for Leiden in Holland to enter the workshop of the master-painter Gerbrandt van Meppel in the condition of leerling (which is called an apprentice in England) for a period of seven years. This was hard for me at first, because we two were very close. But I have never been one to grieve for long, and soon found means to divert myself. My study of anatomy, however, though most fitting for an intending surgeon, none the less caused no small disquiet among my elders and betters. To cut up frogs and herrings bought at the fish market was one thing. But it was another matter entirely for me to procure a small porpoise from the fishermen at Gravelines and by dissecting it, establish that it was not a fish at all but a warm-blooded creature with a heart of four chambers, whereas a fish has two and a snake three, and bore its young alive from a womb like terrestrial creatures, suckling them afterwards at a teat. Which information, when circulated among my classmates at the Latin School, got me soundly whipped for teaching that which is contradicted alike by the writings of Aristotle and Pliny and by Holy Scripture, which is emphatic that the whale which swallowed the Prophet Jonah was "a great fish": and therefore (by the process of syllogism) that whales are fishes.

But my attempt when I was about nine or ten years of age to put together an entire human skeleton was a graver affair even than that, and brought me into the most serious disfavour with my masters spiritual and temporal; not least because it involved my scrabbling about beneath the gallows on the Galgenheuvel and other such places of justice along the highways to find vertebrae and ribs and other items fallen from the carcasses of malefactors as the crows picked them to pieces; likewise in the charnel-house of the abbey church which is where the bones of the poorer parishioners are taken after they have lain in their graves ten or twelve years. By these surreptitious means I assembled myself a pretty well complete skeleton fastened together with wire – though the limbs and bones did not always match left to right, coming from dead people of different sizes – before I was discovered and threatened with excommunication, whippings, exorcism and so forth.

For quickness of wit my only equal at the Latin School was a boy called Ghisbertus Lambrechts, the second son of our town clerk Menno Lambrechts, known among us as "the Moor" on account of his dark complexion and curly black hair, it being rumoured that his true father was a Portuguese sea officer who had been billeted at Gravelines before the Dutch truce. He was three years older than myself and two years younger than my brother, which placed him equidistant between us. He had a most ready wit, and though a Latin scholar of prodigious talent was as restive and turbulent a spirit as can be imagined, for ever in bad odour with our masters for his asking them questions which they would not or could not answer. For if my own questioning was restricted to the area of natural philosophy, his was of a more general nature, to a degree where it already smacked (many said) of heresy or even of atheism. He once enquired loudly, when the Abbé Gosaerts told us that Adam and Eve sewed themselves garments of fig leaves, "So what then did they use for thread?" And on another occasion when the Canon Blanchard was catechising us and told us that heaven was so high above us that a millstone would take a hundred years to fall from it to earth, he enquired how long then it would take for a dead person's soul to rise there in the opposite direction. He and I were rivals at first, and came to blows when he called me an upstart young rogue, he bloodying my nose and I repaying that compliment by blacking his eye. And he would also contrive ill-natured jests that dwelled upon my supposed paternity, the rumours concerning which had never entirely gone away, and had me seized on one occasion in the schoolyard by his subaltern ruffians who most grievously hauled at my arms and legs until my joints were near dislocated, "to put the insolent red-haired dog" (he said) "in memory of his father the regicide, for we know that his name Van Raveyck is but a false beard and a subterfuge", which sport continued until the school proctors came running up and dispersed my tormentors with their dog whips. Yet after I had several times punched his head for him he respected me as a scholar, and congratulated me with every sign of sincerity when I and not he won the school's prize for impromptu Latin oration in the year 1621, so that in the end we became friends.

In that same year the two of us collaborated on a practical demonstration, which was to show that iron will float. For I had observed that although a bar of iron will sink in water, an empty iron kettle of the same weight will float with no difficulty at all, as the most ignorant and unthinking of scullery maids will demonstrate a dozen times a day and not wonder at it in the slightest. Yet one of our masters had observed, treating of Aristotle and occult natures – though I think in truth Aristotle said no such thing – that a ship made of wood will float because the occult nature of wood is to float: and that likewise one made of iron (could such a thing ever be conceived of) would infallibly sink because the occult nature of iron is to sink. So I put up my hand and asked him, "*O præceptor, dis mihi*, how then does an iron pot float when a housemaid goes to the river to draw water, so that she has to tip it over to fill it? Might not a ship made of iron be considered as a larger such pot, and float likewise?" For this I was called to the front of the class and made to lower my breeches, and my tail grievously thrashed with a birch for such impious questioning, and all my classmates taunted me afterwards as "Van Raveyck the fool, who thinks that iron will float", until one or two of the bolder among them essayed to come to blows with me; at which Lambrechts intervened to defend me with his fists, saying that they were all dull-witted bumpkins and indeed I was right and they were wrong and between us we would show them as much. Which we did the half-holiday following, by taking an old rusty iron cashbox which he had procured, removing the lid, stopping the chinks with putty and then going in procession to the banks of the river outside the town walls followed by a jeering crowd of our schoolfellows. Lambrechts invited two of our classmates to come forward and attest that the box was indeed of iron, not of wood painted to look like it. Then he signalled me to place the box in the water; where of course it floated peacefully though the water came pretty near the rim. There was silence, then Lambrechts turned to address the crowd.

"Behold, oh ye of little faith: the chest floats despite being made of iron because, as old Archimedes of Syracuse predicted two thousand years ago and our own countryman Simon Stevin has since reiterated in *De Beghinselen des Waterwichts**, the amount of water that the box forces aside exactly equals its own weight because of the air contained within the box. And likewise if the iron of the chest were melted and cast into an ingot, that would sink, because the volume of water that it pushes aside is

---

* *The Principles of Hydrostatics*, 1586

now less than its own weight as having no air to swell it, and iron itself being heavier than an equivalent volume of water. So you are without excuse, oh ignorant Flemish clodpolls, for not only has one of the greatest of the Greeks explained this to you but also a fellow Netherlander, yet you persist in your rustic ignorance, wallowing like so many complacent hogs in the mud of your own benighted superstitions!"

This was too much for our spectators, who seemed quite happy with their benighted superstitions, and Lambrechts and I were set upon and overpowered, then flung bodily into the river to join our floating chest. This earned us both a whipping when we arrived home all dripping and covered in mud and duckweed. But the two of us were happy none the less to have suffered martyrdom in the cause of learning, and from that day on were the firmest friends and allies.

From all this I made a discovery more important even than causing iron boxes to float or learning by heart the bones of the human body: that in this world most folk are more careful of their lazy comfort than of anything else whatever, and will steadfastly maintain that black is white or that the sun rises in the west rather than suffer the pain of having to revise their ideas about anything in any tittle whatsoever. Or, even if they have wit enough to see that a belief is manifestly wrong, will still maintain it in the face of wind and tide for the sake (as it seems to them) of some greater truth. The whole of my life has been devoted to an unending war against such purblind obstinate folly. For was it not myself, and not Mister Evelyn as he falsely maintains, who first suggested to King Charles of England "*Nullius in verba*"* as a motto for his Royal Society?

★ ★ ★ ★ ★ ★ ★ ★ ★ ★

Before long hard times, never encamped very far from the walls

---

* "Take no man's word for it"

of Houtenburg, returned to lay close siege to the town. On the first day of April of the year 1621 the twelve years' truce between Spain and the Dutch came to an end and was not renewed. Once again, trade with the northern provinces was embargoed while the Scheldt was closed off by the Dutch forts at its mouth, so that Antwerp's commerce soon withered and died and like a tourniqueted limb. As for poor obscure little Houtenburg, its linen thread could no longer reach the accustomed buyers in Haarlem except by pack-horse to Calais and then north to Texel in neutral French vessels, the freight charge for which made the thread too dear for the Dutch market. To be sure, some of it was now needed for the town's own lace-making, since the French market was growing as fashions changed and the old neck-rasping starched ruffs were ceding place at King Louis's court to easy-falling lace collars which allowed men to wear their hair long. But this produced its own discontents within the town since lace-making was exclusively women's work, whereas spinning was men's and women's without distinction. Husbands found themselves sitting idle while lace-maker wives and daughters still had silver in their pockets, which led to all manner of disputes and drunken pummellings, and church sermons on the pride and wantonness of women who demanded proper respect from their menfolk since they were now the breadwinners. In the taverns men began to curse the interfering Widow van Raveyck, who had once thrown herself upon the town's charity as a vagrant and who now repaid its kindness by sowing trouble and discord among them with her affected fransquillon lace-fiddling. They maundered nostalgically over their pewter tankards about their grandfathers' and great-grandfathers' days, when the men of Houtenburg were busy week-in, week-out weaving good woollen broadcloth the thickness of a horse's blanket (which folk wore winter and summer alike, mind you...), when the craft guilds fixed wages and prices, when strong beer was a stuiver the gallon and women knew their place.

The resumption of the Dutch war made itself apparent in other, more directly grievous ways. France was still neutral, having too little money and too many troubles at home to resume its war with the House of Habsburg. But at the same time King Louis XIII was now twenty years of age and wished to cut a brave figure in the world by leading armies in battle, which all men agreed was the most proper and fitting occupation for a monarch. The Dutch were known to be seeking an alliance with France, so the frontier between France and the Spanish Netherlands could no longer be considered safe and must be reinforced insofar as the threadbare finances of the Spanish Netherlands would permit. The result was that in June 1621 the town of Houtenburg had friendly soldiers billetted upon it for the first time rather than hostile ones billetting themselves.

Not that much difference was apparent to the unfortunate townsfolk that summer morning as seven hundred Spanish troops came tramping through the Bergues Gate with trumpets, drums, horses and all the clanking, jingling panoply of war, their muskets sloped across their shoulders with matches burning and their pikes held aloft in intimidatingly perfect order, all dipping as one to pass under the gate-arch. For these were Spanish soldiery in fact as well as in title. Most of the "Spanish" armies who had fought for the past two generations against the Dutch in Flanders were not Spaniards at all but locally recruited Flemings, or German or Swiss or Italian mercenaries, or Irishmen, or even some regiments of English Catholics. But the hard core of the Army of Flanders was still the invincible Spanish tercios. And half of the tercio Guzmán el Bueno, raised around the city of Seville and lately blooded in the Palatinate campaign, was now to be billeted upon the hapless folk of Houtenburg, who would be required not only to provide its board and lodging but also to raise a voluntary contribution among themselves to help pay its wages, since little of the prodigious flood of silver that poured from the mines of Peru ever seemed to get as far as the regimental pay-chests of King Philip's army.

It was plain from the very start that if the tercio's title contained the words "el Bueno", that was about the extent of its benevolence. The soldiers were billeted in threes and fours in the houses of such townsfolk as were either too poor or too lacking in influence to secure themselves an exemption. And veritable tyrants they soon made of themselves, scorning the poor fare and accommodation that the householders could provide for them – mesclin bread, herrings, cheese and beer, which the Spaniards frankly despised – and instead demanding meat, wine and finest wheaten bread; wiping their muddy boots on the bedsheets, hacking the furniture at sword-play or breaking it up to burn. They requisitioned the best feather beds, as often as not ejecting the poor householder and his family to sleep with their livestock in the straw of stables and cowsheds while the dissolute soldiery caroused and played dice in the finest rooms, leaving their gaming and cock-fighting only to molest the women of the household. Any attempt to remonstrate with them would earn the plaintiff a good cudgelling, and any intercession with their officers was met at best with haughty disdain, or more usually answered with a few whacks from the flat of a sword and a kick in the backside, since the meanest of Spanish pikemen esteemed himself a gentleman and therefore entitled to administer a good thrashing to any civilian who vexed him in any way. The soldiery would draw their swords against the townsfolk as readily as against one another – which is to say, very readily indeed – and would not hesitate to run a man through the body if they considered him lacking in respect, so that several unfortunates paid with their lives for failing to step into the miry gutter to let a Spaniard pass. And not just the town's menfolk either: one Wednesday in the Market Place an argument at a fish stall when a Spanish soldier walked off without paying brought his compañeros running to his aid with drawn swords, who slashed the fishwife's skirts off above the knees then plunged her head-first into a barrel of herrings leaving her kicking and struggling with her backside bare for all the town to see, so that the poor woman almost drowned in herring liquor before she was rescued.

Yet for all their roistering blackguardry the Spaniards were ostentatiously pious, every one of them wearing a holy medallion round his neck and falling on his knees before each wayside crucifix in an ecstasy of crossing and mumbled Hail Marys. Whatever one might feel about the Spaniards, there was no denying that when Shrovetide came the Hermandad de las Penitencias to which most of them belonged put on a fine show in the streets of Houtenburg, with its members proceeding to mass in the abbey church naked to the waist despite the cold and flogging one another with knotted cords until their backs were bloody, to the quiet satisfaction of the onlookers, who would cheerfully have done the whipping for them.

Yet for some in Houtenburg the arrival of the Spaniards was not an unmixed bane. Among them was at least one quiet and decent man, Corporal Antonio de Bobadilla y Fuentes. He was a "soldado particular": a gentleman who had joined the tercio (as was the custom) with the rank of common musketeer in order to learn his trade and be promoted to corporal, then sergeant, then ensign as disease and cannonshot thinned its ranks. Though the surgeon's house had not been exempted from billeting, being of the better sort Willenbrouckx and his wife might expect to have officers lodged with them rather than the common soldiery. But until Corporal Bobadilla moved in the Spanish officers sent to them rarely spent more than a day in the house, swearing that the howls of pain and smell of singed flesh from the treatment room downstairs quite put them out of sorts, even though the surgeon and his wife kept a good table and both spoke creditable Spanish. Bobadilla remained because (he said) he preferred to lodge with cultivated folk; and in any case, having lived two years next to a slaughterhouse in Seville before he joined the army the noise of patients undergoing surgery bothered him not in the least.

Before long Willenbrouckx had recruited the good-natured corporal to teach his stepson Spanish, which would be most advantageous to him as a surgeon seeking clients in the Spanish Netherlands or further abroad, and might even qualify him for preferment at court in Brussels. Bobadilla's quiet, scholarly Spanish had the accent of his native Andalusia. But he was well enough educated to teach Frans pure Castilian as well, which the boy, having a great aptitude for languages, picked up very readily and was soon pretty fluent in. Willenbrouckx sometimes wondered what could have made so gentle and studious a man become a soldier when his comrades were for the most part rowdy, drunken, ignorant villains good for nothing but filling grave-pits or adorning gibbets. He wrote poetry and read a good deal, and was knowledgeable in the classical authors, so that priest or librarian seemed more his natural vocation than the profession of arms. The surgeon could only suppose that it must have been a thirst for travel and excitement in his youth; such indeed as had once propelled himself, against all the good advice of his parents and kindred, to enlist as a surgeon's mate with the Invincible Armada. The road of adventure, he feared, is one that though broad and enticing when a man starts out upon it, very soon becomes so narrow that like a salmon in a wicker trap he cannot turn back but must keep on moving forward until he bangs his head against the end of it. He was resolved anyway that neither of his sons would ever follow such a wastrel trade as soldiering if there was anything that he could do to prevent it.

★ ★ ★ ★ ★ ★ ★ ★ ★ ★

My readers will have gathered from all this that as I grew in years and understanding, so too did my regard and admiration increase for my stepfather, who was more to me than the most attentive of natural fathers could ever have been and whose memory I honoured after he was dead by attaching the patronymic "Michielszoon" to my name because, though not my father as regards progeniture, he was more than any man my father as regards mind and spirit. But for all that, one thing still set me apart from my stepfather – though I think that as long as he lived he never suspected anything of it – and that was the small matter of my true paternity. My mother (as our historian has noted above) explained this to me little by little as I grew in years and understanding: first of all that my stepfather was not my father *secundem carnem**, which was easy enough for me to accept, because many of my contemporaries were in the same position after all the wars and plagues that had afflicted our town; then the much more ticklish matter of who my natural father really was. And this, as you might imagine, was a great deal harder news to stomach: that I was the offspring of a regicide put to a foul and shameful death for the murder of the anointed King of France: and not just any King of France one might find in a hedgerow either, but the greatest and most benevolent King of France that ever was, so that it was reported that several of his subjects fell dead from grief at the mere news of his murder.

This particular knowledge first came upon me one afternoon when I was about eight years of age and was standing in the market with my mother, who was buying sprats at the fishmonger's stall while I occupied myself looking at the wares of a bookseller and stationer spread out next to it. A box of copper-plate prints stood on his stall, and as I leafed through them one caught my attention. It showed a naked man spreadeagled on a low wooden scaffold in a town square, his waist pinioned between two upright posts, and four great carthorses harnessed to ropes attached to his limbs as men with whips urged the beasts on. The legend beneath the picture said "*Een Getrouwe Afbeelding vande Vreselijk Terechtstelling vande Afschuwelijk ende Onnatuurlijk Koningsmoordenaer François Ravillac op de Greveplaets in Parijs de xxvii van Mei MDCX*"**. To me it looked at first like some kind of game: perhaps resembling the "touwtrekken" that was held each year in the Market Place during Saint. Wolverga's Fair, where two

---

* According to the flesh
** *A Faithful Depiction of the Terrible Execution of the Detestable and Monstrous Regicide François Ravaillac in the Place de la Grève in Paris on the 27th of May 1610.*

gangs of stout knaves pulled at the two ends of a rope until one of them was forced to give way. So I tugged at my mother's skirts and asked her to explain to me what was taking place. She looked – and at once tears brimmed in her eyes and she dropped her parcel of sprats on the stall, hustling me back to our house with the fishmonger calling after her to say that mevrouw had paid her shilling but not collected her purchase. Once we were home she took me upstairs to the attic, locked the door behind us and kneeling down, told me that the reason for her tears was that the miserable wretch depicted on that print was her one-time husband and my own natural father. And she made me swear then and there, as I loved her and God Almighty, that I would tell no man of it – least of all my stepfather – for fear that I would be thought mad as she had once been. She then described to me the sorry tale of my father's crime as best she could to so young a child, how he had murdered the King of France and afterwards been executed for it, and swore to me that this was all true and not a product of her deranged fancy. Though she owned that it might be a heavy burden for me to carry to know that I was the child of such a father, yet she said she had loved him and knew that he was a good man driven to his terrible deed by an equally great misunderstanding – of which she would tell me fully one day, when I was of an age to understand – and added that in the mean time I was now the sole evidence left upon this earth that he had ever existed, his body having been reduced to ashes and fired from a cannon and even his name declared accursed so that no man might thereafter bear it; and so I had a duty incumbent upon me to become the pious and honourable person he would surely have wanted for a son; and furthermore that I must bear this painful knowledge silently *in pectore* and always comport myself according to his example as though he were watching me from heaven where he must now surely be, having paid in full the price of his terrible crime and died (his confessors reported afterwards) penitently and like a good Christian. Somewhat bemused by all this, I wondered even then what sort of parental example it was that she expected me to follow, if my father's principal deed during his time on this Earth had been to kill his lawful sovereign. But I loved my mother dearly and knew her to be a grave and judicious person not in the slightest given to idle fancies. So I solemnly swore that I would do as she asked and breathe no word of it to any man as long as she lived.

As to how it felt while I was growing up, to know that I was the posthumous son of so notorious a father, I can only say that it seemed natural enough to me since I grew into that knowledge little by little, like my feet into a new pair of shoes, and likewise that it was not vouchsafed to me all at one fell stroke, since I had always known in my heart even before I picked up that copper print in the Market Place that I must be the son of some notable person or other and wondered only who it might be. I suppose likewise that old Henri's son Louis must often have wondered how it fell out that he was chosen among all the infants that were born in France in the year 1600 to become king one day – and I dare say reflected as I did, that some mortal had to perform that office, and the choice had fallen upon him; and that if it had not been him, then it would have been someone else, in which case he might have been the son of an ostler or a charcoal burner. No: through my living every day with even such a terrible knowledge, the sharp edges and corners were rubbed off it and it became smooth and familiar as a pair of old wooden clogs so that it never much galled my feet. That was how matters were; there was nothing that I could do about it – since whatever else he might change, no man can change his paternity or the circumstances of his birth – and I must make my own way in the world as best I could; even draw such solace and encouragement as I might from my private knowledge.

My readers may pause here and wonder, that I should be so depraved a creature as to draw consolation from the fact of my being the son of a king-murderer put to an atrocious death before a great crowd which could scarcely be restrained from tearing him to pieces even before the executioner had done his work. But I think none the less that the deed for which my father suffered – though of course in itself utterly to be condemned – was at the very least a singular one, and likewise competently performed in that he succeeded where so many had failed before him: which has always been for me (I must say) a great deal easier a knowledge to bear than if I had been the offspring of some worthless knave hanged for stealing a five-shilling nag from outside an alehouse. I remember I once maintained as much when I sat at supper one evening with that egregious coxcomb Sir Kenelm Digby, whose own father was hanged and quartered for essaying to blow up King James and his parliament with gunpowder. It was in Paris about the year 1646, by which time I was well enough known for rumours to be current regarding my true paternity, though I neither confirmed nor denied them. After I had cast doubt upon the efficacy of his precious "powder of sympathy", which I said was no more than blue vitriol* ground up small and of as much efficacy as dried hen's droppings, he sneered at me as being "no more than the son of a regicide"; to which I answered that so far as I could see, the only thing worse than being the son of a regicide was to be the son of a *failed* regicide. This boutade of mine set the whole table roaring with laughter, and poor Sir Kenelm was very much out of sorts with me for years afterwards though we were reconciled later on.

* * * * * * * * * *

Despite the war, the Spaniards and the decline of trade, not all was sombre in Houtenburg as the year 1621 neared its end. A certain self-consciousness – even a sort of patriotism – was abroad in Flanders, where dislike of the Spanish protector was only narrowly outweighed by fear of the northern enemy, with its sharp-elbowed commercial practices and its grim-faced Calvinist theo-

---

* Copper sulphate

logians. Even in a down-at-heel little place like Houtenburg one could detect – among the more educated sort at any rate – a growing interest in the town's past. The school of Cynical philosophers in the tap-room of the *Cheval Noir* said that this was because there was precious little else to be proud of nowadays; that in the days of its prosperity the town had not bothered its head about feudal donations and Carolingian charters and suchlike fooleries but just got on with the business of turning sheep's wool into money. But earlier in the year the town clerk Menno Lambrechts had caused a local sensation by publishing in Ypres, at his own expense (for his wife had recently inherited some money), the modest volume *Annales Origorumque Municipium Houtenburgiæ in Comitatu Flandriæ** with an elaborately decorated frontspiece and an obsequious Latin dedication to the Archduke Albert, to whose widow – the Archduke having inconsiderately died in the mean time – the author had the honour of presenting a copy on bended knee at an audience in Brussels (though he got no money from her afterwards as he had hoped, the arciducal treasury being bare as usual). In this work he proved conclusively that Houtenburg was of ancient foundation, having been established by none other than Julius Caesar himself during his Gallic wars, and was in fact the Roman outpost *Noviomagus Belgorum* which earlier antiquaries had placed several miles further to the south-east, towards Cassel. It was indeed true that the horse trough in the Market Place was an old Roman coffin, its funerary inscription almost worn away by centuries of horses rubbing their chests against it as they drank; likewise that part of a Roman altar was visible in the west wall of the abbey church. Until now no one had given much thought to the matter. But before long Præceptor Luytens, the Abbé Gosaerts and Doctor Hooftius were busy of an evening grubbing away in their gardens and orchards looking for pieces of pottery and old coins. Lambrechts even proposed a motion before the town council that the ruinous Calais Gate should be

---

* *Annals and Origins of the Town of Houtenburg in the County of Flanders*

demolished and replaced with a Roman triumphal arch. His proposal, however, got but a frosty reception and was modified to a resolution to have a bust of Julius Caesar added to the town's arms on the front of the Radhuis "whenever funds thereto are available, and a suitable occasion shall next present itself."

A considerable stir was therefore caused in October 1621 when Abbé Gosaerts announced *urbi et orbi* that he had discovered a remarkable Roman artefact while digging in the old abbey orchard behind the presbytery in order to plant a cherry tree. It was a bronze vessel (he said) of great antiquity and wondrously fine workmanship; and furthermore had incised about the rim a cryptic inscription which, when he had translated it, would doubtless prove that the utensil – a deep bowl about the size of a soup tureen, with a handle at each side – was an ancient sacrificial vessel of the old Romans, used no doubt for libations during their religious rites. Had the abbé been a more suspicious man he might perhaps have connected his find with the dim shapes of two boys he had chased out of the orchard some evenings before. But the priest was as unworldly as men of learning usually are, and also too short-sighted from a lifetime of study to associate those two forms glimpsed fleetingly in the twilight as they scrambled over the wall with the impudent young rogue Lambrechts and his red-haired accomplice Van Raveyck. Instead he had set to work like the antiquary and Latin scholar that he was to decipher the mysterious inscription. But when the encrusted dirt had been cleaned off the lettering, it proved much harder to make any sense than the abbé had anticipated. For though it resembled Latin, it was no Latin that any man in Houtenburg or Ypres or Saint Omer could make any sense of, nor even at Louvain University when it was communicated to them by letter. It ran:

C · THETISMÆ · RENGEME · NEPIS · POTENDE ·
VANCO · PERGEMÆ ·

Over the weeks that followed no small quantity of candles,

goose quills and head-scratching were devoted to the inscription by Houtenburg's men of learning, for all recognised that though they could make neither head nor tail of it at first, the very fact that it was so arcane must surely argue for the vessel's antiquity and importance since the Romans would surely not have troubled themselves to adorn some workaday utensil such as a dripping pan or a posset with so mysterious a legend, and its occult meaning must therefore argue all the more strongly for the bowl being a sacred vessel of some kind; which would mean by inference that some great temple had once stood where the abbey cloisters now were, it having most likely been overthrown and burned when the ancient Goths had sacked the place towards the end of the western empire. As to the meaning of the inscription, in the end there were two schools of thought. One faction, led by the Abbé Gosaerts and Canon Blanchard, thought that it must be Latin, but mingled with Greek since *Thetismæ* and *Pergamæ* sounded like barbarous latinifications of the Greek *Thetis* and *Pergamon*, and since the *C* which prefixed the whole undoubtedly stood for "century" (which could be verified from Roman inscriptions elsewhere) it must be a military century of Greek auxiliaries who had come to garrison Houtenburg and somehow forgotten how to write Greek script. The other school however, led Præceptor Luytens, held that it was plainly not Latin or Greek at all but Etruscan or Egyptian rendered in Latin script; which absolved them entirely from trying to make sense of it since it was well known that those two tongues were now lost beyond recall and no meaning might be extracted from them any longer.

In the end, by late October, the question of the bowl's inscription had become so acrimonious and so productive of bad blood that Mayor Cabeljauw referred it to a meeting of the town council after the other business had been discussed, so that all of Houtenburg's more learned heads could exchange their views regarding it and, if no consensus emerged, then the scholars of the Sorbonne in Paris be respectfully asked for an opinion. But the meeting produced so little agreement – indeed such bitter exchanges –

that the municipal surgeon finally asked if he too might have a sight of it. Neither the abbé nor the præceptor was much pleased by this, that a clownish barber-surgeon without a university degree should presume to offer an opinion in matters of scholarship (though Willenbrouckx's Latin was in fact as good as either of theirs), and Doctor Hooftius attempted to have an emergency motion passed "that ignorant mechanicals should henceforth be forbidden to meddle in matters above their degree and station". But the town clerk swiftly quashed this suggestion, and a piece of paper with the inscription written upon it was passed to Willenbrouckx for his consideration. He perused it through screwed-up eyes for some time, holding it at arm's length. Then he cut a strip of paper with scissors and began to write upon it. At last he began to laugh, and so uproariously that in the end he had to be pummelled on the back to stop him from choking. The assembled échevins enquired the reason for such merriment, and wiping the tears from his eyes he said:

"Reverend father, messieurs, it seems to me that you have been most royally cozened with this vessel of yours, because I think that I have now resolved your incription for you. See here: I have removed the dots from between the letters, and written them all upon this ribbon of paper as one long word. Now behold..." and here he held up the strip, "...If I join the two ends together thus, your inscription can be made to read in villainous Latin but wholly honest Flemish, "HET IS MAER EN GEMENE PISPOT ENDE VAN COPER GEMAECT"*.

There was silence for a few moments, then a great roar of laughter, and the abbé and the præceptor afterwards entirely crestfallen, and once the news had spread, barely able to show their faces on the street for a fortnight or so until people had grown tired of telling the tale. In the end the matter was forgotten as some new minor sensation preoccupied the town. But even so, without being aware of it, Michel Willenbrouckx had placed

---

* "It is only a common piss-pot and made from copper"

a keg of gunpowder beneath his household that autumn evening and lit the fuse.

CHAPTER FOUR

By the close of the year 1621 the town of Houtenburg's perennial hard times had lately become a good deal harder, nature conspiring this time with men. After a weeping summer and a poor harvest winter had arrived unusually early, so that already on Martinmas Day the canals were frozen hard enough to bear a man's weight. By the third week in November the plashy meadows about the town, still inundated from the summer's rain, had frozen into a single, mournful sheet of grey ice extending to the bleak ash-grey horizon and broken only by part-submerged clumps of trees and the low mounds on which poor cottages now stood marooned. Great hapless flocks of hungry, bewildered geese waddled to and fro all day across the frozen marshes, honking their discontent at having flown all the way from the Arctic to their winter feeding grounds only to find that the Arctic had got there ahead of them. Folk consulted their almanacs and comforted one another with old threadbare sayings to the effect that if November's ice was thick enough to walk upon the rest of the winter would be mild and wet. But by Saint Lucy's Day, the 13th of December, frost still held the Flanders countryside in its iron grasp, and the coast now likewise, so that every ebb tide left a jagged rubble of dirty sea-ice on the sands at Gravelines. There was already much want among the townsfolk by reason of the war interrupting trade, and the dearness of bread following a meagre harvest; yet for all the town council's pleas to Brussels the burden of taxes and billeting had not been alleviated by a single copper doit. The unseasonable cold made the townspeople careless about drawing their kitchen fires when they went to bed, instead leaving them banked up so as to have some warmth in the house during the night, while their unwanted Spanish guests sought to ward off the dank rheumaticky chill of "Flandria la puta"* by tearing down barns and outhouses to heap up perilously roaring fires in their billets. The result was that every few nights someone's chimney caught fire and the watch had to come running with buckets of water and hooks to pull off the thatch; whilst one freezing night in the last week of November a blaze broke out near the Heilige Bloed Church which consumed the entire street of thirty or forty houses and would surely have gone on to devour the whole town besides if the wind had not suddenly changed direction.

And as if these misfortunes were not enough to be going on with, there was soon sickness abroad as well. In normal times the town bought wheat from Artois and mixed that with rye to make mesclin bread. But the chalk-country harvest had been as mediocre as that in Flanders and the price of corn was high, so the town's millers were obliged to use local rye; much of it already mouldy from having been harvested damp. All were agreed with Doctor Hooftius that such a sudden change to the most basic item of the townsfolk's diet was likely to be highly injurious to their health; and indeed by New Year many of the poorer sort were experiencing visions and curious waking nightmares of flying in the air or seeing strange hideous elves and hobgoblins crouching in the shadows of their poor, cold, dark little houses lit only by a single smoking rushlight. Before long the strange affliction had spread beyond the ranks of the poor: solid and sensible burghers were committed to the Hôtel-Dieu raving the strangest nonsense and complaining that the Devil's imps were nibbling their fingers and toes, or that giant spiders had appeared in their kitchens to communicate messages to them. Hooftius was called to examine them and pronounced in the end – since he could find no obvious explanation in the heavens – that the sufferers had been bewitched.

In normal times witchcraft had never much bothered folk in the Low Countries. In High Germany witches and malevolent

---

* "Flanders the whore"

sprites lurked behind every tree in the endless sombre forests. But here among the flat polderland under the vast rolling skies people had traditionally paid little heed to such morbid fancies; as though the brisk salty North-Sea winds which turned the sails of the mills also blew away the dank woodland miasmas of toadstools and rotting stumps that engendered thoughts of sorcery. Witches there were, to be sure: Holy Scripture was emphatic on that point, and some country folk indeed claimed to be able to cast love spells, find lost door keys or cure sick cattle in return for a few stuivers – though at considerable hazard to themselves, because the most superstitious of platteland boers retained his keen sense of value for money and might well turn up at the door with a cudgel in his hand seeking a refund if the girl married someone else, the key remained lost or the cow died. But as to an organised army of Satan's agents plaguing the populace – witches' covens, flying on broomsticks, kissing the arse of giant black goats and all the rest of it – the countryfolk paid little heed to such babblings and the town magistrates even less. There were occasional convictions and burnings; but fewer and fewer as the years went by, to a point (it was said) where nowadays in the Dutch provinces the courts would not even prosecute unless the complainant could demonstrate that they had suffered material harm; certainly none of the hysterical scenes that travellers reported from Bavaria or Westphalia, where the flimsiest accusation would see suspects thrown into gaol and tortured until they named their accomplices; and the accomplices then arrested and tortured in their turn until they named *their* accomplices, so that in the end half the town might perish at the stake. In Ghent a few years before a tailor had gone around boasting of having sold his soul to the Devil in return for supernatural powers. In the end he was arrested and bound over to keep the peace. He refused and went on with his bragging, so was arrested again and banished from the town for two years to prevent him upsetting folk with his delusional drivellings. He returned none the less, and was given a good whipping – not for the witchcraft but for defying the banishment order – and was banished again, and what was become of him since no one knew; except that in the Palatinate or Alsace mouthing a one-tenth's part of such nonsense would certainly have seen him make a merry bonfire in the marketplace and probably a dozen innocent "accomplices" along with him.

But now in Houtenburg, as the eye-watering January wind drifted the snow in streaks across the ice of the polders and the townsfolk shivered as they supped their thin watery soup of cabbages and parsnips heated over a few handfuls of peat (no fuel barges having been able to reach the town for weeks past on account of the waterways being frozen), people with too much time on their hands began to brood, and feel the strange tinglings in their limbs, and look at the rashes on one another's pallid winter faces, and speculate as to the likely cause of their miseries. Prodigies and singular events were now reported daily from round about the town. A two-headed piglet had been born in Rieteghem (it was said) while two hunters out after hares on the frozen meadows swore that after they had shot at one the animal had run off laughing loudly and calling to them in good Flemish to aim better next time.

Before long the common folk had a powerful ally in their speculations, because at Christmas 1621 a new prevôt had been appointed by the Sovereign Bailiff of Flanders to supervise the administration of justice in the western part of the county. Théophraste de Coqueville was not just a Sorbonne-trained doctor of civil law and an old hand in the ecclesiastical courts, but had also lately served the King of Spain in the province of Franche-Comté, in the foothills of the Alps around the town of Dôle, where witchcraft was taken very seriously indeed and official campaigns against it had led to hundreds of burnings in recent years. His first official visitation to Houtenburg took place just after the Feast of the Three Kings, and saw him arrive on an open horse-drawn sledge despite the bitter weather. This suggested a disturbingly keen sense of duty, which was only confirmed by his subsequent address to the assembled town council.

"Do not seek to persuade me, messieurs, " he said, "that there are no witches in this district, because you might as well try to convince me that it has no frogs or sparrows. Witches are everywhere at all times, a vast invisible army seeking to harm and dismay God's children. And the fact that, according to the records of your seigneurial court, you have not so much as prosecuted one of these hellish malefactors in the past fifty years let alone brought any to justice, does not mean that there are none hereabouts, but rather that you have been scandalously lax and complacent in performing your duties. In Dôle and the regions round about during the ten years that I was royal procurator there we apprehended, tried and burned upwards of two hundred sorcerers both male and female, some of them as young as ten years of age. So there is absolutely nothing that you can tell me about the process of finding these miscreants and bringing them to account."

"Perhaps the region of which you speak is particularly rich in sorcerers?" Mayor Cabeljauw ventured timidly.

The prevôt tipped his head back and gave a creaking, mirthless little lawyer's laugh, so that dust seemed to come out of his mouth.

"Hah! Of course, Monsieur le Maire: how foolish of me not to have seen it. Satan the Prince of Darkness prefers Franche-Comté because of the healthy mountain air, and shuns Flanders for fear that his hooves may sink into its boggy pastures, and the fires of hell perhaps likewise be put out by heaping them up with too many of its damp phlegmatic people." He fixed the mayor with his hard, black little eyes like two shiny buttons of jet, and pulled his fur-trimmed law-doctor's robe closer about him against the chill of the council chamber. "Do not attempt, monsieur, to beguile me with such insipid fooleries: the Devil is abroad throughout this whole sublunary world, and no part of it is less subject than any another to his depredations. Do you not have hailstorms, murrains and plagues of insects as often here in Flanders as anywhere else? Do your infants not fall sick and die? Does your butter not refuse to churn one day where it churned perfectly well the last, nor your beer turn sour in the cask? Do your husbands not prove impotent and your wives barren?" He looked around the winter-worn faces seated about the great council table, searching each in turn and discovering nothing but perplexity: it was indeed difficult to deny that Houtenburg had suffered more than its fair share of the world's misfortunes in recent years; of plagues, of bad weather and of warring armies. De Coqueville smiled and nodded.

"No: you do not deny it, do you? Yet like poor silly sheep in a pen you continue to suffer these calamities instead of seeking after the causes and remedying them; as if our good Doctor... Hooftius is it?" Hooftius nodded. "As if our town physician here, examining a patient, should merely say 'My skill and experience as a doctor of medicine tells me that you are unwell.' And then pack up his bag, bid him adieu and go home instead of letting blood or administering a strong purgative to cure the affliction. Well, messieurs, you may depend upon it that *I* shall not fail in my duty as the physician charged with restoring this part of the county of Flanders to moral health; no, nor likewise flinch from turning surgeon if need be and cutting out the infection with my own hands. For in the gaol at Dôle I once took off my gown, rolled up my sleeves and applied the instruments to a suspect myself, because I saw that the public executioner lacked zeal, and soon had the wretch reeling off names so fast that my clerk could hardly keep pace with her. As to your having no witches in Houtenburg, the reason for that is quite simply that you have failed to look hard enough for them."

"How then do you propose that we begin our enquiries?" the town clerk asked. "Should we perhaps have the constables arrest folk at random in the Market Place and demand to know whether or not they are in league with Satan?"

De Coqueville smiled wearily, wondering at his own patience in dealing with such small-town simpletons.

"No: Monsieur le Greffier, of course not: both the law and natural justice forbid us to proceed thus. To do as you suggest would be mere arbitrariness – and also a complete waste of your time because no witch, even if you chanced to apprehend one, would ever admit to being such. You should rather proceed with cunning and discretion, after long and careful observation, as my officers were schooled by me to do in my last post. First compile a list of suspects: cunning wives, village healers, cow doctors, fortune tellers and so forth. Then wait until some signal misfortune befalls the place where they live: a violent hailstorm in July flattening the crops, a cattle sickness, an army of caterpillars or some such violation of God's natural order – then arrest them and have them put them to the question on suspicion of sorcery. If you proceed thus, then by patient and persistent questioning you will be as surprised as I was at what a web of iniquity you will certainly uncover. I found the process to be rather like unpicking a garment: that finding the right thread to tug at took me some time and trouble, but once I had identified it and began to pull at it the whole conspiracy would suddenly unravel before my eyes. Your first suspect will soon lead you to others. And before long, once they know what you are about, the folk of the district will be bringing you denunciations without your prompting them: that such-and-such an old wife has placed a spell upon them, or someone's neighbour caused their pig to fall sick and die. As learned persons of the better sort we can scarcely imagine what a catalogue of crimes may be covered by the simple and ignorant – sometimes even pious – demeanour of such old village women; that for many years past they have met at regular seasons with other such castaways and had congress with the Devil and his imps. Why, if I persisted long enough when I questioned them, some even confessed that they would regularly fly through the air to attend their meetings."

Willenbrouckx had sat drumming his fingers throughout this harangue, which he found irritated him intensely for reasons that he could not quite define. But now he spoke.

"And what of that, Monsieur le Prevôt? While I cannot, of course, speak for Franche-Comté, here in Flanders we have no law that forbids flying."

Lambrechts and the notary Maître Delvaux harummphed with amusement at this, but quickly stifled their laughter as the lawyer's baleful stare fastened upon them. De Coqueville smiled, displaying his small pointed teeth, like those of a weasel.

"A most amusing sally: I compliment you on your wit. I always consider that a talent for facetious banter greatly adorns those who practise menial trades such as barbering, allowing them to entertain their customers while they clip their hair. But you ask me, 'What of that?' What of it indeed: that people round about — hundreds or perhaps even thousands of them — are in league and solemn compact with Satan, the sworn enemy of God and mankind, who roams day and night like a lion seeking whom he may devour and rejoices at each soul brought to perdition? I reply, a great deal of it. Because when I spoke this afternoon with Doctor Hooftius here and the mayor I learned from them that the people of this town and the countryside round about have been afflicted for weeks past with strange dreams and visions, and tinglings like the pricking of pins in their extremities. Would our learned barber perhaps care to jest *that* away with some flippant remark?"

"I cannot deny that such things have happened," Willenbrouckx replied, "Or make light of them: many have come to me of late complaining of shooting pains in their limbs and strange skin eruptions; some even with signs of early gangrene in their fingers and toes. But are such things to be attributed to enchanters, do you think? Or to poverty and poor food; and lack of fuel in this freezing weather? And the depredations of the rowdy soldiery who force people to sleep in the straw of outhouses in the depths of winter while they appropriate their hearths and their warm beds? Regarding this last point, it seems to me that if Satan the Prince of Darkness and his entire legion of subaltern devils were billeted on the folk of Houtenburg they could scarcely be more of a plague than King Philip's soldiers are. In fact I dare say that Satan might pay his demons more regularly and thereby make them less inclined to plunder and extortion."

The échevins nodded and murmured their agreement to this. But de Coqueville was not abashed.

"Leaving aside the seditious – some might even say treasonable – content of your remarks, you seem to me rather like a town fireman who as the thatch burns and the flames spread to the next street, sits watching with his pot of beer at the tavern door and says, 'What of it? The law does not forbid fire. And anyway this blaze before me is most likely caused by some foolish wife neglecting to cover her hearth when she went to bed and is therefore no concern of mine.' You are paid a stipend by the municipality to maintain the town's health, yet you neglect your duty. And though plainly a man of some wit and learning despite your lowly calling, you seem quite unable to connect effect with cause."

"How do we know that the effects are connected with that particular cause, and not with some other one entirely? Though I am indeed only an ignorant barber-surgeon, as you put it, one of my public duties is to attend the sick in mind in the Hôtel-Dieu. And although over the years I have met with several unfortunates who proudly claim to be witches in league with the Devil, possessed of all manner of supernatural powers, yet when I let the poor wretches talk to me rather than I to them I found them without exception to be deranged rather than wicked; and their delusions of sorcery no more than part of a whole cupboard-full of other such delusions. Even the superhuman powers they laid claim to were directed to paltry and miserable ends like stealing cheeses from window sills and giving their enemies the piles, when if they were real those who possessed them would surely build themselves golden palaces and conjure up volcanoes out of the ground. Until now this town has consigned such poor crazy folk to the hospital and tried to ease them out of their absurd beliefs with kindness and mild conversation. Yet you would have us cast them into prison and apply the thumbscrews until they babble out yet more nonsense in their pain, then use that as evidence to roast them alive and arrest others to be subjected to the same treatment. Is this what you call natural justice? Because for my part I find it neither natural nor just."

Willenbrouckx noticed that throughout this tirade — which seemed to discommode the prevôt not at all — his interlocutor had been scribbling something on a piece of paper. He looked up at last with one eyebrow slightly raised, as though none of this surprised him or was indeed of any great interest. He nodded.

"Hmm. Quite so: just as I would have expected from a small-town medical practitioner: deal with the malady first by denying that it exists; or if we admit that it exists, then deny it to be a malady at all. Thus Satan blinds the eyes of silly men. I hear that in the rebel Dutch provinces the town magistrates are now of much the same mind as yourself, and openly boast that they no longer even prosecute for sorcery let alone burn people for it. Which, if true, only serves to show the ultimate consequences of rebellion against lawful sovereigns: that within a very few decades those who rise up against the ruler set over them by God will inevitably become vassals of Satan instead. No, to deny the existence of witches is not only to deny the truth of Holy Scripture and all learned authority, it might even be taken by one less forbearing than myself as *prima facie* evidence of being a witch yourself, rather than of proud rebellious folly and wilful ignorance. And the fact that, as you seem to imply, there is no evidence of witches being active here — though from what you have just said there seems evidence aplenty — is to me, with no small experience in these matters, merely evidence of just how cunning and full of guile these creatures are, that they take such pains to cover their traces and fling dust in the eyes of those who might pursue them." He stood up, resplendent in his lawyer's robes and red velvet coif.

"And be in no doubt about it, pursue them we will. For if until now the prosecution of witchcraft in west Flanders has been left to legal amateurs; to bumpkin magistrates, idle town clerks and the lazy seigneurs of the courts, it is now in the hands of people like myself who know their business; jurists trained at our most eminent universities and vested with the full power and authority of the law. Awake, I say, from your beer-fuddled Flemish slumbers, for the day of reckoning is at hand. Dame Justicia's sword is drawn from its scabbard. And be in no doubt that its edge is a sharp one!"

The next day, after completing his tour of inspection, the Prevôt de Coqueville summoned Doctor Hooftius, the Abbé Gosaerts and Præceptor Luytens to sup with him in the chambers where he was lodged in the uppermost storey of the Radhuis. Needless to say, those local eminences were only too pleased to obey the prevôt's summons, because being a local notable in a place as small and insignificant as Houtenburg was (quite frankly) a distinction which did not travel very far in the county of Flanders either in medical or in ecclesiastical circles, and an invitation to take supper and – presumably – be consulted on some weighty matter or other by a man of such power and distinction was not one that should be let slip. Besides which it was perishing cold, and to judge by the smoke which had poured all day from the town hall's chimney the prevôt was certainly not a man accustomed to think twice before placing another log on the fire.

The four worthies ate supper together, the physician and the abbé paying great attention to their table manners even though their lack of teeth made it difficult for them not to splutter and mumble on the bones of the roasted capons. Then as wine and cheese were served at the end of the meal – emphatically not a Flemish way of doing things – the prevôt turned suddenly from polite small-talk to what was evidently the purpose of the gathering.

"Messieurs," he said, "my purpose in inviting you to sup with me this evening, as you may already have divined, was so that I might have the opportunity to confer in private with this town's gravest and most learned persons..." he paused so that they might bask in this compliment, which they duly did "...out of the hearing of the rustic clodpolls and *ignorami* who make up the town council." At this they all nodded vigorously to show that no, they were not in the least offended at the prevôt's poor estimation of Houtenburg's better sort; indeed shared it wholeheartedly. "So, with the four liberal arts of theology, medicine, law and philosophy now all present in the same room..." (they smiled at this and tittered obediently) "...I would like you to inform me concerning a certain matter proceeding from my remarks yesterday to the town council concerning witchcraft. Tell me if you will: is it not the case that a woman of this town – to be precise, the wife of that impudent coxcomb of a surgeon of yours – is popularly reputed once to have been the doxy of the villain François Ravaillac, who murdered King Henri of France some twelve years ago? Is this mere vulgar gossip or might there, in your considered opinion, be some substance in the tale?"

The three other representatives of the liberal arts looked perplexed by this question, murmuring among themselves, and it was some time before Doctor Hooftius ventured to speak.

"Monsieur le Prevôt, you were correctly informed that there was indeed a rumour to that effect at the end of the year – when was it? –1610, when the present wife of Meester Willenbrouckx arrived in this town destitute and with child, and gave birth in the cowshed beside the *Cheval Noir* inn, and was later taken in as a servant by the surgeon, and married him some years afterwards. But all wise heads at the time regarded it as a foolish tale circulated among the poor and ignorant sort, and inclined rather to believe that it arose from a mishearing of the woman's married name, 'Van Raveyck', and after a month or two nothing more was heard of it. For myself, I own that I am but little interested in the silly histories of the common people, and heard it only with half an ear from my own household servants, who are endlessly ready to give credence to any fanciful tale that a peddler or a market wife sets before them."

De Coqueville nodded, as though this only confirmed something that he knew already.

"By no means so fanciful a tale, my good doctor, by no means so fanciful. Allow me to inform you of something. When I was the King of Spain's principal law officer in Dôle some seven years ago, a complaint was brought to me by a farmer's wife from the village of Augerans, six or so miles outside the town, that a neighbour of hers, the wife of a wheelwright, had cast spells upon her. And when I investigated the matter I discovered to my astonishment that the woman in question, who had arrived there with her husband and children some five years before none knew from where, was none other than the sister of the regicide: Marguerite Ravaillac, aged around thirty years and a native of the town of Angoulême in France. When I had her seized and questioned her she told me that their entire family had quit the King of France's realms late in 1610 after her father and mother had been banished following her brother's execution, because even though her two surviving brothers had been forced to change their name – and she and her sister of course now bore those of their husbands – it was still impossible for them to continue living in France because all regarded them as the Devil's spawn and would neither buy from them nor sell to them, nor have any commerce with them whatever, so that in the end they were obliged to sell their property through a prêt-nom for a great deal less than it was worth and move to Franche-Comté where her father had already sought refuge, though her mother (she said) had gone instead to Spain and entered a convent there."

"So what was the outcome of it all?" Luytens asked timidly.

The Prevôt smiled his weasel's smile. "Oh, nothing very much; and nowhere near as much as I would have wished. I had her put to the question, and she duly confessed after several days to a most impressive catalogue of *maleficia*: raising whirlwinds, consorting with the Devil, casting spells upon cattle and so forth, and she was burned in Dôle marketplace later that year. But what chagrined me most, I confess, was that for all my questioning of her I entirely failed to lay hold of the rest of her viperous brood; her father and brother and brother-in-law, because I am confident that if I had managed to have them arrested they would have proved a most fruitful source of information. But sadly, the news of her arrest reached them before my officers did, and they packed up their goods one dark night and departed none-knew-where like so many gypsies; in all probability aided in their flight by the Devil their master."

"But surely," the Abbé Gosaerts ventured, "To be the sister or the brother-in-law of even so great a villain as the Ravaillac fellow is no offence in law? The crime he committed was none of their doing, so surely it would be contrary to natural justice to hold them accountable for it. And in any case, was the crime itself so great? King Henri was after all a Protestant heretic only nominally converted to the true Catholic faith, and a notorious whoremonger to boot, and a sworn enemy of our master King Philip of late memory and his father before him. So while I would never for one moment condone regicide, might there still not be degrees of culpability even in that crime?" The prevôt looked shocked.

"Reverend Father," he said, "Remember your calling and pay heed to what you say. Regicide is regicide, the foulest of crimes that a mortal soul can commit short of murdering God Himself. And I must also consider matters as a magistrate charged with the maintenance of civil order rather than like yourself, as a churchman concerned with the salvation of souls. For theology aside, there is no question but that the killing of princes, no matter what their religion, is as abominable a crime as can be in God's eyes and utterly destructive of the polity. Indeed it was for this reason that I was concerned during my time as a magistrate in Franche-Comté to suppress any public veneration of the villain Balthasar Gérard who slew William of Orange, and was a native of Besançon, because although he was paid by the late King Philip, and his victim was as pernicious an enemy of the Holy Catholic Church and of Spain as ever there was, yet he was still a prince and worthy of reverence for that reason if for no other. But as to your more general point, that it was no fault of his kinsfolk that the detestable scoundrel did what he did, I beg leave to differ with you. Do you not think that a crime so foul as regicide argues at the very least tainted blood, and quite possibly a league and solemn pact with the Devil besides? And likewise would not that pact most probably include members of the regicide's family? For heaven's sake,

Reverend Father: if we arrest and burn people for sharing a cottage with someone who casts spells that cause a neighbour's barn to catch fire, then should we not be a thousand times readier to prosecute those who once associated with a villain who murdered his lawful sovereign?" Unable to argue with this reasoning, the three learned men nodded their assent.

"So, messieurs, it proceeds from that by the process of logic, that if we are prepared to burn women for witchcraft by reason of their kinship with a regicide, we should be far readier to burn one who – if the reports are to be credited – consorted with a regicide of her own free will and later bore his child. If you will allow the first premise here, then you must surely allow the conclusions which proceed from it." He folded his napkin to show that the meal was over. "I therefore charge you all, messieurs, to watch this woman closely over the next few weeks and report her doings to me, and likewise what the townspeople have to say about her. I shall then have her arrested and questioned when the time is ripe. As I said yesterday, pull at that single thread and the whole garment will start to unravel."

The prevôt was as good as his word, and the arrests of suspected witches duly began. Within the month a gypsy peddler, fortune teller and mender of cooking pots was seized and confessed under torture to having communed with the Devil and cast spells to cause a snowstorm in January. He was duly sentenced to be burned in the meadow below the Galgenheuvel at such a time as sufficient other malefactors could be assembled to provide a suitable spectacle. In the end the gypsy disappointed the prevôt by inconsiderately dying in prison of a lung congestion brought on by cold and ill-treatment. But news of the trial travelled widely and started a vogue for complaints to the local magistrates; partly from folk who genuinely believed themselves to have been bewitched; partly from those who knew perfectly well that they had not, but feared that their neighbours might soon denounce *them* for sorcery and wished to get their retaliation in first.

It was now late February and the frozen landscape was thawing into a desolate plain of mud and slush beneath a sickly-grey sky. Firing was short, even straw hard to come by, so that people jested bitterly that it was a great pity the gypsy had escaped burning since the onlookers could at least have warmed their hands at the municipality's expense. The diet of even the better sort was now meagre as winter supplies finally ran out: thin pea soup and poor bread made of barley or even beans, fattened with an occasional lump of rancid yellowish-green bacon. Itching boils and carbuncles added to people's miseries and frayed their tempers still further. The first cases of scurvy appeared, then an epidemic of whooping cough carried off child after child until each day saw a steady procession of little coffins and rag-wrapped bundles making its way to the graveyard and the sexton no longer bothered to toll the passing- bell. Yet taxes remained high, with many now in arrears of payment so that the bailiffs came to distrain their few poor sticks of furniture. And the Spaniards likewise were as insolent and quarrelsome as ever – or worse, since they were less accustomed to the sepulchral northern cold and loudly cursed the day that had brought then to this miserable God-forsaken province. Everyone was irritable and wretched, and heaped-up resentments began to discharge themselves upon whoever was closest to hand.

Obviously, not upon those most immediately responsible for the town's misfortunes: it would have been foolhardy in the extreme to seek quarrels with the Spaniards who all carried swords and daggers and were only too ready to use them. Collective anger must instead be vented upon less dangerous targets, and upon less recent newcomers. Despite the singular circumstances in which she had arrived in Houtenburg that winter's night twelve years before, Catherine Willenbrouckx had (it seemed) long since been accepted into local society. But by the time March arrived amid slush and mire, with the days growing longer but little warmer, slumbering old resentments against her and her husband began to stir again like an old wound apparently healed but now bursting open to ooze foul-smelling pus. Who was she (people said) to go around taking charity to the poor when she was herself no more than a maidservant who had married her master? And all that talk years ago about the child of the king murderer Ravaillac: people at the time had put it down to the legendary stupidity of the Sottebecquois, but who could be sure that there might not have been some substance in it? That boy of hers had red hair after all, and was very strange in his ways, conversing with frogs and toads and snakes and suchlike foul creatures, cutting up the carcasses of animals and collecting dead men's bones from beneath the gallows. And that business of causing iron to swim: you had to admit *that* was mighty peculiar, since all men knew that iron had supernatural properties, which is why blacksmiths had such powers to deflect witches' spells. Perhaps the Abbé Gosaerts (who despite his boils, poor man, had now preached several homilies on witchcraft in response to popular demand) was right in declaring from the pulpit last Sunday that a town that tolerated witches in its midst had only itself to blame for its misfortunes. And as for the abbé himself, though he said nothing about it to any man, he still deeply resented the way in which that unlettered coxcomb of a barber-surgeon had so humiliated him in front of the town council the previous autumn over the inscription on the Roman vessel. The fellow deserved to have his cackle silenced – and if his wife was the indirect means to silence him, then the abbé would certainly join in the attack. The faggots were heaping up, and it would require only a spark to light them.

That spark was duly struck on the first day of March 1622 in the form of a deposition made to the clerk of the seigneurial court by a sixteen-year old former scullery maid, Trijntje Lauwereyns from the hamlet of Kapellbroek. The girl had been dismissed some days earlier from the Willenbrouckx household for stealing three silver spoons and attempting to sell them to a pawnbroker in the Visserstraat. The girl did not deny having stolen them, but the surgeon had magnanimously declined to bring the prosecution that would have earned her a public whipping and banishment. Now, though, she wished to make it plain that she had grievances of her own against the surgeon's wife; namely that Mevrouw Willenbrouckx had cast a spell upon her to afflict her with scabies. For did she not converse with cats in French, which certainly no Flemish cat would understand without Satan's help? She added that her former master might also be implicated. After hearing his sermon last Sunday she had gone to the vestry and sought advice from the Abbé Gosaerts (who was plainly most knowledgeable in such matters) and told him that the surgeon had a room full of strange books which, though she was illiterate, she was sure must contain magical spells. And also the son of the house, young Frans, was plainly an apprentice sorcerer since he was always making drawings and casting figures; often of naked women though he was not yet twelve years of age, and likewise mixing all manner of evil-smelling potions and collecting vermin, with a dead man's skull (which fairly gave her goose-pimples each time she had to dust it) on a shelf above his bed and a blind-worm living in box of straw below it. The boy, she said, displayed quite unnatural coldness when confronted with blood, while the surgeon himself practised strange rituals, such as dipping his surgical instruments in a colourless fluid from a bottle and then setting them alight over a candle before he used them. The abbé had advised her to speak at once with a magistrate, which she was now doing, and say that he had sent her.

The clerk asked whether she wished to bring charges against the surgeon as well as his wife. For the moment the girl said no: her present accusation was against her former mistress, because she had concrete evidence against her in the form of the rash on her neck and shoulders. But the matter was left open.

Bored by years of taking depositions regarding overflowing cesspits and bullock carcasses dumped on the public highway, the clerk enquired further over the next two days regarding the servant-girl's accusation. And he found no shortage of people willing to lay accusations of their own against the surgeon's wife. Viewed individually none of them amounted to very much; but taken together they formed a weighty and incriminating dossier. After consulting with the Abbé Gosaerts (whom all men now recognised as the town's expert on witchcraft, which was very gratifying to him) he passed his bundle of papers to the stipendiary magistrate, and the stipendiary magistrate – with an eye perhaps to being promoted out of this hole of a town to a better hole like Ypres or Bailleul – dutifully sent them to the Prevôt de Coqueville who replied with a most gracious letter thanking him for his zeal and assuring him that the matter would receive his closest personal attention, and also be referred to His Grace the Bishop of Saint Omer who would doubtless be appalled to learn what evil-doing been permitted to grow up in his diocese over the years while his attention had been taken up with combatting Protestant heresy, "…as though" (the prevôt wrote) "a man seeking to rid his house of mice should have allowed it to become infested with toads and vipers in their place". Yet the prevôt prided himself on his finesse, and had decided not to act precipitately for fear that the woman's accomplices would take alarm and flee: perhaps across the border into France where – as he had learned during his time in Franche-Comté – the King's officers were scandalously lax and frankly scoffed at talk of witchcraft. For the moment he bade the stipendiary magistrate sit still and observe as a cat would watch a mouse-hole, saying nothing to anyone, but meanwhile preparing to pounce. The suspect in this instance was someone of the better sort with connections and influence, not some poor ignorant gypsy mending pots and pans. But that was all the more reason to arrest her for questioning, since she would undoubtedly have more interesting things to divulge. Her circle of fellow-evildoers might well (he wrote) be drawn from among the local quality, since even among Satan's disciples there must surely be respect for degree and hierarchy, and when they danced naked beneath the dark moon gentlefolk would be most unlikely to caper to the sound of the bagpipes and the hurdy-gurdy in the company of tapsters and ploughboys, but rather dance stately infernal sarabandes among witches of their own rank and condition.

The Willenbrouckx family had little inkling of this in the early days of March, except that people who had once greeted them in the Market Place now seemed anxious to avoid them, while some patients who came to the house complaining of mysteriously unspecific aches and pains were unusually curious about its domestic arrangements, peering into chambers that were none of their business. Meanwhile in the town gaol Nooten the executioner, who was illiterate, puzzled over a mysterious note just arrived from the stipendiary magistrate. He handed it to his assistant Claes Flipkens, who could read and write a little. The youth read the letter, then laughed with his broken, carious teeth.

"Oil up the thumbscrews well, Meester Bartolomeus, because I think we may soon be making much use of them."

"Who do they have in mind this time?" Nooten enquired, without much interest. To him putting people to the question was a matter of indifference: a suspect would be brought from the cells by the town sergeant and his constables as directed in their warrant, and then tortured by him for as long and as energetically as the presiding magistrate instructed and Doctor Hooftius would permit, and no hard feelings afterwards because that was the law and he was only doing his job.

Flipkens guffawed. "Why, are you the only one in Houtenburg not to know? He means the surgeon Willenbrouckx's wife, that stuck-up baggage they say was the murderer Ravaillac's trull and bore his child. Then perhaps Mijnheer Sawbones himself afterwards, if she can be made to denounce him. The same turd-rag, I might remind you, who petitioned the council to have you dismissed from your office and likewise stole all our customers from us. Does the thought of crushing that rogue's fingertips not make your mouth water as it does mine?"

Though not the most imaginative or intelligent of men, Nooten's face brightened suddenly, and he smiled to himself as he considered that pleasing prospect, then set to work at once with a rag and a bottle of oil. The instruments would indeed be gleaming and ready for use when the time came. For once (he thought), he might actually derive some satisfaction from his work.

One evening two weeks after Easter, about nine o'clock, by which time the housekeeper had drawn the fire and gone to bed, there was a knock at the kitchen door of the surgeon's house. Willenbrouckx was still up and about, and went to see who it might be at such an hour.

"Who's there?" he called. "What brings you here? If it's a tooth for drawing, come back in the morning, and in the mean time bite on a wad of tobacco soaked with oil of cloves. And next time please to come to the street door, not the back "

"Let me in," came a muffled voice speaking French, "I must have words with you."

Seizing a poker to defend himself if necessary, Willenbrouckx lifted the oaken bar from its hasps and raised the wooden latch. The door creaked open and a man in a black cloak, riding-booted and with his hat pulled down over his eyes, slipped into the kitchen like a congealed shadow after first looking around to make sure that no one else was present.

"Who are you and what do you want?"

"One that wishes you and your family well – but who has not long to explain why." Willenbrouckx noted that the man was croaking deep in his throat; presumably in order to disguise his voice. His boots and jingling spurs and the fact that he spoke French indicated a person of the better sort.

"What's your business? Who are you, I say…"

"Concern yourself not with who I am, monsieur, but with what I have to tell you. I am a gentleman from round about – I will not say exactly where, for fear that they might squeeze it out of you if they arrest you – and I have certain contacts in the clerk's office at the seigneur's court. I saw today with my own eyes a warrant made out for your wife's arrest on charges of witchcraft, along with a whole sheaf of depositions from fools and rascals who claim that she cast spells on them."

The surgeon was silent a moment. "If what you say is true, then we must go to court and fight the accusations: God will defend the just."

The cloaked man laughed softly. "God might, but no one else will. Let me enlighten you as to what will happen, monsieur, since you seem unfamiliar with the procedure in such cases. Your wife will be taken to the town gaol and there, in front of the examining magistrates, she will be stripped naked by the public hangman and her head and body shaved of all their hair so that they may search her for devil's teats; and this procedure is in itself so disgusting to a respectable woman that she may well confess then and there to whatever they lay to her charge rather than undergo it. But if despite this she maintains her innocence, she will have her thumbs crushed until she names her accomplices. And if even that fails to loosen her tongue, her wrists will be tied behind her back and she will be hoisted up to the ceiling by a pulley with a weight tied to her feet, then be let drop, and afterwards hoisted up again and let fall for as many times as it takes to put her in a different mind. But the purpose behind these torments, I saw in the prevôt's instruction, is to make her incriminate you, so that you may be arrested and a confession extracted from you by the same means. After which the fire awaits you both, and the forfeiture of all your goods, so that your children will be left beggars and taken to the orphanage."

Willenbrouckx was silent for a while. "So what would you have us do?" he said at last. "And why have you come to tell me this?"

"Certain gentlefolk hereabouts who think well of you and are in your debt for healing them have banded together to spirit you and your family away to a place of safety. For this witchcraft nonsense was never current before in Flanders, and if we allow it to take root and flourish here as it has in Germany then no man will be safe. We will move you and your family to France, where the King's justices pay little heed to such twaddle, then petition the Archduchess for the Prevôt de Coqueville's removal."

"To France? If what you say is true then surely the Calais road will be watched?"

"Indeed it will: the prevôt's letter gave detailed orders on that point, and the road to Gravelines likewise, in case you try to escape by sea. But the roads towards Dunkirk and Bergues will not be observed so closely, and we have spoken with certain fishermen who are willing to help us. So as your love your lives, gather together your belongings and money – though no more of either than you can easily carry on foot – and be ready at eight o'clock tomorrow morning to get into a gentleman's coach which will arrive at your door. If any should ask where you are going, say that you are venturing into the countryside near Bergues for a picnic to greet the first of the spring sunshine."

"How do I know they will not come to arrest my wife tomorrow morning at first light, before your coach arrives?"

"Because the prevôt has given express orders to wait until the day after tomorrow. He has been informed that your wife will attend a witches' sabbath on the Mont des Cats tomorrow night when there is no moon. And since the villain is concerned to squeeze the names of her fellow-witches from her, he wants her to have them fresh in her mind; 'and also the Devil's seed still fresh on her thighs', he wrote, which in itself tells you what manner of fellow we are dealing with here".

There was a bumping on the stairs and Catherine's voice. "Michel, for the love of God come to bed. What are you doing down there so late?"

The man turned to go. "Heed well what I say, monsieur. There are still many that love you in this town and wish to help you. But tarry a day longer and there is nothing any mortal man will be able to do for you." And with that he was gone, closing the kitchen door behind him and slipping away into the night with only a cat's mewing to mark his departure.

Willenbrouckx went upstairs to his wife and told her what had passed between them. Disbelieving at first, her eyes wide as saucers in the candlelight, she came after a while to see the force of what he said: people had indeed been behaving strangely towards her these past few weeks, avoiding her as though she carried some invisible contagion. And few in Houtenburg had more reason than herself to know what a mob was capable of. She had escaped then because she was being pursued by an ignorant and irresolute rabble who had been dispersed by a mere toll collector. But what would a mob be like that was led by the powerful and well-educated, with all the resources of justice in their hands?

"So what shall we do, then?" she asked. "And who was this mysterious messenger anyway?"

"I can't be sure, because he disguised his voice. But from his manner and bearing I'm almost certain that it was Guillaume de Roblés, the seigneur's younger son. Last year when he came to have a wart excised he told me that he was training as a magistrate, so he would certainly have the opportunity to see the papers that pass through the greffier's office. But as to what we do next, do you wish us to remain here and know that he spoke the truth only when the faggots are being stacked up around us? I myself was at the meeting with that self-satisfied rascal De Coqueville and saw how his hard little lawyer's eyes bored into me when I challenged his deranged notions. He knows all things in heaven and earth already, having studied them at the Sorbonne, and anything that any man tells him to the contrary merely confirms what he knows already."

"So because of him, are we to drop everything that we have here in Houtenburg and flee like thieves to another country where we know no one and have nothing?"

"Would you sooner stay here and be burned at the stake? When they were to burn the gypsy the magistrates were instructed to contrive a spectacle even more horrible than Nooten might already make it with his bungling. There was to be no bag of gunpowder or slip-knot around the poor wretch's neck, and an order was placed for wet faggots so that the fire would burn as slowly as possible. What do you suppose your fate would be once you were in their hands? Or mine, after they had made you name me as your accomplice? Where sorcery is concerned there are no restrictions on evidence, so they might even take Frans and Henriette and torment *them* until they incriminate us."

"Where will we go if we flee Houtenburg? Will we escape the fire only to die of want in a foreign land, and our children with us?"

"He said that fishermen will take us off the beach between Dunkirk and Gravelines, and from there it's but a short journey down the coast to Calais. I have colleagues and friends there, so we can find lodgings easily enough and I shall earn our living as a surgeon while we wait on events. If this is all exposed as foolery and nonsense then we may well be back here by Pentecost."

In the end Catherine, being a sensible woman, came to acknowledge that their position was indeed perilous in the extreme, and likewise that the most foolhardy course of all might be to sit still and wait upon events. So she dressed in her walking-out clothes and began to fill bags with some clothes for the children and herself while Willenbrouckx got together all the money in the house – fortunately he had still to take the month's fees to the town jeweller for safe keeping – and put together his travelling bag of instruments, with which he was sure that he could earn his family's bread even if they were to find themselves among the Indians of the Americas. And then they both lay down to get what little sleep they could, awaiting the morning.

At six the children were roused and told to make ready for a trip into the countryside. Frans, being a perceptive child, divined from the hurried packing and his parents' nervousness that this would be no ordinary outing. They breakfasted, then gave the housekeeper instructions for the day and also the house keys, saying that they might be away until nightfall. Then they sat and waited. Perhaps it was a foolish jest, Willenbrouckx thought: or maybe even a knavish trick to make them flee so that they could be arrested and their attempt at flight afterwards be presented in court as proof of their guilt. But as the town clock struck eight the iron tyres of a lumbering, creaking coach drawn by four horses trundled to a halt on the brick paving of the street outside. The coachman perched on his box sat silent as Willenbrouckx opened the heavy door and ushered his family into the ponderous vehicle, then put their bags in after them. To his relief only a few street urchins watched them. Then he climbed in himself, shut the door and told the driver to proceed. The man clicked his tongue and cracked his whip, and the coach rumbled away through the streets, swaying on the squeaking leather straps that served for springs, across the Market Place and out through the Bergues Gate.

Just as the nocturnal visitor had predicted, the town gates were being watched. As the vehicle lurched along the rutted, muddy springtime road, past the fork towards Cassel with its gibbet, Willenbrouckx discretely put his head out through the leather curtains of the window and looked back towards Houtenburg. A horseman who had been loitering by the Bergues Gate was now following them at a distance of half a mile or so, matching his speed to that of the coach. He had evidently been instructed to keep the vehicle in his sight but not follow it closely enough to alarm the passengers. The weather was glorious, the first real day of spring and the sun's warmth all the more voluptuous after the bleak ice-bound months that had gone before. The birds chirped and twittered among the roadside thickets, willow catkins shed their yellow dust and the first frogs flopped about in the ponds and ditches after emerging from their wintertime beds in the mud. Then some way past the hamlet of Sint Armboutskappel a very singular thing happened. The road skirted a shallow mere fringed by alder trees and weeping willows, and after the coach had bumped and jolted past them three women emerged from the bushes where they had been hiding, as the gentleman had instructed them to do, and cast off their petticoats to disport themselves naked in the pond "after the manner of water nymphs", with cries of joy – though the water was still rather too chilly for these to be genuine – and with their long henna-dyed tresses unpinned and hanging down their backs. The women were three whores from Bergues, and they had been approached some days before to provide this strange spectacle; which, however, was nothing particularly new to them since they had all posed for painters – or gentlemen who claimed to be such – and only the previous year had appeared in an unclothed state as the Three Graces at a masque to celebrate the new Spanish governor's joyeuse entrée into Dunkirk, to the great enjoyment of His Excellency but the rather more muted appreciation of His Excellency's wife. They cavorted and squealed and splashed one another in the shallow pond as instructed, gritting their teeth together to stop them chattering from the cold. As the solitary horseman approached his eyes popped from his head and he reined his mount to a halt, watching entranced by the spectacle yet at the same time alarmed and fumbling inside the collar of his doublet for his amulet against witchcraft. Old half-remembered fireside tales flitted through his mind concerning the nikkers, the malevolent water sprites of the Flanders meres who lurked below the surface and would seize children's ankles to drown them. After a minute or so of frisking the women looked around as arranged, shrieked in feigned alarm and scrambled into the bushes, covering their modesty among the foliage like one of Meester Rubens's paintings of Diana's nymphs surprised by Actaeon. At that the rider remembered himself and spurred his horse into a gallop to catch up with the coach. But too late: looking back and seeing the horseman come to a halt, the coachman had stopped his vehicle by an alder copse, the surgeon and his family had scrambled out with their bags, then the coach had lumbered off again towards the towers of Bergues in the distance.

The fugitives concealed themselves among the bushes until their pursuer had trotted past them, anxious to close with the coach again and quite unaware that it had ever stopped. Meanwhile, back at the roadside pool, Betje, Grietje and Hentje were getting dressed, shivering from the cold and bargaining vociferously with the mysterious gentleman (who had now appeared as if from nowhere) for a supplement to their agreed fee by reason of the chill, since (they alleged) a man might have seen the goose-pimples on their arses from the top of Dunkirk belfry.

The family crouched among the foliage of the copse, wondering what would happen next as the finches and thrushes sang above them and the frogs croaked in the slimy pools. At last, after half an hour or so of waiting, there was a rustle in the bushes. "Pssst!" It was a village boy of ten or eleven. "The master says you're to follow me."

So they followed the urchin for several hours as the April sun rose in the sky, across semi-liquid meadows and down paths and through thickets, crossing ditches by rotting plank bridges – one of which collapsed under them – and over the main drainage canal in an old duck punt, then across numerous other bridges and down the seemingly endless fenny-black paths of this marshy countryside. At last, muddy-footed and bone-weary, early in the afternoon, they sensed that the land was rising a little beneath their squelching shoes and becoming somewhat drier. They emerged at last from the fenlands, and were soon struggling across scrub-covered sand dunes where plovers piped and gulls screamed in the sky as the sea waves sighed faintly in the distance. At last the boy said "Very well mijne heren, I must leave you here. Ask for the fisherman Matthijs van Loon when you reach the other side." Willenbrouckx tipped the boy a whole silver patagon, and the child then vanished into the landscape like a wisp of smoke, so suddenly and completely that they afterwards wondered whether he had ever existed at all.

They trudged on across the tussocky grass with their bags in their hands, little Henriette sitting astride her father's shoulders, until at last they shuffled wearily to the top of yet another dune, legs aching and feet slipping in the sand, to be confronted suddenly by the level blue-grey expanse of the North Sea with the long white line of the English coast near Dover just visible through the haze in the far distance. On the shore below them three flat-bottomed fishing smacks sat waiting for the incoming tide while men in baggy canvas breeches and wooden shoes busied themselves about them with tarpots and brushes made of unravelled rope.

"Ho there!" Willenbrouckx called to them, shouting to be

heard above the noise of the incoming waves and the screeching of the gulls, "Does one Matthijs van Loon live nearby?"

An old grey-haired man with a face as brown and wrinkled as a leather bag stepped forward unhurriedly, wiping the tar from his hands. A short clay tobacco pipe was clenched between his teeth, bowl downwards. After considering the surgeon for some time he removed the pipe to speak, which was evidently something he did as little as possible.

"He might well do. But equally well he might not. Every man here is called Van Loon, because we all come from Loon village. So why would you want to speak with Matthijs van Loon any more than with more than with Marcus, Lukas or Johannes van Loon? Why him in particular, and not some other?"

Willenbrouckx sensed that this man had a taste for cryptic utterances, and that unless he came straight to the point they might be here all day.

"We were told to speak with one Matthijs van Loon about a sea-passage to Calais: I know no more than that."

The man sniffed loudly, spat, and surveyed them silently from head to foot. "A curious business to be sure," he said at last, "ladies and gentlemen in their town finery, and their children with them, coming out here beyond the dunes to speak with poor mussel gatherers such as ourselves. And carrying baggage too. For all the world as though they might wish to leave Flanders without troubling the coastguards to inspect their pass letters."

"I am sure that if that were indeed the case" the surgeon said, "then those who might carry them would have been informed first of their arrival. And would certainly have been well paid for their trouble."

The man spat again. "Indeed mijnheer, they might. But even so they might need paying still more, to run the risk of spending five years pulling an oar aboard an Ostend galley for having sought to convey the Archduchess's subjects out of her realms in time of war without the necessary permissions. Do you get my meaning?"

Willenbrouckx did get the man's meaning, and pulled out his purse: though only the small pocket one, for fear that the fishermen might sniff the larger and better filled one tied around his waist and knock him on the head for the sake of it once they were well out to sea. An hour later the tide was in and the smack was being pushed out into the waves with the long wooden sweeps so that the red-tanned spritsail could be let down and a course shaped for Calais nine or ten miles down the coast. Off the mouth of the River Aa – the border with France – a coastguard boat approached them: a lugsailed rowing joll with five or six men and a couple of swivel guns. The coxswain demanded to know their business, and was told that they were cockle fishers from Loon going to rake the sands near Calais at low tide. The passengers were well hidden from view below a hatch in the stinking fish-well, so the smack was allowed to pass on unmolested. The wind got up, and blowing against the tide soon raised a short, steep swell so that before long all the family except Michel were disgustingly seasick. Then as darkness fell it started to rain, and they were soon all so soaked and chilled through and beslubbered with vomit and fish slime that they no longer cared whether they lived or died.

Then just after dawn the fishing boat bumped and ground on to a pebbly beach. "At last," Willenbrouckx said, stirring from his half-slumber, "Are we at Calais town or outside it?"

The fisherman laughed. "Who said anything about Calais, mijnheer? This is England, near Dover."

"But we wanted to go to France: we know not a word of English…"

"So much the worse for you, then." the skipper said, "Before darkness fell a Hollander man-of-war sighted us off Gravelines and turned to chase us, so we showed him our arse for fear of ending up prisoners. Then the breeze turned about in the night and blew fairer for the English shore than for Calais, so you'd surely not have expected us to row you there twelve miles or more against the wind."

"But you were paid to take us to Calais!"

"We were paid only to take you out of Flanders, mijnheer, which we've now done, and whether you find yourselves at the end of your passage in France or England or on the coast of Guinea matters not a dried fig to us. So get yourselves and your brats and baggage ashore, I say, without chewing the bacon rind any further, because otherwise we might be tempted to take you all back to Gravelines and hand you over for a reward."

They did as they were told, too weary to argue, and while the fishing boat backed off the steep cobblestone beach into the Channel waves, the fishermen lugging at the sweeps, the family struggled ashore knee-deep in the surf, Catherine with her skirts hitched up about her waist and little Henriette perched on her shoulders. They were now safe from being arrested for witchcraft – but at the price of being cast away on an alien shore with little more than the spray-soaked clothes they stood up in.

Back in Houtenburg next day the whole town was soon abuzz like a beehive with the news of their disappearance. The town constables had arrived at the house with a warrant for the arrest of Catherine Willenbrouckx on a charge of witchcraft – and found no one there except for the perplexed servants, who were promptly arrested and taken to the Bergues Gate for questioning, then released later in the day when it became clear that they had had no part in the escape. No man could provide any rational explanation for the family's disappearance, because the horseman set to follow them swore that he had dutifully followed the coach as far as the marketplace in Bergues and had not seen it stop on the way, yet when he caught up with it the vehicle was inexplicably empty. The coach (he said) had then turned around for no very apparent reason and proceeded back towards the French border near Ardres, which it crossed that afternoon. The prevôt, who was not easily deceived, sniffed bribery or dereliction of duty somewhere in the tale, and in the end threats that the man might be arraigned as an accessory to witchcraft persuaded him to come clean: how he had been led astray and blinded by naked watersprites; no doubt specially sent by the Devil to distract him. As the tale grew during the days that followed, more and more picturesque details were added: that the coachman had no head; that the horses themselves were headless, and likewise had eyes of fire even though (as previously stated) they possessed no heads to keep them in. In the end five or six impeccable witnesses came forward to testify that while they were working in the fields about noon the previous day they had seen a fiery coach drawn by dragons flying through the clouds above Houtenburg; except that they had thought nothing of it at the time, and had thus not mentioned the matter until now. So in the end it was generally accepted that Catherine Willenbrouckx with her husband and children had been snatched from the grasp of justice by her infernal master, then spirited away none-knew-where. Which merely proved how right people had been to suspect her of witchcraft, and her husband too by the look of it. "*Non-lieu: suspect fled with the assistance of the Devil*" was duly entered against her name in the ledger of the seigneur's court. And the investigation was suspended until such time as the Devil saw fit to bring her back again.

These dramatic events brought in their wake certain legal problems of a more mundane nature for Houtenburg's court officials. The surgeon's house and its contents, along with the surgical practice conducted within it, were now vacant though still the lawful property of Michel de Willenbrouckx and his heirs, no warrant for distraint ever having been sought against him. Under the laws of the county of Flanders, for a witch to be found guilty and condemned to death required the suspect to incriminate themselves via a confession – howsoever obtained – because in such cases a conviction could not be secured solely on the testimony of witnesses. So there could be no question here of a trial *in absentia*, because the suspect had fled beyond the reach of the law and therefore no confession could be squeezed out of her. The property of the surgeon and his wife accordingly remained their property, and in their absence must be placed under judicial administration with the rents and emoluments therefrom accruing to their benefit, with only the court's administration costs being deducted. The town attorney, Maître Delvaux, was duly appointed administrator by the court, and the house and surgical practice were let out on successive year-long leases with the monies being carefully collected and held on account. So thus it came about that the very same court of law that would cheerfully have arrested the Willenbrouckx couple, flung them into noisome dungeons, extracted confessions from them under hours or days of torture, then burned them both alive for entirely imaginary crimes, was now acting as their legal agent, taking the most solicitous pains to see that their property was administered for their benefit during their absence and that not one single liard of the rents was misused. Though needless to say, if either of them had reappeared in the town to claim their money the court would have arrested them, flung them into noisome dungeons *et cetera* just as it would have done before, because the arrest warrant for witchcraft still stood and was an entirely separate matter from the administration of property under wardship. The law is truly one of the most remarkable constructions of the human mind, far more wonderful and mysterious in its ways than either music or poetry.

CHAPTER FIVE

So here was a fine tub of herrings we found ourselves in, to be sure: delivered not to Calais as my stepfather had expected and where he had so many friends to succour us, but instead wantonly abandoned on the shores of England like castaways on some Caribbean island full of anthropophages and venomous serpents; entirely ignorant of the tongue of those that dwelt there and bringing with us little more than the clothes we had on our backs. When we set out from Houtenburg that previous morning, being a child of lively apprehension and now eleven years of age, for all that my parents had tried to put a gay face on it by prattling about picnicking among the flowery springtime meadows, I soon enough divined from their anxious mien that this outing of ours into the Flanders countryside was no party of pleasure, and that since we took baggage with us we must be fleeing some imminent peril. So I bore up, and kept myself in good spirits that I might not increase their burdens, and treated it all as an adventure though I knew in my heart that we would not return to our house that evening nor indeed any other evening for some considerable time. My little sister Henriette, though, was very out of sorts and wept piteously as we trudged through the fenny meadows, asking all the time when we might go home; and the same again during our sea voyage, and would not be consoled until after a few days in England she too came to accept that some momentous change had taken place in our family's fortunes and that all must be started over again. Yet I own that as we toiled ashore up that steep and pebbly English beach with our bags slung about us, and the boat that had brought us there stood out to sea once more, I felt a great trepidation and a hollow queasy sensation in my belly, to be entering this unknown kingdom and my new life in it.

The place where we landed was called Saint Margaret's Bay

near the hamlet of Cliffe, about five miles north of the town of Dover, and likewise about five miles down the coast from Deal and Walmer and the great anchorage of the Downs, which was crowded that day with ships, a hundred vessels or more, springtime gales blowing all the previous week having driven them to seek shelter in the lee of the cliffs. Saint Margaret's Bay was a poor little place: no more than a few fishermen's hovels and amid them a wretched ale-hovel built of old masts and ship's timbers washed up by the sea, all lashed together with sun-bleached cordage and bedaubed with tar. A few fishing boats were pulled up above the tidemark, and the semicircular bay was bordered by great cliffs of pure white chalk two hundred feet high or more, which were most prodigious for me to behold, coming from Flanders where the highest things are the church towers and the land otherwise as flat as the sea that laps its shores. Some fishermen were mending their nets or carrying ashore the wicker baskets in which they catch crabs: uncouth savage-looking fellows in red stocking caps, smoking clay pipes as most of the folk now did along this coast, tobacco being plentiful there on account of the people being much engaged in "owling"; which is to say, plying between the Kentish coast and France under the pretence of fishing but in fact carrying English woollen cloth in one direction and French wine and tobacco in the other, with the utmost discretion and under cover of darkness so as to spare King James's customs men the trouble of levying duty on it. They showed little interest in us beyond guffawing at our sorry wet state, and making what were plainly bawdy observations about my mother's bare legs since her skirts were hitched up to her waist, so that she blushed and quickly let them down again when she saw those coarse rascals nudging one another and leering at her.

"What d'ye seek?" one of them shouted at us: but since none of us understood English we could make no reply except by signs. After some time a portly little man in a greasy doublet and a sorry battered felt hat, by his demeanour a petty official of some kind, came bustling down to meet us and grew very vexed and red in the face when he discovered that we could not understand him. At length he called over a fisherman's brat, boxed him about the ears and sent him up to the village to find assistance. After a hour or so the urchin returned with a sailor who, being an owler, spoke a little French. My father explained as best he could that we were fugitives from Flanders, and asked where we might find lodgings. The poor scrofulous little alehouse by the shore had no chambers to let: indeed had but the one chamber to serve all its purposes, and a smoky fire of driftwood and dried sea-wrack burning in the middle of it. So we must tramp with our baggage two miles or more up to the village of Cliffe, then a further couple of miles along villainous muddy roads to the somewhat larger village of Hawkingswould where we found lodgings at the *Blue Lion* inn; not without some difficulty since the innkeeper's wife was mighty suspicious of us and would not consent to let us a room until she had seen my father's money and bitten one of the patagon coins to test it. The officious little fellow who had met us on the beach had meanwhile sent word to the local magistrate to let him know that strangers were entered into King James's realms, since the English on their island are suspicious of all that comes from beyond the sea and none more so than such fellows as he, who was (we learned) no more than a parish constable, but of such great importance in his own eyes that one would think the entire safety of the kingdom rested upon his scurf-powdered shoulders. The whole of England is governed thus by unpaid officers, who in the Low Countries or in France would be officials paid a proper stipend. Their magistrates, called "justices of the peace", are not salaried servants of the crown but local gentlemen who elect one another and serve their prince for no other recompense than the dignity that his commission affords them, which would be inconceivable in any other country. And below them pullulates a whole squirming busybody host of constables, wardens, overseers, vestrymen, aulnagers, beadles, tipstaffs and ale conners who lord it over their fellows by virtue of their petty offices; which though most advantageous for the King of England's pocket, is likewise most oppressive for his private subjects, who must daily be browbeaten at every turn by presumptuous little jacks-in-office amenable neither to reason nor to bribery. But this was merely the first of the many oddities of that island kingdom which would manifest themselves to us in the weeks that followed, and which – since no one would or could explain them to us – we discovered most often by barking our shins against them like pieces of furniture in a darkened room.

Our time at the *Blue Lion* was a dolorous one. Our room was small and the price of it great, while our board – the "ordinary", which we were obliged to eat among ostlers and carters and other such vulgar fellows in the tap-room – was of the poorest sort, consisting of stringy roasted meat (which the English consume in huge amounts, though my mother swore that it came from beasts dead of disease) and noxious pasty bread, and turbid sweetish "ale" which they imbibe lukewarm whereas in Flanders folk drink proper beer made bitter and wholesome with hops, and chill it first in cellars before they drink it. The conversation about the table was loud and coarse, so that my mother declared she was glad she understood no English, and I think "Damn your eyes for a poxy villain" was the first phrase of that language I ever learnt. The innkeeper's wife eyed us all the time with no great affection and muttered to her servants, saying (we gathered) that it was a great shame that old England must be a receptacle for the off-scourings of Europe, and she thought we were no refugees from the Spanish Inquisition at all but must be saltimbanques or cozening gypsies come to chance their fortune among the honest folk of Kent.

On our third day at Hawkingswould a village schoolmaster who spoke some Latin came to us as emissary from the local magistrate to enquire what it was that had brought us to the shores of England. My father, not quite knowing how to account for our arrival early one morning on a remote Kentish beach, said that we were fugitives from persecution in Flanders seeking the protection of King James; though as to what sort of persecution he did not enter into any particulars. This seemed to satisfy our schoolmaster for the moment, and he left saying that after he had conferred with the local justices of the peace we should shortly hear from a charity that existed hereabouts to aid and succour such unfortunates as ourselves. This comforted us somewhat, because although my father intended that we should cross back to Calais at the earliest opportunity, the weather had worsened and contrary gales were blowing which might delay our voyage for some time, and he feared that our money would run out before the wind abated. But it also made our position delicate, since our hosts plainly thought that my parents were Protestants like themselves fleeing to escape being burnt for heretics in Flanders, whereas they were in fact Catholics fleeing to escape being burnt for witchcraft, which was not the same thing by any manner of means. One of the few things my father knew about King James of England (he said to my mother) was that he had written several learned books on witches while he was King of Scotland, and would therefore be the very last prince in Christendom to look indulgently upon persons accused of *veneficium* seeking refuge in his domains: in fact if he ever came to hear of the matter, would probably have us returned straight away to face justice in Flanders. My father's audience with the charity for succouring Flemish Protestants would thus have to be handled very gingerly indeed, not the least of his difficulties being that if he were to be quizzed in any detail on the theological opinions which had brought us into odium with the authorities in Flanders he would be entirely struck dumb, since he swore that he had no knowledge or understanding whatever of that subject, idle speculations about that which could be neither seen nor heard nor touched (he said) never having interested him in the slightest.

My parents were put into an even greater dump at the end of our first week in England when there arrived a sealed letter addressed to my stepfather "quelque-part en Angleterre"*: we never

---

* "Somewhere in England".

learned how or from whom. It said simply that he must not seek to return to Calais or anywhere else in France, because the Prevôt de Coqueville had flown into a mighty rage at our escape and had petitioned the Royal Governor of Picardy, where he thought we must be hiding, to have my parents arrested and returned to face justice. And His Excellency the Governor, France and Spain being at peace – and he likewise a cousin of the De Coquevilles – had unusually granted this favour and issued the necessary warrant. So for better or worse we were now stuck in England, since the only other country where we might seek refuge was the Dutch Provinces, which were at war with Spain, thus causing all manner of trouble for us since we were King Philip's subjects. In the end my stepfather said that we must stick in England for the while and make the best we could of it, since anywhere else might be even worse, and he would do his best in the mean time to dissemble and provide answers that satisfied our hosts.

Our time at that inn otherwise passed tediously enough, with little to divert us children in our poor poky room where my parents slept with my sister in the bed and I on the floor beside them. It drizzled and the wind blew every day we were lodged at the *Blue Lion*, so we could not venture out much. Yet once I had overcome my first dudgeon at the strangeness of it all I found myself in good enough spirits at being in this new country. The English tongue in particular was something that I began to learn almost as soon as my feet touched the shore in Saint Margaret's Bay, for I was always remarkably quick to learn languages, and children are anyway much apter to learn them than grown-ups by reason of their brains being still plastic and unformed. There is in any case about as much difference between Flemish and English as there is between French and Spanish, both of which I had mastered already, and a great deal less than between Flemish and French.

I will not deny, however, that English was passing strange to me during those first few weeks in Kent; and all the more so because in some ways it greatly resembled the speech of Flanders, yet in others seemed but a mangled and bastardised version of it. The tongues of the Netherlanders, the Frisians, the High Germans and the Scandinavians are all kissing cousins, and likewise English once was too, being descended from the speech of the old Anglo-Saxons, whose kings Hengist and Horsa (I later read) had made their first landing in England at Pegwell Bay an hour or so's walk from where we were now lodged. Yet while the other tongues descended from Old Gothic have all kept pretty close company, so that a Hollander may still understand about the half of what a Dane says if he but speak slowly enough, the English language has ploughed its own furrow and nowadays, though lower walls are still the wattle, daub and oaken beams of the old Teutons, the upper storeys of the edifice are a most egregious jumble of broken classical columns and bits of marble pediments looted from Latin and Greek, all promiscuously mortared together with Norman French and I-know-not-what-else into a fantastical dog's breakfast of a language which still sounds in my ears (I must confess) somewhat like the prating of a quacksalver at a Flanders country fair promoting his pills and ointments to the ignorant rustics by larding his speech with macaronic Latin and rogue's hippocrene. In west Flanders most people speak French as well as Flemish, and the better sort often Spanish also. Likewise the Hollanders are most adept linguists: inveterate traders who would surely learn to bark like sea-lions or howl like wolves if they thought that sea-lions or wolves might do business with them. Yet in those polyglot lands the divers tongues are still kept separate, as though people had built walls down the middle of their skulls, and very seldom mingle. But in England, I discovered, Odin and Jupiter Capitolinus sit with their arms round one another's shoulders at the same tavern bench and mingle Germanic ale and Mediterranean wine promiscuously in their cups, so that in the English tongue there are two words for everything: "ox" for the animal (which is cognate to our "oks") yet "beef" for its flesh, from the Latin "bovus", and likewise "bread" for our "brood" yet "pantry" from the Latin "panis" for the room in which bread is kept, whereas we Flemings would call it a "broodruim". But there we are: the English are the English, and their language is their language, and there is nothing that anyone short of God Almighty – and perhaps not even He – can do about either of them. I have always been skilful at accommodating myself to new circumstances however much I might privately deplore them. So before three months had elapsed I could speak English pretty well, and after a year spoke it fluently, though my stepfather (who said that he was now too old for learning languages) never mastered more than a few polite phrases and otherwise got by in French and Latin.

★ ★ ★ ★ ★ ★ ★ ★ ★ ★

In the last week of April 1622 Michel Willenbrouckx received a scribbled note in Latin politely requesting him to "*convenire apud servitorum vestrum obsequisissimum xxvii die aprilis hora decima in vicum Barlingæ juxta Walmerum*". It was signed by the "*reverendissimus Theophilus Knatchbullius Divinitæ Doctoris Cantabriensis*"* who was (it appeared) the rector of the parish of Barlinge and charged by the local justices with the task of assessing refugees arriving on that part of the Kentish coast as regards their fitness to enter the King of England's domains (for though England and Spain had been at peace these past eighteen years, Spain was still Spain and the Pope was still the Antichrist, and in any case one could never be too careful where foreigners were concerned). So the surgeon and his wife brushed their salt-stained and muddy clothes, which still bore traces of the Flanders marshes upon them, blacked their shoes and prepared themselves to be interviewed by the reverend doctor. The children were left for the morning in the care of a chambermaid at the inn while the couple set out along the muddy lanes towards Barlinge, which lay among the chalk downs some miles inland of Walmer.

---

* "meet with your most obedient servant on the 27th day of April at 10 a.m. in the village of Barlinge near Walmer" [...] "The Most Reverend Theophilus Knatchbull DD (Cambridge)".

It began to drizzle almost as soon as they walked out of the door of the inn, and they quickly became lost, unable to ask for directions until a kindly peddler who knew some French took pity on them and led them at last to their destination, by now wet, bespattered with chalky mud and thoroughly dejected. The rectory beside the village church was imposingly large, built of knapped flint, and had a handsome walled garden in front of it surrounded with carefully trimmed box hedges. Their reception though was a chilly one, ushered into the stone-flagged hallway by a servingwoman who swept the mud behind them with a birch broom and pursed lips, muttering under her breath about these foreigners being no better than so many cattle. They were kept sitting there, dripping and without being offered any refreshment, until the rector was ready to receive them. Which ceremony, when he emerged from his study at last, Doctor Knatchbull performed with the fastidious and somewhat pained air of a householder picking up by one leg the corpse of a rat which the cat has deposited on his doormat.

A tall and imposing gentleman of about fifty in a clergyman's gown with a ruff and a coif buttoned round his ears, he ushered them into the oak-panelled study where he had been writing next Sunday's sermon. The interview took place in stilted schoolbench Latin, and with a noticeable lack of warmth, since not only was the reverend doctor evidently a member of the Puritan tendency within the English church but also – more evidently still – a member of that tendency's genteel wing, not in the least inclined to rub shoulders with prophesying cobblers and mystical soap boilers. He was in fact a cousin of Sir Norton Knatchbull of Mersham, no less: a fact that was impressed upon visitors by the family's coat of arms displayed on every available surface, and likewise by the family portraits – most of them execrable, Willenbrouckx considered – that lined the walls of the entrance hall and staircase: successive boot-faced generations of ruffed, doubleted and farthingaled Knatchbulls standing in poses of identical stiffness with their hands on sword hilts or holding infants so tightly swaddled as to resemble little wooden skittles with faces painted on them. The wainscotting, they saw, where it was not adorned with the family arms or a family portrait, was decorated with painted Bible texts like SERVANTS, BE OBEDIENT UNTO YOUR MASTERS (TITUS II, IX) and THE POWERS THAT BE ARE ORDAINED OF GOD (ROMANS XIII, I). All of which was most strange to the surgeon and his wife, since in Catholic Flanders the clergy and the nobility were separate estates and looked it, whereas here in England the lords spiritual and the lords temporal appeared to be one and the same.

"So sir," the rector said at last, "am I to understand that you and your wife have lately fled here from Flanders by reason of your religion?" Since this was approximately true, Willenbrouckx agreed that they had.

Doctor Knatchbull nodded. "I see. And what, precisely, is the nature of the persecution that caused you to flee the King of Spain's realms? You will understand, I am sure, that though a great many of God's elect nation fled from the Low Countries to this part of Kent in good Queen Elizabeth's day when the Duke of Alva was burning the saints in their hundreds, the flow diminished somewhat in the later years of her reign; there being by then, I suppose, very few of them left for him to burn. And since King James ascended the throne and concluded peace with the Spaniard there have been hardly any. Thirty years ago the town of Sandwich had more Netherlandish inhabitants than English ones, and the magistrates there had to seek the Queen's aid to disperse them to other towns around the country. Yet you and your wife, sir, are the first Netherlanders to come ashore here in ten or fifteen years, and though the charitable fund still exists that was set up to aid such unfortunates, no one can remember the last time that it was called upon. So for this reason I have been requested by the trustees to enquire as to your reasons for leaving Flanders. Because if you are Anabaptists, then I would inform you here and now that we in England want no truck with you and would counsel you to depart again as soon as ever you may."

Willenbrouckx was nonplussed: he had not the vaguest notion of Protestant theology, except that it seemed to involve eternal damnation and wearing black; in fact he had not much notion of Catholic theology either since he had only attended Mass on Sundays because the law required it, and had usually sat near the back of the church quietly writing up his surgical notes. So he frankly doubted whether he could plead with any conviction that he and his family had quit the Spanish Netherlands on theological grounds. Then, visible only to himself, the clouds above the rectory suddenly opened and a ray of inspiration shone down through the diamond-paned window.

"*Reverendissimus*," he replied, "we have not left Flanders because we are Protestants, but rather because we are Catholics."

The rector swallowed hard, and stared at him uncomprehending. "Excuse me, sir, but I do not quite understand your meaning…"

"Allow me to explain. Until lately my wife and I were devout Catholics all our lives. But we have come, through diligent study of God's holy scriptures, to realise that the Church of Rome is an invalid church…" The rector nodded, having followed the argument this far. "… And that the Anglican church is in fact the one true authentic church of Christ on earth. Which is why we have come to England to ask to be admitted to it."

Knatchbull gulped in disbelief. "But sir…one does not *become* a member of the *Ecclesia Anglicana*: one either is a member of it, or one is not …"

"But surely, one who is not yet a member of that church may still seek to be admitted to it? Or does the Church of England turn away converts?"

The clergyman considered a while, then spoke. "Indeed so, indeed so: and if you were infidels or Jews or Turks, or the heathen Indians of Virginia, then I suppose that you might be admitted to it by baptism. But since you are both – as I take it – baptised Christians already, then I know of no ritual or form of service by which you might be made *Anglican* Christians. In this country every subject of the King is presumed to be a member of the Church of England by birth and by baptism in infancy; the corollary of this being, I think, that those who are not thus born and baptised, but rather the subjects of some other Christian prince, cannot become Anglicans."

But Willenbrouckx persisted, and in the end the rector got up and consulted Hooker's *Laws of Ecclesiastical Polity* for a while. At last he shut the heavy leather-bound volume with a thump, sending a cloud of dust into the air, and replaced it on the shelf.

"I regret to say that I can find nothing herein for my guidance, and crave only your leave to refer the matter to my bishop. However, it seems to me, speaking but provisionally, that if you were to make public assent to the Thirty-Nine Articles of the Church of England and then take communion according to the Anglican rite, then that would suffice to make you both members of this country's church. But I must seek advice on this, because the matter is outside both my competence and my experience."

So they were shown out by the rector, passing in the hallway his wife and his two ill-favoured daughters, who lowered their heads and folded their hands in proper godly obedience as the reverend doctor passed by, taking no notice of them. The drizzle had by now turned to pelting rain, and they returned to the inn wet through and thoroughly dejected.

"Michel, what have we done?" Catherine asked as she dried her hair with a damp and by now somewhat mouldy towel. "We left Flanders as fugitives from justice, and now we are making ourselves not only castaways in a foreign land but Protestants into the bargain. So if we returned to Houtenburg they might burn us twice over, once for witchcraft and once for heresy."

Willenbrouckx smiled as he pulled off his sodden stockings. "Indeed, my love: and in that case Bartolomeus Nooten might even buy enough faggots to make a proper job of it since he would presumably receive two fees for us not one. No, dearest Catherine: 'Anglican' and 'Catholic' are merest empty words, pure wind, and what matters is how we behave towards one another in the world and not what labels we describe ourselves by; whether we believe bread and wine to become English roast beef and ale, or Spanish sack and chorizo sausage. For my part I care not whether I assent to their Thirty-Nine Articles or three hundred and thirty-nine of them, provided it makes these good folk happy. For from what I have seen of them I doubt very much whether any part of their religion obliges us to become cannibals or to boil infants alive in a cauldron. So do as they say is my advice, and let God decide afterwards whether we have done right or wrong. In Flanders we would face prison and the stake; in France we would be flung into gaol; in Holland we would be enemies of the state; therefore England must now be our home for better or worse. So while we are in England let us be Anglicans, which is no more than good manners on our part."

The following week a letter arrived from Doctor Knatchbull. The See of Canterbury having considered the matter, it was felt that no public declaration of assent to the Thirty-Nine Articles was necessary, only that the family should attend holy communion the following Sunday at the church of the parish in which they currently resided. So the family duly attended divine service at Hawkingswould parish church, and found that the Church of England, though they could not understand the words, at least *looked* reassuringly like a somewhat plainer version of the one they were used to in Flanders. Then next day there arrived another letter, written in even worse Latin and signed by Sir George Yelverton JP, the magistrate at Sandwich which is the chief town in that part of Kent. It informed the Willenbrouckx family that whilst accommodation and work for Flemish refugees was hard to find in east Kent (by which he meant that the poor-rate had charges enough upon it already) he believed that across the Thames in the town of Colchester in Essex there was a long-established community of Netherlanders. He had therefore arranged payment from the poor chest to fund a sea passage from Margate to Colchester where a certain Mijnheer de Gheyn would help them find lodgings and employment. So the next day the family duly boarded the hoy *The Bear's Whelp* bound for Colchester, which was (they were told) somewhere among the wide, marshy rivermouths on the opposite shore of the Thames Estuary.

★ ★ ★ ★ ★ ★ ★ ★ ★ ★

It was early morning as our little vessel made its way on the tide up towards Colchester's port, which is called the Hythe and is a mile or so outside the walls of the town. Though our first approach to that place which would be our new home was humble enough, it filled me none the less with awe and pride to realise that a veritable Roman emperor had once made a triumphal progress up this same river. While we lay at Hawkingswould my stepfather had found me an old dog-eared copy of Suetonius's history *De Vita Cæsarum* to beguile my time at the inn, and I had read therein that this very same Colchester – or *Camulodunum* as it was then called – had been the first Roman capital of the province of Britannia after that country's conquest, and had remained so until the Britons under Boadicea rose in bloody revolt and sacked the place, after which the seat of government was moved to *Londinium*. I read of the Emperor Claudius's visit to Colchester, which Cassius Dio also relates of, to celebrate a triumph with camels and elephants and the building of a great temple in his honour, which now lies beneath the mighty castle that William the Conqueror erected on top of its ruins a thousand years later. This was of great solace to me: that as I travelled with my family towards our new destiny, whatever that might be, I was walking in the footsteps of the ancients.

As our little hoy made its slow way up that winding river through the early-morning mists, borne along on the flood tide with the sailors plying their creaking sweeps since the wind had dropped and the sails now hung limp and wet with dew, it was plain to see why the Romans had so soon grown tired of Colchester as their provincial capital. For the Colne is in truth a paltry cat's piddle of a stream: narrow, muddy and tortuous and not remotely to be compared with the ample Thames, which is so commodious a river that the Pool between London Bridge and the Tower might easily hold a score of the greatest ships that ever were and still have room for others to pass them. And for all its past eminence, nor was Colchester much of a place either, once we had trudged there from the quayside with our bags. Its massy Roman walls still surrounded it, stoutly constructed of brick and flint set together in mortar and of prodigious thickness. But the town inside them was plainly much decayed since that time, and now contained more empty spaces than dwellings. There was some manufacture there: of a woollen stuff called "baize" brought over in Elizabeth's reign by weavers from Flanders. But otherwise it was just an English market town as poor and inconsiderable as the other market towns of England are. That nation, I soon perceived, has not as great a regard for towns as we have in the Low Countries, where the meanest and most inconsiderable municipality will still strive to have a taller church tower and a more splendid radhuis than its neighbours. Though they are numerous and wealthy, the nobility and gentlefolk of England mostly disdain to live in towns and seek instead to build themselves palaces out in the countryside, where they may hunt and cultivate their gardens and pursue other such bucolic pastimes, leaving the towns as mere market places where they come once a quarter for the assizes and to consult with their attorney or their doctor. The consequence is that these towns are commonly very plain and disregarded places; mere necessary offices like a brewhouse or a privy and not joyous works of artifice like the municipalities of the Netherlands or Italy.

At Colchester quay a messenger boy was waiting to conduct us to the house of Mijnheer de Gheyn, a cloth merchant whose parents had come to Colchester forty years earlier from Antwerp when Alva sacked that city, but who still spoke tolerable Flemish as well as French. He found us lodgings and gave us a little money from a charity set up by the Netherlanders in the town, but otherwise left us to shift for ourselves. There were many of our nation living in that part of the town, on its north side around

Stockwell where the ground slopes down towards the walls and the river. All were well established and grown prosperous by their industry, which greatly exceeded that of the English, so that the Dutch weavers now had a cloth hall of their own at the top of the main street in which to sell their wares, and likewise a church to themselves at Saint Giles's just outside the walls. But most were now settled there a generation or more, and plainly viewed us with no small suspicion as the first fugitives to arrive from the Low Countries in some fifteen years or so, suspecting us of being at best vagabonds and ne'er-do-wells imposing upon their charity, or at worst spies for the Spaniards seeking to insinuate ourselves among them and report on their doings. Nor did it escape remark that instead of attending divine service each Sunday in their own Dutch church (which followed the Geneva rite) we chose instead to attend Anglican service in the great town church of Saint Botolph's, so that folk soon muttered among themselves that whatever had brought us to England it was certainly not our theology.

Thus it fell out that for the first few months we languished in our poor little lodging-house (which was built on a hill slope, so that it flooded each time it rained) and scarcely a living soul spoke to us; neither the Dutch who would not nor the English who could not. A small dole given to us each week by the Dutch church's dominie furnished us with bread, and my stepfather found some paltry work with a barber-surgeon trimming beards and holding the basin for blood-lettings while my mother took in sewing. But otherwise we sat idle and disregarded as the money we had brought with us melted away before our eyes like a tallow candle. We now had a fixed abode of sorts, and could send a letter to Regulus in Leiden telling him what had befallen us and that he must not concern himself on our account (though I dare say he concerned himself very much, there being few phrases in any language more disquieting than "you must not concern yourself"). In all other regards though our new home was no great improvement on our room at the *Blue Lion*, except that for the while the charity would pay the rent for it and not ourselves.

All this put my stepfather, who was now fifty-five years of age, into a very melancholy humour. He said that he did not know the language of this country, could not learn it now and had no means of earning our bread in this town, which already seemed well enough stocked with surgeons. My mother though, who had undergone far worse tribulations than this in her time, was more hopeful, and since Dame Fortune smiles most sweetly upon those who go out seeking her rather than those who sit at home waiting for her to pay them a call, she happened one day while shopping in the market upon a certain Madame Lavallanet from the town of Douai in Flanders, whose husband now had a workshop in Colchester which employed nine or ten operatives in the making of silk ribbons. They fell to talking, this being the first time in several months that my mother had been offered the occasion to converse in good French, and the name of Bourchier was mentioned, who were my mother's maternal kindred in Tournai. My mother discovered that she had a cousin Nicholas Bourchier who had grown up in Colchester but was now a wealthy and worshipful silversmith in London, in the parish of Clerkenwell just outside the city walls. Letters were exchanged, and early in August my stepfather was given an introduction to a French physician now practising in the east part of England, one Doctor de Brantôme. Which proved an encounter that made all our fortunes and one that (I now see having cast a figure for that date, time and place) might have been predicted from the planetary conjunctions, since Jupiter and Mercury sat in perfect trine in the sign of Taurus at the very hour of their meeting.

★ ★ ★ ★ ★ ★ ★ ★ ★ ★

Doctor Hercule de Brantôme had arrived in England about the year 1615 and had since built up a sizeable and prosperous practice among the nobility and gentlefolk of the eastern counties, being elegant in person and of exquisite manners, admirably tactful and delicate in treating his patients – especially female ones

– and with an enviable facility for curing or at least alleviating their ills. Which latter skill he owed largely to the fact that his diplomas from the universities of Paris, Basle, Montpellier and Bologna were entirely fraudulent and his licence to practise obtained from the Royal College of Physicians in London by a mixture of bribery and deceit: also from the influence exerted on his behalf by King James's personal physician the Frenchman Sir Théodore Turquet de Mayerne, whose diagnostic skills had plainly been of little help to him when it came to recognising a rogue. For Doctor de Brantôme was, not to mince words, as great a charlatan as the lousiest rascal that ever drew teeth at country fairs or sold pots of pounded woodlice as Egyptian mummy and grand arcanum. Yet if he was a charlatan, he was a charlatan of no mean order. The fact that he had suckled at the teats of none of the *almæ matres* he laid claim to meant that he had at least imbibed none of the often lethally wrong-headed medical theories they dispensed, and was therefore free to proceed on the basis of simple observation and inference, supplemented by native cunning and a powerful desire not to be shackled to a rowing bench aboard one of the King's galleys, which would have been his fate if he had remained in France. His manners were refined, his person debonair and his relations with his patients full of genuine human sympathy. So in practice he healed as much by faith as by the application of poultices; and since he abhorred bleeding and purgatives, was greatly revered by those who sought his aid: especially when they had already suffered grievous martyrdom at the hands of other physicians. Those who would have got better anyway got better, and were grateful and paid their bills with a cheerful heart; those who would have died anyway duly went and died, though mightily comforted by the good doctor's soothing presence; while as for the rest, they enjoyed his ministrations and felt their money to have been well spent in purchasing them the company of so witty and courteous a gentleman who brought a touch of continental refinement and gallantry to the lumpen society of the English shires. No man in England could cast a decumbiture more convincingly, for De

Brantôme was a consummate master of medical astrology and made Jupiter and Saturn, Mars and Venus scurry about the sickroom at his behest as though they were no more than his lackeys carrying out chamber pots and bringing in warming-pans. No physician in the entire Royal College could feel a pulse or palpate a distended belly with a more soulful gaze (even having a servant stand by with a little earthenware hot-water bottle to remove the chill from his fingers), so that many ladies of the quality feigned illness merely for the touch of his delicate, well-manicured hands and the velvet caress of his French-accented English. Nor was any doctor in England more fashionable, wearing his beautiful chestnut hair (now greying a little) long to his shoulders in the style of King Louis' court, with a little moustache and a falling collar of Valenciennes lace in place of the stiff-crackling ruffs that English doctors still wore, which made their grim, close-cropped pates look like John the Baptist's head on a platter.

Much of the doctor's success was likewise due to the fact that he had the good sense to delegate the more manual parts of treatment to his subordinates: a small retinue of surgeons, chiropractors, phlebotomists and apothecaries whose collective wisdom (which was considerable) he gathered together and directed as a singing master might conduct a cathedral choir, making the initial examination and diagnosis himself and then directing his assistants as they applied the treatment, listening to their observations and changing the therapy as circumstances dictated; or even changing the diagnosis itself, which was highly unusual in a physician since most of that profession regarded the patient daring to suffer from anything other than what they had diagnosed as rankest presumption. It had all worked as well as any other way of doing things; indeed had proved most profitable. And now the doctor was in search of a new assistant to expand his practice, which was why he had arranged to meet with Michel Willenbrouckx at an inn in the town of Dunmow, about thirty miles west of Colchester.

"Of course, monsieur," he said as he poured Michel another

glass of wine, "I take the greatest pains in selecting my men – or my partners, as I prefer to call them – and have therefore made the most extensive enquiries concerning you; in particular with Monsieur Lavallière who now practises in Norwich, but was until lately a surgeon at Hazebrouck in Flanders. And I am happy to inform you that his letter of reference speaks most warmly of your character and experience, and in particular of your abilities as a lithotomist. Which is why I have invited you to meet me, since I have at the moment a pressing need for a surgeon skilled in that operation. Tell me, monsieur, are you licensed by the Company of Barber Surgeons in London?"

"I have made application to that body, and must go up to London soon for them to have sight of my surgeon's licence from Flanders." De Brantôme waved his hand as though brushing away a fly and made the little popping noise that the French use to dismiss something of no importance.

"Po! It signifies nothing, and I would counsel you to spare yourself that journey. The writ of those ignorant charcutiers hardly extends outside London, and likewise the surgeons' guilds here in England are but paltry affairs compared with those in France or the Low Countries. Your licence from Ypres and your references will be entirely sufficient for me and for anyone else you are likely to come across outside the capital city. I shall put you to work for a probation of six months. And if during that time more of the patients you cut for the stone have lived than have died, you will become my man for lithotomy and kindred operations." He poured some wine from the pewter flagon and drank it, making a wry face as he did so. "Pouah! Will these English tavern-keepers never learn to decant their wine from the cask into vessels of glass or pottery and not of metal? They were as well serve it in a leathern bottle such as their ploughboys carry to the fields, the taste could hardly be worse. But as I was saying, Monsieur Willenbrouckx, you will be paid your fees less one-quarter coming to me, so your remuneration each year will depend on the number of cuttings that you perform. But I think that I may promise you no shortage of custom. Here in England the better sort are immoderate eaters of flesh, and swallow sweet wine and their detestable sugary ale by the hogshead until a man might think their legs were hollowed out to receive it, all of which is sorely provocative of the stone. Likewise they hugely despise all the salads and fruits that might purify their blood, esteeming them no better than cattle fodder. So for their sins of diet God has smitten them with calculus and the gout more grievously than ever He chastised Pharoah's Egyptians..." He smiled, "...Which, though no doubt mortifying for them, makes good business for us, since to be cut for the stone by a reputable surgeon will cost them forty or fifty English pounds. Tell me, monsieur, do you have an assistant?"

"In Flanders I was assisted in performing lithotomies by my apprentice, who when we left was already in the final year of his indenture. My intention was that when he departed from my service next year my stepson would take his place. But I think that he might as well do so now."

"How old is the boy?"

"Twelve years at Christmastide..." De Brantôme looked doubtful. "...But tall and considerably older in appearance: fourteen or fifteen to look at, and a remarkably discrete and well-conducted young fellow. I would have no misgivings about him assisting me. For several years past he helped me in my practice in Houtenburg and always performed his duties most admirably."

"Is he clean and tidy in his person?"

"Completely, as I am myself."

"Excellent: in my partners I always look particularly for cleanliness and a grave but cheerful demeanour, which reassures the patient's relatives as much as the patient himself. That is why I seek usually to employ operatives from the continent. Most of the English surgeons that I have interviewed are dirty and unkempt in their persons and, as regards their skills, little better than so many sow-gelders. A few of them are admirable, like Master Hillyer who is a very capable young fellow. But most are not, and would only bring my practice into disrepute if I employed them.

You will understand that I must pay the closest attention to our reputation, because a single leg that had to be broken again and reset would outweigh a hundred that were good as new when the splints came off. Our good name is our greatest treasure." De Brantôme smiled slyly, and seemed to hesitate for a few moments, then lowered his voice. "In fact, monsieur, to admit you to a small confidence, I am here in Dunmow today not just to confer with yourself, but also to visit a notable physician, one Doctor Remington, who is highly regarded by the King's favourite the Duke of Buckingham and has already attended him several times at his house near Chelmsford. If I can secure that fellow as one of my associates, we will then have access to the very highest in the land and our fortunes will be made. So you will perhaps see why I am so insistent on the skill and good character of those who work for me."

He paused for a moment, then asked the question that Willenbrouckx had been waiting for. "Tell me, monsieur, what was it that caused you to quit Flanders?" The surgeon drew a deep breath and answered truthfully; for as he would often say, "The trouble with telling lies is that a man must always remember what lie it was that he told last time".

"By reason of the troubled times, monsieur, and for causes quite unconnected with surgery. My wife, though quite innocent of any wrongdoing, was in difficulties with the law, and this would soon have implicated me as well. We had no choice but to leave in haste."

De Brantôme nodded: he quite understood, and it was evident that he would pry no further. Although he never showed it to anyone, his back beneath his fine cambric shirt was crisscrossed with the faint scars left by a whipping in the marketplace at Aurillac in the Auvergne, administered in the year 1613 after a substantial sum of money had disappeared from the office of the notary whose clerk he had been at the time, employed under his baptismal name of Jacques Troudecul. And his ankle beneath its elegant silk stocking still bore the scar of the iron shackle that had galled him so grievously on the subsequent tramp towards Toulon and a sentence of seven years in the King's galleys – except that he had contrived to escape on the way and reached Genoa, then Naples, where he had converted himself so successfully from felon to physician. He still slept habitually with the window open and a knotted rope hanging out of it in case he might once again have to depart in haste, and this had made him remarkably understanding of other people's little difficulties with the law.

"I see", he said at last. "I suppose for reasons of religion, which is usually the case with medical men who arrive here from the continent. Some came even from Holland a few years ago after the Synod of Dort, when the Gomarists crushed the Arminians or the Arminists crushed the Gomarians, I forget which. Monsieur van Roggeveen was among them, and is now my best man for teeth. For myself, I have no opinions whatever in matters of religion and would cheerfully employ a Jew, a Turk or an atheist provided he knew his business and kept his fingernails clean. So when I engage you as a lithotomist, Monsieur Willenbrouckx, I shall find you your patients, and likewise survey your early operations and the patients' convalescence afterwards. And if I am satisfied with your competence I shall thereafter leave the work entirely to you, restricting myself to procuring your patients for you in return for a quarter-share in the fees. Does that seem fair to you?"

"It does: indeed, most generous."

"Good then. But before you commence, here is twenty pounds as an advance against your first fee." He reached into his purse and stacked the sixteen golden jacobus coins on the table, precisely as a physician might, in four piles of four. "See to it that you and your boy have suits of clothes made – elegant but sober: I leave that to your discretion – and also order such instruments as you require, for which I recommend a Swiss craftsman, Master Egersch, in Cheapside who forges blades so fine that they would split a hair four ways and separate a man from his own shadow. As I often say, a sharp blade, a keen eye and a resolute hand are all of a surgeon's wealth."

So on the fifth day of September in the year 1622 Michel Willenbrouckx and his young assistant rode out in their new suits on their hired horses (De Brantôme had been very insistent that they should take the best in the stable and not worn-out nags, which would create a bad impression) to perform their first lithotomy on a subject of His Majesty King James I of England. Their patient was one Sir Robert Hallingbury of Wickermarsh Hall near the town of Halstead, and the operation proceeded – God be praised – with no complications.

Willenbrouckx rolled up his sleeves and donned his kid-leather apron, then washed his hands thoroughly with lavender soap while Frans flamed the instruments in spirits of wine and laid them out neatly on a clean white napkin on a side table, having previously shaved and washed the operation site between the legs of the unfortunate Sir Robert, who now half sat, half lay praying softly to himself, his knees pulled up towards his armpits by a leather strap looped under them then round his neck, and his ankles firmly lashed to his thighs. A copper pan of sand and ashes had been placed below the table ready to catch the blood and urine which would soon pour out. Four burly farm labourers held the patient's arms and legs as his wife sat anxiously on a stool to one side, while the village parson on the other side exhorted him to be of good courage, reading appropriate verses from the Book of Job to fortify him for the ordeal to come. Having first warmed it in a jug of boiled water – for the chill of the instruments (patients had told him) is almost as disagreeable as their cutting and probing – Willenbrouckx first inserted the rounded tip of the long, curved steel sound into the end of the patient's member and pushed it gently but resolutely up the urethra into the bladder, until his sensitive fingers felt the faint "click" of the tip contacting the stone, which he dislodged so that it lay towards the back of the bladder. By now Sir Robert was moaning softly as his wife mopped his brow. Then came the terrible moment of the incision itself: cutting deft and firm into the perineum with a double-edged scalpel to open the wound. The patient writhed in pain as his wife thrust a pad of leather between his teeth for him to chew upon, so that he might not break his teeth or bite his tongue off in his agony. Fast now, as fast as possible: slicing through the prostate gland and into the neck of the bladder to find the tip of the sound. Frans mopped away the blood with a sponge as Willenbrouckx opened the incision about a thumb's length towards the urethra, then withdrew the sound and reached inside the now-gaping bladder with a pair of spoon-bladed forceps. This was the most difficult part for the surgeon, extracting the calculus – or calculi, since there might well be more than one of them – without having to break it up and without tearing the delicate bladder membrane. At last he managed to grasp the slippery stone – about the size of a pigeon's egg – and pulled it out. Wiping off the blood, he saw that one surface of it was worn flat, which meant that there must be another of them.

Sir Robert was now struggling like a snared lion, chewing the gag as though he were trying to kill it or it him. The labourers were having the greatest difficulty in restraining him, so it was troublesome for the surgeon to insert the middle finger of his left hand into the patient's rectum to push against the back wall of the bladder and manoeuvre the remaining stone to where his forceps could grasp it. Sir Robert spat out the gag, and cried loudly for merciful Jesus to deliver him from his agony. The parson, finding Job an insufficiently powerful pain-killer, had meanwhile taken to reciting Latin verses from Horace concerning fortitude and steadfastness. But the sweating, white-faced patient calmed somewhat as Willenbrouckx held up the two stones between his bloodied fingers for him to see. The surgeon made a quick search inside the open bladder with his index finger, to make sure that no other stones or fragments of them remained inside. Then it was a matter of closing the wound and applying pads of lint to staunch the bleeding. Though some surgeons would sew up the incision afterwards, Willenbrouckx saw no need for that: if properly made the cut lay with the grain of the muscles, not across it, which meant that it would close itself naturally if left alone, and in his experience would heal much better than if needles and catgut had caused further damage and inflammation. A perforated silver canula would be left in the wound for a day with the patient lying on his right side and his thighs tied together, so that the blood clots and debris would be washed out, then a catheter would be placed to drain off urine while the bladder and the perineal flesh knitted themselves back together again.

Barely conscious and half dead from pain and loss of blood, Sir Robert was carried away and put to bed while the surgeon and his assistant cleaned up after the operation. They would remain at Wickermarsh Hall for a further four days after the operation in case infection set in. But if all went well – as in this case it did by the grace of God, with only a little pus dribbling from the wound and that all laudable, not dark or stinking – they would depart on the fifth day after bidding farewell to the patient and his family and leaving instructions as to diet and changing of dressings. Considering the anguish that he was required to inflict upon them, operations such as only a public hangman would be required to perform and even he would put the victim out of his misery afterwards, Willenbrouckx never ceased to be astonished that his lithotomy patients were so civil to him when he came to visit them after the operation; indeed sometimes grasped his hand and kissed it when a few hours before it had been slicing into their living flesh and then groping around inside their bladder. But he had witnessed the pain that urinary calculus caused its victims: worse than a hundred stone-cuttings (they said) and if left untreated, then with no relief in prospect until complete strangury and flooding of the kidneys finally brought their sufferings to a miserable end; delirious, bloated, yellow and stinking of urine. Pliny held that only three maladies were so painful that they justified the sufferer in taking his own life; but among those three he awarded bladder stone pride of place. Having by now almost two decades' experience of treating that condition, Willenbrouckx was inclined to agree with him.

The first twelve lithotomies went well, with only one patient dying afterwards and he had been ill for some time already with a dropsical heart. Doctor de Brantôme was well satisfied with his new operative, and after six months advanced him to full partnership in his practice. Meanwhile the fees from the operations – collected if necessary by a man of the doctor's who specialised in such matters, and had a gang of knaves behind him with stout cudgels in case of dispute – began to repair the family's depleted finances. In fact by the spring of 1623 Willenbrouckx was able to rent a fine house in the centre of Colchester, opposite Holy Trinity church, and engage a housekeeper and maidservant; also to hang out his surgeon's sign, which in England was a white pole with a red spiral stripe round it and not a gilded blood-letting basin as in the Low Countries. Bladder stone seemed to afflict people most in springtime, as the vital fluids were drawn upwards by the ascending sun. So it had been agreed with his employer that though Willenbrouckx would give priority to stone-cutting, he would be free at other times to heal such sundry injuries and afflictions as presented themselves to him: broken bones to be set and rotten teeth to be pulled; weeping ulcers to be cauterised and boils to be lanced; and occasionally something more dramatic, like amputation of a leg crushed by a cartwheel and turned gangrenous, though wherever possible Willenbrouckx preferred restoration to wielding the knife, and by skillful splinting and traction with weights and pulleys had saved several limbs which another surgeon would have summarily lopped off like cankered branches in an orchard.

Language was a bother, to be sure, in treating the poorer sort since Willenbrouckx's English was still rudimentary. But among the gentlefolk of the counties of Essex and Suffolk this mattered but little, since most of them spoke some indifferent French or mangled Latin and indeed seemed flattered rather than otherwise to entertain the grave and dignified Flemish surgeon and his handsome young assistant in their houses. All their hosts agreed afterwards that their manners and deportment had been impeccable, and though they were but manual operatives there was not a gentle family in the eastern counties – nor indeed the nobility themselves – who would not be happy to let them dine at their table and have Monsieur Willenbrocks regale them with tales of his service aboard King Philip's galleons in '88, and thereafter in the Low-Country wars in which many local gentlemen had fought on the other side. As for his apprentice, he was a handsome, well-conducted young fellow and already spoke English fluently though with an amusing Flemish accent, so he could always interpret for his master: who also appeared to be his stepfather, though no one was too sure about this, and in any case everyone knew that the familial arrangements of the continentals were peculiar to say the least of it, with brothers freely permitted to marry their sisters and uncles their nieces if the Pope gave them a dispensation for it.

★ ★ ★ ★ ★ ★ ★ ★ ★ ★

By the end of the year 1623, then, as I approached my thirteenth birthday, our family was pretty well set up in England and – or so it seemed at the time – past all our various tribulations. Our practice in lithotomy was now well established, and our fame trumpeted abroad among the nobility and gentry of eastern England so that before long our work had us riding the muddy roads into the neighbouring shires of Hertford and Cambridge, or even once or twice as far afield as Norfolk. By now I had entered a seven-year apprenticeship to my stepfather prior to seeking the Worshipful Company's licence to practise as a surgeon in my own right.

I was an apt pupil, and in addition to the skills of lithotomy quickly mastered the more quotidian surgical procedures such as drawing teeth, letting blood, setting bones and stitching up wounds. I applied myself likewise to the more theoretical part of my trade, profiting here from my father's friendship with the Colchester physician Doctor Francis Mompesson who lived just across Trinity churchyard from us, in the house where Doctor

Gilberd the author of *De Magnete* had once lived, and who allowed me to study in his well furnished library. I was a grave boy and tall for my age (we Netherlanders being generally larger folk than the English), so I usually passed for fifteen or sixteen when we ventured out into the countryside in the springtime to perform our stone-cuttings, the light being better at that time of year and the patients less likely to die afterwards from that lowness of the vital spirits which makes surgery hazardous to attempt in the winter season. My stepfather's sight was now dimming somewhat with age, so that he wore spectacles when he operated and made use of a contrivance of our own devising: four hand-mirrors on swivelling pedestals so that the sun's rays or the light from candles might be focused on to the incision. As he said, I was now his eyes and would soon be his hands as well, and when it came to delicate operations like stitching up a wound he would entrust those to my sharp vision and nimble young fingers and merely guide me as necessary with his instructions, discreetly and in Flemish so as not to alarm the patient and heighten their distress.

Another task that he entrusted to me was to assist him in writing up the notes of his operations, for when he looked behind him my stepfather saw old grinning Death gaining on him with his scythe and hourglass – though he hoped still some way behind him on the road, he said – and wished something of public utility to survive him after he was gone. Which was why he was now intent on writing a treatise on the nature, causes and treatment of bladder stone, *De Natura, Causibus et Curatione Calculorum in Vesica*, which would be the distillation of his many years of experience in the diagnosis and healing of that condition. Part of this task was that, in addition to writing up his notes for him as he dictated them to me, I would also make drawings of all the kinds of stone that we found, and these sketches of mine would then be passed to an engraver to be made into copper plates for the book. Although I was not as skilful a draughtsman as my stepbrother, I still had a passably neat hand and an exact eye for such work. Likewise I had learned from Doctor Mompesson a system of shorthand writing of his own devising which proved very useful, since notes could be dictated to me by my stepfather and I then write them up in fair script for the printer.

While I attended my father performing his lithotomies my knowledge of that procedure increased greatly; of the various complications that might ensue and (by dint of my painstakingly drawing them) the many diverse forms that the calculus might assume. If they survived, which they usually did, our patients would as a matter of course request their stones – which I suppose were their own rightful property, they having invested so much of their wealth over the years in growing them – and have them set in silver or put in a little glass case as a commemoration of their painful deliverance. But before we gave them back to their owners my father would always have me sit down and make a careful drawing and description of them in a notebook. And their variety was extraordinary; not just in size – for some were mere gravel while others were as big as a hen's egg – but also their form and composition: some made largely of a brownish chalky stuff; others of sharp crystals held together by chalk; some smooth and polished while others were jagged and irregular and others still – the most curious of all, and the most exquisitely painful to the patient and troublesome for the surgeon to extract – were covered in sharp spinous outgrowings of crystals like a sea-urchin.

Likewise I would make minute notes on each patient: the diagnosis, the mode of operation that we used and the subsequent course of their recovery or death. This was unusual at the time, though it has since grown more common among physicians, and was a great innovation of my father's into England for which (I have to say) he was considerably derided, as he was likewise for his flaming of the instruments before starting to cut, which was much mocked as a foreign affectation and quite superfluous among red-blooded Englishmen whose constitutions (we were told) were robust enough from a lifetime of ingesting roast beef and ale to resist suppuration of their wounds. Or if not, then they were plainly weaklings and England was better shot of them.

We went mostly to our patients to perform lithotomies rather than have them come to us, because by the time bladder stone had progressed so far that an operation was the last remaining hope the sufferer would commonly be in too great an agony to ever think of sitting astride a horse and riding to Colchester, and in any case would be far better cared for after the operation in his own household and among his servants and family (for it was nearly always a "he" that my stepfather operated upon, only once ever having had to cut a woman patient for the stone, which he thought must be because the female urethra being so much shorter than the male one, the stones are apter to be passed out as gravel). As for ourselves, we were happy enough to be entertained for a few days in the houses of the gentry while we saw how our patient fared. At one or two of the places where we cut for the stone we were afterwards sent to the servants' hall for our board like common lackeys, and to make our bed in the hayloft. But in most we were liberally entertained by the patient's family, who commonly viewed us as saviours and angels sent by God: that is, unless the man's children wished with uncommon fervour for him to die so that they might inherit.

This gave me the opportunity to observe the English better sort from close-to. And very instructive it was for me as well, since I could never as long as I lived have conceived of such folk had I remained in Flanders. The English gentry – or "squires" as people call them – are a race quite unlike anything to be found on the mainland of Europe: prosperous from farming their lands and from trading or even manufacturing ventures (which in England bring no loss of nobility as they do in France or Spain) and likewise inordinately capable and confident of their right to govern others through their service as justices of the peace, which allows them to rule their parish as little monarchs in consultation with the neighbouring little monarchs of their shire at the quarter-sessions, after which they come up to Westminster to sit in Parliament with as much authority (they consider) as the King himself. Their love of horses and dogs is inordinate and their regard for the finer arts correspondingly limited, though some are notable scholars and antiquaries, and in recent years even those that are not have none the less begun to travel in Italy and bring back paintings and broken-nosed marbles to adorn their houses. In the main they are a brutish tribe: violent by nature, fearless, addicted to strong drink and subject often to a kind of quiet melancholia called "humour" which leads them into outlandish behaviour frequently bordering on insanity and which is most probably occasioned by England's drizzly climate and lack of the diversions to be found in continental towns, because for most of them killing wild creatures is their sole amusement. Likewise, though outwardly cordial enough, they have a sovereign contempt for all who are not English, and also for those mortals who are not of their own rank and estate. But there: as I have often remarked, the Devil himself would be civil to a surgeon in case he might have need of him some day to pare his hooves. So my stepfather and I were usually entertained generously enough when we ventured among the English squires. I often suspected that we were being displayed to their guests at table as though we were a pair of baboons: plied with wine and delicacies, but still laughed at for our strange Flemish accents and our curious affected ways like not blowing our noses on the tablecloth and not cutting up the meat on our plate with the knife we last used for trimming our staghound's claws: likewise refraining from breaking wind at table or having loud recourse during the meal to the chamber pot commonly placed behind a screen – or sometimes not, as the case might be – within earshot of the diners. But all in all I found the gentry a most sturdy and vigorous race for all their frequent savagery, and it was no surprise to me years later that King Charles should get the worst of it when he fell to blows with them.

While we were lying at their houses I myself was usually made much of by the families and servants of our patients; and in particular by the young women of the household if there were any, because I was a personable young fellow and gracious in my demeanour. I found it most agreeable after the pain and blood and shrieks of the operating room (which remain distressing even to the most hardened of surgeons) to play blind-man's-buff or hide-and-seek with the daughters and nieces of the family in the long gallery where they would giggle and laugh at my accent and likewise practise their French on me, which they spoke quite villainously for the most part, yet I smiled and complimented them upon their mangling of it. Englishwomen even of the better sort quickly lose their charms once they marry and soon become dowdy and lumpish, quite lacking the modishness and gaiety of our women in France or Flanders. I supposed this must be because, once they have performed their procreative duty and produced a son to continue the line, their husbands grow far more interested in their horses and dogs than in their wives. But while young they are often comely, and undeniably of considerable spirit. And whilst I was perfectly well aware that they regarded me as they would a dancing bear or an ape brought in to entertain them, I was still well enough diverted in their company, and acquired a fondness for the society of the female sex that has never left me: those strange whimsical creatures, so like us but so unlike us withal, and so incalculable in their humours as to be a source of endless curiosity to any man of an enquiring and scientific turn of mind.

In several of these visitations to perform lithotomies Doctor de Brantôme came to supervise us. He would sit in a chair as we operated, observing us with his chin resting on his gold-topped physician's cane and nodding sagely from time to time, as though my stepfather (who had performed a hundred lithotomies and knew that procedure as well as any man living) was a journeyman carrying out his orders. But he had the good sense not to interfere, and never gave instructions nor made any comment other than to murmur his approval. For the truth (I very soon divined) was that he was no more a physician than I was a Carmelite nun, and performed largely by setting others to do his work for him. I must say, though, that I esteemed him none the less for that, because for those who sought his help he was of the greatest service in selecting capable men to treat them. Like most such ingenious rascals he was a mighty acute judge of men's natures, and where he prescribed therapies himself (which was not often) he was blessed with more than his fair share of good luck, so that by accident and the exercise of horse-sense he often hit upon a cure which a more learned man would have missed entirely. Or as my stepfather said, "De Brantôme cures his patients for all the wrong reasons, whereas a veritable doctor of physic would assuredly kill them for all the right ones."

I recall in particular our riding out one day to attend a gentleman near Maplestead who had long been sick of the palsy and for whom our employer, despairing of all other remedies, had prescribed confinement with foxes, since Pliny writes that the stink of a fox is sovereign against that affliction. The gentleman's labourers had trapped eight or nine foxes that winter and locked them in the house with him, so that by the time we got there in the spring the smell of them was so rank that our eyes watered as we entered his bedchamber and most of his servants had quit his employment rather than endure it any longer. By now his foxes were grown tame, coming and going as they pleased through the doors and windows, treating the house as they would their own lair and devouring the partridges and hens they had caught so that the place was all bestrewn with bones and feathers. As for our gentleman, though his palsy had not abated one jot, he had grown as fond of the animals as of his own children and was (he said) as happy as he had ever been in his life, to observe the artful ways of those beasts; and likewise (we supposed) by now grown so accustomed to their rancorous odour that he no longer remarked upon it. As we rode home, hoping that our clothes would have aired somewhat by the time we reached Colchester, my stepfather remarked that thanks to that ignorant rogue De Brantôme the gentleman with the palsy was now a much happier fellow than he would have been from a twelvemonth of bleeding and emetics, "For as Hippocrates observes, the end of all medicine is the well-being of the patient." I enquired whether Hippocrates had in fact said that, since I could not recall seeing it anywhere in his writings. To which my stepfather replied laughing that if Hippocrates had not said it then he certainly should have done, and he would say it for him now.

During this time I myself also grew pretty proficient in the surgeon's art. As an apprentice I might by law only assist my stepfather in his work and perform lesser operations such as sewing wounds up under his supervision. But there were occasions when I was obliged for pity and for charity's sake to attend to patients myself in his absence: as on Christmas Day of the year 1624, my fourteenth birthday, when a woman came a-knocking at the door of our house in Colchester with her face all bound up in a bloody cloth and carrying her own nose packed with snow in a little box. My stepfather being away near Coggeshall attending a patient, I was on my own in the house with my mother and sister; but because of the urgency of her plight I must needs attend to the poor woman myself, there being no one else to help her. She was the wife of a gentleman from near Polstead and her husband had some hours earlier seized a kitchen knife and cut her nose off with it, for it was Christmas morning and he said the goose was underdone. Despite her pain and fright she had sufficient wit to pick up the severed nose and put it with some snow in a box (for she had observed that plucked fowls left out in the snow before being taken to market would not mortify though they hung there for weeks), then bade her servants saddle up a horse for her to ride to Colchester where she had heard there was a Flemish surgeon who might be able to attach the nose back to her face.

She was distraught to find my stepfather not at home, saying that she was quite undone and her beauty would be marred for ever (though in truth she had a face like a horse's rump even with the nose in its proper place). But I calmed her, and ordered every candle in the house to be brought, and set up our mirrors, and then got to work with the finest silver needle we had and the finest silken thread to fix the nose back again, using an everted suture that my stepfather had taught me where the edges of the flesh are pushed outward by the pressure of the stitches instead of being pulled inward, which, though it looks villainous at first, leaves a much less visible scar than an inverting suture once the wound has healed and the scab fallen off. It took me the best part of an hour to perform the operation, working with the utmost delicacy. But words cannot express my joy as the nose warmed in the heat of the room and I saw it change its colour from bluey-grey back to pink as the blood flowed into it once more. I was very apprehensive for the success of this operation. But when the woman came back after four or five days (she having meanwhile taken lodgings at an inn nearby, for fear of her husband) I saw to my delight that the flesh and gristle were knitting together again, leaving a scar that would be scarcely visible two months later. By the end of the week the nose was firmly reunited with her face, and word had spread round the whole of Colchester that young Master Francis Ravick the Flemish surgeon's apprentice had wrought a miracle, so that people who had never noticed me before now doffed their hats and bade me good-day in the market, and the rector of Saint Botolph's Church even preached a sermon in which he likened me to Our Lord who had re-attached the servant's ear in the Garden of Gethsemane after Saint Peter had struck it off with his sword. My stepfather was as proud of me as I of him, that my first essay into surgery had brought renown to us both and lustre to our practice. Sad to relate, though, before long our very fame would be our undoing.

CHAPTER SIX

By the beginning of 1625 Michel Willenbrouckx's surgical practice was pretty well established, and now flourishing to a degree where the surgeon could contemplate retiring in three or four years' time and handing it over to his stepson. Once the witchcraft nonsense had blown itself out he might return to Flanders (he thought); or if not to Flanders, then perhaps to France. Or even remain in England, which for all its rainy climate was – he had found to his surprise – an agreeable enough country with a goodly supply of intelligent and cultivated people to save his brains from turning to soup in his old age, like his neighbours Doctor Mompesson and Mister Wilbye the musician with whom he would hold long colloquies in Latin and French, and perhaps pick out a few airs on the lute.

Each week he penned a letter to Regulus, now approaching the end of his apprenticeship in Leiden, and consigned it by postcourier to the packet boat at Harwich. He even wrote now of the possibility that his son, once he had finished his compagnonage and made his tour of Italy (which was obligatory for aspiring painters nowadays), might afterwards come to London to seek work. There might, he wrote, soon be employment for a capable painter of mythological scenes at the court in London. Old King James was reported to be gravely ill and unlikely to see the year out, and on his death the crown would pass to his son Charles, who was said to be a young man of cultivated and refined taste, already collecting pictures and statuary to the great disgust of the gentry in Parliament, who held that for a king to interest himself in art rather than hunting stags suggested effeminacy at the very least and quite possibly an inclination to popery as well. The surgeon's visits to the greater and lesser country houses of eastern England inclined him to think that there might be considerable opportunities for an accomplished young artist in that quarter as well, "for the family portraits that I see wherever we go" (he wrote) "are commonly no better executed than so many inn signs, and the very worst of our bumpkin-painters in Flanders could do better."

Likewise there was Henriette to be considered: eight years old now and as pert a little demoiselle as could be imagined. A good marriage party might be found for her when she came of age since the English nobility were (it appeared) nothing like as insistent as their French or Spanish counterparts on a daughter-in-law being able to flourish patents of nobility and armorial quarterings, and would pragmatically consider any young woman as a candidate for their son's bed provided that she was healthy, of sound wit, tolerably good-looking and accompanied by a generous dowry, so that many of the English magnates he heard spoken of over the dinner table had a master bricklayer or an innkeeper for their great-grandsire. It seemed, in short, that looking back on those events from the perspective of three years, the family's precipitate flight from Flanders might indeed have been with Satan's assistance, since it had transported them from a life of provincial mediocrity to a whole new world of possibilities in England. Yet there are events gestating in the dark womb of time that we know nothing of, and mighty earthquakes will often betray themselves at first only by the faintest of tremblings, so that cups will scarcely rattle on the shelf when before long the entire roof will come crashing down. The stars and planets move in their habitual courses, and though we may delude ourselves that the clock has stopped and its "tick" will not inexorably be followed by "tock", our present fortune seldom continues for long whether good or ill.

That first premonitory tremor came one evening in the second week of April, about seven o'clock, as the springtime dusk was falling and the townsfolk of Colchester were drawing their hearth fires and retiring to bed. There was a loud insistent banging at the front door of the house. When Jane the servant-girl opened it three men barged their way in wrapped in riding cloaks with their hats pulled down over his eyes, their boots leaving a trail of mud in the hallway and the tips of their scabbards scraping menacingly along the flagstones. Jane demanded to know their business, but they took no notice and shouldered past her in a most arrogant and displeasing fashion, demanding to know where "the stone-cutter fellow" was. She showed them to the treatment room where the master sat, then curtsied and left in an indignant bustle of petticoats.

Frans was with his stepfather, writing up the day's case notes. He rose to greet the visitors.

"How may we be of assistance to you at this hour, sirs? If it's a wound that needs treating we can sew it up now; but if you require a tooth to be pulled we would suggest that you come back in the morning when the light will be better."

The leader of the men replied in a voice that scarcely spoke of wounds or aching teeth. It was evident from his insolent manner that he was a gentleman, though a minor one.

"We have no need either of your needle or your tooth-drawer's tongs, knave. I've been sent to command you to pack up your tools at once and come with me to attend my master."

When Frans relayed these words to his stepfather the surgeon was ruffled.

"Command, sir?", he replied, "Even here in England I scarcely think that 'command' is a word that should be addressed to those you seek to heal you. 'Politely request' might be a more courteous formulation."

"We wipe our arses with your polite requests, sirrah! If you've any sense at all in your Flemish buttercask of a head you'll do as I tell you, for I have four more of my fellows waiting outside ready to enforce my polite request with an even politer cudgelling; in which case you and your lackey here will assuredly wish you'd heeded me the first time. Get dressed, I say, and come with us without further argument – and without telling any of your household where you are going, because I promise you it'll go very badly with you indeed if any word of this ever reaches the ears of the magistrates."

"Might you do me the courtesy, sir, to tell me by what authority you force your way into my house and give me orders?"

The man seized the hilt of his sword and half drew it with a chill scrape of steel.

"By this authority, dolt. Which you'll soon find exercised upon your person if you continue to play the fool with me. You'll be well paid for your trouble, three times your usual fee for a stone-cutting, and returned here without a scratch once the operation has been performed. Come, I say. Or must we drag you with us and burn your house down for good measure?"

So they went; partly from fear of these overbearing ruffians and partly from compassion for their mysterious "master", who although plainly a great villain to have such followers, must also be a fellow mortal in the direst suffering if a surgeon had be found for him by abducting one. Carrying his bag of instruments and with Frans following him bearing the dressings bag, the mirrors and the other accoutrements, Willenbrouckx was led out into the back streets of Colchester, leaving only a scribbled note for Catherine that he and Frans had been called away to an urgent case out in the countryside and might be gone for some time. Outside the town gates, by Saint Botolph's Church, they were each given a saddled horse and told to follow the mysterious gentleman, with two of his followers on each side and four riding behind to prevent escape. They trotted through the spring twilight down the road towards Peldon, and then some way beyond that village were stopped so that they might both be blindfolded and their horses led thereafter by the bridle. They swayed and bumped along thus for a good hour, splashing along muddy trackways between the thorn hedges in blossom, then coming (they perceived by the salty-sour smell and the plaintive piping of curlews) out onto the tidal marshes that fringe the sea behind Mersea Island. Several times the horses' hooves clumped on plank bridges across muddy creeks. Then at last they came to a halt as dogs barked and a voice called "Who goes there?".

"The surgeon, brought from Colchester," came the reply, and a wooden gate creaked open to let the party clip-clop into a cobblestoned courtyard. The gate was slammed shut behind them and barred. They had arrived at Stroodfleet Hall.

The hall was the home and business premises of Sir Thomas Harbrow, *eques in comitatu Essexiæ** and a man distinguished by his villainies even in an age and a country already well stocked with high-handed predatory rascals. Sir Thomas's grandfather, a minor gentleman from near Braintree, had been hanged for rebellion and brigandage by Henry VIII, who always took a firm line on public order, and his father had likewise been banished in Elizabeth's reign, finding employment as a mercenary captain in Italy and subsequently dying of the great pox at Modena. Sir Thomas's elder brother had been killed fighting for the Moors of Sallee against the Portuguese, while his younger brother had taken service with the Uskok pirates in the Adriatic and ended his career in Venice in 1614 along with seven other Uskoks – five of them younger sons of English gentlemen – on a gallows specially erected in their honour on the Piazza San Marco. Meanwhile Sir Thomas had enlisted in an English regiment during the Low-Country wars. But finding the opportunities for pillage, rape and extortion too restricted in the Dutch service (since the Butter Boxes were tiresomely pernickety in these matters and would hang even their own men for looting) he had eventually joined the retinue of the warlord Martin Schenk, who had established his own little brigand-kingdom where the Rhine passes from Germany into Dutch territory just above Nijmegen. It was this which gave him the idea for Stroodfleet Hall, since Schenk had constructed as base and citadel for his operations a great earthen fortress, called the Schenkenschans, on a marshy island where the Rhine divides into the Oude Rijn and the Waal. From this stronghold he had pillaged the countryside round about for several years, to the great

---

* Knight in the county of Essex.

grief of the peasantry whose villages were burned while their cattle were driven off and their daughters taken into prostitution, and had even sought to levy tolls on ships sailing on the Rhine as though he were a ruler anointed by God and not a glorified robber-chieftain.

Schenk was drowned in 1595 at Nijmegen after his men had tried and failed to take the town, seeking to leap in full armour from the quayside into a boat – and missing. But the idea of the Schenkenschans lived on in the head of his English follower, and when he returned to England following the truce of 1609 Sir Thomas had set to work building a similar robber's lair out in the desolate, ague-ridden tidal marshes of Essex, inside the earthen ramparts of an old coastal fort from King Henry's day so that he might avoid a charge of challenging royal authority by building a castle, but still making sure that discretely hidden cannon covered the corners and all lines of approach. And from this base he had commenced a reign of crime and extortion, gathering to him raffish younger sons of the local gentry, disbanded soldiers and all the most dissolute ruffians of eastern England. Complaints to the courts and the Sheriff brought promises of action but no result, since Sir Thomas was a kinsman by marriage to the Lord High Admiral the Earl of Nottingham, and likewise a cousin of Lord Chancellor Bacon, and therefore enjoyed protection at the very highest level. Meanwhile any small man who crossed him could expect swift and certain retribution, his hayricks set ablaze and his cattle hamstrung in the night by marauders who disappeared back into the marshes and creeks whence they came. Piracy off the Flanders coast under the guise of sprat-fishing had been profitable enough, but in recent years the trade in French tobacco had brought better returns, boats arriving in the marshy creeks at dead of night and the contraband being moved inland along dark lanes and through silent hamlets (if the cottagers knew what was good for them) to Tiptree Heath, where a vagabond town of gypsies and horse thieves held a permanent market day of smuggled and stolen goods in open defiance of the King's officers.

But Sir Thomas and his followers were growing old, as even the most insolent ruffians will grow old. And even in the lax and impecunious final years of King James's reign there were limits to how far an audacious villain might go in defying the law. The previous September Sir Thomas had sent a party of his retainers to kidnap a witness about to appear at the assize court in Chelmsford. A riot ensued, a circuit judge was hit by a brickbat, and Sir Thomas was formally declared an outlaw for making affray and assaulting one of the King's puisne judges. So far no one had dared to confront him in his lair at Stroodfleet Hall: troops and even cannon might be needed for that task. But likewise Sir Thomas could no longer venture inland for fear of being arrested, even to seek a surgeon's help for the bladder stone which tormented him day and night. If he was to be operated on – which he must be soon if he were to live – then it would have to be done in secret, for news of his condition might make the authorities bold enough to try arresting him, or a crowd of the little folk he had wronged over the years appear at his gates seeking vengeance. The outlaw knight had taken good care to fortify his lair with more than cannon and walls loopholed for musketry: the whole dreary expanse of saltings between the Colne and the Blackwater was notoriously disease-ridden and offered visitors the prospect of a dose of marsh ague if they lingered more than a few hours. Dank mists hung over the marshes for much of the year, and many a wildfowler caught by the fog had stumbled into a muddy creek and drowned as the tide came in. But there were other sentinels standing guard about Stroodfleet Hall. No county in England was more plagued by witchcraft than Essex, and no part of Essex more than its coastal marshes. In return for his protecting them against the local magistrates Sir Thomas had engaged the services of two of the most notorious local witches, Goody Twinbody of Tolleshunt and Goody Clarke of Wigborough, to cast charms against intruders – and had it well noised abroad that he had done so. The result was that until recently few upland villagers would have dared venture out on to Stroodfleet marshes even if the King in person had bidden them do so. But of late folk had begun to mutter that if the witches' spells were unable to protect Sir Thomas against the bladder stone, what effect would they have against several hundred villagers with staves and cudgels going to speak with him regarding their stolen cattle and pillaged barns? The important thing with terror is always to maintain it: for once a tyrant's mystical aura of impunity starts to fade he is a lost man.

★ ★ ★ ★ ★ ★ ★ ★ ★

When the blindfolds were removed from our eyes we found ourselves in a courtyard surrounded on three sides by stables and by stout brick walls pierced for musketry. On the fourth side was a small manor house of two storeys, made also of brick and likewise with loopholes in the walls. We saw by the light of torches that the courtyard contained a great many idle fellows lounging about on benches drinking ale and smoking churchwarden pipes as though this were some kind of tavern, though it was now near midnight and the air was grown misty. All had about them the insolent, debauched air of soldiers, and most likewise carried swords and firearms: light snaphance muskets which might have been used for hunting wildfowl on the marshes, but which seemed more likely intended for a larger sort of two-legged game. They viewed our arrival with shiftless curiosity and guffawed a great deal among themselves, oafishly buffeting one another about as soldiers are wont to do and making remarks about us which seemed from what I could catch of them to be mighty disobliging. As for the three or four great mastiff dogs that strained at their leashes and snarled at us with foam dripping from their fangs, we divined that if they had their way then it would not be merely their words that were disobliging to us, but their deeds even more so.

We were helped down from our mounts, stiff after so long a ride, and ushered with scant courtesy into the house, then straight up the oaken staircase without being offered refreshment or given time to wash ourselves, into the great bedchamber where our patient lay: the knight and (as we later learned) outlaw Sir Thomas Harbrow: a large, fat, pasty-faced, rheumy-eyed fellow of about sixty years of age with a straggly grey beard and the scar of an old sword-cut across his cheek. He lay in the great bed lit about with candles and bellowed like a bull from pain before we ever came into the room. An attendant pressed to his lips a glass of Dutch brandewijn, which Sir Thomas and his retainers (we saw) were wont to drink like table beer to proof themselves against the damps and agues of their marshy abode. He spluttered, then fixed his bloodshot eyes upon us.

"The surgeon has come, Sir Thomas," his retainer said. "We have fetched the fellow from Colchester as you instructed us."

"The surgeon? May the pox carry you off, Blount, you rogue! Why did you take so long about it when I lie here tormented day and night worse than any dog of a Jesuit was ever racked in the Tower? And what will you have them do with me? Do these rascals propose cutting me?"

The fellow Blount who had burst into our house in Colchester and brought us here seemed to have some authority in Sir Thomas's household, which so far as we could see consisted entirely of men: like a military camp or a monastery, for not a single woman servant did we see the whole time we were there.

"The surgeon cannot understand your questions, Sir Thomas," he replied, "because he is a lousy prating foreigner from Flanders. But his red-headed knave here knows English about as well as such an ape might ever learn it."

Sir Thomas grunted at this and lifted himself up on his elbow, wincing with pain as he did so.

"Brought me nought but a rascally Dutchman, eh? Do you seek to kill me, Blount, you traitorous dog, and make yourself chief here when I'm gone?"

"No Sir Thomas," his adjutant replied, "we your liege-men all love you dearly and desire only that you should live to be a hundred. This surgeon fellow, though but a scurvy Fleming, is reputed to be the most skilful stone cutter in the county and we brought him here in preference even to one from London. But he must examine you first before he sets to work."

So my stepfather lifted Sir Thomas's nightshirt and began to palpate him about the pubic region and between his legs to try and determine how large the calculus was that tormented him and how it might lie. All through this our patient roared and cursed most atrociously, calling us every foul and opprobrious name that he could lay his tongue to for paining him so. And when my father introduced a steel sound (which he had not been given time to warm first) into Sir Thomas's yard to probe for the stone's location in the bladder, the howl he let out must have been heard back in Colchester and caused the fowl that roosted in the marshes round about the house to rise flapping and squawking in alarm. By the time my father had finished his examination some eight of his retainers were sitting on the knight's arms and legs to hold him still.

Mister Blount spoke with us afterwards in his drawling insolent manner and enquired what our diagnosis was, gazing out of a window and examining his fingernails the while as though it was a matter of perfect indifference to him what two such inconsiderable persons as ourselves might think on the matter. My father said that for lack of time to perform a proper examination he could not be entirely sure how large the stone was or how it lay, so the only way to be sure, given the manifest urgency of the patient's case – for Sir Thomas had scarcely passed water all that day – was to cut tomorrow morning at first light. Mister Blount tried to command us in his bullying peremptory way that we should operate immediately, because I suppose he would fain have us out of the house as soon as ever he might in case of an assault on the place by the King's officers next morning. But my father insisted that the light was too poor and the patient must be prepared for the operation. So in the end he relented and we snatched such sleep as we could, getting up before dawn the next day to make the room ready for the operation. As I prepared the instruments my father bade Mister Blount have ready the most stalwart attendants that he could to hold Sir Thomas down during the cutting, and likewise provide stout cords to truss him up with and a gag to prevent him deafening us all with his roaring.

The lithotomy, when we performed it about nine o'clock, was I think scarcely less disagreeable for us doing the cutting than for Sir Thomas who was being cut. My stepfather worked deftly and swiftly enough as our patient howled and struggled, he having been tied up beforehand as firmly as a slaughter-hog with his legs immovably lashed to the bedposts, so that roar and bellow as he might he could not move an inch. As my stepfather cut into his bladder a great cascade of bloody urine poured out, so that I was hard put to it to catch it all in a washtub full of ashes. But as my stepfather reached his middle finger into the incision to find and remove the stone, the forceps having failed to locate it, a look of consternation came over his face. He fumbled a while, then whispered into my ear, "There is no stone here that I can find: only a fleshy lump attached to the bladder wall." From this we deduced that it was no calculus that plagued Sir Thomas but a great polyp or cancer of the bladder about which we could do nothing, for to have cut it out would infallibly have caused him to bleed to death. In the end there was nothing for it but to close the wound again and retreat. As I mopped away the blood and applied an astringent compress to staunch the bleeding my stepfather fumbled in his breeches pocket when Mister Blount was not looking, and hauled out an old calculus which he carried with him always as a charm for good luck: the first stone that he ever cut for, and which the patient, a prebendary of Ypres Cathedral, had not claimed afterwards saying that he was glad to be rid of the cursed pebble that had pained him so much and wished never to set eyes on it as long as he lived. My father held it up now between his gory fingers to show Sir Thomas, who by this time was half swooned from pain and the effusion of blood, and placed it on the bedside stool. Where, unfortunately for us, we inadvertently left it in our haste to pack up our things and be gone now that the operation was over.

My father left instructions for how Sir Thomas was to be tended in the days that followed, since he himself could not remain in the house to care for the patient as was his custom, neither did Sir Thomas's retainers wish us to tarry there. He was very insistent in particular that Sir Thomas should take no strong drink for three days, no matter how much he demanded it, in order that his bladder might heal itself without the scalding of urine heated by winey spirits. But neither of us had much hope that his followers would observe this advice of ours; not when the last thing we saw as we left was an attendant pressing a brandewijn bottle to the knight's lips to revive him. As for ourselves, we were bustled downstairs with scarcely time to rinse the blood from our hands, hoisted into the saddle and blindfolded as before, then led out through the gate and back along the same marshland paths and trackways – except that this time we surmised from the frequent challenges that the guard around Stroodfleet Hall had been doubled during the night for fear of an attack, now that the news had spread of Sir Thomas's indisposition and the disarray of his men. At Peldon the blindfolds were removed and we were told to make the rest of our way to Colchester ourselves on foot, it being (they said) too dangerous for them to approach that town in daylight. So we arrived home early that afternoon, carrying with us a bag containing a hundred pounds in gold coin as payment for our services – and also a parting assurance that if we so much as breathed a word of it to anyone, then we would most infallibly have our tongues cut out and nailed to the town gallows.

★ ★ ★ ★ ★ ★ ★ ★ ★ ★

Sir Thomas Harbrow died two days later from infection of the wound, and from the cancer which had been invading the lymphatic glands in his groin long before the surgeon arrived to cut him. He departed this earthly life in great pain and swearing vengeance against the villainous mountebanks who had hacked him so, consoled only by copious draughts of brandewijn and the assurances of his followers that those two Flemish rascals would surely suffer most grievously for their cozening. For it would have been difficult for Willenbrouckx, had he been challenged in the matter, to maintain that the stone which he left behind had originated in the bladder of Sir Thomas Harbrow, when it could be seen on close inspection to bear the engraved legend IEPER XXVII DIE AUGUSTUS ANNO 1604. For the surgeon and his family a particularly malign conjunction of planets was marshalling in the heavens.

A week later Frans was working with his stepfather in the treatment room of their house, cleaning the instruments and dousing the charcoal brazier after excising a polyp from the neck of a Manningtree harness-maker and cauterising the wound. The smell of singed flesh still lingered as the boy scattered lavender on the glowing coals to sweeten the air before the next patient arrived. In the street outside, by Holy Trinity churchyard, a small crowd had gathered as a band of musicians started to play. There had been an unusual and slightly nervous air of expectancy about the town in recent days. A fortnight before the news had arrived that King James was dead and that the people of Colchester were now the subjects of His Majesty King Charles I, whose reign had been proclaimed by the town crier from the steps of the Moot Hall with three lusty shouts of "God save the King!" and a great deal of cap-waving and huzzahing. There was less apprehension abroad now (people said) than when old Queen Elizabeth had died two decades earlier. Then, there had been no heir of the body and likewise a number of rival claimants to the throne, which always boded ill for the tranquillity of the realm. This time there was a healthy and personable son to succeed the old King, and likewise no pretenders. But even so the deaths and accessions of monarchs figured large in people's lives, public events still being commonly dated as "the such-and-such year of King So-and-So's reign". After twenty-two years of King James – more than half of most people's lives – a certain public unease was only to be expected.

Quite apart from anything else (the harness-maker had said as

Frans made small-talk with him to cover the sound of his father sharpening the scalpel on the leather strop) a new king meant a new parliament, and a new parliament meant elections, which were often rowdy affairs here in England; and all the more so since one of the two members for Colchester was Edward Alford, who was reputed to be no friend of the Duke of Buckingham's and who might therefore expect an attempt to unseat him by the duke's followers bribing or intimidating the town's few hundred voters. "So I would counsel you, sirs," the patient said, "to keep your windows well shuttered during those days. And likewise, as one tradesman to another, to lay in good store of linen bandages and vinegar to bind up all the broken pates that will surely be brought to you. For strong ale and stout cudgels are the customary means by which we elect members to Parliament here in England." But could such nervousness explain the strange looks that Willenbrouckx and Frans had been getting in the streets these past few days? Or the previously cordial folk who now avoided them as though they carried the plague?

It seemed that the assault on Stroodfleet Hall had not in fact taken place: that even on his deathbed Sir Thomas Harbrow had been lucky once more. The Sheriff of Essex and his men were otherwise occupied up near Harwich, where the ragged remnants of Count Mansfeld's* army had just been unceremoniously put ashore by the Dutch and were now robbing villages and farmsteads to support themselves. So for the time being Stroodfleet Hall would have to wait.

---

* The German condottiere Count Guido Mansfeld was contracted by King James's government in 1624 to raise an army to go to the assistance of the King's son-in-law the Elector of the Palatinate who had been turned out of his domains by Spanish troops three years earlier. Ill-equipped and worse-supplied, the army eventually became such a nuisance around Dover that it was shipped across to Holland, where most of its troops died of hunger and disease in the winter of 1624-25 and the rest survived only by begging and theft. In the end the Dutch authorities solved the problem by rounding up the remnants and transporting them back to England.

Frans opened the window to air the room and listen to the musicians out in the street. The tune was *My Cornish Jenny*, which he knew well enough. But as he listened he became aware that something was not quite right about the words:

> "Oh Surgeon Willenbrocks, you would perish of the pox
> And young Frankie on the hangman's ladder,
> Were it not for our dead master, who lies cold as alabaster
> Since you cut and hacked his bladder.
>
> "The rogue who wields his knife to take a beggar's life,
> The law doth rightly abhor him.
> But they who slew our chief, they shall come to greater grief,
> And curse the day their mothers ever bore them.
>
> "Sir Thomas Harbrow, who lies in his grave now,
> While he lived, caused many to quiver.
> But though he's dead and cold his honour we'll uphold
> And his dogs shall eat your liver!
>
> "So Barber Willenbrocks, and your knave with russet locks,
> Your mincing Flemish manners shall not save you.
> And from this life you'll pass with a firework up your arse,
> While the Devil himself doth shave you!"

The crowd in the square laughed uneasily, and the song was repeated; very clearly directed at the surgeon's windows. While the musicians performed a boy distributed leaflets bearing the words of the song. The Flemish surgeon was well respected in Colchester; not least for the charitable clinic which he conducted for the poor on two afternoons each week. But in death as in life, the name of Sir Thomas Harbrow was greatly feared in the locality – and had offered many examples over the years of what condign punishment might fall upon anyone who took it in vain. For the moment, however, nothing untoward happened: the musicians departed into a side street and the crowd dispersed, leaving only a few discarded leaflets lying on the cobbles. Frans went down into the square and picked one up to bring to his stepfather. He translated the title for him: *A True Narration of the Most Villainous Murther (for So It Can Only Be Described) Perpetrated Under the Guise of Surgery the xvi of April Last upon That Worthy Knight Sir Thomas Harbrow at Stroodfleet Hall in the County of Essex by a Pair of Flemish Mountebanks, and a Noted Astrologer's Prediction Concerning the Grievous Fate That Will Surely Befall Those Two Rascals*. It bore a crude woodcut print of "Master Willenbrocks" and "Young Frankie" being dragged down into the fiery mouth of hell by demons while "Sir Thos. Harbrow" looked on approvingly from his bed with a ribbon issuing from his lips bearing the words "*Hola my brave sprites! See to it the villains suffer for their knavery as they so basely served me!*" Willenbrouckx read the pamphlet, then crumpled it and tossed it into the basket of old swabs and blood-crusted bandages.

"Think nothing of it, Frans my boy: mere empty bluster. Sir Thomas is dead now, and his gang of rogues will disperse as all robber bands dissolve when their chief is no more. I might fear their vengeance if we lived in some lonely cottage out in the country. But here in the centre of town the watch will surely protect us. No substantial party of ruffians could pass through the town gates unobserved, so if they came against us we would soon be warned of their approach. This was merely a brag to frighten us and nothing will come of it. I served with the Invincible Armada in '88, and with King Philip's armies thereafter in a dozen campaigns, and a few wastrel younger sons of hedge-squires leading a band of rheumaticky old fellows discharged from their regiments twenty years since put me in no dread at all. They are manifestly a crew of poor, empty braggarts good only for robbing hen-coops; and now that their leader is gone the Lord-Lieutenant's men will soon take and hang the lot of them."

One evening a few days after this Willenbrouckx and Frans sat in the back parlour of their house as the shadows lengthened.

The had eaten supper and the plates had been cleared away, and they now sat picking out a few tunes from a music book: Willenbrouckx on the lute and Frans on the tenor viol, which he already played very competently since he was receiving lessons from Mister Wilbye the composer of madrigals in his house on the other side of the churchyard. They were alone, because Catherine and Henriette had departed the day before to visit Cousin Bourchier in London, riding side-saddle on a hired nag with Henriette perched behind her mother and among a group of travellers for protection against highway robbers. They played a Flemish jig, then Captain Hume's piece *A Soldier's Song* which Frans sang in his clear young voice just starting to break. Willenbrouckx smiled to himself as he read the printed words, which he could now just make sense of:

"*I sing the praise of honour'd wars,
The glory of well-gotten scars,
The bravery of glittering shields,
Of lusty hearts and famous fields.*"

This was no empty boasting: Hume (he knew) had served in the Low-Country wars and, unlike most of the poets who wrote so movingly of battles from the safety of their studies, was no doubt only too well acquainted with that of which he sang. Perhaps it was just that an old military surgeon had a different perspective on these matters, stuck in his tent behind the lines and experiencing none of the mad exhilaration of battle but only dealing with its sorry aftermath. Much (he supposed) as a pox doctor might read lyric poetry addressed to sundry fair mistresses and think rather of sores and purulent discharges.

All was peace as Colchester went to bed and darkness fell. Only a faint clattering came from the scullery at the back of the house, where Jane was scouring the pewter dishes. The surgeon lit the candles and they began a new tune. Then suddenly the world caved in on them: a mighty flash and a deafening bang, then confusion as the moulded plaster ceiling collapsed in a chaos of dust and falling laths. Window glass tinkled in Holy Trinity Church and the houses round about. Dogs barked, people cried in alarm, Jane screamed and the surgeon and Frans, coughing and white as ghosts from plaster-dust, extricated themselves from beneath the fallen ceiling. From the blown-in front of the house there came shouts of "Take the villains, I say!" and "Cut their legs off!" The great oaken front door, barred for the night against intruders, had been blown in by a petard, a keg of gunpowder on the end of a pole, and most of the front of the building with it. It would no doubt have gone very badly with the surgeon and his apprentice if the explosion had not by some merciful dispensation of Providence brought down the hall ceiling as well, blocking the passageway to the rear of the house against the seven or eight ruffians who now rushed in from the street with drawn swords. As they struggled through the fallen beams and plaster rubble there was just time for Willenbrouckx to snatch his cloak and hat.

"Come Frans!" he yelled. "As you love your life, follow me!" They ran out of the back door and into the garden, towards the stable where a horse stood ready saddled, as every evening, with the surgeon's travelling set of instruments in a saddlebag in case he was called out during the night. They got into the alleyway behind the gardens just as Sir Thomas's retainers burst into the parlour. There was no time to reflect, only for Willenbrouckx to climb into the saddle and drag Frans up behind him, then trot down the alley towards the Sheregate postern where (he knew) there was a recently collapsed section of town wall which they might scramble down, leading the horse after them, even though the gate itself was closed for the night.

"Where now?" Frans gasped as they stood below the walls.

"Towards the river: if those villains took the trouble to blow our housefront in with gunpowder they must surely be watching the main roads in case we try to flee." So they made all the haste they could towards Saint Lawrence's Church at the Hythe, hoping to lie low there until morning among the wharfside sheds and then return home. They tried to beat as much of the plaster-dust as they could off one another, so as not to be too conspicuous, but still arrived at the quayside ten minutes later looking like a pair of flour millers.

It was now high tide. Along the waterfront all was quiet except for a few late drinkers returning from the alehouse. Then they heard hoofbeats coming towards them from the direction of the church. It was a party of four or five men galloping in an ominously purposeful manner. Willenbrouckx unstrapped the bag of instruments and set the horse to wander off as they concealed themselves behind a low wall. One of the horsemen reined his mount in and demanded to know whether the tavern-goers had seen a man and a boy dressed in black who spoke with foreign accents. The drinkers said that they had not, but the riders seemed unconvinced and dismounted, then drew their swords to spread out and search among the houses.

"What shall we do?" Frans whispered. "The rogues are armed, and we are not."

Willenbrouckx looked across the road towards the quayside: a dim shape was just discernible.

"Come with me: I see a boat."

First looking about them to make sure they were unobserved, they ran across the road and reached the edge of the wharf. Two seamen were casting off mooring warps from the wooden posts. To his joy Willenbrouckx heard that they spoke Dutch.

"What ship are you, and where are you bound for?" He hissed. The men paused and looked round.

"What's that to you? And what are you doing here at this hour?"

"We'll explain later: just take us aboard and I shall pay you well."

"In trouble with the law, I suppose?" one of the men said. "We'll be in trouble ourselves if we aid men on the run from justice. We ply to Colchester every month and want no unpleasantness with the Port Reeve."

"We are no criminals, only two honest men being pursued by criminals. For the love of God and Christian charity, let us aboard or our throats will be cut before your eyes."

"Oh all right then, come aboard if you must. If we hang about any longer we'll miss our tide." They clambered down on to the deck of the ship: a spritsailed schuit of about forty tons with great leeboards like barn doors, a bluff bow with a rhinoceros-horn stem and a crested rudder like a cock's comb. The master came up on deck.

"What's all this noise?" He asked the mate.

"Two fellows just tumbled aboard, skipper: a man and a boy: both Flemings to judge by their speech, and both gentlemen by their dress but covered in dust and in fear of their lives. They want to come with us."

The captain brought up a candle lantern and examined them.

"On the run from the constables, I suppose." he snapped. "We heard a great bang from the town a half-hour since. Had you a part in that, whatever it was?"

"We had," Willenbrouckx answered. "There are elections afoot to the English parliament."

The skipper nodded. "Yes, I see it all now: the English mad dogs seeking to murder one another as usual: there must be some witch's powder sprinkled in the beer in this country, for I never saw men so violent and quarrelsome. Well mijne heren, can you pay us?"

Willenbrouckx rummaged for his purse. "All we have is three English pounds in silver coin."

"It'll suffice. We're bound for Bergen op Zoom: from there you must find your way as best you can. And the money is solely for your passage, not for your lodging or your food. You must sleep on deck and shift for yourselves; also keep from under the feet of my fellows." Even though he had only the haziest idea where it was, Willenbrouckx said that Bergen op Zoom was perfectly acceptable to him as a destination, so the skipper took the money and disappeared below to his cabin, and that was the last they saw of him as the little ship glided down the river on the ebb tide towards the North Sea.

The schuit *Zwaantje* of Krabbendijk in the province of Zeeland had come from the town of Bergen op Zoom to Colchester to deliver a cargo of earthenware chamber pots, stamped with that town's three crosses and the mark B.O.Z., which had for a time caused a pisspot to be known facetiously as a "boz" among London gallants until fashion changed and it became a "jordan" instead. For return cargo the vessel was carrying seventy casks of Colchester oysters as rations for the garrison of Bergen, since many of them were Englishmen and absolutely disdained to eat the pickled herrings provided for their sustenance by the commissaries of the States-General. Sooner than lose so large a component of the garrison by desertion — which was the usual consequence of discontent over rations among Englishmen in the Dutch service — the fortress commandant, facing an imminent attack by the Spaniards, had decided that instead of hanging a few of the rogues by way of example he would send across to England to bring over a cargo of oysters, which shellfish he understood were relished among the baser sort in that country though he himself detested them. So the schuit's blunt bows were now butting through the muddy grey waves at the southern end of the North Sea, across the sandbanks of the Thames Estuary and headed for the coast of Zeeland. At first light it began to drizzle. The two fugitives sat in the bows wrapped in a damp cloak against the spray and the chill down-draught from the foresail. Hunger already gnawed; but for the entire three days of the voyage they had no other sustenance than rainwater and some crusts of bread begged from the crew, and oysters spilled from a broken cask until they both swore that they would never eat another shellfish again as long as they lived. Then at last the sun came out and their clothes steamed gently in the sunshine. Far away to the east the high coastal sand dunes of the island of Walcheren began to appear above the horizon. Before long the schuit was sailing among the shallows of the Roompot, the southerly channel of the Oosterschelde estuary.

It was Frans's first sight of the Seven United Provinces of the Netherlands. And once they were inland of the coastal dunes a pretty unimpressive spectacle it was too: a dead-straight pencil-line of shore with the sea-dyke above it, broken here and there by a clump of trees and with the occasional windmill or church spire visible in the polders beyond. It was a strange, unsettled, half-formed landscape such as might have prevailed on the third day of creation, before God got around to properly separating the elements of earth, water and air. Beneath the arching dome of the sky the land seemed much like sea and the sea much like land with only the exiguous dykes to draw a boundary between the two. And those were a fragile frontier at best. As the schuit sailed further into the estuary, past Yerseke, she did so with her lee-boards trailing along the bottom to avoid grounding on the shallows despite her meagre draught and the rising tide. This part of the estuary was "het Verdronken Land"*: fields and meadows won from the sea by centuries of dyking and draining in the days of the Dukes of Burgundy – then all lost again one stormy autumn night in 1530 when a spring tide and a gale-driven surge had broken down the dykes, so that by daybreak the entire countryside had been repossessed by its old landlord Neptune and the fishes reinstated as his rightful tenants. Several ruined church towers still protruded above water, while fishermen dredged for mussels where cattle had once grazed, occasionally trawling up old leather shoes, kitchen pots or even dead men's bones to remind them that entire generations of people had once lived their lives where plaice and flounders now swam.

Before long their destination came into view: a long, dark, bevel-edged silhouette of earthen ramparts raised up above the surrounding flatness as though they were floating upon a raft, with a great pepperpot church tower and the brick-pinnacled roofs of buildings visible within the bastions, and the customary windmills spinning in the breeze at each corner of the for-

---

* "The Drowned Land"

tress like drowning men waving their arms for help, or perhaps the motive force of some mysterious pumping mechanism which kept the town afloat so that if the wind stopped blowing it might all sink again. This was the celebrated fortress town of Bergen op Zoom, which had triumphantly withstood a Spanish siege in 1588, and then another one only three years previously in 1622. The States-General had lately invested a great deal of money in the place, employing the very best military engineers from all over Europe to fortify it. And well they might, because as the southernmost Dutch stronghold on the mainland, on the coast of the still-Spanish province of Brabant, Bergen commanded the waterways between the northern provinces and the wealthy city of Antwerp which the Dutch aspired to wrest one day from the King of Spain's grasp. A marvellously complicated system of bastions, lunettes, ravelines, escarpments, demi-lunes and hornworks surrounded the town, blocking any approach from the landward side and supplementing the belt of marshes which had enmired the Spaniards during both sieges, leaving them floundering and struggling in the morass like so many flies caught in a pool of treacle.

Bergen op Zoom in the spring of 1625 was a busy place. Spinola's siege of the town of Breda, only a half-day's ride away, was going well for Spinola and very badly indeed for the Dutch garrison, which was now reported to be entirely cut off and running low on food. If Breda fell the great general's triumphant armies would certainly turn west to lance this vexatious boil which had been allowed to grow on the brow of the Spanish Netherlands. Reinforcements by the shipload were now being brought into Bergen on every tide, and supplies of every kind unloaded at the quaysides as the windmills turned day and night to grind flour for baking biscuit to be laid up against a long siege. Bergen's numerous taverns were meanwhile packed with soldiery of every provenance and coat colour: Scots, Germans, Danes and Englishmen as well as the local sort; drinking beer by the hogshead as they cursed the States-General's rations and their arrears of pay and the lack of action – though suspecting in their hearts the meanwhile that if Breda fell to the Spaniard, they might soon have all the action they wanted and more.

In truth none of these grand strategical considerations figured much in the concerns of the surgeon and his apprentice as they walked across the gangplank on to the cobbled quayside of this town which Willenbrouckx had scarcely heard of before, and where they had now been quite fortuitously set ashore with only a few copper coins to their name, the salt-stained clothes they stood up in and a bag of surgical instruments.

Under the arch of the gateway leading into the town a sergeant sat at a table checking the identities of those seeking to enter. He eyed them suspiciously.

"Flemings, I hear by your voices. What business brings you here?"

"We have not come directly from Flanders: we lived for several years at Colchester in England."

"So why then have you come to Bergen? You look far too old to enlist as a soldier, while your boy here is likewise too young."

"We were fleeing for our lives, from enemies who sought to kill us."

"Indeed? Then if you had men seeking your lives in a country as peaceable as England a suspicious fellow like myself might wonder whether you might not be even greater rogues than those pursuing you. This town is a fortress of the States-General, likely to be under siege before long, and we want no cutpurses or murderers among us. What's your trade, if you have one?"

"I am a surgeon, and this is my apprentice."

The sergeant laughed in that sardonic, mirthless manner that Hollanders often have.

"Ah yes, I see: a surgeon fleeing from his patients. Or their next of kin. I quite understand, for I myself had a broken leg set by a surgeon not five years since – and would cheerfully cut the rascal's throat if I could lay hands on him, since he left me crippled and on half-pay as a result of his ministrations, reduced to sitting here at a desk all day like a scurvy pen licker writing down names and handing out passes to vagrants. I quite understand." He wrote them a pass each and waved them through the gate. "Go on your way then – and may the pox take you both for a pair of cozening rascals. I suspect that England's gibbets have been relieved of your weight only in order to burden our own."

And such was their joyeuse entrée into the town of Bergen op Zoom...

★ ★ ★ ★ ★ ★ ★ ★ ★ ★

Our first few nights in Bergen were spent at a poor sorry inn where my stepfather had persuaded the landlord, who plainly doubted his assurances (such a sorry pair of varlets did we look by now), that he was expecting money from England and desired only a few days' board and lodging on credit. Once installed in our dirty little room, he procured ink and paper and penned a letter to my mother at Cousin Bourchier's house in Clerkenwell explaining our present plight and begging her to forward us money by return so that we might pay our passage home. The letter was put on a boat bound for Den Briel, whence we knew the post for Harwich and London went each week, and we sat down to await a reply. But the days passed without answer, and by the end of the first week our host became mighty importunate with us to pay him or leave; then demanded at last that we leave, because that money of ours was an unconscionable time a-coming from England and for himself he thought we must be two rogues out to defraud him, and would only remit us our bill for board and lodging thus far if my father consented to draw some rotten teeth of his by way of payment.

So, the landlord's teeth once pulled, out into the street we went with nothing but a promise – even harder to extract from him than his molars had been – that he would let us use his inn as an address for our correspondence. As for our lodgings thereafter, the best that we could find by way of chambers was two old herring barrels laid on their sides among the clay-pits and potters' kilns down by the harbour, amid timber stacks and rotten old boats and with none but stray dogs and fellow-vagrants for company. The weather was warm now. But though we had shelter of a kind, and straw for us to lie in, earning our sustenance proved a much greater trouble to us. My stepfather made application to the surgeons' guild of Bergen to be allowed to practise in the town. But they were jealous of their business, and his licence from Ypres lay in the strongbox among his other papers back in Colchester, so they chased us from their doors as a pair of lousy wandering Flemish quacksalvers trying to impose upon them. In the end we were reduced to becoming mountebanks indeed, cutting hair and shaving chins like common barbers and betimes treating those who were too poor to pay a proper surgeon for their cuts, bruises, rotted teeth, boils and stinking horrid ulcers to be attended to. It was a sordid and ill-paying trade, plied all the time in corners and behind fences with myself keeping one eye open for the town constables, since the surgeon's guild were jealous of their custom and absolutely forbade barbers to practise surgery within the town's ramparts. But the few furtive stuivers that we made at it each day allowed us at least to avoid starving to death, able to buy a loaf or some cheese or a few salt herrings and a pint of beer each. So we were duly thankful for it even if it might end up with us being thrown into gaol, then whipped in the marketplace and banished from the town as a pair of rogues.

Several times my stepfather sought to be engaged as a military surgeon serving the garrison. But always there came the same answer; where is your licence then? The best that these endeavours brought us was a few English soldiers coming to us under cover of darkness to be treated for the *morbus gallicus**, which is very widespread among soldiers and which they would otherwise have to pay out of their wages for their regimental surgeon to treat. This was but a thin living, and likewise a mighty unpleasant one

---

* The French disease, i.e. syphilis.

to earn since the mercurial unguents we instructed our soldiers to buy from the apothecary were scarcely less poisonous to us who applied them than to the patients we applied them to. So at the end of a miserable month in that town my stepfather declared that if we were unable to scrape more than a beggar's pittance within Bergen's walls then we might as well chance our fortune inland, in the villages of the platteland where the writ of the surgeons' guild might not extend.

So late in May, with the countryside now in bloom, we walked out through the Landpoort Gate across the bridge and along the road that led inland, then forked towards Breda in one direction and Antwerp in the other. But the land beyond the marshes proved even more unfruitful for us than the town itself: a poor, barren, sandy country of heath and scrubland with only a few meagre villages, and those mostly burned and deserted since this part of Brabant belonged neither to the United Provinces nor to Spain, but had been ravaged and plundered equally by both their armies over many years, until those country boers who had not yet been murdered by the soldiery or perished from want had fled elsewhere. Tumbledown walls and willowherb marked where hamlets had once stood, while the few starvelings that still scratched a living there fled at our approach thinking us to be brigands, for many soldiers had deserted from both armies to rob and plunder on their own account rather than on behalf of King Philip or the States-General.

After a week or so of these bootless wanderings we returned to Bergen very much cast down and enquired at the inn whether any letters had come for us. It seemed that none had: and indeed that none would for a good long time. Not only were the Dunkirk pirates mighty troublesome that summer off the coasts of Holland, taking several Dutch mail packets, but the plague was now reported to be most virulent in London and no packages from England were being allowed ashore at Den Briel for fear of the contagion spreading to Holland. It seemed to us that we were now trapped in this cursed town of Bergen like wasps in a bottle, and would surely die there like wasps in the autumn when the weather grew cold. For all that I could do to keep his spirits up my stepfather became very despondent, saying that he had been chased out of Flanders and now out of England too, and was condemned to be like the Wandering Jew, his beard growing white and his eyes failing as he tramped the roads of foreign lands like a vagabond with nowhere to lay his head.

★ ★ ★ ★ ★ ★ ★ ★ ★

If Michel Willenbrouckx had but known, even more trouble was heading his way in the last days of May 1625. For unbeknown to him and his stepson, eyes had been watching them ever since their arrival in Bergen. The subject was now being discussed in the fortress commandant's chambers within the Markiezenhof; a great palace in the town centre which had once been the residence of the Marquesses of Bergen, but which had been abandoned by them since the religious troubles and now served as a barracks and headquarters for the garrison. The commandant of the town was a colonel of long and honourable service, Anton Willemszoon Wels, Ridder van Grobbendonck, a professional soldier descended from a long line of professional soldiers in the province of Gelderland though his ancestors had come from Flanders. He was a stocky, ruddy-faced, sanguine man in his late fifties with his thick iron-grey hair and beard still clipped short in the style of the 1580s, when he had begun his military career. Because of the warm weather he had put aside his breastplate – which was purely a sign of rank nowadays, being no longer proof even against pistol bullets – but had retained the highly polished steel gorget as a concession to military propriety, since Spinola was only a day's march away and soldierly alertness had to be maintained by example as well as by the threat of punishment. His interlocutor was a German sergeant in his jerkin of oxhide, carrying the half-pike that was the badge of his rank. The sergeant marched in, saluted smartly by clapping the pike to his shoulder, and was bidden to lay it aside by a casual wave of the commandant's hand.

"So Krentz, what have you to tell me?"

Sergeant Krentz spoke creditable Dutch, but still with a heavy Westphalian accent despite his many years in the service of the States-General.

"With respect, colonel, the two Flemings have spent the night sleeping on the south rampart above the Mill Gate."

"So what of that? They must sleep somewhere. Did you expect them to roost like birds in the trees?"

"No, colonel. But they show an interest in the fortifications during the daylight hours as well. The boy is reported to be making drawings in a notebook. Shall I have them arrested now? They've been prowling the town for a good month past. Far be it from me to tell you your business, but we could have cast them into prison long ago and discovered from them what their business here might be."

"Your zeal is commendable, sergeant: without your sharp eyes we would never have suspected two such mean and inconsiderable fellows of wrongdoing. But I have so far resisted your counsel to have them seized, and instead merely had your men follow them around, because I am curious to know what they are about."

"With respect, colonel, I would have thought there was no mystery about that: they are Flemish papists, and they are spies for Spinola. And on both counts they deserve to hang."

"I agree. But if I had thrown them into the Gevangenispoort and set the executioner to loosen their tongues, that might tell us little beyond the fact of their spying on us. What concerns me far more, I confess, as commander of this notable fortress, with Spinola only a day's march away and my garrison not yet strong enough to withstand him, is what precisely is of interest to these two rogues. By which I mean, do they survey the town's defences on the landward side, or do they show more curiosity about the harbour?"

"Does that matter?"

"It matters a great deal to *me*, Krentz. Remember that when

Spinola came against us three years ago it was the Scheldt that defeated him. Because of the river he was never able to close his circumvallation about the town as he has just done at Breda, so he could never starve us out as long as our ships were arriving each day bearing supplies, and his own guns on the shore never quite able to reach them. For him it was like trying to fill up a washtub with a hole in it. Batter as he might at the ramparts, he could never prevail against us, and with the river still open at our backs we might have held the place against him for a hundred years. So if he comes here again he will – indeed must – try to block the approach from the sea. So I thought that our two spies might give us some notion as to how he would go about it." The little man turned and looked out of the bay window on to the palace garden, now in early-summer bloom. Though a soldier all his life, he had always adored flowers.

"Bergen and I are old friends, Krentz. I served here in '88 when Farnese besieged the town." He sighed wistfully. "Yes, that was certainly a siege worthy of the name, fit to stand in the history books alongside that of Ostend or even old Troy itself: six months long, and the best possible school for a young cavalry lieutenant such as I then was, quite inexperienced in the conduct of sieges beyond what I had read of them in the Roman authors." He gave a rueful laugh. "In fact all too good a schooling, I fear, because since then I have scarcely ever swung my leg across a horse to ride into battle, and instead spent most of my career in the service of the States burrowing like a mole. Except for Turnhout , of course, back in '97 – or was it '98; my memory fails me – when we routed a force of Spanish horsemen four times larger than our own by charging them before they were properly drawn up."

Krentz gave a discrete sigh: in recent months he had several times heard the story of the great victory at Turnhout. And a slightly different version of it on each occasion. But the Ridder van Grobbendonck changed course again as deftly and unexpectedly as he had once wheeled his mount in the flower of his youth.

"Yes, a notable siege, that of '88, with Farnese's artillery cannonading us from all sides and only the Scheldt to save us from starvation, which the Spaniard could never cut even though he tried sinking blockships in the channel and building an earthen dyke out from the shore. We held out: and truth to tell, we suffered most of the time more from tedium than from danger, though it was good sport, I confess, to watch the Spaniards digging their saps towards us through the morass and see them turn into canals as fast as they dug them." He chuckled, lost for the moment in his reverie. "In the end, by the middle of August, I remember we were all grown so melancholic from inactivity and the summer's heat that some of us sent a challenge to the Spaniards to meet us on horseback – swords and pistols only; eight fellows per side – on the meadows between our ramparts and their circumvallation. So we rode out, seven of us Dutchmen and one English knight, Sir Matthew Bassingbourne, who served with Norris's regiment. And we met the Spaniards at full gallop like Saladin and Richard the Lionheart. Two of our fellows were cut down, and Sir Matthew thought better of it and ran away, which has left me I confess with an abiding mistrust of the English as allies. But we who remained gave the Spaniards better than we received, killing four of them and driving off the remainder. Quite the best afternoon's work in all my years as a soldier in fact..." He turned round suddenly. "... But what am I doing rambling here like an senile old fool at the fireside. Yes Krentz: your Flemish spies...."

"I await your orders, colonel."

"As you say, the time is now ripe: have them arrested and bring them here to me tomorrow morning."

"Shall I have the executioner prepare them? An hour or two of his company might put them in a more suitable frame of mind before they meet with you."

"No, I think not. Unless they are very obdurate, I suspect more might be got from them by artful questioning than by dislocating their joints. And in any case, I still have my doubts about them."

"Doubts?"

"Indeed, Krentz: doubts. Such as, for example, why Spinola,

if he sent them here to spy on us, sent two shabby starvelings to lodge in old herring barrels and scrape their living as barbers, when he could have dispatched them here with ample coin in their pockets to lodge themselves and purchase information. And I have likewise made enquiry of a bombardier who lived until lately near Colchester in England, and he says that indeed a fellow called Willenbrouckx *did* practise surgery in that town, having arrived there from Flanders about three years before. So the tale they told at the gate about fleeing their enemies might well be true. But no matter: arrest them and bring them here at eight o'clock tomorrow morning, and we shall learn the truth of it or otherwise."

Later that afternoon Sergeant Krentz, with a party of soldiers, seized the surgeon and his apprentice sunning themselves on the ramparts and conducted them to the Gevangenispoort prison in the gateway by the harbour, where they were thrown into the mouldy straw of an underground dungeon along with a dozen or so petty thieves, drunkards and assorted disturbers of the public peace. They spent an uneasy night there, then were woken at dawn and marched through the streets to the Markiezenhof in front of the early-morning passers-by who jeered at them (since a military escort for civilians could only mean spying) and assured them that they would both hang. They looked a sorry enough pair as they stood before the Ridder van Grobbendonck, who was seated behind an oak table with a secretary sitting beside him, quill in hand, ready to take notes of the interrogation. The commandant looked up at them.

"So, mijne heren, what do you have to say for yourselves? Sergeant, show me the boy's notebook."

Krentz handed him the dog-eared notebook which Frans had begged from a stationer's shop some weeks before. Grobbendonck leafed through it, puzzled.

"But Krentz, there is nothing here but pencil drawings of butterflies and beetles. Do these have any military significance to your eye? Because for the life of me, they have none to mine."

"We thought, colonel, that the dots on the wings of the creatures might be joined up to show a trace of the fortifications."

Grobbendonck took a pencil and duly joined up the dots on one sketch, then held the book at arm's length, rotating it and squinting his eyes.

"No, no resemblance that I can see to any ramparts that ever were or ever will be; and though I'm a cavalryman by profession I fancy that I can read an engineer's trace as well as any man living." He snapped the book shut. "So much for the boy spy. Now what about you..." He stopped, gazing into Willenbrouckx's face. "Excuse me, but I think that we may have met already. Were you a surgeon with Verdugo's army before Coevorden back in the year 1592?"

"I was. What of it?"

"And did you set the broken thigh of a young Dutch lieutenant of cavalry brought in from the field that evening?"

"I may well have done, but I cannot recall precisely. It was many years ago and I treated a great crowd of wounded, that day and after a hundred other such encounters. But yes, now that you remind me of it, I do faintly remember one young officer from the army of the States with a comminuted fracture of the femur, so badly broken that pieces of bone protruded from the flesh. The other surgeons wished to amputate because in such cases infection is almost certain, but I thought the limb could be saved and applied traction over several days to reduce the fracture, with a turpentine and egg-white dressing to prevent corruption. But the details are hazy in my mind now after so many years."

"Well permit me to refresh your memory. That young lieutenant was myself..." He stood up and came around the table to clap Willenbrouckx on the shoulder, "And the leg, as you see, healed well and still works perfectly, except that it aches abominably in damp weather. To you, Mijnheer Willenbrouckx, I owe my further military career, since with a leg sawn off I would have been discharged and would now be a dismal squire growing turnips in the Betuwe. Come, sit down, and your boy with you, and tell me what misfortunes brought you here."

The secretary and Sergeant Krentz were dismissed, and an orderly was sent to fetch Madeira wine and almond biscuits on a silver tray. So for the next hour they chatted happily of the campaigns of '92 and '93 in Overijssel, and their lives since: how the Ridder van Grobbendonck had spent six months in Maastricht as a prisoner while his leg healed (for the Spaniards were by then exchanging Dutch prisoners under cartel instead of hanging them as rebels) and was afterwards released to continue his career.

"But why" the colonel asked in the end "have you come here like two vagabonds when you had a prospering practice as a surgeon in England? And why to a fortress town not twenty miles from the enemy, where any stranger was bound to excite suspicion of being a spy? You will surely own that this was foolhardy conduct, and might well have placed a noose around both your necks."

"We had no choice in the matter, colonel: we were set upon by a gang of ruffians in Colchester, the retainers of a great man we had offended, and had to tumble aboard a boat to save our lives without paying much heed to where it was bound for. And since then my letters to my wife in England requesting money to take us home have been fruitless, because the plague now reigns there and the mails have been suspended."

"Well then, might I be of any assistance to you while you wait? I owe you a debt for having saved my leg." Willenbrouckx considered.

"You are very kind. All I would ask of you, if it were possible, is that you might find me and my stepson some work about the garrison until the mails resume and a letter from my wife arrives, so that we may earn our keep like honest men and buy ourselves new clothes. As you see, we are now both very shabby and have not changed our linen in weeks."

"If you wish it, then so it shall be: I shall make enquiry straight away of the surgeon-lieutenant and try to find you both some employment. Depend upon it that I shall see you both set up until such time as you decide to go back to England. I fear, however, that as long as the plague prevails in England letters will not arrive from there, so you may have some time to wait for your fare home – and might in any case be well advised not to return before the autumn, for fear of contagion."

In the end the Ridder van Grobbendonck was not able to find Willenbrouckx and Frans places in the garrison, which was up to establishment with surgeons and indeed somewhat over it. Matters might have looked different if the Spaniards had shown any present intention of moving against Bergen. For the time being, however, they seemed to have their hands full at Breda, and as yet not a sparrow had stirred in the willow thickets between there and the coast. But after a few days a note came to Willenbrouckx and his stepson requesting them to present themselves to the commandant of the garrison without delay.

Grobbendonck shook the surgeon's hand warmly and bade him sit down.

"Mijnheer Willenbrouckx, while I have not managed to secure you a surgeon's place with the garrison – I am, after all, merely its commandant, and you might have done better to find a corporal with some influence – I have spoken with a good friend of mine, a ship's captain, who has need of a surgeon aboard his vessel for the rest of this season: one Captain Loodgieter of the Zeeland ship *Eenhoorn* which serves this garrison as a transport. He wishes to speak with you, and if he thinks well of you will engage you and your boy until the ship pays off in the autumn. This would have the advantage for you both that if this town were to come under siege, being aboard a ship you would be able to return to England when she pays off for the winter instead of being confined here."

"I am most grateful to you. But what of my surgeon's licence? Surely he will wish to see it?"

Grobbendonck waved his hand dismissively. "No matter, no matter: I have had a message from him in which he says that, regarding your abilities as a surgeon, my own recommendation will suffice entirely. So he wishes to see you and your boy the day after tomorrow at nine in the morning at the outer harbour, when his ship docks there, since at the moment they are lying at Zierikzee."

"We are much indebted to you: we will both be there." Willenbrouckx got up to leave.

"Oh, and before you meet him," Grobbendonck said, "pray go to a tailor whose address I shall give you and have suits of clothes made for yourselves, and new linen as well, for you can scarcely wait upon Captain Loodgieter dressed like two scarecrows. His ship is so neatly kept that a man might well eat from her deck-planks without a plate, and he himself most fastidious as to the cleanliness and good ordering of all things aboard her."

"But we have no money; scarcely a stuiver between us…"

"Don't concern yourself in the least regarding that: have the clothes placed on my account with the tailor, and then repay me from your wages once you receive them. This is the smallest favour I can perform for one who once did me so notable a service." The Ridder van Grobbendonck stood up, and began buckling his sword to its hanger. "Very well; you must excuse me now because, as I am sure you understand, I have many urgent matters requiring my attention. Señor Spinola may soon come a-knocking at my door. And my most fervent desire is that we shall be able to accord that worthy gentleman the welcome that his degree and reputation merit."

CHAPTER SEVEN

It had to be admitted that at first glance the pinnace *Eenhoorn*, three hundred tons, master Cornelis Adriaenszoon Loodgieter, was not a particularly imposing sight as she lay at anchor that June morning off the Waterschans, the fort guarding the south side of the channel leading into Bergen op Zoom. In fact, not to mince matters, despite her formal rating as a pinnace and her twenty bronze cannon, the *Eenhoorn* was in reality no more than an armed transport, hired by the Zeeland Admiralty from her civilian owners for a season and superficially converted to a man-of-war, but likely to be unconverted next season if no longer required and return to her humble workaday life carrying barrels of salted herrings from Enkhuizen to Danzig and sacks of rye back from Danzig to Amsterdam. However, it now looked as though an armed transport was all that she would ever need to be. The Spanish threat to Bergen had caused the States-General to instruct each of the two Admiralties concerned, Zeeland and the Maze, to allocate a ship apiece to supply the garrison for the rest of that year's campaigning season, and likewise to deal with any of the Spanish Ostend galleys that might come nosing into the Scheldt bent on mischief. So Captain Loodgieter's *Eenhoorn* and Captain Barentszoon's *Witte Paard* of Rotterdam would now most likely spend the rest of the year transporting barrels of salted beef and sacks of corn to Bergen, thereby missing the opportunities for honour and prize money that might be offered by service in the North Sea against the Dunkirk privateers, or in the Straits of Gibraltar taking Spanish merchantmen.

Not that this appeared to have disheartened Captain Loodgieter in any way that fine summer's morning as he greeted the surgeon and his apprentice clambering up the ship's side in their new suits of black broadcloth still smelling of the tailor's pressing-iron.

Quite the contrary: he seemed as pleased with himself as if he were the very Lieutenant-Admiral of Holland and West Friesland – which indeed he hoped one day to become – welcoming them aboard his flagship. A cheerful, vigorous man of about twenty-five or twenty-six, though only of medium height and not particularly well favoured as regards looks, he had nonetheless a pleasing air of energy and authority about him. Likewise, for the skipper of a mere fluit-ship barely ninety feet long and a warship only by courtesy, he was quite remarkably fashionable in his dress. His hair was worn long to the shoulder, whereas most Dutch skippers of the old school still wore it cropped short in the traditional manner, saying that lice had less purchase on it that way, and likewise he had a little pointed beard and moustache in the French fashion. His doublet and breeches were of the sober black that was de rigueur among the Dutch Republic's sea-captains, who had Calvinist consistories ashore in Enkhuizen and Middelburg only too ready to denounce them for extravagance in dress. But the suit was still cut from elegantly brocaded black velveteen of the highest quality, with immaculate white-lawn cuffs and collar in the latest falling style. And at his hip he wore a short rapier instead of the old basket-handled broadsword which had done such execution in the hands of the Sea-Beggars. But for all his modishness, the man was no fop. Quite the contrary: he was already spoken of as a man to watch among the Republic's sea-officers, in the smoky pot-clanking dockside taverns of Holland and Zeeland where the common sailors debated the strengths and weaknesses of their captains as earnestly as others might discuss racing pigeons or greyhounds – which was entirely to be expected, since all those simple fellows had to sell in the world beside their bare lives was the strength of their arms, their experience and the skill of their calloused hands, and they naturally wished to use those assets as profitably as they could by sailing with the best and luckiest skippers afloat. All connoisseurs of seafaring form agreed that though Loodgieter was much younger than the West India admiral Piet Hein, and a year or two the junior of Marten Harpertszoon of

Den Briel (who now called himself Tromp) and of Harpertszoon's schoolfellow Witte de With (whom all admired for his courage and skill but none liked), he was still a man with a future. True, he had the disadvantage of being a Zeelander when tradition and precedence alike demanded that the most senior flag commands in the Republic's fleet should always go to Hollanders. But against that, though only in his mid-twenties Cornelis Loodgieter already had flair. As a young second mate with Bontekoe's expedition to the East Indies in 1619 he was among the survivors when the ship blew up one bright morning off the coast of Java, and had afterwards made a notable voyage to the Dutch outpost at Bantam with twenty others in an open boat, being almost reduced to cannibalism on the way but winning through by his skill as a seaman and by the courage that kept his companions from falling into despair. And only the year before, in the Straits of Gibraltar, he had famously snatched two richly laden Neapolitan vessels which had just been taken by Algerian pirates, waiting until the Moors had reduced the Neapolitans, then boarding the prizes one after the other and overpowering the Moors, who were later bound hand and foot and tossed overboard (as was the custom) while the crews and passengers – so grateful at having been rescued from the slave markets that they scarcely minded their ships and cargoes being stolen from them – were put ashore at Málaga under flag of truce. The seamen, studious and merciless judges in these matters, said that among the rising captains of the Dutch Republic Loodgieter was a cunning and audacious dog, but at the same time not a tyrant or a reckless fool who would hazard his men's lives for mere bravado's sake. As for his present command aboard the *Eenhoorn*, that was indeed well below his capacities and most likely the result of a difference of opinion the previous year with the Zeeland Admiralty concerning the payment of victualling money. But all were agreed that it was unlikely to be the last that the world would hear of him.

Loodgieter ushered them to the great cabin – though in truth, aboard this little vessel even the great cabin was still a very small one – and bade them sit down at the table while refreshments were brought in. The guests were surprised to see that Loodgieter's servant was a barefooted Moorish boy of fifteen or sixteen wearing a red turban and a long white nightshirt. The Moor placed the tray on the table, then salaamed and left silently after the manner of his people.

"So," Loodgieter said, "I understand from my old friend the fortress commandant" (he spoke as though they were schoolfellows, though the Ridder van Grobbendonck was more than twice his age) "that you seek employment as a surgeon at sea, and your boy here as a barber?"

Being by nature a truthful man, Willenbrouckx felt an urge to say that after his experiences in the summer of 1588 he would sooner seek employment in hell itself or in a dungeon full of toads and vipers than aboard a ship. But he restrained himself, and merely nodded.

"Very well then. To be short with you, I have a pressing need for a surgeon aboard this vessel, the last man having been put ashore by me for reason of drink, and likewise a barber who will also serve as the surgeon's mate. I care greatly for the welfare of my crew, which is the best way to obtain good service from them, and have therefore always taken the utmost pains to engage the best men available for each charge aboard, and likewise pay them generously to retain their love and loyalty. So you, mijnheer, I would propose engaging as surgeon at a monthly wage of twenty-five guilders ..." (Willenbrouckx's eyes fairly popped out at this: eighteen guilders a month was the best that he had dared hope for) "... whilst your boy here, being above fourteen years of age, would serve as barber, surgeon's mate and ziekentrooster* at a man's wage of fifteen guilders per month – though I shall require him also to perform such other duties as I shall assign to him from time to time, with the proviso that these shall be neither menial nor degrading. As for the period of your engagement, that will

---

* Sick-bay attendant

be until the ship pays off at New Year or the end of the present season, whichever is the sooner."

"That sounds admirably fair, captain: we will most certainly accept."

"Good. As to your qualifications to practise, though you have not brought your licence with you from England, and Their Lordships in Middelburg require me to have sight of that before engaging you, I have here a letter of recommendation from the Ridder van Grobbendonck, and for me his word and estimation of you will suffice. The ship's writer Meester Grobelaar will draw up articles for you to sign, and will also raise an imprest for you to stock the medicine chest before we sail. You must also purchase such additional surgical instruments as you require, the costs being deducted from your salary. Having been a ship's surgeon before you will no doubt understand that the medicine chest is the admiralty's property and its medicaments chargeable to the ship as they are used, while the surgeon's chest remains his own property and will leave the ship with him when we pay off. So if you will go now to see the writer in his office I shall speak with your boy."

Willenbrouckx and the Moorish steward went out, leaving Frans alone with the captain.

"What is your name, boy?"

"May it please you, mijnheer, Frans van Raveyck."

Loodgieter laughed, showing a set of remarkably good teeth: very white still since he cleaned them each morning before the looking-glass in his cabin (another modern innovation of his) with finely ground pumice stone and stale urine.

"Frans van Raveyck? Hah! My ears are so dulled by cannonfire I could almost have sworn you said François Ravaillac, the villain who stabbed the King of France and was pulled asunder by horses for his trouble. A most suitable name, I think, for a fellow who will apply a razor to his captain's defenceless throat each morning." Frans laughed uneasily at this jest. "So, young fellow, while I shall require you to spend most of your time aboard cutting hair and assisting your stepfather in his duties, I have other tasks in mind for you to justify you monthly wage, which I need scarcely tell you is high for a lad of...?"

"Fourteen, nearly fifteen, skipper."

"Indeed: fourteen years and a half. So now, if you will, copy out for me this verse from Virgil which I have written here in both Latin and Dutch". Frans took the quill, dipped it in the inkwell and wrote in his fairest hand: "*Arma virumque cano, Troiæ qui primus ab oris Italiam fato profugus Laviniaque venit litora.*"

Then the Dutch translation: "*Ik bezing de heldendaden van een man die vanaf de kusten van Troje als eerste naar Italië, het strand van Lavinium is gekomen, op de vlucht voor het lot.*"* When he had finished Loodgieter took the paper and regarded it critically at arm's length, since like most mariners he was decidedly long-sighted.

"Hmmm, yes. You have a fine neat hand: a most desirable accomplishment. So when not trimming hair and caring for the sick you will be of the greatest assistance to Meester Grobelaar in his endless scribbling of account books and letters to Their Lordships of the Admiralty; because those dogs burden us every day with more paper until I fear the ship may sink beneath the weight of it, every last brown bean now having to be individually accounted for and countersigned by me. Tell me, Van Raveyck, what languages do you know besides Netherlandish?"

"I speak French, mijnheer, because where I come from in the west part of Flanders folk will happily change from French to Flemish and back again in a single sentence. I also speak Latin which I learned at school, and English pretty well from having lived there above three years; likewise Spanish which I was taught by an Andalusian corporal who lodged with us."

Loodgieter raised his eyebrows in mock surprise. "Most impressive. Your talents as a linguist will surely stand us in good

---

* "I sing of arms and the man, who, fleeing the shores of Troy, came first in Italy unto the shores of Lavinium, pursued by fate."

stead, because although I speak French and Spanish, I know no English at all: yet the way that things go now in the world I think we may soon find ourselves allied with those haughty gentlemen who pride themselves on speaking no other language than their own, for all the world as though Adam and Eve spoke English in the Garden of Eden and all the other tongues of mankind are but a corruption of it. We lately transported the soldiers of Mansfeld's army from Rotterdam to Harwich — as base a collection of lousy rascals as ever escaped hanging — and I found myself greatly incommoded by not being able to converse with their officers except in French, which they spoke most villainously, and their Latin even worse. So I am pleased to have aboard my ship someone who can be my English tongue for me. Now: a third matter. Are you skilled at all in music? Because with all your other accomplishments it would not surprise me if you played the lyre like Orpheus himself, and perhaps painted pictures as well."

"I play the viol a little, mijnheer: my stepfather says that for a surgeon some skill in music is most desirable to calm his patients."

Loodgieter laughed. "Your stepfather is right in principle; though I doubt whether in practice you'll have either the time or the inclination to play the fiddle as you saw off limbs and probe for bullets down in the cockpit while the cannon thunder above your head. But now show me a little of your skill: take that viol over there and play me something."

So Frans tool up the viol lying on a bench-seat in the corner of the cabin, tuned it and then applied the bow to the strings: Mister Dowland's piece *The King of Denmark's Galliard*, which he had played so often with Mister Wilbye in Colchester that he knew it pretty well by heart, and which was much jollier than Dowland's other pieces which though as beautiful as anything that was ever written, are most of them so melancholy that a man might go and hang himself after hearing them. Frans scraped away, and Loodgieter tapped his foot merrily, and afterwards clapped to show his appreciation.

"Excellent: better even than I had expected. Just what I was looking for: a fine handsome young fellow to wait on us at table, and then join my other musicians to entertain my guests when they dine aboard with me. I have a small band of players now: our trumpeter, the Norwegian Sigurdsson, who also plays the bass viol and whom you will meet in due course – though I doubt whether you will understand a word he says at first, his Dutch is so criminal – and my manservant Suleiman, who plays the recorder and the riebeck after the manner of his country; and likewise the lute, which he calls "al-ut", which I believe is the Arabic word from which ours is derived. I think it important for a ship's captain of the Republic to keep suitable state no matter what size his vessel, for fear that in foreign havens we Hollanders might otherwise be dismissed as penny-pinching rascals and cheapjacks who, having no king to set us an example, live for all our wealth like the meanest of savages. My intention is to prove them wrong not just as to our martial valour but also as to our munificence and high state, which I think may be as great in a republic as in any kingdom on earth. Anyway, go now and sign your articles, then afterwards have Meester Grobelaar find you someone to show you about the ship, since I divine that you have never been aboard one before."

★ ★ ★ ★ ★ ★ ★ ★ ★

Whilst I never cease to be astonished at the facility and confidence shown by writers of histories in reproducing conversations at which they were never present, and which indeed often took place while they were still in petticoats or not yet born at all, I must say that in this case our chronicler has pretty well set down the gist of my interview that morning with Captain Loodgieter, and indeed refreshed my faltering memory on certain points. The fact of the matter is, that I came out of the great cabin well pleased with myself at the place I had secured even if it was only to be of a few months' duration. I was well enough content that I would no longer have to lodge in a herring barrel like old Diogenes, wearing the same foul linen from week to week and assisting my father in pulling the rotten teeth of beggars or rubbing the malodorous privy members of ruffianly soldiers with cinnabar ointment against the pox. I would now have a roof – albeit a mighty low one – above my head, and my victuals furnished and cooked for me each day; and it seemed likewise that my shipboard duties additional to the trimming of hair and beards would be honourable and even intellectual. As for my stepfather, I knew it must be mighty tiresome for him to find himself once more aboard a ship when he had a surgeon's practice back in England twentyfold less arduous and at the same time twentyfold more profitable. But needs must when the Devil drives, and neither of us was in a position to turn our noses up at this dish which the benevolent stars had so unexpectedly set before us. We hoped at least that by the time the ship paid off in the autumn the plague would have abated in England, and likewise that the rogues who had sought our lives in Colchester would by then all have been hanged or chased out of the county, or have slain one another in their drunken quarrels. Or quite simply have forgotten about the whole business, for I had already observed that the English, though a singularly violent and quarrelsome people and most dangerous in the heat of the moment, are at the same time very little given to lingering rancour and will not nurse grudges for generations as Spaniards or Neapolitans will do, counting it a point of honour to plant a stiletto between a man's shoulderblades because his great-grandsire's goat wandered into their great-grandsire's olive grove.

Meester Grobelaar, our ship's schrijver or writer (which aboard an English vessel would be called a purser), was a stoutish balding fellow of about fifty years with spectacles on his nose for his short sight, which was why he required me to write for him: that he now found it taxing upon his eyes to scribble overlong. I read through and signed the articles he had drawn up, very proud that I could write "Frans van Raveyck" beneath them in my best hand since most of our fellows aboard must make do with an X and a thumbprint. Then I was shown about the ship by the trumpeter Matthias Sigurdsson, who I saw was lame in one foot and hobbled considerably on the ladders. Having never before been aboard any vessel greater than the schuit that had brought us to Bergen, even such an inconsiderable ship as the *Eenhoorn* was a wondrous and (I must confess) somewhat fearful affair to me, most bewildering in its complexity of ropes and blocks and cannon on their carriages and low deck-beams which I – being somewhat tall for my years – continually cracked my head against until I learned to walk stooped over; and the ladders leading up and the ladders leading down; and every surface being at a slope rather than level or perpendicular like floors and walls on land; and even with the vessel lying at anchor the whole edifice full of noise and banging and clumping and creaking (for a ship is nothing but a great wooden box, so that every noise resonates throughout it as through the body of a viol). And this whole structure crammed with noisy raucous fellows – upwards of ninety of them in so small a space once our soldiers were aboard – and those knaves conversing as we squeezed past them in languages that were often quite alien to me: some in Dutch or High German, but many in a tongue which sounded to my ears more like that of wolves than of men, and which I only later came to know was Norwegian. My guide Sigurdsson (who later became my friend and correspondent) seemed at first a very surly fellow and plainly regarded me as a contemptible landlubber, for though he was barely two years older than myself he had been at sea already above a year, and some months before had suffered a crushed foot in an accident with a gun which had blown off its carriage, and had then been promoted to the charge of ship's trumpeter as much for his skill in music as for his present inaptness to run up and down rigging. He indicated each thing to me in single words, such as "the galley", "the mainmast", "the hold" and so forth, as though I were the most complete of blockheads; and in a Dutch that was so like Norwegian as to be scarcely recognisable any longer as Netherlandish, and in which he would attach articles to the ends of words, which is the Scandinavian custom, as well as at the beginnings which is ours, and thus produce manglings like "het rundhus-het".

Though I knew as yet but little of ships, it was plain to me even at first sight that our *Eenhoorn*, which would be my home for the next five or six months, was a well-kept vessel and much loved by her captain, who held that our regard and consideration among the Republic's fleet depended upon our smartness as well as upon our valour. He would sometimes declare to us, in his short peroration for the day after morning prayers, that even if we were to be charged by the States-General with the task of carrying tuns of night-soil, then it would behove us to perform that noisome task with as cheerful a mien as we might (albeit with clothespegs on our noses) and likewise aboard a vessel that was at all times as clean and as smart as she could be made. And he had supported these words of his by dipping his hand into his own pocket; for not only was our little fluit-ship neatly caulked and painted and every rope in its place, but she was also adorned at her captain's expense well beyond what Their Lordships of the Zeeland Admiralty would pay for. At the peak of the stern was a carved and painted arms of the province of Zeeland, with a lion brandishing a sword as it rose from the waves and a gilded scroll beneath with the motto LUCTOR ET EMERGO.* Likewise at the beakhead, where in other ships there would be (at most) a rustically carved red lion bearing the arms of the Republic, there was a very prettily made white unicorn holding with its hooves a shield blazoned with the arms of Zeeland – though this, I later discovered, was retained by wooden pegs so that when the *Eenhoorn* was returned to her owner our captain could have it removed as his personal property. And in all other places likewise the ship was admirably painted and maintained; so that if she was indeed somewhat plain and sober to look at when compared with the war vessels that I saw later on (which have lately become veritable mountains of gilded cherubs and goddesses like floating fair-wagons), she was still comely and pleasing to behold as is the manner in Holland.

* "I struggle and rise above the surface"

There is a misconception very widespread among the English that the Dutch, being mostly Calvinists, are therefore cut from the same sombre cloth as their own Puritans: sworn enemies to all pleasure and gaiety. Yet nothing could be further from the truth, for despite their consistories and their sober black suits the Hollanders are the very greatest devotees of the goddess Hedone and love nothing in the world so much as painted housefronts, silverware and fine tapestries, and carved furniture and pictures, so that in the Dutch provinces even the meanest and least considerable of towns will have its guild of musicians and guild of painters, and even out in the poor platteland villages the doors and windows and the sails of the windmills are handsomely painted and adorned and the doorsteps and pavements sanded, swept and scoured so assiduously that a visitor would think the women of Holland sought to banish sin from the world with their scrubbing brushes. Indeed, even as we installed ourselves aboard the *Eenhoorn* that morning two sailors were out in the vlet (which was the smaller of our two boats) with their paint pots working their way around the ship and painting the strakes between upper and lower wales, where the gunports were, a dull black made by mixing chimney soot and turpentine into the paint. This struck me as strange, though it was undeniably pleasing since it deceived the onlooker's eye into thinking the vessel was somewhat longer than it really was. But I would discover in due course that our skipper's intention in this, as in everything else that he purposed, was quite as much practical as aesthetic.

After Sigurdsson had finished with me and departed, saying he had a tune to practise for dinner that evening, I was able to go and join my stepfather in the surgeon's cabin; which was in fact a dog-kennel affair beneath the quarterdeck, made on three sides with wood and canvas screens and lit by a tiny window six or seven inches square in the ship's side. It was barely six feet long and no more than five feet high, so that we must continually stoop our heads, while as for its width there was scarce room enough for the surgeon's chest – which we would use as our table – and the chest of medicaments. How the two of us were to lie down in it and sleep at the same time, since neither of us stood watches, would therefore have been most questionable if my stepfather had not served in his youth aboard the King of Spain's ships and there become familiar with the hammock, which Columbus's men had imitated from the Caribs but which was still not much used in those days aboard northern ships, the sailors preferring instead to sleep on the bare deck planks. He therefore went straightway to the sailmaker and had him make up a "hang-mat", as he called it. This invention of his was greatly mocked at, but it spared us much discomfort in our tiny chamber since he could sleep in the hammock while I lay below him on top of the two chests laid together, which by good fortune were of the same height. And I was glad that I might do this, because my stepfather was now fifty-eight years old, and aboard a ship once more only from direst necessity, and so long as we were there I was determined that his aged rheumaticky bones should at least not have to bear the rigours of lying all night upon wooden boards.

* * * * * * * * * *

Ashore once more, Willenbrouckx and his assistant went to an apothecary's shop in the Koevoetstraat to restock the *Eenhoorn's* medicine chest according to the prescribed list of medicaments pasted inside the lid. The order was a long one: astringent powders (hare's fur, coarse and fine bolus, red ochre, ashes of dead man's skull); unguents for plasters (apostles' basilic and paste of calendula); essential oils (lily, rose, camomile and linseed); waters (rose, blessed thistle, sage, plantain, scabious and nightshade); balms (mercurial, roseate and parietal); cephalic powders (incense, juniper, myrrh, mastic and lime); laxatives and emetics (powder of rhubarb, senna and agaric); restoratives (fennel, aniseed, fenugreek, lobster's eyes, powder of stag's horn and serpent's blood) and simples (olive oil, turpentine, white beeswax, yellow beeswax and hog's lard). And though the list inside the lid had made no mention of it, Willenbrouckx was careful to add "spirits of wine: two pints" so that he might be able to flame his instruments before operating; and also a pound of blue vitriol ordered by the captain for his own mysterious purposes. Leaving the apothecary to make up the order, they then proceeded to a cutler's shop in the Cromwielstraat, since the surgeon's chest was still lacking in certain necessary instruments such as probes and bullet extractors, and a pair each of crane's-beak and of raven's-beak forceps; likewise elevators for dealing with depressed fractures of the skull, which Willenbrouckx told Frans were very frequent aboard ships by reason of blocks falling from the rigging and braining men standing below on deck.

Then it was back aboard the ship to prepare the surgeon's cockpit down in the hold at the foot of the mainmast. Since the *Eenhoorn's* gun deck had been improvised by planking over the original merchant ship's hold, that space now rose barely five feet above the planking laid on top of the ballast stones, with the water casks and other heavy gear fore and aft of it. With the *Eenhoorn* sailing at present only in coastal waters there was at least more space than there would have been out of sight of land, when the entire hold would be occupied by provisions and water casks. But even so it was a miserable enough hole: dark, cramped and stuffy since light and air had to reach it from two decks above. When he first clambered down the ladder into the dark recesses of the hold, stinking of bilgewater and the accumulated oozings from provision casks, Willenbrouckx suffered a sudden and most painful recollection of the weeks that he had spent down just such a malodorous burrow almost forty years before, in the gale-blown summer of 1588. But there: this time they would be at sea only until the end of November at the latest, and the ship doing nothing more warlike than transporting sacks of brown beans and casks of beer through the winding coastal waterways of Holland and Zeeland where no enemy vessel would ever dare to venture. The worst that was likely to happen on this voyage (he consoled himself) would be a broken leg to set when someone had fallen from aloft or a crushed finger to amputate after some negligent dolt had caught it in the cogs of the windlass.

Indeed if "voyage" it could be called at all, when the *Eenhoorn* would most likely never be out of sight of land, and likewise the vessel itself no more than a workaday fluit-ship hired the previous autumn from her owner in the town of Hoorn in West Friesland. The *Eenhoorn* had never been built for fighting or the pursuit of glory – those two decidedly un-Dutch activities – but rather with an eye to the eminently Dutch preoccupation of making money; one of the hundreds of fluit-ships that now carried the young Republic's blue, white and orange flag to the far ends of the Baltic and the Mediterranean. These were probably the first vessels since a cave dweller hollowed out a tree trunk with a flint to be the product of rational design rather than the result of tiny adaptations made piecemeal, generation after generation, until at last a new kind of vessel emerged: floating testimony to that enterprising and practical spirit which was already making the Dutch Republic such a potent force among the kingdoms of Europe – and likewise an object of instinctive fear and dislike to all states grounded upon precedent, ancient right and the traditional way of doing things. The story (or perhaps the legend, since folk always spin such pretty tales to explain a notable success) was that about the year 1595 a merchant in the town of Hoorn, one Pieter Janszoon Liorne, had purchased a small two-masted merchantman for his growing commerce in citrus fruit with the Italian port of Livorno. And soon discovering that he could easily sell every single orange or lemon that his ship brought back each voyage and still have customers clamouring outside his shop for more, he had given instructions for his ship to be sawn in half amidships, lengthened by twenty feet and stepped with a third mast. This had excited huge disapproval and mockery among the seafaring traditionalists; and fiery sermons from the pulpits in which Hoorn's preachers denounced him for wantonly risking the lives of his employees; and wagers among the dockside idlers as to whether the madman Liorne's floating abortion would founder off Texel or reach the Dover Straits before she sank. But in the event the new ship had entirely stopped the mouths of the scoffers: not only capable of carrying half as much cargo again as she had done before, but also a much better sailer and easier to work, so that fewer hands were needed aboard her and less had to be paid out to them as wages at the end of each voyage. Before long Hoorn's shipwrights, then all the busy-hammering yards of Holland, were building fluit-ships with their characteristic flat bottoms so that they could sit on the mud in tidal harbours, their round tucked-in sterns and also their strange inward-curving sides, since the sharp-witted corn merchants who traded with Danzig realised that the tolls that the King of Denmark levied on ships passing through the narrows at Helsingør were calculated on the width of a vessel's upper deck and not on the capacity of its hold.

But however admirable they might be as cargo carriers, fluits like the *Eenhoorn* still left much to be desired as men-of-war. Constructed with an eye to saving timber, every single stick of which had to be floated down the Rhine from Germany, they were too lightly built to withstand prolonged cannon-battering, their upperworks made of lapstraked pine instead of good sturdy oak planking. And by reason of their upper decks being too narrow to work cannon, most had only a single gun deck; made aboard the *Eenhoorn* by planking over the hold amidships and cutting gunports in her sides. In the end, the only mark of the little ship's status as a naval vessel was the thirty soldiers she carried and the twenty bronze twelve-pounder demi-culverins protruding from the ports in her sides; some of them bearing on their breeches the crest of the Zeeland Admiralty; others the royal arms of Spain and the foundry mark MECHELEN since they had been captured years before from Flemish prizes and rebored to take Dutch roundshot. As he surveyed all this with the critical eye of an Armada veteran Willenbrouckx could only be thankful that the *Eenhoorn* was about as likely to encounter a Spanish vessel as to meet one of the Emperor of China's war junks which he had read about lately in Linschoten's narration of his voyages. Because if it did come to an exchange of broadsides, then he feared that a ship as lightly built and armed as the *Eenhoorn* might be very badly knocked about indeed.

Two days later the *Eenhoorn* received orders to proceed to Hellevoetsluis on the island of Voorne to load a cargo of salt herrings for the Bergen garrison. So at the next high tide – the channel into Bergen being shallow even for a fluit-ship – the anchor was duly weighed, the sailors grunting as they lugged at the windlass bars to the sound of Sigurdsson's fiddle playing the jig *Grietje van Zierikzee*, and was then hoisted dripping to the cathead and the stock swung up to be lashed fast. The wind was a light but steady southerly breeze. The men hauled at the halyards to hoist the fore topsail, then the spritsail, then unbrailed the triangular mizzen. The sheet ropes started to pay lazily through the blocks which clumped along the deck planking as the sails flapped, then filled and began to draw. Imperceptibly at first, the *Eenhoorn* started to move, the turbid, shallow waters of the Oosterschelde rustling at her bow while the gulls screamed and soared above her masttops. The tricolour of the Dutch Republic floated at her stern while the blue-and-white-striped flag of Zeeland waved languidly at the maintop. As they passed the Waterschans fort there was a flash and a puff of white smoke from the ramparts followed by a sonorous boom, and an answering boom and puff of smoke from the *Eenhoorn*. High on the narrow peak of the stern the cripple-footed trumpeter Sigurdsson blew a splendid fanfare, causing the sentries on the walls of the Waterschans to shake their heads and laugh that "the herring-barge skipper Loodgieter" should give himself such airs, as though he were setting off to bring back some foreign princess for the Stadhouder's son to marry and not a few score casks of munition beer for wastrel soldiers to piss against a wall. Before long the fluit-ship's topsails were disappearing from their sight down the estuary, turning north into the Krabbenkreek which separates the island of Tholen from the mainland – or rather, what passes for mainland in that province of Zeeland, where the sea is so shallow and the land so little elevated above it that the two can scarcely be told apart.

As the *Eenhoorn* departed the schuits and pinks and shrimping hoogaars bustled about their business and the sails of the windmills on the town's bastions turned as unconcernedly as before. For who in the whole busy world would remark upon the departure of so inconsiderable a vessel, or even notice it? The defenders of Breda were now marching out of the town's gates with their drums beating and their matches lit, as specified in Spinola's generous terms of surrender; many of them now to enlist in the Ejército Real, eat cats and be left unpaid for years on end on behalf of the King of Spain exactly as they had previously eaten cats and been left unpaid for years on end in the service of the Dutch Republic. In London the creaking dead-carts were already collecting four or five hundred corpses each night as the hand of pestilence tightened its bony grip on the capital. In Canterbury (on account of the plague in London) the young King Charles was marrying the even younger French princess Henrietta Maria. In Saxony and the Palatinate soldiers engaged in that confused series of campaigns which historians would later call the Thirty Years' War were burning villages and ravishing their female inhabitants, whose shrieks travelled for a second or two then faded and were lost amid the early-summer twittering of birds and buzzing of insects. At Braunsberg in East Prussia two witches were being burned in the market place. And in a room in Pisa Galileo Galilei scribbled away at the first draft of his *Dialogo Sopra i Due Massimi Sistemi del Mondo**. The sun rose, the sun reached its zenith and the sun set in its annual progress through the zodiac whilst all things in the sublunary world continued much as they always had. And in all probability always would.

The *Eenhoorn* glided serenely northwards along the Krabbenkreek, between the flat meadows on either shore where cows grazed belly-deep in the lush June grass, unperturbed by the sight of ship's sails passing along above the dyke top. Michel Willen-

---

* *Dialogue Concerning the Two Chief World Systems*

brouckx meanwhile sat down on the surgeon's chest in his tiny cabin to slit open a letter which bore his wife's neat, small handwriting and which he had collected from the inn just before the ship sailed. Grubby and tattered, the letter had obviously been quite some time on its way from England to Bergen op Zoom. He also noted that it was crinkled and smelled of vinegar; presumably from having been disinfected against the plague somewhere along its route. It was brief and to the point:

Sweet love,

I was quite distracted with worry when Jane sent to tell me of those ruffians assaulting the house and blowing in the front of it in with gunpowder that night, thinking that they must have dragged you and Frans away and cut your throats. But then afterwards I learned that you were safe in Zeeland, so I did not worry and, to pay for your return, have now given order for money to be remitted to you at Bergen op Zoom.

We are presently living out in the country at a place called Hoddesden which is near the town of Hertford a half-day's ride from Clerkenwell, Cousin Bourchier having sent us all here because of the plague which grows daily in London, though he has elected to remain there for the sake of his business. Our landlord in Colchester demands compensation from us for the damage to his property, and swears that it was all your fault that you so angered some local great man or other. But good Doctor Mompesson has sent a letter to say that he will manage this and your other affairs in Colchester until we all return there – though this may not be yet awhile, primo, because the doctor writes that the plague is now arrived in Colchester from London so we were best remain where we are for the present, and secundo, because poor Henriette is ill with measles so we could not travel even if we would.

I sometimes think that the stars must be set against us two, that we must so often flee and change our place of abode. But as the sun remains true to the moon, and the two constant to one

another despite all their wandering about the heavens, so do I remain constant in my love to you and to my son.
Adieu until we meet again
Your loving Catherine
Written at Hoddesdon Manor, xxivimo day of May anno 1625

Willenbrouckx placed the letter with the other papers in his chest, thankful that his wife and daughter were safe now in the countryside where the plague was unlikely to reach them. But he roundly cursed the luck that had caused him to sign the articles condemning him and Frans to five or six months aboard this dismal tub when, if they had known two days ago that succour was at hand, they could now have been on their way back to England. There it was though: his signature on a contract was his signature, so there was nothing now but to make the best of it and hold out until the autumn, when they might return to Colchester and resume their rudely interrupted lives. Some weeks before he had written to Doctor de Brantôme to explain their sudden disappearance. He had so far received no reply, which was not to be wondered at with the posts so disrupted. But it worried him little, for though an honest man the surgeon was a sufficiently shrewd judge of character to suspect that that worthy physician had himself been obliged more than once in his career to depart under cover of darkness without leaving a forwarding address. For the time being he could hope only for a tranquil spell of duty and a rapid paying-off at the season's end. It looked like being a tedious summer and autumn before they could return home. But other things being equal (he considered), being bored for a few months was greatly preferable to being murdered by Sir Thomas Harbrow's retainers or dying of the plague. His main concern for the moment was that the ship aboard which they now found themselves might have a skipper and a mate competent enough to keep them all from ending up on a lee shore in an autumnal gale; an ever-present hazard amid these cursed Dutch shallows with the westerly winds blowing on to them.

Regarding this latter point, the surgeon need not have feared in the slightest. When it came to selecting a crew Captain Cornelis Adriaenszoon Loodgieter had complete authority delegated to him by the Zeeland Admiralty; and whilst he had not chosen them all – the mate Ellert Hendrickssen had come with the *Eenhoorn* when she was chartered, and Meester Grobelaar had been directly appointed by Their Lordships as a precaution against false accounting – he had enlisted the rest of the crew himself, and selected the best even if it had meant paying them somewhat above the wages that the Admiralty pay-scales laid down. The drum had been beaten that spring in the towns and villages of Zeeland to announce that the pinnace *Eenhoorn*, Captain Loodgieter, was lying at Middelburg seeking men, and this had raised about a third of the required crew of ninety-five. Thirty of the complement were soldiers, supplied by the admiralty with a corporal to lead them. And of the remainder nearly half were Norwegians: all from the same few villages around Hardanger Fjord and enlisted together under a foreman, Thomas Jesperssen, who spoke tolerable Dutch and was therefore appointed to negotiate for them. They had been in the Dutch service for three years now, and as well as being admirable seamen were abstemious and well conducted, remitting most of their wages back to their families instead of pouring them down their throats in the dockside taverns. They spoke Norwegian still among themselves, which a Zeelander could half understand if it was spoken slowly enough, but most had now mastered sufficient Dutch to comprehend the bo'sun's commands and get along with their shipmates, even if they preferred to congregate in their own messes at mealtimes. They were smart about their business, and the most that anyone could reproach them with was having an excessive number of lice in their long, usually blond hair, which they regarded as a sign of good health since headlice will forsake a sick man. Most had likewise plaited some of their hair into a long, thin lock against elves and goblins, of which they seemed inordinately afraid, every man of them carrying several talismans against witchcraft. The Norwegians were strange and sometimes seemed slightly mad, though that was perhaps from being so long away from their families, which they seemed to have long since given up any hope of ever seeing again. But everyone knew there was no remedy for that: the fleet of the Republic must employ them and Danes and Scots and Danzigers and all manner of other foreigners besides. Unlike England or Spain, Holland had no press to force seamen to serve aboard its ships, and could only induce them to sign articles by offering good wages. Or, if even that failed, recruit foreigners to make up the numbers.

Next morning at the end of the first watch the *Eenhoorn* rounded the western tip of Overflakee Island and turned to run towards Hellevoetsluis on the tide, with only the cry of the leadsman in the foremast shrouds to break the faint rush of wind down from the sails and the constant chorus of creaking as the ship rolled and pitched gently on the estuarine swell. Ashore the sails of the windmills turned, cows lowed to be milked in the flowery meadows and the smoke of breakfast fires rose from cottage chimneys invisible behind the dykes as the haymakers made their way out into the fields with their scythes over their shoulders. It was a fine morning in early summer, and the world went about its quotidian business. Around the port of Hellevoetsluis men were already at work as the *Eenhoorn* approached: hundreds of labourers delving with shovels, picks and wheelbarrows, piling up the sticky clay of Voorne Island to construct ramparts around the little fishing haven which the States-General had recently decreed would become the Republic's principle naval base, surrounded by bastions to make it impregnable against attack from land or sea and containing not only a dock large enough to hold the Republic's entire war fleet but also the provision warehouses and powder magazines, the roperies and biscuit bakeries and breweries and slaughterhouses and cannon foundries to maintain it at sea. The town of Den Briel had been considered for a while – but the mouth of the Maas was clogging with silt, so that no amount of raking and dredging could keep the channel deep enough for great ships. So Hellevoetsluis was being taken in hand and transformed into a mighty naval arsenal. Some of the older captains rubbed their chins and declared that it was rankest folly to put all the Republic's ships into one harbour where they might be trapped like wasps in a bottle by contrary winds or ice in winter, or an enemy fleet lying out in the Goeree Roads. Yet it was still an impressive sight to see the gangs of labourers that morning as they swarmed like so many ants over the bare new ramparts round the harbour: part of that centuries-long epic struggle with spades and wheelbarrows that had caused Holland to rise from the sea – but which could now only keep the sea at bay by constant labour, as the tides and winter storms ate away at the dykes and the melted snows coming down the Rhine in springtime threatened to drown the land once more. "God made heaven and earth but the Dutch made Holland", people would say with pride; omitting to mention that on the seventh day God had sat back and rested from his labours, whereas the Hollanders were now condemned to toil like old Sisyphus day and night until the very end of time to retain what they had so impudently snatched from Neptune's grasp.

Moored to the smart new brick quayside at Hellevoetsluis, it was to work at once for the *Eenhoorn*'s crew in order to load two hundred casks of salt herring. The barrels were stacked on their sides in two layers in the hold and chocked up with baulks of wood, then in another layer standing on their ends in the middle of the main deck to allow enough room around them to work the guns, because although it was unlikely that the enemy's larger ships would venture amid the coastal islands, it was not unheard of for Ostend galleys to come raiding into the winding channels of the coastline, and not three months before a fluit-ship had been boarded and taken in broad daylight by a Spanish galley off Zierikzee thanks to the complacency of her crew. The herrings were duly signed for, and the *Eenhoorn* set sail on the evening tide, this time heading out to sea to take advantage of the wind, then down the coast round Goeree and Schouwen to head back into the Roompot and the Oosterschelde on the starboard tack.

Her arrival back at Bergen was as little remarked upon as her departure, noticed only by the commissariat officials and a few dockside idlers as the herring casks were trundled noisily up the timber barrelway through the Hampoort gate to be stowed in the garrison's fish warehouse. The German and Scandinavian mercenaries in the service of the States-General would eat Enkhuizen herring readily enough, and likewise the Scots, albeit with some reluctance. But the English soldiery heartily detested it and regarded being fed raw fish as part of their rations as tantamount to breach of contract – though they would eagerly swallow oysters, which were every bit as uncooked and far more liable to cause fluxes and distempers. A jeering crowd of Englishmen gathered as the casks made their way through the streets and swore that they would sooner hang than eat such filth, and next morning a salt herring was found dangling from the town gallows with an offensive note to the fortress commandant pinned to it:

"*Who feeds poor soldiers but fishes and bread,
Will end up like Lord Jesus, dead.
Who gives his men raw herrings to eat,
Shall be declared a cozening cheat.*"

Shown this libel, the Ridder van Grobbendonck considered having a few of the rascals strung up for discipline's sake, since in his experience English mercenary soldiers were worth less than German ones and a great deal less than the Scots, who were admirable fellows in every respect. But on more mature reflection and in view of Breda's surrender, news of which had reached him that very morning, he came to the view that even the most insubordinate of soldiers who could fire a musket was likely to be more use to him than a corpse dangling from the gallows. So for the time being, in the wider interests of the Dutch Republic, he decided that he must swallow the insult as though it had never been offered. For the truth of the matter was that the fortress's position now looked perilous indeed, since Spinola would surely not rest upon his laurels after such a notable victory but instead turn his victorious army against some new objective while the campaigning season lasted; either against Geertruidenberg on the Maas (the strategists thought) or against Bergen which was the more enticing prize of the two since its capture would secure the approaches to Antwerp. Another siege seemed imminent.

So as soon as the *Eenhoorn* had discharged her load of herrings it was back to sea on the next tide; this time to Delfshaven on the Maas just west of Rotterdam in order to pick up a far more delicate cargo: three hundred twenty-pound kegs of gunpowder brought down by barge from the province of Holland's powder mills at Delft. It was with the greatest care and circumspection that the carefully made oaken casks, lined with brown paper against leakages and bound with brass hoops to prevent sparks being struck on the cobbles, were rolled up the gangplank and bedded down below decks by sailors who were either barefoot or wearing old woollen stockings over their shoes. Except for the stern lantern with a sentry to guard it, all lights aboard were extinguished for the duration of the voyage. The galley fire was out, so everyone had to subsist for three days on bread, cheese and beer. Yet all considered the lack of candles and hot food well worth the trouble; and none more so than Captain Loodgieter, who not many years before had found himself swimming in the Java Sea among the fragments of his ship as a result of gunpowder being negligently handled. The perilous cargo was duly landed at Bergen and consigned to the fortress magazines with a collective sigh of relief, and the galley fire was lit once more to prepare a great kettle of pea soup. Then it was new orders; this time to embark live cargo.

Two mornings later the town of Dort* came into view in the clear dawn air, seemingly afloat upon its island in the middle of the great waters where the Maas and the Merwede joined into something like an inland sea; that proud and ancient municipality – first among the towns of Holland by right of precedence, it claimed – with its lofty church towers, its fine merchant's houses, its vast timber stacks and its splendid new harbour gateway adorned with the town's arms and the blond-haired Hollandsche Maagd seated inside a wattle fence around the Hollandsche Tuin**. The *Eenhoorn* moored at the quayside, the gangplank was let down; and along the cobbled roadway through the echoing brick arch beneath the portcullis there came tramping at a steady pace a company of two hundred and fifty Swiss mercenaries led by a drummer and a fife player, their captain and sergeants at their head, their muskets sloped over their shoulders in immaculate order, all clad in dark grey serge, enlisted in the Valais canton that spring and brought down the Rhine from Basle by river barge. Their captain, Balthasar Krauschli, saluted Loodgieter with his sword at the head of the gangplank and was formally welcomed aboard, followed by his men, who then fitted themselves in as best they might aboard so small a vessel: on the main deck for those more senior in rank, and down in the hold – which still stank of herrings – for those of lesser degree.

There was some dissatisfaction among the crew at having soldiers aboard, since they were but passengers and though they ate the ship's rations, neither could nor would help with the ship's work. The *Eenhoorn's* own soldiers had by now been trained out of their original savage and uncouth state into some semblance of humanity, able to walk on their hind legs and even capable under the bo'sun's direction of performing a few laborious but mentally undemanding tasks like raising the anchor or walking back a halyard. But these Switzers were plainly no more than so much lumber, their presence aboard all the more tiresome since they were mostly French-speakers and it was therefore troublesome to communicate with them; especially when they were served with

---

* Dordrecht
** The Dutch Maid and the Dutch Garden, a popular emblem of the day.

oatmeal groats or good Dutch pea soup from the ship's kettle, paid for out of the ship's victualling allowance by courtesy of the Zeeland Admiralty, yet still looked upon it as though it was mere swill for pigs and they were used to much better fare at home. But the ship was under orders and commissioned by Their Lorships to transport either goods or livestock. So the best must be made of it, and the foolish fellows be delivered as quickly as possible to Bergen to be put ashore, and good riddance to them.

However, it seemed that the *Eenhoorn* was not to be so quickly rid of her unwanted guests; for as soon as the ship moored to Dort's quayside a profound summertime calm had descended over southern Holland. The water around the town turned glassy-smooth beneath a cloudless blue sky in which swallows turned and darted, the only disturbance of its mirror-like calm the occasional "flop!" of a fish come up on the flood tide and breaking surface to try and take a fly. After embarking her passengers the ship was towed out into the Merwede again and dropped anchor, because the town's busy quays had to be kept clear for commerce. But there was no prospect of her moving any further until the wind got up again, which at this season of the year might well be days or even weeks. Boredom spread insidiously among the soldiery, packed together below decks with scarcely room to move and all the gunports open for ventilation in the oppressive summer heat. Loodgieter (who spoke French fluently) was soon in conversation with Captain Krauschli about finding means to divert his men during their unlooked-for spell at anchor in the Merwede and prevent the spreading of melancholic humours. The Swiss were all musketeers? Very well: he would furnish sport and practice for them in an exercise of his own devising, which could not but sharpen their military skills and prevent them from falling into slothful dissipation, idling away their days at dice and cards to their own undoing and that of his crew, who (he said), being but simple sailors and innocent as so many children, would soon gamble away their wages and the very clothes from their backs if they came into contact with soldiers.

The exercise that Loodgieter set up next day was an elaborate one: as intricate as a ballet in a court masque and frankly of questionable military value, but none the less highly diverting both for the soldiers taking part and for the seamen looking on curiously from the rigging. Fifty of the most proficient marksmen in Krauschli's company lined the starboard bulwark in the waist, shoulder to shoulder with their muskets pointed over the side. And kneeling in file behind each of them were two of their fellows, with the rest of the company down on the gun deck beneath the hatchway with their ramrods, bullet bags and powder flasks ready to load and prime. At the command "Donnez le feu!" the musketeers made as if to discharge their weapons (though for the time being the exercise would take place without lighted match, since it concerned only the handling of arms). Each man then passed the musket which he had just supposedly fired backwards with his left arm, while seizing with his right a fresh musket proferred by the man kneeling behind, who at the same time passed the empty musket back to the man behind him so that it would end up below decks to be reloaded, then be passed back again to the shooters at the bulwark. And in this way Loodgieter said that a force of fifty men standing at a fortress courtine with a hundred or so of their fellows behind them as loaders might, if well enough drilled, fire off ten or even fifteen shots in a minute instead of the two that was the most that even the most proficient musketeer could discharge while loading and priming for himself. "For I have observed in the course of my military career" Loodgieter informed Captain Krauschli – who had doubtless been under fire a hundred times more often than the Dutchman, but out of politeness tried not to show it – "that the important thing in battles is not who can fire the first volley, for any set of poltroons may do as much, but who fires the second and the third, once fellows have fallen to the enemy's reply, the ranks are in disarray and each man is astounded with the din and smoke of battle." Krauschli nodded his agreement, since this did indeed pretty well bear out his own long experience of battles even if he doubted a mere sailor's credentials for saying so. "I think, therefore," Loodgieter continued, "that to train your fellows in giving such sustained fire, though it will not often be applicable, may still be of some utility when they are defending a gateway or a breach in a wall where only a limited number of them have shoulder room to stand and face the enemy. So let them continue to exercise, and when they are perfect in their movements I shall make powder and shot available so that they may discharge their muskets in reality, and not in pantomime as at present." He smiled, and Krauschli thanked him for his generosity and his consideration for his men's welfare. They were hardened warriors, from a strongly Calvinist part of Switzerland and as proud of their Protestant faith as of their fearsome reputation on the battlefield. But even so, practising this drill evolution could only be good for them, and would at the very least give them some useful occupation while they languished in this cursed muddy ditch.

★ ★ ★ ★ ★ ★ ★ ★ ★ ★

It was indeed a sight for us to behold that next morning, when our Switzers made their first essay of this rolling method of fire with their muskets loaded with powder and ball and their matches lit. For two whole days now they had perfected this precise and intricate muster, and their corporals had each worn out several canes with their beating of the soldiers to instruct them out of their faults. But now they were as perfect in their evolutions as the mechanism of a newly oiled clock, each subaltern cogwheel turning in faultless harmony with the others, which was most wondrous for the sailors to behold since military drills are unknown aboard ships except in the service of their cannon, each man priding himself on knowing precisely what to do without anyone shouting commands at him as though he had a boiled cauliflower inside his skull. An old rotten boat had been procured for a few stuivers, and this was now towed past some twenty yards abeam by our own vlet while we all looked on with great curiosity from the foc'sle and poop or (like myself, for I was by now pretty confident aloft) hanging out along the yardarms for a better view. At Captain Krauschli's word of command his fifty marksmen popped up from behind the bulwark like so many jack-in-a-boxes and gave fire with a great rippling crackle of musketry like a drum roll or a man-of-war's mainsail being rent asunder by the hands of a giant. White smoke rose up in a cloud and hung in the still air above the river as each man passed back the spent weapon and seized a charged one from behind him, then shouldered it and at the word of command, fired again. And thus for eight whole volleys fired (I should think) in the space of less than a minute, so that when the smoke cleared we saw that there was no boat any more, just our vlet towing a line with only the shattered stem attached to it, and a patch of splinters floating on the water where the boat had been. And meanwhile the other soldiers beneath the hatchway had been most diligently loading the empty muskets passed back to them, so that when the Switzers ceased their firing they still had a store of loaded muskets at their backs and could easily have fired off as many volleys again.

At dinner our captain professed himself well pleased with this demonstration, and swore that if the Switzers afterwards applied this drill of his in a narrow space then no man would be able to stand against them. So he counted the expenditure of our own powder and shot (he said) of no matter to have given our honoured guests the opportunity to have exercised themselves at so useful a skill. For himself he thought it of but limited application aboard ships, because of the danger of lighted matches trailing negligently etc. etc., which was why our own soldiers had snaphance muskets instead of matchlocks and why he had given order that the decks and cordage should first be well doused with water. However, there was no question in his mind but that it might prove mighty useful on the walls of a fortress. Meester Grobelaar, though, was less persuaded of our captain's benevolence when he had me make an entry afterwards in the ship's account ledger: *"For powder, ball, match and wadding ex-*

pended by Captain Krauschli's Swiss for exercise while lying at Dort: ten guilders and seventeen stuivers. Chargeable to the captain's own account." "Mark my words, young Frans," he said (for we had already formed a certain amity), "for our skipper to spend above ten guilders from his own pocket for this soldiers' lark – which is a third of my own monthly wage less emoluments – is most unlike him unless he has some further aim in mind. The man scarcely sneezes or scratches his nose without thinking first how he may turn it to his profit. So before either of us is much older we may expect something to come of it."

On our last evening lying at Dort there came aboard to dine with our captain the skipper of a Rouen wine ship which had arrived just before the calm descended. Once the dishes were cleared away the two of them dismissed us all and held a most earnest discussion in French behind closed doors, calling only for me to bring them sea charts to pore over and our copy of Waghener's pilotage book from the mate's cabin. As Meester Grobelaar had prophesied, some great business was plainly afoot.

CHAPTER EIGHT

On the afternoon of the fourth day the glassy summer calm was broken by a light southerly breeze ruffling the waters around the town of Dort. The *Eenhoorn* duly weighed anchor to depart, everyone glad to be moving again after days of being packed together like herrings in a barrel aboard so small a vessel in such sultry weather. The shortest way back to Bergen op Zoom, Ellert Hendrikssen said, would be to tack southwards into the Hollands Diep and then towards Willemstad before turning south into the Volkerak. But the captain overruled him, saying that laveering to and fro in the narrow channels between the islands would be too laborious in the fickle summer airs, so the ship would instead sail down the Maas on the port tack to reach the sea past Den Briel, then for a day or so out to sea, then run back into the Oosterschelde on the starboard tack. Which of course is all perfectly feasible in Holland, to sail through the middle of the country as though it were the open sea, since the land below Nijmegen is so flat that nothing hinders the wind and a vessel sailing along a river will often be higher than the fields on either side. So down the river they went, past Zwijndrecht and Spijkenisse, then Den Briel with its massive church tower, then out on to the wide North Sea which the Swiss were intrigued to behold, having never before in all their lives set eyes upon salt water. As Loodgieter had predicted it might, the breeze dropped the next afternoon and a salty, clinging sea mist descended upon them. The *Eenhoorn* drifted while Sigurdsson blew his trumpet every minute or so by way of warning, since the waters hereabouts were crowded with ships likewise becalmed; some drifting along with the current but others, bound for Rotterdam and Delfshaven, lying at anchor for fear that they might be carried past the entrance to the Maas before the fog lifted. As the late twilight of midsummer descended they were still rolling gently on the sea swell, the mist forming beads on the limp sails and dripping to make puddles on the decks while trumpets, cow-horns, bells, drums and the occasional musket shot sounded around them as invisible tokens of mysterious vessels they would never see, having drifted miles away from them by the time the fog cleared.

The mist lifted just after dawn as a light summer breeze blew up from the north-west. By the middle of the forenoon watch the *Eenhoorn* was ambling along at a steady three or four knots down the coast, about fifteen miles out from the shore. The sea was now empty of ships. North of the Flanders Banks there was sufficient depth of water close inshore, so vessels heading for the Maas and Texel preferred to hug the coast and use the tops of the church towers beyond the dunes as leading marks. Yet for all the apparent tranquillity, something was clearly afoot. Loodgieter had changed from his normal day clothes into an old russet coat, and replaced his elegant beaver-felt hat with a battered woollen klapmuts, the brim drooping down on each side of his head like a sow's ears. He had likewise given orders that the ship should be "beslordigt": ropes slackened rather than triced up, falls left trailing loose instead of being smartly belayed, and – most puzzling of all – the unicorn figurehead at the bow and the Zeeland coat of arms at the stern unpegged and stowed below. The captain meanwhile paced the sloping deck at the narrow peak of the poop below the lantern, barely wide enough for two men to stand together, carrying with him his much-derided "kijkglas" which he had lately had made at considerable expense by an Italian lens grinder in Haarlem who manufactured such devices. It was a pretty enough toy, to be sure: a wooden tube pleasingly decorated with pearl and tortoiseshell, and a lens in each end of it, and was greatly admired by the captain's dinner guests though the mate swore in private that if skippers needed discs of glass to supplement their eyes, then they were plainly blind moles fitter for libraries or counting-houses than the decks of ships. About six bells of the forenoon watch the captain peered intently through the tube after the lookout had shouted down from the masthead that a topsail could be seen above the horizon to north-westward. The *Eenhoorn* held her tranquil, inoffensive course, and the lower sails of the other ship soon became visible. She was moving faster than they were, and had evidently altered course to close with them. After another half-hour the stranger's hull was visible. It was a man-of-war; and plainly not a Dutch one either: a low, lean vessel of about twenty-four guns. Before long the matter was resolved beyond any doubt. The white flag of Burgundy with the ragged red saltire flew from her jackstaff, but the royal banner of Spain fluttered at the head of her mainmast. So this was a king's ship and no Dunkirk privateer, and the stories they had heard from the Rouen wine ship lying at Dort were true: one of the new and much-feared Spanish fraga-tas was indeed cruising off the Dutch rivermouths like a kestrel hovering above a summer meadow, and falling upon such poor unwary fieldmice as neglected to keep one eye turned skywards. The French vessel had herself been stopped by the Spaniard some days before, and only allowed to go on her way after her skipper had shown his papers to prove that the ship was neither Dutch-owned nor carrying a contraband cargo.

Aboard the *Eenhoorn* all was abuzz with preparations. An old sail had been hung above the waist as though it was being patched, so as to conceal the Swiss musketeers now crouched on deck. And down below the guns were loaded with their crews kneeling about them, matches lit and placed over tubs of water for safety, but the port lids still closed and the guns not run out. A sailor was sent aloft to the maintop carrying something wrapped in a sack. Meanwhile down in the hold the surgeon and his apprentice prepared their dressings and laid out the instruments. Willenbrouckx's confident prediction that their seeing action this voyage was as likely as swallows at Christmastide looked set fair to be blown full of shot-holes in the very near future. Yet all this was done with the greatest discretion, so that no single clue might reveal to a sharp-eyed lookout that the *Eenhoorn* was anything other than a harmless fluit-ship with a half-dozen small guns and a crew of twenty men and boys. The gunports in her sides, which would have betrayed her as a warship, were now painted dull black, surrounded by the dull black of the midwales of the hull, and therefore invisible to anyone standing beyond musket shot.

The frigate *Nuestra Señora de las Vírgenes* was indeed a formidable little vessel, built the previous year at La Coruña as part of the great design of the Count-Duke Olivares for constructing a Spanish fleet that could carry the war to the Hollanders, rather than merely sit helpless as a target for the Hollanders' guns. After forty years of defeats at sea it had dawned at last upon Spain's naval officials that towering, unwieldy galleons were of little use against the nimble Dutchmen, and that the rowing galleys which had served so well against the Turk at Lepanto were something worse than useless on the brutal grey waves of the North Sea. Spain had many fine shipwrights and experienced sea captains, even if it had hitherto paid but little heed to them, and the fragata was the result of their collective wisdom: a long, narrow vessel with three masts, low in the water, with a single deck of close-spaced guns and carrying a crew of two hundred gunners and musketeers: more than sufficient to overawe any Dutch merchantman they might come across. So the frigate's captain, Don Hernando-Felipe Velado de Córdoba y Quevedo, was entirely confident that morning of yet another easy prize to add to the bag of seven Dutch vessels that his ship had taken in these waters over the previous five weeks; all of them unwary fluit-ships imprudently thinking themselves out of danger once they were past Dunkirk and the Flanders Banks; in fact often falling out of convoy contrary to orders so that they could make port a day earlier than the rest and thus steal an advantage in the marketplace. Though not a man much addicted to jests – as a Spanish nobleman and a sea officer of King Philip he abhorred frivolity of any kind – Don Hernando had been moved a few days before to suggest to his Flemish sailing master over dinner that their ship's name should perhaps be changed to *Nuestra*

Señora de las Siete Vírgenes Insensatas.* This eighth victim, though, looked unlikely to be as profitable as the others once the admiralty court in Brussels had adjudicated upon her. She was visibly high in the water, and therefore sailing unladen, so once she was lying at Dunkirk only the vessel itself could be auctioned and her crew held in gaol until a ransom was paid for their release; which was likely to be a modest one since they were evidently poor silly bumpkin-sailors from some benighted mud-hole of a town in West Friesland. But there: if it damaged the commerce of the Dutch rebels even an empty fluit-ship was a prize worth the trouble, and one (it had to be said) worthier of a king's ship commanded by a nobleman than their wretched stinking herring busses, which were fit only for Dunkirk privateer ships commanded by greasy dishonourable Flemish scoundrels. Does an eagle prey upon flies, or a lion upon rabbits?

The two vessels were now within hailing distance.

"Who are you, and where are you bound for?" Don Hernando called through a speaking-trumpet; in French, since the fluit-ship flew no ensign and therefore might conceivably be a Calais or a Rochelle vessel now that French owners were having their ships built in Dutch yards. In the present somewhat strained state of relations between France and Spain it was advisable to establish this early on and thus avoid later unpleasantness with the Flanders Admiralty, as Don Hernando had prudently done with the Rouen wine ship some days before though his crew were pressing him to board her.

Standing on the *Eenhoorn*'s poop, Loodgieter affected not to understand, instead holding one hand to his ear in an exagerrated manner like the fool in a rustic comedy. So the question was repeated in bad Dutch.

Loodgieter answered in good Spanish.

"May it please vuestra merced, we are the fluit-ship *Eenhoorn* of the town of Hoorn in West Friesland. Which together is two

---

* *Our Lady of the Seven Foolish Virgins.*

horns – and therefore, one would have thought, a most appropriate vessel for Your Excellency to encounter." He then held his hands up to his head with the fingers extended to mimic a stag's antlers, after which insult he doffed his hat with an exagerrated courtly flourish. "Pray tell me, señor, how does my lady your wife divert herself in Your Excellency's absence?"

Don Hernando flushed dark red and reached instinctively for his sword hilt despite their being thirty yards apart.

"You will pay dearly for your insolence, you Hollander dog!" he shouted back, "For I swear upon my honour that after we have taken you I shall make you swallow your own testicles at swordpoint!" He turned to his sailing master. "Buyskens, give the order to grapple and board them."

"Shall we give them a broadside first by way of preparation?" the Fleming asked.

"No, that will only batter their miserable barge and make it less saleable at auction – and the prize money will be little enough as it is, with no cargo to sell and only two dozen worthless rascals to ransom – less their skipper, who will surely go overboard with a roundshot tied to his feet for his impertinence. Just grapple them and board. The other seven struck their colours before any of our men had so much as crossed the rail. These Dutchmen are cowardly mercantile maggots, made pale and rheumy by their beer and cheese and herrings and such cold moist foods. They know only too well what manner of men we Spaniards are, with fire infused into our veins by wine and garlic."

The two ships bumped against one another, grinding side to side as they rolled on the summer swell. Aboard the *Nuestra Señora* a hundred boarders stood in the waist with swords and pikes ready to swarm across as the grappling irons were thrown out – though, the ship being high in the water and sailing light, the *Eenhoorn's* rail was a good nine feet above that of the low-slung Spanish vessel. Meanwhile on the *Nuestra Señora's* quarterdeck two dozen musketeers, Genoese mercenaries, stood ready to give the boarders covering fire. But they never got the chance: instead a sudden blaze of light blinded them as the sailor in the *Eenhoorn's* maintop aimed the midday sun's rays into their faces with the aid of the looking-glass from the great cabin. Then a deadly blast of musket balls tore into them as Captain Krauschli's Swiss musketeers bobbed up above the *Eenhoorn's* rail and opened fire. Confused and shaken, their eyes dazzled by the light, those Genoese still standing tried to return fire, but were smitten by a second volley, then a third and fourth, until the deck was strewn with dead and dying and the survivors could only take cover and fire snap-shots in reply. Meanwhile the boarding party in the waist was in utter confusion and disarray, most of its men now dead or wounded and the remnant stumbling about in confusion.

Seeing this, Captain Krauschli roared "Prenez-les, mes enfants!" His grey-clad soldiers threw aside their muskets, drew their short swords and followed him as he scrambled over the *Eenhorn's* rail and down the sloping side, then leaped across on to the Spanish frigate's corpse-strewn, blood-slippery deck. Before long the Swiss were hacking and parrying and thrusting their way like a troop of devils across the *Nuestra Señora's* decks – then below decks as the Spaniards, outnumbered two to one, were driven down the companionways to fight as best they could among the cannon of the main deck. Within five minutes it was all over: one of the *Eenhoorn's* men climbed to the *Nuestra Señora's* masthead and tore down the Spanish royal banner to replace it with the Dutch tricolour. A few Spaniards and Genoese still fought on in the hold, until they were promised their lives and threw down their arms. But from the great cabin there was only silence as Loodgieter made his way aft to demand the ship's surrender, bloodied sword in hand and panting from exertion. He pushed against the door, and found it blocked by something lying on the deck. Inside the great cabin brains and skull fragments were spattered across the deck-beams where Don Hernando had put a pistol to his head, having first (it seemed) tried to fall upon his sword in the Roman manner but found the weapon too long for that purpose.

Loodgieter behaved like a fellow seafarer and a good Christian, albeit a Protestant one, and in his account of the action for the Zeeland Admiralty wrote that he and the Spanish captain had met in single combat and that he had wounded him in the belly, then shot him after he refused an offer of quarter. The *Nuestra Señora's* surviving crew were battened below decks and a prize crew was put aboard to sail the vessel to Vlissingen. As for Don Hernando, his body was later embalmed and handed over to the Spaniards at Aardenberg under flag of truce. It was solemnly buried in a splendid marble tomb in the Church of Saint Carlo Borromeo in Antwerp, with a long Latin epitaph listing the deceased's exploits on land and at sea; but tactfully omitting to mention his final engagement in which pride and rashness had proved his undoing.

★ ★ ★ ★ ★ ★ ★ ★ ★ ★

We had seen nothing of the action hitherto, only felt the great jarring shudder of our first contact with the Spanish ship, then heard the din of musketry come down the hatches to us from above. But then it became unnaturally still, as though our ship were deserted, because after the Switzers had boarded the enemy vessel our gunners too were ordered up from the main deck to follow them, with our soldiers meanwhile firing their muskets to aid them. No wounded men were brought for us to dress until the fight was over and the Spanish frigate had surrendered. Their surgeon, a Fleming called Pelsaert, came across to us since he was now our prisoner; though my stepfather magnanimously forwent his right under the rules and customs of war to appropriate his chest of instruments, saying that whatever the usages might specify it would be entirely improper for one Flemish surgeon to despoil another (though I think what he really meant was, that he would have one chest of instruments to dispose of at the end of our commission, and had no wish to encumber himself with two of them). As for the men that were hurt in the fight, the lesser wounds gave us little trouble, my stepfather and Meester Pelsaert between them probing and applying compresses to bullet wounds and stitching up sword gashes with the greatest dispatch, then leaving me to dress them afterwards as well as bandaging broken heads and performing other such minor tasks. Some, though, were plainly beyond our help. Bullet wounds to the chest or abdomen (my stepfather told me) were always infernally difficult to treat. Though in this encounter the distance was so short that the ball had in most cases gone clean through the body and out the other side, punctures of the body cavities nearly always turned septic (he said) from shreds of dirty clothing being carried in with the bullet even if it touched no major blood vessel or vital organ. The best we could do with shot-wounds through a lung was lie the poor fellow on his side for the blood and rheum to drain out through a canula inserted into the wound, then later apply a thick emplastre to close the thorax against air whistling into it through the bullet hole as the man breathed, in which manner my stepfather said he had saved one or two in the past whose lives had been despaired of.

There was only one amputation to be performed: a Genoese corporal whose left arm had been smashed at the elbow by a musket ball. The two surgeons examined his arm, agreed that the limb was beyond saving, and so placed a tourniquet to staunch the blood vessels then set to work with dismembering knife and bone saw to remove the arm above the elbow while their patient was still half-numbed with shock. As they went about this melancholy task I had the job of pulling out the severed blood vessels a half-inch or so with a tenaculum then ligating them with twine, since although we had the charcoal brazier burning, and cauterizing irons heating in it, we were not in any haste now and might therefore dispense with searing the veins and arteries shut, which, though a speedy method when there is a great press of wounded to be attended to, is painful alike to suffer and to witness and makes the stump much slower to heal afterwards. After about two minutes the limb was off and lying forlornly on the bloody table as though it expected to rejoin the patient's body one day, though it would never do so now until the general resurrection. The corporal bore this ordeal with great fortitude, like a true soldier, and scarcely cried out. But once I had dressed the stump and we had laid him on a straw mattress and placed a blanket over him (for he was now white from loss of blood and shivering mightily) he seemed quite broken and wept openly as I knelt and endeavoured to give him some wine to restore him. I think that perhaps the poor fellow suspected that this was all a nightmare and not real at all, and that he would wake presently to find his arm still attached to him, which would make his deception all the crueller when he found that it was gone for good and he would now be discharged from the army with a miserly pension and no trade open to him other than begging. As I departed from him I was mighty glad – and remain so to this day – that the profession of arms has never held the smallest attraction for me. For no man knows better than a military surgeon what hecatombs of sacrifice the god Mars demands from his votaries in the darkness of his sanctuary, behind all the pretty tinsel banners, the gaudy apparel, the banging of drums and the braying of trumpets which beguile the foolish multitude gathered in front of his temple.

We reached Vlissingen the following day, on the next tide after our prize, and were welcomed like the heroes of antiquity, with cheering and flags and much firing of cannon. The whole town had come out to throng the harbourmouth and the shore on either side of it and fête our arrival. The reason for all this jubilation was not far to seek. The year 1625 had thus far not been an auspicious one for the Dutch Republic, and the goddess Bellona had as yet placed precious few bay leaves upon the brows of the Hollandsche Maagd. Prince Maurits had died in May; the town of Breda had fallen to Spinola in June; and since the shipping season began the provinces of Holland and Zeeland had lost between them upwards of fifty merchantmen to the Dunkirkers and the Spaniards, and likewise a good hundred and fifty fishing vessels and their crews, which was greatly disruptive of the trade in salt herrings which furnished so much of the Republics' wealth, since for every herring buss that was taken or sunk two more would cut loose their nets and run when a privateer's sails appeared over the horizon. There were few triumphs to brag of that year and a great many setbacks. So now that we had taken a war vessel from the enemy the people of Vlissingen were intent on making as great a festival of it as they could.

It might indeed have proved a bloody holocaust like those with which the Indians of Mexico were wont to celebrate their triumphs before Cortés landed upon those shores. Vlissingen had suffered more grievously from the Dunkirkers that summer than most other Dutch towns, the herring fisheries being the greatest part of its wealth, and hundreds of men from there and the villages round about now sat in the mouldy insalubrious dungeons of Dunkirk citadel waiting to be ransomed. So the womenfolk of the town, learning that the *Nuestra Señora's* prisoners were to be put ashore, had gathered on the quayside with their hatchets and fish-gutting knives intent on butchering them and tossing their dismembered carcasses into the harbour, and it was only after the town's governor addressed them – emphasising his words with a row of musketeers standing behind him with lighted matches – that they repented of this murderous resolve. He informed them that whilst Dunkirkers from privateer ships might properly be hanged as pirates without further process, this was a king's ship and its crew were therefore lawful prisoners who must be treated according to the customs and usages of war.

Our captives were duly escorted by the musketeers to the town gaol amid much fist-shaking and throwing of dead cats and herring offals. As for ourselves though, every man, woman, child and stray dog in Vlissingen town wished to be our friend and buy us pots of beer. A Roman triumphal arch of wood and cardboard decorated with wreaths of greenery was set up before the town hall, and the master of the town's rederijkers pronounced a long Latin oration in our honour likening us to Hector, Achilles, Julius Caesar, Alexander, Pompey, Regulus, Horatius, Scipio Africanus and every other antique hero he could remember from his schooldays, informing us that we Batavians (as Tacitus writes) were regarded by the Romans as their equals, not their vassals, and acknowledged by them to be a people as valiant and martial as themselves. Until Captain Krauschli – who I saw was much put out of sorts by all this – snorted loudly, *"Non Batavii fortii erunt, sed Helvetii"** and stumped away in a huff.

★ ★ ★ ★ ★ ★ ★ ★ ★ ★

Once the *Nuestra Señora* was safely docked at Vlissingen the ponderous, creaking wheels of naval administration began to turn with unwonted speed. The frigate's crew held in the town gaol were questioned by the Zeeland Admiralty's fiscal advocate sent from Middelburg. Those who wished to continue in the Spanish service were loaded aboard a schuit and taken across the Scheldt to Breskens, then to the town of Aardenburg, where they were exchanged for Dutch prisoners under flag of truce. As for the eighty or so Genoese soldiers, after some negotiation between the advocate and their lieutenant they consented to enter the service of the States-General on land at a monthly wage equivalent to that which the King of Spain had paid them – which they were only too happy to do, they said, since sea service had turned out to be tedious with bad food and cramped lodgings and a vainglorious fool to lead them, and had likewise offered precious few opportunities for the plunder that led men to enlist as soldiers.

So in the end only seven prisoners were left: sorry fellows – mostly Flemings – whom several witnesses remembered having been taken prisoner already, at the end of 1624 when a Spanish ship was blown ashore near Westkapelle, and who had been exchanged under cartel on condition of their swearing not to fight against the Dutch Republic for a year and a day afterwards. The matter was investigated, and in the end six of them were hanged for oath-breaking in front of a jeering crowd on the greensward by the entrance to Vlissingen harbour. The whole of society ran

---

* "It was not the Dutch that were brave but the Swiss."

on a man's word being his bond, and if oaths could be broken with impunity then all right-thinking folk agreed that civilisation would collapse.

The object of the Zeeland Admiralty's interest, however, was not the *Nuestra Señora's* crew but the vessel herself. And word soon spread beyond the province of Zeeland, because the very next day the ornate little statenjachts of the Maze and Holland Admiralties appeared in Vlissingen harbour bearing high-ranking officials and master shipwrights to inspect this precious capture. The officials were conducted around the vessel, its decks still spattered with dried blood, while the shipwrights scrambled about in the hold measuring and taking notes. Then the next day a still more splendid statenjacht arrived amid a great pomp of trumpets, drums and salutes fired from the harbourmouth forts. It was Anthonis Duyck, Grand Pensionary of the United Provinces, the Republic's highest salaried official, accompanied by the Maze vice-admiral Jasper Liefhebber. They were shown around the *Nuestra Señora* and were suitably impressed.

"The trouble, Your Excellency," Liefhebber explained, "is that the vessels of our own fleet cannot compare with such ships as this either in speed or in handiness."

"Why should this be so, admiral? You will appreciate that I am a jurist by training and not a sailor."

"Our ships, Your Excellency, are cargo vessels which we charter from their owners as needed and then convert into warships. They are seaworthy enough; but they sail clumsily to windward and are slow running before the wind, and are in no way to be compared with vessels such as this, which have been designed for fighting and for no other purpose. To set one of our vessels in pursuit of one such as this is like a cow giving chase to a hare."

"So how come one of our lumbering Dutch cows took this Spanish hare?"

"Speaking with Captain Loodgieter, Your Excellency, I think that it was rather by guile and good luck, and the chance that our ship happened to be transporting a company of Swiss musketeers who quite overwhelmed the Spanish crew with their fire once they were foolish enough to try boarding. He freely confessed that if the Spanish captain had stood off and used his guns then it might have gone very badly with them indeed."

"What do you conclude from this, then, admiral?"

"I conclude, Your Excellency, that if we wish to have the upper hand over the Spaniard on the sea – which is our republic's life-blood and its only sustenance – then we must build vessels such as this one. To which end I would respectfully suggest that Their Excellencies the States-General purchase this ship as quickly as possible from the Admiralty of Zeeland, whose property she now is, tow her to Amsterdam and carefully take her to pieces so that shipwrights may measure all her timbers and make drawings of them, then copy those drawings and notes and publish them to each of our five admiralties with an instruction that they build as close copies of the vessel as they can. For if we wait for fashion among shipwrights to change as it does now, from father to son, then I fear that our grandchildren will all be mumbling Hail Marys in Spanish."

The result was that the *Nuestra Señora* was judged lawful prize the very next day and put up for auction the following week with the States-General the only bidder, paying an inflated price of fifteen thousand guilders in order to forestall an attempt by the Zeelanders to retain the vessel for their own fleet. And the prize having been sold, the prize money had to be distributed according to the customary rules: that is to say, one third to the admiralty and the remaining two thirds to be divided into three-hundredth parts, with each member of the *Eenhoorn's* crew receiving the number of such parts specified in his articles of engagement. Loodgieter would receive twelve parts; the mate eight, Meester Grobelaar six, the surgeon four and Frans himself one, which at thirty-three guilders was equivalent to two months' wages. So all things considered the *Eenhoorn's* crew had reason to be well pleased with their captain at the end of this adventure: a rich prize taken at minimal cost in blood (since only two of the *Eenhoorn's* men had been killed in the action and three hurt, none of them seriously), and a considerable sum due to them when the ship paid off.

And in addition to the pecuniary benefit there was the glory, several three-hundredths of which might rub off on the lowliest lamp trimmer or cook's mate. Loodgieter was invited to Middelburg where the admiralty and the thankful ship owners of Zeeland presented him with a handsome gold medal on a silver-gilt chain, while the States-General voted him a commemorative sword. And within the week a pamphlet went on sale relating *The Memorable and Heroic Action Lately Taken Place off the Shores of Walcheren in Which the Zeeland Pinnace 'Eenhoorn' of Captain Cornelis Adriaenszoon Loodgieter Took the Spanish Royal Frigate 'Nuestra Señora de las Vírgenes' and Brought Her Captive into Vlissingen*, adorned with a fine copper-plate engraving of Captain Loodgieter wearing a somewhat incongruous laurel wreath and holding a trident, being drawn across the waves in a nautilus-shell chariot pulled by seahorses and surrounded by ample-bosomed tritons blowing on conch shells with garlands of seaweed entwined in their hair.

Yet within a few days a discordant note was audible amid all this trumpeting and loud jubilation. Captain Krauschli's Swiss, who had lost five men in the action and as many again wounded, were now lodged in Vlissingen waiting for transport onwards to Bergen op Zoom. And their disgruntlement was great when it was explained to them by the fiscal advocate that although they had done most of the fighting to capture the *Nuestra Señora*, they would have no part in the subsequent distribution of the spoils since the prize court's terms of reference clearly named "the crew" as beneficiaries and not any passengers who might have been aboard at the time. The soldiers, after all, had engaged to fight the enemy on behalf of the States-General; an enemy had presented himself; they had duly fought him; and they had therefore fulfilled their terms of contract and should be content with their agreed daily wage. Like (the advocate added, heaping insult upon injury) the labourers in the vineyard in Saint Matthew's

Gospel Chapter XX, verses 1 to 16, which parable plainly showed Our Lord's high and eminently Dutch regard for the sanctity of contract above mere equity and natural justice. This reasonable conclusion – perfectly self-evident to any properly trained Dutch jurist – quite failed to satisfy the gallant Swiss captain when it was presented to him; in fact it threw him into a rage worthy of Achilles himself in which he swore and fulminated in both French and High German throughout all the taverns of Vlissingen that his brave fellows had been shamefully cozened by these pusillanimous Dutch cheese maggots into doing their fighting for them, then defrauded afterwards of their just reward by a collection of quill-scratching Hollander lawyers who would not know a soldier's honour from an old woman's petticoat. And furthermore that Captain Cornelis Adriaenszoon Loodgieter in particular was a perfidious hound and a base deceitful fellow who had artfully contrived the encounter with the Spaniard knowing that it was other men who would do the fighting and not his own worthless crew, for was it not Krauschli's own valorous musketeers who had boarded the enemy vessel, with the Dutchmen following them only when it was safe to do so?

Which contumelious words could not but eventually come to the ears of Captain Cornelis Adriaenszoon Loodgieter. The result was a confrontation in the Market Place in which Captain Krauschli made his accusation to the face of Captain Loodgieter before a hundred or so witnesses, then arranged to meet with him early next morning on the grassy sward by the harbour gate, not far from the town gibbet where the gulls now flapped and screeched over the dangling bodies of the recently hanged oath breakers.

Despite the early hour the whole of Vlissingen turned out to watch the duel, perched on the town walls and the housetops by the harbourmouth as though a brigand chief or some notable person was to be executed. The two duellists appeared, removed their doublets and saluted one another curtly; Krauschli with his basket-hilted military sword and Loodgieter with his somewhat shorter sailor's "degen" which he had elected to keep despite the captain's chivalrous offer to send for a longer weapon. They crossed swords, circling one another cautiously at first and making a few feigned passes. Then Krauschli lunged suddenly like a striking adder, and though Loodgieter managed to step aside the soldier's blade grazed his left arm above the elbow, causing a sudden spreading dark patch on his white linen shirt. Loodgieter grunted, but waved aside all offers of bandaging and returned to the attack.

And so they continued for fifteen minutes or more with the crowd cheering every thrust and parry, the combatants equal in skill so that it might well have continued thus all day until both were exhausted. The words uttered (all men agreed) had been too insulting for there to be any thought of declaring a draw once blood had been shed, and one or other of them must necessarily die. Then at last, stepping backwards to avoid a sudden thrust, Krauschli caught his heel on a molehill and lost his poise for a moment. The Dutch captain's blade darted forward and, though it missed Krauschli's windpipe, cut a finger's depth into his throat below his left ear, severing the jugular vein. Spuming blood and with his hand pressed to his throat, the captain fought on valiantly for another half-minute or so, until he stumbled and fell to his knees, then slumped over on the grass. Loodgieter was upon him at once and could have despatched him there and then – but instead dropped his sword and knelt to raise the Swiss captain up, calling for a surgeon. Willenbrouckx came running over and tried to apply a compress to staunch the bleeding. But it was too late. The captain looked up at them with his glaucous pale blue eyes, seeing them all but far off and vaguely now as he drifted away towards the land whence no man ever returns. He tried to say something, then died as the previously roaring crowd fell silent at the pity of the spectacle.

Loodgieter stood up, panting from his exertions and in tears. "Poor fellow," he said at last, "poor silly fellow. I've killed not a few men in my time, but never one as fair and as gallant as this. God grant him rest." The captain's body with a wreath of bay leaves on its head was placed on a richly decorated bier and carried in state to the Jacobskerk where it lay on public view for two days with the whole of Vlissingen filing past to honour it, before being buried in a tomb beneath a marble tablet paid for by Loodgieter himself with Latin verses singing the dead man's valour and accomplishments. Even in an age when all men held their lives cheap but their honour dear, the affair of the Swiss captain was remembered and held up to successive generations of Zeelanders as an example of how a man should comport himself. Until, in the course of time, long after both were turned to dust, Loodgieter and Krauschli became in local legend two bosom friends compelled by a careless word to fight until both of them lay dead.

As for the rest of the Swiss, they were left in an even more bilious humour than before, their captain not just dead but slain by the hand of a mere sailor, which for a soldier is as humiliating an end as can be imagined. After smashing up several of the town's taverns that evening, much heated by drink, they marched down to the foreshore and cut loose a number of fishing boats to row themselves across the Scheldt in the moonlight to land near Breskens. Once ashore they marched south to the village of Sintjanspolder, which they plundered most meticulously in lieu of back pay and prize money, then crossed the lines to the Spanish side under flag of truce to offer their services to King Philip, who, though a papist idolater and a sworn enemy of God and His holy elect people, might at least be a more honest employer than the States-General of the Seven United Provinces.

★ ★ ★ ★ ★ ★ ★ ★ ★ ★

We lay three weeks at Vlissingen while the lawyers of the admiralty court wrangled about our prize and the amount of money that we would be paid for it; which sum, being decided at last, occasioned Meester Grobelaar and myself no small clacking of abacus beads to calculate the amount of it due to each man, and likewise a considerable expenditure of ink and goose quills entering those sums into the ship's account ledger and writing out the promissory notes which would (we were assured) miraculously transubstantiate themselves from paper into silver coin when presented at the admiralty's pay office in Middelburg. For himself though, Meester Grobelaar privately confessed to being mighty doubtful concerning this last point, seeing the great difficulty and slowness of obtaining payment from Their Lordships for even the most lawful and urgent of our expenditures, which he swore was like drawing teeth from a crocodile.

But all this to-do fell somewhat into abeyance as June turned into July. Spinola had not in the end moved against either Bergen or Geetruidenberg after Breda had fallen to him, since according to our intelligence his pay-chest was empty and his men mutinous for want of the money that had been promised him by Madrid but never sent. The imminent peril to Bergen having therefore passed – and the States-General, moreover, being as short of funds as Spinola was – there was no urgency any more to send soldiers and munitions to Bergen, which had quite enough of both for any likely contingency, but rather to dispatch them to the borders of Germany where the fortress of Grol* was now menaced by the Spaniard. As for ourselves, Their Lordships had decided that we should spend the rest of the season with Vice-Admiral Hollaer's blockading squadron off Dunkirk, where three Zeeland ships already cruised with five from Amsterdam and four from the Maze to hinder that town's privateer ships from breaking out and vexing the Republic's commerce and fisheries. This news was greeted with a groan by all aboard who had any experience of blockading work, for it was (they swore) a tedious and unprofitable duty in the extreme: cruising off a lee shore battered by wind and waves, with our anchors liable to drag because of the poor holding and ourselves, if we escaped drowning and got ashore, likely to be summarily hanged by the Dunkirkers as repayment for all their

---

* Groenlo

fellows we had thrown overboard as pirates.

We discovered that blockading was indeed most wearisome work, once we had arrived off Dunkirk at the beginning of July. So great was the hurt that the Dunkirk privateers had done us at sea since the truce ended that Their Excellencies the States-General and the Amsterdam merchants considered it well worth keeping a good half of the Republic's fleet lying off that harbour month in, month out in an endeavour to prevent their ships from putting to sea. But it was from the very start a most futile undertaking (as anyone will readily comprehend who knows anything of that Flanders shore) and altogether like trying to imprison coneys in their warren by sitting in front of it and uttering threats against them. Well nigh impregnable from the landward side by reason of its marshes and the numerous forts the Spaniards had placed among them, Dunkirk town was likewise admirably defended on its seaward aspect both by artifice and by nature. The waters thereabouts are shallow, and great sandbanks extend parallel to the shore for some two miles each side of the harbour-mouth, so that a vessel of even as modest a draught as our own would have been mighty ill-advised to try crossing them except at the very top of the spring tides. The harbour entrance had been extended by the Spaniards a half-mile out to sea with wooden groynes, to prevent the sands from blocking it, and puissant batteries of cannon had been mounted on top of these structures to hold us in respect. But since Don Ambrogio Spinola had become governor in Flanders, even those formidable obstacles had been further strengthened by that most able and vigorous of generals. In particular, the approaches to the harbourmouth had lately been made a hundred times more hazardous by an ingenious work devised (we were told) by the Italian engineer Pompeio Targone who later directed the siege works at La Rochelle. The principal channel of the approach, called the Scheurtje, runs parallel to the shore from westward near Gravelines, passing the fort of Mardyck among the dunes, and is flanked to seaward by a long sandbank, the Braek, which is nearly dry at low tide and which has insufficient water above it even at high tide for any large ship to pass across it. And to cover this channel more effectively, there had been raised some two years before a most singular edifice called the "Houten Wambuis".* Since no stone fort could be built upon the shifting sands, Signor Targone had had great piles of elm wood driven down into the seabed and a massive fort then constructed entirely of timber on top of them, its double oaken walls each thicker than those of the stoutest man-of-war and with shingle packed in between them to deaden cannon-shot. On top of this structure he then placed twenty or so cannon of the heaviest weight, and all around it wooden posts were driven into the sand to arrest any fireship that we might send drifting down upon the fort in an endeavour to set it ablaze. The artfulness of his conception was that the Braek hindered our ships from getting close enough to pummel the Houten Wambuis with their broadsides; yet if they approached it along the Scheurtje channel they must do so in keel-water line, with the leading vessel exposed to the full fury of the fort's cannon while unable to reply itself, so that it would infallibly be smashed to toothpicks long before it could bring its guns to bear. Meester Grobelaar (who fancied himself expert in these matters, having served under Prince Maurits on land in his youth) summed it all up most justly as we surveyed that formidable redoubt from a distance on our first morning lying off Dunkirk: "We cannot take their confounded fort unless we first get ashore. And likewise we cannot get ashore unless we first take their confounded fort."

So all that summer long (which seemed to us more like eight whole years than as many weeks) we must content ourselves with impotently cruising to and fro off Dunkirk town, its bastions and the great belfry and Saint Eloi's Church so close that we fancied we might reach out and touch them, and also people walking among the dunes to look at us, and the sentries pacing on the ramparts of the forts; yet all of this as distant and unattainable to

---

* "The Wooden Doublet"

us as a bullfinch in a cage hanging from the kitchen ceiling is to a cat licking its chops on the table below it. We saw ships depart and ships enter; those that returned often bringing Dutch prizes in with them. Sometimes we would see the masts of twenty or thirty vessels together lying in Dunkirk harbour, their number seeming to grow and diminish without the smallest regard to anything that we might do about it. Yet we had no means to hurt them, since the Dunkirk vessels were shallower than ours and handier to windward, and likewise the Dunkirkers themselves no mean seafarers, with much better knowledge than our own concerning the lie of the sandbanks and channels around their port, which moved and shifted all the time as though they were alive. Their privateer frigates would set sail as bold as you please in broad daylight, and our admiral would detach a couple of ships in pursuit. But by the time our vessels had reached the end of the Zuydcoote Pass where they could safely cross the banks and close with their quarry, the Dunkirker would be well ahead of them and out into the open sea beyond the banks, whereafter he might go whithersoever in the world he pleased. Every now and then, at the top of a spring tide, one of our ships might venture in across the sandbanks close enough for their forts to fire at them, and they fire a few shots back; but all of this more from bravado than from any hope of harming them. Most of the time we merely cruised to and fro and ate up our stores, and hoped that if our presence did not entirely prevent the depredations of the Dunkirkers (which only occupying the place and blowing it up with gunpowder could do for certain) then at least it diminished the hurt that the Republic's commerce might otherwise suffer from those injurious rascals.

It was a most tedious service, and very unpopular with the more ambitious of our captains since it offered great labour and no small peril, but precious little prospect either of action or of prize money, the Dunkirkers being concerned to give us the slip and avoid battle with us. Though we might rail against them as cowards and lackeys who refused to fight with us, and sometimes send bottles drifting ashore with opprobrious messages to that effect, they merely laughed in our faces; for they knew only too well that the Republic's lifeblood was its trade; that the more East India ships or herring busses they took the thinner Holland's purse would be, and the States-General less able to hire the soldiers it required to fight the Spaniard on land. We all of us laugh at that honourable hidalgo Don Quixote charging at his windmills. Yet if they had been Dutch windmills and not Castilian ones that he levelled his lance against then there might have been some method in his madness withal; for if the busy windmills of Holland were ever to stop turning then the whole country would drown or go bankrupt within the month. Yet while we could do little harm to the Dunkirkers, the Dunkirkers could still reach out and tweak our noses whenever it pleased them. They had numerous small rowing galleys which were shallow enough to cross the sandbanks, and these would often sally forth at night to try and cut out one of our vessels. From the very first night we lay off that port our captain posted a strong deck guard of soldiers with muskets and gave order that the crew's weapons were always to be stacked ready to hand in case the villains tried boarding us.

Like ourselves, the Dunkirkers and their Spanish masters no doubt grew melancholic from kicking their heels all the length of the summer days, impotently staring at us out on the sea beyond the reach of their cannon, as impotently as we stared back at them. So from time to time – to lift their spirits I suppose – they would essay some notable mischief against us. As soon as our ship joined the squadron we were warned to have hoses rigged to the pump and keep the fire buckets ready at night in case the perfidious dogs sent fireships to drift upon us, which they had attempted several times already and indeed set one vessel ablaze though her crew managed to put out the flames. But fireships, though most fearsome to behold, are very visible withal, and if a ship has sea room enough to manoeuvre she may easily evade them. And we would soon discover that our enemies had more subtle engines of malice at their disposal.

One night late in July we lay at anchor about two miles off the harbourmouth. There were five of our vessels there that night, the Holland ships having gone down-Channel to the Dover Straits to escort the great annual return fleet of East Indiamen bound from Java for Texel. As for the rest of us, we had been commanded to lie moored in a half-circle between bow and stern anchors with our guns loaded and facing the town, since our admiral had received intelligence that nine or ten of the enemy might break out that night when there was no moon and a spring tide, and likewise a light breeze from the east which would carry them across the sandbanks. Since we lay at anchor the crew were permitted to sleep, except for the watch on deck. All was still as we lay there moored between the *Halve Maen* of Medemblik ahead of us and the *Fortuijn* of Vlaardingen astern. My stepfather and I slumbered in our tiny cabin, he in the hammock above and myself on a straw mattress laid on top of the two chests. Then all of a sudden, midway through the hondewacht about two in the morning, there was a most violent detonation which blew in the tiny window of our cabin and threw him clean out of his hammock to land on top of me. All was commotion as our men seized their weapons and scrambled to their appointed stations, thinking we would be boarded. But when my stepfather and I came up on deck all was calm again; naught at all to see but a great cloud of smoke astern of us rising into the night sky to obscure the stars, and the windows of the great cabin blown in, and the *Fortuijn* drifting broadside to us held by her stern anchor with her bowsprit blown away and most of her beakhead along with it. Next morning we helped them fish for their lost anchor (which would otherwise have been chargeable to them), and when we had grappled up the end of the cable, saw that it was all burned and with a curious hook hanging from it made of iron wires twisted together.

No one could venture any explanation of this mighty thunderclap in the dark, until a few days later a Spanish soldier was snatched by one of our boats from the sands near Mardyck where he was out fishing for shrimps at low tide. He told us that his comrades, vexed beyond measure by watching us day after day, had filled an old boat with two or three hundred pounds of gunpowder and then fixed around it wooden arms bearing wire grapples connected by strings to the lock of a pistol, so that if any of the grapples tangled against some object the tug at the cord would snap the hammer and send sparks flying into the powder. They had painted their boat black to be invisible in the darkness, and stepped in its bows a mast and a square sail made likewise of black stuff, then set it to drift towards us, where this devilish engine would infallibly have sunk the *Fortuijn* had it not chanced to snag against her anchor cable instead. Thereafter order was given that our ships must not lie at anchor but instead traipse to and fro day and night in all weathers like melancholics in a madhouse, which was vexing and also very fatiguing for the sailors since our ship was too small to have three watches such as the greater Dutch vessels have nowadays, but only two, so that watch-on, watch-off every four hours was the rule: the Prinsenkwartier then the Graf Mauritskwartier then the Prinsenkwartier again *usque ad consummationem sæculi amen**.

There was little enough to do apart from handling the ship, which was no very great labour in the light summer airs, and the quotidian works aboard such as caulking the deck seams (the planks shrinking greatly in the dry weather), painting and sail-patching and similar tasks. And less even than that for us two medical men, given that our ship's folk were well enough nourished from sailing close to home, so that there was no scurvy among them or any other of the distempers attendant upon long voyages, while the summer warmth likewise disfavoured the rheumatisms and lung inflammations that mariners are subject to in winter from being constantly wet. I clipped hair and shaved chins as requested, but otherwise spent most of my days with Meester Grobelaar attending to the ship's accounts since we were soon due a visit from the admiralty's auditors to inspect our ledgers and, if there were a discrepancy of two or three stuivers (he said), then

---

* Even unto the end of the world amen

we might depend upon it those dogs would sniff it out and apply the thumbscrews to him to discover what was become of them.

As for my stepfather – "Vader Willenbrouckx" as the crew called him out of respect for his venerable age – though he stood at the foot of the mainmast with the medicine chest at four bells after evening prayers and called out "Kreupelen zieken en blinden, kom laat ghij verbinden!"* as prescribed by regulation and immemorial custom, there were few that required his services: some boils to be lanced and sores to be plastered, and sometimes a wood splinter to be extracted or a cut to be sewn up where one of our soldiers had hacked another while exercising with their swords. But otherwise little to speak of, and each day exactly like the next and the one before it; only Sundays to mark the passing of the weeks, when the blockade squadron's chaplain would come aboard to celebrate divine service and offer communion; which we were discretely permitted to refuse, being of the Catholic persuasion, though we had to attend service for propriety's sake and roar out the Genevan psalms like everyone else, and my stepfather likewise read the lesson by reason of his age and superior education.

The life that I must perforce lead aboard ship was very strange and unfamiliar to me at first, its customs and mores as outlandish as those of any savage tribe in any remote land of this Earth whatsoever and the mariners, by reason of their being cut off most of the time from land, like men half divorced from the rest of the human race, so that it was no wonder at all to me when I later read that the old Greeks were in some uncertainty whether to number them among the living or the dead. I was fortunate that I was a vrijslaaper, not required to stand watches, and worked instead only from dawn until nightfall, then might sleep undisturbed except for the constant clumping and banging of gear and men's feet on deck, the melancholy bell clanging out every half-hour as the sand-glass was turned by the binnacle, and the trill-

---

* "Cripples, sick and blind, come to be bound up!"

ing pipe of the bo'sun. But even so, my manner of life was very singular: my bedchamber narrow as a coffin and my bed a sack filled with straw; my toilette each morning a sluice-down in a pail of sea-water, without benefit of soap since I soon discovered that the soapballs I had brought with me turned to a sticky paste in salt water. Washing my linen was as great a trouble to me as washing my person, because soap would no more wash clothing in salt water than it would skin, and the best that could be contrived was for us to trample our filthy shirts in a tub full of old urine to dissolve the greasy dirt, then rinse them out in seawater and leave the sun to bleach them. But there: as the Latin poet observes, "*Ubi omnes foetent, nemo odet*"*, so I resolved to lay my nose aside for as long as we were at sea.

As for my daily board, it was most literally that: a pine plank suspended by ropes from the deck-beams with a great wooden bowl to eat from, dipping my spoon into it in competition with six others, and a pewter flap-can of one quart's capacity as my drinking cup. I must confess here that although I am (I hope) no lady's lap-dog as regards my victuals and have often fared much worse, my diet was at first very gross and monotonous to one accustomed to more delicate meats at home; though I dare say at the same time agreeable enough to my messmates, who were used to no better fare ashore, and that commonly with less regularity and in far smaller quantity. We were fortunate aboard the *Eenhoorn* that our skipper did not feed us badly. The custom aboard our Dutch ships was that the admiralty paid the skipper a "kostgeld" or provender money of twelve stuivers per man *per diem*, and from this sum he was required to purchase victuals and drink for them for three months at a time; so there was great temptation for a captain to line his own pocket by scraping the bellies of his men. Our Captain Loodgieter knew though that ill-fed sailors will not fight willingly – indeed may not be able to fight at all if the food be nasty or meagre enough – and so took care that our provi-

---

* "Where all stink, no man smells" (Source unknown).

sions were of good quality and likewise supplied according to the victualling scales ordained by the Zeeland Admiralty, so that if we scarcely feasted like old Lucullus neither did we go hungry.

But even so it was mighty hard for me at first to accustom my stomach to so coarse and unvarying a diet. Our breakfast, at eight bells of the morning watch, was oatmeal groats with some prunes mixed in it and then bacon fat poured overall. Our dinner at midday was every day, for each mess of seven men, one wooden pail of brown beans or the grey chickpeas that we call kapucijners; to which was added on Mondays, Tuesdays, Wednesdays, Fridays and Saturdays a half-pound per man of boiled stockfish with a sauce made with mustard, butter, flour and vinegar (since to eat boiled stockfish without a sauce would be like chewing and swallowing a deal board) and on Thursdays and Sundays a half-pound of bacon instead. Our supper was ship's biscuit; of which one pound per man each day, and beer; of which one gallon per man per day for as long as stocks lasted. And in addition to the above, each mess to receive every calendar month a firkin of butter; and for each man besides on the first day of every month a sweet-milk cheese of four pounds' weight, though this was usually gone by the end of the first week.

While my stepfather dined with the captain and the other officers in the great cabin, I was part of a mess of seven with the carpenter's mate, the other ziekentrooster, the bottelier's assistant, the captain's servant Suleiman the Moor, the drummer-boy and of course Matthias Sigurdsson the trumpeter. Every mess aboard either adopted a name or had one bestowed upon it, such as "de Remonstranten" or "de Zeeadvocaaten". And ours being the youngest, we were christened "de Snotapen".* So we sat at our table slung from the deck beams and ate our pea soup with lumps of boiled bacon, or our brown beans with stockfish, and talked of this and that. Our sailors were for the most part uneducated, simple fellows who could barely write their own names; as well

---

* "The Snot-Apes"

they might be, since they had been put to work by their parents as soon as they could walk and had been sent or run away to sea almost as soon as they were into breeches. But Siggurdsson was cut from different stuff, and though he was a taciturn and suspicious fellow we two soon recognised one another as young men of education and discernment with preoccupations in the world other than beer, harlots and playing at dice.

He was a year or so older than myself and was (I learned) the son of a Lutheran village pastor from a place called Kinsarvik on Hardanger Fjord northwards of Bergen, which long inlet of the sea was where most of our other Norwegians came from. Though he was plainly of good upbringing and education, his knowledge of the Latin authors being as extensive as my own, there was about him a strange wild quality, as though he was a child of elves or a wolf that had entered the body of a man. Nor could I ever induce him to say other than in the most general terms what had driven him to sea, he talking always of "we" in this matter (meaning him and his fellow countrymen) rather than "I". "All of us are fisherfolk," he would say, "so we know boats and ships well. But many now in our villages are hungry every year: the winters colder than ever and the summers shorter so that the corn never ripens and men must make bread from the bark of birch trees. Every summer the isbreen" (by which he meant those prodigious rivers of ice in their mountain valleys) "come down lower and swallow up farms. So we must earn our bread on the sea or starve like so many dogs. For there are villages in the mountains around the fjord where folk have been driven by hunger to turn cannibals, and now waylay travellers to kill and eat them." And these discourses of his about his native country would fairly freeze my blood with the terror of its dark lowering mountains of granite and its everlasting fields of ice, and its gloomy silent forests haunted by all manner of monsters and malignant sprites which they call trolls. Which imaginings were well borne out years later when I had cause to go there myself in the King of Denmark's service, and wondered greatly that men should ever have chosen to dwell in such a terrible wilderness rather than abandon it to the wolves and the bears. Yet Siggurdsson was often a jolly, whimsical fellow as well, despite his crippled foot, and a most capable musician, so that when we and Suleiman were called upon to play for our captain's guests as they dined in the great cabin he always took the lead and we two followed him.

Suleiman the Moor was likewise a puzzle to me. He was aboard one of the Salee rover galleys that Loodgieter had boarded off Gibraltar after they had taken the Neapolitan ships, and though the Moors that survived had afterwards been summarily knocked on the head and tossed overboard as is the custom, our captain took pity on the boy because he was such a handsome child, and made him his own servant. Suleiman could by now speak Dutch pretty well and served as our captain's special cook when we had guests aboard – which was very often, for Captain Loodgieter loved society and would send out invitations indiscriminately to any vessel that lay near us. Among those who knew him these dinners of his were mighty popular, because instead of the usual sea-fare of salt flesh and dull boiled puddings he would serve all manner of fragrant dishes confected by Suleiman over a charcoal brazier in the steward's pantry after the manner of the Moors: messes of rice with herbs and spices and strange seasonings held in little tin boxes. As for Suleiman himself, though he was a merry rogue and full of knavery, yet it made me scratch my head a little to observe the relish with which he devoured his half-pound of bacon on Thursdays and Sundays and downed his daily gallon of beer, since my stepfather (who had once been in Tangier during his Spanish service) told me that the Mahometans abhor swine's flesh and strong drink and would cheerfully suffer death rather than partake of either. When I quizzed Suleiman about this he laughed and showed his fine white teeth, saying that Jesus and Mahomet were alike a pair of cozening rascals, and for his part he was glad to live now in Holland where men cared little for the one and nothing at all for the other.

Siggurdsson was the one man aboard (apart from my stepfather and the captain) who did not scoff at the means by which I beguiled my idle hours, which were wearisomely many despite all my various duties aboard. For I very soon grew curious concerning the fishes that swam below us among the Flanders sandbanks. Our Norwegians were great fishermen, that having been the trade of most of them before they entered the Republic's service, and were much more adept at fishing with a hook than our Dutchmen, who were accustomed rather to taking flatfish with nets in the shallows, or eels and salmon with traps in the rivers. They trailed their lines overboard day and night (since different sorts of fish are to be taken in daylight and in darkness) and thus enlightened me as well as varying their own diet, since I soon persuaded them to give me first sight of their catch and also to instruct me in what they knew of each particular fish and its habits; likewise to sell me for a stuiver or two any unfamiliar fish they had taken so that I might cut it up and make drawings of it in my notebook. Some I knew pretty well already, such as cod and ling and whiting and haddock, as well as the small flatfish like plaice and sole and flounder which are commonly to be seen in fish markets: also the great flat-fishes like the skate and the ray which they took from time to time. But others there were that were most outlandish in their appearance, all spines and fins and goggle eyes and strange colours, and many of them with venomous barbs withal so that I must be wary how I handled them. Likewise there was the dogfish or hondshaai, which I concluded after dissecting one must be kindred of the skate from the configuration of its mouth and the nature of its bones, which were of gristle rather than hard chalky matter. I made this observation to Sigurdsson as he stood over me at my table, since he took an interest in all this; unlike my other shipmates who scoffed and said that there were only two kinds of fish: those that were good for eating, and those that were not. I pointed out to him the resemblances between the dogfish and the skate, both of which I had laid out before me, and said that it was as if, rather than Almighty God having created both dogfish and skates on the fifth day and they having remained thus unchanged for five or six thousand years since, they might both have started out as the same kind of fish and the one become flat or the other round-bodied over the course of time according to their mode of life, since our Norwegians informed me that the one might be taken with hooks dangled in mid-water but the other only on the sea-bottom, where to have a flat body for hiding beneath sand might be a considerable advantage. Sigurdsson grew grave at this and told me to avoid such follies; or, if I entertained them, at least to hold my tongue about them, since it was speculations of that kind which had obliged him to come seeking his bread upon the waters rather than casting it there as Our Lord instructs us.

Throughout the weeks we lay off Dunkirk we were cut off from the rest of mankind as effectively as Saint Simon on his pillar in the Egyptian desert. But from time to time some communication would reach us when the provisioning vessel came from Middelburg to replenish us and brought papers for our captain. Among this correspondence at the end of August was a letter addressed to my stepfather at the tavern in Bergen op Zoom. It was from Doctor de Brantôme, and had taken eleven or twelve weeks to reach us. In it he wrote that like ourselves he had been in some tribulation of late and was now (but temporarily, he hoped) lodged in another kingdom. He said that it was all because of his associate the physician Doctor Remington of Dunmow; the man who was a protégé of the Duke of Buckingham's. When old King James fell ill of an ague at Theobalds House in March, Buckingham had Doctor Remington come there and examine him, telling the King that he himself had taken much benefit from the doctor's ministrations. In particular, a certain emplastre of Remington's devising was applied to His Majesty by the Duke himself, who chased the King's own physicians out of the room before he did it. And soon afterwards the King's illness grew much worse and he sank into the palsy from which he died a week later. Though the plaster could not be found afterwards, it was soon whispered that it must have contained arsenic or some such insidious poison, and that Buckingham had applied it to rid himself of the old king and put

Prince Charles on the throne, and have at last his war with Spain which King James had always set his face against. These murmurings had grown when Parliament met, De Brantôme said, and before long it was being urged by the honourable members – Buckingham himself being at present too great a stag for the hounds to drag down – that Doctor Remington and his associates should be arrested and taken to the Tower to discover what they knew of the matter. And while stretching a free-born Englishman on the rack without a warrant to do so from the Privy Council might (he wrote) occasion some quibbling among the lawyers, no such scruples would apply to a prating French mountebank such as himself. So to cut matters short, he had thought it politic to discover pressing business that must be attended to in France, and was now lodged in the town of Boulogne waiting on events. He hoped that by the autumn the plague would have abated and Parliament forgotten about the matter, and that we might all be able to return quietly to England and resume our practice. But for the time being, like ourselves, he must sit where he was and kick his heels till Sirius the dog star no longer ruled the heavens and summer was at an end.

CHAPTER NINE

Even though he must dip into his own pocket to pay for it, Cornelis Adriaenszoon Loodgieter liked to keep high state aboard his vessel, regarding it as an eminently worthwhile investment in his career as a sea officer of the Dutch Republic to build up his credit and acquaintance and keep himself au courant with events in the great wide world outside the Dunkirk blockade squadron. So whenever a ship dropped anchor near by to repair a broken mast or staunch a leak he would send across a note presenting his compliments and inviting her skipper to dine with him that evening. Some were Dutch men-of-war arriving amid a great flutter of bunting and cannon salutes, or straggling East India ships on the last leg of their weary seven- or eight-month voyage home from Batavia and detained in the Dover Straits by contrary winds. But most were Danes or Hamburgers or Swedes, who as neutrals had little to fear from the Dunkirk privateers. One such was a French vessel of three or four hundred tons bound from Nantes to Copenhagen with a cargo of wine and captained by a Huguenot from La Rochelle, a client of the Duke of Soubise currently in rebellion against the French King, and therefore with a most lively and personal concern to make friends with his Dutch fellow Calvinists.

They dined pleasantly in the great cabin, the windows open to the evening breeze, as Frans and his fellow musicians played sweet airs for them.

"Of course, my dear captain," the Frenchman said as he took another slice of plum tart (made with fresh plums generously sent over by himself earlier in the day), "things cannot continue thus for ever."

"Forgive me, monsieur, but to us here off Dunkirk it often seems that things *will* continue like this for ever, and that perhaps time itself has stopped like a broken clock. Even the weather seems in abeyance of late: September already, and still neither a cloud in the sky nor the merest puff of a west wind. This cursed easterly blows off the land day after day and keeps us on our guard at all hours against the Dunkirkers drifting fireships towards us, or coming out and boarding us."

"Indeed. And likewise the conjunction of the planets breeds pestilence. I heard at Dover that the plague still rages in London and that King Charles and his Parliament remain at Oxford, which greatly impedes the conduct of business and delays the whole war with Spain."

"Excuse me monsieur, but what do you mean, 'delays the war with Spain'? There *is* war with Spain already, which is why we are here."

"I meant, that there will soon be war between Spain and England also. Young King Charles and Milord Buckingham" (he pronounced it "Bouquinquant") "both yearn for a war to prove themselves great captains, and likewise the gentlemen in Parliament rail against the King Philip and the Pope and the Jesuits as they did when they were young fellows in Queen Elizabeth's day, though they are now toothless old pantaloons who can barely retain their water, and there have been two further King Philips since the one they have in mind. They plainly believe that a war with Spain will restore the youthful heat to their palsied rheumaticky old limbs as Abishag the Shunamite did to King David's. So all things drive towards it. An army is already assembled at Plymouth and ships have been chartered for the venture. But King Charles still dithers like an old woman considering the purchase of a penny ribbon at a haberdasher's stall: sometimes yes and sometimes no. I spoke lately with their Captain Pennington at Le Havre, who was sent there with two of the King's ships to serve King Louis against my master Soubise. And he was fairly distracted by the want of consistency in his orders: sometimes to proceed against Soubise, sometimes to come home again, and at others to hand his vessels over to the King of France. He confided to me that he could make neither head nor tail of what it is that His Majesty wishes him to do, and is half-minded to resign his commission and return home."

"So how might all this affect us here, monsieur? No more than a hailstorm in Hungary, I would think."

"I would not be so sure of that, my dear Loodgieter. If the English enter the war on the side of the Dutch Republic – as soon they must, let King Charles dither as he will – then an expedition will have to be sent against Spain this very year, for fear that if they are left undisturbed King Philip and Count Olivares will prepare another Invincible Armada to send next spring against England and Holland. So if you have had a flat summer, I think that you may still have a very busy autumn."

It was indeed as the French captain had predicted. As the fluit-ship *Eenhoorn* rolled in the languid late-summer swell off Dunkirk, at the centre of her little disc of sea and sky and distant sand dunes, events were moving in the great world beyond; and likewise among the immutable silent stars that shape the destinies of kingdoms on land and those miniature wooden kingdoms on the water that we call ships. King Charles had decided at last on war with Spain, despite his treasury being just as whistlingly empty as it had been under King James, and Parliament no more inclined now than it had been then to vote taxes to replenish it. An army of ten thousand men had been recruited that summer by combing the county gaols and rounding up vagrants from the hedgerows, and this great congregation of worthless rascals was now encamped outside the town of Plymouth robbing hen-roosts, tumbling milkmaids, stealing cheeses from windowsills and purloining bedsheets from the drying-hedges as cheerfully as if it were already on Spanish soil. In the royal dockyard at Chatham old, rotten ships left over from Queen Elizabeth's reign were being patched up and refitted with sails and cordage that had lain half a lifetime mouldering in musty warehouses, then provisioned from the victualling yard at Deptford with sacks of ancient biscuit in which a hundred generations of mice had lived and died, and casks of beef containing the flesh of animals slaughtered fifteen or twenty years before, and old gunpowder all clumped into cakes from damp so that it had to be broken up with a mallet. Rusty old cannon were being scoured up and painted to pass for new, with no man ready to test them for fear they would blow apart.

And meanwhile in Devon and Cornwall Sir James Bagg, Comptroller of the Navy and admiral of those two counties, was sending out his horsemen to press sailors for the king's service; even into the poor fishing villages around Looe which had been raided the previous year by Algerian pirates and their inhabitants carried off into slavery, with no cannon to repulse them and no King's ships to chase them since Sir James had pocketed the money allocated for that purpose and used it to build himself a great house at Saltram. The accounts were now being audited after twenty years of neglect and wholesale embezzlement at every level from the Lord High Admiral down to the meanest of Chatham carpenters who spent his days converting the King's timber into cupboards and linen presses for private sale, remembering his royal master only at midday when the dockyard bell rang to summon him to dine upon the King's beef and drink his beer.

If King Charles was bent on war with Spain he would have need of allies. France was plainly disinclined, having problems enough of its own to contend with. So there was nothing for it but for the young king to swallow his inborn distaste for republics and seek an alliance with Holland. The treaty was duly signed at Southampton in the second week of September and, despite Dutch misgivings about an expedition so late in the year, it specified that the Republic would provide twenty ships towards a force that would attack the Spaniard at a time and place yet to be decided upon. It was plain that the Dutch too would have preferred France as their ally. But any friend is better than none when wars are going badly; especially for a tiny country like Holland struggling for its very existence against the world's greatest empire. For lack of butter dripping must do, and as the black-suited plenipotentiaries made their way back to The Hague it was reassuring to know that Holland now had at least one ally. For even if that partner was frankly of questionable value as regards its army and fleet, it would at least be convenient for the Dunkirk blockade squadron to have friendly harbours at its back when the autumnal storms began to batter the Flanders coast.

For the crew of the *Eenhoorn* the first sign that events were stirring was the arrival alongside early one September morning of a schuit bringing supplies from Middelburg: fresh water (which was always a problem in the blockade squadron, and already starting to run low), beer in fifty-gallon casks, and – of particular interest to the crew – two hundred cheeses to provide each man with his monthly ration as specified in the admiralty's victualling scales. While these were being passed from hand to hand down into the reeking cheese room, to be stowed like cannon balls on the wooden racks, a packet of papers was being taken to the great cabin where the captain sat at breakfast. He broke the seal, and took out the order written in careful chancellery script. He read it, then called the mate in.

"So, Meester Hendrickssen, it seems that we shall be bidding farewell at last to Dunkirk belfry, the dunes and our weary tramping from Gravelines to Zuydcoote and back again. 'Proceed at once to Plymouth and there await further orders'. What do you think that might signify?"

Hendrickssen rubbed his whiskery chin: the day-to-day running of the ship was work enough for him, and grand strategy as high above his simple sailor's head as the stars in the night sky: also of considerably less practical value, since a man may at least use the stars to find his way whereas politics are of interest to none but kings and their courtiers.

"I think it means, skipper, that we're off to fight the Spaniard somewhere other than here; and this time in the company of Jan Engelschman, as our French captain predicted. But beyond that I don't trouble my head about it overmuch – except to hope that it'll be somewhere warmer and less windy than the Flanders coast once the autumn gales start to blow. Do you know Plymouth at all, and do we have a chart for it? I can lay a course to take us there, but as for entering the haven I've no knowledge of it at all."

"I was at Plymouth once, when Bontekoe's ship took refuge there from a storm on our way out to the Indies. But I recall little enough of it beyond there being a great rock in the middle of the harbour entrance. However, Van Barendrecht of the *Vliegende Hert* knows it well, I believe, so I shall visit him and take a sketch of his chart. For the time being, then, merely lay me a course from here to Plymouth."

That evening the *Eenhoorn* and the *Vliegende Hert* bade a thankful farewell to the blockade squadron and shaped their course down the English Channel; across towards Dover with the breeze astern, then turned to keep well south of the treacherous Goodwin Sands, then west again towards Dungeness. One by one the headlands of the English Channel coast passed by: the great looming white mass of Beachy Head gleaming in the sun at dawn, then Saint Catherine's Point that evening, then Portland Bill, staying well out to sea to avoid the vicious tidal race. It was fine sailing in the balmy early-autumn weather, the little ship butting into the steel-blue Channel waves as though she was as glad as her crew to have escaped at last from the futile treadmill of the Dunkirk blockade and the turbid waters swirling over the Flanders Banks. The sails drew steadily, and the number of leagues run each watch accumulated on the slate beside the helmsman as he swung his creaking staff to move the rudder, feeling the ship's movement beneath his feet and its shuddering through his hands, making constant tiny adjustments to its course as a good helmsman should, anticipating the vessel's behaviour rather than reacting to it, and keeping one eye all the time on the sails above him. Ships passed them bound up-channel; English, Dutch and French, firing their guns and dipping their topsail yards in salute if they were close enough. Off the Isle of Wight a couple of suspicious-looking vessels without flags came close to the two fluits, but then sheered away again without returning their salute: probably pirates, but it was difficult to be sure and mattered little anyway since they had clearly thought better of it.

The hulking grey shoulder of Start Point passed on the evening of the second day, and the two ships dropped anchor in Lannacombe Bay to wait for next morning's tide to take them into Plymouth Sound. On the land above the shore stubble fires flickered in the September dusk, filling the air with the smell of burning straw and covering the decks with black smuts. Cattle lowed in the fields at milking time while women on the beach collected baskets of seaweed for manure. Then at dawn the anchor was raised and it was on into Plymouth Sound, where England's great armada lay at anchor: eighty ships and sixteen thousand men assembled ready to perform their royal master's bidding.

★ ★ ★ ★ ★ ★ ★ ★ ★ ★

I thought that until then I had never seen a braver sight in all the world than King Charles's fleet lying there that morning in the Sound of Plymouth, which is a fine deep inlet of the sea reaching six or seven miles into the land and surrounded by wooded hills and green pastures, with the town of Plymouth perched on a rocky bluff at the head of the harbour where the Sound divides into two lesser arms. Yet this haven was altogether disproportionate (I saw at once) to the settlements about it, which are no more than a few paltry villages and Plymouth itself, which is a mean and inconsiderable little place. We all of us wondered greatly at this incongruity: that in the Low Countries every tortuous mudcreek with scarce enough water to haul a barge at high tide still has some great and prosperous town at the head of it, and even Amsterdam's approaches are so shallow that the larger ships must discharge their cargoes before they can cross the Pampus shoal, yet this splendid haven, which could accommodate all the ships in the world and still have room left over, is home only to a few poor fishermen. This spoke much (we felt) for the commercial genius of our people, and correspondingly little for that of the English, who enjoy such signal advantages over us Netherlanders as regards harbours and winds and depth of water and abundance of timber for building their ships, yet seem to draw so little profit from them.

The vessels lying there that morning were mostly no greater than our own because (Meester Hendrickssen informed me) they were collier ships chartered for King Charles's service: vessels of about three or four hundred tons' burden which normally ply between Newcastle and London carrying seacoals, wood having long been so expensive in that city that its inhabitants nowadays warm themselves and dress their victuals with fires of stone coal which though its smoke greatly befouls the air, sustains a fleet of several hundred ships to carry it down the east coast from the coal pits along the Tyne. Being very knowledgeable in all matters concerning commerce, he told me that the coal trade was presently slack because of the hot summer weather; and the carriage of wine from Spain and Portugal, which would otherwise keep the colliers busy all summer, was in abeyance because of the plague in London which had caused the magistrates there to close the taverns. So the coal-ship owners had been happy enough in April or May to charter their vessels to the King, having no other employment for them. But winter now approached, and the plague was abating somewhat, and the coal trade was soon likely to pick up again; so our collier captains (he thought) would now be mighty reluctant to hazard their vessels and the integrity of their skins fighting the Spaniard in distant waters when there was better money to be earned elsewhere at far less risk. Which prediction of his, though made without the help of astrology, proved quite remarkably accurate.

They none the less made a most festive sight as they lay there in Plymouth Sound that morning, a great concourse of eighty or more vessels bobbing upon the sparkling waters with their boats bustling about them and their cannon banging out in salute as we passed. Of king's ships there were few: only five or six, by reason of the great decay which England's navy had fallen into under King James once the war with Spain was over. The greatest of them was the *Ann Royal* which we passed close by as we made our way up towards Plymouth town and the anchoring place the port admiral had allotted to us. A mighty vessel of over a thousand tons with sixty guns, she was quite the largest ship I had ever set eyes upon until then: distinguished from the rest by having two mizzen masts, each with a triangular sail; a fashion permitted by her great length, but which was still very odd to my eye and which I afterwards never saw again. She was the admiral's ship of this great armada, flying his red flag at her maintop, and likewise much decorated with carving and giltwork: too much, I think, for our more sober Dutch taste which though it likes adornment and painted carvings on housefronts, disapproves of them on ships, where they merely increase top-weight to no useful purpose and likewise draught of water, which is a very ticklish matter amid our coastal shallows.

Beheld from far off the *Ann Royal* was indeed a most splendid and martial sight. But a fair mask will often belie a pox-raddled countenance below it, and the great ship, we saw as we passed close by, was like some powdered and painted old beldame of the King's court: not near so enticing at close quarters as from a distance. The mate swore frankly that if our own modest vessel were as badly caulked as the great English galleon, then he would have her bo'sun whipped for a rogue and put ashore with a wooden ladle hung round his neck. "And do you see the pump spout?" he said. "The old tub gushes water like a boar pissing in its stall even though we are now midway between watches. I'll wager my eyeteeth that she leaks like a basket and the English have the pump working day and night to keep down the water in the hold. And behold her masts..." We looked up as we passed, for the great ship's masts and spars towered above our own. And indeed even I could see that they were in a poor state: slubbered down lately with grease and linseed oil to give them the appearance of newness, but much cracked and split, and underneath, the grey-black colour of rotten trees leaning against one another in a wood where the wind blew them over years ago but the woodcutters have not yet quit the alehouse to clear them away.

Nor were the other English men-of-war that we passed in much better case: the *Swiftsure*, which was the Earl of Essex's ship, and the *Saint Andrew* which was the Earl of Denbigh's. All were plainly old and rotten, because for want of money and lack of enemies only one or two new vessels had been built during King James's reign, and a great ship laid up in ordinary with only watchmen to care for her decays faster than a herring in August – which was why Their Excellencies the States-General were so reluctant to spend money on warships and preferred instead to hire them in as needed; because they knew full well that the outlay on building and fitting out the vessel would be a bare half or one-third part of the money they must spend on her, the rest going on her upkeep.

When we reached our anchoring place in the Cattewater, which is the arm of the haven eastward of Plymouth town and the debouchure of a small river, we found two Dutch fluit-ships waiting for us; the *Basilisk* and the *Dolfijn* of Enkhuizen, which had been dispatched straight from Texel to Plymouth after the alliance was signed. When we had anchored our captain changed from his sea clothes into his best suit, hung over his shoulder his new trophy sword on its belt – which he said was too pretty a toy to kill a man with, but good enough for visiting withal – and put on his best plumed beaver hat, then bade me accompany him ashore to be his interpreter.

Plymouth, I saw, was a paltry little place compared even with Colchester: dirty unpaved streets; poor sordid houses of timber and plaster with roofs of thatch; no more than two or three thousand souls living by fishing and coastal trade – and now caught between six thousand rough sailors in their ships out on the Sound and ten thousand rowdy wastrel soldiers encamped about the town or (what was far worse) billeted to live in their houses, which was like lodging weasels in a dovecote. But for all the depredations of the soldiery the town's mayor and its governor were still doing their best to appear willing and loyal subjects, for King Charles and his queen were expected in the town the following day after conducting a great review of the army on a common some way inland. We conducted our business in the Guild Hall, which concerned watering and supplies, then made our way back to our ship, the captain remarking that there was little reason to tarry there since a man might see all there was to be seen in Plymouth in the course of five minutes and still have time left over to ease his bladder, and he must speak with the port admiral about us finding us some convenient shallow place to heel and bream our ship, whose bottom had grown foul with weed while we were off Dunkirk.

Our way back aboard the *Eenhoorn* took us past the *Ann Royal* lying at anchor below the headland called the Battery. As we passed about fifty yards off her starboard bow we saw two fellows in their shirts and breeches clamber out of a gunport near the bow and slip into the water, then begin to swim away from the ship, until a sentinel in the bow saw them too and raised a shout, then shouldered his musket and fired at them so that the bullet splashed into the water between them and our boat. Then other men came running up on the *Ann's* foc'sle and shot at them as well, until the smoke obscured their view. The two swimmers were by now near our boat and waved for us to pick them up, which we did out of Christian charity, hauling them over the gunwale like two great fish to lie gasping for breath and streaming water on the bottom boards. We looked at our captain, wondering what to do, but he merely signalled us to row on towards our own ship as though nothing had happened. It seemed that in the smoke and confusion the English sentinels had not seen us take the two men aboard, for a jolly-boat of their own full of armed men went rowing along past us following the course our two fugitives would have taken towards the shore.

When they were gone Loodgieter had me question the two Englishmen. I learned that they were poor fishermen from the county of Cornwall, lately pressed (as the English call forcing men for the King's service) and now confined aboard the *Ann Royal* as though they were in a gaol with no wages and with food (they vowed) scarcely fit for dogs, and not just that but the old ship so leaky and perished withal that they must pump day and night to keep down the water in the hold; likewise her cordage and sails so decayed that her mainsail was more patch than sail and all would surely come crashing down at the first capful of wind. They swore, in short, that though they were no cowards and would loyally serve their prince in aught that they could, yet likewise they were not suicides, and would sooner be hanged than venture out to sea in so rotten a vessel; and all the more so since they had wives and infants at home who would starve if they were drowned (for though there was a fund to support the widows and children of sailors lost in the King's service, yet Sir James Bagg had already engrossed it to build himself a fine house, and would cheerfully let their widows and orphans die of want at his gate). I related all this to our captain, and he commanded that we row on towards our ship to allay suspicion, then turn towards the strand and put the two men ashore to fare as best they could. "For it seems to me," he said, "that although they are plainly base rascals, yet I would never wish to have men serve under me that were forced to do so against their will; because when things grow hot such poor fellows are merely a hindrance and discouragement to those around them who are of more resolute spirit. So I think myself that King Charles is better quit than rich of them, and will not assist him in dragging them back so unwillingly to his service."

Since our ship was to be heeled next day in the shallows for her bottom to be cleaned, which process would last several days, my stepfather and I resolved to hire a room at an inn for as long as we lay at Plymouth, since (he said) at his age he was not so enamoured of the lodging and ordinary to be found on ships that he would willingly sojourn aboard one if the chance offered itself of sleeping in a cow byre ashore and dining with pigs at a trough. So we took an attic room at the *Brindled Bull* inn outside the town walls; at extortionate price since the King's army was now encamped about the town and all the rooms in Plymouth had been taken by its officers.

And a mighty singular army it was to be sure, when we were vouchsafed our first look at it. England had been at peace now above twenty years, and the profession of arms was therefore greatly decayed, since the only means that men had of exercising it during the years of the Dutch truce with Spain was to enlist for service with foreign princes as far afield as Poland or Muscovy. We gathered from what we heard at our meals that few of King Charles's captains had any military experience to boast of. His chief general of this expedition, Sir Edward Cecil, had never commanded more than a regiment of cavalry, while most of his subaltern officers were English gentlemen who for all their martial swaggering, had never smelt powder except at the annual exercises of the county militias which were then the nearest thing England had to an army: a collection of feeble old fellows dressed up in antique corselets got together by the parish vestries, shouldering pikes half eaten-through with woodworm and rusty old arquebuses from King Henry's day. Their officers were for the most part loud, roistering, empty-headed fellows, and vowed every evening in the tap-room of our inn among many toasts that, by God, they would singe King Philip's beard for him as surely as ever their fathers did, and kick the Pope's arse likewise for a cozening rascal. But, listening to their drunken braying as we lay endeavouring to sleep in the room above, I wondered how many of them would prove good coin and not counterfeits when the bullets began to fly.

As for the men, they were pretty much of a piece with the officers; which is to say, such a collection of good-for-nothings as surely the world never witnessed before, as though all the lousiest vagabonds and most worthless rascals of England had been swept up by the scavengers and deposited at Plymouth under the designation of an army. We learned over supper that commissions of array had been sent out that summer to all the lords-lieutenant and justices of the peace in every county of England, that they should seize all vagrants and idlers of the male sex and between the ages of sixteen and fifty years in their parishes, and convey them under close guard to the nearest town to be enlisted: likewise to all the town magistrates that they should clear their gaols and, instead of condemning felons to be hanged, should send them off to be soldiers instead. One of the officers that ate at table with us swore that a fellow in his company had been standing on the ladder with the noose around his neck saying his prayers and waiting for the hangman to turn him off when the King's commissioner rode up to snatch him from death's embrace. Not to be outdone, another officer said that this was nothing: a fellow in *his* company had been tipped off the ladder already and was dangling by the neck with his legs kicking when the muster sergeant arrived to cut him down and revive him, then pack him off to the army. At which a third laughed uproariously and swore that by the look of them his own company had been hanged already and left some weeks on the gibbet for the crows to pick before they were enlisted for soldiers. Which may give my readers some idea of the peculiar temper of the English, that they find such matters a fit subject for jesting over supper and seem always to take a perverse delight in the direness of things, so that nothing in this whole world is so bad but they will tell you with relish of something even worse.

We had ocular proof of this on our third morning there, because our inn stood by an area of common land where the soldiers were wont to drill; which is a grand word to dignify the evolutions performed by such a sorry collection of ragamuffins who were most of them still without soldier's coats or shoes (because none had yet been provided for them, nor probably ever would be) and had staves instead of pikes to drill with. Yet still their sergeants were doing their best to teach them the fundamentals of the military art, such as how to shoulder their pikes – that is, when they received pikes to shoulder – and form a column of march, then how to unshoulder their putative pikes once more and assume a defensive posture. All day the common rang to their shouting as the sergeants and corporals drilled their men and sauced them with blows and curses for their many faults of muster. But that morning, for some of them at least it was not broomsticks serving the office of pikes but real muskets. Powder and ball had been furnished for this exercise, so we heard a great deal of shouting and swearing from the sergeants as they instructed their men how to load and prime their weapons and keep their matches alight. We heard a spattering volley of shots, then more shouting and cursing as they were shown how to reload, then another volley somewhat less disorderly than the first, then reloading and another volley some five or six times so that we no longer paid any heed to it and got on with eating our breakfast.

Then all on a sudden there was a great pounding at the door and cries of "A surgeon! A surgeon!" The door opened, and the soldiers carried in a poor bloodied wretch stricken white with shock, his face begrimed with gunpowder and his left arm all shattered above the wrist; the hand gone, the bones of the forearm exposed with the flesh hanging in rags and the sleeve of his shirt burned and tattered up to the elbow. We laid him down on a bench and I did my best to calm him (for he was blubbering and sobbing with terror and pain) while my stepfather placed a tourniquet on his arm to staunch the bleeding. In the end we had to cut off what remained of the arm midway between wrist and elbow and then dress the stump. We asked the lieutenant of the man's company what had caused this, and he said that the musketeer was a poor dribbling idiot boy of eighteen or nineteen enlisted into the King's service from a madhouse in the county of Chester, then sent to Plymouth with a dozen other such simpletons and lunatic fellows by the magistrates in order to disburden the poor-chest. When they were exercising he had conscientiously performed each successive loading of powder, wadding and bullet (since fools commonly delight in such repetitive actions) but without his match being lit, which his corporal had failed to notice, so that at each command to fire nothing happened when the fellow applied his match to the touch-hole, yet he still went ahead afterwards and loaded his weapon until he had seven or eight charges packed on top of one another in the barrel. The corporal then saw that his match was out and lit it for him; so when he next pressed the trigger the weapon's barrel blew apart like a grenado and carried away his left hand with it.

After we had performed the operation and the poor idiot boy had been led away, still babbling to himself, the lieutenant thanked my father and offered to pay him for the service, though he could give us only a promissory note since no money had yet been furnished to pay or victual his men, so that everything must be done by credit or the men stealing it for themselves. He said that as yet his regiment lacked a surgeon for want of money to engage one. My father courteously waved this offer aside and said that he had performed the amputation *gratis*, out of human compassion. The officer thanked him most earnestly for this and pressed his hand by way of thanks. But we still thought it a mighty strange way to conduct an army, that it should be dependent for its medical services upon the charity of passers-by.

We went each day to the ship, lying on her side on the Cattewater mudflats, to attend to our sick and injured if there were any and see how the work of breaming her bottom progressed, which is the burning-off of the weeds and barnacles that had grown thereon with torches of reeds, then painting those same bottom planks with "witstof", which is a mixture of train-oil with beeswax and of a greyey-whitish colour. This was slubberly work and most tiresome for the crew, who must splatch about bare-legged on planks laid in the mud, but very necessary withal since the growth of weed by now greatly hindered the ship's passage through the water. Our captain, we learned, had given order that the pound of blue vitriol which he had had us buy from the apothecary's shop in Bergen should be mingled with a quantity of the witstof, which gave it a greeny-bluish colour, and this mixture then be applied to a patch of the bottom exactly two yards square. And the reason for this was (he said) that he had lately heard from a Hamburg skipper that blue vitriol is sovereign against the growth of weed and barnacles, and to put this to the test he would apply some of it to the ship's bottom, then heel her after six months to see whether there were any less such growth on the patch than around it; and if there was then he would know that it was the blue vitriol that was the reason for it and not some other effectual cause; which may give my readers some notion of just what a rational and enquiring spirit it was that we had here, because most skippers would merely have daubed the bottom all over with the greeny-blue witstof and then concluded if less weed grew thereupon, that it was the blue vitriol that was the agent when it was in fact the saltiness or the coldness of the water or some other such adventitious reason. And this principle of his is one which I have myself applied ever since in my chymical experiments.

★ ★ ★ ★ ★ ★ ★ ★ ★ ★

The autumnal equinox came, and the leaves began to turn colour in the Devonshire hedgerows as the great armada got ready to depart for a field of honour yet to be decided upon. The soldiery exercised on the fields and commons round about Plymouth, and began to take on the outward semblance of an army, though even to a non-military eye their lack of clothing and shoes was still very apparent. Likewise, many were deciding that military life was not for them and running away, so that the magistrates of Devon and Somerset had been instructed to place blocks on the main roads and arrest any sturdy vagrant who looked as though he *might* be a deserter, regardless of whether he was one or not. At Plymouth quayside there was a constant bustle of waggons and boats as provisions and stores were loaded aboard the ships: great casks of salted beef and sacks of biscuit, and powder and wadding and thousands of yards of match for muskets, and weapons and tools and horseshoes and a thousand other items, all loaded into the waiting longboats amid prodigious swearing and confusion to be rowed out, swung aboard amid yet more swearing and confusion, then stowed in no particular order in the holds of the collier ships which were to act as transports for this mighty host; the largest (men said) that had ever left England's shores.

Those few elderly quartermasters with any experience of such matters complained that the stores provided were inadequate to maintain a fleet and army in harbour, let alone at sea; also that the quality of them was very poor and much of the beef and beer already spoiled when it came aboard. But there was no time to bother now with such trifles. The monies voted by Parliament (everyone knew) were insufficient to fund a war against Spain. It was even reported that the King had pawned some of his Crown Jewels to finance this expedition, and likewise diverted much of the money which he had lately received from King Louis of France as dowry for the king's sister. But if wishes were horses beggars would ride, and suits must be cut according to their cloth; and if His Majesty purposed war against Spain then his loyal subjects were obliged to do his bidding with whatever means were to hand since (all men agreed) waging war and leading armies was the primary purpose that God had anointed kings for.

As for the Dutch contingent, the ships lay at anchor in the Cattewater and replenished their supplies as best they could for the coming voyage. The *Eenhoorn* was now back afloat on an even keel, the galley fire was alight once more and the captain was writing up the log for the previous day from the running log on the slate. He smiled as he dipped his pen in the inkwell, then paused.

"There, Meester Hendrickssen: I am just about to write 'the twenty-fifth of September'. But I understand from the surgeon's boy Van Raveyck, who is a mine of information on such matters from his having lived in England, that ashore in Plymouth it's only the fifteenth of September, the reason being that whereas we adopted Pope Gregory's calendar fifty or more years ago, the English kept to Julius Caesar's saying the new one 'smelt of Rome', for all the world as though old Julius dwelled in some other city; in consequence of which their dates are now trailing ten days astern of ours. A trifling enough matter, I suppose; except I fear that in their insular pride they believe that the heavens and the weather must conform to the English calendar, according to which we are not even properly into autumn yet. Anyway, tomorrow is the twenty-sixth of September – or the sixteenth if you prefer it so –

and King Charles will be in the town with his queen and My Lord Buckingham. So I shall be going ashore to see him, since I have never before set eyes on a reigning monarch."

The next day it rained a little in the morning as King Charles reviewed his army outside the town walls. Those few troops who had proper coats and shoes were put on the outsides of the columns, and the ragged barefoot starvelings were kept towards the middle. The regimental colours with the red cross of Saint George fluttered bravely in the damp breeze while plentiful cannon-firing provided smoke like incense round the elevation of the host to hide the spectacle from more sceptical eyes than those of the young King, whose military experience had thus far been limited to playing war games with an army of lead soldiers. Then His Majesty came into the town in the afternoon to meet with his principal captains, the latter hoping that the aim of this expedition might at last be revealed to them. In so far as he had any opinions in the matter the King seemed to echo My Lord Buckingham, that the expedition should cross the Atlantic to attack the Spaniards in the West Indies, perhaps even paying for itself by taking the Mexico silver fleet. But others with greater experience and more caution urged that the season was now too far advanced for that: that the hurricanes were already blowing in those distant waters; that the silver fleet would surely have left Vera Cruz already; and that the ships and men were anyway too ill-prepared for such a hazardous venture. The autumnal gales blowing on to the Flanders coast precluded an expedition to take Dunkirk. So in the end it seemed by default that the armada must head for the coasts of Spain; though where precisely, and what it would do once it arrived there, were matters to be resolved at some later date. Nothing much at all having been decided after two hours or more of talking, His Majesty then departed to review his fleet.

★ ★ ★ ★ ★ ★ ★ ★ ★ ★

I was there on the quayside as King Charles and his attendants stepped down into the barge that would take them out to review the ships and dine afterwards aboard the *Ann Royal*. This was the first king that I had ever seen, and in truth he seemed to me an ordinary enough young fellow: small of stature and slightly built, comely enough of countenance with light brown hair and beard, but with a stiffness about him that was forbidding and likewise he walked somewhat awkwardly from an inflammation of the leg-joints (a bystander told me) when he was a child. Buckingham followed close behind him: a pretty young man who had (it seemed) much appealed to old King James, who was inordinately fond of such handsome youths. Behind them came the King's lieutenant-general Sir Edward Cecil, of whom I would see a good deal later on. He was a tall, grey-haired man of about fifty-five years, but seemed far older from having been much worn down lately by the cares of preparing so great an expedition with such slender means. His thin grey hair and beard straggled like those of an old man, his shoulders were stooped and his eyes drooped sadly at the corners like those of a beaten dog. For all his top-boots and his half-armour, his plumed helmet and his baton of office, he seemed to me more like a threadbare attorney or a schoolmaster than a general. They all took their places in the barge; the trumpets sounded; the cannon boomed out from the ramparts of Plymouth Castle; and the rowers lay to their oars to propel the vessel out to where the ships rode at anchor, their rigging full of seamen swarming like bees ready to cheer their king as he passed by. And our Dutch ships also were dressed overall with bunting, the orange, white and blue flag floating at their jackstaffs and the admiralty flags at their maintops so that, for all their modest size, they presented quite as gay a spectacle as the English vessels.

Yet on the quayside the crowd did not disperse once King Charles and his officers had departed, for there was a large knot of ladies gathered there still, and I heard that all of them were conversing in French. I perceived also that they were much better and more stylishly dressed than the dames of the local notables drawn up to see their king. The French ladies took no notice of the English ones, and seemed preoccupied by one in their midst as they now formed a procession to make their way back to the Guild Hall. I asked a bystander who this might be, and he told me that it was King Charles's young queen, Henrietta Maria of France, who would not accompany her husband out to the ships because she detested boats and water after being seasick on her way to Dover that summer to marry the King, and anyway had been in a great sulk ever since she arrived in Plymouth, for no reason that anyone could discover, except that the local ladies of the quality were much put out by it and thought that now she was their queen she might show more interest in them.

The procession set off as I stood in the front row of the crowd, and we all doffed our hats and knelt. Then to my surprise I saw that they had stopped — and that the Queen was looking directly at me, having (I suppose) been told by her attendants that it behoved a Queen of England to make some attempt at conversation with her loyal subjects; except that she had not as yet learned any English, having brought her entire retinue with her from France and been shut up with them until now in a house far away from London by reason of the plague. I cast down my eyes as ceremony required, thinking as I did so that it must have been my reddy-gold hair that caused her to single me out among the crowd.

"Et you, garçon, 'oo ees you?", she said.

I stood up, and made a low obeisance as I had been taught to do at dancing school in Houtenburg. She was a small, black-haired girl of about sixteen with spots on her face and teeth that stuck out like clothes pegs: not at all majestic as I would have expected a queen to be. And as I beheld her, a strange and troubling thought came to me: that this was the woman my father's terrible deed fifteen years before had robbed of her own father. It was as though a knife had pierced my own chest as well. But I replied as graciously as I was able.

"S'il-vous plaît, Votre Majesté, je m'appelle Frans van Raveyck.", I said, pronouncing the words clearly and distinctly since I thought that for cause of her late father, my name said hurriedly might discommode her by its resemblance to "François Ravaillac". But I need not have feared on that score, for her sombre discomfitted face – what in French is called "boudeuse" – suddenly became animated and cheerful.

"Aha? But what a pleasure for me to find someone who speaks good French, and not the English mangling of it, which is though a dog had chewed it and spat it out." Her ladies laughed at this and wagged their fans, though the English ones who knew some French looked mighty offended. "But what misfortune brings such a handsome young fellow as yourself to this miserable crapaudière of Plee-moot? Are you one of Soubise's men?" (For the Duke of Soubise's ships, in rebellion against her brother, were at that time lying in the Ham Oaze not far away).

"If it please Your Majesty", I answered, "I am here aboard one of the Dutch ships, come to assist His Majesty your husband against the Spaniards."

"For a Hollandais, you speak excellent French." She said. "How is this so?"

"Your Majesty, though I serve the United Provinces I come from a part of Flanders near the border with King Louis' domains, where we all speak French as readily as we do Flemish."

She smiled most graciously at this. "Then Flanders is fortunate indeed to be blessed with such well-favoured young fellows – and these dowdy Englishwomen luckier than they deserve to have one in their midst."

"Your Majesty is most kind," I said, to which she replied

"De rien, jeune homme. Adieu," and with those words passed on up the street, leaving me feeling very strange: that I had just spoken with a king's wife, and the daughter of a king, and the sister of a king, yet all that had come into my mind as I conversed with her was a strange thought that if she were God's anointed – or if not exactly that, then almost so – and not made of the same base stuff as ordinary folk, then it was mighty remiss of God to have given her such bad teeth and so spotty a complexion; much worse than that of most milkmaids in the platteland villages around Houtenburg. Her imperious manner set her apart from the common sort. Yet I did not feel myself to be in any way of the common sort when I spoke with her, and instead answered her as frankly and cordially as I would any lady that I had met: as though we were equals in station and not just in age. Considering the matter afterwards I thought it passing strange likewise, that King Charles's thaumaturgic power bestowed upon him by the donation of Saint Remigius should not extend, apparently, to touching his wife for her pimples, and wondered idly whether that power of touching might be inefficacious on other royalty, much as scorpions (Pliny writes) are immune to their own venom.

The townsfolk said afterwards among themselves that although King Charles was a fair and handsome enough young fellow, his wife was a silly affected creature with scarce a civil word to say to anyone, and her French ladies-in-waiting even worse than herself with their rolling eyes and their fans and oh-la-la's and their disobliging remarks about the gowns of the local ladies, which one had been overheard to say looked as though old Queen Elizabeth had been dug up from her grave to provide a mannequin for them. They murmured that it augured ill for young King Charles to have to share his bed each night with such a petulant baggage and one so lacking in courtesy, and all felt that it would be as well if her husband took a stout willow stick and beat some respect into her, selon la mode anglaise, before it was too late.

Back at our inn that evening, and bursting to tell my stepfather of my conversation with England's Queen (which is scarcely an everyday occurrence for surgeon's mates) I found him sitting on the bed quite motionless and astounded like a man smitten with the palsy. I asked him what was the matter, and he made no reply but to indicate with his finger a letter that had come for him among a parcel of documents brought to Plymouth by a Dutch ship arrived that morning. I picked it up, feeling the blood drain from me as though all my veins had been opened at once. It was from Cousin Bourchier's wife at Hoddesden, dated the fifteenth day of August. From it I learned with a horror which I cannot readily describe that my dear mother had died of the plague at Chelmsford in Essex about the eleventh of that month: that Cousin Bourchier having fallen sick in his shop in Clerkenwell at the end of July – though not with the plague as was feared but with some more benign calenture – my mother had gone back to London to nurse him, all his servants having fled. And once the worst was over and he was on the mend, she had elected not to return straightway to Hoddesden, but go instead to Colchester where there was business to attend to with the landlord of our house about the frontage being rebuilt. But coming to Chelmsford, which is about halfway, she was detained because the road had been barred by the Essex magistrates to prevent the plague from spreading. She took lodging in an inn, fell sick there next day and was cast out of the house from fear of the plague to die unattended in a field by the roadside, her body afterwards being interred in a common pit with other strangers; and if it were not for the charity of a local clergyman who collected up her belongings and sent them to Hoddesden we would surely never have known what was become of her.

So I was now motherless, and my sister Henriette with me, and my stepfather a widower for the second time, which cast him down utterly after so many other tribulations that year and left him for a while quite unmanned, since he had loved my mother dearly for her goodness and honesty. I thought for a time that this would be the final misfortune that put him into his grave. I tended him as best I could those next few days and forced food into his mouth like a baby, because I feared that he would cease to eat and starve himself to death, and also saw to it that he washed and combed his hair and beard. He got up and went about his duties around the ship, holding his spreekuur each morning and evening as usual, and bound up the quotidian injuries as before. Yet I sensed that the heart was gone out of him and that he performed these actions now like some clockwork automaton, muttering to me that there was now no sense in living; that he might as well take a cannon bullet from the shot racks and cast himself overboard, and that all that prevented him from having done so already was the shallowness of our anchorage in the Cattewater and the discourtesy to our English hosts in obliging them to retrieve his corpse and bury it. I bade him bear up and think of Henriette, who was still to be looked after; likewise that we would soon be at sea, and that a voyage to foreign lands would give him a change of air and scenery and revive his spirits. But he said that that was the trouble: that he had seen too many foreign lands now and was sick of them and his endless gadding about, and that he was an old man and had wished only to retire to the country with his beloved wife, who was now dead and lying jumbled together with poor naked wretches in a common pit. But he seemed to revive a little in spirits as the days passed and we made ready for sea, so I supposed that the worst was over and that he was now on the mend. I hoped only that our voyage, wherever it would take us, would soon be over and that we might return to England before New Year. Of which, however, there seemed to be little prospect since it was now agreed by all our Delphic Oracles around their mess tables that we were bound for the south of Spain or perhaps the Mediterranean Sea.

For myself, I confess that though it was very hard for me in the days that followed to reconcile myself to my mother's death, and likewise to the forlorn manner of it, alone in a field beneath the indifferent sky with none to attend her and far from her loved ones, the prospect of sailing for foreign parts distracted me somewhat from my sorrow and was by no means as detestable a prospect for me as it was for my stepfather. For even if I settled down afterwards to be a surgeon in England and was not in the smallest degree inclined to a soldier's life, I still thought that it might be well to have in my past some small military experience that I could brag of when others were bragging likewise; to have heard bullets fly – provided they flew on past me – and bring back a few tales of battles and distant lands with which to divert my patients from their sufferings as I lanced their boils or pulled out their teeth. And all the better, I thought, that it should be now, when I was not yet fifteen years old, rather than making a great interruption in my life once I had gained my licence, as had been the case with my stepfather. But I saw that for him this voyage of ours was anything but a welcome diversion, he having already (he said) had his bellyful of ships and dying men's groans when he was young and they were the very last thing he desired now that he was an old man. Before the news arrived of my mother's death he had mused aloud in our room at the inn that we might both simply bid the whole business adieu: hire horses and ride out of Plymouth one fine evening and let the Zeeland Admiralty find someone else to be surgeon aboard their wretched ship. But we knew that the roads out of Plymouth were closely watched for deserters now that the army was about to embark, and that two Dutchmen seeking to leave the town would be suspected at once of absconding. And he was in any case a man of utter integrity, wholly incapable of breaking his word once he had given it. Now, though, he seemed to abandon even the thought of such stratagems, saying that we had no one to return to, so it was all perfectly indifferent to him if we sailed to Peru or Japan and remained there a hundred years. Such despondency made me fearful for him, because a prisoner is a prisoner indeed who no longer even dreams of escape. I could only hope that having business to occupy him now that we were making ready to depart would revive and animate him, and the Biscay gales disperse the melancholic fogs that clouded his mind.

On the third day of October, which was a Friday, and my father and I already back aboard preparatory to our ship's departure, we were diverted early in the morning by a great to-do and banging of guns all down the length of Plymouth Sound. The remaining sixteen of the twenty Dutch vessels promised by the treaty had arrived, led by two lions: the *Geluckige Leeuw*, which was the flagship of the Jonker Willem van Nassau van der Leck, Lieutenant-Admiral of Holland and West Friesland, and the *Gouden Leeuw* which bore the flag of his vice-admiral, Doctor Laurens Reael. They came to anchor as our guns spewed out flame and smoke like bronze dragons and our sailors perched in the rigging cheered and waved their caps while Matthias Sigurdsson blew a most ornate fanfare on his silver trumpet. Their longboats rowed our two admirals ashore to be received by the Governor of Plymouth, then a signal was hoisted that all the other Dutch captains were to join them: I suppose to make a better show with our allies. So I was bidden change into my best suit and accompany our skipper ashore.

The Jonker Willem was greeted *pro forma* by the English notables, then came to speak with his own captains. A scion of the princely house of Orange, he was a bastard son of the late Prince Maurits; about twenty-four or twenty-five years of age and a comely enough young fellow with a sensitive, delicate, somewhat melancholic face such as one might see on a poet or a scholar. But no matter: his deputy and our effectual leader was our vice-admiral, Doctor Reael, who had lately been the Company's Governor-General of the East Indies before Jan Pieterszoon Coen occupied that office, and was a man as skilled and valiant in war as he was learned in jurisprudence, which had been his first study. They both greeted us all most cordially and hoped that they might rely on us in whatever enterprises we should undertake. For (Doctor Reael told us) it had still not been decided with the English where this expedition of ours was bound for, and he hoped very much that this small matter would be resolved by King Charles and My Lord Buckingham in the days to come.

★ ★ ★ ★ ★ ★ ★ ★ ★ ★

Though in deepest mourning for his mother, Frans still had his quotidian duties to perform, from which there could be no compassionate leave granted aboard a ship on the eve of sailing; and certainly not in a world where sudden bereavement was the earthly lot of every mortal man, woman and child until Death at last snatched them away as well. So that evening, though his heart sat cold and inert like a lump of lead within his chest, he was still obliged to wait at table in the great cabin, then make cheerful music with Matthias Sigurdsson and Suleiman the Moor for the entertainment of the diners. For important guests had come to sup aboard: none other than the Jonker Willem and Doctor Reael. The young prince desired that while they lay at Plymouth he should dine with each of his captains in turn, that he might come to know them better. And the signal favour and honour of being first for a princely visit was to be accorded to Captain Cornelis Adriaenszoon Loodgieter, in recognition of his late feat of arms in taking the Spanish frigate *Nuestra Señora*. In addition to which the captain's table and entertainment were widely spoken of in the fleet, and the Jonker Willem had already (in truth) grown somewhat tired of shipboard fare, which seemed to consist entirely of boiled bacon and kapucijner peas. After supper had been served – a curious but fragrant confection of rice with sundry meats and vegetables which Captain Loodgieter had come to relish in the East Indies – the musicians played their galliards and alemands as the drizzle of an autumn evening pattered against the glass of the stern windows. The conversation had already turned from affable pleasantries to serious business.

"King Charles was most cordial to us when we met with him last evening at Saltram House," the Jonker Willem said, "which is the seat of Sir James Bagg: built, we understand, from the proceeds of pilfering and grand larceny in supplying the English navy so that the rogue is widely known among our allies as 'Bottomless Bagg', which signifies 'bodemlos zak' in our tongue." The assembled company tittered sedately at this, as befits a princely witticism. "But as to his queen, Henrietta Maria," the Jonker Willem continued, "I must say that she was far less agreeable than His Majesty and seemed to be in a great huff with all the world – and most of all with her husband, for whom she could scarcely spare a civil word. It causes me to fear greatly for their future."

"Tell me, Your Highness," Loodgieter said, "Were you able to discover from King Charles any hint as to where this expedition of ours might be bound?"

"I fear not: despite all our pleading and the representations of our ambassador the English have bluntly refused us permission to take part in their councils except by invitation. We Netherlanders, it seems, are merely to do whatever they decide, without first having had any say in deciding it, on the grounds that we are supplying ships for this venture but not soldiers and must therefore be subordinate to the English in all matters regarding the disposition of the army. But I think the real reason for the aim of this expedition having not yet been declared to us, is quite simply that there is none."

The table fell silent. Loodgieter spoke at last.

"But this is scarcely to be credited: that we are here on the very eve of departure, with the soldiers preparing to embark, yet no one has decided where we are to go."

"Indeed, captain", Doctor Reael said. "It beggars belief that the English should have assembled ten regiments of a thousand men each, and six thousand mariners, and a hundred vessels, yet still have no idea what they wish to do with them. But such we understand the case to be. Though they bar us from their councils we still have our eyes and ears to report on their deliberations, and my intelligence from the council they lately held here at Plymouth is that there was great discord among their senior officers as to the purpose of this venture. All of them – Sir Edward Cecil, the Earl of Essex, Lord Delaware, the Earl of Denbigh and the rest – are land soldiers with not a single week's sea service to share between them. And even among these land-rats it appears that only Sir Edward, whom His Majesty created Viscount Wimbledon while we were at Saltram House, has any military experience worthy of the name, he having for some years commanded a regiment of horse in our own army. The rest are soldiers by title only and entirely lack the experience to direct so great a force. I fear things will go badly with this venture, and am thankful only that our ambassador managed to dissuade the English from their insane project to take the whole force off to the West Indies so that it might be wrecked by some hurricane on the shores of Cuba."

"So does that mean we are to be wrecked on the coast of Spain instead?"

Reael smiled. "Try not to be so gloomy, Captain Loodgieter: as valiant an officer as yourself should surely be more positive. Yes, you are certainly correct in supposing that when we leave Plymouth we shall head for Spain. But this is our destination only by default, as it were, all the others having already been disqualified by reason of one difficulty or another. However, where we are to go and what we are to do when we get there has not yet even been discussed, let alone settled upon. His Majesty and My Lord Buckingham, it seems, consider that such decisions may reasonably be put off until nearer the day. Or in other words, the fleet will only know where it is bound for once it has arrived there."

"This is indeed a most singular way to conduct a war," Loodgieter said. "We might as well sail out of Plymouth with blindfolds round our eyes and navigate by sticking pins in the chart, or by casting dice."

"Quite so. And if we were putting soldiers ashore alongside the English we would certainly demand a greater say in their employment. But as things are, our capability to hurt the Spaniard away from our own shores is limited by the blockading of Dunkirk which occupies so much of our fleet. So to carry the war to our enemy we must perforce go along with the English, whose navy is so much greater than our own, as a smaller but cleverer brother will accompany a larger but more stupid one. If we were to happen on our own upon the Spanish Mexico fleet, which must surely be on its way home by now, then we could never hope to take it with our mere twenty vessels. But with a hundred we well might, covering the costs of this expedition out of our share of the booty and likewise depriving Spinola of the wherewithal to pay his men, thereby doubling the benefit to us. Such an outcome would repay our trouble a hundred times over."

"Could the States-General not have furnished an army as great as the English one, so that we might have more say in this enterprise?"

"Captain, you know as well as I do that England is a country two or three times more populous than our own little frog-patch; likewise that the general lack of ability among the English as regards commerce and manufacture means that a great proportion of their people are idlers and dissolute rascals. So when King Charles wishes to raise an army, he need only send out his sheriffs to gather up all their vagabonds and sturdy beggars like so many stray dogs and clap soldier's coats on them; whereas in our own busy little country such fellows would already be employed from morning to night weaving cloth or building ships so that they could not be spared, and the States-General would have to vote whole bargeloads of silver to hire soldiers from abroad. The two cases are not comparable."

When the two exalted guests got up at last from the table, about ten o'clock, to make their way back to their own ships, the Jonker Willem paused as befits a prince's son to thank the musicians and tip them each with a gold coin for their playing, which he said was excellent and rivalled that of the most accomplished players ashore. He likewise exchanged a few princely banalities with each, enquiring of Suleiman whether he had always been so black and of Sigurdsson whether he was born lame. Then he came to Frans.

"You are a handsome young fellow, to be sure. From what town in Holland do you come?"

"From none in Holland, Your Highness. I am from Houtenburg in Flanders."

"Aha, a Fleming. And do you speak French?"

"As well as I do Dutch, Your Highness; and English and Spanish likewise."

"Most interesting. How well do you know English?"

"Pretty well, Your Highness: I lived for three years in the town of Colchester."

"Splendid!" The Jonker Willem turned to Loodgieter. "Captain, you must lend me this excellent young fellow when I request him. I speak no word of English, and they speak abominable French, and the interpreter they gave me when we left Texel is a dingy hunchbacked fellow who would sit more fittingly among baboons in a fairground cage than at a conference table. This handsome young man would not only ease my communication with Sir Edward and his captains but also do us credit among them. They sneer at us Hollanders as plebeian cheesemongers who dress in canvas breeches and wooden shoes out of meanness. So we must show them that though we have no king to rule over us, we still have as regal a bearing and state as themselves."

* * * * * * * * * *

The next morning the embarkation of troops began. Though still very low after learning of my mother's death, my spirits had at least been somewhat raised by His Highness's kind words addressed to me after dinner, which proved to me yet again that which had already been demonstrated by my earlier meeting with King Charles's queen: that though I was at present but of low degree in the estimation of my equals and those below me, in the eyes of the great I stood out from the ordinary run of mankind and readily attracted their notice. But I had other affairs anyway to occupy my thoughts that morning, for we were making ready for sea and the ship was all a-bustle with activity. We had as yet no news regarding where we were bound for – that is, if Sir Edward and his captains had yet give any thought to that small matter. But seafarers are philosophical folk, I had discovered, and Spitsbergen or the coast of Guinea pretty well alike to them as destinations. Our ship was well found and adequately provisioned, our sailors competent and our captain a man of the greatest discretion and experience. So our fears were only those normal for ninety-five mortal men venturing out upon the great ocean in a wooden box at the stormiest season of the year, there to face a potent foe by no means to be despised as regards cunning and martial valour.

At first it was intended that our ship would carry neither soldiers nor horses nor supplies, being a private vessel bringing naught but her guns to the party, and we could therefore watch the embarkation taking place all around us with complete equanimity as being no concern of ours. And it must be admitted that it was a most extraordinary spectacle that unfolded itself before us there in Plymouth Sound as King Charles's army boarded the ships that were to take it to do his bidding at some destination yet to be announced. For it was indeed a prodigious force assembled there: above ten thousand soldiers and five or six thousand seamen, with twelve great battering guns and twenty horses apiece to draw them, and all the stores and paraphernalia that attend so mighty a host, now being put aboard in the very greatest confusion so that we all wondered, having seen the stuff go into the ships amid such disorder in a peaceful English haven, how much greater that disorder would be when it must all come out again with the Spanish cannon-shot flying round our ears. Then at last, the provision casks and sacks of biscuit and kegs of powder having all been put aboard, it was time to embark the soldiers, rowed out to the ships a hundred at a time in the longboats and urged up the swaying wooden sides with much shouting and cursing from their sergeants and prodding of backsides from below with their halberds by way of encouragement. Those boats that passed near us were filled for the most part (we observed) with very wretched and unmartial soldiers: poor ragged starvelings, some of them in soldiers' coats and hats but likewise many not, and still wearing the miserable lousy garments in which they had been delivered from their gaols and poorhouses. As they were being put aboard the longboats on the beach we saw certain of them try to slip away unnoticed, or simply run for their liberty, so that horsemen patrolled the hills above the shore to catch the fugitives, who were soundly cudgelled for their trouble then flung aboard the boats to be taken out to the waiting ships with such encouraging words as "You'll find our wooden gaols are stronger than the stone ones you came from, you villains, and not so easy to escape from either, as having a wider moat about them!"

The English ships being crowded to bursting with troops by

Saturday afternoon, and their supplies of food and water already insufficient for such a multitude, our fluit-ships *Eendracht* and *Vliegende Hert* were commanded to each take aboard a company of English soldiers, which request the Jonker Willem had consented to out of readiness to oblige our allies. But no sooner had their passengers been got aboard than the captains of those two ships requested him that they all be taken off again for fear of the spotted fever (for all were lousy and some were sick already) and because those that were still healthy fell immediately to pilfering the ship's gear with such alacrity that as Captain van Barendrecht of the *Vliegende Hert* declared later to our skipper, he feared that by Sunday morning his men would all be naked, their clothes having been stolen in the night, and his ship likewise falling apart by reason of the very nails having been filched from her timbers. He vowed to our skipper that this whole expedition was surely no military venture at all but a cunning scheme on the part of King Charles and his ministers to disembarrass England of its most grievous rogues and beggars by transporting them all to the coasts of Morocco, putting them ashore and then sailing away in the night, it being (he added) scarce worth the trouble of taking them to the slave markets of Algiers since the Moors were discerning buyers, and the price to be obtained for such poor varlets was unlikely to repay the cost of their transport.

It was therefore with much dismay that we learned late on the Sunday afternoon that we too were to transport a company of English soldiers, about one hundred and fifty men, which had just arrived at Plymouth after marching down from the middle of the country. But as they came alongside we saw that our fears were baseless, for these men did not in the least resemble the dissolute rogues aboard the *Vliegende Hert*, savage and uncouth as a troop of apes. Instead they sat motionless on the longboat's benches in silence and perfect order, in gleaming helmets and corselets with green coats beneath them, and in the hands of each, dressed perfectly vertical, a short pike about ten feet long with what appeared to be another pike lashed to it, but which turned out on closer inspection to be a shooting-bow. As they clambered aboard we perceived likewise that they were a great deal older than the other English soldiers: men of at least forty years, and some above fifty, rather than youths of eighteen or twenty. Many indeed lacked teeth, and climbed over the rail mighty stiffly by reason of their rheumaticky joints. But as they formed their ranks in the waist and were dressed off by their sergeant and his corporals, it reassured us greatly to see that their bearing was soldierly and their discipline as immaculate as that of Roman legionaries, which led us to hope that their conduct aboard would be as honest and sober as their demeanour on parade. The soldiers were told off to their quarters down in the hold and their gear was got below decks. Then their commander came aft to present his compliments to our skipper.

For all his courtesy and his martial posture, Captain William Neades had about him the air of being a soldier by occasion rather than by calling: a long, lean fellow with hair like straw and a hungry countenance with eyes deep-sunk in their sockets: a gentleman to be sure, but one whose military service hitherto had most likely been (we thought) with a county trained band in peacetime and not in some Low-Country fortress under siege or facing the Turk in Hungary. He thanked our captain for receiving him and his men, and promised that during the voyage, be it never so long, his men would be impeccably behaved and their corporals would punish the smallest wrongdoing: likewise that they would be obedient to the ship's officers and bo'suns in all matters concerning the vessel's handling and their own quartering and sustenance; though in this last matter he begged our indulgence, since he and his men knew no word of Dutch, and instructions would therefore have to be conveyed to them by way of myself.

Captain Loodgieter replied that he quite understood the difficulties that might arise from this; but was sure that with such a good and amicable spirit on both sides their stay aboard would be harmonious and the voyage as pleasant as we could make it. He then enquired out of politeness what manner of troops these were, whether pike or shot, because he saw that they carried both pikes and shooting-bows, and he wondered which of them they would use? At this Captain Neades grew mighty animated and had one of his corporals come to demonstrate to us the weapon they carried, which was (we saw) a pike combined with a bow by a swivelling joint of brass which attached the middle of the bow to a point about five feet above the pike's heel. This, Mister Neades proudly told us, was his own invention: a weapon that would make a revolution in the conduct of wars by combining the offensive power of shot with the defensive power of the pike, yet with none of the great discommodities of muskets such as the powder being spoiled, the match being put out by rain, and of course the lamentable slowness of their loading. "For one of my fellows", he told us with his eyes shining like John the Baptist's, "can easily loose off five arrows in the time that it takes a musketeer to fire a single shot, and with as much distance and wounding force as any bullet; and all at a fraction of the cost to His Majesty, since a dozen bows may be manufactured for the price of one musket, not to speak of its crutch and all the slow-matches, powder horns, bandoliers, bullet moulds, touch-hole prickers and other such fallals as are necessary for a musket's service. And then when the enemy's horse come against him – or such of them as are not already lying in the dust all full of arrows like so many pincushions – he may quickly unstring his bow and swivel it round… thus…to rest against the shaft of the pike, then set the heel of his pike into the ground and slope it, so that not even the most intrepid rider will be able to break through the hedge. Your musketeers need pikemen to protect them, and your pikemen need musketeers to pepper the enemy. But my soldiers can perform both those offices for themselves."

Our captain marvelled greatly when I had translated all this for him (though it was difficult for me to keep up with Mister Neades in full flow). "Most remarkable," he said at last. "But might I ask a question as a simple sailor unacquainted with military matters? You are but a hundred and fifty men among this whole army. So do you suppose that a few flights of arrows will discommode the King of Spain's soldiers? To be perfectly frank with you, in Holland we gave up the use of bows and arrows long ago except as a toy for children or for shooting popinjays at country fairs." I thought it best to moderate these words as I relayed them, for I knew enough of the English to suspect that our Dutch candour, though kindly meant, might still cause needless hurt. But that gentleman was not so easily to be put off.

"Indeed, good sir, we are few in number. But I hope that before long we may grow to be a mighty host and form the whole shot of the King of England's army, quite doing away with that noisy uncouth foreign innovation of gunpowder which requires us to bring shiploads of saltpetre from abroad each year to make it, and in its place return Englishmen to the honest and healthful exercise of the longbow which has so often struck dread into the King's enemies. I have made it my aim and purpose in the world to restore the practice of archery, and devoted my life and fortune to it. Indeed I lately wrote and had printed at my own expense a treatise on the subject, called *The Double-Armed Man*, which I have dedicated to His Majesty, and have likewise raised an equipped at my own expense this company of militia, which gave a demonstration to His Majesty at Oxford last week and so impressed him that he straightway commanded we should take part in this expedition. Which is why we were so late arriving at Plymouth, that we had to march all the way down from Oxford to get here."

"That must have been taxing for your men," our captain remarked, "for I see that they are somewhat more advanced in years than the generality of King Charles's soldiers."

Captain Neades (who was himself about thirty years old, I should think) nodded sadly in agreement.

"Alas, I fear that what you say is true: that although they are as bold and as stout-hearted a band of fellows as ever ate roasted venison and drank good ale with Robin Hood and Maid Marian in the greenwood, and of indomitable valour, they are indeed well declined into the vale of years; the reason for this being that shooting with the longbow has so much decayed these past twenty or thirty years through the laxity of our magistrates in not enforcing the law commanding practice at the butts every Sunday after church. So the only men I could find that were still proficient in its use are most of them fellows that were young in good Queen Bess's day." At this he smiled and his face brightened. "But I still fancy that once they are face to face with the Spaniard they will give as good an account of themselves as men half their age. For a valiant heart overcomes creaking joints, and one good English yeoman fed on beef and beer, whatever his age, will see off a dozen miserable Dons brought up on garlic and Hail-Marys as surely as his great-grandfather saw off the chivalry of France at Crécy and Poitiers."

We both perceived from this that Mister Neades was a great enthusiast and thus not to be argued against, for such fellows as he are beyond persuasion and only the most brutal experience – if indeed even that – will shift them in their opinions, while rational argument merely confirms them in their folly. But as our captain remarked to me afterwards, "Though the fellow is plainly a notable fool and his fellows marching to their perdition with such a zany to lead them, yet he and they are honest and well-conducted folk and not the thieving good-for-nothings that Van Barendrecht has aboard his ship. So we must be properly thankful for that, and see that they are used with all courtesy during their time with us. I shall invite Mister Neades to dine with me each evening, and instruct the mate and the writer to double up so that he may have a cabin to himself as befits a gentleman. These Englishmen of ours must be well looked after while they are aboard. For I fear that if they offer battle to the Spaniard armed only with their bows and arrows, then not nearly as many of them will be coming back with us as we first took out."

CHAPTER TEN

It was Monday morning, the 13th of October aboard the Dutch ships – though still only the 3rd of October aboard the English ones. The embarkation of the troops was now complete and the armada ready to sail from Plymouth Sound. Yet as the tide turned, still no order came for the ships to weigh anchor. Aboard the crowded vessels men fretted and grew impatient, and by midday boats were being sent ashore, clean contrary to orders, to fill water casks and complete such other mundane tasks as had been neglected in the bustle to get the troops aboard. That evening the Earl of Essex's blue squadron of forty vessels was instructed to leave on the tide for Falmouth and wait there for the rest. But aboard the remainder of the fleet sour inactivity reigned all that evening and the next day likewise, until in the wardrooms and about the mess tables the mariners began to mutter about "Sir Edward Sit-Still"* and speculate whether their general, who had never been at sea before except for crossing to and from Holland by packet boat, had any comprehension whatsoever of such matters as winds and tides. For the breeze, which had been favourable for getting out of the Sound all of Monday and most of Tuesday, had veered southwards by Tuesday evening so that the ships would now have it blowing in their faces and be obliged to tack their way out past Saint Nicholas's Island: no simple matter for such high-sided, clumsy vessels in so crowded an anchorage. Meanwhile, aboard the *Ann Royal* the cooks reported that when the casks were brought up from the hold and opened to prepare dinner (since the ships were now on sea rations) much of the salted beef was discovered to be tainted so that it had to be thrown overboard; likewise that some of the beer was already turned sour

---

* His family name, "Cecil", was often pronounced "Sissle" at this period.

and the water putrid from lying in butts made from unseasoned wood. Meanwhile Sir Francis Stewart of the *Lion* sent a message to the newly created Viscount Wimbledon respectfully wishing to draw His Lordship's attention to the fact that his ship now had three feet of water in the hold despite the pump being manned day and night, and that ordering her to sea with the rest would be no less than wilful murder on His Lordship's part since she was so old and rotten that the bottom would surely fall out of her before she ever passed Eddystone Rock.

A fretful night passed, with the soldiers packed together on the dark, ill-ventilated orlop decks trying as best they could to sleep on the bare planks. Anchor cables creaked in the hawse holes and chafed on the bitts as the sixty or more vessels swung round like so many great lumbering wooden seagulls to face into the wind now blowing straight into the haven. Every half-hour the bells chimed in a peal down the length of Plymouth Sound as the officers of the watch turned the sand-glasses. Lamps burned dimly in the lanterns on sixty high sterns as the autumn dawn came up, turbid and sullen with the promise of a storm later in the day. Then at six bells of the day watch the lookouts all shouted down to the deck as one man that a blue flag had just unfurled from the *Ann Royal's* mainmast head. A cannon banged from the flagship in confirmation of the order. And on sixty decks the seamen were soon at work, running back the halyards to hoist sail as their companions below tramped round the capstans to haul in the dripping hemp cables, slimy now with the weed that had grown on them during a month or more lying at anchor.

For the moment the anchors were merely broken out of the bottom and left lying there. The *Ann Royal* would proceed out to sea first as befitted the fleet flagship, tacking her ungainly way down the Sound past the rows of still-moored vessels as guns boomed out their salutes and brazen trumpets blared. Despite the early hour, up on the rocky headlands and hills around Plymouth Sound thousands of country folk had gathered to watch the great fleet set sail, so that they could tell their children and grandchildren that they had witnessed Sir Edward Cecil's men depart; just as their own parents and grandparents had told them how they had stood on those same headlands one summer's afternoon half a century before and seen the great menacing crescent of King Philip's armada appear over the southern horizon. And had also watched on the Hoe just outside the town (though surely they could not have walked there so quickly nor so many have stood there all at once) as good Sir Francis Drake played bowls before sallying out on the evening tide to harry the Dons up the Channel.

When the flagship was past Saint Nicholas's Island – narrowly missing it, since the old tub had always steered badly even when she was new – the rest of the fleet began to weigh anchor and follow. But it was all done in a most disorderly fashion, with ships running foul of one another as they tacked to and fro into the freshening wind, so that it was a matter for wonder that none of them actually collided rather than merely brushing yard-arms. At length, about eight o'clock, the wind had got up so much that the *Ann Royal*, having laboriously beaten to windward as far as Penlee Point, put her helm up and ran back into the Sound, signalling the others to follow her. Many of the vessels trying to stand out to sea failed to see the signal and continued their tacking back and forth, while others dutifully went about, causing even greater confusion than before. On the shore the spectators looked at one another in bewilderment, unable to comprehend why part of the fleet was putting to sea and the other part returning to harbour. In the end, by midday, with a sorry drizzle being drifted along by the wind, most of the ships were back at anchor in the Sound, apart from a few which had persevered and were now almost out of sight on the waters of the Channel wondering why the rest had not followed them. An order went out from the *Ann Royal* commanding the ships to anchor in the outer harbour and forbidding their men to go ashore for fear of desertion. But as the weeping autumn dusk descended, boats could be seen making their furtive way to Plymouth quayside. Aboard the *Ann Royal*

Sir Edward, seeing this from far off, demanded of his captain Sir Thomas Love to know who the defaulters were so that he might have them punished for insubordination. Sir Thomas turned to his sailing master for assistance, since he himself was captain only of the flagship and not vice-admiral of the fleet. Master Siddall said that it was too far off for him to tell, and that the light was fading, and that he could not recognise the vessels (which had no names painted on their sides), and that the *Ann's* jolly-boat was already employed running messages so he could not send an officer to demand their names; but he would most surely look into the matter later on when he had more leisure. Which was the last that was ever heard of it.

★ ★ ★ ★ ★ ★ ★ ★ ★ ★

We spent Thursday thus, and Friday likewise, lying at anchor in the Cattewater as we had for nearly three weeks past, all ready to sail but no nearer sailing than we had been at the beginning. Our captain fretted and fumed and wondered aloud what manner of fools these Englishmen were that they could not even put to sea in an orderly manner, for word had come to us of the great disorderly mêlée in the entrance to Plymouth Sound the day before as part of their ships tried to get out while the other part tried to get back in again. So we sat where we were awaiting further orders, and meanwhile went about our daily business as patiently as seamen are accustomed to do, their lives being always at the disposition of others, to go where they are directed by admirals and owners as it shall please those gentlemen, and being anyway subject in all things to winds and tides which take no more heed of petty men's wishes and designs than the stars in the sky above. We might sail on the next tide; we might sail in a week's or a hundred years' time; or we might never sail at all; and that was all there was to be said on the matter.

About three in the afternoon of the next day, which was a Saturday, there was once more a great commotion and banging of guns out in the Sound, and we gathered that we were all to put to sea except for five of our ships which the Jonker Willem and the English had decided would return to blockading Dunkirk, which we later heard caused no small uproar aboard those vessels since they had wished to come with us in the hope of plunder and prize money. Aboard our ships there was great activity, to get everything ready for when our turn came, because being so far into the harbour, we would be the last out; the English having placed us there (we suspected) because they were less fearful of our men deserting than their own. We waited with the anchor broken out and the sails brailed up ready to be set, for the sun had now come out again and the wind veered round to the north-east, which was the most favourable quarter for blowing us out of the harbour. Yet it was not until evening that we set sail, the confusion and disorder in the mouth of the Sound being once again very great so that two of their colliers collided and another went aground, and the tide was already back on the flood by the time we passed the rocky island that lies athwart the harbour entrance. By nightfall our Dutch squadron was at last clear of Plymouth Sound with our stern lamps burning and all the great host of English ships discernible out on the open sea ahead of us by their myriad lanterns in the dusk like so many glow-worms. Yet as we came down the Sound we saw that a good dozen of the English colliers had remained at anchor, which perplexed us greatly to see such open contempt for orders, and also that one of the king's ships (the *Lion*, someone said) was now very low in the water and likely to sink before long, her men already getting into the boats and taking her gear ashore while they could.

The next morning dawned bright and clear and found us off the haven of Falmouth at the tip of Cornwall, where we met with the Earl of Essex's ships. By now we were sailing in a great square formation, ninety-six ships in all, with our fifteen Dutchmen in their own block on the right flank and Sir Edward's flagship and the red squadron about two miles away to larboard. The wind continued to blow fair all that day and we lost sight of land. But during the night the wind fell away to nothing, so that the next sunrise found our entire fleet becalmed somewhere west of the Scilly Islands, which we had passed during the night: all that mighty concourse of vessels sitting motionless as ducks on a farm pond with the sapphire-blue sea as smooth as a looking-glass and the faint swell below it causing us to rise and fall so gently that the motion was barely perceptible. Our hundreds of flax-grey sails hung limp as bedsheets on a clothes line as we lay there; a great town of fifteen or sixteen thousand inhabitants (which is as large as Norwich or Bristol) floating motionless on the water with depths scarcely to be imagined below us full of strange fishes and monsters, and soaring above us the cloudless blue vault of the heavens.

It was then that a sudden sentiment first struck me – though I would often have it again later in my life – of how little and insignificant men are in this world; that we poor tiny insects venture out upon the deep in our fragile nutshells which are no more than so many wheat-husks or specks of sawdust upon the face of the waters, yet with as foolish an assurance as though we walked down the street outside our own house and as nonchalantly as a stonemason will eat his boterham at midday perched on a plank at the top of a cathedral spire, scarcely paying heed to his fellow ants scurrying about their business five hundred feet below the soles of his boots. Yet no one that I could see shared these reflections of mine – or if they did, showed any sign of it. From all around us came the busy sounds of life aboard ships, very audible in the still morning air; the shouting of commands, the trilling of the bo'sun's pipes, trumpet calls and the beating of drums, the resonant clump of feet on wooden decks and the squeaking of blocks, the clanking of ladles in iron kettles as the cooks served out breakfast, the creaking of windlasses, the chink-chink of blacksmith's hammers on anvils. And every half-hour, passing from one ship to the next, the strokes of the bells; until at noon a gun aboard the *Ann Royal* fired to signal that her sailing master had observed the sun at its zenith, so that all the other sailing masters, hearing the cannon's report, could turn their sandglasses all at once and midday aboard all our ships would thus be synchronous. As for the latitude observed at noonday aboard each ship, while I do not know what the English custom was, the order in our Dutch squadron was that this should be noted down and rowed across immediately to the *Geluckige Leeuw* so that her skipper could calculate an arithmetical mean to compare with his own observation, which experience had taught us was the surest method when sailing in squadron, since whilst one captain may easily make an error, it is most improbable that all the captains will make the same error. Meanwhile the calm continued all that day, and the next day as well, the only small difference of latitude in the noon observations being the result (we imagined) of the current having drifted us all along by a league or so. And as is the way at sea, we soon forgot that there was or ever had been any such thing as a wind in all the history of the world.

★ ★ ★ ★ ★ ★ ★ ★ ★ ★

On the second day that the fleet was becalmed off the Scillies Sir Edward Cecil, now Viscount Wimbledon, mindful of the great responsibilities entrusted to him along with his peerage, decided that it was time to summon his first war council, His Majesty and the Duke of Buckingham having enjoined him before they left Plymouth that he should take no decision without first debating it with his senior officers and coming to a resolution upon which all might agree. Likewise, though Sir Edward was plainly a man of sound judgement and some experience in military matters, his vice-admiral the Earl of Essex, his rear-admiral the Earl of Denbigh and several other of his senior officers took precedence over him as peers of the realm, he being Viscount Wimbledon for less than a week past and that only by His Majesty's special favour, with his elevation to that dignity only titular and still to be confirmed by Parliament. The fact that he was a grandson of Elizabeth's great minister Lord Burghley was nowadays of little consequence to anyone less than fifty years old. So it would be as well (he thought) for him to assert his authority as His Majesty's lieutenant-general now rather than later on.

The white council flag was duly hoisted to the *Ann Royal's* maintop and a cannon was fired to draw attention to it, and aboard the other king's ships longboats were soon being brought to the gangway so that the admirals and their captains could board them to be rowed across to the flagship, which was distinguishable among the other vessels by reason of her great size and her fourth mast, like a goose floating on a millpond amid a flock of ducks. And now Sir Edward sat in the state room beneath the stern of the old ship, at the great oaken council table among the brocade hangings (which he had supplied at his own expense) with the autumn sunlight streaming in through the cabin windows. To add dignity to the gathering Sir Edward wore his breastplate and gorget with their gilt-decorated edges, of finest Milanese work though they made it plaguey difficult for a man to sit at table and write while wearing them. His plumed general's helmet with its visor open rested on a side table next to a copy of Julius Caesar's *De Bello Gallico* and his general's baton, while his sword hung over the back of the chair in a tableau such as befitted the room of a great captain and would have furnished a pretty subject for a still-life painter if any painter of still-lives might be found two hundred miles out upon the Atlantic Ocean.

The principal officers and their retinues made their entrance with a perfunctory obeisance to their commander. First came the vice-admiral, the Earl of Essex; a pudgy-faced morose fellow who could (Sir Edward considered) have been any age between twenty and fifty though he was in fact in his mid-thirties. He plainly suffered from the curse of being the mediocre son of an illustrious father: Elizabeth's glittering favourite Robert Devereux, the wick of whose brief candle had been summarily trimmed by the headsman's axe on Tower Hill after a bungled attempt at armed insurrection. As for the rest of them, they were frankly a sorry crew as he surveyed them seated round the council table: William Feilding, Earl of Denbigh, who had been raised from Warwickshire squire to knight along with several hundred other such starveling adventurers by King James during his progress southwards from Scotland at the start of his reign, then later elevated to the peerage with equal undeserving on the strength of his being the upstart Buckingham's brother-in-law. And touching military experience, had never so much as led a trained-band company at annual muster before he came out here to be admiral of the blue squadron. Likewise Henry Power, Viscount Valentia, admiral of the white, bickering and jostling as usual with My Lord Delaware for the precedence of being the greater nincompoop of the two. And snapping behind them as ever Thomas, Baron Cromwell. There seemed to be little love lost between any of them: and likewise (Sir Edward considered) about as much military capacity as might be found in a dame-school. He rapped the table to bring the meeting to order.

"My lords, gentlemen; I have convened this meeting so that we may turn this unexpected calm to our profit, which though it delays us on our way to do His Majesty's bidding, offers us the opportunity to debate and settle certain matters which it may be inconvenient to discuss later on. So to start our deliberations, Mister Glanville will distribute among you an aide-mémoire of mine concerning the disposition of our fleet." Sir Edward's secretary stood up and began handing out sheets of paper on which stencilled ships, like little flat-irons, had been marshalled into a neat square. "I had my clerks sit up all night to copy it" Sir Edward said with modest pride, "so I hope that it may prove useful to us as setting out my preliminary thoughts on the conduct of this enterprise."

The soldiers stared at it bemused: to them it might as well have been in Arabic despite the three neatly coloured-in divisional flags: red for the admiral's squadron; blue for the vice-admiral's and white for the rear-admiral's, with names written beside each ship and a vague fourth column labelled "*The Dutch ships*" to the right of the other three. Sir Samuel Argall of the *Swiftsure*, a mariner since his youth, regarded it at arm's length and made little tooth-sucking noises before speaking at last.

"My Lord, might I make so bold as to enquire what exactly is intended here?"

"Why Captain Argall, I would have thought that that was obvious: I have drawn up a battle formation for our fleet, should we encounter the Spaniard at sea." Argall looked unconvinced.

"Then might I enquire why Your Lordship chose this particular formation? Because I freely confess, it looks like nothing that I have ever seen before in all my years as a sailor."

If he was annoyed at this boorishness, Sir Edward managed not to show it.

"Indeed? Then perhaps you never sailed before in so great a fleet. To me it was obvious that with eighty-one English vessels at my disposal, that number being a perfect arithmetical square, the most commodious formation would be to dispose our vessels in a square made up of three columns, and each of those columns containing twenty-seven ships in three divisions of nine apiece. Which, if equal distances are preserved between the vessels in each rank and file, will give us a square as broad as it is long."

Argall rolled up his eyes and drummed his fingers on the table: plainly tact was not his strongest point. He spoke at last.

"My Lord, I would respectfully suggest that while such a formation might perfectly answer for a regiment of horse, it will serve uncommonly ill for a fleet of ships."

"How so, sir? Please explain yourself."

"I would remind Your Lordship of that which he will doubtless recollect from his service in the Low-Country wars: that a horseman's pistols and sword have their greatest effect in front of him and scarcely any to his sides. But with ships the opposite is the case. They have at most two guns disposed to fire ahead, and the rest along each beam to fire sideways. Therefore, in this formation which your lordship proposes, neat though it is and of great geometrical perfection, only eighteen guns out of three or four hundred could be brought to bear upon the Spaniard if he were ahead of us, though he might at the same time batter us with a hundred or more of his own. And if he were on either side of us our case would be little better, since the nine vessels on either flank could bring to bear perhaps ten guns apiece, with the remaining two or three hundred pieces impotent to do any hurt since they would all be on the wrong side or masked by our own vessels. Likewise the sea is a fluid and changeable element and not solid ground beneath our feet. The smallest shift in the wind would make the whole thing a nonsense if it forced us to beat to windward, since no admiral on earth could prevent vessels so tightly massed together from running foul of one another." Sir Edward looked nonplussed at all this, understanding very little of it but comprehending dimly that the plan which he had distilled so conscientiously from his experience as a cavalry commander was in some mysterious way defective when applied to ships. But being an intelligent man and not a blustering numbskull who would maintain that two and two made five or the sun rose in the west rather than admit his ignorance, he retreated with as much good grace as he could muster.

"Very well them, Captain Argall. I am greatly indebted to you for your advice and crave only your indulgence for not having completely understood these matters at first sight. 'Better wise late than a fool forever' is a sound motto." He shuffled his papers. "So, my lords, regarding this plan of mine, it seems that while there may be certain practical objections to my enjoining it upon all our captains as a matter of discipline, yet it still has value as begetting in them a right understanding of the conception and intent contained in it; so that with an honest endeavour to come as near as they can to performing it – rather than their performing it minutely in every last detail – it may none the less be of merit in preserving us from confusion in general. You will see, when we come later to my general instructions, that I have allowed that the Dutch ships may keep their own formation as seems best to them and fight according to their own methods. And I shall now apply this liberty to our own vessels as well, requiring my captains to observe this formation here only insofar as they may."

At this there was a considerable exchanging of puzzled looks among the sea-captains present, with one or two shrugging their shoulders when Sir Edward was not looking in their direction. And meanwhile the noble Lords Essex and Denbigh gazed on as bewildered as two jackdaw chicks in their nest, having scarcely comprehended a single word of it.

The meeting then moved on to the next item, which was where the fleet was bound for and with what aim. On this point Sir Edward could offer little enlightenment beyond what had been common knowledge while they lay at Plymouth: that they were to proceed against the coast of Spain with the intention of taking the Mexico silver fleet when it arrived there some time towards the end of October. But as to the precise when, where and how of all this, Sir Edward said that these questions would be decided at a later council once they were nearer their destination. But now they were at sea he could reveal what His Majesty and My Lord Buckingham had vouchsafed to him while they were still at Plymouth, but he had kept secret until now for fear of spies: that besides waiting for the plate fleet – which aim was self-evident – the expedition was to take and hold a Spanish port to lie in for the winter; though again, which one precisely would be decided later on. On the matter of sending scouts ahead to look for the silver fleet, Sir Edward was adamant that for the time being all vessels must keep the closest formation possible and not give chase without his permission even if Spanish vessels were sighted. No answer was given to Captain Argall's question "How, then, shall we know when to look for the treasure ships, if we have already sailed past them in the night?"

The only remaining matter of urgency was that of rations, the ships' captains reporting that beer was already so short and so much of the provisions spoiled in their casks that from now on five men would have to be placed on the rations of four until such time as the ships could be revictualled at the enemy's expense. Mister Glanville scribbled diligently throughout the meeting, and at last thankfully concluded his note "*And so the council was dissolved*"; resisting as usual the temptation to add "*having decided nothing very much.*" As the admirals and captains departed back to their ships they were (it must be confessed) not much the wiser than when they came aboard. The secretaries were busy meanwhile in their office aboard the *Ann Royal* transcribing Sir Edward's general instruction to the vessels of the fleet: a copy for each ship, which would take them most of the rest of that day and the one after it. As their quills scratched away the ink in their inkwells began to slop gently from side to side. After the two days of prenatural calm the wind was blowing up and dark clouds were boiling over the western horizon. Ropes began to pay through squeaking sheet blocks as the sails of ninety-five vessels flapped and swelled. The floating city had turned once more into a fleet under sail.

★ ★ ★ ★ ★ ★ ★ ★ ★ ★

It was next morning during the dagwacht, as we were at breakfast, that the longboat from the *Geluckige Leeuw* came alongside with a package. I was spooning my groats from the bowl with the other Snotapen when the bo'sun's call came down the hatchway like the voice of the Archangel Gabriel: "Van Raveyck, to the captain!" I sprang up, wiping the bacon grease off my mouth and fingers, and made my way to the great cabin where our captain sat reading four or five sheets of paper.

"Ah, Van Raveyck, I have a task for you", he said. "The Jonker Willem received this missive from Sir Edward at six bells, and since neither he nor Doctor Reael can read a single word of English, and their clerk for these matters is lying sick, he has sent them here for you to translate as soon as you may, because I see that they are numbered items and may therefore be of importance."

So I sat down and translated Sir Edward's thirty-one *Articles Touching the Form of a Sea-Fight Performed Against Any Fleet or*

Ships of the King of Spain or Other Enemy, and Some Directions to be Observed for Better Preparation to be Made for Such a Fight and the Better Managing Thereof. And such stuff they were too: as long-winded as their title and many items worded with the utmost obscurity, as though their author had deliberately set out to cloak his thoughts in verbiage, while others were clear enough in their intention, but so banal withal that any laundrywoman in Houtenburg could have done as well had she been given the task. The note that covered them said that they were not instructions to us – for Sir Edward was graciously pleased to let our Dutch ships keep their own formation and fight as they pleased – but merely an aide-mémoire to tell us how the English proposed ordering their part of the fleet. As I translated and wrote them down in my best hand our captain stood watching me with great interest, taking up the sheets to peruse as I finished each of them. He rubbed his chin at last.

"Hmm, these are fine instructions to be sure: '*Article XXIV: That the master or boatswain of every ship, by command of the captain, should appoint a sufficient and select number of seamen to stand by and attend the sails.*' And again '*Article XXV: That they should by like command appoint sufficient helmsmen to steer the ship.*'" He laid down the paper. "It seems to me that Sir Edward might well append the following items: '*Article XXXII: That all aboard shall drink their beer from a can and not a sieve*' and '*Article XXXIII: The bottoms of all vessels shall be properly planked to keep the water out.*' These are indeed most excellent instructions he has given us here, and without equal for teaching eels to swim and eggs to be wiser than the hens that laid them. I hope only that the Jonker Willem will treat them as they deserve and hang them on a nail in the roundhouse, for all to peruse as they sit there."

I sent off the instructions to the *Geluckige Leeuw* and we heard no more of them; except to learn to my great satisfaction that the Jonker Willem would use my services again the next time the English held a council, because he had learned that I could write shorthand and was very desirous to have a Dutchman there to observe the proceedings under pretence of taking a note. I was very gratified by this, to see that among all his people he considered me, in despite of my tender years and lowly estate, to be a person of such discretion and gravity that I might attend a council of the great without incongruity, which I took to be as much a compliment to my bearing and deportment as to my knowledge of the English tongue and my skill at writing notes of meetings.

By next evening though, such petty scrivener's concerns as councils and minutes and instructions had been rudely scattered by those loud old ruffians Neptune and Boreas overturning his letter-writer's stall like two roaring boys in a marketplace. The tempest that had been brewing since the previous day fell upon us from the north-west, and with such a ferocity that even our oldest mariners said afterwards they had seldom seen the like of it. For myself, inexperienced as I was at sea, it was a trial most terrifying at first since I had never before been out in anything more than a topgallant breeze, and was sure that in such a blast as this we would all infallibly be drowned. For two whole days and nights our little ship scudded before the storm under a goose-winged fore course while the wind screamed in the rigging under the tempest-racked skies and great waves the height of town houses with salt spray tearing from their crests came chasing us one after another, each in turn seeming like to be the one that would crash over our poop and sink us. Yet our little vessel rode well to the sea, and after a few hours of inexpressible terror I came to see that so long as we kept our stern to the waves and were not broached and rolled over, then we were safe enough so long as we had sea-room to run in; which was most likely the case since we had been two hundred miles out from the continent when the storm came upon us and the wind had veered north-east in the mean time, so that we now had the whole wide ocean to run in rather than being driven into the Bay of Biscay. Our captain had us hoist the longboat aboard when the wind first blew up and lash it down securely in the waist, then replace it with a drogue of old spars tied in a bundle and towed astern, which (he said) would both keep our stern to the sea and slow our headlong progress, since our bottom was cleaner than those of the other Dutch vessels and we might otherwise run ahead of them and lose them. We later learned that to perform the same office the English ships had persisted in towing their longboats as the storm got up, and in consequence had lost nearly all of them from their swamping or their painters chafing through, which loss would greatly incommode our expedition later on.

Those two stormy days were nevertheless a great ordeal for us all. Myself, though I was pretty well hardened to the seasickness now after several months afloat, I still felt queasy from the continual violent pitching and rolling which made every action troublesome. As for Captain Neades and his bowmen down in the hold, they surely suffered more grievously than martyrs ever did in the Roman Coliseum, groaning and spewing into a stinking tub until it was a-brim and all the while damning their cursed fate and praying that the ship might founder and put an end to their sufferings. They could eat nothing, nor keep it down for long if they did. But neither did the rest of us fare much better, because the galley fire could not be lit on account of the rain and spray, nor would the great copper cauldron stay filled by reason of the ship's rolling and pitching. So we subsisted on biscuit, butter and cheese as best we could, which was an additional tribulation for us not to have warm food since we were soaked and shivering the whole time.

But even the most vehement tempest will blow itself out, and on the morning of the 24th of October, which was a Friday, the gale blew down and the seas subsided, changing from ragged-edged angry waves to the great smooth-rolling surge of an old sea no longer driven along by the wind and too tired to work any further mischief. We scanned the horizon round about us and saw the sails of three vessels; all of them Dutch fluit-ships and the English nowhere in sight. We sent to question them and discovered them to be the *Fortuijn*, the *Pelikaan* and the *Vliegende Hert* which had been our companions in the Dunkirk squadron, and were therefore mighty pleased with ourselves that despite the violent weather and having been driven so far by the wind we had all kept pretty good station and suffered no damage other than the *Pelikaan's* fore topsail having been split by the wind while they were taking it in. Meester Hendrickssen took observation with his cross-staff at midday, the sun now being visible, and discovered our latitude to be forty-four degrees and four minutes. So given that the north shore of Spain runs along about the fourty-fourth parallel and no land was to be seen south of us, that meant that we were some good way out into the ocean to the west of Finistere, having run eight or nine leagues per watch by reason of the wind's force. From this we concluded that even the greatest evils have some good within them, and that the tempest, while it had scattered our ships and most likely done notable damage to them, had at least borne us all a good way further towards the shores of Spain.

Later that day we began to see other sails above the horizon as the vessels gathered together, for the rule in such cases is that one ship seeing another will steer towards it, and then another ship seeing two vessels will steer towards them, and in this way they congregate once more, as motes of straw are mysteriously drawn together when they float in a cup of water. At first it was our fellow-Dutchmen, then the English in twos and threes, until at last the great shape of the *Ann Royal* with her four masts came into sight, accompanied by Lord Delaware's *Saint George* and fifteen or sixteen of the colliers. The *Ann*, we saw, had her main topmast broken, which the sailors were busy sending down, and was likewise much battered by the waves with some of her decorations torn away. We learned that the seas had burst through one of her hatches and poured below decks, so that much of her biscuit and some of her powder was spoiled, while two guns broke free in her battery through being insecurely lashed up and rolled to and fro causing much detriment. All aboard her swore that they had never seen such a storm before and expected every minute to founder and be drowned, though by God's sovereign mercy they had all been miraculously spared from the tempest's wrath; which led me (I confess) to wonder why then God had sent it in the first place. But next day we learned that our fleet had not escaped without signal damage. The collier *Robert* of Ipswich had foundered with a hundred and thirty-eight souls and – what was far worse for our expedition – with the ninety or so draught horses that were to have pulled our great siege cannon. There was no doubt concerning this, because the collier *Bonaventure* of Hull had been in company with them when the tempest knocked them over, and despite the raging seas had sent a boat over to try and rescue her men, but the vessel had foundered too quickly for them to save anyone and the boat's crew could only listen to the distracted neighing of the horses drowning in the darkness below decks, which woeful sound I had no doubt would haunt their ears until their dying day. That loss meant that when our army disembarked and wished to take any walled town it would either have to find horses to pull the guns, or sit impotently waiting for more to be sent out from England. Which was a lesson to me for my later life: never so far as lay in my power to let the whole success of an enterprise be dependent upon one fallible part of it, as an entire chain may be rendered useless by the snapping of its feeblest link.

★ ★ ★ ★ ★ ★ ★ ★ ★ ★

As he surveyed the ruins of the *Ann Royal's* great cabin Viscount Wimbledon (though he still had to keep reminding himself of that latter dignity) wondered what monstrous sin he had ever committed in his – so far as he could see – largely blameless fifty-three years of earthly existence, that there should have been laid upon his shoulders so onerous a charge as directing this sorry broken-backed expedition to nowhere. The panes of a good half of the stern windows had been dashed in by the waves as the great ship ran before the wind, so that the carpenters were now boarding them up. The wall-hangings were spoiled by sea-water, and likewise the chairs and benches all tossed about and battered one against another. Though he was no seaman and freely confessed that he had no knowledge of that art, being entirely content to rest upon Captain Love's counsel in such matters, he still wondered why it was that the king's ships should offer so much smashable glass to the wind and waves at precisely that part of the vessel where it was most likely to be smashed, and why it would not be possible to contrive their sterns as he saw the Dutchmen did, with a rounded tucked-up shape to deflect the waves and little windows set in the sides high above the water. But the sea (he realised) is a place as full of such arcanæ as it is of fish, and only those high priests in Neptune's temple the mariners fully conversant – or so they would have men believe – with its sacred mysteries, so that there was no request of his so simple that they were unable to find some excellent reason for not doing it, claiming that the wind or the tides or the construction of their vessels would not allow it, and telling him to his face that landsmen such as himself had no understanding in these matters. For this reason he now frankly detested ships and everything to do with them. They stank; they rolled and pitched abominably; they would not go where they were supposed to go; and something or other was always amiss with them so that they could not perform their required office; like Lady Cecil's precious case-watch which he had bought in Holland at her request and which was always wrong or out of order, so that he had once excited her wrath by telling her that now it was entirely stopped she might console herself that it was right at least twice a day, and suggesting for good measure that she use an honest sundial such as had sufficed for her grand-dam. Before this voyage his experience of seafaring had been limited to the packets taking him to and from his regiment in Holland, which were disagreeable enough to be sure, and the two or three days at sea had always seemed like as many years, but he could always console himself as he lay groaning and spewing in his bunk that his sufferings would shortly be at an end and dry land under his feet once more. This time, though, it seemed that he had been condemned to suffer for all eternity aboard this evil-smelling hulk; racked by nausea (though that was a somewhat abated now) and revolted still further by the odours of tar and bilgewater and gross victuals boiling in the cauldron, yet still be required to direct a great expedition upon which his master's honour and credit might depend among the princes of Christendom.

And plagued not just by such minor inconveniences as seasickness and a leaking ship either (which an old soldier ought not to complain of), but called upon to execute the King's wishes without experienced commanders or seasoned troops to serve under him, or proper supplies, or even any clear notion of what it was that His Majesty and My Lord Buckingham (who was frankly an impertinent coxcomb) required him to achieve. Having seen considerable service in the Low-Country wars in Queen Elizabeth's day, he had pressed King James the previous summer to reinforce Count Mansfeld's army at Dover and send it across to fight alongside the Dutch, whom he knew to be solid and dependable allies. But after whole wagonloads of money had been spent upon that sorry force, it had been allowed to rot away from sickness and desertion, and instead Buckingham and the Parliament had persuaded His Majesty for this present lame-witted scheme, to hurt the Spaniards in their own country and perhaps take their treasure fleet so that the whole thing would pay for itself. Except that no man knew whether that fleet was on its way, or had arrived yet, or had even left Vera Cruz; whilst as for the rest there was no agreement at all among his captains where they might best put the army ashore.

Because go ashore they soon must. The winter gales were approaching – of which the past two days were but a foretaste – and likewise the victuals were much of them already rotten, and fresh water running short, and the soldiers likely to decay and sicken the more with every day they spent rolling upon the waves. Sir William Saint Leger of the king's ship *Convertive* had in fact just sent him a most disquieting message in which he wrote that he feared he had the plague aboard his vessel, and would therefore not be able to attend the next council for fear of bringing the contagion with him. No, there was no question of it: they must land at the first opportunity and have done with ships. Sea campaigns were best left to mariners, who understood these matters, and for himself he would be happy to be back as soon as he could fighting the only kind of war that he properly understood; on good solid land which did not roll and heave and shift its place the whole time.

He was old now, and his joints ached, and such few teeth as were left to him pained him day and night, and he feared that he might already have the stone in his kidneys. That previous storm-racked night as he lay in his rolling cabin-bed (which was but a coffin with curtains) hanging on to the sides for fear of being thrown from it and leaning out from time to time to make use of the wooden pail which his manservant had placed at his bedside, he had dreamed in between bouts of vomiting of cara Italia where he had studied as a young man; the warm lemon groves in the sunshine, and the brown-skinned contadina who had charitably instructed him in certain matters among the olive trees that day near Fiesole – though he hastened to assure himself that since he married Lady Cecil he had been entirely faithful to her despite his many long absences. But he quickly thrust aside such idle and unmanning reveries: his name was Cecil, and to be a Cecil was to serve, which was his family's business and fortune and without which they would still be no more than impoverished hedge-squires in the Welsh borders. He still sometimes wondered though, in the dark hours of the early morning, whether the profession of arms was the only way to serve, or even the best one, and whether perhaps the law or scholarship or even the Church might not have been a wiser choice. But enough of these unprofitable maunderings: he was who he was; and he was where he was, in the great cabin of one of His Majesty's ships a hundred miles off the coast of Spain – about the latitude of La Coruña, Captain Love thought – with sixteen thousand men and ninety-six vessels under his command and great things to be accomplished in the days ahead. But still His Majesty's last words to him at Plymouth rang in his ears like the echo inside the cathedral dome in Florence: "Remember always and bear foremost in your thoughts, Wimbledon, that our ships are the principal bulwark of our kingdom, and that if we lose them we stand naked against the King of Spain. As the Delphic oracle told Pericles of Athens, 'the walls of your city are made of wood'." His Majesty was right: he must be audacious. But at the same time, not *too* audacious.

★ ★ ★ ★ ★ ★ ★ ★ ★ ★

Once the gross of our fleet was reassembled – though Lord Essex's ships were still nowhere to be seen – we turned south by south-east to bring us back in towards the coast of Portugal, which was in those days but a province and dependency of Spain. The wind still blew north by north-east, but moderately now so that we were sailing on our most favourable quarter and made good progress. The weather was turned fine again, and the seas likewise warmer now that we were so far south. As we sailed along through the sunlit waves dolphins came to join us, which are a sign of good fortune, and swam along all day beneath the bows of our vessels, leaping and rolling after their manner as though they had sought out our company and now delighted in it. Sigurdsson told me that he had heard from fishermen in Norway that those creatures take pleasure in men's music, as Pliny also relates; so for a trial he took his viol to the beakhead one midday after dinner and played them a merry jig, then a sad air, so that we might see what the effect would be. But we observed none, our four or five dolphins sporting along as before, so we concluded that their ears must be adapted to hear sounds in the water but not in the air above it.

Next day in the forenoon watch the ships on the larboard flank of our armada all started signalling by firing guns and dipping topsails that their lookouts had sighted land, which we supposed to be some way south of Lisbon since our noon observation gave us a latitude of thirty-eight degrees and four minutes. By the middle of the afternoon watch we could plainly see the coast about six miles distant: a hilly shore with sandy cliffs which Meester Hendrickssen (who knew this coast well from the salt trade, that having been our ship's business before she was chartered) thought must be Cape Espichel south of the Tagus estuary. But if we could see the shore, the shore could likewise see us. Before long columns of dark smoke were ascending into the sky as beacons were lit one after another to signal our arrival. This was mighty disconcerting to us, since beacon fires are not got together and lit in an hour but have to be heaped up days before, and likewise watchmen camped nearby to light them; which plainly meant that the enemy was expecting our approach – and most probably on that part of the coast as well, since the shores of Iberia are exceeding long and to place beacons along the whole extent of them would be a most costly undertaking.

Our captain declared at supper that since we had now been nine days away from Plymouth, and that a fishing smack might cross to France in a night or to the shores of Galicia in two days, and a messenger then gallop by relays to Madrid in four or five days, it was entirely probable that our armada was expected, and Rey Felipe would surely have hot dishes ready to be served to us as soon as we came knocking at the door of his inn. Yet we saw that far from being daunted by that prospect, he regarded it with relish, and indeed hoped that the Spaniards would be there to greet us as we came ashore rather than our landing like caitiffs on some miserable desert island and claiming we had conquered it. "My own surmise," he informed us as we cleared the dishes away, "is that once the English have dithered a season as is their custom, we shall make either for Cadiz on the Atlantic shore or for Málaga in the Mediterranean. Gibraltar is too strong a fortress for us to attempt without siege artillery; so those other two harbours are the only ones close by that are capacious enough to hold our ships through the winter. Myself though, if any man would listen to so lowly a fellow as the skipper of a Dutch fluit-ship, I would counsel taking the haven of Ceuta on the African side, which would give us just as great opportunity to plague the Spaniards next year, and likewise be much less accessible to them taking it back from us since the country inland of it belongs to the Barbary Moors, who would assuredly cut up any Spanish army that landed there and feed it to their dogs." At which Suleiman showed us his white teeth and assured the captain that yes they would, en de kloten van de Spaansche varken wel ook op vleespinnen braaien en vreten.*

But seeing my somewhat morose countenance (since for my father's sake I had hoped that we would be home by the year's end and not marooned on the shores of Spain) he slapped my shoulder to hearten me. "Come, Van Raveyck, my brave young fellow: with all your learning in the classical authors, does not a season ashore in their towns that were once Roman and Greek cities entice you at all? I can assure you from my own observation that many temples and amphitheatres from those days are still to be seen there and await a draughtsman's pencil. And likewise wine, and olives, and many a dark-eyed señorita sighing behind the grille of her window at the sight of a handsome young Dutchman in the street outside. I'll wager that if we occupy one of their towns for the winter, then by Easter your privy member will be weighed down by all the maidenheads it's claimed like an orchard bough in October creaking under the burden of apples." Seeing my discomposure at this bawdy frankness, he laughed heartily. "Remember always, jongen: the Republic's service at sea is a hard one and a sailor-man takes many a knock. But none the less our life has its small consolations – and my advice to you is to take them while you can, for they may not come your way again."

I was somewhat discomfited by this cheerful bluntness of his, even though the Hollanders are commonly franker in their speech than we are in Flanders, and seamen in general but little given to delicacy in their discourse. But I saw that though coarse, his advice was kindly meant. And indeed, to tell the truth, I had felt lately that my blood had started to bubble inside my veins like fer-

---

* ...and roast the testicles of the Spanish pigs on skewers and eat them up.

menting cider; and likewise begun to have curious but agreeable early-morning dreams in which fair ladies and book-engravings of Greek nymphs often figured, though as yet I had no idea why.

One thing that eased my heart not a little as we sailed southwards was, that for all his lamentations at being obliged once more to venture upon the great ocean though his hair and beard were now white as snow, borne to the galleys (he said) like old blind Anchises upon the shoulders of his son Aeneas (though I think that herein he rather exaggerated matters for effect), my stepfather appeared somewhat pulled out of the dump into which he had fallen upon receiving news of my mother's death, and I thought that the change of air and surroundings might indeed have worked to his betterment; likewise the busy purposeful watch-on-watch life of a ship at sea, which is far less generative of melancholic humours than lying at anchor awaiting orders. He was by no means his old self: a wistful sadness still surrounded him and he no longer cracked jokes or told stories to entertain the company at dinner. But neither did he seem as utterly cast down as he had been at Plymouth, and went about his duties briskly and with every outward sign of courageous resolution so I thought that he must be on the mend.

He agreed with me that it was his duty not to make an end of himself; if only for the sake of my poor little sister Henriette who, though she was now lodged with the Bourchier family at Hoddesden who would surely be loving and attentive kindred to her, would likewise scarcely thank him for being turned so soon from a half-orphan into a whole one. But that evening as we sailed along past Cape Espichel and it was plain that we would soon make a landing, he remarked to me as we observed the sun sinking below the ocean horizon, and I said to him how fine a spectacle it was, that he could not see it because he was dead: that though his eyes registered the sight his head took no cognisance of it. Thinking that he jested with me, I enquired how that might be, since he plainly walked and breathed. To which he replied that whilst he might display all the outward signs of life, it was but an empty pantomime, as a dead body might still twitch and its limbs convulse several hours after life has departed. Not a little alarmed to hear such talk, I asked him then, if he was now dead, how did he still perform his duties aboard the ship, and might it not be viewed as a fraud against the Admiralty of Zeeland if he remained on the ship's muster roll and continued to be paid his wages each month, and perhaps he should request Meester Grobelaar to strike his name from the pay ledger? At which he smiled faintly, like the sun trying to shine through clouds, and said that I must not be at all disquieted on his account: that though he was now a dead man, yet he still fancied that he was as punctilious dead as he had been when he was still alive, and would faithfully perform his duties as surgeon for as long as the voyage lasted, after which I might take him ashore and bury him whenever I pleased. "For it is plain for any fool to see," he said, "that we shall soon be in the middle of what in French is called 'une partie de cassepipe', and that of no mean order withal. And many hundreds – nay, thousands – of poor deluded young fellows that sought glory and honour on foreign fields, or were pressed for their prince's service, will be lying all torn and mangled, crying most piteously for a surgeon's help. So though I am now myself dead, my final task in this world of sorrows will be to ease their doleful lot as best I can. For I see clearly, now my life is over, that fame and honour, wealth and love and religion and learning and all the rest were but fleeting shadows, and that in the end the best we can do is to help one another hobble along the sorry path that leads from our cradles to our graves, and try to make the miserable lot we are all born to somewhat less unbearable. Because nothing else has any sense at all." And though these words of his disturbed me not a little, since I knew him to be a man of the utmost resolution, and consequential in all that he did, my fears were at least allayed that he might cast himself overboard one dark night.

It was during those balmy days as our fleet sailed down the coast of Portugal that I came to make the acquaintance of one of Captain Neades's bowmen. Our English passengers mostly kept well clear of us Dutchmen, for though they were courteous and well-behaved enough, being men of mature years who had laboured all their lives to earn their bread and not rowdy dissolute young wastrels such as soldiers commonly are, they still kept their own company and saw us only at mealtimes when they came up to collect their food from the galley. Now that the weather was turned fine again they would congregate under the direction of their corporals on some part of the deck out of our way, and sit there to scour up their corselets with fine sand and scraps of old canvas until the steel gleamed like silver. And this was no discourtesy on their part, for scarcely a man of our crew knew any English, and they likewise no other language, so fellowship between us would have been limited by the lack of words to express it in. I would act as intermediary for them when it was required; but for the most part they kept themselves to themselves.

But there was one among them who took a special liking to me: a corporal called Will Shefford who was a merry humorous old rascal of (I should think) nearer sixty years than fifty and almost without teeth and hair. He was a wheelwright, he told me, in a village in the county of Buckingham called Whaddon and had many grandchildren, though he was now a widower. I quickly perceived, though, that his amity towards me had as much to do with my possession of a key to the beer cask (which I had in my capacity as ziekentrooster, so that I could draw beer for the sick) as with my own good parts. We and the English soldiers alike should each have received a gallon of beer per day as part of our rations. But our complement having been more than doubled by their coming aboard, the ration had been reduced to a half-gallon per day and the rest "beveraas", which is a mixture of cask-water with vinegar. Corporal Shefford, however, held that because his two or three remaining teeth made it troublesome for him to chew ship's biscuit he was therefore entitled to more liquid sustenance than the rest by way of compensation.

"For depend upon it, young Frankie," he said as I brought a surreptitious flap-can of beer to him while he sat sunning himself on the foc'sle, "no man ever perished yet from excess of ale; and though the rest of our fellows think little of your Hollander's beer, saying it both looks and tastes like horse's piss, myself I esteem it a good wholesome beverage – and now gratefully drink your health in it, and that of your king likewise."

"We have no king, Master Shefford" I said. "We are a republic, and our prince is the Stadhouder Frederik-Hendrik of Nassau." He looked at me in puzzlement, then winked and raised his can.

"Here's a health, then," he said, "to the Stoat-Holder Hederik-Fendrik of Mousehole and all his heirs and successors, and to all Dutchmen both aboard this vessel and wheresoever else they be in the world; for they brew good beer and are therefore honest fellows in my sight. But I pray you, cease to address me as Master Shefford and just call me Will, which is how all other men name me when I am out of my harness and my military duty. And you, young Frankie, how does it fall out that you speak English so well?"

"I lived three years at Colchester in Essex," I replied, "where my stepfather practised as a surgeon. He spoke mostly in French, saying that he was too old to learn other tongues. But I soon became pretty fluent in your language, which anyway has many points of resemblance with Dutch."

"True enough," he said with great gravity, "and I can already converse well enough with your fellows about such matters as bruin brood, boter and groene kaas.* Tell me, do they shoot with the longbow there in Essex, or in Holland?"

"To tell you the truth," I said, "not a great deal: the practice of archery is long extinct in those eastern counties of England, while in the Low Countries it was never much practised at all."

He nodded sagely and gurgled down some beer, afterwards wiping the foam from his mouth with the back of his hand.

"That would agree well enough," he said. "Away from the woodland shires, Englishmen shoot but little with the bow these

---

* Brown bread, butter and green cheese.

days. But where I live we still have great forests of beech and oak. And there in the leafy fastnesses of Whaddon Chase men still sally forth of a summer's morning when the dew lies on the grass of the greenwood glades to hunt the timorous deer as their great-grandfathers did in the olden time." Here he held up his bow, which he had detached from the pike so he could oil it with linseed. "This good instrument here, young Frankie, was old England's bulwark and protection in days of yore – and will be for as long as there are Englishmen with strong right arms to draw it. Away, I say, with your villainous new-fangled gunpowder and the stinking tubes that discharge such noxious farts of the Devil. The longbow is every whit as fatal to man or beast as a musket from just as far off and..." (here lowered his voice, as though telling me some momentous secret) "...has the great and sovereign virtue of silence, for the noise of a gun will startle all the deer for a mile or more about even if a man misses the mark. But the bow is so stealthy and insidious that a fine fat buck or a scurvy papist Spaniard may fall dead with an arrow through his heart, and his companion grazing beside him not even be aware of it."

He nodded, and paused to drink some more beer. And I nodded likewise since I thought my assent was required, though I still could not rid my mind of a sudden fantastical vision of my old friend Corporal Bobadilla placidly cropping the grass while another Spanish soldier lay beside him transfixed by an arrow.

"Depend upon it, young fellow," he said, "though we are but a small company and all old men, we shall none the less perform such deeds in Spain as our posterity will surely sing of around the fireside along with their ballads of bold Robin Hood and his merry men, and King Arthur and Ranulf Earl of Chester and all the other worthy heroes that our island race has produced. For be sure that Englishmen, though they are not accustomed to brag and boast as Frenchmen or Spaniards will..." (I shook my head here, as if to say, "Perish the thought") "...are nonetheless of dauntless heart and will not bend their necks before the Pope or the King of Spain any such foreign tyrant, as we have proved on a hundred fields such as Poiticourt and Agitiers" (I think he meant here Poitiers and Agincourt, but our Dutch beer was more potent than their ale, and his bald old head perhaps not as strong as other men's to resist it).

"In which campaigns did you serve then?" I asked him, since at fifty-five or sixty years old he would be about the same age as my stepfather, and was therefore likely enough a veteran of the Low-Country wars in Elizabeth's reign. But at this he cast down his eyes and sighed, and returned to polishing his bow, so I thought that perhaps I had spoken amiss and that his memories were painful to him, as the scars left by his recollections on an old soldier's mind are sometimes more hurtful than those he bears upon his body.

He answered at last. "I had the honour, young Frankie, to serve in my youth in the great Armada campaign of '88."

And I thought he must mean by this, at sea with Drake and Hawkins, and was about to tell him that my stepfather had also served in that campaign though on the other side. But he spoke first, as though confessing to a crime before the accusation of it was even levelled.

"I served on land, at Tilbury where we paraded before Good Queen Bess of blessed memory, then latterly at Dover Cliffs in Kent, where I saw the great host of their ships sail up the Channel towards Gravelines with our vessels snapping at their heels, and each of their galleons carrying a rack in the hold ready to make us abjure the true Protestant religion when they came ashore, and likewise great store of stakes and faggots for their fat villainous friars to burn us with. By God's merciful providence they never set foot ashore in England. But if they had, we were waiting for them with our bows and our quivers full of good clothyard arrows, to convince them of their error and send Parma* scurrying back to Flanders with his trunks all full of our barbs like a porcu-

---

* The great Spanish general Alessandro Farnese, Duke of Parma was usually known as "Parma" in England but as "Farnese" in continental Europe.

pine's quills. So I count myself a veteran of that campaign. And though I was never called upon to shed my blood for England, yet I would have done so as readily as any man — and for all my years and my grey hairs will do still upon the fields of Spain in vindication of King Charles's honour, and the Protestant religion, and the puissant longbow. For though some wiseacres say that an arrow is not as efficacious as a musket bullet in piercing plate, we hope to show them wrong. Here, let me give you a demonstration: take that old breastplate over there, which Mister Neades told us to throw overboard as unserviceable, and stand it against the fence-thing down there" (by which I divined he meant the beakhead rail, near to the planks with holes in them on which the sailors sat to ease themselves). I did as he instructed me with some apprehension, because playing with bows and arrows aboard a ship is a dangerous pastime. But the hands were all below at their dinner and few men were about, it being fine sailing weather and little work required on deck.

I returned to him as he took an arrow from his case, which I think is called a quiver in English. He fitted the notch in the end to the bowstring and pulled it back with a prodigious creaking, because the bow-stave of yew-wood was thicker than a broomstick and very stiff to bend. He squinted along the arrow, then let fly, the bowstring slapping the leather brace on his left forearm with a mighty crack. The arrowhead struck the breastplate with a resounding clang — but, failing to penetrate it, flew off at an angle into the sea. This was a considerable relief to me, because if it had stuck into the ship's timbers and the bo'sun had seen it then Will Shefford might very well have been ducked from the yardarm for indiscipline and endangering his fellows, which punishment at his age would most likely have been the end of him.

But as I retrieved the breastplate (which was dented but not pierced) I saw to my dismay that there was a great commotion in the water alongside and that the waves were red with blood. The glancing arrow had struck one of our attendant dolphins just as it leaped and wounded it mortally, so that the creature was now thrashing about in its heart's blood while its fellows looked on. They fell astern and I saw no more of them. But after that the dolphins would have no further truck with us and shunned the company of our entire fleet, word having spread among them that we had used one of their number so villainously and without the smallest provocation. And this, I think, was the start of our undoing, since all seafarers reverence dolphins and regard them as bringers of good fortune; so that when they leave they take good fortune with them.

CHAPTER ELEVEN

The next day, which was the 30th of October, just after midday and at thirty-six degrees of latitude, we sighted a great many sails over the horizon to westward. We thought at first that we must have stumbled unwitting upon the Spanish plate fleet – and wondered in that case how we might take it, given that we had but thirty-four vessels, whilst the Spaniards would certainly be twice or three times as many. But two of our ketches having been sent to reconnoitre, we soon learned that they were the Earl of Essex's ships together with those of the Earl of Denbigh, fifty-one vessels in all, which had been scattered by the storm but had reassembled some fifty leagues to the west of Cape Saint Vincent. With them were four small fishing carracks out of Lisbon which they had taken the day before, one of which had been blown out to sea the previous week and was in such desperate necessity when they came upon her that her crew were drinking their own urine for lack of water. The Portugalers told us that the silver fleet was indeed on its way, and that four of its galleons had already arrived at Lisbon ahead of the rest. Sir Edward (we heard) was mighty suspicious of this intelligence, and thought the carracks might have been sent out on purpose to beguile us. But at least our armada was together once more, so it might now proceed to business.

And what that business was to be, might at last be decided upon since we were in Spanish waters and the weather likewise calm enough to summon a council. So at four bells of the forenoon watch an order came from the *Geluckige Leeuw* that I was to change into my best clothes and betake myself aboard the *Ann Royal* where a council of war was convened, and there make a note of the proceedings so that the Jonker Willem and Doctor Reael might peruse it afterwards to see what it was that our allies purposed, they themselves not being privy to their plans in the event that they had any. I duly clambered down into the *Leeuw's* longboat with my notebook under my arm and my pen-case and inkhorn in my pocket, and was saluted by the boat's coxswain like a person of consideration (which I will confess was not a little gratifying to me) and then rowed across to the flagship where I was most cordially received by Lord Wimbledon's secretary Mister Glanville and allocated a place at a table in the great cabin alongside one of his own clerks. "And if you need to know who any of the speakers is, or have any other such question," he said, "you need only to ask Mister Hopkins here, who will gladly assist you."

The council this time was not a war council, consisting only of Sir Edward and his principal captains, but a *magnum concilium* of the entire English fleet comprising not only the admiral, the vice- and rear-admirals and the colonels of the army regiments, but also the captains of the collier ships; which made altogether about a hundred persons crowded into that room. We all stood up and removed our hats as Sir Edward entered with his principal officers following him, Mister Hopkins kindly whispering to me who each of them was, such as "The podgy-faced fool is My Lord Essex". Sir Edward sat at the head of the table with Essex and Denbigh beside him, then the others were seated around it according to their degree and precedence, with the rest on benches behind them or standing up against the walls. So before long it was mighty close in the cabin, the stern windows having mostly been boarded up; the atmosphere thick with the smell of unwashed bodies and with tobacco smoke since many of the collier captains persisted in puffing at their clay pipes, until from foulness of the air the rest prevailed upon them to put them out. Then we proceeded to business.

And such a council it was too, as I have never seen the like of before or since: more like a hospital ward for the feeble-witted in plenary session than a grave discussion among statesmen and captains such as I had read of in the antique authors; where Pompey and then Crassus each address the Roman Senate in measured cadences of faultless Latin prose and are listened to by the assembled *patres* in their togas with grave attention, then another stands up and agrees with them or gives rebuttal, and all as orderly and calm as you please until the venerable senators, having heard and weighed the arguments for and against, come after due deliberation to a motion which is then put to the vote. Or perhaps the antique historians put a fair face on it all, and the proceedings of the old Romans were in fact as muddled and inconsequential as our own; I cannot tell. I know only that it was mighty hard work for me to keep up with it all and produce a fair shorthand record to write my report from, and I often had to turn to Mister Hopkins and enquire in a whisper who such-and-such a speaker was and what exactly had he just said? And was told by him as often as not that he could make no sense of it either.

Though no agenda had been drawn up for the meeting (which Sir Edward owned was a grave defect and occasioned by the pressure of business upon his clerks) we divined in the end that its purpose was to decide what we should do next, we having come all this way and no particular enterprise being yet in prospect. He revealed that His Majesty's secret commission to him at Plymouth, besides taking the Mexico fleet, was to capture and hold some convenient port on the coasts of Spain where our vessels might pass the winter and come out again in the spring to harry the enemy's shipping. And though His Majesty had not been over-precise in the matter (geography and pilotage not being the principal business of monarchs) he himself considered, having taken the advice of his most senior sea-captains, that we should head for San Lucar, which was at the mouth of the Guadalquivir River, and capture that town, which would give us alike a safe haven for the winter and a base whence our soldiers might advance inland to take Jerez and Seville, which were not far away and would give them good opportunity for plunder since not a man among them had yet received a single farthing of his wages.

At these words of his you would have thought a fox had got into a hen-house, to see the commotion and dismay among the assembled collier captains who all fell to wailing and lamenting in a manner most pitiable to behold, fairly rending their garments and pouring dust on their heads after the manner of the ancient Jews. They all swore most vehemently and as one man that if San Lucar were to be our aim, why then surely we were all undone, because it was a most villainous haven and in no way convenient as an anchorage for so great a fleet; that it was shallow, and the river mouth full of treacherous sand-bars which shifted from day to day; and was likewise exposed to any gale of wind from the south-west so that ships lying there would have no shelter from the seas and with their anchors dragging in the sandy bottom, would infallibly be cast ashore and lost: that in short, if Viscount Wimbledon had asked them to nominate the very worst haven that might be found upon all the coasts of Europe, then they would have been unanimous in choosing San Lucar; and if he commanded them to anchor therein then he was no better than a heathen Tartar and they would all surely be drowned and their wives left widows and their children orphans. And so on and so forth, so that you would have thought from their wailing that San Lucar was the very mouth of hell or that Sir Edward was commanding them to stick their heads into a lion's jaws.

When they had quietened somewhat Sir Edward enquired how it was that they knew all this? And they told him that they were well acquainted with that port because the London sea-coal trade being slack in the summer months, they had been accustomed each year between May and September to employ their vessels carrying from San Lucar a sweet wine called "sack" which is produced in that region, and which the English are inordinately fond of though it conduces greatly to bladder stone and the gout. So they knew the place pretty well (they said). And esteemed it a most detestable hole.

"So then, sirs," said Sir Edward at last, who I could see was struggling to contain his annoyance, "Why did you not inform us of this when we were with His Majesty at Plymouth? We spoke of San Lucar then, and you had naught to say against it. So why do you now tell me that the place is so villainous a haven? Either you were wrong then, or you are wrong now."

And at this the captains fell once more to wailing and bemoaning; until one of them, Captain Brigstocke of Hartlepool, a great pocky-faced fellow, spoke for the rest.

"My Lord, when we were with His Majesty and My Lord Buckingham at Plymouth we indeed told them how ill a harbour San Lucar is for great ships to lie in; but they paid no heed to us, we being but persons of lowly degree. But now we are here, and winter already close with all its storms and hazards, we are put in greater and more vivid a mind of how evil a haven that place is than when we were so far distant from it in England. We crave only Your Lordship's pardon that we did not make this plainer at the time."

Sir Edward harrumphed, and gave Master Brigstocke a look as though he did not believe him but was too much a gentleman to say so. Then he sighed and returned wearily to shuffling his papers.

"Well then, my good sirs." he said at last, "Where else might we land upon these coasts, if geography denies San Lucar to us? In this I depend entirely upon your advice, for I freely admit that I am a land soldier and know nothing at all of the sea, so that if you assured me our ships could come out of the water and advance to Seville on wheels I would be compelled by my own ignorance to believe you." There was silence at this. "Come, sirs, what do you advise?" he asked, looking about the table.

There was murmuring and whispering for some time, and nothing could be made of it by me. So I turned to Mister Hopkins to seek his opinion. "Do all Sir Edward's councils proceed thus?" I whispered.

He laughed. "Pretty well all. Though a just and honest master, he lacks force and therefore allows matters to drift along willy-nilly for want of a firm hand and prior preparation. I have sat to take the minutes at five of his councils now, at Plymouth and on the way here, and at each of them Mister Glanville and I were in the greatest perplexity afterwards to discover what had been decided upon – or, indeed, what had been debated."

"Why then are the collier captains so fearful?" I said. "They scarcely strike me as timorous men by nature, yet now they sound like so many old maids in breeches."

"Indeed they do." he replied, "And the reason for that is that their vessels are on charter to King Charles, and they rightly fear that if they are lost or damaged and themselves killed or wounded, then they will have to whistle for their compensation, it being notorious that England's treasury is empty. The lords and gentlemen desire a fight, because war is their trade and their dignity and port depends upon it, and they have fortunes and lands to support their families if they are slain or maimed. These poor mariners, though, have nothing but their lives to hazard, and the ships which are their livelihoods, and so will be utterly undone if either suffer hurt. But hark, the meeting resumes…"

While we conferred Captain Argall (who commanded Essex's ship *Swiftsure*) had been consulting among the sailors and had made himself their spokesman.

"My Lord," he said, "after considering the matter somewhat we have concluded that the only ports accessible to us on this coast are Cadiz on the ocean side, or Málaga in the Mediterranean Sea, or Gibraltar which lies in the straits that separate the two. So we would respectfully suggest that Your Lordship considers each of these three with a view to selecting the most suitable." At this Captain Love of the *Ann Royal* interrupted him.

"Sir Samuel," he said, "while I hesitate to correct a fellow mariner, I would add that should Cadiz town prove too strong for us, I am informed that the bay behind it still contains a tolerable harbour on its north side called Puerto Santa María which might serve our purpose equally well." At this he stood up and looked round the great cabin. "Does anyone here present know anything of this place, for I confess I have never visited it." There was silence at this: it appeared that no one knew anything of Puerto Santa María (though when I related this later to our mate

Ellert Hendrickssen he was incredulous and said that the English collier captains were plainly mendacious rascals or very forgetful, because their ships plied from there quite as much as from San Lucar, and their seafarers commonly called the place Saint Mary Port as though it was one of their own harbours). Sir Edward spoke at last:

"Very well then." he said, "It seems to me that from ignorance of this Puerto whatever-it-is place we must debate the choice of Cadiz, Gibraltar and...what was the third place, Mister Glanville?...Ah yes, Málaga. So what can you tell me of them?"

Concerning Gibraltar, the opinion among all the army commanders was that though it was a fair haven and commodiously placed for harrying the enemy's shipping, it was likewise too strong a fortress for us to attempt with the weak means at our disposal, having no horses now to drag our siege guns. Málaga was then considered, but dismissed in the end as being too far into the Mediterranean, so that our armada might be bottled up there next spring by contrary winds and unable to get home again if King Philip dispatched his fleet against England. So in the end Cadiz was chosen, not as being the most suitable goal, but rather the least unsuitable. Or of course Puerto Santa María across the bay if Cadiz proved too strong; so that in the end no one seemed any the wiser as to which of these two we would attempt first. In the end, after about two hours, the meeting ended – or rather expired – and all those present returned to their ships amid a great deal of snorting and God-damn-me-sir-ing that so little should have been decided for so great an expenditure of time and breath.

★ ★ ★ ★ ★ ★ ★ ★ ★ ★

Next morning, the last day of October, the coast of Spain near Cape Granado came in sight: a low, sandy shore of dunes and scrub where the great Atlantic rollers broke on lonely beaches, with none to hear their incessant roaring since there was hardly a fisherman's hut between the Guadalaquivir mouth and Cadiz Bay.

But at least this time no plumes of smoke announced the great fleet's arrival, so there was still some small hope that Cadiz might be taken by surprise before messengers arrived to warn the town of its peril. This was indeed a reasonable enough surmise, because as the great concourse of topsails appeared over the horizon, gleaming white in the afternoon sunshine, and it became clear that this was not the Mexico fleet which would surely have sent messengers ahead of it, panic broke out among the folk of Cadiz, who remembered only too well how the English had sacked and burned the town during their last visit thirty years before. Gathering together such belongings as they could carry, people began to flee down the road that runs along the sandy isthmus that connects Cadiz to the mainland. The town had in it a mere four hundred soldiers, mostly elderly militiamen who would be of little use against regular troops, and no more than five barrels of powder. But Cadiz possessed a resource greater than either men or munitions in the person of its governor Don Fernando Girón de Salcedo y Brivesca. Though above sixty years of age and half crippled by gout, he was carried out of his palace in a chair borne on two poles and taken to the main gate where he stemmed the rush out of the town, allowing the women and children to depart so as to reduce the number of mouths to feed but detaining all men of fighting age. He dispatched a messenger on horseback to warn the Corregidor of Jerez that the English were approaching, then sent the five rowing galleys at his disposal across the bay to Puerto Santa María to bring over soldiers and supplies as these arrived from the country round about. As the autumn dusk fell he was still being carried about the town by torchlight to instruct his captains, and was up again before dawn next morning as the first troops came ashore from the galleys.

By midday of the 1st of November, All Saints' Day, the garrison had doubled in size. The town's white Moorish walls and crenellated towers bristled with cannon and musket barrels, and a thousand pairs of eyes peered seaward to make out what it was the English intended doing, ominously massed in the bay to the north of the harbour entrance about a mile distant. The sight of so great a fleet would surely daunt the stoutest of hearts. But the day wore on, and the English quite inexplicably did nothing; only sat there and missed two successive tides which would have taken them into Cadiz Bay. Around forty sailing ships and galleys had been trapped in the bay by their arrival; but these now profited from their foe's hesitation by weighing anchor and moving up on the flood tide into the innermost recesses of the bay, sinking blockships full of stones to close the channels behind them.

Meanwhile, aboard the *Ann Royal*, Sir Edward Cecil was deliberating with his secretary upon weighty matters. For it was plain that the long-smouldering enmity between the Earl of Denbigh and Baron Cromwell on one side and the Lords Delaware and Valentia on the other had at last broken out into flame.

"Mister Glanville," he said wearily, "Please refresh my memory, if you will, concerning this matter." Sir Edward was wan and bleary-eyed from having sat up all the previous night dictating orders to his secretaries and consulting with the regimental colonels and ordnance masters.

"It concerns Your Lordship's decision to replace Sir Francis Stewart as your rear-admiral of the fleet — and therefore admiral of the fleet's white squadron — after his ship was found unserviceable when we departed from Plymouth."

"Yes? And what of it? I replaced him with the Earl of Denbigh as the rear-admiral of the fleet. And if that also makes him admiral of the white squadron as well then I can only say, so be it if the sailors would have it that way. For myself, I would never have thought to command a regiment of horse in such a convoluted manner, where the cornet who leads my right-flank squadron also becomes in some mysterious fashion a captain so far as that squadron is concerned, and likewise all his corporals sergeants by virtue of the fact."

"Quite so, my lord: the mariners have their own way of ordering their affairs and we landsmen must accommodate ourselves to them as best we can. But the rub in this particular case is, that when My Lord Denbigh became your rear-admiral he hoisted a white flag with a Saint George's cross at his maintop to signify the fact."

"Yes, I understand that: Captain Love was kind enough to explain to me this business of squadrons and colours while we still lay at Plymouth."

"Excellent. So Your Lordship will therefore understand that as a consequence of My Lord Denbigh's promotion, My Lord Delaware became vice-admiral of your own squadron – that is to say, the red one – to take his place, and now flies at his foretop a red flag with the Saint George's cross on a square of white."

"By foretop, do you mean the summit of the pole-thing at the front end of the ship? I confess myself little versed in such matters."

"I do, my lord."

"Good. So what grieves him in that?"

" It grieves My Lords Valentia and Cromwell that My Lord Delaware, who is but an English baron and therefore of lower precedence than themselves, they both being Irish viscounts, should have been promoted out of turn by yourself to take the place of an earl as vice-admiral of the red, when by right of precedence My Lord Valentia should have filled that charge, and My Lord Cromwell have been moved to replace him as vice-admiral of the blue squadron."

Cecil sighed, and tried his best to remain patient and collected amid this bewildering whirl of flags, mastheads and noble ranks. He spoke at last with the strained air of a man trying to control himself.

"Mister Glanville, I would remind My Lords Valentia and Cromwell that having been entrusted by His Majesty with the charge of lieutenant-general for this expedition, I have perfect and sufficient authority vested in me to make whomsoever I please the vice-admiral of my squadron, and might perfectly well appoint my cook or my barber to that office if I were so minded; or indeed create green, yellow, pink and purple squadrons if it pleased me to do so. In any case, regarding his degree Sir Francis Stewart was but a knight, and I still had him as my vice-admiral without any objection from the noble lords. So what troubles them about this promotion?"

"For the sake of harmony and the success of our expedition, my lord, the two noble lords were prepared to overlook the offence against precedence. And Your Lordship will recall that he himself consented, when the matter was discussed with them after the council of war held off the Scillies on the thirteenth of this month, that to satisfy their honour My Lord Valentia might also fly a plain red flag, My Lord Cromwell a plain blue one and My Lord Delaware a plain white one from whichever of their mast-tops was not already occupied by an admiral's flag. But they complain now that My Lord Delaware flies not only the red flag with the Saint George cross at his foretop, which signifies the substantive charge that he now occupies, but also the plain white flag at his maintop whereupon he has without authority placed a red cross to distinguish it, saying that a plain white flag is the mark of one seeking to surrender, or of a French royal ship, and he will not be thought either a coward or a Frenchman. So in consequence, they say, it might appear to an uninformed observer that we have two admirals and not one to the white squadron. And this, they say, is not only contrary to all discipline, but My Lord Delaware not presently being on English soil, he cannot even claim precedence over My Lord Cromwell by virtue of the former noble lord being an Irish viscount and the latter one an English baron, which he might be minded to do were we still lying at Plymouth ."

Sir Edward fought back an urge to go into his closet and hang himself.

"What then would the noble lords have me do about this, with us now at Cadiz – which I believe is a port in Spain, or we have all been mightily deceived – and the enemy barely a mile distant from us? Even if I were minded to do so I could scarcely demote My Lord Delaware from his present charge without causing the very gravest confusion in the fleet; and likewise I can hardly clamber up the mast of his ship and rip off the offending cross with my own hands. What do you advise, Mister Glanville? Can we resolve this dispute by the exercise of common sense, or must it come to Their Lordships fighting a three-cornered duel on my quarterdeck while the Spaniards look on?"

"I have taken the trouble, my lord, to consult the late King James's instructions concerning precedence, a copy of which was brought aboard when we were at Plymouth. And I see therein that when Parliament's late subsidy in aid was voted, the name of Lord Carew, who is an English baron, appeared in the list above that of Lord Grandison, who is an Irish viscount. So that at least may settle the question of degree for the moment."

Sir Edward sat for some time slumped at the table with his face in his hands, shaking his head in disbelief. He spoke at last.

"Dear God, how extraordinary! What foresight is revealed here, Mister Glanville: what perfection. We have rotten beef and sour beer and spoiled biscuit and wet powder, and the ordnance master informs me that many of the cannon shot are too large to fit the cannon, and likewise some of the muskets lately supplied to us by the contractors are without touch-holes so that they cannot be fired but only swung like a club. And to complete our misfortunes, two hundred men aboard this vessel now lie sick with the spotted fever and I know not how many aboard the other ships. Yet we must be of good heart and not despair, because we have aboard a copy of His Late Majesty's instructions concerning precedence among peers of the realm. But what of this wretched flag? For myself, so long as the noble lords obey my orders then I care not a fig whether they fly a hundred flags of every colour of the rainbow, or no flags at all."

"Quite so, my lord: my own sentiments precisely. But the noble lords are none the less much exercised on the matter: and say likewise – though I hesitate to mention this – that though Your Lordship is His Majesty's lieutenant-general as regards his military office, he is otherwise but a viscount of very recent creation, his elevation to that rank not yet confirmed by Parliament, and he is therefore unqualified to resolve questions of honour by virtue of his own superior precedence, so that the Garter King of Arms in London must be consulted for a definitive opinion. So the solution that I would now respectfully suggest to Your Lordship, *ad tempus*, is that My Lord Valentia shall carry the red flag at his maintop with a Saint George's cross bordered with white superimposed upon the whole expanse of it, as your supernumerary chief deputy or vice-admiral, and My Lord Cromwell likewise a blue such flag at his maintop to signify that he is your supernumerary second-chief deputy or rear-admiral, and furthermore that…"

There was a sudden great rushing noise and a splintering crash above them, followed by a shower of debris falling past the cabin windows.

"Dear God!" Cecil cried, "What was that…? He called through the cabin door, "Captain Love, what is happening up there?"

After a while Love came into the great cabin, still white-faced and trembling from a cannon ball having recently passed close enough to knock him and those around him off their feet before smashing out a section of the taffrail.

"My lord, we must move away from the town. The Dons plainly have at least one cannon large enough to touch us."

"But you assured me that we were beyond shot…"

"Indeed I did, my lord. But evidently they have at least one piece large enough to touch us: most probably a long culverin which though it throws a ball of only twelve pounds or so, can throw it an exceedingly long way."

"Are we in peril of being struck again?"

"I think they hit us only at a venture, because at so long a distance the aim is very uncertain. But so long as we sit here we will be a cock-shy for them. We must either enter the bay on the next tide or fall back to seaward. We thought we might engage them when we pleased. But they have just engaged us."

At this point there was a noise of bos'un's whistles at the gangway as important visitors came aboard. It was the Jonker Willem and Doctor Reael, followed by Frans with his notebook tucked under his arm.

★ ★ ★ ★ ★ ★ ★ ★ ★

Cadiz as I first saw it that midday from the *Geluckige Leeuw's* longboat was a town surrounded by high walls, whitewashed after the fashion of the Moors and with many turrets along them so that its appearance was very singular and quite unlike that of any town that I had ever seen before in Flanders or in England. Its situation, though, was humdrum enough, on a low island at the tip of the long sandy isthmus that separates Cadiz Bay from the ocean. We came within four or five cable lengths of its walls, but at no great danger to ourselves (the boat's coxswain assured me) since we were well beyond musket shot. From time to time the Spaniards would fire off a great gun, and the bullet would plump into the sea three or four hundred yards short of the English vessels, and one or other of the English ships would then fire back at them with similar result. But this was only for bravado's sake, as two herring-wives will hurl abuse at one another *pro forma* from opposite ends of the fish quay without ever intending to come to blows. The Spaniards in the town were prudently husbanding their powder while observing us to see what it was that we intended. That is, if our captains themselves knew what it was that they intended, which was altogether somewhat debatable and the reason for our Dutch admirals going now to parley with them. For though our fleet had arrived off Cadiz the previous afternoon, it had made no attempt to enter the bay except for the Earl of Essex aboard the *Swiftsure*, who had gone in on the first of the flood and engaged the ships lying there, but finding that none followed him, had been obliged to let the enemy slip through his fingers and take refuge further up into the bay. Cadiz Bay itself, I saw (having consulted our Waghener's pilotage book, left lying on the cabin table after breakfast) was like a sack or poke, or a man's stomach in an anatomy book viewed posteriorly, and was about five miles across from east to west by three miles from north to south. The narrow sandy isthmus leading to Cadiz town separates it from the ocean, and inside the bay the entrance or gullet is between the peninsula of the Trocadero on the mainland side, and a small promontory called Puntal on the isthmus. And on this low promontory a fort, called San Lorenzo de Puntal, stands to guard the entrance to the inner bay. The Bay of Cadiz itself is not at all any great spectacle to look at, since its shores on every side are low and marshy, and the water in it likewise too shallow for great ships except along a channel in the middle leading to Puerto Real and Carraca at its easternmost extremities, which was where the Spanish ships were now anchored beyond our reach, they having sunk blockships in the channels. Cadiz Bay is not a very commodious anchorage at all except that its location makes it so, there being no other or better haven along all that straight, sandy coast between Faro and Gibraltar.

We were nearing the *Ann Royal* as the cannon ball struck her. It was the first time I had witnessed a vessel under fire, since during our engagement with the Spanish frigate that summer I had spent the entire action below in the surgeon's cockpit. So though I was diverted by the sudden puff of smoke from the ramparts and the burning wad flying out of it, then the boom coming to us across the water, I did not associate the sudden rushing noise with any peril until I saw the *Ann's* taffrail suddenly fly in pieces with a loud crash and the ball splash into the water some way beyond, then heard a great noise of cheering and trumpets come to us across the water as the Spaniards saw they had touched their target. I then realised with a sudden chill that if they could hit the English flagship, then they could also hit the longboat in which I now sat.

"So," Doctor Reael remarked (who was surely no novice as regards the enemy's fire), "Jan Spek* has drawn first blood. Your Highness must urge these English blockheads to cease their dith-

---

* "John Bacon": the Dutch sailor's nickname for a Spaniard.

ering and decide whether they wish to take the town, or enter the bay, or take Puerto Santa María, or go home instead. For I see that the Spanish ships which lay here when we arrived are now well beyond our reach."

"And what of that, Doctor Reael?" the Jonker Willem answered. "Surely we have them trapped in the bay and therefore hors de combat?"

"Indeed, Your Highness," he said, "but we still have them at our backs to bother us. From my questioning of the Spanish fishermen we took this morning I learned that the ships here are mostly Neapolitans, while the Spanish main fleet lies either at Gibraltar or at Cartagena. If they come against us, then we might find ourselves caught between two fires: the Naples ships inside the bay and the Spanish ones outside it. Your Highness must be firm with Sir Edward, or Viscount Wimbledon or whatever he now calls himself, and insist that he makes his mind up, because as matters stand we are likely to find ourselves – if Your Higness will pardon the expression – with our arse between two stools and sitting on neither."

Our stay aboard the *Ann Royal* was but a short one, it having already been decided by Sir Edward since the last council that, contrary to what we thought had been agreed there, Puerto Santa María was too shallow a haven to be useful to us (which I thought he might easily have discovered by consulting a pilotage book, but the ways of generals were still new and mysterious to me). So the only course for us now, it seemed, was to enter Cadiz Bay and anchor there beyond reach of the town's guns, then put our soldiers ashore to march up the isthmus and take the town from landward. But Fort Puntal guarding the narrows would first have to be reduced; so it was agreed by Sir Edward and our admirals that a force of five Dutch fluit-ships and twenty English colliers would first bombard the place, the water thereabouts being too shallow for the great ships. That matter having been settled (or so we thought) we bade Sir Edward goodbye and climbed down to our longboat waiting alongside. As we were rowed back the

Jonker Willem thanked me for my services.

"We are most grateful to you, Van Raveyck, for your assistance to us", he said, "But for the time being we have no further need of your services, our business having now been decided with Viscount Wimbledon insofar as such a thing is possible. So we shall take you back to the *Eenhoorn*. Your ship will shortly see action against Fort Puntal, and you must be aboard her to assist her surgeon. But rest assured that we have not forgotten you, and will send for you again should the need arise. So please to accept this as a small token of our gratitude." He then handed me a small gilt medallion of himself on a chain which I have to this day and treasure as a sign of princely favour; for though he himself was sadly slain two years after this at the siege of Grol, I still honour his memory as one possessed of that generosity and largeness of spirit which characterises great captains, and think that had he lived, he might have gone on to perform deeds as notable as those of his father Prince Maurits. He then fell back to talking with the vice-admiral and I was forgotten, to be left with my thoughts touching the coming action.

Back aboard the *Eenhoorn* I changed into my sea-clothes in great haste and went below to assist my stepfather in making the surgeon's cockpit ready for the coming battle. The ship was now all a-bustle and clearing for action, a message having already been sent to our squadron that five of us were to attempt Puntal along with the English colliers: our own ship, the *Fortuijn*, the *Halve Maen*, the *Basilisk* and the *Pelikaan*. Our captain eagerly solicited from Doctor Reael the privilege of leading the assault, knowing that a successful action would greatly advance his credit and reputation even if it left half his crew dead. But the reply came back that the *Fortuijn* and the *Pelikaan* would sail up to Puntal first to reconnoitre: to see what the true depth of water was since this was by no means certain from the chart which had been drawn for us by an English wine merchant resident in Cadiz, a Mister Jenkinson, who claimed to know these waters like his own breeches pocket – though this was most questionable, and our captain said afterwards that like the back of his neck was nearer the truth.

So about six o'clock that evening, as it grew dark, the two fluit-ships ventured up towards Puntal on the flood tide and were warmly received, the *Fortuijn* stranding on a mud bank within range of the fort and being most grievously knocked about before the water rose enough to float her off. Her skipper Captain Douwes was slain, his both legs being taken off above the knees by a cannon bullet so that he bled to death, and about thirty of her fellows were also killed, until the *Pelikaan*, as befits that most charitable bird, came up to cover her with her own fire, making the Spanish gunners keep their heads below the parapet while her men got a warp aboard the *Fortuijn* to tow her clear.

That night we lay at anchor off Cadiz town and awaited the coming day, which bade fair to be a hot one. Supper was served in the great cabin, with an empty place set at the table in memory of Captain Douwes, and all the fluit-ship skippers came aboard to confer about the morrow's action. There also sat down to sup with them an English army officer, one Captain John Palethorpe from the Earl of Denbigh's Regiment who had business aboard with Captain Neades since his bowmen, for want of any better employment – and I suppose to keep them out of harm's way – were to be assigned to the left flank of Captain Palethorpe's company. He was a Lincolnshire gentleman of cheerful ruddy countenance, about twenty-four or twenty-five years of age, who had already served three years as a lieutenant in the armies of the States-General and in consequence spoke pretty creditable Dutch, which was very singular in an Englishman since however long they served with us they mostly disdained to learn our language and expected us to learn theirs instead. The conversation over supper fell to our generals and their capacity or lack of it. To the great surprise of all present Mister Palethorpe – perhaps feeling freer in Dutch than he would in his native tongue – frankly owned that our commanders were, in his opinion and that of the other regimental officers, no more than a collection of worn-out old boobies left over from Queen Elizabeth's day and directed (insofar as any man directed them) by the Duke of Buckingham, whom he esteemed an entirely worthless person fit for nothing but to be a tailor's mannequin, and who owed his present dignity only to having been King James's catamite. Sir Edward Cecil (he said) had been chosen to lead this expedition merely by default, because King Charles could not decide between Sir Robert Mansell, who was advanced in years but a sea-officer and still energetic, and a younger but experienced land-officer like Sir Horace Vere or Ferdinando Fairfax. As to Sir James Bagg, who was Buckingham's creature and had been charged by him with provisioning and fitting out this expedition, he roundly declared that the rogues whose carcasses presently decorated England's gibbets were most of them hanged for lesser felonies than his. And touching the Earl of Essex, he said that there was much disquiet as to that noble lord's fitness to command: that he was a peevish undecided fellow and though none knew any positive *harm* of him, yet the command of armies required more qualities than the mere absence of vices, otherwise any country curate or pious lady's maid might equally well be appointed a general. He said likewise that it was widely rumoured in the army that Essex lacked the manly vigour that soldiering demands, having some ten years before had his marriage dissolved on grounds of its non-consummation though his wife was as comely a baggage as could be wished (and mighty lascivious withal) and would surely cause the greatest eunuch that ever was to stand up and salute her. "Here," he said, "I shall sing you a ditty that was current then, and which is now much sung again in our messes". At which he took Suleiman's lute that lay on the side table, tuned it, and then (having some skill as a musician, and a fine tenor voice) sang us a most salacious catch entitled *Sweet Frances Howard of Hornchurch Town**, which my readers

---

* In 1606, when he was 15 and she was 13, Robert Devereux, Earl of Essex was married to Frances Howard, daughter of the Earl of Suffolk. By 1613 the marriage was still unconsummated, and was finally annulled under pressure from King James on the grounds that her Essex was impotent and his wife still

would surely blush to hear in full, but the chorus of which was:

"Sweet Frances Howard of Hornchurch town,
Her shift went up but his yard hung down.
A virgin still though a wife and a whore,
Was ever the like of it seen before?"

And concluded with the lines

"Now back in Essex poor Bob doth chafe,
And at his horns all men do laugh."

This bawdy song of his diverted the company not a little once Mister Palethorpe had translated the words for them, though Mister Neades (who was plainly of a more serious temper) looked pained throughout. But even so I think we were privately somewhat shocked and disconcerted that among our allies their disrespect — not to say contempt — for their commanders went so far as to touch upon such intimate matters. We Hollanders are also mighty satirical towards our great ones: not least because whereas in England a man may still be stood in the pillory and have his ears sliced off if his words displease the mighty, in the Dutch provinces there is no such constraint from the law, and a libeller is at hazard only of receiving the libellee's rapier through his guts if a gentleman or being soundly cudgelled by his servants and tossed into a canal if of lower degree. Each year our printing presses disgorge hundreds of "spotprenten", which are droll commentaries in verse on our affairs and those of our neighbours and often very nicely illustrated by our finest engravers. But I never saw one of these that would debate whether Such-and-such was able to perform the marital devoir or not, and soon realised that where satires are

---

a virgin, though she was known to have had several lovers in the mean time. She then married the king's Scottish favourite Robert Carr. In 1615 Carr and his wife were implicated in a murder and were banished from court. But Essex's reputation never recovered from the affair, and gibes about sexual inadequacy pursued him for the rest of his life. Hornchurch is a small town in Essex.

concerned the English are unique among the nations in combining their dissidence with ribaldry. They are a folk that will tolerate any brutality or incompetence whatever in their rulers, provided only that they *look* like rulers; and conversely find nothing more contemptible in them than the appearance of lacking vigour. Yet from what we witnessed of the later conduct of that expedition, we were forced to admit that there might be something in the captain's song withal, and that fumbling incapacity in the service of Venus might indeed make King Charles's generals less than apt as votaries of Mars. For, as the English say, to fight and to fornicate are close cousins.

We were all up at three o'clock next morning as the tide turned, making ready to go up into the bay and resume our bombardment of Fort Puntal. To replace the *Fortuijn*, now so grievously battered as to be unserviceable and her crew taken off her, we were joined by the Zeeland ship the *Zeeridder* of Captain Johan Evertsen, who later won great renown in the Republic's service and was slain in the Two Days' Battle against the English. We all of us felt no small trepidation, because we had seen the previous evening from the essay of the *Fortuijn* and the *Pelikaan* that though of small size, Puntal fort might prove a nut the cracking of which would cost us several broken teeth. But even so we were all eager to make a start on our work, waiting for battle to commence being the most trying of vigils. So our gunners lay to their guns, eight men to each, and saw that all was made ready that was requisite for the service of those bronze gods: round shot in the racks to hand; cartouches of powder and wadding placed ready; tubs of water for sponging out and for the lintstocks to be laid over when the slow-matches were lit. At four o'clock, though it was still dark, the vlootpredikant* Dominie van Elst came aboard to conduct divine service because it was Sunday morning, and likewise to dispense us all from the sin of Sabbath-breaking, because (he said) there was God's work to be done and the Spaniards were notorious

---

* Fleet chaplain

enemies of His elect nation, so that drubbing them of a Sunday morning was no sin and might even be considered meritorious in the Lord's sight.

It began to grow light, and the water being judged by now to have risen high enough above the muddy shoals of the bay, we weighed our anchor and moved up towards Puntal on the tide with a light westerly breeze filling our sails, in line ahead with the *Basilisk* leading and ourselves second, the *Zeeridder* astern of us and then the *Halve Maen* and the *Pelikaan* bringing up the rear. For my own part, I was not immediately required below, all things having been made ready in the surgeon's cockpit, so our captain bade me come up on deck to convey his instructions to Mister Neades and his archers if the need should arise. The Englishmen were (he confessed to me) a great nuisance to him since we were the only ship of our squadron that was carrying land soldiers, there having been no opportunity yet to put them ashore. He had most earnestly counselled Captain Neades to keep his men below in the hold throughout the coming action, there being no advantage whatever in having them on deck, for if we were beyond musket shot what use would bows and arrows be against a fortress? But that gallant gentleman had insisted most vehemently that his men should be on deck to face the enemy's shot instead of skulking below like caitiffs while their Dutch hosts hazarded themselves to the Spaniard's fire. So with a sigh Captain Loodgieter had consented at last that if it pleased them so, and it did not hinder the working of the ship, then they should all stand drawn up in their ranks in the waist like so many skittles outside a tavern and have their foolish old heads knocked off to no purpose.

So as we sailed up towards Puntal in the first light of morning our pikemen-archers stood in the waist, drawn up in ranks in their corselets and gleaming helmets, with their pikes dressed with perfect perpendicularity and each of them as uniform and martial as though they had all been cast in green wax from the same mould. Mister Neades told me that it would be good for them and harden them, to face the enemy's fire even though they had no means of returning it, for he said that for many of them it was a long time since they had last been in battle – by which I took him to mean "never" – and that while a soldier soon grows accustomed to the idea that men who have never met him actively seek his death, this is a disturbing conceit at first and better for them to get it over with now than later.

It was soon apparent to us that the Spaniards were up early as well, because as the *Basilisk*, which was about two cables' distance ahead of us, came within range of Puntal the fort's guns crashed out in welcome, the orange flame from the muzzles all the brighter in the half-darkness. The *Basilisk* replied with a rolling broadside of her ten guns on the starboard battery, and the Spaniards likewise. As the smoke drifted away on the breeze I saw in the dim light that Fort Puntal was what military engineers call a quadrangular sconce; which is to say a low, square structure about a hundred foot across, with a pentagonal bastion at each corner and embrasures below the parapet which gave two tiers of cannon: about sixteen or twenty pieces in all, we thought, though it was later revealed to us that the fort was being refitted when we arrived and had only eight pieces able to fire. It was built of brownish stone, not earth or brick, and it was plain likewise that it lay on a low sandy peninsula with a moat dug across it which would cut it off from the mainland at high tide, thus making it very troublesome to be taken from landward (which we supposed to be Sir Edward's intention) until low water, which would be about five o' clock that afternoon. Having discharged her guns the *Basilisk* sailed on past the fort, and we came up, matches lit and cannon ready to fire. Our captain up on the poop turned to the mate and said

"Meester Hendrickssen, do you see any sign of our allies?"

Our mate peered astern, past the three vessels that followed us, and replied "Neither hide nor hair of them, skipper. What's become of the lazy dogs? You said that there were twenty of them promised to join us."

"Indeed I did: this was firmly agreed yesterday between our

admirals and Viscount Wimbledon at their meeting. The Jonker Willem sent a note afterwards to inform me of it. So what are they doing? Do they still lie abed in honour of Sunday morning?" Then he shrugged and turned back to the business in hand. "Anyway, colliers or no colliers, we are here now and each of us must do his best. We shall pound Jan Spek as best we can, and hope only that Jan Engelschman will see fit to join the party later on. Make ready to fire!"

We drew level with the fort, and as its guns banged out so did ours, in a broadside that made the whole ship to tremble: not a sudden single thunderclap but a leisurely rolling of detonations as the captain had instructed the master gunner; not each gun captain applying his match to the touch-hole when he saw the piece to right of him leap backwards as was the custom when engaging another ship, but each to count up to five then discharge his cannon so that the entire broadside lasted a minute or more and the fellows towards the stern were already reloading as the forwardmost gun gave fire. As for the enemy's shots at us, we perceived that they were more disordered now and worse-aimed than those they had fired at the *Basilisk*, so that one knocked out a piece of the fret beneath our beakhead and another hit the side well aft, while another aimed too high tore a rent in the mizzen sail and passed on with a great roaring noise, but most of their bullets merely splashed in the water about us. For myself, standing there beside our skipper, it was as Mister Neades had predicted a most disagreeable reflection at first that the bullet that had just ripped through the sail twenty feet above my head would infallibly, if aimed a half-degree or so lower, have knocked me all to bloody gobbets; and myself a surgeon's mate withal, with no more mortal weapon about my person than a fleam in my pocket for letting blood. But as Mister Neades had likewise predicted, the sensation quickly passed, and it seemed before long quite normal to me and perfectly comprehensible that those unseen rascals in the fort over there should be seeking to kill me though I had never offered them the smallest offence. And throughout all this din and peril our English bowmen stood like so many statues in the waist, never flinching even when shot whizzed overhead, until I think that their rheumaticky old calves must have grown tired with the standing.

Our starboard battery discharged and we having received (we ascertained) but small hurt in return, we sailed on past Puntal as our gunners reloaded, then ran the starboard guns in and shut and barred the port-lids since to have more gunports than necessary open during an action is always hazardous. About ten cables beyond the fort, as the *Zeeridder* fired at it, we put up our helm and went about. The wind blew steady from the west, so we could proceed past the fort on the starboard tack while discharging our starboard battery, then turn and pass back the other way on the larboard tack giving them the benefit of the guns on that side. This was the *modus operandi* that our captains had agreed the previous evening aboard the *Eenhoorn*: that each ship would begin firing as the vessel ahead ceased, and those coming back on the larboard tack likewise; and in this way Fort Puntal would be steadily battered over several hours or as long as it took to reduce the place; not with a sudden hurricane of shot from all our ships at once, which might only serve to inflame the courage and martial ardour of the defenders, but rather with a steady drizzle of fire to dampen it, each ship in its turn sousing the fort in passing like drunkards pissing against a stone outside a tavern, and in this manner subject their courage and mood to slow attrition, as a steady drip will wear away a stone more efficaciously than a sudden torrent.

Despite the danger to my person (which was most likely not very great so long as our ship kept moving and did not run aground like the unfortunate *Fortuijn*) I must confess that this first real battle that I had witnessed was a mighty imposing spectacle: the thundering of the cannon, the sulphurous white smoke, the flying banners all gaily coloured that fluttered from our mastheads, the red "bloedvlag" at the stern which our Dutch ships would hoist when going into battle as a sign of their earnest; and above all this the shrilling of trumpets and rat-tattling of drums which we kept up to encourage our own fellows and dishearten the enemy. And so this noisy pageant continued all the morning, our five vessels (for there was still no sign of the English colliers) discharging broadside after broadside at Fort Puntal, whose own guns had by now fallen silent, though they still loosed off a shot now and then to show us that they were not entirely reduced. As the tide rose Essex's *Swiftsure* came up with us and being too deep to come close in to the fort, dropped anchor with a spring-cable at her stern to manoeuvre herself and added her fire to ours, though more to hearten us than anything else since she was too far distant for it to have much effect. Yet as we came close at each pass and the smoke cleared I perceived that though it was now almost noon and the top of the tide, and we had fired off (by my computation) close on two thousand shots between us, yet still the little fort remained largely intact: a corner of wall knocked off here and there and the parapet edges somewhat dilapidated, and shot-marks on the walls, but the main structure still solid and intact as ever, which was very curious to me because I had always been told by the military wiseacres and alehouse strategists who abound alike in Flanders and in England that stone walls would not stand up to cannon and that only earth (by its softness) or brickwork (by its close-knit texture) would resist being battered by cannonfire without crumbling away to rubble. But this fort was patently built of stone, yet it seemed of adamantine toughness and utterly resistant to all that we might hurl against it, which I found most troublesome to account for.

★ ★ ★ ★ ★ ★ ★ ★ ★

It was seven o'clock in the morning aboard the *Ann Royal*. As the guns flashed and thundered a mile away divine service was being celebrated by the fleet chaplain Doctor Brundell, the seamen and soldiers drawn up in their ranks in the waist and Sir Edward and his officers on the quarterdeck above them to hear the Bible reading (Saint Paul's Letter to the Ephesians, Chapter 7, concerning obedience to lawful rulers) and to bellow out the psalms with the rest, then hear the doctor's sermon – likewise on obedience to lawful rulers – then take communion. The same scene was being enacted by Doctor Brundell's curates aboard all the king's ships, so Cadiz Bay was filled for the while by the sounds of an English Sunday morning as the defenders on the ramparts gazed across the water at them: impotently now that the English vessels had prudently withdrawn beyond the reach of the long culverin *Juanita* which had knocked a corner off their flagship the previous day. In Cadiz town too the aid of God was being invoked: or in this case Deo, assisted by La Virgene María and her son, and Todos los Santos for good measure. And men who might be dead or maimed by nightfall were being assured just like their English counterparts of the perfect divine justice of their cause, and therefore how pleasing an offering to the deity their own death or mutilation would be. Down the steps of the cathedral, surrounded by the smoke of incense, swaying precariously on her bier borne on the shoulders of barefoot members of the Brotherhood of Penitents in their pointed hoods, the image of the Blessed Virgin Mary began her journey around the town's narrow, malodorous streets before crowds of soldiers and townspeople who knelt in the filth and crossed themselves at her approach. And behind her, also borne on poles resting on the shoulders of his attendants, came the Blessed Virgin Mary's local agent Don Fernando de Girón in half-armour (though the weight of it plagued his gouty old joints more than he could well describe), raising his hand in acknowledgement of the blessings and encouragement that came from all sides.

The procession, though, was merely to put heart into the people: the real work had already been done without the assistance of the Virgin Mary or the communion of saints. All the previous night under cover of darkness the galleys had been plying to and fro across the bay between Cadiz and Puerto Santa María ferrying soldiers across a hundred at a time, and barrels of powder and kegs of musket balls, their oars creaking as their stems sliced through the calm waters, the manacles of their sweating slaves chinking in rhythmical chorus punctuated by the crack of the garda-chusma's whips – for the rowers were becoming tired – and yelps of pain from those whose backs were licked by them. It puzzled Girón that the English had made no attempt to interfere with this traffic across the bay, which had already raised the strength of the town's garrison from four hundred to nearly three thousand men. But the English (all men knew) were a strange people and their actions – or in this case, the lack of them – entirely inscrutable to rational beings. For his own part, though he regarded himself as an upright and honourable man, Don Fernando had likewise been a soldier long enough not to have any scruples about profiting from an enemy's folly and negligence. So in his heart he now joined the townsfolk in thanking the Blessed Virgin Mary, protectress of all Catholics and likewise Saint James of Compostella, patron saint of Spain, for having answered his prayers and smitten King Philip's enemies not with blindness or boils but with that strange paralysis of the will which in Spanish is called "abulia".

Halfway through Doctor Brundell's sermon aboard the *Ann Royal* there was a commotion at the gangway. The master-at-arms came up and whispered to Sir Edward that a boat from the *Geluckige Leeuw* had just come alongside bringing the Jonker Willem van Nassau, who urgently desire to speak with him. Sir Edward excused himself and hurried aft just in time to meet the Jonker Willem coming aboard followed by two of his aides. The princeling had no interpreter with him this time, so he spoke in French which Sir Edward (though he was fluent in Italian) understood but with a hop and a skip, having not studied that language since his far-distant schooldays. He made a bow of a depth appropriate to the Jonker Willem's princely rank, but the Dutchman did not return it. He was plainly much agitated.

"Milord de Wimbledon, il faut que je parle avec vous – en urgence!

"Erm...naturallemente... je serais enchanté de obligare Vestra

Altesse. And in what might I be of service to you?"

"Sir Edward, what is the meaning of this? Our Dutch ships have already been engaged with the enemy for two hours, yet there is still not a sign of the English collier vessels you promised to aid them. They have not so much as raised anchor, les lâches, and while Dutchmen shed their blood in this common enterprise you English stand singing your psalms as though you were still lying at anchor in Plymouth Sound. C'est pas honnête de vôtre part, pour le moins dire…"

Sir Edward understood barely the half of all this, but still saw that the young nobleman was highly displeased and fairly beside himself with anger.

"Er…je ne connais pas niente de tout cela. Pray be patient, my good prince…" He turned to Captain Love, who had by now joined him. "Sir Thomas, His Highness says that the ships we promised him yesterday for reducing Puntal are still riding at anchor and have not budged. Please to get a boat ready at once, that I may go and discover the meaning of this. And which are the vessels guilty of this dereliction, so that I may convene a court-martial for their captains?"

"I regret, my lord, but I have no knowledge of that: Captain Argall of the *Swiftsure* was appointed to detail which colliers would take part. And the *Swiftsure*, as your lordship will observe, has already weighed anchor and gone up into the bay on the tide. So we must go and interrogate each of the colliers in turn to discover whether they received such orders from him, and if so why they have ignored them."

So Sir Edward clambered down into the longboat with Captain Love and was rowed out across the early-morning water to the colliers, which were anchored a half-mile off, over in the shallows towards the Trocadero peninsula. They arrived to find the ships half awake, with that somnolent air of vessels lying in harbour early on a Sunday morning, for all the world as though the smoke and banging of gunfire less than a mile distant was no concern of theirs whatever. Sir Edward stood up in the stern sheets, sword in hand and red silken general's sash draped about his gorget and breastplate.

"Ho there! I would speak with the captain of this vessel." The mate of the collier-ship *Amity* of Middlesborough looked down at his visitors and continued to smoke his clay pipe, then took it out of his mouth at last.

"And who might you be when you're at home, sir?"

"How dare you address me thus, you insolent dog! I am Sir Edward Cecil, Viscount Wimbledon; His Majesty King Charles's lieutenant-general and commander of this expedition. Bring me your captain at once, or it'll be the worse for you!"

The mate scratched himself. "Begging your pardon: no offence intended." Then he strolled aft to the cabin and roused Captain William Skipwith from his sleep. "Skipper: there's a zany-headed fellow come alongside in a boat waving a sword and says as how he's the Fly-Hound Bimblebum or Bumble-bee or some such nonsense. He says he wants to speak with you."

The captain tumbled out of his bunk, groaning and tousled, and came forward to the gangway.

"What's all this commotion. Can't a man even lie in of a Sunday morning?"

"Are you the master of this ship?"

"Aye: happen I am."

"Then why have you not moved up to assist the Dutch vessels that currently bombard Fort Puntal?"

"Because no man ever told me that I should. We were instructed by the *Swiftsure* to drop anchor here on Friday evening, and not a word since. I reckon you must be wanting the *Bonaventure*: a boat came alongside them yesterday in the first dog watch, so it must be them as received the instruction and not us."

"Where are they?" Sir Edward demanded.

Skipwith pointed to a group of colliers anchored about two cable-lengths away . "More than likely it's that lot over there. For our part, if no one tells us to sling our hook and move, then it concerns us no more than last year's snow if the Butter-Boxes wish to spend Sabbath morning cracking their skulls against the walls of a fort. By all accounts those blackguards lately used our fellows uncommonly ill at Amboyna in the Indies*. So if they wish to make amends now by fighting the Spaniard for us then I think that only fitting reparation. I bid you good-day now, sir, for my breakfast awaits me"

Spluttering with rage (though he was not naturally a choleric man) Sir Edward was rowed across to the other colliers, where he received much the same reception: denials of ever having been given any such order, and directions to go and speak with someone else if he would be any the wiser concerning it. By the time he had questioned his third lot of collier captains Sir Edward was in a fine fury, inveighing against "these pusillanimous wretches that take the king's coin and eat his bread, but refuse to move a finger in vindication of his honour", and assuring each skipper in turn, sword in hand, that if he did not weigh anchor forthwith and move up towards Puntal he would infallibly be court martialled and hanged from the *Ann Royal's* yardarm for mutiny and dereliction of duty and afterwards left there for the fowls of the air to devour like Pharoah's baker. Yet after he had rowed on not a single vessel moved from her station, and Captain Love's pencilled list of defaulters contained several such entries as "*The collier-ship Whim-Wham of Gotham: master Captain Robin Hood*" and "*The collier-ship The Moon of Coventry: master Captain Mann*". In the end only the king's ships of Essex's squadron moved up on the tide to support the Dutch. And likewise – though no one had given order for her to do so – the Hartlepool collier *Great Sapphire* of the red squadron came up about eight o'clock to join the

---

* In 1623 the Dutch East India Company's traders at Ambon in the Moluccas eliminated their English rivals by arresting them on a charge of plotting against the Company, torturing them to extract the confessions required under Dutch law for capital crimes, then beheading them. The affair rankled for many years afterward, and rejection of a claim for compensation was one of the pretexts for the First Anglo-Dutch War in 1652.

party, her master Captain Raymond declaring that it was great shame that Englishmen should lie in their bunks while Dutchmen shed their blood in a common venture; for all that he could see that was common about it was that the Hollanders (whom he greatly respected, his adored wife Saskia being of that nation) should be graciously allowed to push the cart up the hill, while the English would push it down the other side. He took his ship in even closer to the fort than the Dutch vessels, and was killed about midday along with his mate Master Kenton by one of the last shots that the Spaniards fired, both smitten dead by the wind of the ball passing between them as they stood together on the poop deck. Which was a sad end for so gallant a seaman who had demonstrated that though of lowly degree he was still not insensible to the call of honour.

CHAPTER TWELVE

By about three o'clock in the afternoon, the tide by then approaching half-ebb, we had battered Fort Puntal until our ears were dull from the constant thundering, which after a while ceased to be single detonations and became instead a kind of basso continuo in the background. Thus far, praise God, our ship had suffered no man hurt, though three or four shots had struck her and as many more come close. As for the fort, it had now ceased its firing. Much of the parapet lay in ruins and cannon had been knocked off their carriages so that the barrels stuck up in the air. But still no sign came that its defenders wished to surrender, though we had several times ceased our cannonading so that they might have time to reflect on the matter.

About half-past three o'clock, the tide by then having ebbed sufficiently to reunite Puntal with the mainland, it was therefore decided by the Earl of Essex that soldiers must be put ashore to finish the job. Word of this was conveyed to us, whereupon Captain Neades sprang forward immediately and entreated me to send word back to My Lord Essex that he and his bowmen ardently solicited the privilege of making the first assault on the fort. I assured him that I would – but afterwards our captain took me aside and told me to do no such thing: that Mister Neades was plainly a gallant gentleman but also a very great fool, and to send his arthritical old fellows armed only with their bows and arrows against a well-defended fort would be as culpable a murder as King Herod ever perpetrated on the Holy Innocents. In the end a company of musketeers led by Captain Bromingham was put ashore from the *Swiftsure* on the beach just beyond shot of the fort and then, about four o'clock, essayed to take it from the landward side. As they waded across the moat they were hotly received with musketry and a shower of stones, and in the end were forced to fall back again since they lacked ladders with which to scale the ramparts. They then sent a message back to us, did anyone among us speak Spanish so that Captain Bromingham might explain to the defenders the hopelessness of their case? In the end, no one aboard Essex's ships apparently having that skill, Captain Loodgieter called me to him as his interpreter, and Matthias Sigurdsson with his trumpet, and had us all rowed across to join Mister Bromingham and his men.

We crouched in the ditch of the fort just out of the defenders' sight as Sigurdsson blew the chamade, which under the laws and usages of war is the formal summons for a fortress to surrender, and which if ignored three times allows the position afterwards to be stormed and its defenders put to the sword for having occasioned needless effusion of Christian blood. Our captain, whose Spanish was fluent and natural, then raised a white cloth tied to an oar to show that we wished to parley.

"Soldados del Rey Felipe", he shouted, "you have defended your position most gallantly these past eight hours and withstood a battering that would have daunted lesser men. But you will see from the great host surrounding you that your position is hopeless. Surrender now, and you will be treated with all the honours of war: allowed to keep your colours and weapons and conveyed across the bay in our boats under flag of truce to rejoin your fellows. Continue to resist, though, and when we have taken the place by storm your throats will all be cut for having occasioned so pointless a slaughter." He then turned around and said, "Sigurdsson, blow the chamade a second time." Sigurdsson put the trumpet to his lips and blew a fine clear blast. There was silence for a while, then muskets with white handkerchiefs tied to their muzzles began to appear from the fort's embrasures. We could hear shouting from within, and gathered from this that there was some disagreement among them about what to do next. At last a head in a plumed helmet appeared over the rampart. It was their commander, one Don Francisco de Bustamente; a very gallant gentleman who, towards the end of our late bombardment, had loaded and fired the cannon himself after his men had sought refuge in the cellars.

"Señore, what are your terms for surrender?" he shouted.

"As I said, vuestra merced," our captain called back, "your gallant fellows will be allowed to march out of the fort with their colours flying and their matches burning, led by their trumpeters and drummers, and will then be conveyed across the bay in our boats to be set at liberty on the other side."

There was a pause, then at last: "This seems fair and just, because our powder is low and we cannot resist much longer. But I myself, having been charged by His Excellency the Governor of Cadiz with defending this fort to the death, will require from you a certificate attesting that its further defence was hopeless."

"That attestation, señor, I will freely and gladly give you", Loodgieter shouted back.

So the gate opened at last and the Spaniards marched out of Fort Puntal, then Captain Bromingham's men marched in. As promised, they were embarked – about two hundred men in all, mostly local militiamen and not regular soldiers – in our boats and were rowed across to Trocadero to be put ashore. Meanwhile Don Francisco came up to us and, saluting our captain, offered him his sword, which I saw was mighty galling to Captain Bromingham whose men had done most of the fighting. But Loodgieter refused it and said that he could not take the sword of so valiant a gentleman (though he told me afterwards that he had no mind to have the weapon, which though finely decorated was too long for use aboard a ship, and likewise liable to rust in the salty air from being made of Toledo steel).

Back aboard the *Eenhoorn* he treated the Spanish officer with all courtesy, and had Suleiman bring him wine and refreshments; also a basin and ewer with a towel since his face was all begrimed with sweat and powder-smoke. In the mean time he had me sit and draw up a document in Spanish, on parchment and in my fairest hand, attesting that Don Francisco Iacinto Jesus-María de Bustamente y Suárez, captain of the Royal Army of Spain, had defended the fort of San Lorenzo de Puntal for the space of twenty hours on the first and second days of November in the year sixteen hundred and twenty-five against a greatly superior Dutch and English force, and had surrendered it only when his ammunition was used up and all hope of relief had vanished; and likewise how all aboard the Dutch ships had wondered greatly that so small a fort could resist so valiantly and cause such great loss to its assailants (which was not true at all). And in a word, how no man in the world could have given greater and truer service to his prince than this fort's gallant commander. Our captain then signed this with a great flourish "*Cornelis Adriaenszoon Loodgieter, capitano del peniche 'Unicorno' en servicias del Almirantazgo de Zelandia y de los Estados-Generales de los Siete Provincias Unidas de los Países Bajos*" and had me affix the ship's seal thereunder.

Don Francisco seemed well enough content with this certificate of good conduct, which we supposed he required to protect him if questions were to be raised afterwards, since the Spaniards are a people mighty tender of their honour and, save only for cuckoldry, no accusation is more galling to them than that of cowardice. He departed with our bo'sun's pipes to trill him to the longboat, and sat with a very grave mien in the stern as he was rowed across to Trocadero, so that proud Achilles himself could not have appeared more martial.

"So farewell then to our brave Spanish fool," our captain remarked once he had seen him off. "I had to credit him with deeds that would have graced a ballad book, as though he and his fellows had held the bridge like Horatius against all the hordes of Tuscany, which is gross exaggeration even if their defence *was* creditable enough. But if I had not flattered his vanity so shamelessly he might have had them resist further; and in the end perhaps tossed a match into their powder room and blown us all into the clouds, which such proud honourable hidalgos as he are perfectly well capable of. But it was worth it, for more wasps are caught with a spoonful of honey than with a barrelful of vinegar."

After the Spanish had marched out of Fort Puntal I had a brief opportunity to examine that edifice a little, because I was curious to know how it had so long withstood our ships' cannonading though constructed all of stone and not from earth. And I saw that the stone was of a hard, brownish, puddingy kind made from pebbles and seashells all conglomerated together, and without layers along which it might fracture as the shot struck it; likewise that the blocks were not just laid in mortar but most ingeniously keyed together with nubs on some that fitted into rebates in those beneath, and also iron bars the thickness of my wrist that morticed the stones one to another. All of which was no doubt most costly to King Philip's treasury, but gave him in exchange for it a fort which though small, was most obdurate against the enemy's cannonfire. I saw also that among the ruins of the fort and all round about it there lay thousands of our cannon bullets. This being reported to Meester Grobelaar, he at once sent the longboat and a dozen seamen across to gather up as many of them as they might, so that he could restock our shot-room with them at no charge to the Zeeland Admiralty and (I supposed) pocket the difference for himself. I heard later though that, having tried one in a cannon's muzzle, he discovered that all of them had been banged ovoid by their striking the walls of the fort (for if the stone would not cede, then the iron must) and were fit for nothing but to be used as ballast.

Fort Puntal having been reduced – though very tardy and late in the day, for with the twenty English colliers to help us we would certainly have taken the place by mid-morning – our fleet now had at least a sheltered and deep enough anchorage for it to ride in. The Neapolitan ships and the Spanish galleys that still lurked within the bay were a thorn in our foot which would certainly have to be plucked out before we could sleep safe at night; but for the moment we could put the soldiers ashore at last, which was very needful for them after three weeks at sea, our ships all being by now short of water, and sickness very widespread aboard the English ones from having so many men cooped up below decks for so long in foul air and on a diet of sour beer and tainted beef.

When our longboat passed under the bows of the *Swiftsure* that afternoon we saw how great icicles of filth hung beneath her beakhead from all the men aboard her that were now afflicted with distempers and fluxes of the bowels caused by their bad victuals. Likewise the previous evening their longboat had borne fifteen or twenty dead men wrapped in canvas to be dropped overboard further out in the bay where the water was deeper: poor fellows who had been carried off that day by the *morbus campestris** which was now cutting a wide swathe through them.

About six o' clock that Sunday evening the disembarkation began. And such a landing it was too, as surely never mortal man had previously witnessed for its disorderliness and confusion, so that our captain viewing it remarked that his own grandmother could have conducted it better: which I dare say was true enough, for Dutchwomen are famed for their practicality and good sense, and that worthy dame would have seen to it also that they disembarked in fresh linen washed, starched and ironed to perfection, and complained only that the soldiers sullied her nice clean-swept beach with their muddy shoes. The best that can be said of the whole affair is, that though it was a notable shambles, without the assistance of our Dutch ships it would have been an even worse one, because we Hollanders had at least some experience in the landing of men and stores more recently acquired than half a century before. The reason for our being requested to help the English ships carry their army ashore was that (as I have already related) they had most of them lost their longboats in the great Biscay storm. So all of that evening and most of the night (which was very inconvenient because there was no moon to see by) our sailors, all begrimed with powder and their heads still ringing from the banging of cannon, were obliged to row back and forth between the ships and the shore at Puntal where Sir Edward had now set up his headquarters. Our Dutch longboats carried in the end several thousand men, and also great store of munitions and

---

* Camp fever, also known as gaol fever: i.e. typhus.

provender which our fellows set down all higgledy-piggledy on the waterline – having no time to do otherwise, for they must then row back for more – and trusted that the English quartermasters would have it moved further up the beach. But we saw that whenever their sergeants tried to enlist some of their fellows to carry it, they were shunned and made mock of by the men, who vowed that they had enlisted to serve King Charles as soldiers and not as market porters.

But still we carried them across from their ships and put them ashore, then went back for more of them until our seamen, worn out and their hands all blistered from much rowing, requested that some of the English seamen might replace them, or perhaps compel the English soldiery to do some oar-pulling instead of having us row them along in state like the Doge of Venice in his galley. But at this the mate of the first English collier we approached swore that it was no business of theirs; *primo*, because the soldiers answered to their officers alone, and they themselves (being but civilians under charter) could compel them to nothing; and *secundo*, that by conveying the rogues to Spanish waters they had fulfilled their terms of contract and how the lousy villains got ashore thereafter was their own affair. But so long as they went somewhere he himself (he said) would be well enough content, for their vessel was now bespewed from stem to stern with soldier's vomit and not a dark corner but there was a turd lying in it – for they never could train the caitiffs to use the heads – so that a Turk would be sick to have to clean it up; and every seaman's chest likewise robbed bare by the rogues; and that how they got to dry land now was quite immaterial, and for himself he desired only that King Philip's men would slay them all to save him and his crew the trouble of having to transport them back again. At the end of this philippic he was joined by his skipper, who likewise swore most vehemently that since his own longboat had been borrowed by the *Swiftsure* (those lubbers having carelessly lost their own) he had no means of rowing his passengers ashore even if his men were inclined to do it. We replied that he might then borrow our longboat and have his own fellows do the rowing instead of us. But at this he vowed that his crew had no skill in the handling of "Dutch floaty-boats" (as he called our craft), for they were mariners on blue water not brown and disdained to paddle about in a washerwoman's scow like ours. Which remark I confess had some justice in it, for our own longboat was very much after the Dutch manner: shallow and broad with a raised prow and stern and two leeboards instead of a keel, and a spritsail instead of a lug such as the English use, so I supposed that it might indeed have been troublesome for them to manage at first.

It began to drizzle about seven o'clock, which put us all on edge for fear that the Spaniards might profit from the murk to set fireships drifting down to us on the ebb or send their galleys in amongst us in the dark to do us mischief. But as regards the naval part of our expedition, our fighting seemed to be over now that Puntal had been reduced and the army put ashore; and unless the Spanish ships in the bay attempted to break out there was for us Dutchmen but little prospect of further action. But at six bells of the second platvoet watch a message arrived from one of Doctor Reael's adjutants aboard the *Gouden Leeuw* commanding me that I prepare myself to go ashore next morning, having first furnished myself with suitable clothing and shoes along with a drawing book, pencils, rulers, compasses and other such items requisite for the making of maps; all these and two days' rations besides to be carried in a good stout satchel. It seemed that word had reached the ears of our vice-admiral of my skill in draughtsmanship as well as in the English language and the taking of shorthand notes, so I was to accompany a military officer called Captain Martinius van der Hulst on a surveying expedition ashore; partly as his interpreter in dealing with the English, and also as his amanuensis in drawing fortress traces, since the year before three fingers had been shot off his right hand before Breda and he could no longer hold a pencil for himself. He would collect me in the *Leeuw's* longboat (the note said) at eight bells of the morning watch. I therefore collected my drawing instruments and rations together into a satchel as instructed, then suppered and said farewell to my stepfather, telling him that I expected to be back aboard in a day or so, which I was very anxious I should because it pained me to leave him on his own. But he said that I must not trouble myself on his account, and told me to take care, then embraced me and kissed me farewell, which was singular of him and (in retrospect) as though he had been vouchsafed some premonition that he would not see me again.

I soon discovered next morning that the true reason for my going ashore with Captain van der Hulst was somewhat different from that which is given in the written annals of the Cadiz expedition, from which I suspect our chronicler has drawn most of his information, which will perhaps teach him not to credit all that he comes across in state papers and great men's memoirs. The Jonker Willem and Doctor Reael did indeed wish to place a Dutch land officer with the English to learn what it was they intended doing, they having thus far proved themselves most negligent about disclosing their plans to us even when they had any. But their real reason for sending Captain van der Hulst ashore was, that they wished to see what might be done to fortify our position now that the English troops were ashore. Over the past three days they had become greatly concerned by Sir Edward's manifest want of capacity to command so great an expedition, he and his generals plainly being men too feckless to come in out of the rain and too myopic to foresee Easter on Good Friday.

This dilatoriness of theirs had already cost us Cadiz town, for thanks to the ceaseless plying to and fro of their galleys over the intervening three days – which the English ships had done nothing whatever to hinder – the Spaniards must now have three or four thousand men in the town and good enough store of victuals and munitions to make our taking it now a very doubtful enterprise, though the place might have been ours for the asking when we first arrived in the bay. Both being men of astute understanding and Doctor Reael of great experience likewise, our admirals saw plainly enough that once the English army was ashore it would be sitting on a barren sandy isthmus five miles long and scarce five hundred yards wide, between the ocean on one side and Cadiz Bay on the other, with an unreduced town on their one flank and the Spanish mainland on the other, which might see our expedition end amid great slaughter if the garrison of Cadiz sallied forth against us while the King of Spain's army arrived at the landward end of the isthmus. They wished therefore to put a Dutch military engineer ashore to survey the land and draw up a proposal for fortifying some nearby part of Spain to serve as an encampment during the winter months. For they had the most lively apprehension that if we Dutch did not make such preparations for ourselves, then Sir Edward would neglect to do so and this whole expedition, which the States-General had invested a great deal of money in and weakened its blockade of Dunkirk to support, would be utterly undone after having achieved nothing. I was assured of all this by Meester Grobelaar over breakfast, he having once been a land soldier in his youth and therefore having (he claimed) understanding of these matters.

"Depend upon it, young Frans," he told me, "if it comes to a fight with Jan Spek on land, which is his element as the sea is ours, then he will surely have the better of us. The Spanish kingdom might nowadays be much decayed from what it was a hundred years ago. But I served with Prince Maurits at Nieuwpoort, Grave and Ostend, and the Spanish tercios are still greatly to be feared; this sorry English rabble no more against them than so many stray dogs yapping at a lion. Their discipline at Nieuwpoort was so stern that they stood there in their squares among the dunes an hour or more while our shot rained upon them, and not a man of them moving except to fall over dead, and then when at last their drummers beat the advance it was as though fortresses were moving forward on legs. If the English come up against them in their present array, without even horse or artillery, then we are all most certainly undone."

These opinions of Meester Grobelaar, that grand strategist of the cheese room, were pretty well confirmed to me by Captain van der Hulst when I joined him in the *Gouden Leeuw's* longboat just before eight bells that Monday morning. He was a saturnine man of about forty years of age; a military engineer and artillerist and of great renown who had accompanied Doctor Reael to the Indies during his governorship there and had done him signal service in fortifying the East India Company's trading post at Selembang so that it was able to withstand a siege of above six months by the Portuguese and the sultan of that locality. Our vice-admiral was still warmly mindful of the services the captain had rendered on that occasion, and now desired that he should go ashore for two or three days with the English army to survey the ground well forward towards the mainland and see what could be done to fortify it. "For the merest fool can see," the captain informed me as we sat together in the stern sheets, "that while our force, being only ten thousand strong, is quite insufficient to invade so vast a country as Spain, it might still be able to hold the island of León for the winter, which would afford our army shelter when the gales and rain come. Because otherwise they will have to lie out in the open on this barren sandy peninsula for three or four months with nothing but tent canvas over their heads and nothing but miserable dune grass to burn for fuel, which will infallibly lead to the spreading of disease, and in the end there will not be soil enough there to bury the dead. But if we can hold the Isle of León with ships to supply us through the winter, then in the spring we might cross to the mainland and take Jerez or Seville." And he indicated to me on the map he had with him the Isle of León that he spoke of, which is divided from the Spanish mainland by a muddy, winding tidal channel called the Caño Sancti Petri, flanked by marshes on both shores. Our purpose, he said, was to survey the island side of this channel and see what would be required to fortify it: how many men for how many days with picks and shovels; how much timber for palisados and revetments; how many cannon brought ashore from the ships to cover all the approaches and angles of fire, *et cetera, et cetera*. And the results of our survey once we had made it would be most forcibly presented to Viscount Wimbledon by our two admirals, who would insist that he put it into effect. And (he hoped) cudgel the old fool to within an inch of his life if he demurred.

When we stepped ashore on to the beach by Fort Puntal it was indeed a most dismaying spectacle that greeted us. Some of the sundry stores we had put ashore the previous evening had been moved up the beach by the English as the tide came in. But most had not, and now lay ruined and utterly spoiled by their immersion: sacks of biscuit, kegs of gunpowder, tents, arms and a hundred other items now soaked and rendered good for nothing. The night had passed uneasily, with a great deal of banging and shouting coming to us across the water as the English soldiers endeavoured to sort themselves out into their companies and regiments, for they had all been put ashore pell-mell at divers places, and for them to re-form themselves in the darkness and drizzle was like replacing the contents of my lady's sewing basket which has been upset and then played with by her cat , but in a dark cellar and without a candle.

The disembarkation had resumed at first light, yet their officers and sergeants seemed as impotent as before to bring any order to it. And if the expedition's stores were in a sorry state, with the men the case was plainly even worse. For if King Charles's men had seemed to us an unsoldierly enough crew of rascals when they embarked at Plymouth, their martial aspect had been in no wise improved by three weeks at sea, crammed together like so many pilchards on the airless, leaky orlop decks of vessels rolling and pitching as the tempests buffeted them; fed on the rotten victuals and worse beer supplied by the rascally contractors and liberally spewed over by comrades as seasick as themselves. A miserable enough collection of starvelings even when freshly delivered from their gaols and poorhouses, they now looked like ghosts or corpses exhumed from the graveyards: pallid from their long confinement and so unsteady on their legs from want of movement that many of them fell over when they first stepped ashore. But there (the captain observed): they were soldiers of a sort, carrying weapons and with two legs, two arms and a head apiece; so perhaps something might be made of them now they were back on *terra firma* at last.

I was pleased however to see that Captain Neades and his bowmen were disembarking from the *Eenhorn's* longboat and forming themselves into orderly ranks and files upon the strand as composed and resolute as the heroes of antiquity, which was very reassuring for us to behold, to see some discipline and soldierly bearing even amid such disorder, though Captain van der Hulst remarked to me when we were out of earshot that such decayed toothless old fellows would be better employed guarding the geese on a village green than playing at soldiers, carrying their silly ineffectual bows and arrows and accoutred likewise in their cheap corselets of sheet-iron that a Spanish musket would knock a hole through at two hundred paces. As they clambered out of the boats in their breastplates and morion helmets and the tassets on the fronts of their thighs – which last item of harness plainly encumbered them greatly – I saw my old friend Will Shefford porting his pike-bow and called out to him, wishing him Godspeed. Recognising my voice, he turned and laughed with his toothless old gums. "And God be with you as well, young Frankie. For my part I come ashore with a glad heart, that we are off at last to fisticuffs with King Philip and his inquisitors and the friars who seek to burn us. Mind yourself, young fellow, and when I see you again I shall be carrying the King of Spain's beard at my belt."

A few of the other English companies ashore were likewise orderly and well conducted: those whose officers, like our Captain Palethorpe, had served in the continental campaigns. But most of the regiments were very slovenly and ragged from their lack of officers; and likewise from the lack of experience among those officers they *did* have, who were plainly gentlemen and not much else. The result was that insubordination was widespread, and for all the officers shouting and threatening and the sergeants belabouring men with their halberds, there seemed no immediate means to remedy it. But an even greater deficiency (the captain remarked as he surveyed them with evident distaste) was their lack of cavalry, the few horses that had not drowned on the way or died from ill-feeding in the ship's holds having been requisitioned by Sir Edward and his staff as soon as they came ashore. "And this," he told me, "will be mighty inconvenient to them later; for you may depend upon it that though the Spaniard is at present insufficient in strength to confront us on the Isle of León, yet he will still not take to his heels and scamper in terror all the way back to Madrid, but rather retreat in good order towards the mainland as we advance and wait there for reinforcements to come up. Without cavalry to scout ahead of them the English will not know where their foes are or how many face them, which may well be their undoing when it comes to a fight, since Sir Edward will not know whether he should give battle or refuse it. I understand that he hopes that mounts may be requisitioned from the country people as we advance. But I am well acquainted with Andalusia and I see little prospect of that. Cuirassiers mounted upon mules or plough-oxen make but a sorry sight, and they would be better off walking".

We soon discovered that from lack of horses for us to ride on we too would be obliged to make our way on foot with the English vanguard as they advanced down the isthmus towards the mainland; for it seemed to be Sir Edward's intention that the entire army should do so now that he had realised that, without siege guns and scaling ladders and even such petty munitions as grenados, an assault upon Cadiz town would be futile and that the best we could hope for now was to blockade the place and reduce it by hunger. So the captain and I went and sought among the great disorderly milling mob of soldiery for someone to assign us to a company with which we could march. We flourished our passe-partout letters countersigned by Sir Edward, and in the end we were attached to a company of the Duke of Buckingham's Regiment led by a young Suffolk gentleman called Lieutenant Bullock. He accepted us cheerfully enough when he saw that we would be no encumbrance to him, and put us with his own company at the head of his men as they formed up behind their colours and their drummers for the march south. They had spent a miserable damp night lying out among the scrubby dunes under the drizzle without tents to shelter them, but seemed glad enough even so to have firm soil beneath their feet once more and not the heaving deck of a ship. They were hungry however, they having been given no more victuals since the previous afternoon than a few ship's biscuits to gnaw upon, and likewise thirsty because the rain that had fallen during the night had sunk straight into the sand instead of making puddles which they might drink from. Many among them now complained most piteously that their heartless officers had put them ashore on this sandy barren peninsula with neither meat nor drink to sustain them like so many castaways on a desert island. As for Captain van der Hulst and myself, we had with us a leather knapsack with provision of ship's biscuit and cheese for two days, and two curious Spanish leathern bottles he had brought with him made from goat's skin and called "botas", shaped like a comma with a sort of wooden nipple at one end and (he told me) a direct descendant of the old Roman wineskin, the *uter*, though in our case the captain had filled them with a quart each of ship's beer, and gave me one of them to hang over my shoulder on a cord. As for our armament, he carried only a dirk and a wheel-lock pistol (which he gave me to carry), saying that we would be keeping close company with the English all the way and their pikes and muskets would protect us if we came up against the enemy's skirmishers.

About ten o'clock our column moved off at last down the isthmus towards the Isle of León, after much delay caused by the circumstance that none of their commanders (who seemed to us more and more to resemble the seven foolish virgins of the parable) had thought to bring with them any map of the region, so that all we had to navigate by was a sketch that the Captain had taken the previous evening from Waghener's pilotage book. So we commenced our trudge of four or five miles down that sandy spit with the ocean breakers rolling on to the shore on one side and the shallow waters of Cadiz Bay on the other. At first it looked fair to be no considerable journey, but soon fell out to be a most wearisome trudge which seemed ten times as far as it was in reality. Mister Bullock's two companies (there being too few officers to assign a lieutenant to each company) consisted of about a hundred musketeers, who marched in the van, and an equal number of pikemen behind them. We set out bravely enough with the drums rat-tat-tatting and the fifes squeaking a tune as the regiment's colours fluttered boldly in the salty breeze. But from the very outset the going was heavy and laborious, for the paved road – built by the Romans I should think, for *Gades* was one of their chiefest towns in the province of *Hispania* – was in a bad state from many centuries of neglect, and in divers places completely overblown and buried by the sand that a thousand winter storms had drifted up from the shore. This made it very tedious for us to tramp along it, our shoes soon filling up with the sharp grit, and dust likewise rising in clouds to choke us as the sun got up in the sky and dispelled the morning's misty vapours.

There was little on this desolate shore to divert us from our discomforts: only the waves thundering on the ocean beach, and otherwise naught but dunes, thin grass and wind, and the gulls shrieking above us. As we tramped along we passed some overgrown ruins among the scrub just beyond the place where a decrepit wooden bridge took the road over a creek. Captain van der Hulst, who was a very learned gentleman as befits a military engineer, told me that these were all that remained of the great temple of Hercules that Herodotus writes of as being built by the Phoenecians, and that its two great bronze pillars were the originals of the Pillars of Hercules that marked the western limit of the world for the ancients and still figure on the royal arms of Spain; likewise that some scholars believed Hercules himself might lie buried there, but no man might now know the truth or otherwise of this, because the Moors when they came across to Spain from Africa were at great pains to burn down and make a ruin of the place. This heartened me and lifted up my spirits in no small measure as I trudged down that weary road; to know that I might be passing within a few yards of the veritable bones of one of the great heroes of antiquity, and to reflect that these worthies were not just fables in storybooks written for the oppression of schoolboys, but had once lived and breathed as I now lived and breathed and done great deeds that I myself might one day emulate. For no doubt old Hercules had been vexed by the weariness of his limbs and galled by the rubbing of grit in his sandals and the chafing of his massy club on his shoulder as he went from each of his twelve labours to perform the next. Yet still he went on and performed them.

Before long though, we all of us stood in the direst need of whatever encouragement Hercules or any other of the ancient heroes could offer us, because by midday Lieutenant Bullock's company was in a sorry plight indeed. We had marched only three miles or so down the isthmus, but the men were by now fatigued almost to dropping. When the sun first rose in the heavens that morning it had delighted our companions; that their clothes wet from the night's drizzle were being dried and warmed by its rays, so that a visible cloud of vapour hung over our company as it tramped along and the salty air reeked of damp woollen cloth. But as he neared the zenith Phoebus had long since turned from benevolent friend to cruel tyrant. The soldiers were weak from their long confinement aboard ship, and many of them further undermined by fluxes and colics resulting from putrid food and drink. Their burdens were likewise heavy. Each musketeer carried his musket and its crutch, which might together weigh twenty pounds, and in addition to this a short pattern-sword at his hip, a bandolier of chargers, a bag of bullets, a horn of priming powder and a knapsack with necessaries, plus such other sundries like tent poles and digging tools as it might please his corporal to make him carry. As for the pikemen that marched behind us, their state was even worse since they were burdened down with a helmet, and with breast- and backplates, and with tassets in front of their thighs as well as their sixteen-foot pike and their sword, and their knapsack and other accoutrements. The pike did not have the wide-brimmed felt hats worn by the shot, so they suffered cruelly from the sun as they toiled along, steaming like fresh-boiled lobsters inside their iron carapaces.

Before long the drummers and fifemen had ceased their playing and the column trudged along the sandy road in silence like some procession of penitents or slaves destined for the galleys amid an eerie sound composed of panting for breath, feet shuffling in the sand, cursing as men stumbled, the clanking of the pikemens' corselets, and above it all the strange rattling noise made by the shot. Our musketeers carried twelve little wooden bottles each holding a single charge of powder, suspended by strings from a bandolier, and the noise of several thousands of these clacking against one another as we marched along was most singular to hear and gave our army's column a sound like some enormous serpent a mile or more long rattling its scales. We toiled and stumbled along, cursing the sand that clogged our shoes, and with each furlong that we marched a louder and more insistent grumbling arose against the tyrant officers and their subaltern bullies the sergeants and corporals who made them to suffer thus like so many cattle driven to the slaughter. Yet we could not halt for to rest until we reached the Isle of León, because the road was narrow and the isthmus likewise, and there would have been nowhere for us to sit down and regain our breath without blocking the highway for those behind us.

Thirst soon compounded our miseries, because the soldiers had no drink bottles with them (money being short and the army's commissariat not having thought to provide such fripperies) and the dust kicked up from the road clogged our mouths to grit between our teeth while the sea-spray carried by the wind dried on our lips and parched us still further. The soldiers nearest us began to cast envious looks at our wineskins and to mutter about uncomradely Dutch dogs who would not spare a cup to wet the throats of their fellows – though if we had distributed our small store of beer among so great a multitude, then unless Captain van der Hulst could have emulated the miracle of the loaves and fishes there would have been scarce a single drop of it for each man. Yet out of decency he and I were unable to slake our own thirst for fear that the sight of us drinking would merely increase the distress of our companions.

By now the sandy isthmus was broadening out to become the Isle of León, where a cluster of fishermen's hovels and a tower was marked upon our map as "*Torre Gorda*". And from this place onwards a fresh torment was added to those that we already had to endure, because the marshy shores on either side of the roadway were covered with salt-workings: great shallow rectangular pans divided from one another by low dykes of earth and with little wooden gates at their seaward ends, so that every few days seawater could be admitted at high tide to flood the pans, then the sluices closed again to let the sunshine and wind evaporate the water, then more seawater let in, and in this way to accumulate stronger and stronger brine until the floors of the pans were covered with a thick crust of pure crystalline salt which was then raked up into great mounds of dazzling silvery whiteness. The sun's reflection glaring from the salt was very trying to us as we marched, and likewise the briny dust raised by the breeze made our skins to prickle and our lips and tongues to parch even worse than before. Soon men began to fall out of the column exhausted, some pikemen divesting themselves of their corselets and flinging them into the ditches by the road then sitting down to nurse their bleeding feet, for the shoes which the commissariat had supplied them with were plainly very hard and ill-made and galled them cruelly. Likewise our musketeers were by now complaining most vehemently at being so used; to be conscripted against their will just because they were poor men and of lowly degree (for gentlemen and yeomen, they saw, were never pressed for soldiers) then packed into the holds of foul-smelling ships and fed on stony biscuit and stinking beef that the very dogs at a bear pit would scorn if it were thrown down for them, then put ashore in this desert place and herded along like the vilest of felons under the burning sun without food or drink to sustain them. Four or five of them declared loudly that even Chester Gaol (which it seemed had been their previous lodging) was to be preferred to this torment, since at least they had been given bread and water twice a day and did not have to march along in the sun carrying heavy loads like poor silly mules.

After another ten minutes or so one of these fellows, bolder than the rest, cried out that by God, he would endure it no longer and King Charles and the Duke of Buckingham might kiss his arse as regards further service. He then divested himself of his musket and bandolier to fling them aside, which his companions imitated, and set off with them towards the ocean shore saying that they would first cool their martyred feet then set off back towards Cadiz to find a ship that would take them home – and if they found none, why then they would enlist with the Spaniards who could scarcely treat them any worse. Seeing this, Lieutenant Bullock called to them to come back, then drew his sword to run after them. They took to their heels, but he caught up with them at the water's edge and accosted their ringleader. As we watched the man made as if to draw his own sword in defence – at which the lieutenant ran him clean through the body at about the height of his kidneys so that we saw the blade protrude from the fellow's back. The man goggled astonished for a moment, then fell to his knees clutching his midriff as Mister Bullock pulled the sword out again. The soldier slumped over, then lay still in a puddle of red as the waves lapped around him and his fellow fugitives ran for their lives back in the direction of Cadiz. The officer returned to us panting from exertion and wiped his bloodied sword with a handful of dune grass. "There," he said, "that caitiff abandoned his weapon in the face of the enemy, deserted his column and offered violence to an officer, each of which is a hanging matter. So all I have done is spare the provost-major the trouble of finding a tree to suspend him from. As for the other scoundrels, when they are taken they will be hanged as deserters without further process. So take heed all of you, that as I lately used that fellow, so would

I do to any one of you." And with that he sheathed his sword and we marched on in silence.

About this place the road swung northwards towards the crossing from the Isle of León to the mainland at Zuazo Bridge. The isle itself appeared to be a low sort of place except for some slight hills along its spine, so insignificant that they would have been unremarked upon even in the flattest parts of Flanders. The island, which was about four miles long by three broad, seemed fertile enough however, inland of the salt marshes that fringed it, and had numerous vineyards and olive groves. But cottages were few, and all that we came upon along the road were deserted, the Spaniards having plainly removed all the country people and their cattle to the mainland ahead of us. Of the enemy we saw nothing, save for a few horsemen in the distance who were plainly scouts reporting our progress and who avoided tangling with us. A mile or two distant, at the highest point of the island, there was a square white tower which Captain van der Hulst said was an old Moorish fort, and all around us in the countryside were the whitewashed buildings of the substantial farms or manor houses that the Spaniards call haciendas. But there were too many of these buildings and too large to be answerable solely to the island's wealth, and it was only later on – too late – that their true purpose would become clear to us.

We came about one o'clock in the afternoon to a tide-creek that cuts into the island from the Bay of Cadiz. There a surprise awaited us: a longboat from the English collier *Perseverance* of Hull moored by the bridge where the road crossed the creek and bearing provisions for us.

"Are you the Duke of Buckingham's Regiment?" the coxswain shouted to us. Mister Bullock replied that we were. "Then we have food and drink for you – and may you all be graciously pleased to choke on it for having caused us to row it here for you in this confounded sun."

And with that his sailors negligently tumbled some canvas sacks and two firkins of beer into the mud beside the creek, then backed their oars and pulled away. We retrieved the provisions and found the sacks to contain ship's biscuit and a quantity of beef, a hundred pounds or so in weight, still warm from the ship's cauldron and plainly none the better for having lain above six months in pickle, since the smell of it was most rank and offensive despite its having been recently boiled. Mister Bullock commanded his sergeant to have this equitably cut up and distributed among the men along with a biscuit apiece. As for the beer – the smell of which was little more enticing than the beef once we had tapped the casks – there was only twenty gallons or so, which meant that each man of our two companies received a bare cupful and no more. Our companions sat down gratefully enough to devour this meagre fare and nurse their lacerated feet, and the captain and I meanwhile ate some of our biscuit and cheese with a few swigs of beer each. But before long it became plain that the provisions sent to us had made the men's case worse rather than better. The flesh, besides being high and still half raw from its cursory boiling, was extremely salty from not having first been steeped for a day in fresh water, the order to cook it having been given (we supposed) only that morning because no one had thought of it previously. The soldiers devoured it at first like dogs worrying carrion in a ditch. But before long they were spitting it out half-chewed and saying that it parched their throats and made them unable to swallow their ration of biscuit. So when after twenty minutes or so Lieutenant Bullock had the trumpeter blow the command to get up and form column of march once more, our state was little better than it had previously been.

As we prepared to resume our march the captain picked up a discarded gobbet of the beef and examined it with some curiosity. "What the rascals have done here," he said, "is put the beef into the brine casks without first draining the blood from it, then salting it a day to draw from it the remainder of the blood and the more watery humours. So small wonder it has gone putrid during the weeks at sea. And likewise this year was plainly one in which the contractors should have taken double care over the salting of their beef, because Jupiter and the warm, watery stars which engendered the plague among men in England no doubt had much the same influence on cattle, so that their flesh when slaughtered would be bloodier and moister than usual and therefore more liable to corrupt." And with that he tossed the piece of beef into the creek. I remarked that I wondered greatly that a military engineer should be knowledgeable in such trivial matters as the provision of salted beef. At which he smiled, and said that a military engineer worthy of that name must concern himself not just with the building of fortifications but with their munition as well, because what use is the strongest fortress that ever was if the men inside it have naught to line their bellies with? For he supposed (he said) from his diligent study of the ancient and the modern authors that for every fortress that ever fell to direct assault, three or four must have succumbed to starvation or to sickness caused by rotten victuals.

★ ★ ★ ★ ★ ★ ★ ★ ★ ★

By three o'clock in the afternoon the column, now much reduced by stragglers falling out along the way, had reached what might be termed the more solid part of the Isle of León (so much of it being salt marshes) and was approaching a substantial hacienda set well back from the road behind an ornate whitewashed gateway and a drive shaded with plane trees. As it did so a messenger on horseback came up with an order for Lieutenant Bullock. Sir Edward earnestly desired that the first English soldiers to get there would turn aside to the house, which appeared to be the largest on the island, and occupy it without delay so that the general and his staff could use it as their headquarters when they came up from Puntal. So the sergeants duly pointed their halberds, and the column wheeled right in a disorderly fashion to march up the road towards the house, finally coming to a halt in the courtyard amid a great collective sigh of relief and the men then breaking ranks (without any order being given) to slake their thirst at a horse trough, which they drank dry in less than a minute.

As Frans and Captain van der Hulst came up the driveway with the first of the soldiers a dismal sight had greeted them. Two men – Spanish soldiers by their dress, though they now had only shirts and breeches – dangled lifeless by their necks from one of the trees, with flies already swarming around their protruding blue tongues and their goggling bloodshot eyes. There was no indication what they had been hanged for, but that scarcely mattered: it was quite probably for some entirely petty offence since the renowned iron discipline of the Spanish tercios was maintained by liberal use of the strapado and the halter (...and a great pity, Lieutenant Bullock remarked, that King Charles's army did not do likewise, because then something might perhaps be made of the rascals). The sight of the two corpses was nevertheless a dispiriting one for men who might soon themselves be in battle, so the lieutenant commanded that they should be cut down and buried at once to avoid depressing the spirits of his men any further.

Though the house itself appeared deserted, the English advance guard circled it cautiously at first half expecting a volley of shots from its windows, which were small and set very high up in the walls in the Moorish fashion. It seemed to have a wing for dwelling in, and alongside that two great buildings without windows which looked like storehouses of some kind, but were surely too large to be granaries on so small an island. Likewise there was a kind of railway of wooden baulks laid end to end leading from the storehouses down beside the driveway towards the road and the bay beyond. The soldiers were set to work at once to secure the house for the arrival of Viscount Wimbledon and his staff, while Frans and the captain were left to their own devices to do a little exploring. "If we find great store of grain lying here after the late harvest," Van der Hulst declared, "then our task becomes a great deal easier, since all we need do is construct a few windmills to grind it and our army will then have bread for the whole winter." They pushed against a great ponderous oaken door which had been left ajar, and as it creaked open on its massive iron hinges they peered inside the building. Once their eyes had become accustomed to the gloom after the blinding sunshine outside they saw that the building was stacked to the roof with oaken casks of ox-head size, each holding a hundred gallons or more. One of these was leaking, and fluid dripped from it to form a dark pool on the stone-flagged floor. The captain knelt down to dip a finger in it and taste it.

"Wine," he said, "and but lately pressed too: only a month or so since. This building must be a winestore for the Spaniards to provision their Mexico fleet, which would explain that railway down to the bay: they must roll these casks along it to some jetty, then load them into boats to take them out to the ships lying at anchor. By the look of it there must be an entire year's ration here, brought in no doubt from the countryside round about and waiting for next spring when their fleet returns to Vera Cruz. We must inform Lieutenant Bullock of this at once and have sentinels placed, because if that rabble outside gets a sniff of it then no man will be able to restrain them. New wine, as Saint Luke informs us, is doubly intoxicating because the windy air of fermentation in it combines with the heat of the vinous spirit to invade men's brains and make them mad. So run at once and inform him."

Frans ran and told this news to Mister Bullock. He waved the boy aside, saying that he had more urgent matters to attend to than such trifles as wine, and he should speak with a sergeant. But when Frans had at last found a sergeant willing to take heed (the others being more concerned to fortify the building as soon as possible) the man said that this was indeed welcome news: that his fellows would have something to put them in good heart again after their weary march. He would see to it that water was drawn from the well in the courtyard to mix with the wine pint for pint, and each man would then receive two pints of this beverage under the supervision of the corporals to avoid drunkenness. He then asked Frans, since he seemed to be such an inquisitive young fellow, to tell him of anything else he might come across that would be useful.

When Frans rejoined the captain he found that others had already got wind of their discovery, sniffing out the smell of wine on the air from far off as wasps will detect the scent of ripe pears on a windowsill. A crowd had gathered before the doorway of the great warehouse and was remonstrating loudly with a corporal and two musketeers who sought to bar the entrance, declaring that it was great shame upon King Charles that he should bring them all here to fight his enemies for him, but the scurvy knaves of sergeants then debar them from partaking in the rightful spoils of victory so that the greedy villains could have more of it for themselves, and the poor soldiers be left with nought but puddle water to slake their thirst. "Aye," one said, "and the wine be later shipped back to England so that the Duke of Buckingham and Sir James Bagg may sell it to their great profit and enrichment. For though we are but poor men, still we are not fools and know well what manner of cozenage is intended here!" At which a great cheer went up, and the sergeants in the end came along and (in order to avoid further indiscipline, there being no officer at hand) consented that each man should be given two pints of wine to drink unmixed with water; which was foolhardy in the extreme, but hardly to be avoided when two sergeants with their halberds faced several hundred men armed with muskets and pikes.

Our two Dutchmen had meanwhile reconnoitred further about the place and besides some storehouses with sacks of garbanzo peas and casks of bacon in pickle, which might also be useful, they had discovered that the hacienda was not entirely deserted: there was still an old man there, a servant about the house, who had stayed behind when the others fled the previous evening since his wife was ill with dropsy and bedridden and he would not leave her. They conducted the man to Lieutenant Bullock to be questioned, Frans assuring him meanwhile that though they were indeed heréticos luteranos they would not harm him. He said that the house belonged to one Don Luis de Soto who was the principal landowner hereabouts, and also the main contractor for supplying wine to His Majesty's Indies fleet; furthermore that the whole Isle of León was effectively one great victualling yard for that fleet and full of storehouses for wine and other provisions. When the Spanish soldiers (of whom he thought there must be about a thousand) had withdrawn to the mainland the previous evening they had set fire to the biscuit store a mile or so further along the road, but had not had time to destroy any of the other warehouses. In the end the old man was released, and Lieutenant Bullock, being a just man if a severe one, ordered that a sentinel be placed at the door of his cottage to prevent him and his wife from being molested.

Once they had rested a little and refreshed themselves, Captain van der Hulst declared that there was no sense in their waiting any longer for the arrival of Sir Edward and his staff, because they had plainly been delayed by the press of men along the road down the isthmus. It was now mid-afternoon and there would only be a few more hours of daylight, so they would go and begin their survey, return to the house at nightfall to sleep there under the protection of the English, then complete their task next morning. They refilled their botas with a mixture of wine and water, since the captain said that undiluted wine is very deleterious in the heat of the day and cuts a man's legs from under him. Before leaving the hacienda they enquired of Mister Bullock what the password for the day was to be – and were told there was none since no thought had been given to that matter, which the captain plainly considered highly unprofessional, but nothing was to be done about it. Then they set off down towards the tidal channel that separates the Isle of León from the mainland.

Their way led them through fields and olive groves where cicadas chirped in the afternoon warmth and chameleons stalked unwary flies on the stone walls. The Caño Sancti Petri when they reached it was a shallow, winding channel about two hundred yards wide, muddy at low tide and fringed on either side with a wide expanse of marshes and salt pans, so that in order to set foot on the Isle of León an attacker would first have to struggle through a good a half-mile of swamps on the mainland side, then cross the muddy channel, then negotiate another half-mile of swamps to reach dry ground. A mile or so away was the Puente Zuazo, which Frans saw was in fact more of a causeway than a bridge – the remains of an old Roman aqueduct, the captain said – with two great culverts to let the tide through and a break in the middle with a drawbridge to allow the passage of vessels. At both the island and the mainland ends of the bridge there were earthen forts to guard the crossing, and on the island side there was likewise a small, squarish, whitewashed castle plainly of Moorish origin. To judge by the cooking-fire smoke that rose from them and the sentries visible on their battlements all these strongholds were manned. But for the rest, all that they saw of the enemy was two horsemen cantering through the fields over on the mainland side, stopping to gaze across and make out how far the English had advanced, then galloping away again in a cloud of dust.

★ ★ ★ ★ ★ ★ ★ ★ ★

We spent the rest of that afternoon walking along the edge of the high ground that overlooks the Caño Sancti Petri, stopping at intervals for me to make pencil sketches of how it lay with all its salients and re-entrants and for the captain to dictate to me the most favourable placement of batteries, the number of guns and the amount of building materials that he considered would be necessary to fortify each spot. And in the intervals of doing this, while he was busy with his own calculations, I had the opportunity to examine the flora of the island, which was most diverting for me since I had never before visited the Mediterranean lands with their vineyards and olive trees, though I had read much of them in the classical authors. There were not just the customary olives, grapes, figs and pomegranates either, but stranger plants even than they, since Cadiz and the Isle of León had long been Spain's principal port for the Americas and many curious herbs had come back from Mexico and Peru to take root in its soil: like cactuses, which are a sort of single great fleshy leaf native to desert places and all covered with sharp barbs and spines; and likewise cultivated plants such as potatoes, and a curious vegetable which I had never seen before which was called the egg-plant: bluey-black in colour and shiny, and entirely edible (the Captain assured me) though at first sight it looks as poisonous a fruit as can be by reason of its colour. Potatoes were already somewhat familiar to me, because in Flanders the country folk had already started to grow them but only as food for swine, holding that they cause leprosy in men. But the potato's close cousin the paradise-apple or tomato I had hardly seen at all before except as a freak in herbalists' shops, and knew invincibly that its red berries were as deadly poisonous as those of nightshade, which I think must be its European kindred by the shape of the leaves (though I could never make out why the one should grow only in the Americas and the other only in the Old World). When we sat down to take refreshment the captain bade me sample one, saying that they are not noxious in the least or why would the Spaniards be growing fields full of them? So I essayed one of these red apples – but very gingerly – and found it to have a curious taste but not at all disagreeable: sour yet sweet and with an earthy savour as though it were intermediate between fruits and vegetables.

"Do you think that the Spaniards could cross this channel?" I asked the captain as we walked along the escarpment edge above the Caño Sancti Petri.

He laughed at this. "They could, young man. But whether they *would* is another barrel of herrings entirely. From what I can see standing here, if we were to further fortify the bridge at Zuazo – or demolish it altogether – and construct a few batteries of cannon along the edge of this island to cover the most propitious places for fording the channel, then we might sit here a century undisturbed by King Philip's armies, be they never so great. But the problem for us, I see now, will be to obtain from Viscount Wimbledon the means for constructing those batteries: the soldiers to dig them – for the ones the English have here appear to me a most worthless crew of fellows, and there are no countryfolk for us to conscript as labourers – and likewise the necessary picks and spades, since the English have neglected to bring any with them, and the wood to make revetments and floors beneath the cannon, which we would have to break up some ships to obtain since there is barely a stick of timber on this island. I fear that when I have drawn up a plan for the defences and the Jonker Willem goes to Sir Edward with it, he will be told that if we Dutchmen devised the scheme, then we must carry it out ourselves and it is no concern of theirs."

I must say that I was immensely gratified to be taken so soon into the confidence of so distinguished an officer, as though I was a colleague and equal of his and no mere clerk. Before long I came to see that he was instructing me in the military engineer's art as we went along, setting me problems and asking me how I would solve them, such as "Do you think that might be dead ground there in the hollow of that slope, and if so how would you suggest we cover it?". So it was no surprise to me later on when he asked me, was I intent on becoming a surgeon when I reached man's estate? I replied that I had never considered anything else, since that was my stepfather's trade. To which he said, "That, then, is a great pity, because I see from the precision of your drawing that you have the makings of a very capable military engineer, and thought that I might appoint you my secretary and apprentice once this present business is over, and train you up to my own profession." And this, I have found in my life, is one of the most authentic marks of great men: that they seek always to share their knowledge and foster ability wherever they find it, whereas mean-spirited fellows will always endeavour to hold information to their own bosom and impart as little of it as possible, for fear that their pupils might prove greater than they are.

The sun by now sinking towards the ocean horizon, and we mighty hungry after all our walking about, we returned towards the hacienda where we supposed Sir Edward would now be established with his staff. We intended coming back next morning to complete our survey, for there was one difficult place the captain said might need his particular attention since it had a creek running in from the Caño Sancti Petri beneath a low bluff, which might necessitate a separate fieldwork being dug there to cover it against an enemy vessel coming up the creek at high tide and enfilading (which was a new word to me) the neighbouring battery.

As we approached the house along a lane a shout of "Who goes there?" from behind a stone wall brought us to a sudden stop; likewise the barrels of five or six muskets pointing over the top of it at us. It was fortunate for us that I knew English, because I think that on his own the captain might have continued and been shot full of holes like a colander for his trouble. I conveyed the sentinel's challenge to him, and he told me to reply, "A Dutch officer and his assistant."

This I did, and the answer came back: "Give the password, then."

"What password?" I enquired. "Before we left the house we were told that there was none for today..."

My words were interrupted by a bang and a flash, and a musket ball whistled past my ear to smash against the stones on the other side of the lane. We both hid in the lee of the wall as more shots rang out, then at last heard the voice of Lieutenant Bullock asking what was the Devil was the matter here and were the Dons attacking us? He bade us advance and be recognised, and saw at last that we were who we said we were. Captain van der Hulst was most indignant that the pair of us had come near being riddled with musket balls as a result of this misunderstanding. Mister Bullock apologised and said that yes, while no password had been set before we departed, Sir Edward had since arrived at the house and given one, which (for our future information and the integrity of our hides) was "heaven bless us." I conveyed this information to the captain, who harrumphed and said that so far as he could see, "God help us" might be more apposite.

Coming up to the house at last we saw that his words were prophetic, and that matters must have gone uncommonly ill during our absence; that in fact a riot was taking place there, with fires burning, men milling round outside the wine store and other men on horseback riding in amongst them, belabouring them with the flats of their swords amid a great deal of noise and shouting and singing and musket shots fired into the air. We saw one officer dragged from his horse to be kicked and pummelled by the soldiery as he lay on the ground; then, as we came closer, Sir Edward himself in his breastplate, gorget and plumed helmet, sword in hand, coming out from the house to restore order. From within the great cavernous wine store there came a monstrous racket of yelling, singing, spewing and brawling as if all the demons in hell were inside carousing to mark the Devil's birthday. All around us men lay helpless with drink or staggered about and fought with one another. A dark red rivulet of wine flowed out through the doorway of the storehouse and into the gutter, and men knelt to lap it up from the puddles like dogs.

We peered into the building, and saw that it was crowded with fellows smashing in the ends of the casks with their musket butts and endeavouring to collect the wine that gushed forth in their hats, or simply lying down beneath and letting it fill their open mouths. Two knaves were swimming in a great wine vat they had filled, while others were hanging head-first and motionless over the edges of a broached cask stood on its end, they having seemingly drowned in their toping. We drew back as quickly as we could, neither wishing nor daring to enter upon this vile bacchanalia. Meanwhile Sir Edward and his adjutants had arrived outside the doorway.

"What is this swinish rout?" Sir Edward yelled as he laid about him with his sword, "What is the meaning of this foul debauchery? Return to your duty at once, you insubordinate hounds, or I swear you'll all hang, every last one of you!"

The revellers paused, some looking sheepish and abashed. Then one insolent fellow bolder than the rest stepped forward from the crowd, swaying and staggering, with his face flushed purple from wine. He doffed his hat and made a mocking low obeisance, nearly falling over as he did so.

"My Lord of Wimbledon...Your excellency..." he said, "Might my lord be so good as to accept our compliments, and tell us what brings him here among us?"

"I am your general, you injurious scoundrel," Sir Edward replied, "and His Majesty's lieutenant here, entrusted with the summary power of life and death over you. Return to your obedience at once, or I promise you that you'll hang within the hour without benefit of court martial."

"Hang, my lord?" the fellow answered, not one whit abashed. "Why, 'hang' is surely a mighty discourteous word to use to poor soldier-men who have come all this way to fight the King's enemies, just because they choose to wet their whistles with a cup or two of Spanish wine." Here he looked round to see whether or not his comrades supported him in this opinion. And seeing that they plainly did, he turned back to face Sir Edward. "For we, my noble lord, are free-born Englishmen and King Charles's soldiers, and we obey none but him. As for hanging anyone, is there a tree, a rope, a ladder or a hangman to be seen hereabouts? Where we are so many, and the officers so few? Speak not of hanging, my gentle lord. Because as matters stand it's far more likely that we should hang *you*, rather than you hang us."

At this Sir Edward brought up his sword, and I thought for a moment that he would run the fellow through with it as Lieutenant Bullock had done with the deserter earlier that day on the seashore. There was stillness, and an uneasy humming noise such as bees make in a hive. Then Sir Edward tilted his head forward a little – and the visor of his helmet fell shut with a clang. At this all the men roared out with laughter at the absurdity of the scene, as their general struggled to lift the visor again (it having become jammed in its falling) and in the end had to have one of his adjutants open it for him. By the time he could see and speak once more the moment for executing summary discipline had plainly passed, for it must be uncommonly difficult to run someone through the body with suitable *gravitas* when all around are laughing at you. So he merely paused a few moments in silence and glowered at the man – who seemed no whit discomfitted by it – then lowered his sword and thrust it back into its scabbard with an angry motion, and turned on his heel to pass through the silent men and return crestfallen to the house, bidding his officers restore order because he had more important matters to attend to (he said) than maintaining discipline in the ranks, which was work for corporals not generals.

He was followed by the jeers and catcalls of the men, who saw that they had plainly prevailed against him, and slapped their late spokesman on the back to congratulate him for having put the presumptuous old booby in his place. Captain van der Hulst looked at me and I at him. But we said nothing, for there was no need. We both knew that in those few brief moments our whole great expedition to Cadiz had come to naught and that all was now up with it; that unless Sir Edward was replaced at once (but by whom?) there was nothing for it but to re-embark the troops and go home. For a general who cannot face down the meanest of his musketeers and make the man do his bidding, but walks away from the encounter browbeaten and vanquished, is no more than a walking corpse as far as his authority is concerned no matter how many viscountcies might be conferred upon him and how many coloured plumes there are on his helmet; and indeed if the King were to dub him Tamburlaine or Pompey the Great that would but increase his abjection and make it more manifest that the stuff of command was not in him.

I reflected before I fell asleep that night, and likewise often in the years afterwards, what a very curious thing it is that the English should have so many among their notables like Sir Edward – but so many also that were his complete antipodes: all the greedy beef-faced ruffians like Sir Robert Holmes or Sir Edward Spragge who later caused us Dutchmen so much mischief and who, were a lion to cross their path, would surely strangle it to death with their bare hands. It was as if Sir Edward and his like were their shadows or their images in a mirror; or the mould for a bronze statue which is exactly like the statue at all points, but a negative of it and defined by the statue's absence. I would sometimes think later on when I beheld English commanders of Viscount Wimbledon's ilk (as I often did) that a surgeon had opened their veins and drained from them all the blood which gives a man heat, and also their livers to remove the bile which imparts courage and martial anger, and had then infused these two fluids into someone like Holmes so that the one fellow had none of them at all, but the other a double ration. Among our Dutch captains courage and discretion were pretty evenly distributed, so that none of them (I think) had too much or too little of either. But among the English I saw that these were either entirely absent, or present in superlative measure. And in military affairs, of course, the excess is greatly to be preferred to the absence, for while the soundest-conceived plans will mostly miscarry for lack of forcefulness in their execution, bad ones may still sometimes succeed if pursued with sufficient vigour, if for no other reason than that the foe is astonished that anyone should be mad enough to attempt them. I do not mean by this that Sir Edward was a poltroon: nothing could be further from my intention, for he was a most honourable gentleman and I am sure would cheerfully have charged into a breach sword in hand in the face of a hundred cannon if his prince's honour had demanded it. It was rather that his actions were all so nerveless and lacking in urgency that they were doomed from the outset to miscarry, as though in his heart he expected them to fail even before he embarked upon them. He commanded, but none would obey his commands though he had in one hand a drawn sword and in the other a general's baton, and a viscount's title and an ancient lineage, because he lacked within him that invisible quality which is called authority and which no amount of gilded armour or patents of nobility can confer. Our Captain Loodgieter, who was the son of a shoemaker in Brouwershaven, seldom raised his voice to shout or to bluster, and his commands had about them more the air of polite requests. Yet no man aboard the *Eenhoorn* would have thought one single instant to disobey him, and I think that if he had ordered us to grapple and board the moon itself we would have done our best to obey him.

I wondered why this should be so, since even then in my adolescence the driving springs of men's understandings and actions intrigued me quite as much as the anatomies of fishes and fowls. But it was not until I became learned in the motions of the stars and planets that I began to comprehend these matters. It was about the year 1640 or 1641 that I found myself once more in England: in the shires of Huntingdon and Lincoln where I had been engaged as an engineer by a company formed to drain those morasses that the English call the Fens. Visiting the town of Stamford on business and having time to spare, I devised to be shown around the great house of Burghley nearby which is the seat of the Cecils. And I thought to enquire of the domestics, did anyone recollect the birth of Sir Edward Cecil (who was by this time dead and buried several years) which I thought must have been about 1570? Quite by chance, an old crone happened to be there, about eighty years of age, who had been a serving girl attending My Lady Burghley's lying-in, and she told me that it was the year 1572, on the 29th day of February (which I afterwards verified from the flyleaf of the great household Bible in the hall where the names and birth-dates of all the family's children were written), and that Sir Edward was born about nine o'clock in the morning which she well remembered, because she had brought hot water from the kitchens and the house clock struck the hour as the baby gave its first cry. Back at my lodgings I used this information to cast a natal horoscope for Sir Edward. And the results were intriguing, since they exactly predicted all that I had witnessed years before at Cadiz. With the Sun in the sign of Pisces and the Moon in Taurus the child would be mild and gentle-natured; cautious and inclined to seek security rather than being drawn to hazard. Likewise with the ascendant in Taurus (which is an earthy sign) and Venus (whose ruling metal is copper) in the twelfth house at that hour and place it was predictable that he would be a solid and incorruptible, always equable and little inclined to shows of anger, but likewise a dull and plodding fellow: conscientious and honest in the performance of his duty but little inclined to pursue it outside the well-trodden pathways. With the Moon in the first house at that hour it was forseeable that Sir Edward would be inclined always to conciliate and gain agreement, so fearful of discord and of bruising the feelings of others that he would rather let them persist in a wrong course than force them to a right one (which is why his threats that men would hang were ignored by those they were uttered against as so much bluster, because it was manifest that he would never be savage enough to do it). Saturn in the sixth house and opposing the ascendant showed that he would always be readier to defend than to attack; whilst the Sun in the eleventh house and Venus in the twelfth ordained respectively that he would enjoy much preferment in his life through the patronage of the great (which was palpable, because King Charles preferred him to lead the Cadiz expedition over several more capable and experienced captains) and that he would be at all times tactful and discrete: more suited to be a courtier or an ambassador (in which latter trade the best course is often to say nothing) than a general, where not to speak or act in time is frequently ruination. This exercise heartened me beyond measure, that albeit retrospectively and years after the hurt, I had accurately forecast it through methodical study of the stars, and it set me on my later course of collection the nativities and subsequent annals of great men in order to compare them and deduce general rules from them which would turn astrology from mere quackery to a true and demonstrable science like mechanics or geometry, based on general axioms that are applicable at all times and places.

CHAPTER THIRTEEN

Darkness fell at last, and the captain and I retired to sleep under sacks in a hayloft, intending to be up and about our surveying at first light next morning, then back aboard ship as fast as ever we could. I fell asleep to the noise of the English soldiers about their campfires bellowing out their roistering bawdy songs, which I was thankful the captain could not understand because if he could, it would surely cause him to think even iller of our allies than he did already. We took the precaution of sleeping by watches, two hours each, with the loaded pistol ready to hand, because it seemed entirely possible (the captain said) that, having got wind of our army's debauched and incapable state, the Spanish cavalry might beat up the place in the night, and he doubted very much whether the English would have troubled themselves to place pickets about the house since they were currently preoccupied with drinking the wine store dry and ransacking the rest of the buildings.

As the sun rose next morning all was quiet about the house, apart from the crackling and hissing of embers where the drunken soldiery had the previous night fired a barn for their sport. I went to draw water from the well in the courtyard while all about me King Charles's myrmidons lay fast asleep and snoring loudly – and some of them so fast asleep withal that they would plainly never stir again, lying motionless in puddles of blood after being hacked with swords or shot with muskets. Inside the great wine store, now silent, two or three fellows floated with their faces downwards in the great vat full of wine like so many dead wasps, having plainly drowned therein. Some that lay about the place, I think, must simply have burst their bellies with their toping. Weapons and accoutrements lay everywhere amid puddles of winey vomit and urine. Some of the officers and sergeants were up now, kicking the sleepers awake and part exhorting, part threatening them to take up their arms once more as they loved their lives, because the rattle of musketry could be heard not far off and the Spanish might be upon us at any moment. But wine had plainly unmanned even those few that were still willing to fight, because they stumbled about helplessly like so many bullocks with the brain-staggers, the crapulent pounding inside their skulls so loud that it was audible to me twenty paces distant.

I found us some biscuit for breakfast, and a few onions, and likewise the remains of a smoked ham. But wine, though abundant there as rainwater, no longer savoured much to either of us, and indeed it was years before I could drink that beverage without tasting in it the bitter flavour of disaster and swinish rout. As we ate the clatter of musketry in the distance grew louder and more insistent; so we finished as quickly as we could and set off to complete our survey, hoping to be safe back aboard our ships by the afternoon – though whether our survey would be of much utility was now most questionable.

As we walked towards the Caño Sancti Petri through the morning fields with the autumn dew still fresh upon them we saw that gunsmoke rose in a haze above Zuazo Bridge a mile or so away and that horsemen were galloping across it, while in the channel a rowing galleas full of musketeers was engaging (we supposed) the English attacking the fort at the island end of the bridge.

"Pay no heed: they are too far off to concern us," the captain said, and instructed me what to draw as he had done the previous evening, pacing out the distance of each trace, judging its alignment with his pocket compass and then calling its length and aspect to me to write down. The galleas had meanwhile rowed down the channel from the bridge and was now no more than three hundred paces distant from us. The Spaniards aboard her caught sight of us, and musket balls were soon plopping all about us like great leaden raindrops.

"Let the fools blaze off their powder if it amuses them," the captain said, "they can do us no hurt at this distance." And with that he turned back to his pacing. "Hornwork number fifteen; south by south-east face; twenty-five yards!" he called out, then came back towards me counting his steps. As he neared me there was a sudden flash and a puff of white smoke from the Spanish vessel, followed by a loud bang – then a sound like an axe striking a rotten tree stump, and a shower of bloody fragments spattering all over and about me. Wiping a gory scrap of flesh out of my eye, I saw the captain stand an instant goggle-eyed and dumbstruck, a great hole blown clean through his chest so that for a moment daylight was visible on the other side of it. Then the top part of him collapsed, his backbone being shot through, and he staggered a pace or two then toppled forwards to lie still. Some yards beyond, his heart lay still palpitating on the dewy morning grass amid fragments of his ribs and sternum, and some yards beyond that, half embedded in the ground and still smoking, the falconet bullet of about three pounds' weight which had struck him squarely between the shoulderblades and knocked his heart out through his breastbone. A great cheer went up from the soldiers aboard the galleas when they saw that they had brought down one of the enemy; which, however, I attribute to pure good fortune on their part and ill on ours, because a cannon is impossible to aim even as precisely as a musket.

Astonished at first and frighted beyond words so that I stood for a while rooted to the spot, I came to my wits at last, gathered up the satchel and scurried for shelter in a ditch, then when the galleas has passed on, made my way back to the house as fast as my trembling legs would carry me, my heart still thumping with fright. It had just been made graphically plain to me that war is the most dangerous and unpredictable of sports, and all things considered I found that I liked it very little. The captain would now no longer be able to make me his secretary and apprentice as he had suggested. But if this was war, to be conversing with a man one moment and bespattered all over with bloody gobbets of him the next, then I felt it would be no great loss to me if I were not to be trained up after all to that honourable profession.

I arrived back at the house still quivering from the shock of what I had just witnessed. But this time no sentries challenged me: the place was quite deserted except for some stragglers and the dead men or dead-drunk that lay all about. Sir Edward and his staff had plainly decided to fall back on Puntal, able neither to advance any further, nor even to hold the place with such a worthless rabble if the Spaniards came against them. Beyond the gateway of the hacienda a troop of riders galloped along the road towards Cadiz in a great cloud of dust: Spanish cavalry I supposed, since the English had no horse with them. They passed by without sending men to inspect the house, so I went to the kitchens to find some provisions for my journey back to my ship, which I determined would be as soon as possible and by the directest route I could find.

As I rummaged in cupboards the kitchen door creaked open. I fumbled for the pistol in my satchel, wondering as I did so how I would cock and fire it since it had to be wound up first with a key. But there staggered into the kitchen none other than our Captain Palethorpe, all bloody and blackened with gunpowder smoke and a dirty rag bound about his head. I gave him some wine to drink and unbound and examined the sword-cut across his brow, then washed it and sewed it up with the needle and silk thread which were contained in the hollow handle of the fleam which I carried in my pocket. As I worked he related what had happened.

"It was yesterday evening," he said, "and our army visibly melting away in drunkenness and riot. I had the drums beaten for volunteers so that we might attempt Zuazo Bridge at dawn, reasoning that if we took and held it, then this island would be secure for the moment and we might have respite to return our soldiers to their proper obedience. About two hundred brave fellows came forward; some of them gentlemen volunteers but for the most part common soldiers disgusted by the rout they saw all about them. And at dawn I led them against the redoubt at the island end of the bridge with our drums beating the forlorn hope. We took the place with some considerable loss. But no sooner had

I sent word back to inform Sir Edward of it, than there came up a messenger on horseback with an order from him to withdraw or find ourselves abandoned there, because he had commanded our army – or what was left of it – to fall back on Puntal. So we quit the fort not a half-hour after taking it, leaving seventy or eighty of our brave fellows lying dead behind us, and the Spaniards reoccupied it so that their men could march unmolested across the bridge which might have been ours for the asking. It makes me heart-sick to tell you of it." He paused to swallow some wine, then wiped his mouth with his cuff. "Hah! He's a brave fellow to be sure, this Viscount Wimble-Wambledon of ours. I think that if he sought to lead his men into an alehouse they would decline to follow him, even though he promised to pay the score from his own pocket." Yet he said these bitter words of his with a smile, and seemed not at all crestfallen or dispirited by what had happened but ready to engage the enemy again as soon as ever he could.

This, I have found, is very much the temper of the English and was most puzzling to me at first: that though a bold and resolute people when well led, instead of making great boast of their valour they seek always to dissemble it by grumbling that all goes ill; indeed seem never happier than when things go badly, which however does not discompose them at all or cast them down because (they say) they never expected that things would go well in the first place, and that given the incapacity of their commanders they are surprised that they have not gone even worse. And this is a great secret resource of theirs.

Having dressed Captain Palethorpe's wound, I offered to try and find a horse for him to make his way back to Puntal. But he declared that he would rather go on foot among his soldiers who waited outside, they being well able (he said) to defend themselves against the Spanish horsemen who now snapped at the retreating army's heels, but had only swords and pistols and would therefore be little inclined to pick a quarrel with a resolute body of musketeers and pikemen. He waved me goodbye as he set off with his men, who I saw were begrimed and battle-stained as himself, but triumphantly carrying with them a Spanish standard they had taken. They offered to take me along with them. But being unarmed except for the captain's pistol, and entirely unskilled in the use of a musket, I said that I would rather make my own way back to the ships which were plainly visible in the distance only two or three miles off, and which I thought I might easily reach by swimming if I could find no boat, the water being calm and warm, and I having besides the two botas which I could inflate to support me. It seemed to me that if the English commanders had as much brains as earwax – though I confess that this was by now mighty debatable – they would try to hold Torre Gorda where the isthmus joins the Isle of León; which meant that if I tried to gain Fort Puntal by that road I might find myself in the midst of a battle, and most likely in as much in peril of being wantonly shot down by the English as of being cut down by the Spaniards. But the watery route, though shorter and seemingly less perilous, had the disadvantage that I must needs go some way northwards towards the white tower on the hill, then from there to a promontory which reached into Cadiz Bay and which seemed, being somewhat higher than the shore on either side, to offer the prospect of my not having to struggle through marshes and salt pans to reach the water's edge. So I set off up the road towards the tower, keeping a sharp lookout meanwhile for horsemen and with my ears cocked for the sound of hoofbeats.

After about a mile I came upon the first dismal signs of a battle having been fought there a few hours earlier. Dead men lay strewn about beside the road and in the fields on either side of it, with crows already hopping gingerly about them to make sure that life was extinct before they sat down to dine after their manner, which is first to pluck out the dead man's eyeballs which they esteem as great delicacies. As I progressed up the road I saw to my dismay that more and more of the dead wore the green coats of Captain Neades's archers, and lay about either singly or heaped together where they had stood to defend themselves with their bow-pikes. As I passed by, one of these sad figures croaked and reached out to grasp my legs.

"Give me to drink, for sweet Jesu's sake." I knelt down – and saw that it was Will Shefford. I unslung my bota and pressed it to his lips.

"What ails you?" I asked – though it was perfectly plain that what ailed him was lead poisoning: *scilicet*,* two ounces of that metal lodged in his liver, as might be seen from the hole the musket ball had punched through his breastplate on the right side about halfway up. I lifted him up and unstrapped his corselet to examine the wound. Beneath the breastplate his doublet and shirt were all sodden with blood. "What happened to you?" I asked.

"Captain Neades was told to hold this crossroads against the Dons when their horsemen came up from the bridge, after they took the fort there," he said. "We drove off their first charge under a pretty rain of arrows – but then the dogs came back at us in open order so that our shooting had less effect, wheeling and caracolling then gathering into a block at last to charge us when they saw our arrows were all spent. They did us much harm with their pistols, because our pikes were too short to hold them in respect. And then there came up behind them a company of their musketeers, who gave us a couple of volleys to which we could make no reply. Our fellows broke at the second volley and ran away, though Captain Neades tried to stem them. And having been hit already, I was left behind." He pulled at my sleeve. "Sweet Frankie, as you love your old friend Will: make an end of me before the Dons come upon me. I fear if those evil papist curs find me alive they'll have much sport with me before they knock me on the head. Do this for me as a last favour and token of affection."

So I took out my fleam, rolled up his sleeve and opened the vein in his left forearm, then that in his left ankle as well, but so deftly from long practice in phlebotomy that I am sure he felt nothing. He was dead within five minutes, having already lost most of the blood in him from his wound. I held his hand as he

---

* "That is to say"

shivered from the heat leaving his body and his fingertips turned blue, and he fell still at last. Then I closed his eyelids and disposed his limbs in as seemly a fashion as I could, and said a *Paternoster* and an *Ave* for the repose of his soul which I thought he might mind being a Protestant, but I could remember no others and felt that God would surely understand. Then I left him with the crows, already flapping and cawing over their breakfast. I had no thought now other than to make my way as fast as I could towards the waters of the bay, gleaming blue in the morning sunshine, and our ships riding at anchor in the distance.

★ ★ ★ ★ ★ ★ ★ ★ ★ ★

As he made his way towards the shore of the bay Frans was once or twice obliged to hide from cavalry patrols. But they passed far off without seeing him, and he reached the water's edge about mid-afternoon. There he discovered that, as he had surmised, the tip of the low promontory was separated from the water only by a narrow shore of muddy sand. Above the beach was a fishermen's hamlet of three or four tumbledown cottages, with frames for drying nets and with eel spears, oars and mussel rakes leaning against the walls – but no sign of any boat, though several had plainly been there not long before, because there were rings for tying them up, and the tracks their bottoms had left across the beach as they were dragged down to the water. The place was deserted except for one or two stray dogs which yapped and snarled at him but came no closer. Resolved to strip off his clothes and swim out to the ships if he could find no boat, Frans peered into one hovel, the door of which was banging fretfully in the breeze, but saw in it no oars or other gear that might indicate a boat hidden somewhere nearby. He tried the next cottage, lifting the wooden latch and pushing open the door – only to find the point of a boathook levelled at his chest.

"¿A dónde vas?" At the other end of the boathook was a stocky, black-eyed woman of about thirty or thirty-five, with blue-black hair hanging loose over her shoulders and wearing a dress of coarse russet stuff. The expression on her face was determined – and anything but welcoming. "Who are you?" she hissed, "What do you seek here?" Her words had a malevolent rattle to them. Frans was glad now that his tutor in Spanish had been from Andalusia, because if he had learned the pure Castilian Spanish current among the better sort in Flanders he would scarcely have understood a word the woman said.

"Buena mujer*, I am… " She ignored him, jabbing the boathook against his breast and plainly quite prepared to do far more drastic things with it. "Are you an inglés? A luterano?" Frans explained as best as he could that he was not an Englishman or a Protestant but a Hollander, pointing towards the ships out in the bay to underline his meaning. In fact, he said, he was not a Hollander but from Flanders: a Catholic like herself.

This seemed to reassure the woman somewhat, and the boathook was lowered provisionally, though she continued to glare at him. She swept the hair back from her eyes with one hand.

"What do you seek here?" she asked. In all decency, being a well brought-up youth, Frans could hardly tell her that he was looking for a boat to steal. But she seemed to know that already. "Were the soldiers chasing you? Have they seen you come here? Are there any others with you?"

Frans said that so far as he was aware, no one had watched him come this way. And as for companions, he was completely alone. So in the end it seemed that there were just the two of them, the Dutch fugitive and the Spanish fisherwoman.

"Is there anyone else here in this village?" he enquired.

"No," she said, "only me. I was raking mussels on the mudflats at low tide on Sunday afternoon after Mass when the soldiers came here to command us all to leave. They said the Corregidor of Jerez had ordered that we must cross to the mainland, taking all our cattle with us, so that the English pirates would not have

---

* Goodwife

them."

Being even then of a sceptical disposition, Frans wondered how she would have known this if she was working away from the village at the time. But perhaps (he thought) the woman had simply felt unable to abandon her poor cottage and meagre belongings to the plundering soldiery and had stayed behind, or slipped out of the refugee column later on and returned. He wondered whether she might now betray him to the horsemen who would be out looking for stragglers from Sir Edward's hapless army. Or, even worse, to her neighbours when they returned; for a soldier cut off from his fellows on the enemy's territory is the forlornest of creatures and only too likely to be hunted down by the country folk and put to some cruel death for their amusement, like the young English soldier near Houtenburg in 1592 who was caught and had his eyes gouged out by the villagers incensed at the plundering of their homes, and was then flayed alive for good measure by the village butcher and his hide nailed to the door of the parish church. However, they were two miles or more from the nearest settlement, so if she wished to turn him in she would have to hitch up her skirts and run there for assistance, which would give him plenty of time to escape.

But the woman seemed peaceably enough disposed, now that her first alarm had passed. She put aside the boathook and motioned him to enter the cottage, which was a wretched low building with a reed-thatched roof and only a wooden table, a cupboard and two benches for furnishing. The woman poked the fire of driftwood beneath an iron cauldron that hung from a chain over the hearth. Before long a smell of lentil pottage reminded Frans that he had eaten no hot food for the past three days. She bade him sit down at the table, ladled the stew of lentils and bacon into an earthenware dish, then gave him a wooden spoon to eat with. He thanked her as graciously as he could, knowing that the Spanish were very fond of elaborate courtesies, and likewise addressed her as "buena mujer" even though she was barefooted and plainly of lower degree than himself. He took good care as he ate to face the doorway and listen all the time for the sound of approaching hoofbeats. But the woman showed no malicious or hostile intent, and instead sat down with a quizzical smile to watch him eat, chin cupped in hand and her elbow resting on the table, much as a proud mother might observe her favourite son.

"Where do you come from, boy?" she asked.

"May it please you, buena mujer, I was born and grew up in a small town called Houtenburg in Flanders. But I lived for some years in England, and I now serve aboard a Dutch vessel here as part of the expedition."

"What do you do aboard your ship? Are you a common sailor?"

"No, I am apprentice to the vessel's surgeon, who is also my stepfather."

"If you are a ship's surgeon, what are you doing here ashore? Are our Spanish teeth so rotten that we need Hollanders to come and draw them for us?"

"I came ashore with a Dutch military engineer to assist him in making a survey, because I have some skill in drawing maps. But he was slain by a chance cannon-shot, so now I must make my way back to my ship as best I can."

She sat silent for a while, gazing at him. Then she spoke. "So you came here to steal a boat, I suppose?"

Frans nodded: there seemed to be little point in denying something so obvious.

"Well, my fine young Flamenco, you are likely to be disappointed in that design, because the soldiers commanded our menfolk to untie the boats and row them round to La Carraca to keep them out of the hands of the English. But…" she paused, "I might still be able to assist you. Because you're a handsome youth to be sure, and evidently of good family, and it would pain me to think of so fair a young fellow having his throat cut by the soldiers or being sent to pull an oar in King Philip's galleys when by rights some lucky Flemish girl should have him to her bed. So when you have finished I shall lead you down to the marsh and reveal to you a skiff, which is so well hidden among the creeks that without my help you would never find it even if you searched a hundred years. And with this you will be free to row back to your ship out in the bay – if you promise me to leave the boat and its gear behind when you sail, because it would be a shabby thing for a wealthy people like the Hollanders to steal from poor fisher-folk like us who have no other means to earn our bread."

Frans nodded vigorously to assure her that he would take every care of the boat, and leave it moored by a stone tied to the painter when he was done with it.

"...But that will be on tonight's high tide, because the ebb has started now and the boat is too heavy for us to drag out of the creek. So in the meantime, my handsome Flamenco, you must perform me a small service by way of payment." She stood up, and without a further word unfastened the buttons of her dress to let it fall about her ankles, standing there quite naked since she was wearing no shift underneath.

Frans goggled in disbelief, spoon poised in mid-air, blushing crimson from perplexity and having not the slightest idea what to do or to say.

The woman smiled, and folded her arms behind her head to lift her breasts, which were as heavy and rustic as her hips but still pleasing enough to look at.

"There, young fellow, have you seen many women who look so well at thirty-four years old? Or thirty-five: I can't say which, except that I remember watching in my father's arms from across the bay when the English burned Cadiz in old King Philip's day. But still, though I say it myself, with a figure that many a young girl would be glad of. Does it not please you?"

Frans blushed again, which plainly amused her, and nodded to signify that she was indeed well-shaped; though his experience in these matters was extremely limited; restricted to certain much-thumbed plates in Vesalius's *De Corporis* and to cherished book-engravings of classical nymphs and goddesses.

She sighed, and looked down at her breasts. "Yes indeed; thirty-four years old now. And the years pass. Without children. And no man now to my bed to keep me warm on the cold winter nights."

"But what about your husband?" Frans stammered, because though young he still knew enough of the world to fear that the master of the house might suddenly appear in the doorway and take a less than indulgent view of his wife displaying her person to a vagrant Dutch sailor.

"My husband?" she snorted. "I scarcely remember him now, except when my tongue feels the gap left by a tooth he once knocked out, among all the black eyes and bruises that he gave me. They pressed him two years since to fight the Hollanders aboard a king's ship in the northern seas, the frigate *Nuestra Señora de las Vírgenes*, and I've heard nothing of him since. The Corregidor's clerk gives me some money from his pay now and then. But otherwise never a word whether he lives or is dead. Who speaks now of husbands? And anyway, to us poor women does it matter whether the cocks that are stuck into us are Spanish or English or Dutch ones, and lawfully wedded to us or not?"

Frans was somewhat shocked by this bluntness; but Spanish (he knew) is a notably foul language where merda and coño rub shoulders every moment with Jesús and el santo sacramento.

"Come my fine young Flamenco", she said, "There's a tribute you must pay me before I lead you to the boat."

"What tribute, buena mujer?"

"What tribute do you think, fool? To scratch my back for me? No, young man: I want you to leave me with child when you row away to your ship. You look of an age to be capable of doing so."

"With child...?"

"That's what I said: with child. Twelve years I've been married, and never a sign of a baby, so that the village women mock me and call me a barren mule. Yet I think my husband may be the one wanting in that respect, and not me."

"But what will your husband say if he returns after two years at sea and finds you with child, or with an infant in your arms? And your neighbours likewise?"

She laughed. "Simple enough: I would tell them that the English soldiers ravished me, which is credible since the folk around Cadiz know better than any in Spain that the English are rapists without scruple or respect for any woman, worse than the most lascivious of stray dogs. And I will tell them that though I scratched and bit as best I could to defend my honour, they overpowered me at last and had their way with me, and that the child is the innocent fruit of that crime. Who could possibly quarrel with that?" She smiled. "Or if the baby has your fine red-gold hair, I could always tell them that an angel of the Lord passed by and made me pregnant. Either way I'll get a good beating for it from my husband, I know that well enough. But I'd probably receive a good beating from him for falling pregnant even if he *was* the child's father, so what difference does it make? A babe sucking at my breast after so many years would still be cheap at ten times the price."

She put her bare arms around his shoulders, and despite his embarrassment he felt a stirring in his loins, as though a weasel or some other small creature were waking from its sleep. She pulled him to his feet and started to unbutton his breeches, then his shirt, running her hands across his skin and standing back to regard him critically. "Yes, a fine well-shaped young fellow indeed, and a shameful waste for him to be left lying dead in some field for the crows to pick. Come my young Flamenco, to my bed. Tonight is the new moon, which is the season most favourable for the planting of seed. If the soldiers take you they'll most surely hang you, or send you to rot in the galleys if it pleases them to spare your life. So consider that this modest expenditure of your generative fluid is purchasing you your life."

Frans was pulled to the low truckle bed, and then into it, and was deftly relieved of his virginity at the hands of an expert: hands that took him and gently guided him into her. It surprised him afterwards, his head still spinning, that he had known what to do without ever having been taught or shown it, or even told of it, and that his body had seemed to assume command and direct matters without his conscious involvement, so that he felt as though he had become a spectator of himself. Afterwards, as he lay gasping and spent between her breasts, the woman stroked his hair, and laughed at how light his skin was alongside her own – "like a white hen's egg beside a brown one" – and kissed him with motherly solicitude, and asked him about his family and his life in Flanders. She never once enquired as to his name, though, which he thought afterwards must have been deliberate, so that at confession she could tell the priest in good conscience that the father of the child now in her belly was unknown to her. Then after a while for him to recover himself, she made him perform the same actions, but more leisurely than before: the timeless actions that are the origin of us all; mundane and marvellous alike; every time different and every time the same. And so on until darkness was long fallen and the required tribute had been paid three times over. Though to what effect only time would reveal.

Meanwhile the thin fingernail-paring of the new moon had risen to take its place amid the autumnal stars above the Bay of Cadiz, shedding its faint silvery light indiscriminately upon the cottage where the two of them lay in one another's arms, and on the grimacing dead lying stiff and cold on the battlefield barely a mile away; on those poor mortals whose earthly troubles were now at an end; and perhaps (if the sowing had been efficacious) upon one poor mortal for whom they were only just beginning. On the battlements of Cadiz Don Fernando Girón de Salcedo y Brivesca, who had had himself carried up there by his attendants even though the evening chill aggravated his gout, looked out towards the ships in the bay and then towards Fort Puntal where the lanterns could be seen and the faint shouting heard which signalled that the English were re-embarking after having marched to Zuazo Bridge the day before, then unaccountably marched all the way back again. Nothing in his considerable military experience could throw any light upon this strange behaviour. But no matter: they had returned in evident disorder, and tomorrow morning he felt that he might risk a sally out of Cadiz to disorder the rascals even more.

Behind the stone wall of an olive grove near Puntal Captain Palethorpe and his band of volunteers tried to catch such sleep as they could against the morrow, which looked as though it might be a busy one. They were tired, but well pleased with themselves after having ambushed a Spanish cavalry squadron just before dusk and driven them off with considerable loss. They had been detailed to fight in the rearguard tomorrow if the Spaniards tried to harass the re-embarkation of the army. But that prospect was not at all displeasing to them, and they felt confident of giving a good account of themselves. Meanwhile aboard the fluit-ship *Eenhoorn* out in the bay, her surgeon leaned on the rail and gazed towards the land. Frans had been due back with Captain van der Hulst that afternoon. So what could have delayed them?

About ten o'clock hooves thudded on the track outside the fisherman's cottage, and there was a jingling of steel, then loud voices. The door was kicked open, and three men rushed in with a candle-lantern and drawn swords. The woman screamed and leaped out of bed, holding up a blanket to cover her modesty, and began to weep profusely, her hair all dishevelled and thanking the Blessed Virgin Mary for answering an honest woman's prayers, that good honourable Spanish soldiers had arrived at last to rescue her from a beastly foreign ravisher. The men dragged Frans from the bed and berated him as a *pero* and a *ladróne* while beating him conscientiously with the flats of their swords. Meanwhile the woman sobbed as the corporal in charge of the patrol comforted her.

"Calm yourself, woman. What happened?"

"The Hollander pig broke into my house at midday and forced me at pistol point." She wailed, "Three times he ravished me and robbed me of my honour – and me a married woman too, old enough to be his mother! The shame of it will kill me, to have been so foully used!"

"Núñez, tell this Dutch dog to get his shirt and breeches on.

Then bind his wrists and put a halter round his neck."

"Shall we hang him up outside, cabo? There's a frame for fishing nets strong enough to serve as a gallows. And string the bastard up naked as he is and we won't have the trouble of stripping him of his clothes afterwards."

The corporal had meanwhile found the leather satchel and was rummaging in it, examining the drawings and notes.

"No, let him get dressed. This is plainly no common foot-soldier that we have here but a fellow that can read and write; perhaps an officer of some kind, or a spy. The Corregidor was arriving at San Romualdo just as we left, so he may want to question him in the morning."

Frans was pummelled some more, so that the soldiers could show their proper military and Catholic disapproval of invading heretical rapists, then dragged outside and a bowline placed round his neck. The other end of the rope was then hitched to a saddle pommel, and he was dragged off through the night towards the castle of San Romualdo near Zuazo Bridge. Even as he stumbled along the stony roads on his bleeding feet, and fell, and was cursed and dragged back to his feet again, and stumbled on further, Frans found that he held no rancour in his heart towards the woman for having seduced him then denounced him as a rapist when the soldiers arrived. He knew that the Spanish were extremely jealous of the honour of their womenfolk – though they treated them like dogs in every other respect – and might have been very unpleasant towards her if they had suspected that she had willingly lain with a foreigner and a heretic. No: he was grateful to her and wished her well, and fancied he would now take the consequences of his deeds with as much equanimity as Marcus Aurelius himself.

After being half driven, half dragged by his captors several miles through the darkness to San Romualdo, Frans's numbed wrists were unbound at last. He was pushed unceremoniously into a dark cell, and the heavy oaken door was slammed shut and barred behind him. An indeterminate number of prisoners already lay there, and as he landed among them they cursed him drowsily in English as a blackguard and a whoreson villain, then went back to sleep. Exhausted by his barefoot canter along the country roads, the boy dozed a little until the first anaemic light of morning glimmered through an iron grille high up in the wall, revealing thirty or so other unfortunates snoring amid the musty straw.

About six o'clock the door opened and two guards entered. They seized Frans one under each armpit and dragged him on to his lacerated feet, then out into the chill autumnal early-morning air of the courtyard. A fire was burning in a brazier and a group of elegantly dressed officers was gathered around it, holding an impromptu staff conference while breakfasting; some standing, some on horseback and others seated at a table writing out orders in a tableau that would have gladdened the heart of any painter of military scenes. At the centre of the group one officer – plainly having authority among them to judge by his finely gilded half-suit of armour and the deference with which he was treated – sat nonchalantly on the end of the table studying a map with one gauntleted hand while drinking a cup of warmed wine with the other. This was Don Luís de Portocarrero, the Corregidor of Jerez, who for three whole days had never slept or been out of his clothes as he assembled the makeshift force which had been intended only to delay the English army until regular troops arrived from Seville – but which now seemed quite inexplicably to be chasing them back towards Puntal. When the English ships were first sighted off Cadiz it had been on his initiative that messengers were sent on horseback around the towns and villages of Andalusia to call the local gentry to arms. And that policy now seemed to have paid off handsomely, since more than a thousand gentlemen – many of them veterans of His Majesty's wars in Flanders – had mustered next morning at Chiclana de la Frontera with their swords and pistols and three days' rations to be formed into an impromptu regiment of cavalry; good only for skirmishing, since as hidalgos their discipline was sadly not the equal of their loyalty, but still more than enough (it seemed) to see off the English.

The gaoler propelled Frans towards the Corregidor. "May it please Your Excellency, here's the Dutch youth the patrol took prisoner last night."

Don Luís looked up from his map. His eyes were red-rimmed from lack of sleep, but still those of a man thoroughly in command of events: stern magistrate and judicious military commander rolled into one. He surveyed the dishevelled captive from his bare, bleeding feet via his torn breeches and filthy shirt to his tousled hair. It was plain that what he saw was neither pleasing to him nor of any great interest. He sighed.

"Why should this dirty fellow be of any concern to me? I am a field officer of His Majesty King Philip the Fourth on campaign, not a village constable rounding up vagrants."

"Your Excellency, the Hollander was caught in the act of ravishing a local woman and would have been hanged on the spot without troubling you. But the corporal leading the patrol thought you might wish to question the fellow, because he had these papers with him, and also this fine wheel-lock pistol which is certainly of a quality befitting a gentleman. Likewise he speaks good Spanish. So the cabo considered that whoever he might be, he is certainly no common soldier, and might even possess useful intelligence."

The Corregidor opened the satchel and shuffled through Captain van der Hulst's drawings and notes, then nodded at last, and surveyed Frans again much as a hawk might sit in judgement upon a mouse.

"Who are you then, young man?" he said, "I warn you now, answer my questions truthfully, because you were caught in the act of rape; you have plans and notes with you concerning fortifications; and if you speak Spanish as well, then you are quite probably a spy. I could have you hanged without further ado on each or all of those charges. But as His Majesty's corregidor for the county of Jerez I also have the power of clemency vested in me."

"May it please Your Excellency," Frans answered, "my name is

Frans van Raveyck, and I served aboard a Dutch ship as barber and surgeon's mate. I came ashore the day before yesterday with a Dutch military officer to assist him in surveying the island with a view to fortifying it, but only as a secretary to take notes and make drawings for him. He was struck dead yesterday morning by a cannonshot fired from a galley. So the English army having now retreated, I sought to find a boat on the shore and rejoin my ship."

"...Pausing only to do a little ravishing of our womenfolk on the way, naturally enough?"

Frans hesitated. "Er...indeed, your excellency: unfortunately my instincts got the better of me, so I forced the lady, which I now deeply regret, but she was very comely and I had been at sea for many months. Your Excellency will surely understand."

Don Luís nodded and smiled bleakly as though he did understand – and was sure that the hangman would understand as well.

"Where did you learn to speak Spanish so fluently?" he asked, "And for what purpose? In my experience draughtsmanship and foreign tongues are not everyday accomplishments among ship's-barbers-turned-rapists."

"May it please Your Excellency, in Flanders where I was born. My stepfather thought that Spanish would be useful to me in my later life. I was taught by a corporal of a Spanish regiment quartered there."

Don Luís's eyebrows flicked up in a menacing sort of way, much as a snake might raise its eyebrows before striking if snakes possessed eyebrows.

"Indeed? A Fleming? And therefore a subject of King Philip now enlisted in the service of his enemies: yet a fourth reason for me to hang you, if you had four necks for me to hang you by. Your plight looks graver by the minute. Tell me now, boy, as you value your life: how many men do the English have ashore here, and how many still afloat?"

His knees knocking together by now, Frans replied that so far as he knew there were about ten thousand men in the English army, and that all of them were now ashore.

"And your Hollanders, do they also have soldiers here?"

"Your Excellency, we have only fifteen or so ships here to assist the English: there are no Dutch troops ashore or afloat."

Don Luís nodded as though to himself. "Yes" he said, "that would tally with what we know already. Tell me now, to the best of your knowledge: do the English intend to lay siege to Cadiz town? And if so, have they the means to do it?"

"By your leave, I doubt it: they have only ten or twelve siege guns and no horses to drag them with, the ship carrying them having been lost in a storm on the way here. And it was widely complained of among their officers that they had brought no scaling ladders or digging tools."

The Corregidor smiled. "Hmm, I see then that you kept some company with the expedition's officers – or at least listened to their conversations while trimming their beards. Tell me, boy: the Vizconde de Vimbledón: what manner of man is he, and how is he spoken of in your fleet?"

Frans marvelled that the news of Sir Edward's viscountcy should have travelled so quickly to Spain. But he still thought carefully before he answered, knowing that a person of so lowly an estate as himself expressing too frank an opinion about another nobleman, albeit an English one, might well earn him a beating from Don Luís on grounds of class solidarity.

"Your excellency, while all men know Viscount Wimbledon to be a most honourable gentleman and as faithful a servant as any prince in Christendom ever had, it is also widely said that he lacks the necessary vigour to take timely actions, and likewise the authority to make men do his bidding, so that he commonly gives his orders too late and half convinced before he even utters them no man will pay any heed to them." Don Luís nodded.

"That would certainly explain a great deal, and I had already gathered as much for myself. I thought at first yesterday morning that the English falling back so suddenly from Zuazo Bridge just after they had taken it might be a trap, to entice us to advance on to the island in pursuit of them and then cut us off, which is why I withdrew my musketeers back across the bridge for a time. But then my scouts informed me that the English were indeed scurrying back towards Puntal leaving all behind them. So what you have told me confirms what has since become plain: that they behave thus because they cannot behave otherwise, and their general has no control over them."

"Indeed, your excellency," one of the officers added, "to let thirsty men loose upon a storehouse containing fifty thousand gallons of new wine is surely not the act of a prudent commander or one who has authority over his men. This must surely be the first military campaign since the world began in which more have fallen to the darts of Bacchus than those of Mars." They all laughed uproariously at this, as soldiers are wont to do when one of them displays a little more wit and learning than the rest. Even Don Luís gave a thin smile, as befitted a man with a sound classical education. When the laughter had died down he resumed his questioning.

"So tell me now, young man: what was spoken aboard your ship concerning the silver fleet from Mexico? Was that not the reason why King Charles and Milord Buckingham sent you here?"

Frans forebore to reply that a mole with its eyes sewn shut could see this was the reason for their coming here to Cadiz.

"Your excellency, it was indeed the plan to come here and take Cadiz town, then await the treasure fleet's arrival; that much was evident to all of us aboard."

"When you left your ship, to the best of your knowledge did the English have any intelligence concerning the silver fleet? You seem to me to be of livelier wit than the common run of seamen, and came ashore to assist a Dutch officer, so I think that you might well have overheard something concerning this. Be sure that you tell me the truth though, because you still have a noose around your neck and only I can remove it."

"Your excellency, we had no knowledge of the plate fleet's approach beyond what was gained from the fishermen My Lord Essex's ships took off the coast of Portugal. There was never any talk of scouts being dispatched to search for it – though our Dutch admirals pressed for them to be sent out – and I think that the intention was and still is to sit in Cadiz Bay until the fleet arrives and falls unsuspecting into our lap."

Don Luís turned to his officers. "Very good then, señore, the English are plainly every whit as much a troop of clowns as their actions proclaim them to be, and I think that we may safely assume that their unsoldierly bumbling is no pantomime meant to beguile us, but rather a true expression of their incapacity." He turned back to Frans. "There is still one thing I would ask you, young man, if I thought that you could satisfy my idle curiosity. Which is why Rey Carlos of England has thought fit to insult the King my master by sending such a pitiful rabble to face the finest soldiers in Christendom; some of them poor doddering old fools armed only with bows and arrows like the naked Indians of the Americas, which is a thing I would never have credited unless I had seen it with my own eyes. Did the English perhaps hope to make us all die of laughter at their buffoonery?" He snapped his mapcase shut. "I think, though, that only Viscount Wimbledon himself can answer that question for me, and regrettably he is not present among us – though I confess it would not surprise me in the least if he were now to be led in here a captive with his breeches round his ankles, having been taken at stool in some privy house." The officers once more laughed at this.

Then the Corregidor stood up "Enough of this prattling, señore: we have business to attend to. I think we can now be confident that the English are indeed as inept soldiers as they appear – and more important, that the Hollanders have no troops here to support them, who might have given us a deal more trouble. The main thing is that the Mexico fleet is now reported safe, Girón having had the wit as soon as the English appeared off Cadiz to dispatch vessels to look for it and warn its admiral to head for Gibraltar. So let us now press onwards towards Puntal and hope to cut off these worthless rascals and destroy them before they are able to embark. I shall now send word to Cadiz to inform Girón that he may send his men out in a sally to give this English rabble yet more reasons why should depart from our shores and never return." Don Luís took the pen and paper proferred by an orderly and began to write.

"Your excellency..."

He looked up. "Yes, what is it?"

"The Dutch youth: what shall we do with him?"

Don Luís sighed wearily. "Ah, yes: the young Flamenco with a taste for violating our women. By rights he should hang. But I promised him his life for being frank with me, which I think he was. So send him to the galleys for five years instead. He's a pretty youth, and a season chained naked to a rowing bench among several hundred Turks and convicted sodomites may perhaps dampen his enthusiasm for rape and send him back to Flanders a sorer but wiser man. Who says that the Corregidor of Jerez pays no heed to the reformation of felons?"

The assembled staff officers laughed at this bon mot (as staff officers will laugh at any jest on the part of their superiors) and Frans was conducted back to prison.

★ ★ ★ ★ ★ ★ ★ ★ ★

My companions in that dungeon at San Romualdo fort were fifteen or so English soldiers: stragglers from Lord Wimbledon's army who, through some oversight or whim, had not been summarily cut down by the horsemen who overtook them on the road and being noblemen, were in general but little disposed to spare the lives of lowly foot-soldiers for whom no ransom could be obtained. Some of them were wounded – though more probably by their own side in their drunken brawling than by the Spaniards in battle – so I cleaned and dressed their injuries as best I could, tearing up an old shirt for bandages. Later that morning we were rousted out by our guards, who said they had work for us to do, which was to go about the Isle of León with ox-carts collecting up the English dead (of whom there were about three hundred I should think) in order to cleanse and disembarrass Spain's holy soil of their heretical carcasses. But once we had gathered up the poor corpses and stripped them of their harness, their shoes and other such items which might be of use, a command came to us not to dig a pit somewhere and bury them with quicklime as we had expected, but instead to cart them down to the shore of the bay and load them aboard the hulk of our Dutch fluit-ship the *Fortuijn*, which had been abandoned some days before after the fight at Puntal and left to run aground in a creek. When we had dragged aboard the dead bodies (which was most disagreeable work, since they were already bloated and starting to stink) the hulk was towed out into the bay and set ablaze, then left to drift down on that evening's ebb tide towards the English fleet anchored two or so miles distant off Puntal. We watched as the burning vessel drifted away into the autumn twilight beneath a great cloud of smoke and sparks. At last, when the ship was about a mile distant from us, there was a sudden mighty boom as the flames reached her powder room. Burning timbers and fragments of dead men's bodies fell all about her, and her blazing mainmast was projected up into the sky to turn end over end like a fire-swallower's torch before it fell back into the water.

When the smoke cleared there were only some burning fragments of wood left floating on the water. By this time the vessels of our fleet, thinking no doubt that fireships were being sent against them on the ebb, had weighed anchor and were quitting the bay as fast as ever they could. We watched glum-faced from the shore, seeing the ships which had brought us to Spain now departing to leave us behind; prisoners condemned to an indeterminate season of oar-lugging in King Philip's galleys. As the ship burned, then exploded, I said a silent *Salve Regina* (which I was sure he would not mind) for the intention of poor Will Shefford, whose body I had placed aboard with as much reverence as possible, but whose shoes were now on my own feet, I having surreptitiously removed them when our overseer's back was turned.

That would be his posthumous gift to me during what I expected would be a long and wearisome march towards the galley port of Cartagena, which I thought must be two or three hundred miles distant on the Mediterranean shore.

My own thoughts on this latter point were far from agreeable, since I had not merely been abandoned to captivity on the shores of Spain but condemned for good measure as a felon to five years' servitude in the King's galleys. I knew from my stepfather's accounts – he having spent a year as a surgeon to the Flanders galleys at Sluis towards the end of his time in the Spanish service – that the life of a rower aboard a galley, though hard, is not the very worst fate that might befall a man; that those vessels commonly spend only four or five weeks a year at sea, and that the rest of the time their rowers are employed as labourers ashore working upon fortifications *et cetera*. But whereas the servitude of my English fellows might last only a few months until prisoners were exchanged under cartel, I myself had been condemned for the crime of rape and might therefore never see the end of my sentence, the mortality from sickness aboard the galleys being very high from so many being crowded together in such great filth, and the hazards of battle likewise considerable since those vessels are but lightly constructed and have no bulwarks to protect the rowers, and if they burn or sink then the slaves will burn or sink with them from being chained to their benches. But there was nothing to be done about it, I thought, so I must needs submit to the destiny the stars prescribed for me and meanwhile use such wit and adroitness as I possessed to better my lot. At least my Spanish was fluent and I could write, and I was likewise skilled in surgery; so I fancied I might very soon find myself elevated aboard my galley from common rower to the charge of surgeon's mate or clerk to the captain. But it still seemed likely to be a very far cry from my earlier life in Colchester town, to have passed within a mere eight months from the honoured estate of surgeon's apprentice to that of a felon shackled to a bench aboard a galley, and only went to show just how swiftly and unpredictably the goddess Fortuna's wheel may spin.

Our journey of two days from the Isle of León to the prison in Jerez, though no more than twenty miles, was a tiresome one because my English companions and I were shackled together by a long chain, as is the custom with men condemned to servitude in the galleys, and this dragged along chinking in the dust of the road and galled our ankles us we walked. But our guards (I must confess) were cordial enough towards us: two old bumpkin militiamen armed with rusty halberds who might have been poor Will Shefford's Spanish half-brothers, and though they would not unlock us from the chain so that we might obey the needs of nature, for fear that we would flee or overpower them, they were otherwise kindly disposed and saw to it that we were properly fed with coarse barley-bread, and given water to drink whenever we came upon a well; likewise not forced to trudge along in the full heat of the day but permitted to take a siesta with them under the shade of the roadside trees. The country round about was low and sandy, and as we passed through each village the rustic folk, who looked more like Moors than Spaniards, came out from their mud-walled hovels to stare at us as heréticos and luteranos, which is what they call all Protestants in that country. Yet though they touched our white skin and marvelled at my red hair (which is very uncommon in that part of Spain) they did not molest us or pelt us with filth or set their dogs on us as we had feared, but only remarked that it was great pity that Rey Carlos our master should have sent us so far to fight on his behalf then sailed away again and left us. From which we surmised that our fleet must already have stood out to sea and be no longer visible from the coast, and that we had indeed been abandoned to our fate since there was now no prospect that our army might defeat the Spaniards in battle and set us free. For better or worse, it seemed that we had come to Spain not just for a visit but for a more lengthy sojourn.

CHAPTER FOURTEEN

Beheld from far off as we shuffled towards it along the dusty road from Zuazo, Jerez was a town most characteristic of that Andalusian province of Spain: a close-packed array of square white towers and flat red-tiled roofs set on a hill among vineyards and olive groves with many palm trees among them; most picturesque to behold and of a Mahometan rather than a Christian aspect even though it had a great basilica in the middle of it, and also several very splendid churches. But its comeliness or lack of it concerned us but little as we made our dejected entry through the Cadiz Gate that evening, because a great crowd had gathered to jeer at us, the townspeople having been in mortal fear until only the day before that the English would march on the place and sack it. Their relief at having escaped this fate was now turned to a great contumely for those who might have done the sacking but were now at their mercy; as dogs will bark and snarl most gallantly against a lion in a cage whom they would never dare to face were he still at liberty. They shook their fists at us, spat, pelted us with rotten fruit and denounced us as ladrones, and would no doubt have handled us even worse if there had not been a sufficient number of soldiers to guard us. We were taken to the town's fortress, which is called the Alcázar and was once the palace and citadel of the Moors when they ruled over Andalusia, and there we were unshackled and cast into a large vaulted dungeon along with forty or fifty other prisoners.

When we woke next morning, scratching our many fleabites, the head gaoler, the alcaide, came in and commanded "the red-haired Hollander dog" to come and assist the under-gaoler to draw water from the well for our breakfast, since it was already known that I alone of the prisoners from Cadiz spoke any Spanish. I emerged from the noisome dungeon into the clear morning air and followed him to the well in the courtyard, which was arcaded all about in the Moorish manner. I let the bucket down into the well, which was prodigiously deep, and while it was filling with water I looked up, seeing that someone stood by me and expecting a blow from the under-gaoler for not being smart enough about my task. I stared dumbfounded; and Corporal Antonio Bobadilla y Fuentes likewise stared dumbfounded back at me. Once he had overcome his astonishment at seeing me there (for though it was almost four years since we had last met he still recognised me) he greeted me with the greatest amity, embracing and kissing me, and asked how in the name of the Blessed Virgin and all the company of saints it fell out that I came to be in such a place, and were the tales then true that had been current in Houtenburg which credited our family with the ability to change our shape and fly through the air as we pleased? And if so, why had I chosen to fly to a gaol in Andalusia of all places on the Earth?

I explained to him as best I could – though in truth it was a long and tangled tale, and I had to omit much of it alike for brevity and for decency's sake – that I was at Cadiz as part of Viscount Wimbledon's late expedition, and that while ashore I had been left behind by the sudden rout of the English, and was now a prisoner destined for a spell in the galleys. I asked likewise how he did and what brought him back to Spain, and he told me that he was a sergeant now, but that his preferment had been purchased at a heavy price: that he had been wounded in the forearm by a sword-cut at Breda some seven months since leading a forlorn hope, as a result of which two of the fingers on his right hand were now palsied and useless so that he could no longer hold a sword or discharge a musket; but in view of his long and valorous service and exemplary character the colonel of his regiment had found him a place as a recruiting officer here in Jerez.

But he was (he said ruefully) in truth more a gaoler than a recruiting officer, since his task was to pick through the catch which the puissant nets of justice disgorged into the Alcázar's dungeons each day and extract from among the pullulating ruck of slimy worthless creatures those few silvery fishes which might be of greater service to His Majesty on some foreign field than pulling an oar in his galleys or decorating one of his gibbets. He told me that this was a most onerous charge, since although the daily haul of malvados and picarones and ladronillos brought in by the constables was indeed a prodigious one – the entire kingdom of Spain now crawling with worthless rascals, he said, as a beggar's shirt is infested with lice – the number of them that were like to be of any use in the King's service was so small as to make the exercise scarcely worth the trouble. For (he said) the profession of soldier, if it is to be at all well performed, demands as much integrity and good character as any other, and the discipline that can be imposed on rogues and cutpurses by the threat of the gallows and the strapado is worth little alongside that which proceeds from inside a man himself; so that an army composed entirely of felons will be no more than one great gaol moving about on legs.

"But there, young Francisco", he said with a sigh, "A man who has but one hand to eat with cannot be over-nice as to which table he dines at, and if I did not earn my bread here endeavouring to turn hares and apes into soldiers, then I would now most certainly be begging for it beneath the town gate." I enquired how his arm was, and he rolled up his cuff to show the scar to me, saying that though deep enough to cut the bone it had healed well though he still had shooting pains in it, and he was now well enough practised to be able to write with his left hand since his work entailed much drawing up of muster rolls. He asked what was to become of me, and I replied that so far as I could tell my English companions and I were to serve in the galleys until an exchange of prisoners could be negotiated – though as for myself, I omitted to mention that my spell pulling an oar might be longer than theirs since I had been sentenced by the Corregidor of Jerez as a common felon. We were parted at last by the under-gaoler upbraiding me for not being fast enough about drawing the water. But as I returned to our dungeon with two pails of water and our daily ration of barley bread in a sack I was already in better heart, knowing that in this alien country I now had at least one friend.

Since I spoke Spanish and they did not, my English companions were soon clamouring to know what was likely to become of them, for a rumour was current among them that as Protestant heretics we were all to be handed over for the Inquisition to deal with, which news had them fairly soiling their breeches at the prospect of finding themselves in the hands of that redoubtable body which (as all good Protestant Englishmen know from their cradle upwards) has no other purpose in the world than that of stretching good Protestant Englishmen on the rack to make them abjure their heresy, and if they refuse, then burning them for their obstinacy. I tried to still their fears as best I could, saying that they were soldiers of King Charles taken captive on the field of battle, and that anyway – for I was knowledgeable in these matters, or at least gave the appearance of being so – the treaty signed years before between King James and the Spaniards was quite specific that his subjects on Spanish soil would no longer be molested for being Protestants provided they made no public display of it. But I was secretly less sure of this than I sounded, and feared that King Charles's waging war on Spain might have abrogated that part of the treaty as well as the rest, and that we might therefore indeed have to reckon with the Holy Office. This put me in a fear scarcely less than that of my companions, because although the Inquisition did not operate in Flanders, what I had heard of its activities elsewhere was very little to its credit. My stepfather told me once of a burning he had witnessed in Santander where the executioner took a pitchfork and thrust a bundle of flaming brushwood into the condemned man's face until his nose and lips were all burned away, to the great amusement and satisfaction of the onlookers who sang solemn *Te Deums* throughout the whole horrid spectacle.

As is so often the case with Goodwife Rumour, her intelligence turned out to be half true and half not. The next day we were ordered to get up and move to a dungeon of our own, which was no small relief to us because our Spanish companions were a company of cozening villains such as the Devil himself would have refused to rub shoulders with unless he wished to be relieved of his pitchfork, and probably his horns and tail as well, since they stole everything that came within reach of their fingers and would assuredly have robbed us all naked as new-born infants if we had passed another night among them. Then when we were lodged in our new quarters, the governor of the Alcázar himself came to address us: a very haughty and fine gentleman in a plumed hat, from time to time sniffing an orange stuck with cloves to ward off the foul gaolhouse miasma that hung about us. He made us a grand proclamation, which I had the task of interpreting for my fellows, to the effect that though we were but scurvy heretical English dogs who merited the gallows for having come here to plunder and despoil King Philip's peaceful subjects, yet His Most Catholic Majesty, out of the infinite mercy and forbearance that is the mark of a Christian monarch, had ordained that any Englishman taken prisoner under arms would be offered the choice of either being sent to the galleys until such time as an exchange of prisoners took place, or being converted to the one true Catholic religion and enlisting as a soldier in his army at the same rate of pay and under the same conditions as one of His Majesty's subjects by birth, thereafter to serve him loyally wherever he might be sent, and following his discharge be permitted to settle in His Majesty's domains either in the Old World or the New. And we would (the governor said in conclusion) be given a day to reflect upon this most magnanimous offer.

My English companions asked me afterwards what I thought of it, and what would I counsel them to do? I said that they would be well advised to consider becoming Catholics and enlisting as soldiers, for the life of a galley slave, be it only for space of one or two years, was a hard one with more knocks than rewards, and a goodly chance withal of dying from sickness or wounds or shipwreck before they could be exchanged. Whereas the King of Spain's service on land, while certainly no picnic of pleasure, would assuredly be no worse as regards pay and treatment than what they had just experienced wearing the King of England's coat. To which last point they all assented most vigorously, saying that no man had paid them a copper halfpenny since they were pressed, whilst as regards their victuals, many an English gentleman's staghounds dined on better fare than they had sat down to each day. On the matter of their committing treason by enlisting in the armies of King Charles's enemies, I said that that only applied while they were under their colours bearing arms, and that now they were prisoners they were no longer under military obedience and might therefore enlist where they pleased like the many other Englishmen, Scots and Irishmen who currently served in the armies of Spain. As for their becoming Catholics when they enlisted, though I did not say so, I scarcely thought that would bother them overmuch since they were plainly persons of the poorest and meanest sort, born in ditches and sheepcotes and as ignorant of the doctrines of the Anglican Church as so many jackdaws, so that they might just as well become Mahometans or Hindus of the Coromandel and suffer no injury to their religious principles since they had none to start with. I might likewise have added – though out of kindness I forbore to do so – that if one is born to sleep under hedges in the rain and trudge the muddy highways, then it might as well be in a soldier's coat as in a beggar's rags; and if in a soldier's coat, then the precise colour of it would be of little consequence to such poor starvelings as these; likewise that if one's ultimate fate is to be stripped of that coat and tumbled into a common pit along with a hundred other poor naked wretches, then whether that pit be in Flanders, in the Palatinate or on the Isle of León would also be a matter of supremest indifference. For soldiers (I had already perceived) are like money: to be gained and saved up by princes and then expended with no further thought for what becomes of it afterwards. A rare golden ducat is a fine coin and handsomely chiselled with the arms of Spain or France or England, so that a man may hold it up and admire it for its artistry as much as for the worth of its metal. But poor grubby copper farthings are myriad, and will serve for small change just as well in one kingdom as in another.

As for myself, before the governor departed I presented myself before him and asked of him in my best Spanish with much grovelling and many courtesies, were Dutch prisoners to be included among those to whom Rey Felipe's generous offer was extended? The alcaide cuffed me for my presumption in directly addressing so great a personage, but the governor graciously deigned to look at me, filthy and ragged though I was.

"What Dutch prisoners?" he said, and turned to the alcaide to demand the list. He perused it for some time, then nodded and said at last, "Ah yes, I see here on this list sixteen English soldiers taken at Cadiz, and one Dutch sailor, which I presume to be yourself. So although His Majesty's decreto makes no mention of it, I would assume that the offer applies to Hollanders as well."

At this the alcaide cuffed me for wasting His Excellency's time with my foolish questions. But for myself I breathed a mighty sigh of relief and gratitude, though I took great care not to let either of them see any sign of it. It appeared that the kind Fates had interceded on my behalf and that an error had been made in drawing up the list – or perhaps I had merely been included in the wrong party of prisoners – and I had thereby escaped five years' slavery in the galleys. I was mighty anxious all the same that I should be safe with my regiment before the error was discovered. For if trailing a pike through Flanders or Italy might not be a very desirable trade compared with that of surgeon's apprentice, honoured and respected with a fine velvet suit and clean linen to wear and a feather bed to sleep in, it was still greatly to be preferred to lugging at a galley's oar with the driver's whip at my back, shackled to a bench among four or five hundred of the most iniquitous rogues that God ever permitted to walk upon the face of the Earth. No: I was determined that if nothing better were offered I would don King Philip's coat for the time being and hope to use my fluency in Spanish and my skill in surgery to secure the most comfortable place I could in my regiment, then desert when an opportunity offered itself and make my way back to England. As for conversion to the Catholic religion, that condition caused me no disquiet at all. Though I had attended Anglican service with my parents for some years past in Colchester town I had been baptised and brought up a Catholic in Flanders and could therefore claim to be one still, with no man able to gainsay me since if need be I could still rattle off the *Ave Maria*, the *Paternoster* and the *Confiteor* as glibly as the Holy Father himself.

When the governor came to us again next morning to hear what my English companions and I had decided, I respectfully informed him that as one man we had all elected to become Catholics and enlist in King Philip's armies according to His Majesty's most gracious offer. At which His Excellency fairly wept for joy, to see how through the application of kindness rather than chastisement even so brutish and savage a people as the English could be brought to see reason and the truth of the Holy Catholic Church's eternal claims, and how there was no wild beast so uncouth (he said) nor any man so devoid of reason and the urgings of conscience that gentleness would not tame them, nor a plain statement of the truth convert them from their lamentable errors. He said that as to our acceptance into the Catholic Church, instruction in its doctrines would be given us by one Fray Anselmo, a Dominican friar long resident in Jerez though an Englishman by birth, and we would afterwards be received into the bosom of Holy Mother Church at a solemn Mass in the great basilica. His Excellency then announced that in recognition of our new and honourable estate as recruits to the armies of His Catholic Majesty, we would be set at liberty and given our coat-and-conduct money until such time as we could go up to Seville, where our regiment was being raised, to take the oath and swear fealty to our regimental colours. In conclusion he felt sure (he said) that such lusty fellows as ourselves would bring further glory to the arms of Spain on whatever fields our prince bade us fight. And in conclusion, begged leave to remind us that the hangman stood ready behind us should we display any reluctance in the matter.

This "liberty" of His Excellency's was in the event but little distinguishable from our earlier captivity. Sergeant Bobadilla having given us our coat-and-conduct money of two ducats apiece, which was to dress us and transport us to our regiment and feed us in the mean time, the fear that we might then vanish with the money as so many had done before us led to our being shut up in another wing of the Alcázar until such time as sufficient recruits had been assembled for a party to go up to Seville. We now had straw paliasses to sleep on, and a bodega within the walls to buy wine from, and we might have food brought in from a cookshop outside; but all this was behind stout iron grilles over the windows and with watchful sentinels posted on the walls to shoot us dead if we tried to escape.

As for the society we had in that place, however, it was but little improved on what we had enjoyed before in our dungeon: a collection of fifty or so loud roistering good-for-nothings playing at dice and cards all day and most of the night too, and thinking little else than of wine, of whores (for strumpets from the town were permitted to visit them and relieve them of some of their money in exchange for divers foul diseases) and devising subterfuges by which they might escape from the Alcázar with their two ducats and then re-enlist in some other town, which several boasted they had done half a dozen times already. Yet the guard was close day and night, and those who sought to escape disguised dressed in women's clothes as bawds or washerwomen were all detected and given the bastinado until they shrieked for mercy. The thought (I confess) that I must pass several years in the company of such vile wastrels, unless a musket shot put an end to me first, filled me with a sadness that grew rather than diminished with each day that passed. Seafarers are a rough enough set of fellows to be sure. But they are for the most part honest, since a thief aboard a ship is every man's enemy and he will likewise have nowhere to hide or to spend his loot. Also they are commonly to be relied upon in an extremity, since the sea is so plainly *hostis humanæ generis** that if one man should fail to perform his duty then all will surely drown.

But among these rascals there was little such intrinsic honour or dependability be found. The kingdom of Spain had in recent years (Sergeant Bobadilla informed me) become quite overrun with worthless rogues, the old manufactories of that country having greatly decayed by reason of the annual flood of silver from the Americas allowing it to purchase whatever it needed from foreigners rather than make it at home. Likewise Spain's endless wars (he said) had been very deleterious in draining away its finest young men for three or four generations past, so that only the weaklings and imbeciles rejected by the recruiting officers were left behind to breed from. The result, he vowed, was a country full from the Pyrenees to Gibraltar of idle knaves who had never done a day's honest work, nor ever would if they could help it (since all held themselves to be gentlemen by birth and above such sordid concerns), and were good only for the gaol, the army or the gallows. And such fine birds I now found myself cooped among, with their dicing, brawling, singing, pilfering and quarrelling at all hours of the day and night, and I having no function among them except to be a butt for their cozenage – for I was invited to play at cards or dice with them twenty times a day – and to bandage their sorry heads after they had cracked them in their drunken quarrels. Though I knew only too well what must await me in my regiment at Seville, I began to long that we might arrive there so that if nothing else the sergeants' halberds and the threat of the strapado or worse might instil some honesty into them.

Apart from my occasional conversations with Sergeant Bobadilla, my only diversion in all this was the arrival of Fray Anselmo to conduct the catechetical classes for my English companions, whom I was by now seeking to instruct in the essentials of the Spanish language – and found most inapt for this, since their grasp of their own language was pretty tenuous, they preferring

---

* "Enemy of the human race"

to communicate instead by grunts and bellows like beasts of the field, which greatly disabled them from the learning of any other tongue. One of them, called Ned Tyrell, from the county of Warwickshire, was a youth of eighteen or nineteen years who seemed of livelier understanding than the rest despite his mean birth and might (I thought) rise to corporal or even sergeant in the King of Spain's service if he lived long enough. But the rest of them were a sorry set of varlets, and I doubted they would ever serve for anything much except to bolster out the ranks of a tercio and then fill a pit afterwards. Fray Anselmo tried his best to instil the rudiments of the Christian religion into their sorry pates; but in the end the best he could do was to perjure himself by attesting that they could recite and understand the Catechism, and that they were therefore fit to be admitted to the communion of the Catholic Church.

As for Fray Anselmo himself, it soon became evident to me that though as kindly-natured a fellow as a man could be and still serve the Holy Inquisition, he was himself of no great mental acuity either. We fell to talking together after he had wearied himself half a morning endeavouring to explain the doctrine of the Holy Trinity to my English companions, and had finally abandoned the attempt in despair saying that he would find a livelier understanding among the savages of Tierra del Fuego. He was a tall, thin, pale fellow of about thirty-five years with a balding pate which showed even through his Dominican's tonsure, and watery goggle-eyes of a pale blue colour. He enquired how it fell out that I, though a Fleming, spoke such good English, and I said that I had lived above three years in England, at Colchester.

He sighed, and said that he too came from the county of Essex; from Canfield over near Dunmow where his family the Fitches were lords of the manor and his brother William had become a Capuchin monk in France under the name of Benoît de Canfield, where he wrote a devotional book called *La Règle de Perfection*, which I later essayed to read out of curiosity, and found such tedious and inspid stuff that once I had laid it aside I could never force myself to pick it up again. He himself, though he had entered the Jesuit college at Douai (he said) and sought to become a missionary priest to England, had parted company with that order – by which I think he meant, that he was rejected as being too stupid to join it – and had later become a Dominican in Flanders, then come to Spain and entered a religious house in Jerez where he now was, with very little to do unless, as happened from time to time, the Inquisition sent him an English herético to work upon; which was usually some drunken roaring sailor off a wine ship apprehended for brawling in a tavern and blackguarding the Pope or pissing over an image of the Virgin Mary, which offence the magistrates construing as a breach of King James's treaty with Spain, they would hand him over to the religious authority not the secular one to deal with and, in short, cause everyone a great deal of needless bother and pen-scratching. He said that in such cases the most he could do to save such loud foolish braggarts from the galleys or the stake was to persuade them to make a recantation, which he commonly did – since they were all full of bluster and bravado at first as Englishmen abroad commonly are – by conducting the interview in an underground vault of the bishop's prison, with an old rack which had not been used these forty years past lying in the shadows, and the hangman's assistant standing by in his black mask with his arms folded as though he waited only for Fray Anselmo's word to demonstrate the working of that device. This pantomime (he said) usually sufficed to put the poor silly fellow into such a fright that he would make public amends before the cathedral in his shirt with a lighted taper in his hand and a noose hung round his neck, then receive a moderate whipping for the offence, and afterwards be expelled from the country aboard the next ship.

Fray Anselmo asked me all on a sudden one morning, did I intend returning to England or to Flanders once my military service was over? Since I felt that I might be franker with him than with a Spaniard-born, I replied that my vocation was as a surgeon not a soldier, and that I intended returning to Colchester at the very earliest opportunity to take up my apprenticeship once more under my stepfather, since only the chance of my having been separated from my ship at Cadiz and taken prisoner had obliged me to enter the King of Spain's service.

At this he rubbed his chin thoughtfully, and at length said, "Then there is something that I must tell you of – though in the closest confidence, because if it became known then these miserable rascals would desert at once even if they had to tear the walls of the Alcázar apart with their bare hands to do it."

"And what is that, reverend brother?" I asked, my heart suddenly thumping in my breast.

"The regiment which you are to join at Seville," he whispered, "is being raised for service not in Flanders, as you were told, but in the Philippine Islands at Manila. If you become a soldier in it, then you will be away from Europe for a good long time – six or seven years at least – and indeed may never return, because quite apart from the hazards of battle against the Dutch and the local tribes the climate of those islands is most pestilential and the mortality from agues and fluxes very great among those who serve there. This regiment is only being raised now to replace one that went out from Seville two years since, and is now so wasted away from disease that it has been struck from the list. Sergeant Bobadilla, who is a good friend of mine, told me this news not an hour since."

This was dire intelligence indeed. Once I had been inducted into the regiment there would be precious little opportunity for me to give it the slip thereafter. The route by which Spanish regiments went to the Philippines (I knew) was a very long and tedious one: by galleon from Cadiz to Vera Cruz and then on foot across Mexico, then from Acapulco on the Pacific Ocean side to Manila by another galleon, which voyage might take six months or more and occasion still more losses from disease and scurvy. Most of the journey would be aboard a ship, from which there is but little opportunity to desert, and once we were arrived at Manila there would be none at all unless I wished to end my days being roasted and eaten by the natives. So once I had sworn the oath in front of the regiment's colours, I saw that I would be imprisoned more effectively than in the deepest dungeon in the strongest of fortresses. I therefore asked Fray Anselmo, out of Christian charity what he would counsel me to do. He answered that I must show the proper resignation of a child of God in the face of tribulation, and also the loyalty due from of a subject of the King of Spain (which I was by birth) towards my prince, which would also be pleasing to God since had not Our Lord himself counselled his followers to pay to Caesar that which was Caesar's, and likewise told servants that they must obey their lawful masters? Which is pretty well what I had expected he would say, and no help to me whatsoever in my present plight. He then departed, and left me to spend an even more unquiet night than usual, kept awake by the drunken carousing of my companions, who had learned from the guards that we were to go up to Seville in three or four days' time and be made soldiers of, and were thus set upon making the most of their remaining freedom before the tercio's ranks shut around them like the walls of a prison.

★ ★ ★ ★ ★ ★ ★ ★ ★ ★

Next morning Frans received a scribbled note telling him to report to the recruiting officer at the Alcázar of Jerez. Which was of course none other than Sergeant Bobadilla.

"You are indeed in a pretty plight, young Francisco," Bobadilla said. "Fray Anselmo told me of it yesterday after he spoke with you."

"It seems that we are to be sent to the Philippine islands once our regiment has formed at Seville?"

"Indeed you are: that perfidious hound of a paymaster told me at first that it was for service in Flanders; but that was merely to beguile me, since if I had let slip to these rascals where they were bound for, then any of them with enough brains to stop the eye of a needle would gladly dash them out against the nearest wall sooner than go there. But after speaking with the reverend brother, whom I know well and consider to be a good man, we have between us devised a way for you to escape."

"How can I do that? I have received my coat-and-conduct money and been inscribed on the muster roll, though not yet sworn as a soldier."

"Indeed. But Fray Anselmo has discovered a way to keep you here when the others are sent up to Seville. Tell me, did you attend Protestant religious services when you were in England, or aboard your Dutch ship?"

"I did: my stepfather had us attend service at Saint Botolph's church in Colchester every Sunday – though he said that he cared not a bone button for any of it and only did it to maintain his credit in the eyes of his patients. And aboard the *Eenhoorn* we had prayers twice daily according to the rite of the Dutch Reformed Church, and divine service each Sunday at which my stepfather read the lesson."

"Splendid. Fray Anselmo asks likewise, did you ever take communion with them?"

"I did a few times: the Anglican church prescribes communion once a quarter."

"Even better. According to the reverend brother that, then, would make you a renegado in the eyes of the Inquisition: that though baptised and confirmed a Catholic, and of the age of reason, you have taken part in the blasphemous Protestant parody of the Mass where the bread and wine are declared to be the body and blood of Christ though no such transformation takes place. I confess that none of this is very clear to me as a soldier. But if you are a renegado as Fray Anselmo says, then in the eyes of the Inquisition you have committed a very grave fault which needs to be further investigated, and if you are found guilty you will have to to make recantation and be punished for the good of your eternal soul."

Frans turned pale. "So I would exchange the army and the Philippines for a prison cell again, except this time the Inquisition's? Excuse me, Don Antonio, but I fail to see how that would help my case, because to me it sounds like curing a cold by catching the plague."

Bobadilla smiled at this, and Frans divined that as like many men of lively understanding who have found themselves imprisoned for life inside the army or the Church, he derived a quiet satisfaction from making a fool of the institution whose coat he wore and whose bread he ate.

"Not so hasty, young Francisco, not so hasty. You would indeed be moved from your present lodgings to the bishop's prison and questioned for some time concerning the matter. But Fray Anselmo says that he is busy at present, so the examination might have to wait a good while. Likewise witnesses would be difficult to procure, and the papers might take a considerable time to be got together once the case was opened. So he thinks it quite possible that by the time your case is heard your regiment might already be halfway to Manila."

"And what then?"

"If the case against you is ill-prepared enough, he is confident that you would be acquitted and set free. And even if the Inquisition were to convict you, the penalty would be no more than making a public penance and receiving a dozen strokes of the whip on your bare back. After which you would be expelled from Spain and free to return to England and your old trade."

"Might the Ejército Real not still have some claim upon me?"

The sergeant smiled. "Ah, Francisco: innocent youth that you are, take the word of an old soldier for it. Armies are all alike in being mighty proficient at losing people who might cause them trouble and an excess of scribbling. The pockets of Mars's breeches are full of holes – he being too proud and idle a dog to sew them up – whilst as for Dame Justice, being blindfolded she is ill-equipped to go scrabbling around the floor after him looking for the small coins that may fall through those holes. Depend upon it, if Fray Anselmo and I set our minds to it, then so far as King Philip's service is concerned the two of us can contrive to lose you as effectually as if you had never existed at all."

Frans thanked Bobadilla for this kindness, and the Sergeant replied that he should think nothing of it: that he himself had chosen the wastrel life of a soldier when he was young and now had nothing to show for it but his right hand palsied and useless and an ill-paid place as a provincial gaoler. He was determined (he vowed) that if he could at all help it so dismal a fate would not befall such a goodly and ingenious youth as Frans was, since such fine young fellows as he was were not to be wasted on an idle worthless trade like soldiering. Ten-a-penny hobnails (he said in conclusion) commonly being made from iron and not from gold.

The next morning the alcaide appeared and roared out above the hubbub that the red-headed Dutchman was to get his belongings together and accompany him to the bishop's prison, which was in the Augustinian priory on the other side of the town. At this all the company who understood Spanish howled with merriment, assuring Frans that he would be stretched on the rack to twice his present length and then burned at the stake as a miserable heretic, and that they would all come to the auto da fé to drink a health to him as he sizzled like a bacon rasher on the coals. For which Frans thanked them all with a low obeisance, and assured them that on the contrary, long before he was burned for heresy they would all themselves be rotting amid the ricefields of Luzon Island, bristling like so many porcupines with the poisoned arrows of the natives. Which sally caused them to fall silent all of a sudden, thinking that he might be party to information hitherto denied to them...

Frans spent ten days in the Inquisition's prison, in which he had a cell all to himself and two blankets to sleep under as well as a straw mattress. Which was just as well, for it was now past the middle of November and the weather had suddenly turned cold and exceedingly wet. Outside the barred window of his cell the wind blustered and rain poured down day and night without ceasing as old Boreas, after beating up Viscount Wimbledon's hapless ships out on the Atlantic, sent his rain-laden gales inland to drench the Iberian countryside. Apart from his gaoler's twice-daily visits to bring him his meals and take away his slop-pail – another amenity not granted to prisoners of the secular arm – Frans saw no one and was able to speak with no one. So it was almost a welcome diversion for him when after a week of confinement he was ushered to spend a session with Fray Anselmo and a notary so that the facts of the case against him might be established: that though a baptised and confirmed Catholic, he had by his own admission at divers times and places wilfully entered into communion with Protestant heretics and had therefore made himself a renegado and an apostate: one who had knowingly abjured the true Catholic faith in favour of heresy. Which if he was convicted of (the notary said) might expose him to a penalty of penance and a public whipping, followed by banishment, with the stake waiting for him afterwards in the event of his relapsing into error and falling once more into the Inquisition's hands.

At the end of the session Fray Anselmo solemnly closed the folder and tied it with the attached red ribbons, saying that these were most grave and damnable matters, and that he would therefore have to send to Seville to consult with the bishop since he himself was a Dominican and his immediate superior here in Jerez was an Augustinian. After that the matter might have to be referred for an opinion to the Inquisitor General's office in Madrid, which would certainly take many weeks or even months, given the badness of the roads in winter. But in the meantime he felt himself not to be competent to deal with the case here in Jerez, and would therefore make arrangements to have Frans moved to the bishop's prison in Seville; which would now have to be by river since the journey was some fifty miles and the road entirely impassable by reason of the autumn rains as well as the countryside being plagued with brigands. So next morning Frans set off again; this time in the company of two tipstaffs of the bishop's prison, to walk the fifteen or so miles to the port of San Lucar at the mouth of the Guadalquivir, where they would board a packet boat to take them up to Seville.

When they set off the weather was sunny, though the road was exceedingly miry after a fortnight of rain. The way ran across the usual low, sandy hills of the Andalusian coast through a countryside very little populated or not at all. As they approached San Lucar the land turned to marshes and reed-beds, with the road – which was evidently but little frequented – sometimes disappearing altogether. Frans was chained by the wrist to the elder of the two guards; a portly, wheezing old fellow called Jacinto who seemed to be related in some way to the other tipstaff, Lodovico, who carried the key to the manacles in his own pocket for fear that Frans might filch it from the older man and escape, thus exposing the pair of them to serious penalties since the Holy Office was famously solicitous of its prisoners and would certainly take a very poor view of petty officials who had lost one of them. Though they argued volubly enough with one another in their thick Andalusian dialect, the two men were little disposed to talk with Frans; in fact seemed decidedly resentful that they were having to take so much trouble on his behalf tramping the plashy roads at such an inclement season of the year.

They trudged on most of the day, because the going was indeed very bad, and in the afternoon it started to drizzle. As the November afternoon was turning to dusk they came to a crude bridge of rotten logs across a marshy stream swollen with rainwater. While the two tipstaffs were debating how best to cross it – for the water was high and the current fast, and it was by no means certain that the bridge could bear the weight of one man let alone three – they heard a shout and hoofbeats, and turned to see two men splashing up the muddy trackway behind them on horseback.

"What can they want?" Jacinto asked, "shouting and hallooing like fools out here in the middle of nowhere."

"I suppose they might be brigands," Lodovico replied, "but I can't see what they'd want with poor fellows like us, and only two of them as well."

Jacinto laughed. "Well, if they're robbers they can have this poxy Hollander of ours and welcome to him. My poor old feet are martyring me from having to tramp round the countryside shackled by the wrist to him, and in weather like this as well. Why couldn't the inquisitors just burn the bugger in Jerez and have done with it?"

At last the two men came up with them. From their confident demeanour they were plainly no brigands but persons having authority of some kind or other – though in Spain that was almost as bad. One was armed with a cavalryman's carbine, both wore short swords, and both had coiled whips hanging at their belts. They had about them the grimly purposeful look of the sort of men one would rather not meet with at that particular time and place – nor indeed at any other.

"And how may we be of assistance to you, vuestras mercedes? the younger tipstaff asked with exaggerated politeness, doffing his hat and making a low bow.

"We seek a felon escaped from His Majesty's galleys at Puerto Santa María – or rather, a felon who never joined His Majesty's galleys in the first place, having absconded on the way. And I think that we may have found him at last. The description we have is of a tall, well-built, red-haired Hollander youth of about fifteen or sixteen – and the fellow you have chained to your wrist there seems to fit that description pretty well." He addressed himself to Frans. "Say after me, knave, 'Pablito clavó un clavito.¿Qué clase de clavo clavó Pablito?'"*. Frans repeated the tongue twister. And good though his Spanish was, his Flemish accent betrayed itself at once.

The man nodded."The very bird we were hunting, then. Unshackle him at once, so that we may have him and claim the bounty. As for the Dutchman though, I don't envy him one bit. The penalty for convicts who escape from the King's galleys is to have their noses cut off before the entire company of rowers, as a warning to the rest, then be given a good flogging before being

---

* "Pablito hammered in a little nail. What type of nail did Pablito hammer?"

chained to a bench for the rest of their days."

But Jacinto was evidently not going to hand his charge over so easily.

"Not so fast, amigo. And who are you to give us orders anyway? This man is a prisoner of the Holy Office, on his way to be questioned in the bishop's prison in Seville. I have a written warrant here in my pocket saying so – or so we were told in Jerez, because neither of us can read it."

The man with the carbine laughed. "For all I care he could be Judas Iscariot himself; the Corregidor of Jerez sentenced the fellow to five years' servitude for rape, or so *our* warrant says, but the rogue managed to wriggle himself in among a party of English prisoners taken at Cadiz and gave us the slip, being conveyed with them to Jerez when he should have been on his way to Puerto Santa María. So as far as we're concerned, His Majesty's Lieutenant-General of the Galleys owns the worthless rascal – and we as his officers of the garda-chusma duly claim his property back for him."

"Go bite your backside, brigand!" Jacinto replied, "We're the Bishop of Seville's tipstaffs, eating his bread and wearing his badge here on our sleeves. While conveying a prisoner of the Inquisition we are agents of the Holy Office itself, and if we handed him over to two highwaymen like yourselves – who might be anyone at all – we'd like as not end up with our own arses being toasted over a slow fire for dereliction of duty. If you want him that badly, come with us to Seville and argue your case in front of the bishop's court."

The other garda-chusma had by now dismounted and seized Frans's unmanacled wrist. He pulled at it – and Jacinto pulled the other way on the chain, so that Frans's shoulders were almost dislocated. As the two men struggled and grunted, their feet slithering in the mud, Lodovico suddenly burst out laughing, looking up at the man with the carbine still seated on his horse.

"Why, God bless my soul if it isn't Jesus-Cristo López of the village of Cuartillos! Who was himself sentenced to the galleys for five years in his youth after being caught buggering a jack-mule behind Don Alvaredo's barn one Sunday while the rest of the people were at Mass. You were always said to be a prime piece of ordure: so no doubt you became a garda-chusma after your sentence expired, as having the qualities of character desirable for that most honourable charge."

By now Jacinto had ceased his tugging at Frans's wrist and stood listening to this diatribe. Then he too fell to laughing.

"Yes, indeed, I remember it now as well: all the countryside round Jerez spoke of nothing else for a fortnight or more. And all men swore that you addressed yourself to the back-end a jack-mule because you were so ugly a scoundrel that no jenny-mule would have you." López glowered at this, his pock-marked face turning a deep mottled plum colour. "And what a pity likewise," Jacinto added , "that after your mule-fucking career was over and you returned from the galleys you married one of the daughters of men and not a nanny goat..." he paused for effect. "...because then the pair of you would have horns, and not just the one!"

López's answer to this witty sally was simple and to the point: he lowered his carbine, cocked the hammer, then fired. The bullet hit Jacinto squarely in the middle of his chest, killing him at once and sending him staggering backwards to fall over in the mud, dragging Frans down with him. The bang and flash of the shot sent the other garda-chusma's horse galloping away whinnying in terror. Lodovico stood dumbstruck for a moment – then drew his dagger and hurled himself at the dismounted man who had meanwhile drawn his own sword and was moving towards him. Avoiding the first thrust of his sword, the tipstaff grappled with the man, stabbing him twice beneath the ribs. Clutching his belly and then raising his bloodied fingers to look at them in disbelief, the garda-chusma tottered forward, then stumbled and fell into the stream beside the bridge with a great splash. Lodovico ignored him, and instead leaped at López, stabbing him several times in the thigh and trying to drag him from his horse as the murderer flailed at him with the butt of his gun. The mounted garda-chusma spurred his horse, and the animal galloped away dragging the furious Lodovico along still clinging to López's leg and plunging his knife into the man's flesh, vowing by the entire calendar of saints that he would cut the murdering son of a whore's entrails out and feed them to the crows. They disappeared among the reed-beds, still fighting like wildcats, and that was the last that Frans saw of them: either Lodovico had killed López, or López had killed Lodovico, or both had succeeded in killing one another, because neither came back to the scene of the crime. As dusk fell he found himself alone by the roadside as the rain poured down, shackled by the wrist to a corpse and with not a living soul to come to his aid.

* * * * * * * * * *

My plight was indeed most lamentable, for not only was it growing dark but a great storm of rain and wind had blown up from the north-west and I had neither shelter nor fire to warm me, nor even any clothes of my own beyond the pair of rope-soled sandals and the coarse hempen shirt and drawers which I had been given to wear in the bishop's prison at Jerez. As the rain poured down mixed with icy hail and the bullying wind roared around me I contrived to strip my dead companion of some of his clothes and put them on, and also use the sizeable bulk of his carcass to shelter behind. But with him still manacled to my wrist I was quite unable to move from where he lay, and must remain there at least until the morning, unable to drag him along behind me because of his ponderous weight and likewise unable to free myself from him, since no matter how minutely I searched through the pockets and lining of his doublet and breeches I could not find the key to unlock my fetters and supposed that he must have given it to his companion Lodovico to keep it out of my reach – except that Lodovico had now disappeared fighting with the garda-chusma who had fired the shot, while the other garda he had stabbed and who had fallen into the stream, had now been borne away by the current.

Not finding the key wherewith to unlock myself, my next thought was to procure a knife and cut the dead man's hand off so that I could slip the manacle off his wrist. But as with the key, he seemed likewise to have entrusted his dagger to his companion for fear (I suppose) that I might purloin it and hold it to his throat until he freed me. So I had no means at all to separate myself from his corpse, and must needs either wait until it was light and hope that I might find a stone or a log of wood within reach which I could use to break the bones of his hand all to pulp and get the fetter off that way, or – which was a most disgusting thought to me – gnaw through the tendons and ligaments of his wrist with my own teeth. But what (I thought) would become of me thereafter even if I steeled myself to perform that horrible task? I would only be free to roam this desolate marshland in prisoner's garb with a chain dangling from my wrist, until such time as I either perished from cold and hunger or some band of rustics with staves and pitchforks apprehended me as an escaped galley slave so that I might be sent to Puerto Santa María to be whipped and have my nose cut off, then be chained to an oar for the rest of my life. Or perhaps – they not having any other culprit available – be tried for the murder of my guards and be broken on the wheel for it, and my spreadeagled carcass afterwards be set on top of a post here by the wayside and left to rot as a warning to others.

But such considerations must wait until daybreak, and for the moment there was nothing to be done but to seek what shelter I might from the storm. So I dozed a while, shivering and wet through from the freezing rain, frighted by the thunder and lightning (for it was a prodigious storm) until at last the sky began to lighten somewhat in the east as the day announced itself. Then I heard voices, and the sound of footsteps plashing along the muddy road. There was a sudden flicker of lightning, and I had a glimpse of two men coming towards me shrouded in squares of canvas against the driving rain. As they drew nearer, I heard to my astonishment that they were speaking Flemish, and saw by the light of another flash in the sky that they were both wearing the garb of seafarers.

"The pox on this filthy storm!" one of the men said, "And the pox plus the clap multiplied by the plague on that old halfwit Coussemakker for having us tramp three leagues all the way to Puerto Santa María and back in such weather. And on a fool's errand as well."

"True enough," the other said, "But what else were we to do? There was no credit to be had in San Lucar, so there was nothing for it but to go to Puerto and beg it from the agent there."

"And he likewise bade us kiss his arse and sent us on our way empty-handed," the first man said, "because if you're a privateer and your owner goes bankrupt, then no man wishes to know you, and we can count ourselves lucky that Don Matteo chose not to set his dogs on us or have his servants give us a good beating for our trouble."

"Anyway," his companion answered, "there's nothing for it now but to get ourselves back aboard as soon as we may and weigh anchor to take us away from this filthy country...But what's this here?"

The two men stopped, and looked at me lying shivering in the mud, by now so wet through and cold that I was heedless of whether I lived or died. One of them stirred the body of the tipstaff Jacinto with his foot.

"A young fellow chained by the wrist to a fat old man. And a dead one too, by the looks of it."

"Best to leave them where they are, then" the first man said (who seemed to be the more senior of them). "The whole of Spain is full of lunatic scoundrels and scoundrel lunatics from one end to the other, and no part of it more so than here in Andalusia. A dead man lying by the roadside is no great matter in these parts, so leave the rogue where he is and be on our way is my advice. If he's chained to a corpse then the villain is probably some slave who cut his master's throat while on his way to be sold, and we were best have nothing to do with it for fear that we might end up in court as witnesses, or even be accused of the crime ourselves."

At this I found the strength to croak, "Mijne heren, would you leave a fellow countryman in such a plight? For sweet charity's sake, at least cut me free so that I may go on my way."

The two men knelt beside me.

"He speaks Flemish," the one said to the other, then asked me, "So how do you come to be lying here?"

While abridging my tale considerably – because this was neither the time nor the place to recount it in full – I explained that I was a prisoner being conveyed to Seville for trial, and that we had been set upon by brigands who had afterwards fled. The elder of the two sailors rubbed his chin. "Brigands attacking a prisoner under escort, you say?" he replied. "Mighty stupid brigands by the sound of it, then. But that scarcely matters, Mijnheer Whatever-your-name-is. You're in trouble sure enough to have fallen into the hands of these Spanish villains, because from what I know of the blackguards, their law officers are scarcely less criminal than the rogues they hang and my first thought would be to aid anyone trying to escape from them. But then again, we might likewise find ourselves in a deal of trouble for helping you."

At this the younger man interrupted, "Oh come on, Bart, he's from Flanders like us, and he's no more than a boy, and he's like to end up with his thumbs being crushed by those sons of bitches to make him confess to crimes he like as not never committed, which is their manner of doing things here. After the way the Spanish dogs have treated *us*, is that not reason enough for us to help him escape from them?"

At this the man called Bart sighed, and drew his sailor's knife out of its sheath, hanging from his belt in the small of his back as is the fashion with seafarers, so that either hand can reach for it equally well. He began hacking through the ligaments of the tipstaff's wrist, and at last the dead man's hand was off so that I was free of him. Between them they then lifted Jacinto's corpse and tipped it into the stream to be carried away by the current, saying that it might be better for us all if there were no tokens left behind of what had taken place. They then picked me up beneath my armpits one on each side (for I scarcely had strength any longer to move my limbs), gave me a swig from a leather flask of brandewijn which one carried in his pocket, then half dragged, half carried me along the road in the pelting rain the last few miles to the shore of the Guadalquivir River just to seaward of San Lucar, since I had the fetter still dangling from my wrist and would certainly have attracted notice if they had taken me through the streets of the town.

They bade me hide myself among the reed beds by the shore and wrapped one of their squares of tarpaulin about me to shelter me from the rain, then went to board their vessel, saying they would send a boat to fetch me. So round about eight bells of the morning watch I found myself being hauled up the side of a ship with a bowline under my armpits, because I was by now too weak to climb aboard for myself.

CHAPTER FIFTEEN

Captain Jacques Dirckszoon Coussemakker sat at the table in his cabin and considered the present melancholy state of his affairs. A ponderous, doughy-faced man of fifty-nine, already suffering from rheumy lungs and inflammation of the heart, he felt old, heavy and tired beyond his years; worn down alike by the steady advance of Chronos, and by this late lamentable season which, one way or another, seemed destined to be his last. For even if most of the *Zwarte Hond's* misfortunes over the previous seven months could be attributed to bad luck rather than bad judgement, that still did not exonerate him as the vessel's skipper. A Dunkirk privateer captain was not appointed by some distant admiralty or through a courtier's patronage, as would be the case aboard a king's ship, but was instead selected to occupy that charge alike by the owner of the ship, and the shareholders who financed the voyage, and even (in a sense) by the vessel's crew, who signed articles to sail under his command and would have signed articles to sail with someone else if they had lacked confidence in him. If he had been chosen for his proven competence as a fighting seaman – which went without saying – he had equally been selected for his record of being lucky. So a privateer captain pleading bad luck to excuse his failure was, not to mince words, as pitiful a creature as a blind portrait painter or a surgeon who faints at the sight of blood. In the end it mattered not a jot whether he was born unlucky, or whether his previous good fortune had simply turned sour and dribbled away as good fortune always does in the end: once it was gone there was nothing that could save him. For a privateer skipper had no articles of war to read out, with their list of ferocious punishments appended to them to keep the crew mindful of their duty, and likewise neither courts martial nor prisons nor gallows ashore to hold his men in awe of him. Aboard a naval ship an inadequate captain might have his crumbling authority propped up for a while by the structures of naval discipline, until his crew petitioned the admiralty to remove him or simply jumped ship at the next port. A privateer captain, however, had only his own personal aura to rely upon (supplemented where necessary by a smart whack with a belaying-pin) and once his *magisterium* faltered, could soon expect to be overthrown – and count himself lucky not to be thrown overboard as well, which was a fate that had befallen more than one Dunkirk skipper who had lost his men's confidence.

Over the past forty years privateering had become that town's staple industry – not least because there were precious few other ways for it to earn its living once the rapacious Hollanders had elbowed the Dunkirk boats out of the North Sea herring fisheries. Many a fine house on the town's streets and in the platteland round about had been built on the proceeds of licensed piracy. True, business had slumped somewhat during the twelve years of the Dutch truce with Spain, so that many of the town's privateers had been obliged to become unlicensed pirates in order to earn their daily bread. But now, four years into the resumed war, things were going nicely once more, the town's quays a bustle of eager activity each spring as the ships fitted out for the coming season and the seamen signed their articles on tavern benches and upturned barrels at the dockside. During the winter months, while the North Sea gales pounded against the dunes and filled the streets with salty spray, the form of privateer captains would be as eagerly debated in the dockside taverns as that of fighting cocks, because no man would willingly ship with a mediocre skipper or one whose tally of prizes the previous year was below expectations. So whilst successful skippers were treated as temporary nobility and had all men doffing their hats to them as they passed, ones who had failed as abjectly as he now had could expect to be whistled through the streets by the urchins and pelted with offals by the irate fishwives on the quays, whose husbands had returned from eight or nine months at sea with nothing to show for it.

Coussemakker knew all this, because he had once been a skipper blessed with good luck above all other men. In the early years of his career the goddess Fortuna had seemingly gone out of her way to bestow her smiles upon the gallant, handsome young privateer captain from the town of Hondschoote. In an epic fight off Gravelines in 1595 he had famously taken the English pirate Sir Barnaby Rawlings, returning from the Canaries with a ship so laden down with treasure that the water lapped the sills of the lower gunports. And had afterwards seen Rawlings and his eighty or so surviving villains dance their last jig dangling from a fine multiple gallows specially erected for them on the dunes outside the town, and their carcasses left afterwards for the gulls to squabble over while Coussemakker and his men rode in triumph through the streets to a magnificent reception in the town hall, behind thirteen wagons loaded with silks and precious metals. In the campaigning season of 1602 had he not done such signal damage to the Dutch herring fleet that the States-General in plenary session had placed a price of five thousand guilders upon his head? And had he not likewise seen off all those who sought to claim it, killing the Dutch admiral Willem Roelofssen in single combat on the quarterdeck of his own ship off Zuydcoote, then hoisting his victim's head to the maintop in a wicker basket?

Though he found it hard to credit now, he had once cut a most dashing figure, his portrait being painted by young Meester Rubens himself and all the ship owners of Flanders seeking him as a marriage partner for their daughters. But now he was old and washed out, his luck all perished and sagging like the sorry dropsical carcass that he was forced to inhabit. He wondered idly what price the States-General would place on his head now if the matter came to be debated: probably no more than a stuiver or two for its value to a soap-boiler, since he still wore his grey hair and beard cut short in the old style and his thin old locks would therefore fetch but little as cushion stuffing. Age and widowerhood had made him heavy; and the body's slowness, and gout, and the kidney stone which plagued most sea captains after a lifetime of salt meat and biscuit with no fresh vegetables to cleanse the blood and too little fresh water to rinse out their systems. According to the ship's writer Guyot, who was a learned fellow and took an interest in such matters, his trouble was that Saturn was dominant in his horoscope; though what precisely he was supposed to do about *that* nearly sixty years after the event was something upon which the writer could offer no useful suggestions. Saturn, the planet of old age and decrepitude; dry, cold and heavy as lead; presiding over the degeneration of the bladder and joints; weighing down his calves when he stood up as though he was wearing stockings knitted from leaden wool. Lead: sullen, dull and grey, with no resonance to it when struck. No longer the brave young captain who had snatched the beautiful Diana Tindemans from under the noses of a dozen rival suitors. And she alike now wrapped in Saturn's metal these seven years past, in the mouldy damp vaults below Saint Eloi's Church, worn out by too many pregnancies and too many miscarriages. Only two of their ten children had survived: one of them, young Guillaume, now serving aboard the *Zwarte Hond* as acting second mate, with fire in his veins and gnawing the ends of his adolescent moustache in frustration at his father's lack of success, which was beginning to tarnish the credit of the entire Coussemakker family. A son had a duty of love and obedience to his father over and above that which a mate owed to his captain. But even that would infallibly be eroded by a long enough run of bad fortune. In fact they were now so down on their luck that he had been obliged to send the bo'sun Bart Coymans trudging on foot to Puerto Santa María despite the vile weather to see whether he could wheedle some credit out of the owner's agent in that port. But even that had failed, it seemed, and he had returned empty-handed except for some allegedly Flemish vagabond they had scooped up along the way: as if the *Zwarte Hond's* store of troubles were not already sufficient. These melancholy thoughts were interrupted by the mate knocking on the cabin door.

"Do you wish to see the boy now, skipper?"

"Ah, yes: send him in. In all decency we can hardly tip the rogue overboard, so I suppose I shall have to find him some employment. Does he look able-bodied?"

"Perfectly so, skipper, though famished and half dead with cold and wet. He seems a sturdy enough youth, tall and well built for his age, of reasonable wit and evidently of good family. He can read and write and says that he was a surgeon's mate aboard a Hollander ship at Cadiz. So I dare say we can find work enough for him to earn his keep."

"Very well then; send him in. I'll speak with him and then hand him over to the bo'sun, because I wish to confer with the ship's officers here at eight bells."

Frans was ushered in, dressed now in a shirt and breeches from the ship's slop chest, but with the iron fetter still hanging from his wrist, so that he was obliged to carry the free end of it in his left hand. He had been given soup to eat by the bo'sun and some wine to drink, and was now no longer shivering as violently as when he was hoisted aboard.

"Et alors, mon jeune homme, veux-tu parler flamand?" the captain enquired. Frans nodded to signify that he did, and added that he was a Fleming by birth, from the town of Houtenburg just inland of Dunkirk.

Coussemakker regarded him with a mixture of curiosity and suspicion. The youth certainly *looked* respectable enough, despite his bedraggled state, and was likewise well spoken. But the iron chain dangling from his wrist was a singular sort of bracelet and not worn (he suspected) as personal adornment. Even privateer ships had standards to maintain; not to speak of the trouble that might ensue with the local magistrates from aiding the escape of a convicted felon. The *Zwarte Hond* was already in bad enough odour with the court officials here at San Lucar without his adding to it by helping fugitives from justice.

"So who are you, young fellow, and what brings you aboard my ship in your present state?"

"My name, mijnheer, is Frans van Raveyck and though I was

born and grew up in Houtenburg, my family moved to Colchester in England some three years ago, where my stepfather later practised his trade of surgeon, and I was his apprentice. Following a succession of misfortunes which it would be too long to relate, he and I engaged aboard a Dutch fluit-ship, which is how I came to be at Cadiz with the English, and was taken prisoner while ashore."

"What's your family's name?"

"My stepfather is called Michel Willenbrouckx, born in the town of Poperinghe."

"The name is not familiar to me. And your mother's family?"

"My mother, mijnheer, is – or rather was, since she died last summer of the plague – Catherine Maertens from the town of Tournai. But my stepfather's first wife was called Laetitia Collaerts, and she dying in 1614, my stepfather afterwards married my mother, who had been a servant in his household."

Coussemakker's face brightened a little at this news. "Collaerts, do you say? Well, that makes you a distant cousin of mine even if only by adoption, because my mother was also of that family. So I suppose that if nothing else the bond of kinship obliges me to help you. But that chain of yours: so far as I am aware, the Spanish are not in the habit of shackling their prisoners of war, or of sending them tramping round the countryside manacled to the wrist of a guard. Is it possible that you might have been convicted of some graver offence and been on your way to prison, or to the galleys at Puerto Santa María? In our present difficulties I have no wish to make myself even more *persona non grata* with King Philip's officers than I am already by aiding the escape of convicts."

Frans felt here that making a clean breast of things might be better than telling half-truths which would rebound upon him later.

"I was in fact a prisoner of the Inquisition being taken from Jerez to the bishop's prison in Seville, and my guards fell in on the way with two fellows who claimed that I was an escaped galley slave, as a result of which the man I was chained to was shot dead while the other ran off in pursuit of the murderer and vanished..." He saw that Coussemakker's pallid face had turned several shades paler at the mention of the word "Inquisition". But he persisted. "My arraignment by the Holy Office was purely *pro forma*, though, to save me from being sent to the Philippines as a soldier. It was contrived between a Dominican monk of English birth called Fray Anselmo, who took pity on me ..." Frans could already see as he recited this improbable-sounding narrative that Coussemakker was beginning to wonder whether it might have been a madhouse and not a prison that he had escaped from, but he persevered "...and by the recruiting sergeant in Jerez, who is an old friend of my family and taught me Spanish when he was in Flanders."

He saw to his relief that the privateer captain's face had suddenly warmed, as though a watery sun had come out after a rainstorm.

"What was the name of this sergeant of whom you speak?"

"Antonio Bobadilla y Fuentes, of the tercio Guzmán el Bueno."

"Why then, a particularly fortunate constellation of stars must have gathered above your cradle when you were born, young man, because Sergeant Bobadilla and I happen to be brothers-in-law, he having married my youngest sister after she was widowed, and brought her back here to Spain with him. He is a gallant and honourable gentleman, and if it were not for his influence with the King's officials in this town I dare say I might now be sitting in prison for debt. But the fact that you were – or so you say – in the hands of the Inquisition disturbs me greatly, because there's no calling off those black-frocked dogs once they get their fangs into a man's leg, and no amount of bribery or influence will ever make them let go. If it were not for the name of Collaerts and my friendship with Sergeant Bobadilla I might be minded to tip you back over the side and leave you to your fate. But there we are: we sail on the morning tide and are bound for Dunkirk to pay off, so I dare say that I can risk keeping you hidden below until we are well out to sea." He sighed, and got up from the table slowly and with a noticeable effort. "But anyway, young fellow, it seems that I now have to find some employment for you aboard this vessel. You say that you were a barber-surgeon's apprentice. So do I take it that you have some skill in hair-cutting as well as in surgery?"

"May it please you, my charge aboard the ship was that of barber, surgeon's mate and ziekentrooster. I am not yet licensed to practice surgery, but I have already served three years of my apprenticeship and think that I can perform most operations with some assurance."

Coussemakker snorted. "Your 'think I can perform' is something that will no doubt reassure me beyond all measure when you have the bone-saw in your hands, and I'm lying on the table before you with a leg to be taken off. But there we are: for want of butter, oil must serve. Our own surgeon went ashore while we lay at Tangier, being discontented with his share and the Bey there having offered him better employment aboard one of their pirate galleys. So rather than leave my crew without anyone to cut their hair and lance their boils during the remainder of this voyage, I must find someone to fill that charge. But I have to tell you here and now that the best I can offer you by way of payment is your passage back to Flanders and your bare board and lodging for as long as you are with us. I freely confess that this voyage has been a singularly thin one and not profitable in the least. If I now offered you a share in its proceeds as is the custom, it would be no more than a tithe of candle-ends and mouse droppings, and might indeed leave you in the end owing money to the shareholders."

"My passage to Dunkirk with board and lodging would be perfectly sufficient, mijnheer."

"Very good then: I shall have the writer draw up articles for you to sign. Your duties, as I have said, will be to cut hair, to shave beards, to let blood and to attend to such other ailments and hurts as may be presented for your attention, and likewise to perform such divers duties as the mate may see fit to assign to you. Your articles will commence today, and will expire on the first day of January or when the ship pays off, whichever is the sooner."

Frans bowed, because he had no hat to doff, and turned to leave.

"Oh, and by the way... Van Raveyck, is it?" Coussemakker said. "Tell the bo'sun to have that manacle struck off your wrist as soon as he can find time to do it. Having members of my crew trailing their fetters about the deck not only looks most unseamanlike, it also puts me most uncomfortably in mind of the lodging that probably awaits me when we get home."

Frans duly signed his articles and was handed over to the bo'sun to be shown to his bedchamber, which would also be his place of work. It was a dingy, dark hole at the foot of the mainmast with scarcely enough headroom for him to straighten his back, and no footing beneath his feet but the ballast shingle. As to the tools and consumable stores of his trade, in deserting at Tangier the previous surgeon had taken with him not only the surgeon's chest, which was his own property, but the contents of the medicine chest as well – though out of residual decency he had left the chest itself behind. There was no money left in the ship's cash box to purchase replacements, so any surgery would have to be performed with such tools as could be borrowed from the carpenter, and ailments likewise treated with whatever medicaments were to hand, such as Stockholm tar or linseed oil or turpentine or mustard (which in truth, though, was no great hazard since most of the pharmacopoeia of the day was either useless or downright poisonous, and those homely remedies were at least no more harmful than the rest of what was commonly forced down the throats of the sick or slapped upon them as poultices). The bo'sun meanwhile informed Frans that the breeches and shirt he had been given when he came aboard were the ship's property and would have to be given back when they paid off; ditto the doublet and hat with which he would be provided, though those would cost less than their new price since they had been worn already by two successive members of the crew, both of them now dead.

As they spoke a shout came down from above, then a confused hubbub of feet on the deck planks, then more shouts and the sounds of blows being exchanged. A boat had come alongside with seven or eight armed men in it, and they were now attempting to come aboard while being stoutly resisted by the *Zwarte Hond*'s crew. The bo'sun bundled Frans behind a tier of casks in the hold and told him to lie still and make no sound, then went up on deck. The boy lay a half-hour or so on the ballast shingle quaking for fear that he would be seized by the Inquisition's officers and returned to face justice. But after a while all was silent again, and he sensed by its rising-and-falling motion and the creaking of its timbers that the ship was now under way and standing out to sea.

At last he went up on deck and thanked Captain Coussemakker and his new shipmates, several of whom were now nursing bruises and broken heads, for having so stoutly resisted the Inquisition's attempts to snatch him back, and said that he thought such behaviour comradely in the highest degree. Coussemakker brushed his thanks aside with contempt.

"Inquisition, you fool?," he snorted, "Do you think we'd exchange blows with the Holy Office on *your* behalf, you conceited young whelp? Why, those fellows in the boat were court bailiffs come out with a warrant to distrain the ship for debt. We chased the dogs off, and cut our anchor cable, and are now heading out to sea beyond their reach. But assaulting the King's officers in the performance of their duty is no light matter, and from now on if we put into any port on the coasts of Spain or Portugal we'll most assuredly be arrested and flung into gaol and the ship sold at auction. Our plight was bad enough before they came alongside, but now it's ten times worse!" He flung his hat to the deck and stamped on it in his fury "*And* we've lost a perfectly good anchor into the bargain, which will now be charged to my account!"

As Frans would discover over the coming days and weeks, the privateer frigate *Zwarte Hond*, one hundred and fifty tons, was by no means a fortunate ship. A sleek, low-lying little vessel armed with sixteen twelve-pounder guns, all mounted on the upper deck, the frigate was built, like all the Dunkirk privateers, to be rowed as well as sailed, pushed along during calms by great twenty-foot sweeps run out through scuttles on each side, four men to each sweep, which though wearisome for the rowers was most convenient for stealing up on victims lying becalmed, or for escaping from Dutch men-of-war which were far too heavy, broad-beamed and high-sided to be propelled under oars. Unlike the *Eenhoorn*, which was a merchant vessel converted for naval service, the *Zwarte Hond* had been designed and built with but one purpose in mind: that of chasing and capturing vessels weaker and slower than herself while running away from stronger ones. But all things in this world have their price, and the single-mindedness of her design brought penalties of its own. Narrow and fine-lined for speed, she was likewise shallow for creeping across the Flanders Banks where deeper vessels could not follow, and for lying in Dunkirk's sandy harbour, where larger vessels would ground at low tide to the great detriment of their hulls. But this meant that the little ship heeled heavily in a breeze, so that the lee side's scuppers were awash and its guns menaced the fishes whilst those on the weather side pointed at the clouds. Being low enough in the water to be propelled by oars meant that waves swilled and washed over her deck in anything stronger than a stiff breeze, pouring through hatches and dripping between the deck planks no matter how carefully the seams had been caulked, so that in bad weather everything below decks was permanently wet. And being lightly built for speed meant that the vessel worked all the time in a seaway from her scantlings being too meagre, water trickling through the hull seams so that the pump had to be manned day and night to keep her hold clear. All in all she was a ship built for running, not for fighting: too fragile and lightly gunned to escape being knocked to pieces in an exchange of broadsides with a man-of-war, and good only for terrorising merchant skippers into striking their colours from fear of the Dunkirkers and their evil repute. Which, though invisible, was the most potent of her weapons; for as soon as the white flag with its ragged red saltire broke out at the masthead and the trumpeter blew the summons to surrender, all but the most resolute skippers of fluit-ships and herring busses would strike their colours for fear of what might otherwise befall them, as a woman will submit to being ravished for fear of worse outrages if she resists.

By November of the year 1625 though, the *Zwarte Hond* would have been hard pressed to intimidate a prize into surrendering even if she were able to find one. Her complement, in fact, now numbered a mere seventy-three men and boys: less than half the number she had sailed from Dunkirk with in April. Privateer ships needed a large crew marshalled on deck, brandishing their muskets and boarding pikes to intimidate their prey into striking – or if that failed, then to be sure of overpowering their victim if it came to boarding, because no self-respecting privateer captain would willingly resort to gunfire, which might leave the prize too battered to fetch a good price at auction while squandering shot and powder which would later have to be offset against the profits of the voyage.

The *Zwarte Hond's* crew had numbered one hundred and sixty-three when the ship left Dunkirk that Easter Sunday morning, slipping out of the harbour entrance on the high tide as the bells of Saint Eloi's Church rang echoing through the town's narrow streets, then turning with the spring breeze filling her sails to glide along the Scheurtje channel under the protecting guns of Mardyck fort, her flags fluttering bravely and her trumpeters blowing derision at the two clumsy Dutch fluit-ships that dutifully detached themselves from the blockade squadron and pursued her as close inshore as they dared, their shot falling a good two hundred yards short and kicking up spurts of sandy water in the shallows. Past Gravelines they turned north-eastwards, heading for the white cliffs on the English shore, with the fat-arsed Hollanders lumbering along in their wake like two portly village constables pursuing a nimble-footed beggar urchin, falling ever further astern until they finally abandoned the chase. Two captures soon followed: a Huguenot merchantman from La Rochelle laden with wine and olives bound for Rotterdam, and then a Bordeaux ship bound for Enkhuizen with a cargo of Biscay salt for packing herrings. But three weeks later the news had reached Coussemakker that the Admiralty Court in Brussels, anxious not to offend the King of France, had judged the vessels not to be lawful prize although both were carrying cargoes destined for Dutch Protestant heretics, and had therefore ordered their release, with compensation to be paid to their owners out of the bond that the *Zwarte Hond's* owner Antoine Ryckx had lodged with the Flanders Admiralty in exchange for his letter of marque.

A few Dutch herring busses were attempted east of Lowestoft at the beginning of May – but two Hollander men-of-war had appeared on the scene, so the prizes were abandoned rather than risk an unequal fight. Later that month off Shetland the *Zwarte Hond* had sighted a more promising prize: the East Indiaman *Wapen van Medemblik* which had fallen out of her return convoy to put in at Royan and repair a broken mast, and was now sailing for Texel round the north of Scotland rather than risk the Dover Straits. Returning Indiamen sailing out of convoy were a tempting prize: richly laden, and often so worn after nine months at sea and their crews so wasted by disease that they could offer little resistance. But not in this case. The outcome was a humiliating drubbing, with the *Zwarte Hond's* boarders repulsed, three men dead and two more maimed, and the ship herself obliged to put in at Kristiansand on the coast of Norway for repairs made even more expensive by having to bribe the town's governor to turn a blind eye to their presence in a neutral harbour.

After that, no prizes having materialised during two fruitless weeks of cruising off Shetland, they had sailed across to Bergen hoping to surprise some unwary Dutch fluit-ship laden with fir trunks, which if not exactly a rich cargo, would at least be a saleable one at auction. But the timber ships from Norway to Texel were now being convoyed by warships; so after an exchange of gunfire with a Dutch vessel – which cost them a further two men dead – they had headed for the Øresund in Denmark in search of fat, slow Amsterdam grain ships carrying rye from Danzig; except that the one vessel they took turned out to be chartered to a Copenhagen merchant and not lawful prize. Coussemakkers was politely advised by the Danish warship's captain who took the prize back again that he would do well to quit Denmark's territorial waters as fast as ever he could, or he and his crew might enjoy a fine though brief view of the Øresund from the commodious gallows which His Majesty King Christian maintained on the ramparts of Kronborg Castle.

After this Coussemakker had tried his luck once more in the Channel, having received word that the Dutch blockade squadron off Dunkirk was being reduced so that ships could be sent to join the English at Plymouth. But only disappointments followed; until, with the nights lengthening past the equinox and the autumn gales starting to blow, the *Zwarte Hond* headed south to try and recoup the losses of a meagre season in the Straits of Gibraltar, where Dutch or English vessels would be unconvoyed and off their guard, not expecting to meet Dunkirkers in such distant waters. Things had looked promising on the morning of the 21st of October off Ceuta: a fluit-ship deep in the water with a cargo of Sicilian oranges ambling along on the morning breeze blowing down from the Atlas Mountains, with the Dutch tricolour floating at her stern and never a care in the world. But as luck would have it two Salee pirate galleys had also spotted the Dutchman and given chase – and objected most vehemently to Flemish infidels meddling in local piracy. The outcome was that the larger of the Salee galleys took the fluit-ship while the smaller engaged the *Zwarte Hond*, attempted to board her, then stood off and knocked her about with her guns, which was most unusual for a Salee pirate, but the vessel had several English renegados aboard who were skilled in the use of artillery.

Sorely battered, with thirteen more of her crew dead, the privateer put in to Tangier – only to suffer the further humiliation of being refused credit for repairs. The news had just arrived that Antoine Ryckx had been declared bankrupt, so his agent in that port was no longer honouring his promissory notes. This final misfortune prompted the surgeon, the second mate and thirty of the crew to walk ashore declaring that the owner's insolvency meant that they were released from their contracts, and anyway they would have nothing further to do with such an ill-starred voyage; indeed were taking service with the Moors, who evidently possessed a greater flair for piracy than Couseemakker did. All that the *Zwarte Hond* could do was limp across to San Lucar on the Spanish coast; just in time to be trapped there by the arrival of Viscount Wimbledon's fleet.

It was by now evident as a post above water that the Dunkirk poorhouse was more likely to be the destination of the *Zwarte Hond's* remaining crew once they got home than some neat little farmhouse out in the polders with an apple orchard and a herd of dairy cattle. Most of them were younger sons or debtors seeking to restore their fortunes, who had been obliged to borrow money to buy their share in the voyage and outfit themselves for it – and who would soon have to repay the money advanced to them. And even if death and desertion had increased the shares in the voyage for those that remained aboard, the dullest-witted foc'sle hand could soon work out that six-fifteenths of nothing comes to no more handsome a sum than three-fifteenths of nothing. The season was now far spent, with not a copper doit to show for it. The clothes provided by Dunkirk's fournisseurs that spring hung now in grimy rags, there having been no opportunity to replace them from the sea-chests of their victims, which was the usual means by which privateer-men changed their linen. The sails were patched, and the hemp cordage frayed and rotten from too much sun and salt, silvery grey with a sickly pallid shine on it like the bloom on the face of a consumptive. The provisions were nearly spent, now that the news of Ryckx's insolvency had reached Spain and San Lucar's victuallers would no longer offer credit. The crew had long since been reduced to a paltry diet of garbanzo beans, olive oil and crumbling mouldy biscuit washed down with "breuvage" of vinegar and cask water, beer being now no more than a wistful memory. And after a long series of fruitless engagements powder and shot were likewise too low for the *Zwarte Hond* to attempt any but the weakest of prizes. The crew were dispirited, wishing now for nothing more than a speedy return to Dunkirk in the hope of recouping their losses with a better season in 1626 – that is, if they could get home soon enough to sign articles with a more capable captain than old turnip-face Coussemakker, and not find themselves haunting the docksides in March or April looking for a ship that still needed hands, all the most desirable berths already being occupied.

Eight bells rang out: time for Coussemakker to confer with his remaining officers. They clumped noisily into his cabin – all now wore clogs in order to spare their leather boots – and at his bidding removed their hats and sat down on the benches on either side of the table. There was a palpable air of nothing very much being expected any longer, all those present having long since abandoned any hope that their captain might produce any ideas more profitable than those which had already been tried and found wanting.

"So messieurs", Coussemakker concluded with a sigh after a few minutes of half-debate, "it seems to me that we must now decide whether to search again for prizes in the waters between here and Gibraltar, or instead turn for home before the winter storms set in. Biscay in December is likely to be a mighty uncomfortable place for a vessel as small and as ill-found as ours."

"Judging by the clouds this morning at first light the winter storms have already set in, captain", the mate said. "Because of them there'll soon be few enough prizes to seek in these waters, as the Dutch and English vessels lay up for the winter. In any case, the present war will surely make the London vintners look elsewhere than Jerez this year for their store of Christmastide sack, and cause any English merchantmen that were in Spanish waters to return home in company with Wimbledon's fleet."

"What word do we have of them?" Coussemakker enquired.

"Little new, save that the skipper of a fishing boat that came into San Lucar just before we sailed said that they were sighted two days ago off Cape Saint Vincent, steering a course north by north-west. The Mexico fleet is now safely anchored under the guns of Gibraltar, having given Milord Wimbledon the slip and been the occasion of a solemn *Te Deum* in all the churches of Spain by way of thanksgiving. So having failed to take the silver fleet, and having likewise failed to take Cadiz but instead been chased off with their arses hanging in tatters, there now seems little enough hereabouts that might cause the English to tarry off a lee shore as the ocean gales start to blow."

"And for good measure they seem to have been smitten by sickness," young Guillaume Coussemakker added. "I spoke yesterday with the customs master of San Lucar and he told me that many dead Englishmen were being washed ashore with the marks of spotted fever on them. The galley slaves from Puerto Santa María were being put to work, he said, to collect them up and burn them on the beaches for fear of infection."

"If Wimbledon is now on his way home," Coussemakker said, "for us that means a sea empty of prizes until next spring. As you say, we might try our luck once more in the Straits. But would you recommend that with the shot-room nearly empty and only six barrels of powder to our name, and the Spanish ports now closed to us too by reason of our having assaulted the King's bailiffs? And if we tried to dock, then Ryckx's creditors lining the quayside waving writs for distraint at us by way of greeting?" He turned to the writer. "What do you advise, Meester Guyot? You study the stars, I believe?"

"I do, skipper: and more to the point, I also keep the ship's accounts. Leaving aside the Ephemerids and Ptolemy's *Tetrabiblos* for the moment, and considering only the state of our ledger book, it seems to me as a man of business that our sole recourse now is to turn for home, and hope that on the way back the stars will cause a rich and easy prize to cross our path. For I fear that otherwise, when the final accounts for this voyage are drawn up, we shall all find ourselves owing the shareholders money rather than them owing money to us. Thanks to Mijnheer Ryckx's failure our credit is quite gone locally, and I could only buy us garbanzos and olive oil yesterday in San Lucar by pawning the gilt chain that the Archduke once gave you for taking the Englishman Rawlings."

Coussemakker nodded sadly: that chain had indeed been precious to him as a memento of happier days.

"Very well then," Coussemakker said at last, "cutting our losses and heading for the Channel seems the only course left to us. But we must keep close in to the French coast from Barfleur point to the mouth of the Seine. France is still neutral in this war, but both English and Dutch vessels ply their trade with her, so perhaps even at this late season we may happen upon a prize rich enough to at least to pay off our creditors. Because otherwise I fear that the Hôtel-Dieu awaits the crew, and the debtors' prison myself."

By nightfall Cape Saint Vincent had been rounded, and the *Zwarte Hond* was shaping course for Sagres. Next morning the storm predicted by the mate duly blew up. This was indeed no time of the year to be loitering off the Atlantic coasts of Spain. The Bay of Biscay was crossed, rougher than ever; and on the 28th of November, midway through the morning watch, the Isle of Ushant loomed in sight through the rain squalls, and next morning Alderney and Cape de la Hogue. They were back in home waters.

★ ★ ★ ★ ★ ★ ★ ★ ★ ★

It was now the last days of November, and Sagittarius the Archer galloped through the nocturnal sky shooting his windy darts across the Biscay waves. Having little enough to do aboard the *Zwarte Hond* other than barbering and such odd menial tasks as the mate assigned to me, the days being short and myself but little inclined to spend my time playing at dice like the rest — and the *Zwarte Hond's* leaky main deck likewise being scarcely less wet and cold than the one above it, open to the heavens — I spent much of my time in the company of Meester Guyot, the ship's writer – or Maître Guyot, as he preferred that I call him, since he felt more at ease in French than in Flemish and valued my company because (he said) I was plainly a young fellow of wit and education rather than some lumpen caboteur in clogs, and spoke French easily and naturally instead of mangling it as the Dunkirkers did who would pronounce his name "Ghhhowee-yott" with their Netherlandish coughing G, which he said sounded like a cat vomiting up a mouse it had swallowed.

We would sit together through the long stormy evenings in his cubby-hole of an office near the stern, which though it had barely enough room for the two of us to sit in, was at least tolerably dry and moreover warmed a little – though at the same time made villainously smoky – by the one tallow candle allotted to him by the bottelier each evening to illuminate his quill-scratchings in the ship's ledger. There we talked of all that had befallen me, which he was very curious to learn about since I think that he was by nature a timorous fellow, being a failed attorney from Béthune in Artois driven to sea only by necessity, and relished hearing of adventures which he would have been too fearful ever to have undertaken for himself. For my part I was (I must confess) pretty pleased with myself, having lately escaped so many perils at Cadiz though not yet fifteen years of age, and now fancied myself a mighty hard-bitten and seasoned fellow, having not only heard bullets fly about my ears and seen men die before me, but quite fortuitously enjoyed the favours of a woman at an age when my schoolfellows were still at their desks construing their Virgil and Seneca (though naturally enough I said nothing to him concerning this latter episode, so as to excite neither his censure nor his envy).

Maître Guyot listened with particular interest over several evenings to my narrative of the late expedition to Cadiz, remarking at last that so far as he could see, it was fated and ordained in advance that the whole sorry venture should miscarry, since Viscount Wimbledon had plainly chosen a signally unpropitious season for it. I enquired what he meant by this, so he took out his much-thumbed book of ephemerids and began to cast an astrologer's chart for the enterprise, which was very curious for me to behold since I had until then little notion that such things could be done at all, let alone how to do them.

"When did things finally go amiss, do you think?" he asked me.

I considered awhile, and opined at last that although the venture had not gone particularly well earlier on, to say the least of it, we had still taken Fort Puntal by the afternoon of the second day of November, and put the army ashore by midday on the third; so matters had not taken an irrevocable turn for the worse (I thought) until that same evening, when Sir Edward's soldiery broke into the wine warehouse and became so helplessly drunk that Julius Caesar himself could have done nothing further with them. So he cast his chart for five o'clock in the afternoon of the 3rd of November, taking the latitude and longitude of Cadiz from Waghener's pilotage book. He made his calculations with a great deal of humming and hawing, writing in the aspects of the stars and planets on his chart, which was square with a lozenge inside it, then another square inside the lozenge, so that in the end there were twelve triangles corresponding to the twelve astrological houses. At last he was finished, and looked across the table at me with a smile of satisfaction.

"There, young François: precisely as I would have expected. The configuration of the heavens at that place and time plainly foretold some event that would be fatal to the whole enterprise; and if your Lord Wimbledon had had the wit to take an astrologer with him on this expedition of his, then he might have chosen a more propitious day and hour and the whole venture would then have slid along as smoothly as butter upon butter. In the first place, mark here that the Sun was at that hour in perfect opposition to the ascendant sign, which was Taurus. Duty, which is ruled by the earthy bull, and authority which is the Sun's quality, were therefore in direct conflict. So men's brains at that hour and that latitude were already mazed by the opposition between the two and thus rendered like sponges waiting only for wine to be poured upon them. Likewise the Sun was in Scorpio, which is a watery, fickle sign in direct conflict with it. And moreover Mercury and the Moon, those two great waverers and vagabonds of the heavens, were in perfect quadrature with Mars the ruler of war, and Venus the governor of reason and judgement. So it was entirely to be predicted that discipline and duty would be subject to dissolution and the whole enterprise cast adrift upon the waters, since the very heavens themselves were in flux at that hour and delivered over to the rule of caprice and giddy inconstancy." He laid aside his paper. "In fact it surprises me, looking at the chart I have just cast here, that Wimbledon's soldiers needed wine to provoke them to insubordination, since the stars alone should have sufficed to make them skittish and intractible as a herd of cattle tormented by gadflies."

I was much in awe of this reasoning of his, so magisterial and confident did it sound. But being even then a tiresome quizzical fellow, I enquired of him how it fell out that the Spaniards, who were present at precisely the same time and place, should have escaped this malign influence of the stars; in fact seemed from what I could see of it to have comported themselves with the most admirable discipline and resolution. To which he replied, with the patient sigh of one explaining long division to an idiot-boy, that the stars do not influence all equally, because otherwise we would be like a shoal of herrings or a flock of starlings, all turning at the same moment; which is patently not the case with men, each of whom has a reason, a conscience and a bodily temperament of his own. He explained that instead the stars work on men and nations differently according to their underlying humoral dispositions; and in this case Leo the lion (which is the sign that rules England) was plainly in the descendant and subject to the watery powers, and its soldiers therefore feeble and unmanned, while Taurus the bull (which is the ruler of Spain) was in the ascendant under the fiery signs, and its men made resolute thereby and filled with high courage. So all in all he did not see how it could have turned out otherwise than it did, and deplored only that Sir Edward had not consulted the stars before putting his warriors ashore, which action he likened to that of a man who goes swimming in January – because he did so in July and took no harm of it – and catches his death of cold.

"So do you believe, then, " I enquired, "that all the affairs of men are thus governed by the stars and planets?" I asked, because though I knew of astrology and its usefulness in physic, I had at that time little practical acquaintance with it, its application to surgery being limited since a surgeon usually has not the luxury of choosing the most propitious time to ligate a femoral artery cut through by a mower's scythe, but must do it immediately regardless of the Sun's position in the zodiac otherwise the patient will bleed to death.

"Perfectly and absolutely," he declared. "All my studies over many years have convinced me of it; that we and the planets and the world of living things are all bound up in one great whole, and everything we do is occasioned by that which happens elsewhere in the cosmos. The rub is, that while we know intuitively that all things in the heavens and on Earth work together, we do not as yet have any very good understanding of the mechanism by which they do so; much as a Carib or a Huron Indian might marvel at the intricacy and regularity of a clock, and perceive dimly that the wheels all work together in some mysterious fashion, yet be entirely ignorant of the spring that drives it and of which wheel propels which subordinate cog to produce the observable motion of the hands going round the dial. I have therefore devoted my life to this study, and hope in the end to produce a grand hermetic philosophy that will explain all things. Because as it is, we learned men each cultivate our own little plant-bed – which we call physic or mechanics or geometry – and pay no heed to the garden of knowledge as a whole, since we stand too close to discern it among the thousand individual herbs."

This discourse of his gave me great cause for thought, and made me see all on a sudden, as with a flash of lightning that illuminates an entire landscape, that the stars had been uncommonly kind to me in ordaining our precipitate flight from Colchester, then my enlistment aboard the *Eenhoorn*, then the whole sorry business of the Cadiz expedition, then my deliverance from the Inquisition afterwards, which had resulted at last in my being brought into proximity with this great and unusual intelligence who – though I heard he was hanged a year or two afterwards at Ghent for false coining – first set my youthful feet on the path of enquiry that I have followed all my life since. There we were, he and I, aboard a leaky privateer ship bucketing about on the Biscay waves with a crew of hungry and raggedy-elbowed piratical ruffians for company, conducting our learned colloquies each evening by the light of a smoky tallow candle with naught but garbanzos and breuvage to line our bellies and dead men's clothes on our backs, and scarce a doit between us to scratch our backsides with. Yet we talked of the great forces that move kingdoms and empires, and to which monarchs in their palaces were every bit as much subject as we ourselves; the only difference between them and us being that we sought to understand those powers, and they did not.

It was then that I first began to comprehend the port of the phrase, "the republic of learning" and to account myself a citizen of it, seeing that so long as we have a brain inside our skulls and a sheet of paper and a pencil to write with – or failing that a patch of sand to draw figures in like Archimedes of Syracuse – then the whole universe can be ours, and all the princes and potentates of the earth, all the lieutenant-generals and lord high admirals and pensionaries and corregidors in their sad gaudy finery, can go drown themselves in a horse-pond as imagining themselves to be the authors and rulers of events, when in reality those events rule *them*. For who in truth would not sooner be Eratosthenes of Alexandria, quietly calculating the Earth's circumference with two sticks and a piece of string, than Alexander the Great with his hundred thousand spearmen, seeking to engross the whole world in an empire that barely survived his own death?

★ ★ ★ ★ ★ ★ ★ ★ ★ ★

Dawn on the 15th of December found the *Zwarte Hond* butting through the cold easterly chop off Dungeness Point, heading north-east for the Downs and the host of vessels that lay there at anchor, sheltering from the winter gales between the high chalk cliffs and the Goodwin Sands. Trying to snatch a prize from the Downs would have been foolhardy in the extreme: that anchorage was well surveyed from Deal Castle at one end and Sandwich Castle at the other and Walmer Castle in between, and England and Spain now being at war a vigilant watch was no doubt being kept for prowling Dunkirkers, which were recognisable from far off by their low-lying hulls and their characteristic rig. But vessels continually left the Downs to proceed elsewhere, as wind, tides and owners' instructions dictated, so it would surely not be too difficult for a wolf surveying the flock from far off to single out a fat complacent ewe, then run after her and drag her down once the silly creature had quit the sheepfold. Just a little luck and they might all be home for New Year, if not rich men then at least with a few coins chinking in their pockets and new clothes on their backs. The early-December gales had now given way to bright, cold weather in which objects that were far off appeared close and sharp. The crew's breath steamed in the air and they shivered in their threadbare garments as the biting east wind out of France whipped spray from the wave crests. They could see Calais belfry now in the distance and felt suddenly homesick, to be so near their families but still so far away. Yet the hope of gain kept them at sea – and fear of the shame of returning empty-handed after eight months away, to be hooted through the streets of Dunkirk as poltroons and duck-pond sailors.

But once again the fickle goddess intervened to the *Zwarte Hond's* disfavour. During the night of the 15th a flat calm descended, and with it a dense, freezing fog that shrouded the mouth of the Thames and the Essex sandbanks. A hundred or more vessels now lay becalmed on the oily swell with hoar-frost crusting their rigging and their hanging sails frozen stiff as cardboard. Bells rang and drums tapped in the swirling murk as ships sought to warn one another of their presence. Not a vessel was moving now except as the tide bore them along; but since some were drifting while others rode at anchor there was always the risk of a collision. All were still except for one. Since first light the Zwarte Hond had had her sweeps out and was now creeping northwards through the freezing murk off the North Foreland; slowly and with great effort – since a hundred and fifty tons is a ponderous weight to be moved by men's arms alone – but still making headway with the tide behind her at about two leagues each hour. Her oarports were muffled with wads of sacking and woollen rags to deaden the creaking, for why would a ship proceed under oars in a fog if not with dishonest intent? Round about her trumpets and cowhorns sounded from time to time, and once or twice the booming cannon of some great ship warning others to keep clear. But in so dense a fog all sounds seem equally close, so those unseen vessels might just as well have been a cable's length or five miles distant. Every few minutes Coussemakker and the mate would signal the rowers to stop, listening as intently as two foxes outside their earth, then motion them to start rowing again, lugging wearily at the ash-wood sweeps which blistered their hands and made their shoulders ache as their bellies rumbled with hunger. At last, about eleven o'clock, a musket shot was heard close by. Coussemakker signalled the rowers to pause, and they stopped at once, thankful to have the chance to blow on their frozen hands and slap themselves about the body with their arms to generate some warmth.

"What do you think?" Coussemakker murmured softly to the mate. "A man-of-war?"

"I doubt it. A warship would fire off a cannon not a musket. The king's powder is no charge to them, so they expend it like beach-sand."

"A merchantman, then?"

"I doubt that likewise. A merchant skipper would hardly keep a musketeer on deck, but instead blow a horn or beat an iron kettle. My guess is for a packet boat; probably the one between Queenborough and Vlissingen. But hark..." They both strained their ears to catch the sound of voices perhaps fifty yards away. "A packet for sure then, " the mate said. "Only passengers would prattle so on deck. Mariners would either be about their work in silence, or below round the galley fire to warm themselves."

So the guns were made ready and weapons prepared as the *Zwarte Hond* slid silently through the fog towards the mysterious vessel. Another musket shot cracked in the still air, nearer this time so that the orange flash from the muzzle could be seen faintly through the wreathing greyness. Coussemakker cupped his hands and called out at last.

"Qui va là? Who are you?"

After a pause a call came back, in accented English, "Ze *Coque d'Or* out off Oshtend. 'Oo are jouw?"

"Speak Flemish before we believe you."

There was silence, and distant murmuring, then a call back: "Wel zo – en wie bent ghij?" The accent was certainly authentic for Ostend, or perhaps Nieuwpoort.

"The fishing boat *Witte Zwaan* of Zuydcoote," Coussemakker called back. "But where are you bound for? Spain and England being at war, why do you sail between England and Flanders?"

"We have thirty English Catholic gentlemen aboard going to fight for King Philip and the true faith. Here, listen." There was another pause, then English voices singing in unison:

"Salve, Regina, Mater misericordiæ,
Vita, dulcedo, et spes nostra, salve.
Ad te clamamus, exsules filii Evæ,
Ad te suspiramus, gementes et flentes
In hac lacrimarum valle..."

Coussemakker shrugged in resignation and turned to the mate. "That settles the matter then: no Englishmen nowadays would know the *Salve Regina* unless he were a Catholic." He called out,

"God speed you all, then."

The boat full of English volunteers fell astern unmolested as the *Zwarte Hond's* crew cursed their ill luck, and rowed onwards through the fog.

Next morning the mists had been dispersed by a north-westerly breeze. They turned east near the Gunfleet Sand and pointed the *Zwarte Hond's* bows for the Flanders Banks. The wind bellied out the sails as the first wet snowflakes of winter fluttered through the air. By evening they had reached the Wielingen channel and the entrance to the Scheldt, where an unwary fluit-ship or even a belated East Indiaman might perhaps be found sailing out of convoy. If no suitable victim presented itself Coussemakker had already determined to give up and return to Dunkirk and the debtors' prison that probably awaited him. If this last throw of the dice failed as all the others had done, then he must conclude that the whole venture had been at the very least ill-starred from the outset and quite possibly bewitched as well. But by now he felt too old and too ill to care much any longer. Young Van Raveyck examined him each day and treated the sores where his swollen dropsical ankles overlapped his clogs. But what could a mere boy still full of life and hope know about the weary afflictions of old age? One way or another, he was sure that this would be his final voyage, and regretted only that he had not retired from privateering and become a landed gentleman while he was still at the height of his fame. In his mind he could already see the satirical pamphlets with their woodcuts depicting him pulling out the linings of his empty pockets above the legend "*Jacquou-le-Brédouille*", or sitting in an armchair on his quarterdeck with a pair of spectacles on his nose knitting stockings.* The sweet heady wine of renown, he knew, is liable to turn very quickly indeed into the vinegar of public contempt, and those who turn out to cheer a man through the streets would most of them cheer just as loudly at his hanging.

---

* "Empty-Handed Jim". "Coussemakker" means "stocking maker" in Flemish.

★ ★ ★ ★ ★ ★ ★ ★ ★

When the call came down from the lookout that morning off the mouth of the Scheldt I was sitting with Maître Guyot in his office with a posset of breuvage which we had heated over the galley fire to put some warmth into us, but which only made it taste (he declared) like horse's urine fresh from the horse instead of horse's urine left to grow cold. We talked of his study of the stars, and of how any great man should always have an astrological chart cast before embarking upon any important venture.

"Yes, indeed," he said with a sigh, "it would have been as well for King Henri of France to have listened to Père Brossard and not to his court astrologer Thomassin that afternoon before he ventured out from the Louvre in his coach, because the prognostication which old Brossard gave him was by all accounts a villainous bad one, though of but a few hours' duration, and if old Henri had paid heed to it and remained at home for the rest of that day he might still be with us now." He paused and drank from the posset, making a wry face as he did so, then put the cup down. "Ah yes, young François, that was a curious business altogether, King Henri's murder. And there is much that I could tell you concerning it that you will certainly never read of in any of the histories."

At this you may be sure I pricked my ears up, because although I doubted very much whether Maître Guyot was anything more than a provincial wiseacre (the Most Christian Kings of France not usually being in the habit of consulting attorney's clerks from small towns in Artois) I had, as you may imagine, a considerable desire to learn anything that I might concerning my father's abominable crime and the circumstances that surrounded it; particularly since my mother was dead and would now never be able to fulfil her promise to tell me the whole story of it when I came of age. So I displayed some mild curiosity, and asked him politely to enlarge upon what he had just said.

"Indeed: King Henri's murder and all that followed upon that notable crime. I was well acquainted with the assassin Ravaillac, you know?"

I nodded to signal my assent to this, as though for me being on terms of intimacy with a regicide was the most usual thing in the whole world, and bade him go on, all agog by now though I tried to show no sign of it.

"Yes, he and I studied law together for a season at the Sorbonne when we were young, about 1595 or '96. He was a great blundering mazy-headed youth from out in the Angoumois, I remember: innocent as a babe in some matters – they say he once walked to Fontainbleau and back to repay a debt of three sous – yet cunning as a magpie in others, so we never quite knew what to make of him and all thought that his roof must need thatching. And a great Leaguer as well: so devout he would never miss attending a procession or an exposition of the blessed sacrament, and crossed himself and said grace at every mouthful he took though it was but a sprat's head on a bread-crust. He kept company with others as pious as himself, and likewise with some Jesuits who haunted about the Sorbonne and were their special confessors and confidants. He shared his lodgings for a time with Jean Châtel, who was stark mad and beset all the time with visions of hell, and in the end took a dagger to the King because he said that the Holy Spirit had commanded him to do it, but missed his mark and only cut His Majesty's lip open, and was pulled asunder by four horses for the crime of lèse-majesté the following day, though many said his execution so soon afterwards was to shut his mouth for fear that he might name those who had placed the knife in his hand. Our brave Ravaillac fairly fouled his breeches at this, and left Paris for a while for fear that he would be arrested as an accomplice. But I heard later that after Châtel's remains were burned and the ashes fired from a cannon, Ravaillac obtained one of his teeth and wore it round his neck in a locket as a holy relic, telling all who would listen that the poor deluded fellow was a saint and a martyr."

"He sounds to have been a great fanatic", I said. "But did you see or hear of him after that?"

"Not for a long time," he replied. "He left the university after a year or two and returned to Angoulême: some said because his father had lost his place in the law courts there by reason of drunkenness and could no longer pay for his studies, though his uncles were canons of the cathedral, I believe, and his mother of good family. I took my master's degree that year and returned to Artois so that I could enter articles. But I did see him again, about 1607 or perhaps '08, I forget which year, by which time I was a practicien in the Procurator's Court in Brussels. I met him one day in the street – he being very visible by reason of his size and his red hair – and asked him how he did. He was very mysterious with me and avoided my questions, and refused to say what business had brought him there. But I heard afterwards that he had spoken with people that were highly placed in the Archduke's court. And when I met him his face was all freckled and sunburned, though it was but March, from which I concluded that he might lately have spent much time out of doors in a southern climate, perhaps as a soldier. Then some time afterwards I heard from one who also knew him in Paris that he had been at Bruges and stayed some time in a monastery there, which led me to suspect…."

At this he broke off, because a call had come down from the lookout at the mast head, then an imperative rolling of the drum. A vessel had been sighted, and we were to clear the ship for action. As I made my way below Maître Guyot assured me that he would tell me more about all this later on. But the stars had ordained that he would never have the chance to do so.

I must go below at once to prepare the cockpit, so all that I saw of the fluit-ship was her masts and sails. Had I been granted a sight of her hull, which was still below the rim of the horizon, then I would most certainly have remarked upon it and the whole affair might have taken a very different turn. But so does posterity make fools of us all; and in any case, Captain Coussemakker's hunger for a prize would in all likelihood have got the better of his judgement whatever I had said. For the truth is that he and his men were now as ardent to take a ship as street dogs are to leap upon a bitch in heat, being otherwise faced with the prospect of returning to Dunkirk after nine months' absence with their pockets empty and nothing but a poor thin fire of bailiff's warrants to warm their hands at over Christmas. Famine will make a rat bold to attempt even a cat, so I fancy that if even one of Haireddin Barbarossa's galleys crowded with janissaries had been in the offing they would still have been disposed to try taking her, driven alike by cupidity and by desperation. The fluit-ship (I heard the mate say up on deck) was plainly no more than that: dawdling along with her boat trailing behind; but with the Dutch flag floating at her stern, which offered some hope that this time our victim would be lawful prize.

Down below in the hold I had much to occupy me, setting up the trestle table to lay out my instruments and prepare dressings, lighting the charcoal brazier to heat the cauterizing irons *et cetera*. For surgeon's mate I had Jaap Zoetermelk, the cook's helper, a boy of my own age who was plainly simple-minded, but tractable withal and would do as I instructed him if I spoke plainly enough; and anyway there was no better assistant for me with our crew so depleted and every man that could hold a boarding-axe required on deck to make as brave a show as we could. I was less than confident of my ability to perform an amputation or other major surgery if I had to, for though I had seen limbs cut off several times I had never carried out that operation myself, my part in it having been limited to the subordinate operations like tying off the blood vessels and dressing the stump afterwards. My instruments likewise were a sorry collection: an old carpenter's saw scoured up and fitted with a new handle, and a number of knives and pincers begged from the carpenter and the armourer which I had mended with wire as best I could and sharpened up to their proper offices. The best that I could hope for was that our fluit-ship would see the hopelessness of her plight at once and not make a fight of it.

While I and my assistant strove to complete our preparations, on the deck above our heads there was a great dragging and bumping and stamping of feet as the guns were made ready and the cartridges and shot brought up from below. At last all fell silent, and we knew that the hour of decision was at hand. Our Dutchman might elect to strike his colours at the first summons of the trumpet, knowing the evil fame of the Dunkirkers and deeming a month or two in Dunkirk Citadel awaiting ransom preferable to being summarily cast overboard. But nothing was certain here: the Hollanders are widely famed as a stiff-necked and intransigent folk, so that even a fluit-ship captain in a patched coat and canvas breeches with clogs on his feet might still fancy himself a hero and make a fight of it.

At last there was a sudden great shuddering, crashing sound, and dirt and cobwebs showering on our heads as our larboard guns bellowed out one after the other. It seemed that our summons to surrender had been rejected. But in what terms was only made plain thereafter, when a mighty thunderous splintering tumult above our heads, and howls of alarm and dismay, told us that the Dutch ship had given answer in a voice as loud as our own. But no injured men were brought down for us to attend to, because a cavernous boom set the deck lurching beneath our feet as the two vessels bumped together side by side, and a great shouting and rushing of feet from above told us that our captain had elected to grapple the Dutchman and board him, our store of powder and shot being insufficient for more than two or three broadsides. Then there was quiet for a while, broken only by the groans of the injured, who had been left on the main deck as our entire crew leaped across to the Dutch ship. Zoetermelk and I went up to attend to them as best we could, and found them lying dead and injured amid a great jumble of overturned carriages and fallen gear. We saw at once that the Dutch broadside had been too weighty and too well aimed to have come from some poor peacable merchantman. Between us we carried some of the injured below to the cockpit, though most were already beyond our help. Before long though there was a great commotion of shouting and pistol shots and swords clashing alongside, and it dawned upon us that no wounded men were being brought for us to dress, which was a mighty bad omen since it meant that those of ours who fell hurt, were falling hurt upon the Dutchman's deck with none to carry them across. At last seven or eight of our own fellows came scrambling down the companion ladder all bloodied like butchers, begrimed with powder-smoke and their eyes full of terror and apprehension.

"Quickly!" they shouted, "Close the hatch above us, for all is lost. The Dutchman is no fluit-ship but a man-of-war tricked out to seem like one, and packed to the deck-beams with armed men! May the Devil roast old Coussemakker's arse on a gridiron for misleading us so!. The Hollanders were upon us like a nestful of hornets as soon as we had a leg over the rail!"

They slammed the hatch shut above them – though what refuge they hoped to find in the hold when the rest of our ship was in Dutch hands was a mystery to me; I suppose only that fear is so imperious a master that it makes men clutch at the smallest and most illusory hope, as hares in a cornfield at harvest time will seek refuge from the mowers in a patch of standing corn which in the end is scarce large enough to conceal them.

"Where's the captain?" I asked one of them, hoping that he might have fallen back aboard our ship to rally his men and yet save the day, for the name of Jacques Coussemakker was a talisman that still had some power to put heart into those who sailed with him.

"Dead already," he replied, "before we even came to grips with the Hollanders. He groaned and seized his chest, then fell to his knees, and we thought he had been shot; but instead his heart had burst within him and he fell over and lay still. Then the mate was brought low with a musket ball through his head, and all went awry from then onwards with none to lead us…"

A Dutch voice boomed from above like that of the Archangel Gabriel on Judgement Day.

"Give yourselves up, you Flemish dogs, or we'll toss a stinkpot in among you and smoke you all out like so many wasps!"

One of our fellows replied: "Promise us our lives and we'll come up."

To which the voice shouted, "We promise you nothing but this, you vermin!" Following which a pot of burning brimstone was dropped down through a skylight, and very soon filled the hold with its stinking fumes which set us all a-coughing and our eyes streaming so that no man could have withstood it for long, and after five minutes we all came up and were seized to have our wrists bound behind us, then be dragged across the bloody deck amid a great many cuffs and kicks and flung like so many sacks of meal aboard the fluit-ship. As for myself, my head was banged against the rail on my way across and quite dazed me, so that when I came to myself again I was lying face-down on the fluit-ship's deck. Yet as I looked about me amid all the confusion of gear and men's legs, the view seemed a curiously familiar one, so that I thought at first that I must be dreaming. And only slowly came to realise that I was back aboard the *Eenhoorn* after an absence of six weeks.

As you may well imagine, this was somewhat troubling for me, my articles aboard that vessel still having some three weeks to run, so that I was guilty of breaking my contract merely by serving aboard any other vessel during that time, let alone an enemy privateer-ship. But as I was pulled up by the collar and propped against the bulwark with my fellow captives, the thirty or so of our men who had survived the encounter, I soon divined that having violated my articles of engagement was the very least of the matters for which I must now answer. For it was as plain as a post above water that our captors were not in the least well-disposed towards us. The Hollanders frankly viewed all Dunkirk privateer ships as pirates even if they possessed a letter of marque from the Flanders Admiralty. The *Zwarte Hond* now possessed no such letter, it having expired with the owner Ryckx's bankruptcy. But it was evident now that all was up with us even if we had presented our captors with decree signed alike by the Pope and the

Holy Roman Emperor and a golden seal affixed thereunto. The Dutch Republic (we afterwards learned) had had a famously bad autumn of it with the Dunkirkers, twenty-five or more of whom had broken out during the high tides in October (the blockade fleet having been much weakened by gales and in favour of the Cadiz venture) and caused great mischief both to the Norway trade and to the herring fisheries. So the crew of any Dunkirk privateer that was taken by the Hollanders would have even less expectation than before of being given quarter; which is to say, none at all.

"What went amiss?" I asked Maître Guyot who sat bound beside me, with a sword-cut across his cheek tied up with a dirty rag, he having been pressed for service as a boarder though I should think that few men on Earth were less apt for the bearing of arms.

He laughed at this, as though he found it amusing. "Everything. And with Mercury in opposition to Mars it could scarcely have gone otherwise, as I took the liberty of warning old Coussemakker this very morning, but he only brushed me aside as a star-gazing pen licker with no experience of the sea. This vessel turned out once we had boarded her not just to be a man-of-war, but to have twice the normal crew of a man-of-war, the people from another fluit-ship having been taken aboard her at Cadiz. They outnumbered our fellows three or four to one."

"So what do you suppose will become of us now?" I asked.

"I suppose", he said, "that they'll either they take us ashore and hang us at Vlissingen for the amusement of the fishermen's wives whose husbands now languish in Dunkirk Citadel – or worse still, throw us bound hand and foot to the same herring wives so that they can have their sport on us with their gutting knives. Or they may put us all back aboard our ship and nail down the hatches then set her alight, rather than go to the trouble of towing her back as a prize. But either way it's all up with us now, young François. So say your prayers while you still have time."

I myself was soon the object of particular interest among my former shipmates once they realised who I was, buffeted and cursed as a schelm and a verraderlijk schurk,* since all had imagined me slain or taken prisoner at Cadiz, and now here I was serving aboard a Dunkirk privateer. I asked to see my stepfather, whom I imagined was down below treating the wounded. But I was told curtly that he was no longer aboard the *Eenhoorn*, which caused me the most acute apprehension as to what was become of him. Only Matthias Siggurdsson and Suleiman the Moor showed me any kindness, bringing me some beer and placing it to my lips for me to drink when no one was watching. But before I could ask them what was become of my stepfather they were jostled aside, and Captain Loodgieter stood before us, all dishevelled and black with powder-smoke, and with a gory sword still in his hand, but his face flushed with triumph to have concluded so good a season by taking yet another prize and bringing to an end the piratical career of Jacques Coussemakker. He strode down the row of defeated and crestfallen wretches sitting propped against the bulwark with bound hands.

"So, my fine fellows," he said, "You thought to take a dove, and found it to be a hawk in dove's feathers. If it might still profit Captain Coussemakker for me to tell him so, I would strongly recommend that he invest in a kijkglas such as I possess, which for all its shortcomings is unequalled for examining a prize from beyond cannonshot before attempting to take it, and thus amply repays the initial expense. But as for you, my Flemish friends, I fear that advice comes too late, for your privateering days are over. I compliment you all on having put up a gallant fight, for you defended yourselves as stoutly as any men could against such odds. But you have been vanquished none the less..." He paused in front of me, then swept his hat off with a flourish in a mocking obeisance. "Aha, Mijnheer van Raveyck I see? How honoured we are to have you back aboard with us after so long an absence. And what do you have to say for yourself, you perfidious young hound?"

* Blackguard and traitorous scoundrel

I explained as best I could that I had been taken by the Spaniards on the Isle of León after Captain van der Hulst was slain, and had taken service aboard the Dunkirker only in order to escape the worse fates of a galley or the Spanish Army. But he brushed this aside as a cock-and-bull story, and said that I was nothing but a common deserter who had willingly taken service aboard an enemy vessel in contempt of his articles of engagement – and not aboard one of the King of Spain's ships either, for which there might be some excuse if I had been pressed as one of his subjects by birth, but a vulgar pirate vessel where all aboard her (as was common knowledge) were leagued together in crime by virtue of their having shares in the venture, and were therefore in his opinion no better than brigands were on land, entirely answerable for their actions and without any protection whatever from the laws and customs of war. I asked him that he might at least for charity's sake tell me what was become of my stepfather. But his reply to this was curt:

"Your stepfather is a good and honourable man, and may count it a signal blessing that he is no longer aboard this vessel to see what manner of devious untrustworthy rascal it was that he once so foolishly took to be his son. The French say that 'bon sang ne saurait mentir'*. Well, I would say that by the same token bad blood cannot lie either, and that a base-born varlet's whelp scooped up from a roadside ditch will grow up to be a base-born varlet in his turn, no matter how much money is spent trying to make a gentleman of him."

"Tell me at least then, what then has become of my stepfather" I insisted, made bold by the hopelessness of my plight and fearing that some harm might have befallen him. At this Loodgieter relented somewhat.

"Vader Willenbrouckx was given leave by me to serve aboard the *Ann Royal* when we left Cadiz. They had many sick and wounded aboard and their surgeon, being overwhelmed by the

---

* "Good blood cannot lie"

number of them, begged that he might have your stepfather to help him since he knew him of old and thought highly of him. We had the *Fortuijn's* surgeon aboard along with the rest of her people, so I granted him a dispensation from his articles and he left us on secondment, though he remains part of the crew according to the muster roll. For all that I know he may now be back in Plymouth, because the last we heard of Lord Wimbledon's ships they were off the Scillies and in a most pitiable state from sickness and stress of weather. But all that matters not a jot to you in your present plight, which is a grave one indeed."

I derived some little comfort from this at least, that my stepfather was still alive, though either aboard another ship or even returned now to England, and (as Loodgieter had observed) that he was not there to see me in my present sorry and abject state, which would have been most distressing for him.

So we sat there awhile, with our bonds chafing and in great distress for want of drink since fighting and excitement make the mouth very dry. But when we begged some water from our captors for humanity's sake, they merely laughed, and swore that we would soon have more to drink than ever we wanted. At last we were hauled to our feet and bundled overboard, our hands still bound behind us, down into the *Eenhoorn's* longboat, where we lay on the bottom boards like so many sacks of turnips, which hardly seemed to augur well for our future. I wondered whether drowning were as painful a death as hanging, and thought in the end that there was probably little to choose between the two, only hoping that it would be over as soon as possible. I thought it a scurvy jest though, that I should be dealt with thus when I was still not quite fifteen years of age. But the rule aboard ships is that a boy becomes a man at fourteen years, and I had been paid a man's wage. So however much I might privately deplore my own death, matters were all fair and square according to the customs and usages of the sea. Then I heard from the voices forward that Captain Loodgieter had come with us in person to witness our execution. And I considered this very low conduct on his part, that he should not only command the death of his vanquished foes but come to see the sentence being carried out like a vindictive and unworthy person.

Still a faint hope lingered within my breast that since we had been put into the longboat rather than simply being tossed overboard, then the intention might be to land us at Vlissingen or some other Dutch port. And I hoped that if this were the case, then if we came before the magistrates ashore my youth might weigh in my favour and I be reprieved. Yet as soon as I had thought that thought, I unthought it again, for though I am no hero and never have been, it seemed to me on reflection that it would be a shabby thing, if I were to escape the gallows yet see my Dunkirker companions – who though pirates, had been my shipmates and would doubtless have stood by me in any fight – all strung up before my eyes for no other reason than that they were a month or two older than myself. And I resolved that I would sooner die with them than reproach myself for ever afterwards that, though as guilty as they were, I had escaped hanging when they had not.

At last after a half-hour or so the oars ceased to creak in the rowlocks and our longboat came to a stop. Then the casting overboard began. The fellows lying on the bottom boards nearest the stern were picked up one after another beneath the armpits by two lusty hands armed with stout cudgels – which they plied readily to quieten any struggling – and dragged to the raised platform at the stern, where they were flung overboard with a great splash, the two knaves then coming back for another one. I said the *Confiteor* to myself, knowing that my hour had come, and murmured a farewell to Maître Guyot who lay next to me, and he also to me, saying that I was a brave young fellow and it was great shame that I should end my days so prematurely, because he himself was an old man and his life almost over whereas I had all mine still before me; but if the stars ordained it, then so it must be. They took him, and overboard he went.

Then they picked me up, and I felt no fear but only a kind of peaceful stillness, as though death had half claimed me already, and wondered only whether I should exhale the air in my lungs all at once or fight to retain it as long as I could with the water darkening over my head and the curious fishes swimming about me as I sank into the depths, now examining me in their element as I had so often examined them in mine. As I neared the boat's stern sheets I saw that Captain Loodgieter was standing to watch with a great smile on his face, and this sickened me more than I can readily express.

"Look sharp about it!" he said. "There are still eight more of them and darkness will be upon us soon. Ah, Van Raveyck at last? Overboard with him, I say! One so young and from so good a family should have been more careful as to the company he kept. If the knave had lived longer he would doubtless have proved an even greater villain!"

"You injurious wretch!" I cried, "Not content with treating us worse than a cannibal would, you come to gloat over our drowning. You are a cruel and cowardly dog for all your finery, bloodier-handed than Nero or Caligula. I thought you once a hero, but now see you for a vain malicious coxcomb!" For these observations of mine I received a kick in the belly from one of the hands, which clean knocked the wind out of me, and was then flung overboard and landed in the water with a mighty splash.

At first the chill shock of it took my breath away and confusion filled my head as water did my mouth and lungs. I felt myself go under as the air left my garments, and relinquished my hold on life. But then after sinking somewhat, I realised with no small surprise that I was sinking no further: that my feet were supported, and that I was struggling myself upright and breathing air once more, not salt water. In the end, once the water had streamed from my eyes and I had coughed and spat out a great quantity of it, I discovered that I was standing up to my chest in a calm sea with oozy sand or fine gravel beneath my feet, and eight or so fellows about me in a similar plight with new ones being pitched into the sea to join us.

At last all had been heaved overboard, and we stood there shivering with cold and fright while Captain Loodgieter addressed us from the stern of the longboat like Christ preaching to the multitude on the Sea of Galilee.

"My apologies, mijne heren," he said, "for having treated you thus rudely, but I fear that my orders were quite specific. When I received my commission from the Zeeland Admiralty I had to swear an oath that in the event of my taking a Dunkirk privateer ship I would 'rinse the feet' of any that we took captive; and likewise that if I failed to do so I would be relieved of my command. However, the oath made no mention of the depth of water in which your feet were so to be rinsed; so I consider that I have now fulfilled both the exact terms of my oath, and the requirements of Christian charity. The tide is presently on the ebb with about two hours left to run, and the shore…" (here he pointed away behind us) "…is less than a mile distant, with the sands hereabouts so flat and firm you should have no difficulty wading ashore. The place is near Knokke on the Flanders coast, and that mound which you see in the distance on top of the dunes is Fort San Pablo which is the last Spanish outpost before our lines. So on your way then, you villains, before you all perish of cold. And thank your benevolent stars that it was Cornelis Adriaenszoon Loodgieter's ship that you so imprudently boarded and not my colleague Witte de With's, because Dubbelwitt would surely have strung you all from his yard-arms like so many partridges while his musicians played a merry jig to accompany your dancing. Adieu."

Here he gave us a farewell sweep of his hat, and replaced it as he made to sit down in the stern sheets. Then he turned back to us. "Oh, one small matter that I forgot: Van Raveyck, I will ignore your late remarks about me as having been uttered in the heat of the moment, and would remind you that your wages will be calculated by Meester Grobelaar up the date of your being taken prisoner at Cadiz. They and your stepfather's may be collected from the Admiralty in Middelburg after we pay off, which should be next week or the one thereafter. Likewise your notebook concerning the anatomy of fishes and other such creatures will be waiting there for you. Farewell then, and good fortune."

Before long the *Eenhoorn's* boat had dwindled to a speck in the distance. But we paid it no heed as we wallowed and splashed our way towards the Flanders shore, which exertion at least generated some animal heat to prevent us all perishing from the wintry chill of the water. Crabs several times pinched our feet, and we likewise stumbled into runnels and creeks in the sandy bottom, one man going under never to emerge again. But after an hour or so of wading across that flat, broad sandbank which is called the Paardenmarkt, we emerged at last, streaming water and with our teeth chattering, onto dry land. One of our fellows found the bonds around his wrists coming loose from their soaking, and was therefore able to untie the rest of us. Our salvation – because we would otherwise surely have perished from cold – was a fire lit on the strand by the soldiers from Fort San Pablo to boil cockles over, since they were wont to rake those shellfish up from the sands at low tide and sell them in the market at Bruges to make up the wages which (they said) had not been paid them for the past two years or more.

When we were warmed somewhat and had stopped shivering, our soaking-wet clothes steaming in the winter air, these same soldiers, who were Irishmen from Tyrconnell's Regiment and very hospitable to us poor castaways, took us up to the fort and gave us hot soup to eat and also a liquor called "uskebog" to revive us, which in their Celtic tongue means "water of life", though for me it was almost water of death when I swallowed a gulp of it, they having distilled it themselves from fermented potatoes to keep the Flanders ague at bay. Our hosts generously sent a messenger running ahead to the Governor of Bruges to tell him that we were come ashore naked and destitute, and requesting that he might send clothing and shoes for us. To which a reply came back next morning that we were a privateer crew and not from one of King Philip's ships; and that so as far as he was concerned we might therefore all go hang, adding (there being little love lost between those two towns) that it was no part of his duties to divert monies from the Bruges poor-chest to indemnify Dunkirk's failed business ventures. So we set off, shivering from cold and with our feet bound up in rags, to walk down the coast to Dunkirk.

A cold welcome awaited us there also, from the principal shareholders who had sunk much money into the *Zwarte Hond's* voyage and now had nothing to show for it: not even the ship itself, which we heard later was towed into Middelburg and auctioned as a prize. Their chagrin at us was so great, in fact, that they contrived to have us all arrested by the town magistrates and cast into prison on suspicion of having mutinied and murdered our officers, then burned the ship; and it was only when news came from Holland on Christmas Eve that the vessel had indeed been overmastered in a fight that they grudgingly set us free and allowed us to return penniless and in rags to our homes.

I was more fortunate than the rest of my companions in that I had a friendly house not far off to receive me. For the greffier's clerk who came to Dunkirk Gaol with the warrant for our release was none other than my old schoolmate Ghisbertus Lambrechts, who was earning some money from that office in order to fund his study of medicine at Louvain, his father (he told me) having the previous year suffered no small damage to his purse by reason of the government in Brussels defaulting on a contract for him to supply shoes to Spinola's army – which was news to me, that Houtenberg's most honourable town clerk was lately become a cobbler, but Lambrechts said that his father's part in it was but to furnish money on credit for others to manufacture the shoes, having himself first borrowed the money on the security of the very same shoes that were yet to be made; which I confess I found almost mysterious, but such are the ways of finance. The upshot of our meeting was that he took me with him back to Houtenburg, and there I spent the Christmas season staying with his family in their house on the Langestraat, which seemed no whit the poorer (I must say) for his father's recent troubles, though I later discovered that an outhouse was indeed packed to the rafters with soldiers' shoes. Mijnheer and Mevrouw Lambrechts treated me with every consideration, as though I were a long-lost son of their own now miraculously returned to them, giving me new clothes and shoes — several pairs of them in fact — to wear because I was now as ragged as the lousiest of vagrants and almost naked to the winter wind. And thus I spent the Christmas season with them in ease and jollity.

For all the warmth of my reception in their household, I was still in some trepidation as to how I would be received by the rest of Houtenburg. My recent deliverance from the Inquisition, and that I was a theoretical deserter from the army, bothered me not at all because the King of Spain's officials in Jerez had no idea (I surmised) of what had become of me and my guards during our journey to San Lucar, and must surely suppose us all to have been murdered by brigands along the way. And even if they did think to enquire after me in Flanders (which I doubted they ever would) it would take months for any warrant to arrive there. No, my concern had more to do with the sudden disappearance of my family almost four years previously, and with — for aught that I knew of it — the accusation of witchcraft still hanging over my parents' heads.

Though so far as I knew no charges attached to my own person, I having been a minor according to the law at the time of the offence, I still feared that I might be seized and questioned by the magistrates regarding my parents' flight. I discovered, though, to my great relief that nothing much of the affair seemed to have lingered in the town beyond a tavern-bench tale of the municipal surgeon and his wife and children being snatched away by the Devil one morning on the Bergues road; which though a foolish story, was no more foolish than all the rest of the ignorant fancies with which the vulgar sort commonly divert themselves; of ghosts, hobgoblins, buried treasure and wonders of every kind. I learned that word had very soon got back to the more sober part of the townspeople that we were now resident in England; and since fleeing to another town to avoid arrest for crimes like doodslag* was an everyday affair in the Low Countries, it seemed no great wonder that people might do it likewise to escape arrest for witchcraft.

People greeted me on the streets with every sign of amity and remarked how I was grown into a fine handsome young fellow during my time in England where the air and diet plainly suited me, and how did it go with Mijnheer Willenbrouckx and my lady your mother: both of whom they would no doubt have watched a few years before being roasted alive on the meadow below the Galgenheuvel with perfect equanimity. As to the charge of witchcraft against my mother – who was now dead anyway – I discovered that this had soon fallen into abeyance from the lack of anyone much interested in prosecuting it. The Prevôt de Coqueville was now likewise dead some two years or more, having suffered a sudden apoplexy while presiding over a witch-burning in Cassel, which the onlookers took to be an infallible sign from God of the woman's innocence and had rushed to pour buckets of water over the flames.

After a few days in Houtenburg recovering my spirits – for to have been tossed overboard to drown is a mighty unsettling matter, say what you will – I went to our family's attorney Maître Delvaux to enquire after our affairs, which he had faithfully overseen during my stepfather's absence.

"Well, young fellow," he said as I sat in his office, "you are certainly not without the means to support yourself if you choose to remain with us in Houtenburg. Your stepfather's surgical practice was rented out following his sudden departure, and the monies derived therefrom – and also from the farm at Langebroek which he received as dowry from his first wife – have accumulated in my coffers over the three years, deductions being made each quarter only to pay the stipend to your half-brother in Leiden."

"So might my stepfather now return to Houtenburg?" I enquired.

---

* Involuntary homicide.

"Of course", he replied, "The warrant for arrest on suspicion of witchcraft was against your poor late mother, not against Monsieur Willenbrouckx himself. She is dead now and beyond the law, so the only charge that might persist against him is that of having aided the escape of a suspect. But I am sure that with the Prevôt de Coqueville now dead as well, the seigneur's court would be little inclined to pursue the warrant, and applying a little tincture of silver to the itching palms of certain court officials would soon resolve the matter beyond all peradventure. But where is your stepfather at the moment, if I might ask?"

I replied that so far as I knew, he was aboard the English flagship the *Ann Royal*, which had been reported off the Scillies two weeks before, and was now presumably lying at Plymouth, so that I thought we would soon have word from him, his intention being to return to Colchester as soon as he was ashore, be reunited with my sister who was presently lodged with Cousin Bourchier's household, then take up once more the surgical practice that he had been forced to abandon that spring.

"And what are your own intentions?" he asked.

I said that after all the upheavals and commotions of the last eight months I desired nothing so fervently in all the world as to rejoin my stepfather just as soon as ever I could and resume my apprenticeship with him; not least because his eyesight was beginning to grow dim and I would soon be required to take over the business from him. As to the house in Houtenburg and the lands nearby, I thought that he would probably wish for these to go on being rented out until such time as Regulus finished his apprenticeship, but we might then sell them and move our entire estate across to England, my stepfather having prospered there beyond all expectation because of the prevalence of bladder stone in that country, which seemed like to go on furnishing us with good business for as long as we lived.

"I am sorry to hear that," he said at last, "Your stepfather was an ornament to this town, as was your poor late mother despite the foolish calumnies that were raised against her. A fine young fellow such as yourself might one day grace the office of town surgeon, and your stepbrother's skill as a painter might likewise help to restore Houtenburg's battered fortunes were he to set up his workshop here, as Meester Rubens has lately done in Antwerp. But having so foolishly driven you all out with their gossip and malicious tittle-tattle, these Flanders péquenauds can scarcely complain if you now choose to dwell in another country. All I can say of the matter is, that Houtenburg's loss is Colchester's gain."

★ ★ ★ ★ ★ ★ ★ ★ ★ ★

Frans left Maître Delvaux and returned to the house of the Lambrechts family; not least (it must be admitted) out of a desire to be once again in the company of Ghisbertus's pretty young sister Artemise, a bright little creature of thirteen years with merry dark brown eyes like those of a robin and the beginnings of a woman's figure. Two days passed in pleasant dalliance and the making of music, for Artemise already played exquisitely upon the virginals while Frans accompanied her on the bass viol. But on the morning of the Feast of the Three Kings there was an urgent banging on the street door. It was a boy with a message from Maître Delvaux, politely requesting that Frans should come to see him at once on a matter of some gravity.

Frans laid aside his viol, seized his cloak (for it was now snowing hard) and strode through the icy streets to the maître's house, where he was greeted with a solemn countenance that boded little good.

"Sit down if you will, young man," The attorney had already poured a glass of madeira wine for him, which seemed to augur even worse. "I fear that I have bad news for you, and you must brace yourself to hear it." He picked up a paper from his desk and adjusted his reading spectacles. "I have here a letter that came to me this morning from Calais. It was written some three weeks ago at a place called Kinsale, which I believe is on the southern coast of Ireland, and was penned by the chaplain of the king's ship

Ann Royal, a certain Doctor Brundell, who seems to be a learned gentleman since he writes Latin so elegantly." He swallowed hard, and drew breath. "He writes, that your stepfather is dead."

He looked up to see that as he expected, the colour had suddenly drained from Frans's normally rosy countenance. "Permit me to read to you what he writes," He coughed:

"Written aboard His Majesty's ship 'Ann Royal' lying at Kinsale the 26th day of December anno domini 1625.

To whom it may concern
It is my sad duty, being chaplain to the fleet and aboard this vessel lately engaged in the expedition to Cadiz on the coast of Spain, to report the death of that excellent man and most esteemed friend Mister Michel de Willenbrouckx of Colchester in Essex and Houtenburg in the county of Flanders, who quit this earthly life on the evening of the twenty-fourth of December here at Kinsale, carried off by the spotted fever that has in recent weeks claimed so many others throughout this fleet now arrived, by God's mercy, in safe harbour after so many tribulations.

Mister Willenbrouckx came aboard this vessel of his own inestimable Christian charity and by special invitation of Viscount Wimbledon when we lay off Cadiz, having previously been surgeon aboard a Dutch vessel, by reason of the great numbers of sick and wounded that were to be cared for, which quite surpassed the capacity of our own surgeons and their assistants. This task he performed with most admirable devotion, winning the esteem of all around him even to the common soldiers and seamen, whom he treated alike, dressing their wounds and comforting the dying without the smallest regard to their rank or degree.

We reached the Scilly Islands after being sorely battered all the way by storm and tempest, and thought we were safe at last. But there he fell sick, and died the same evening that we dropped an-

chor here at Kinsale. He was taken ashore to be buried along with many others in Kinsale churchyard, and it was my sad last duty as his friend and companion in misfortune to accompany him to his resting place, and afterwards to gather up his belongings, which I shall consign to his heirs once I have an address to which they may be sent.

In God's grace
William Brundell, Divinitatis Doctoris"

He put down the letter, then got up to walk round his desk and place his arm round the shoulders of the boy, who was by now weeping bitterly.

"There, there young fellow, all that lives is fated to die; good men just as surely as scoundrels. You stepfather, may God rest his soul, died as he lived and as I am sure he would have wished to have died, in the service of others and caring for his fellow sufferers in this vale of tears – but I am sure making less noise than many another philanthropist would do, since he told me it always made him sick to see how those who succoured the poor made such a great show of it. But come back here tomorrow when you are recovered a little from your grief, and we shall talk about how to order your stepfather's affairs. With both your parents dead your half-brother is now head of the family, and must be apprised of the fact as soon as a letter can be got to him in Leiden. He will need to come here to talk with me concerning your father's will and the disposition of his property, and also the arrangements to be made for your sister until she comes of age. Tell me, is it your wish to have a chantry endowed for the saying of Masses for the repose of your parents' souls?" Frans gulped through his sobs that he had no thoughts as yet in the matter. At which the lawyer, seeing that enough had been said for the moment, ushered him out into the frozen streets of the little town.

A cutting east wind blew and snow fell earnestly from the low slate-coloured sky as he made his way back to the Lambrechts' house. As he entered and shook the snow off his cloak Artemise greeted him with joy – but saw at once that something was dreadfully wrong. "What ails you?" she asked as she took his cloak. Without saying a word he thrust the letter into her hands, which she being a well-educated girl who knew not only Latin but also Greek and some Hebrew, took and read with eyes that widened in dismay. She laid the letter aside; but being as tactful as she was wise, said nothing and only clasped his hands in hers. He brushed her aside without a word, then took the bass viol and bow from the side table where he had left them, adjusted the strings and sat down to play. It was Mister Dowland's sad, sweet pavane *Lachrimæ Antiquæ* which had become so popular over the previous twenty years that every musician in Christendom knew it by heart. And without saying anything (for words would have been superfluous) she adjusted her skirts and sat down to the virginals to accompany him, since she also knew that piece well enough to have no need of a music book.

And so they played together as the short winter's day faded into evening. Far away, beneath two feet of hastily shovelled earth in an Irish graveyard, Michel Willenbrouckx lay stiff and cold amid a tangle of dead men's limbs all mottled blue and green, tumbled together into the pit naked but for their filthy shirts and without even shrouds let alone coffins, so great was the multitude of them: some dead of gangrenous wounds, others poisoned by rotten food or worn out by weeks of labouring cold and wet aboard the leaking storm-battered ships – but most of them from the spotted fever which had come aboard at Plymouth with the gaolbirds delivered in their lousy rags, and which had then spread stealthily as dry rot through the crowded orlop decks to explode like a bomb on the return journey among the ill-nourished, dispirited wretches packed together in their great creaking wooden prisons. The ones interred on land at Kinsale were but the afterthought and remnants; those unfortunate enough not to have succumbed earlier and been put over the side out in the Bay of Biscay. The fleet's processional route back from Cadiz to the Scillies was now lined with King Charles's soldiers: in the black depths of the ocean a mile or more down where they stood swaying in the current with ballast stones tied to their feet to spare the expense of roundshot, the hagfish already stripping the flesh from their bones, and the crabs then ready to devour the bones themselves so that before long nothing would remain to mark their twenty or thirty years of earthly existence but two hastily scratched entries; one in a parish register and the other on a muster roll; the latter now with a line drawn through it.

Fifteen thousand had sailed from Plymouth that October morning. And now less than ten thousand had returned, and even those disease-ridden and famished, put ashore at last unpaid and in rags to make their way home as best they could, spreading beggary, disease and highway robbery throughout the counties of Devon and Somerset so that before long troops of armed gentlemen on horseback had to be raised by the local magistrates to deal with them, much as the Corregidor of Jerez had raised troops of armed gentlemen on horseback to deal with them at Cadiz. It was a sorry end to the young King's first essay in foreign policy, and in Parliament when it reassembled after New Year those who had once been loudest in calling for war with Spain – though usually the most reluctant to dig into their pockets to finance it – now called for Buckingham's impeachment as the price for his mismanagement; or failing that, then at least the hanging of his familiars and accomplices such as Sir James Bagg, whose rotten provisions (men said) had killed a score for every one that the Spaniard slew.

In the great cabin of his weather-battered, crumbling old flagship now lying at anchor in the Downs with six feet of water in her hold; tired, ill and haggard by failure, Viscount Wimbledon sat down to pen a letter to his sovereign – though as much in answer to the street balladeers and those in Parliament who were now calling for his head to be forfeit. It concluded:

"... *For more ignorant captains and officers Your Majesty could hardly have found, or men more careless of Your Majesty's honour and profit as though they were rather your enemies than servants, studying their own ease and commodity above all other things, which had they not done then we might have accomplished far more; the sea-officers being so bent upon thievery and cozenage that they have rather combined in knavery with their mariners than corrected them."*

The letter was duly signed, sealed and sent ashore, and arrived two days later at Whitehall Palace where it was placed on the King's desk by his Secretary of State Sir John Coke. The King glanced through it in that disconcertingly offhand way that he had, as though none of it were really any concern of his, then put it down with a petulant little sigh of resignation, as if to say that it was no more than he would have expected. His only comment was, "Plainly, Wimbledon has not such qualities as we would have wished for in a general." In any case, he had more pressing matters to attend to now than failed expeditions. The war with Spain having gone so ill, My Lord Buckingham – on whose advice the King relied implicitly in all matters – now proposed to remedy the situation by seeking war with France as well...

And in a small house in a street in Wapping by the Thames a woman sat waiting for the return of her sailor husband, a master gunner aboard Sir William Saint Leger's *Convertive*; now dead from spotted fever and put over the side several weeks before, though that news had still to reach her. She sang a lullaby to her baby lying in its cradle:

"There was a monkey climbed a tree,
When he fell down then down fell he.
There was a crow perched on a stone,
When he flew off, then perched there none.
There was a fleet went out to Spain,
It went there and came back again."

CHAPTER SIXTEEN

I will not deny that the news of my stepfather's forlorn death there off the coast of Ireland unmanned me and left me prostrated by my grief for several days afterwards, so that all the consolations that the Lambrechts household could offer were in vain. I refused all nourishment and would surely have starved to death, had it not been for the distraction of music that sweet Artemise provided me with (for words, however kindly meant, would merely have deepened my sadness) which dragged me at last of the slough of despair into which I had sunk. My readers may consider this unmanly of me to confess. But so great was the love and reverence with which I had come to regard my stepfather that his death was to me as though all on a sudden the sun had been extinguished in the heavens and darkness was fallen over all the Earth. But I was now just turned fifteen years of age, on the edge of man's estate, fair of countenance and vigorous in body, with the whole wide world before me; and the vital fluids will rise in a young tree in springtime though all the branches have been lopped off the previous autumn. By the Feast of Saint Agnes I was pretty well myself again: an orphan now to be sure, but reconciled to that estate since I still had a half-brother and full-sister whom I loved dearly; and was likewise far from having been left destitute and naked in the world by my parents dying within five months one of the other, but instead had a sizeable inheritance to support me. So in the end, though my grief while it lasted was very profound, I spent but little time a-grieving, and resolved rather to proceed with my life as bravely as I could, which I thought was what my stepfather and my mother would both have wanted, they both being folk of a practical disposition and neither of them much inclined to spend their days in vain languishing.

Some practical matters, however, had first to be set in order in Houtenburg, in which the Maître Delvaux was of the greatest assistance to me as we rustled among dusty old parchments concerning the farm at Langebroek. By the middle of February all was settled at last; so my most pressing concern now was to make my way to Leiden to consult with Regulus, with whom at present I could only communicate but indirectly and laboriously by reason of the war, my letters having to go to Calais, thence to Margate, then by the packet boat to Vlissingen, which meant that they might take several weeks on their journey if the winds were contrary.

The main question now at issue was that of my own future, for I was still but three years into my seven years' apprenticeship as a surgeon, and had now been made masterless by the death of my stepfather, which meant that to continue my studies and gain my licence I would have to find myself another master for the four years that remained. Money was not the rub here: I was assured of an income from the rents of the family's property in Houtenburg. But the surgical practice in Colchester was now plainly defunct by reason of my father's death. Doctor de Brantôme was most cordial when I wrote to him (he having by now returned to England), and assured me that I would be welcome to work for him once I had my licence; but I must obtain that first. So in the end I elected to seek a new master in the Dutch provinces; for preference in Leiden where I was assured of lodgings with Regulus and where I might afterwards go on to study physic at the university. My reason for deciding this was that my long colloquies with Maître Guyot aboard the *Zwarte Hond* concerning his hermetic philosophy had led me to see that medicine and surgery are two faces of the same healing art, not the one a learned science and the other a mere empirical craft as the physicians maintain, and that to practise the one of them to good effect I must needs be familiar with the other; yes, and even the manual trade of pharmacy as well, since I had already observed that as many patients are hurt as are healed by a physician's ignorant prescriptions made up by an equally ignorant apothecary.

Mijnheer and Mevrouw Lambrechts beseeched me to remain in Flanders and apprentice myself to a surgeon in Ypres or some such nearby town so that I might stay among them. They had already noticed the affection and affinity that Artemise and I had for one another, and foresaw that I might make a suitable marriage party for her once I had my surgeon's licence in my pocket, since they greatly loved their daughter and desired her happiness as much as her material comfort. But Flanders had no university nearer than Louvain, which was reputed – and Ghisbertus Lambrechts confirmed as much to me – to be very encrusted and old-fashioned in its teaching of physic, condemning Paracelsus entirely out of hand and scarce admitting even Vesalius through its doors. Leiden's anatomists, by contrast, were now renowned as the most learned in Europe. So I resisted the blandishments of my hosts, well-meaning though they were, and set my gaze towards the north, beyond the ramparts and entrenchments along the Scheldt where Spain and the United Provinces fought their interminable battles, quarrelling and snarling over the petty townships of Flanders and Brabant like two curs in the gutter disputing a bone. If I remained among the willow groves and fenny meadows around Houtenburg I would (I perceived) remain for the rest of my days a bumpkin surgeon among bumpkins in a poor little bumpkin town, pulling their rotten bumpkin teeth and stitching up their bumpkin heads cracked in bumpkin brawls outside bumpkin alehouses; tending hurts caused just as often by their own clownish stupidity as by blind misfortune. I was fluent not just in Flemish and French but in English, Spanish and Latin as well, of lively understanding and quick perception, and likewise now become (or so at least I fancied myself) an erudite and much travelled man of the world who had braved all manner of perils on land and at sea. Though I was fond of Artemise and she likewise of me, I still envisaged a prospect for myself somewhat more elevated that that of being one day municipal surgeon in Hazendonck or Wustwezel with the townsfolk doffing their hats to me in the market and bidding me good-morrow Meester van

Raveyck, while I wondered how I might best cajole them towards settling their bill.

During my weeks in Houtenberg, once I had recovered from my bitter grief, I was a great celebrity with the Lambrecht household and the whole of the town's better sort beside, gentlefolk coming in their carriages from far afield of an evening to have me recount to them my adventures with Viscount Wimbledon's expedition, in gaol in Jerez and aboard the *Zwarte Hond* etc. etc. They all sat wide-eyed listening to me as I related all this – or at least, *almost* all of it, for naturally out of respect for the modesty of the female portion of my audience, and likewise for Artemise's good opinion of me, I omitted to mention my transactions with the fisherman's wife on the Isle of León (since for a boy of fifteen to admit to having lain with a woman twice his age would have been considered most scandalous) and likewise my condemnation to five years' servitude in the galleys, which should it become public knowledge in Houtenburg, might well put me in bad odour with the law. For my audience, though, the fact that I had served aboard ships of the Dutch Republic against our sovereign lord King Philip IV, and was likewise a fugitive from his army, seemed not to offend them in the slightest. The lately resumed war with the Hollanders – and now a new war with England for good measure – were proving most deleterious to the trade and prosperity of Flanders which had been dragged (they said) into a brawl not of its own formenting, and was now required to pay heavy taxes to support King Philip's army as well as suffering all the depredations and wanton violence of his soldiers billeted on its towns and villages, so that folk already muttered beneath their breath that the Spanish Netherlands might do well to be shot of Spain once and for all like the Hollanders, and it was only the thought of their being obliged to throw in their lot with those money-grubbing Calvinistic blackguards north of the Scheldt that had prevented them from doing it already.

But beneath all the admiration and wonderment of the townspeople, I detected that there was some envy and resentment against me as well, which is commonly the lot of those who escape from petty little towns into the great wide world and then return to them again. All manner of calumnies began to spread like weeds in the cracks between paving stones: the story of my mother's accusation for witchcraft, and behind it the old half-remembered tales of my being Ravaillac's child, the red-haired offspring of that monstrous regicide. Some people made the sign of the cross as I passed them in the street, or flourished talismans against sorcery. And when I went to Saint Wulverga's Church to arrange for a regular chantry Mass to be said for the repose of my parents' souls, the young canon there (who was new to his post and a great fanatic, having studied divinity at Salamanca) spurned the money I offered him and instead told me roundly that my stepfather was a godless heretic (for word of his attending Anglican services in England had reached Houtenberg some time since) and was now roasting for ever in a pit of hell so deep that no amount of money and chantry masses might ever buy him out of it. Whilst concerning my late mother, that most godly young man declared that from what he had heard of her she was plainly a witch (though never actually convicted and burnt as such, more was the pity) and was widely known to have had congress with Satan himself in the guise of the vile king-murderer Ravaillac, of which foul coupling I myself was commonly reputed to be the fruit, and furthermore that I had red hair like my iniquitous father as a mark of my reprobation. And (he added for good measure) his predecessor Canon Blanchard had assured him that when I was baptised at the church's font, the water in it turned to blood and the effigy of Our Lord fell from its cross above the altar. All of which I took to be a refusal on his part, so I thanked him politely for his time and patience, and went instead to the Church of the Holy Blood down the street where the priest fairly snatched my hand off with the coins still in it, and I think would have done the same if the Devil himself had requested a chantry Mass.

* * * * * * * * *

In the final days of February 1626 Frans said farewell to the Lambrechts family, thanking them for their hospitality, and set out to walk to Calais. From there he took ship for Dover, then sailed aboard a hoy to Queenborough on the Medway, where he boarded the packet for Vlissingen. The vessel reached the coast of Zeeland three days later, and he came ashore to make his way on foot to the town of Middelburg in order to collect his own back wages and his stepfather's from the admiralty pay office. The *Eenhoorn*, he learned, had now landed her guns at the arsenal quay and paid off for the winter. Her crew, however, still lingered in Middelburg waiting for Their Lordships of the Admiralty College to find the money to redeem their pay tickets, and likewise disgorge the prize money due from the captures of the *Nuestra Señora* and the *Zwarte Hond*. This latter victory had contributed a sizeable sum since, in addition to the normal prize money, the States-General's bounty on the head of Jacques Coussemakker still stood despite the lapse of twenty-three years. Captain Loodgieter was reported to have journeyed to The Hague carrying that grisly trophy with him in a bag to display to Their Excellencies gathered in plenary session – and mighty glad the weather was so cold too (Master Grobelaar said) because the head was already starting to smell and to ooze putrescent fluids despite having been left outside over Christmastide packed with snow in a butter-firkin.

Frans went next day to the admiralty pay office on the Loskade – and found that the entire complement of the *Eenhoorn* was gathered there in the street as well, along with the crews of a dozen other ships besides: all of them in an ugly and restive mood because they had just been informed that there was no money to pay them and they must come back the following week; or at Eastertide; or at Midsummer; or at the next blue moon. Stones were already flying and window glass tinkling on to the cobblestones as an official arrived from the admiralty building further up the quay, ominously accompanied by a dozen musketeers with lighted matches. And just in time as well, because some sailors were manoeuvring a twelve-pounder cannon up on to the canal dyke opposite the pay office, and were only prevented from firing it by the local shopkeepers refusing to sell them gunpowder. Being as silver-tongued a rascal as jurists usually are, the official beguiled the simple mariners with promises of payment the following week when abundant coin (he said) would arrive from The Hague, and they dispersed, grumbling mightily the while and saying it was great shame that poor sailor men should be treated so, who had risked their necks and strained their backs in the Republic's service lying out on the yards in all weathers and facing the enemy's shot. So for the time being Frans took a room at an inn, sharing the cost with Matthias Sigurdsson and two of his fellow Norwegians. Then at last, the following Tuesday, word came to them that chests of Spanish silver reals had just been delivered to the pay office under armed guard, and they must all hasten there to redeem their tickets before Their Lordships thought better of it. After several hours of standing in line in the bitter weather with sweaty fellows smoking clay pipes and spitting into the gutter, Frans came at last to the massive oaken screen and the little window covered by a stout iron grille.

"Name?" the pay clerk demanded.

"I would like to draw pay for two persons…

"So would we all; and that rainwater were beer and there were two Sundays in every week. I asked you your name."

"Van Raveyck: Frans."

"Your ship and your charge aboard her?"

"The pinnace *Eenhoorn* of Captain Loodgieter. And in the offices of barber, surgeon's mate and ziekentrooster."

The clerk ran his ink-stained finger down the list of names.

"Yes, here we are: four full months at eighteen guilders the month. And two short months totalling eighteen days, since you are listed here as absent, believed dead or captive, on the 4th of November. So that makes eighty-two guilders and nineteen stuivers to your account." The clerk wrote out a ticket, and Frans took it then started to move towards another queue which would take him eventually to the even more heavily grilled window where the money would be paid out.

"Not so fast, young fellow" the clerk said, calling him back. "There's the small matter of prize money as well. I see here that the sum of thirty-three guilders is listed against your name in respect of the frigate *Nuestra Señora*. And a further twenty-two for the Dunkirk privateer *Zwarte Hond*."

Frans was speechless for a moment, then said bewildered, "But I was not aboard the *Eenhoorn* when the Dunkirker was taken..." (omitting, however, to mention the small fact that on that occasion he had been aboard the ship which was taken, not the one which had been doing the taking).

The clerk snorted with impatience: he had stood here all morning explaining the workings of the pay office to these dull-witted tarpaulins who could barely count to ten, or perhaps twenty if they first removed their shoes and stockings. Yet again he drew a deep breath.

"Whether or not you were *aboard* the vessel in bodily form at that time makes no difference as far as the calculation of prize money is concerned: you were listed on the ship's muster roll, so you are entitled to your share as stated in your articles and that's the end of the matter."

"Er...thank you: you are most kind..."

The clerk lifted his eyes to the ceiling and drummed his fingers on the desk with exasperation.

"Don't *thank* me, jongen: the money is yours by right, otherwise you wouldn't be receiving it."

"I apologise; but I was not aboard the *Eenhoorn* at the time, so I failed to see how I could be entitled to prize money."

The clerk gazed into his eyes, pitying. "Young fellow, let me tell you something that may be of use to you in later life. You will often be punished without your being guilty of any dereliction, because the regulations for service at sea laid down by the Their Excellencies the States-General and Their Lordships of the Zeeland Admiralty work that way. So on the rare occasions when those same regulations that punish you without deserving, also operate to reward you without merit, my advice is to take what they give you in a suitably grateful spirit and ask no questions. Now, did you say something about collecting pay on behalf of a second party?"

"I did: for my stepfather who is now dead."

"Do you have proof of his decease?"

Frans handed the pay clerk Doctor Brundell's letter written at Kinsale, thrusting it beneath the grille. The clerk screwed up his eyes and made a face – plainly his Latin was rusty from long disuse – but at last he pushed it back and made the entry *A.D.*, signifying "afgemonsterd dood"* against the name "*Michel Willenbrouckx: chirurgijn*" on the *Eenhoorn's* muster roll. He then wrote out a ticket for no less than one hundred and fifty-five guilders, plus one hundred and sixty-two guilders' prize money, and pushed his quill pen through the grille so that Frans might counter-sign the entry in the ledger. Their Lordships of the Admiralty College of the Province of Zeeland had no further call upon the services of either the deceased surgeon or his relict apprentice, and both were now free to make their way wheresoever they pleased in this world or the next.

★ ★ ★ ★ ★ ★ ★ ★ ★ ★

In the third week of February, while I was still lodged with the Lambrechts household in Houtenburg, there came a letter from my half-brother Regulus. Learning of our father's death and the consequent breaking of my apprenticeship only three years into it, he had made enquiry in Leiden and had found me a place as an apprentice for four years to a surgeon of that town who had lately lost his own apprentice, almost the same age as myself, through the accident of the boy falling through a hole in the ice while skating on a canal and dying of the cold before he could be pulled out.

---

* Discharged dead.

Even though my thoughts might (he wrote) incline me to study in Paris or in London, Leiden, though a small place and lacking the prestige of those two royal cities, was home nowadays to some of the most accomplished surgeons in the whole world; and likewise to a university school of anatomy which far from debarring mere vulgar mechanicals as the Sorbonne or Louvain still did, instead encouraged them *pro bono publico* to attend dissections in its fine new anatomy theatre. Also (he added) Leiden had an unrivalled supply of subjects for anatomising, since Holland was a small province and its waterways provided quick transportation, and its climate was likewise cool enough to slow the process of decomposition, and the magistrates were nowadays most accommodating of the needs of anatomists in having malefactors wherever possible hanged rather than broken on the wheel or burned, which penalties rendered their bodies quite unfit for dissecting afterwards. In short, Regulus considered that a surgeon's licence issued by the Leiden guild would be as prestigious as any that could be obtained in the world, and he had therefore secured me a meeting with Meester Lukas van Backhuysen, a surgeon practising on the Boterstraat in that town. So after I had collected my own wages and my father's from the pay office in Middelburg, pausing only to remit the money we owed him to the Ridder van Grobbendonck in Bergen op Zoom along with a letter of thanks, I departed next morning on the packet schuit for Schiedam on the River Maas en route for Leiden.

As I stepped ashore on the quayside of Leiden by the Galgewater I found Regulus waiting there for me, which is one of the many advantages of those Dutch beurtvaart ships departing at regular and published times (which was never the case before): that folk, knowing more or less when they will depart, also know more or less when they will arrive. We fell into one another's arms and wept for joy, having not seen one another in nearly five years. Then we went straight to his lodgings on the Mandenmakerssteeg near the Weigh House which he had been renting since the previous autumn, he being now in the final year of his apprenticeship and Meester van Meppel having granted him a derogation from those terms in his indenture which obliged him to sleep under his master's roof and eat at his table.

Regulus was now almost twenty years old and grown quite the man; very grave and handsome in his suit of black velveteen with the neatly starched ruff, which was in truth a little démodé now, but suited him well enough and made him look somewhat older than his years with his blond beard and close-cropped hair. He said that to be a painter here in Holland was a serious and worthy trade like that of shipwright or master glazier, and that if he wished to be admitted to the Guild of Saint Luke next year then he must dress as soberly as the town's other painters did and not trick himself out in ribbons and lace like some gadabout dice player and frequenter of taverns. His not attending divine service each Sunday (he being still a steadfast Catholic) had been remarked upon, and though the Guild was disposed to look through its fingers since he was from Flanders and had therefore been born and brought up in the popish confession (which is not persecuted in the Dutch provinces, but Catholics had still better be mighty discreet about it), he must needs be on his best behaviour in all other respects.

Though we were still in mourning for our parents, he sent out to a cookshop nearby to have a supper brought for us, and also a jug of wine since he said that the Prodigal Son having returned, it behoved him to kill the fatted calf (which I took to be part of the store of scriptural allusions that he was laying up for future employment in his paintings, along with a whole attic full of ones drawn from the Greek and Roman authors). So we spent that evening and the days that followed in merriment and good companionship as he showed me round the town and all its sights; and in particular the university with its host of students from all nations, for though scarce half a century old the place was already much renowned for the excellence of its teaching. We went to the anatomy theatre, where we saw a hanged criminal dissected by the famous Doctor Jan Deijman, and were shown the tanned hide of another felon, and also a wondrous array of the mounted skeletons of men and beasts; likewise the *hortus botannicus**, the astronomical observatory and all the other appurtenances and purlieus of learning, which together made a very great impression on me since I had never before seen a town so devoted to the pursuit of knowledge. Leiden is not itself of very large size: about the extent of Colchester I should think, and ringed round by its canals or "grachten" with a great mound in the middle, the Burcht, said once to have had a Roman fort on top of it, on the banks of the Old Rhine River which now loses itself inconsequentially among the sand dunes behind Katwijk, but in the days when it debouched straight into the North Sea, was the northern frontier of their empire.

For all its modest size Leiden is a prodigiously busy place by reason of its university and likewise because of its draperies: the weaving of wool and linen, and also lately of cotton fibres brought from the Levant. And these cotton stuffs are woven and dyed by the townsfolk with such niceness and ingenuity that the weavers and dyers in those countries where the cotton grows could scarce do it better. The populousness and constant bustle of Leiden were very attractive to me, having never lived before in so industrious a place; and Colchester was but a sleepy market town by comparison. Everything there was new, the whole town forever rebuilding itself, while the looms clacked day and night, with scarce an idle person to be seen anywhere; not least because if any man or woman so much as paused on street corner to scratch their ear the Leiden magistrates would seize them for idleness and fling them into the Tuchthuis (which is a sort of house of correction for beggars) to earn their bread by rasping brazil wood to powder for the cloth dyers with a great saw. In that remarkable town even the whores have the outward aspect of busy housewives, so great is the public horror of laziness, and when they go soliciting must needs do so with a basket under their arm as though they were on their

---

* Botanical garden

way to market, though they signal their true business – which is offering goods for sale, not buying them – by a quick twitching aside of their apron.

It disquieted me somewhat at first that my brother seemed already to be on cordial terms with several of these harlots, and I wondered also why it was that their faces, when he greeted them in the market, appeared strangely familiar to me already – until I realised that they were the models for the goddesses and nymphs in the paintings that lined the walls of Meester van Meppel's workshop, and perceived that they were harder for me to recognise with their clothes on than with them off. Thus I did not at first connect the canvas on the wall of my brother's chambers and its demure Saint Catherine with her eyes turned heavenwards as the executioner stood by, sword in hand, with the furious doxy we passed the next evening by the Galgewater as she belaboured a drunken sailor about the head and shoulders with a malt shovel "... because the poxy son of a whore had torn her ruff, and she would whack his lousy head for it until the pus from his boils spattered the walls or her name was not Antje Kwaadekont!"* My stepbrother bade her good evening, she paused in her beating to curtsy and bid him good-evening Meester Willenbrouckx, then resumed her drubbing of the sailor with such ferocity that I wondered how the executioner would have fared if she had been the *real* St Catherine.

Regulus considered, though, that despite the many attractions of Leiden, he would return to Flanders for his compagnonage, because he suspected that in the longer run that province might be more favourable to his muse than the Dutch Republic, since his own taste (he confessed) inclined towards the grand antique style full of gods and shepherdesses, whereas the Hollanders, having no royal court to guide and uplift them by its example, were nowadays much besotted with idle depictions of herring merchants and their fat blowsy wives or boors carousing in wayside taverns

---

* "Bad-arse Annie"

to the great detriment of true painting, the purpose of which is to exalt the spectator by the depiction of high moral precepts and scenes of ancient virtue, rather than offering maltsters and cheesemongers a looking-glass in which to behold the reflection of their own foolish faces. He acknowledged that the Dutch painters were mighty skilful rogues and could depict an apple so perfectly that a man might reach out and try to take a bite from it before he realised it was but a simulacrum. But the purpose of painting (he maintained) was not just the artfulness with which an object is represented, but also the judicious choice of that object. Or as he expressed it, "a turd painted with the most exquisite skill that ever was, is still but a turd, and only directs our thoughts downwards that we may not step in it, whereas a *Hector and Achilles* or a *Samaritan Woman at the Well*, be it never so clumsily painted, lifts our gaze upwards and arouses us to virtuous emulation." But he freely admitted that there was much to learn from the Hollanders as regards technique, so he thought he would stay among them for the time being and acquire all the skills that he could, then bid them adieu and move to Antwerp or Brussels where there were far more lucrative commissions to be had from the Archduchess's court and the Church than might ever be found in a republic full of plebeian merchants.

On the Thursday of that week, having taken several days to re-acquaint myself with my stepbrother after so long a separation (which I hope the reader will forgive in two such young men who had not seen one another for several years, and me having so much to relate of my own adventures) I betook myself once more to serious business, and brushed up my clothes, donned a freshly starched and ironed collar of suitably sober cut, then set out to meet with Meester van Backhuysen the surgeon in his fine brick house *De Krokodijl* on the Boterstraat. He greeted me most cordially, and had the housemaid (for he was a widower) bring Canary wine and some almond biscuits to refresh me, which I considered very hospitable of him until I saw that the girl had also deposited a little Delft-ware saucer on the table beside the tray, and when I asked her the purpose of it, was told that I was expected to put a couple of stuivers into it by way of payment, which is the custom among the Hollanders and was (I confess) not a little repugnant to me at first, used as I was to our freer and more open-handed ways in Flanders. I perceived meanwhile by the howls from the operating room that my prospective master was at work, and had to wait fifteen or twenty minutes before he finished his task, which was the excising of a polyp from a fishmonger's neck and then cauterising it, and came to speak with me still in his leather apron, wiping his bloody hands on a towel. He was a short, bald-headed fellow of about forty and already wore spectacles to correct his sight. He asked about my antecedents, and read a number of letters of reference, including one from Doctor de Brantôme (which I saw impressed him in no small measure since it was written in French and in finest court script) testifying to my gravity and manual dexterity, and to my knowledge in the area of lithotomy which had been my late stepfather's particular art: likewise making reference to the gentleman's wife whose nose I had so deftly stitched back on again the previous Christmas when I was but fourteen.

"You must realise of course, young fellow," he said, "that we perform little enough lithotomy here in Leiden. That procedure is more common in the great sea-ports like Amsterdam, since mariners are particularly liable to the stone by reason of the saltiness of their diet, of too little fresh water and too much strong drink and – though I hesitate to mention it to one so young, yet we are surgeons and must be men of the world – of the prevalence among them of a certain infection of the urinary tract acquired through loose conduct while ashore, which we in Holland call the druiper and the French the chaude-pisse.* But your skill in the repair of noses might be of considerable interest to me, since there are now many in this province whose countenances have been ravaged by the great pox and who would pay handsomely to have them made

---

* Gonorrhea.

whole again; likewise the drawing of rotten teeth, which has become a staple of my business in recent years now that the voyages of our ships and the growing taste for luxury among our people mean that folk season their food with all manner of spices, which erode their teeth far more than was ever seen in the days when even the better sort subsisted on rye bread and herrings."

Without asking my leave, he then palpated my wrists and forearms as a butcher might feel the shoulders and rump of a slaughter ox. "Yes," he said at last, "fine solid limbs such as are required for pulling teeth: in a tooth drawer as in a public executioner, strength and resoluteness are the guarantors of a good outcome far more than finesse and delicacy. I had a patient last week, a farmer from Voorschoten, whose wisdom tooth was so securely anchored in his jaw that I almost pulled his head off before I had it out, and had to call in my serving-man to kneel on the fellow's shoulders while I lugged at the tooth, and he roared so loudly that folk for several streets about laid down their work to come and see what was afoot, fearing that some atrocious murder was being committed. Anyway, young man, what would be your terms?"

I replied that the terms that I sought were those that I had before, insofar as that were possible; and that each year of my apprenticeship my father's estate would provide a fee of one hundred and fifty guilders to cover my board, lodging and tuition. To which he replied curtly that it would be two hundred guilders each year, and my board would be paid for over and above that since the price of victuals was higher in Holland than in either England or Flanders; likewise that I would be obliged to work on all the principal public holidays since a hundred Dutchmen (he said) is a hundred knives; and a hundred knives plus a hundred pots of beer at Saint Pancras's Fair equals a hundred wounds to be dressed; and though this was good business for him, what use would his apprentice be to him if he were absent all that day roistering with the other wastrels? I said that in that case, though I saw his reasoning and understood it perfectly, I would require five or six days' holiday a year in lieu. To which he replied curtly that

that was not his intention.

I saw here at once that I had to deal with a notable skinflint and a hard taskmaster, and reflected whether I wished to bind myself for four years to such a cheese-paring rogue, since if this was how things went at our first meeting, what would he be like later on? But in view of Leiden's primacy in the study of anatomy, and the opportunities that it offered for me to pursue physic as well, I swallowed my pride and said that his terms would be acceptable to me. After all (I reflected) with my brother living only three streets off I need not endure his company the whole time, whilst as for the substance of my surgical studies it was undeniable that he was widely reputed as one of the most knowledgeable surgeons in all Holland and soon likely to be elected deputy president of the Leiden guild, which might greatly advance my career later on if I remained in his favour. So I agreed there and then to enter into four years' apprenticeship with him, starting on the first day of March, living for the first two years of that time under his roof, though I might later lodge on my own if I wished.

★ ★ ★ ★ ★ ★ ★ ★ ★

March arrived, with the last of the winter ice melting in the polder-land ditches and the willow catkins starting to appear along the canal banks. And Frans Michielszoon van Raveyck, fifteen years of age, native of the town of Houtenburg in the county of Flanders, was duly installed as apprentice to the surgeon Lukas van Backhuysen at his premises *De Krokodijl* on the Boterstraat in the town of Leiden, his articles of indenture being afterwards registered with the Surgeons' Guild of Saints Cosmo and Damian in that town and a bond of two hundred and fifty guilders lodged there as security. Things could scarcely have looked better for him: financially secure now, rich in experience for one of such tender years, and with every reason to anticipate a bright future as a surgeon in Holland, Flanders, France or any other country of Christendom he might choose to dwell in.

Meanwhile back in Houtenburg, in the parlour of the Lambrechts household, Artemise paused in the writing of her twice-weekly letter to him (in French, which she considered so much more distingué than Flemish) and surreptitiously pulled forward the neckline of her bodice to examine with detached but critical curiosity the two embryonic breasts that were beginning to bud beneath her shift. She was only thirteen now. But by the time cher François gained his surgeon's licence she would be seventeen, going on eighteen, and her parents would be seeking a suitable marriage party for her. And she would most assuredly see to it that when the time came there were no other contenders, even if she had to administer ratsbane to each of them with her own hand.

Yet nothing is fixed or certain aboard this giddy cosmic ship that we call the Earth, spinning like a humming top as it hurtles along its reckless annual course about the sun while the inconstant moon and the planets move about it through the zodiac, conjoining and drawing apart in their perpetual, silent sarabande as we petty mortals seek to keep our balance standing on a three-legged stool poised on the edge of a table which a blind epileptic pushes in a wheelbarrow along a greasy fraying tightrope stretched above a bottomless chasm. Kings wage war against one another and conclude treaties of peace, then break those treaties and wage war again; armies march and countermarch and fleets of ships plough the seas to do the bidding of their princes. Harvests prosper and fail, plagues wax and diminish, regicides whet their daggers and seas break through dykes to flood the land, while in the heavens above us the immutable stars exert their mysterious influence over the sublunary world. There are always fresh adventures and misadventures simmering in the dark cauldron of time, and nothing in this whole world is certain except that, save only for death, all things are uncertain.